MW00528122

EVERYMAN'S   LIBRARY

EVERYMAN,
I WILL GO WITH THEE,
AND BE THY GUIDE,
IN THY MOST NEED
TO GO BY THY SIDE

CHESTER HIMES

THE ESSENTIAL HARLEM DETECTIVES

A RAGE IN HARLEM
THE REAL COOL KILLERS
THE CRAZY KILL
COTTON COMES TO HARLEM

WITH AN INTRODUCTION
BY S. A. COSBY

EVERYMAN'S LIBRARY
Alfred A. Knopf New York London Toronto

417

THIS IS A BORZOI BOOK
PUBLISHED BY ALFRED A. KNOPF

First included in Everyman's Library, 2024

US copyright information:

A Rage in Harlem
Copyright © 1957 by Chester Himes, copyright renewed 1985 by Lesley Himes
The Real Cool Killers
Copyright © 1959 by Chester Himes, copyright renewed 1987 by Lesley Himes
The Crazy Kill
Copyright © 1959 by Chester Himes, copyright renewed 1987 by Lesley Himes
Cotton Comes to Harlem
Copyright © 1965 by Chester Himes, copyright renewed 1993 by Lesley Himes

UK copyright information:

A Rage in Harlem
Copyright © Chester Himes, 1957, 1985
The Real Cool Killers
Copyright © Chester Himes, 1959
The Crazy Kill
Copyright © Chester Himes, 1959
Cotton Comes to Harlem
Copyright © Chester Himes, 1965

Introduction copyright © 2024 by S. A. Cosby
Bibliography and Chronology copyright © 2024 by Everyman's Library

A Rage in Harlem originally published in the USA in 1957 as *For Love of Imabelle* by Fawcett World Library. First published in Great Britain (as *A Rage in Harlem*) by Allison & Busby, 1985. *The Real Cool Killers* originally published in France in 1958 as *Il pleut des coups durs*. First published in the USA in 1959 by Avon and in Great Britain in 1969 by Panther Books. *The Crazy Kill* originally published in France in 1959 as *Couché dans le pain*. First published in the USA in 1959 by Avon and in Great Britain in 1968 by Panther Books. *Cotton Comes to Harlem* first published in France in 1964 as *Retour en Afrique*; first published in the USA in 1965 by G. P. Putnam's Sons and in Great Britain in 1966 by Frederick Muller.

All rights reserved. Published in the United States by Alfred A. Knopf, a division of Penguin Random House LLC, New York, and in Canada by Penguin Random House Canada Limited, Toronto. Distributed by Penguin Random House LLC, New York. Published in the United Kingdom by Everyman's Library, 50 Albemarle Street, London W1S 4BD and distributed by Penguin Random House UK, 20 Vauxhall Bridge Road, London SW1V 2SA.

everymanslibrary.com
www.everymanslibrary.co.uk

ISBN: 978-1-101-90839-6 (US)
978-1-84159-417-0 (UK)

A CIP catalogue reference for this book is available from the British Library

Typography by Peter B. Willberg

Book design by Barbara de Wilde and Carol Devine Carson

Typeset in the UK by Input Data Services Ltd, Bridgwater, Somerset

Printed and bound in Germany by GGP Media GmbH, Pössneck

THE ESSENTIAL
HARLEM DETECTIVES

INTRODUCTION

When I was twelve years old, my uncle gave me a copy of *The Real Cool Killers* by Chester Himes. For a nerdy kid who cut his crime fiction teeth on Chandler, Hammett and Macdonald (Ross and John D.), seeing this book written by a Black man about Black people—Black cops and con men, Black madams and Black ministers—this unapologetic zenith of Black identity was a revelation in every sense of the word. It felt both spiritual and inspirational. In short, it changed my life. Even though I was a poor boy from rural Virginia who had never stepped foot in Harlem, Himes spoke to me with a wild and powerful clarion call that can only be heard when an elder speaks.

If Chandler is considered the poet of crime fiction and Hammett its great journalist, then Himes is the songwriter of the downtrodden. His stories sing with a fire and light that comes from a simmering sense of loss. A loss of respect, of humanity, of honor.

Grave Digger Jones and Coffin Ed Johnson are not private eyes. They are police detectives and carry with them all the psychological and sociological caveats that come with that occupation in the Black community. And yet Himes is able to garner sympathy and adulation for these two men who, within the world of Himes' Harlem, try their best to mete out justice equally under an inherently unjust system. They use abhorrent techniques to get information from abhorrent people. They never make the mistake of thinking they are the good guys. To quote another fictional policeman, Rust Cohle, they are "the bad men that keep other bad men from the door."

But Coffin Ed and Grave Digger don't have the luxury of white privilege to assuage their conscience. There is no system in place that assures them the ends justify the means. They are self-aware in a way that few characters in a crime fiction novel were in the Golden Age of Literary Noir. They realized they were not heroes. They were the protagonists; they were among the first antiheroes in crime fiction. But unlike Mike Hammer, they never lied to themselves about who or what they were.

vii

I had never encountered anything like the world or the words of Chester Himes. But I knew I wanted more. The next book I devoured was *Blind Man with a Pistol,* a deeply twisted and morally ambiguous novel about the senseless nature of violence. A work that is both terrifying and philosophical, it was a watershed moment for this young wannabe writer that also just happens to have one of the most fearless endings in crime fiction history.

As I read more of Himes' work, I came to understand he wasn't just a great Black crime fiction novelist.

He was a great novelist.

On par not only with his contemporaries in the crime fiction world but also with the great novelists of his time regardless of genre. He is a contemporary of Ralph Ellison and Richard Wright, Langston Hughes and William Gardner Smith, of Hemingway and Fitzgerald.

His implacable drive to examine the Black experience, the disingenuous nature of the American Dream, the reality of pain and sorrow and what it does to the soul, that is what makes him the bard of the existential African American psyche.

Himes' life was a tangible journey through that psyche. The son of educators, Himes had his first, but sadly not his last, experience with the vile nature of racism in America at the age of thirteen. Because of some misbehavior on his part, his mother kept him from attending school to help his brother in a science demonstration that used gunpowder as an active agent. Tragically, his brother was blinded in that experiment and then was refused treatment at a white hospital. Himes reflected upon that moment later, saying "White clad doctors and attendants appeared. I remember sitting in the back seat with Joe watching the pantomime being enacted in the car's bright lights. A white man refusing; my father was pleading. Dejectedly my father turned away; he was crying like a baby. My mother was fumbling in her handbag for a handkerchief; I hoped it was for a pistol."

Later, after the family had moved north to Ohio, Himes found a wildness in the streets of Cleveland that spoke to something wild within himself. Arrested and incarcerated for eight years for armed robbery, Himes literally wrote himself out of that Tartarus, finding his voice and his implacable drive within the confines of that stone and iron dungeon. Those years he spent behind bars, cut off from the rest of the world, shaped not only his literary point of view but also his world view. "It seemed so illogical to punish some poor criminal for doing something that civilization taught him how to do so he could have something that civilization taught him how to want. It seemed to him as wrong as if they had hung the gun that shot the man."

. Himes' was a life lived at every level and within every hierarchy of the African American experience. From middle class stability to painful poverty to disillusioned expatriate, his life was a parallel to the African American experience of the early twentieth century, and he used this in his work time and time again.

Himes inspired countless writers, but he was a touchstone for Black writers specifically. His ferocious tenacity in the face of racism and prejudice laid the foundation for the path many of us have walked in the years since he published his first novel. On the family tree of African American crime fiction, there is a direct genealogical link from Coffin Ed Johnson and Grave Digger Jones to Easy Rawlins and John Shaft, to Aaron Gunner, to Blanche White, to Marti MacAlister, to Larry Cole, to Cass Raines and Dayna Anderson. Although Himes wrote in multiple genres and disciplines, including social criticism with novels like *If He Hollers Let Him Go* and *Lonely Crusade*, he is most well-known for his Harlem Cycle with its mordant and fatalistic recreation of a Harlem that existed but was embellished and made mythic by Himes' razor-sharp prose. "The Harlem of my books was never meant to be real; I never called it real; I just wanted to take it away from the white man if only in my books."

That is not to say Himes is a humorless, all-knowing guru. His books brim with hilarity, hard-won intimacy, and steely camaraderie. My mother always beamed with the light of memory when she regaled me and my brother with the story of her first date with my father. They'd gone to see the movie *Cotton Comes to Harlem*, based on Himes' book of the same name. Years later, I would take a date to see another Himes adaptation, *A Rage in Harlem*. That kind of serendipity is a magical thing that seems to happen often when one discusses the work of Chester Himes. It's Black Magic, made with Missouri red clay and Cleveland smokestacks and sprinkled with love, laughter and a smattering of philosophy.

That's the power of his words. He helped many generations create memories through a shared connection to his work, a sort of sacred tapestry that weaves its way through souls. His books were the catalyst for this kind of shared consciousness. His work centered Black people and Black life like few artists before him. A broad panoply of feelings, ideas and emotions integral to the Black experience in America filters through the prism of his crime fiction novels.

I often say crime fiction is the gospel of the dispossessed. If that's true, it's in the Book of Himes that we find the parables and the sermons that cry out with unbridled, righteous rage at the unfairness of life in general, and the particular type of unfairness Black people have and continue to experience.

But in the end, it's his unflinching portrayal of the rage that lived inside the heart of one who is not simply dismissed but never acknowledged in the first place. As he says in one of his more famous quotes:

There is an indomitable quality within the human spirit that cannot be destroyed; a face deep within the human personality that is impregnable to all assaults.

Chester Himes knew this intimately. He lived it. He sat down and articulated it in a way that was neither saccharine nor servile. Just magnificent.

That is his legacy.

That is his gift to all of us.

S. A. Cosby

S. A. COSBY is an Anthony Award-winning writer from Southeastern Virginia. He is the author of the *New York Times* bestsellers *All the Sinners Bleed* and *Razorblade Tears*, and the highly acclaimed *Blacktop Wasteland*, winner of the *Los Angeles Times* Book Prize.

SELECT BIBLIOGRAPHY

BIOGRAPHY AND CRITICISM

CAMPBELL, JAMES, *Exiled in Paris* (New York: Scribner, 1995).

DAVIS, URSULA BROSCHKE, *Paris Without Regret: James Baldwin, Kenny Clarke, Chester Himes, and Donald Byrd* (Iowa City: University of Iowa Press, 1986).

FABRE, MICHEL, ROBERT E. SKINNER, and LESTER SULLIVAN, *Chester Himes: An Annotated Primary and Secondary Bibliography* (Westport CT: Greenwood Press, 1992).

FABRE, MICHEL, and ROBERT E. SKINNER (eds.), *Conversations with Chester Himes* (Jackson MS: University Press of Mississippi, 1995).

HARRIS, TRUDIER, *Exorcising Blackness: Historical Literary Lynching and Burning Rituals* (Bloomington: Indiana University Press, 1984).

JACKSON, LAWRENCE P., *Chester B. Himes: A Biography* (New York: W. W. Norton, 2017).

MARGOLIES, EDWARD, and MICHEL FABRE, *The Several Lives of Chester Himes* (Jackson MS: University Press of Mississippi, 1997).

MILLIKEN, STEPHEN F., *Chester Himes: A Critical Appraisal* (Columbia: University of Missouri Press, 1976.)

SALLIS, JAMES, *Chester Himes: A Life* (New York: Walker & Company, 2000).

SILET, CHARLES L. P. (ed.), *The Critical Response to Chester Himes* (Westport CT: Greenwood Press, 1999).

SKINNER, ROBERT E., *Two Guns from Harlem: The Detective Fiction of Chester Himes* (Bowling Green OH: Popular Press, 1989).

ANTHOLOGIES

CLARKE, JOHN HENRIK (ed.), *Harlem: Voices from the Soul of Black America* (New York: Signet Books, 1970).

FRANKLIN, H. BRUCE (ed.), *Prison Writing in 20th-century America* (New York: Penguin, 1998).

GALBÁN, EUGENIO SUÁREZ (ed.), *The Last Good Land: Spain in American Literature* (Amsterdam: Rodopi, 2011).

Hard-Boiled Dicks no. 8–9: *Les Durs-à-cuire Spécial Chester Himes* (Paris: L'Introuvable, December 1983).

JARRETT, GENE ANDREW (ed.), *African American Literature beyond Race: An Alternative Reader* (New York: New York University Press, 2006).

The Payback Sampler: New Titles Spring 97 (Edinburgh: Payback Press, 1997).

POLITO, ROBERT (ed.), *Crime Novels: American Noir of the 1950s* (New York: Library of America, 1997).

PRONZINI, BILL, and JACK ADRIAN (eds.), *Hard Boiled: An Anthology of American Crime Stories* (New York: Oxford University Press, 1995).

TRUEBLOOD, KATHRYN, ISHMAEL REED, and SHAWN WONG (eds.), *The Before Columbus Foundation Fiction Anthology* (New York: W. W. Norton, 1992).

ULIN, DAVID L., *Writing Los Angeles: A Literary Anthology* (New York: Library of America, 2002).

WILLIAMS, JOHN A., "My Man Himes: An interview with Chester Himes" in *Amistad 1: Writings on Black History and Culture*, ed. John A. Williams and Charles F. Harris (New York: Vintage, 1970).

WORKS BY CHESTER HIMES

If He Hollers Let Him Go (New York: Doubleday, 1945).

Lonely Crusade (New York: Alfred A. Knopf, 1947).

Cast the First Stone (New York: Coward-McCann, 1952). See also *Yesterday Will Make You Cry.*

The Third Generation (New York: New American Library, 1954).

The Primitive (New York: New American Library, 1955). Later revised in 1990 to *The End of a Primitive*.

For Love of Imabelle (Greenwich CT: Fawcett, 1957). Later revised in 1965 to *A Rage in Harlem*.

The Real Cool Killers (New York: Avon, 1959).

The Crazy Kill (New York: Avon, 1959).

The Big Gold Dream (New York: Avon, 1960).

All Shot Up (New York: Avon, 1960).

Pinktoes (Paris: Olympia Press, 1961).

Cotton Comes to Harlem (New York: G. P. Putnam, 1965).

The Heat's On (New York: G. P. Putnam, 1966).

Run Man Run (New York: G. P. Putnam, 1966).

Blind Man with a Pistol (New York: William Morrow, 1969).

The Quality of Hurt: The Autobiography of Chester Himes, volume 1 (Garden City NY: Doubleday, 1972).

Black on Black (New York: Doubleday, 1973).

My Life of Absurdity: The Autobiography of Chester Himes, volume 2 (Garden City NY: Doubleday, 1976).

A Case of Rape (New York: Targ Editions, 1980; Washington, D.C.: Howard University Press, 1984).

SELECT BIBLIOGRAPHY

The Collected Stories of Chester Himes (New York: Thunder's Mouth Press, 1990).

Plan B, edited and with an introduction by Michel Fabre and Robert E. Skinner (Jackson: University Press of Mississippi, 1993).

Yesterday Will Make You Cry (New York: W. W. Norton, 1998).

Dear Chester, Dear John: Letters between Chester Himes and John A. Williams, compiled and edited by John A. and Lori Williams (Detroit: Wayne State University Press, 2008).

CHRONOLOGY

DATE	AUTHOR'S LIFE	LITERARY CONTEXT
1909	Birth of Chester Bomar Himes on July 29 in Jefferson City, Missouri to Joseph Sandy Himes and Estelle Bomar Himes.	W. E. B. Du Bois: *John Brown: A Biography.* Gertrude Stein: *Three Lives.* Booker T. Washington: *The Story of the Negro.*
1910		Jane Addams: *Twenty Years of Hull House.* E. M. Forster: *Howards End.* Deaths of Leo Tolstoy, Mark Twain.
1911		Du Bois: *The Quest of the Silver Fleece.* Ezra Pound: *Canzoni.*
1912		Thomas Mann: *Death in Venice.*
1913		Willa Cather: *O Pioneers!* Edith Wharton: *The Custom of the Country.*
1914		E. Burroughs: *Tarzan of the Apes.* James Joyce: *Dubliners.*
1915		Du Bois: *The Negro.* Charlotte Perkins Gilman: *Herland.* Arthur Conan Doyle: *The Valley of Fear.* D. H. Lawrence: *The Rainbow.*
1916		*Journal of Negro History* founded. Alain Locke: *Race Contacts and Interracial Relations.* Joyce: *A Portrait of the Artist as a Young Man.*
1917		William Carlos Williams: *A Book of Poems: Al Que Quiere!*
1918		Cather: *My Ántonia.* Lola Ridge: *The Ghetto and Other Poems.*

Rise of "Progressive" movement in US. National Negro Committee formed, reorganized in 1910 as the National Association for the Advancement of Colored People (NAACP).

Mann Act abolishes white slave trafficking. China abolishes slavery. Mexican Revolution (to 1920).

Roald Amundsen reaches South Pole.

Textile workers strike in Lawrence, Massachusetts. W. C. Handy's revolutionary "Memphis Blues." Sinking of RMS *Titanic*. New Mexico and Arizona become US states. War in the Balkans.
Woodrow Wilson becomes US president. First Woman's Suffrage procession in Washington on the eve of his inauguration. Death of Harriet Tubman.

Beginning of World War I. President Wilson proclaims US neutrality. Panama Canal opens.

Revival of the Ku Klux Klan in Georgia. Death of Booker T. Washington. World War I rages in Europe. US begins its occupation of Haiti (to 1934).

Battles of Verdun, the Somme, Jutland. Marcus Garvey arrives in US. "Organic Act" creates National Park Service. First jazz recording.

US declares war on Germany (April 6) and Austria-Hungary (Dec 7). Bolshevik Revolution in Russia. Red Scare in US (to 1920).
Wilson's Fourteen Points for world peace. World War I ends (Nov 11). Collapse of German, Habsburg and Ottoman empires. Worldwide flu epidemic kills millions (to 1920). Major anti-Black riots in US. Leonidas C. Dyer introduces Anti-Lynching Bill. Women over thirty gain the vote in UK.

DATE	AUTHOR'S LIFE	LITERARY CONTEXT
1919		Sherwood Anderson: *Winesburg, Ohio.* Birth of J. D. Salinger.
1920	Himeses move to St. Louis, Missouri (summer) and then to Pine Bluff, Arkansas (fall). His father takes a job teaching mechanical trades and African American history at Branch Normal College.	F. Scott Fitzgerald: *This Side of Paradise.* Sinclair Lewis: *Main Street.* Wharton: *The Age of Innocence.* Lawrence: *Women in Love.*
1921		John Dos Passos: *Three Soldiers.* PEN, international association of writers, founded.
1922		T. S. Eliot: *The Waste Land.* Lewis: *Babbitt.* Claude McKay: *Harlem Shadows.* Eugene O'Neill: *The Hairy Ape.* Carl Van Vechten: *Peter Whiffle.* Joyce: *Ulysses.*
1923	Chester's brother, Joseph Jr., is blinded after an accident in a chemistry demonstration at school and is refused treatment at a whites-only hospital. Remembering this incident in the first of his two autobiographies, Himes wrote, "That one moment in my life hurt me as much as all the others put together." His mother takes Joseph back to Missouri to be treated, and they stay in St. Louis.	Jean Toomer: *Cane.* Williams: *Spring and All.*
1924	Chester and his father move back to Missouri with his mother and brother before the family relocate to Cleveland, Ohio in 1925. They live with Chester's aunt, Fannie, and her husband during a time of financial difficulty.	Jessie Redmon Fauset: *There Is Confusion.* Walter White: *The Fire in the Flint.* Birth of James Baldwin.

CHRONOLOGY

Paris Peace Conference (to 1920). US Senate refuses to ratify Treaty of Versailles. Punitive war reparations imposed on Germany. German Workers' Party (later the Nazi Party) founded in Munich. Savage anti-Black riots in Chicago and Washington. Wartime strike wave (1916–22) peaks, with over four million US workers on strike. 18th Amendment ratified, prohibiting alcoholic beverages. US Communist Party organized. League of Nations created, without US participation. 19th Amendment ratified (women's suffrage). Marcus Garvey speaks in Madison Square Garden. Gandhi launches non-cooperation campaign against British rule in India.

Warren G. Harding US president. Quota laws restrict immigration. Margaret Sanger founds American Birth Control League. Thompson ("Tommy") machine gun goes into production ("the gun that made the Twenties roar"). Oxford Group founded: beginning of "Moral Re-armament" movement in US. Charlie Chaplin's first film (*The Kid*). Harlem Renaissance. Coal mine and railway strikes. Oklahoma under martial law after Ku Klux Klan terrorism. US Senate votes against Anti-Lynching Bill (no anti-lynching legislation is passed by both Houses until 2022). Broadcasting boom in US: 500 stations operating by end of year. Mussolini marches on Rome; fascist government formed in Italy. USSR established.

Calvin Coolidge becomes president after Harding's death. Tri-state conclave of Ku Klux Klan in Indiana, 200,000 members attend. Automatic traffic light developed by Garrett A. Morgan. "The Charleston" song and dance composed, first performed in hit Broadway musical *Runnin' Wild*. German hyperinflation. Hitler's Munich Putsch fails.

US Congress grants indigenous people right to citizenship. Gershwin's *Rhapsody in Blue*. Duke Ellington's first recording. Death of Lenin; Stalin's rise to power. First Labour government in UK.

CHESTER HIMES

DATE	AUTHOR'S LIFE	LITERARY CONTEXT
1925	Himeses buy new house in a predominantly white neighborhood (Oct).	Countee Cullen: *Color*. Fitzgerald: *The Great Gatsby*. Alain Leroy Locke: *The New Negro: An Interpretation*. Franz Kafka: *The Trial*.
1926	Himes graduates high school. Attends Ohio State University with hopes of becoming a medical doctor. Joins fraternity Alpha Phi Alpha. Suffers serious injury whilst working at a hotel, falling down an elevator shaft.	Ernest Hemingway: *The Sun Also Rises*. Langston Hughes: *The Weary Blues*. Van Vechten: *Nigger Heaven*.
1927	Brings fellow students to a brothel he frequents and is asked to withdraw from college due to "ill health and failing grades." Sent to prison for committing fraud (September). Mother and father separate permanently, divorcing in 1928.	Cather: *Death Comes for the Archbishop*. Hughes: *Fine Clothes to the Jew*. Thornton Wilder: *The Bridge of San Luis Rey*. Virginia Woolf: *To the Lighthouse*.
1928	Commits armed robbery and sent to prison in Ohio. Serves eight years of a twenty-year sentence. His injury suffered two years previously exempts him from hard labor and he can dedicate time to writing in prison.	Du Bois: *Dark Princess: A Romance*. Fauset: *Plum Bun*. Rudolph Fisher: *The Walls of Jericho*. McKay: *Home to Harlem*. Woolf: *Orlando*.
1929		Cullen: *The Black Christ*. William Faulkner: *The Sound and the Fury*. Dashiell Hammett: *Red Harvest* and *The Dain Curse*. Hemingway: *A Farewell to Arms*. Thomas Wolfe: *Look Homeward, Angel*.
1930	Witnesses the Ohio State Prison fire that kills 322 prisoners.	Dos Passos: *U.S.A. Trilogy* (to 1936). Faulkner: *As I Lay Dying*. Hammett: *The Maltese Falcon*.
1931		Robert Frost: *Collected Poems*. Hammett: *The Glass Key*. Toomer: *Essentials*. Birth of Toni Morrison.

CHRONOLOGY

Scopes "Monkey" trial in Tennessee. Sweet trials in Detroit: Clarence Darrow successfully defends eleven Black men charged with murder when protecting their home and lives against a white mob. Louis Armstrong's first recording. Birth of Malcolm Little ("Malcolm X"). Hitler publishes *Mein Kampf.*
Foundation of the Harlem Globetrotters. John Logie Baird demonstrates the television. Fascist youth organizations set up in Germany and Italy. General Strike in UK.

Charles Lindbergh completes the first non-stop solo transatlantic flight. Transatlantic telephone service inaugurated for commercial use. Sacco and Vanzetti executed. First full-length movie with sound sequences, *The Jazz Singer.*

Oscar De Priest of Illinois becomes the first African American to serve in Congress since 1901. *The Lights of New York*, first all-talking motion picture. Stalin's first Five-Year Plan.

Stock market crash. Herbert Hoover US president. Birth of Martin Luther King, Jr. Museum of Modern Art founded in New York. Charles Hamilton Houston develops outstanding program in law at Howard University (to 1935), training Black attorneys who will lead the battle to end segregation. John Hope becomes president of Atlanta University, which establishes the first graduate school for Black people.

US tariff raised to levels which damage world trade. Gandhi drafts the Declaration of Indian Independence and embarks on his "Salt March." Nazi Party makes great gains in German elections.

Scottsboro case: nine young Afro-Americans charged with rape of two white women in Alabama, provoking major civil rights controversy. Trial of Al Capone. Increasing financial panic and unemployment in US. Empire State Building completed.

DATE	AUTHOR'S LIFE	LITERARY CONTEXT
1932	Chester's father remarries. Brother graduates from Oberlin.	Faulkner: *Light in August*. Fisher: *The Conjure Man Dies*. Aldous Huxley: *Brave New World*.
1933	Meets Prince Rico, romantic affair begins whilst in prison. Begins sending short stories to magazines from prison. "Prison Mass" published in *Abbott's Weekly*. "A Cup of Tea" published in *Atlanta Daily World*.	James Weldon Johnson: *Along This Way*. George Orwell: *Down and Out in Paris and London*.
1934	"Crazy Stir" and "To What Red Hell" published by *Esquire* magazine, Himes strikes up a working relationship with its founder, Arnold Gingrich. "The Black Man Has Red Blood" published by *Chicago Defender*.	James M. Cain: *The Postman Always Rings Twice*. Fitzgerald: *Tender Is the Night*. Hammett: *The Thin Man*. Hughes: *The Ways of White Folks*. Zora Neale Hurston: *Jonah's Gourd Vine*. Agatha Christie: *Murder on the Orient Express*.
1935		Du Bois: *Black Reconstruction in America* Hughes: *Mulatto*. John Steinbeck: *Tortilla Flat*. Wolfe: *Of Time and the River*.
1936	Released from prison on parole (April). Meets writer Langston Hughes.	Arna Bontemps: *Black Thunder*. Faulkner: *Absalom! Absalom!*
1937	Marries his first wife, Jean Johnson (July).	Hurston: *Their Eyes Were Watching God*. Steinbeck: *Of Mice and Men*. Christie: *Death on the Nile*.
1938	Begins work as research assistant and writer for Cleveland Public Library Project.	Wilder: *Our Town*. Richard Wright: *Uncle Tom's Children*.
1939		Raymond Chandler: *The Big Sleep*. Steinbeck: *The Grapes of Wrath*. Joyce: *Finnegans Wake*.
1940	Fifteen prose poems published in the *Cleveland News*.	Chandler: *Farewell, My Lovely*. Hemingway: *For Whom the Bell Tolls*. Wright: *Native Son*. Graham Greene: *The Power and the Glory*.

CHRONOLOGY

Landslide victory for Democrat F. D. Roosevelt in US presidential election. Amelia Earhart first woman to fly solo across the Atlantic. Nazis become largest single party in German Reichstag.

Roosevelt launches "New Deal" recovery program. By this year 11,000 of the 25,000 banks in the US have failed. Unemployment peaks at nearly thirteen million (nearly a quarter of the workforce). 21st Amendment repeals Prohibition. Hitler appointed Chancellor of Germany; Albert Einstein and other émigrés flee to US. Nazi book burnings.

US tariff reduced. Mao Zedong's Long March. USSR admitted to League of Nations. Stalin's Great Terror begins (to 1939). Hitler becomes German Führer.

National Labor Relations Act gives workers right to form or join unions. Category 5 Labor Day Hurricane hits Florida Keys. Nuremberg Laws in Germany, legitimizing persecution of Jews. Italy invades Abyssinia.

Dust bowl drought, tremendous losses for farmers. Spanish Civil War. German troops occupy Rhineland.

Joe Louis wins heavyweight championship bout. Picasso paints *Guernica*. Japanese invasion of China.

Munich Pact: Britain, France and Italy agree to German partition of Czechoslovakia. Fair Labor Standards Act sets first minimum wage in US.

Germany invades Poland causing Britain and France to declare war on Germany. World War II begins. End of the Spanish Civil War. Britain and France recognize the Franco regime as Spain's government.

Franklin D. Roosevelt wins the US election. Winston Churchill becomes British prime minister. Battle of Dunkirk; evacuation of British forces; fall of France. Hattie McDaniel first African American actor to win an Academy Award.

DATE	AUTHOR'S LIFE	LITERARY CONTEXT
1941	"Face in the Moonlight" published in *Coronet*. Works as a butler at Malabar Farm (summer) under Louis Bromfield. Bromfield persuades Chester and Jean to relocate to Los Angeles, offering to pitch novel by Himes, *Black Sheep*, to film producers. (The novel is eventually published as *Cast the First Stone* then later, unabridged, as *Yesterday Will Make You Cry*.)	Eudora Welty: *A Curtain of Green*. W. Somerset Maugham: *Up at the Villa*. Deaths of James Joyce, Virginia Woolf.
1942	Gains entry-level writing position at Warner Brothers until Jack L. Warner learns that Himes is Black, uses a racial slur against him and has him terminated immediately.	Mary McCarthy: *The Company She Keeps*.
1943	Publishes several short stories in NAACP's *Crisis* magazine. Starts writing column in union magazine *War Worker*.	Chandler: *The Lady in the Lake*. Antoine de Saint-Exupéry: *The Little Prince*.
1944	Receives year-long writing fellowship from the Rosenwald Fund, approved by Vandi Haygood. Moves to New York, stays in Harlem with his cousin, Jean remains in LA.	Saul Bellow: *Dangling Man*. Lillian Smith: *Strange Fruit*.
1945	First novel, *If He Hollers Let Him Go*, published. Meets Ralph Ellison and Richard Wright. Death of Himes' mother, Estelle.	Robert Penn Warren: *All the King's Men*. Wright: *Black Boy*. Orwell: *Animal Farm*. Evelyn Waugh: *Brideshead Revisited*.
1946	Meets Carl Van Vechten. Article in *Chicago Defender* names Himes, Ellison and Wright as "blues school of writers."	Death of Willa Cather.
1947	*Lonely Crusade* published.	Arthur Miller: *All My Sons*. Greene: *The Heart of the Matter*.
1948	Receives a scholarship from the Yaddo artists' community where he stays and works (April). Meets Patricia Highsmith.	William Gardner Smith: *Last of the Conquerors*. Orwell: *Nineteen Eighty-Four*.

CHRONOLOGY

Japanese Navy launches a surprise attack on the United States at Pearl Harbor. US enters World War II. British cryptologists break the Enigma code.

American success at the Battle of Midway is a major victory. The Declaration of the United Nations is signed. Manhattan Project begins.

Allied forces take back North Africa. Mussolini ousted and arrested; Italy surrenders to Allied Forces. The United States Congress passes the War Labor Disputes Act.

The Siege of Leningrad ends after 872 days. Allied forces land in Normandy during the D-Day invasion. Paris is liberated from Nazi occupation. Franklin D. Roosevelt becomes the only US president to be elected for a fourth term.

President Roosevelt dies, succeeded by Harry S. Truman (April). Germany surrenders. War in Europe ends on VE Day (May 8). Atomic bombs dropped on Hiroshima and Nagasaki. VJ Day (Aug 15).

United Nations' first meeting held in London.

US Secretary of State George C. Marshall announces the "Marshall Plan" to help rebuild Europe. The Cold War begins.

Israeli declaration of independence. Soviet blockade of Berlin and Allied airlift (to 1949).

DATE	AUTHOR'S LIFE	LITERARY CONTEXT
1949	"Journey Out of the Fear" published in journal *Tomorrow*. "Mama's Missionary Money" published in *The Crisis*.	Simone de Beauvoir: *The Second Sex*.
1950	Lectures at North Carolina College for Negroes. *Black Sheep*, the novel based on his prison experience which was initially accepted by Henry Holt, is rejected when he arrives to sign the contract.	
1951		Frost: *The Complete Poems*. J. D. Salinger: *The Catcher in the Rye*.
1952	Separates from first wife, Jean. *Cast the First Stone* published (unexpurgated text published in a new edition, *Yesterday Will Make You Cry*, in 1998).	James Baldwin: *Go Tell It on the Mountain*. Ralph Ellison: *Invisible Man*.
1953	Chester's father dies (January). Rekindles friendship with Richard Wright. Travels to France by boat, settles in Paris (April). Meets James Baldwin. Spends three months in London (from July).	Bellow: *The Adventures of Augie March*. Chandler: *The Long Goodbye*. Wright: *The Outsider*. Samuel Beckett: *Waiting for Godot*.
1954	*The Third Generation* published.	Kingsley Amis: *Lucky Jim*.
1955	Travels back to New York (January). Leaves New York for France, never to live in US again (December). *The Primitive* published (new edition, *The End of a Primitive*, published in 1990 with Himes' original introduction).	Vladimir Nabokov: *Lolita*.
1956	Writers' colony, La Ciotat (till June).	Baldwin: *Giovanni's Room*. John Osborne: *Look Back in Anger*.
1957	First installment of the Harlem Detective series, *For Love of Imabelle* (republished as *A Rage in Harlem*, 1965).	Jack Kerouac: *On the Road*. Boris Pasternak: *Doctor Zhivago*.

CHRONOLOGY

Senator Joseph McCarthy's Communist "witch-hunt" begins. Communist leader Mao Zedong establishes the People's Republic of China. The Fourth Geneva Convention is agreed.

President Truman sends US military personnel to assist French forces in Vietnam. Korean War (to 1953).

US government begins Nevada nuclear tests. Development of birth control pill. First color television pictures broadcast from the Empire State Building.

57,000 children are paralyzed by polio in the US.

Dwight D. Eisenhower inaugurated as US president.

McCarthy is censured by the Senate. Ellis Island closes as an immigration station. Brown vs Board of Education: US Supreme Court rules that segregation in education is illegal, though this proves difficult to enforce. French defeat in Vietnam at battle of Dien Bien Phu; peace talks in Geneva; French withdrawal; Vietnam divided into North and South. Rosa Parks arrested after refusing to give up her bus seat to a white passenger.

Suez crisis in Egypt caused by nationalization of the Suez Canal (to 1957). French colonial rule ends in Tunisia and Morocco. USSR invades Hungary. Khrushchev denounces Stalin. European Economic Community founded (France, Belgium, Italy, Luxembourg, the Netherlands, West Germany). "Little Rock Nine": Governor of Arkansas calls in National Guard to prevent nine African American students from entering the Central High School;

DATE	AUTHOR'S LIFE	LITERARY CONTEXT
1957 cont.		
1958	*For the Love of Imabelle* is translated as *La Reine des pommes*, and published in Gallimard's Série noire, followed by *Il pleut des coups durs* (French version of *The Real Cool Killers*). *La Reine des pommes* receives the Grand Prix de Littérature Policière for the best detective fiction in French.	Chinua Achebe: *Things Fall Apart*.
1959	*The Real Cool Killers* published in the US. French (*Couché dans le pain*) and US editions of *The Crazy Kill* published. Lesley Packard meets Himes to interview him for *The Herald Tribune* (spring). They move in together by winter in the south of France. Suffers the first of several strokes that will occur over the course of his life.	Bellow: *Henderson the Rain King*.
1960	*All Shot Up* and *The Big Gold Dream* published.	Harper Lee: *To Kill a Mockingbird*. John Updike: *Rabbit, Run*. Death of Richard Wright.
1961	*Pinktoes* published in French (in English, 1965). Meets Pablo Picasso. Meets with Arthur Cohn and accepts $4000 deal for a screenplay – begins writing *Baby Sister*, retracts deal following April, suspicious of Cohn's treatment of director and friend Pierre-Dominique Gaisseau.	Joseph Heller: *Catch-22*. V. S. Naipaul: *A House for Mr. Biswas*. Frantz Fanon: *The Wretched of the Earth*.
1962	Assists on a French documentary in Harlem. Meets Malcolm X.	Nabokov: *Pale Fire*.
1963	*Une Affair de viol* (*A Case of Rape*) published in French. "Harlem: An American Cancer" published by *Présence Africaine*.	Baldwin: *The Fire Next Time*. McCarthy: *The Group*. Sylvia Plath: *The Bell Jar*.

CHRONOLOGY

President Eisenhower calls Federal troops to escort them in. Beginning of communist insurgency in Vietnam. USSR launches Sputnik 1, beginning the Space Race.

Fall of Fourth Republic in France, result of Algerian crisis. Charles de Gaulle returns to power (Fifth Republic), elected as president. Recession in the US brings large increase in unemployment. NASA created. US launches Explorer 1 satellite, USSR launches Sputnik 3.

Fidel Castro comes to power in Cuba. US vice-president Richard Nixon and USSR premier Nikita Khrushchev engage in the impromptu "Kitchen Debate," arguing the merits of capitalism and communism. Resnais and Truffaut spearhead "New Wave" cinema in France.

The US sends its first troops to Vietnam to fight. France conducts nuclear weapons tests, Algeria. "Sit In" movement to oppose segregation spreads from North Carolina to colleges throughout the country; the Student Nonviolent Coordinating Committee (SNCC) founded.

John F. Kennedy becomes US president. SNCC organizes "Freedom Rides" in the South. Erection of Berlin Wall. Algerian demonstrators killed by Paris police.

Algeria wins independence from France. Cuban Missile Crisis.

Assassination of President Kennedy. Lyndon B. Johnson becomes US president. Protest march on Washington; Martin Luther King Jr.'s "I have a dream" speech. De Gaulle vetoes British entry into the EEC. Nelson Mandela jailed for life, South Africa (released 1990).

DATE	AUTHOR'S LIFE	LITERARY CONTEXT
1964	*Retour en Afrique* (*Cotton Comes to Harlem*) published in France (in US, 1965). Meets Carlos Moore. Himes featured on front cover of French magazine, *Adam*.	Bellow: *Herzog*. Carl Van Vechten dies.
1965	*Pinktoes* is a bestseller after publication in US.	Baldwin: *Going to Meet the Man*. Claude Brown: *Manchild in the Promised Land*. Martin Luther King: *Why We Can't Wait*. Malcom X: *The Autobiography of Malcolm X*.
1966	*Run Man Run* and *The Heat's On* published.	Truman Capote: *In Cold Blood*. Thomas Pynchon: *The Crying of Lot 49*. Achebe: *A Man of the People*.
1967	Builds house in Moraira, Spain after much searching for the right spot with Lesley.	John A. Williams: *The Man Who Cried I Am*. Gabriel García Márquez: *One Hundred Years of Solitude*.
1968	*If He Hollers, Let Him Go!* released as a film, directed by Charles Martin.	Eldridge Cleaver: *Soul on Ice*. Alexander Solzhenitsyn: *Cancer Ward*.
1969	*Blind Man with a Pistol* published.	Maya Angelou: *I Know Why the Caged Bird Sings*. Ray Bradbury: *I Sing the Body Electric*. James Alan McPherson: *Hue and Cry: Stories*. Mario Puzo: *The Godfather*.
1970	*Cotton Comes to Harlem* film released, directed by Ossie Davis, breaks box office records in New York, Chicago, Washington D.C., and Detroit. Meets Maya Angelou.	Toni Morrison: *The Bluest Eye*.
1971		Toni Cade Bambara: *Blues Ain't No Mocking Bird*. Flannery O'Connor: *The Complete Stories*.
1972	*The Quality of Hurt, The Autobiography of Chester Himes* (volume 1) published.	Ishmael Reed: *Mumbo Jumbo*. Hunter S. Thompson: *Fear and Loathing in Las Vegas*.

CHRONOLOGY

HISTORICAL EVENTS

Civil Rights Act prohibits discrimination in US. Brezhnev becomes Communist Party General Secretary in USSR.

De Gaulle re-elected. US bombing in Vietnam begins. Malcolm X assassinated.

Mao's Cultural Revolution launched, China. Race riots across US.

Arab-Israeli Six-Day War. President Johnson commissions a report on racial violence in US. De Gaulle visits Canada. First heart transplant operation.

National strike sparked, France, by student protest. Anti-Vietnam War demonstrations across US. Martin Luther King assassinated. Civil Rights Act prohibiting housing discrimination based on race, religion, national origin and sex in the US, signed. Soviet invasion of Czechoslovakia.
Moon landing. De Gaulle resigns. Pompidou elected president of France. Richard Nixon becomes president of US.

De Gaulle dies. US invades Cambodia.

Four Power Agreement on Berlin signed.

Strategic Arms Limitation Treaty (SALT) signed by USSR and US. Watergate Scandal: Democratic National Committee headquarters burgled. Nixon visits China. US bombs Hanoi. Shirley Chisholm first black person to

DATE	AUTHOR'S LIFE	LITERARY CONTEXT
1972 cont.	Come Back, Charleston Blue (based on The Heat's On) released as a film, directed by Mark Warren. Television interview on Soul. Suffers from a stroke (December).	
1973	Black on Black, collection of short work, published.	Pynchon: Gravity's Rainbow. Alice Walker: In Love and Trouble: Stories of Black Women.
1974		Henry Dumas: Ark of Bones and Other Stories. Heller: Something Happened. Erica Jong: Fear of Flying. Robert Persig: Zen and the Art of Motorcycle Maintenance. Reed: The Last Days of Louisiana Red.
1975		Bellow: Humboldt's Gift. Gayl Jones: Corregidora.
1976	My Life of Absurdity, The Autobiography of Chester Himes (volume 2) published.	Raymond Carver: Will You Please Be Quiet, Please? Alex Haley: Roots.
1977		Stephen King: The Shining. McPherson: Elbow Room: Stories. Morrison: Song of Solomon.
1978	After a long engagement, Himes marries Lesley.	John Cheever: Collected Stories. Marilyn French: The Women's Room. John Irving: The World According to Garp.
1979		Octavia Butler: Kindred. Jayne Anne Phillips: Black Tickets. Gilbert Sorrentino: Mulligan Stew. William Styron: Sophie's Choice. Updike: Too Far to Go. Italo Calvino: If on a winter's night a traveler.
1980	A Case of Rape published in the US.	Cade Bambara: The Salt Eaters. Marilynne Robinson: Housekeeping. Eudora Welty: Collected Stories.

CHRONOLOGY

bid for the Democratic presidential nomination: is unsuccessful.

Arab-Israeli War. Middle East oil embargo – power crisis in West. France instigates Messmer Plan for nuclear power expansion. Spanish prime minister Carrero Blanco killed by Basque separatists. US troops leave Vietnam. Pompidou dies, Giscard d'Estaing president. Nixon resigns after Watergate scandal. Gerald Ford becomes US president.

Vietnam war ends. Death of Franco, succeeded as Spanish head of state by King Juan Carlos; transition from dictatorship to democracy begins. Jimmy Carter elected US president. Chairman Mao dies. First Apple computer.

Elvis Presley dies. First free elections in Spain for four decades.

Camp David Agreement signed by Carter, President Sadat of Egypt and Israeli prime minister Menachem Begin.

Soviet troops occupy Afghanistan. Carter and Brezhnev sign SALT II. Shah of Iran forced into exile; Ayatollah Khomeini establishes an Islamic state; American embassy siege in Tehran. Margaret Thatcher becomes the UK's first woman prime minister.

Ronald Reagan elected US President. Iran–Iraq War begins (to 1988).

DATE	AUTHOR'S LIFE	LITERARY CONTEXT
1981		Carver: *What We Talk About When We Talk About Love.* Updike: *Rabbit Is Rich.* Salman Rushdie: *Midnight's Children.*
1982	Wins Before Columbus Foundation's American Book Award for Lifetime Achievement.	Audre Lorde: *Zami: A New Spelling of My Name.* Gloria Naylor: *The Women of Brewster Place.* Walker: *The Color Purple.* García Márquez: *Chronicle of a Death Foretold.* Primo Levi: *If not Now, When?*
1983	Final installment of Harlem Detective Series, *Plan B*, published (unfinished).	Carver: *Cathedral.* Bobbie Ann Mason: *Shiloh and Other Stories.*
1984	Death of Chester Himes, aged 75 (November 12), buried in Moraira.	Phillips: *Machine Dreams.* Updike: *The Witches of Eastwick.*

CHRONOLOGY

A Rage in Harlem

I

HANK COUNTED THE stack of money. It was a lot of money—a hundred and fifty brand-new ten-dollar bills. He looked at Jackson through cold yellow eyes.

"You give me fifteen C's—right?"

He wanted it straight. It was strictly business.

He was a small, dapper man with mottled brown skin and thin straightened hair. He looked like business.

"That's right," Jackson said. "Fifteen hundred bucks."

It was strictly business with Jackson too.

Jackson was a short, black, fat man with purple-red gums and pearly white teeth made for laughing, but Jackson wasn't laughing. It was too serious for Jackson to be laughing. Jackson was only twenty-eight years old, but it was such serious business that he looked a good ten years older.

"You want me to make you fifteen G's—right?" Hank kept after him.

"That's right," Jackson said. "Fifteen thousand bucks."

He tried to sound happy, but he was scared. Sweat was trickling from his short kinky hair. His round black face was glistening like an eight-ball.

"My cut'll be ten percent—fifteen C's—right?"

"That's right. I pays you fifteen hundred bucks for the deal."

"I take five percent for my end," Jodie said. "That's seven hundred and fifty. Okay?"

Jodie was a working stiff, a medium-sized, root-colored, rough-skinned, muscular boy, dressed in a leather jacket and GI pants. His long, thick hair was straightened on the ends and burnt red, and nappy at the roots where it grew out black. It hadn't been cut since New Year's Eve and this was already the middle of February. One look at Jodie was enough to tell that he was strictly a square.

"Okay," Jackson said. "You gets seven hundred and fifty for your end."

It was Jodie who had got Hank to make all this money for him.

"I gets the rest," Imabelle said.

The others laughed.

Imabelle was Jackson's woman. She was a cushioned-lipped, hot-bodied, banana-skin chick with the speckled-brown eyes of a teaser and the high-arched, ball-bearing hips of a natural-born *amante*. Jackson was as crazy about her as moose for doe.

They were standing around the kitchen table. The window looked out on 142nd Street. Snow was falling on the ice-locked piles of garbage stretching like levees along the gutters as far as the eye could see.

Jackson and Imabelle lived in a room down the hall. Their landlady was at work and the other roomers were absent. They had the place to themselves.

Hank was going to turn Jackson's hundred and fifty ten-dollar bills into a hundred and fifty hundred-dollar bills.

Jackson watched Hank roll each bill carefully into a sheet of chemical paper, stick the roll into a cardboard tube shaped like a firecracker, and stack the tubes in the oven of the new gas stove.

Jackson's eyes were red with suspicion.

"You sure you're using the right paper?"

"I ought to know it. I made it," Hank said.

Hank was the only man in the world who possessed the chemically treated paper that was capable of raising the denomination of money. He had developed it himself.

Nevertheless Jackson watched Hank's every move. He even studied the back of Hank's head when Hank turned to put the money into the oven.

"Don't you be so worried, Daddy," Imabelle said, putting her smooth yellow arm about his black-coated shoulder. "You know it can't fail. You saw him do it before."

Jackson had seen him do it before, true enough. Hank had given him a demonstration two days before. He had turned a ten into a hundred right before Jackson's eyes. Jackson had taken the hundred to the bank. He had told the clerk he had won it shooting dice and had asked the clerk if it was good. The clerk had said it was as good as if it had been made in the mint. Hank had had the hundred changed and had given Jackson back his ten. Jackson knew that Hank could do it.

But this time it was for keeps.

That was all the money Jackson had in the world. All the money he'd saved in the five years he'd worked for Mr. H. Exodus Clay, the undertaker. And that hadn't come easy. He drove the limousines for the funerals, brought in the dead in the pickup hearse, cleaned the chapel, washed the bodies and swept out the embalming room, hauled away the garbage cans of clotted blood, trimmed meat and rotten guts.

All the money he could get Mr. Clay to advance him on his salary. All the money he could borrow from his friends. He'd pawned his good clothes, his gold watch and his imitation diamond stickpin and the gold signet ring he'd found in a dead man's pocket. Jackson didn't want anything to happen.

"I ain't worried," Jackson said. "I'm just nervous, that's all. I don't want to get caught."

"How're we goin' to get caught, Daddy? Ain't nobody got no idea what we're doing here."

Hank closed the oven door and lit the gas.

"Now I make you a rich man, Jackson."

"Thank the Lord. Amen," Jackson said, crossing himself.

He wasn't a Catholic. He was a Baptist, a member of the First Baptist Church of Harlem. But he was a very religious young man. Whenever he was troubled he crossed himself just to be on the safe side.

"Set down, Daddy," Imabelle said. "Your knees are shakin'."

Jackson sat down at the table and stared at the stove. Imabelle stood beside him, drew his head tight against her bosom. Hank consulted his watch. Jodie stood to one side, his mouth wide open.

"Ain't it done yet?" Jackson asked.

"Just one more minute," Hank said.

He moved to the sink to get a drink of water.

"Ain't the minute up yet?" Jackson asked.

At that instant the stove exploded with such force it blew the door off.

"Great balls of fire!" Jackson yelled. He came up from his chair as if the seat of his pants had blown up.

"Look out, Daddy!" Imabelle screamed and hugged Jackson so hard she threw him flat on his back.

"Hold it, in the name of the law!" a new voice shouted.

A tall, slim colored man with a cop's scowl rushed into the kitchen. He had a pistol in his right hand and a gold-plated badge in his left.

"I'm a United States marshal. I'm shooting the first one who moves."

He looked as if he meant it.

The kitchen had filled with smoke and stunk like black gunpowder. Gas was pouring from the stove. The scorched cardboard tubes that had been cooking in the oven were scattered over the floor.

"It's the law!" Imabelle screamed.

"I heard him!" Jackson yelled.

"Let's beat it!" Jodie shouted.

He tripped the marshal into the table and made for the door. Hank got there before him and Jodie went out on Hank's back. The marshal sprawled across the table top.

"Run, Daddy!" Imabelle said.

"Don't wait for me," Jackson replied.

He was on his hands and knees, trying as hard as he could to get to his feet. But Imabelle was running so hard she stumbled over him and knocked him down again as she made for the door.

Before the marshal could straighten up all three of them had escaped.

"Don't you move!" he shouted at Jackson.

"I ain't moving, Marshal."

When the marshal finally got his feet underneath him he yanked Jackson erect and snapped a pair of handcuffs about his wrists.

"Trying to make a fool out of me! You'll get ten years for this."

Jackson turned a battleship gray.

"I ain't done nothing, Marshal. I swear to God."

Jackson had attended a Negro college in the South, but whenever he was excited or scared he began talking in his native dialect.

"Sit down and shut up," the marshal ordered.

He shut off the gas and began picking up the cardboard tubes for evidence. He opened one, took out a brand-new hundred-dollar bill and held it up toward the light.

"Raised from a ten. The markings are still on it."

Jackson had started to sit down but he stopped suddenly and began to plead.

"It wasn't me what done that, Marshal. I swear to God. It was them two fellows who got away. All I done was come into the kitchen to get a drink of water."

"Don't lie to me, Jackson. I know you. I've got the goods on you, man. I've been watching you three counterfeiters for days."

Tears welled up in Jackson's eyes, he was so scared.

"Listen, Marshal, I swear to God I didn't have nothing to do with that. I don't even know how to do it. The little man called Hank who got away is the counterfeiter. He's the only one who's got the paper."

"Don't worry about them, Jackson. I'll get them too. But I've already got you, and I'm taking you down to the Federal Building. So I'm warning you, anything you say to me will be used against you in court."

Jackson slid from the chair and got down on his knees.

"Leave me go just this once, Marshal." The tears began streaming down his face. "Just this once, Marshal. I've never been arrested before. I'm a church man, I ain't dishonest. I confess, I put up the money for Hank to raise, but it was him who was breaking the law, not me. I ain't done nothing wouldn't nobody do if they had a chance to make a pile of money."

"Get up, Jackson, and take your punishment like a man," the marshal said. "You're just as guilty as the others. If you hadn't put up the tens, Hank couldn't have changed them into hundreds."

Jackson saw himself serving ten years in prison. Ten years away from Imabelle. Jackson had only had Imabelle for eleven months, but he couldn't live without her. He was going to marry her as soon as she got her divorce from that man down South she was still married to. If he went to prison for ten years, by then she'd have another man and would have forgotten all about him. He'd come out of prison an old man, thirty-eight years old, dried up. No one would give him a job. No woman would want him. He'd be a bum, hungry, skinny, begging on the streets of Harlem, sleeping in doorways, drinking canned heat to keep warm. Mama Jackson hadn't raised a son for that, struggled to send him through the college for Negroes, just to have him become a convict. He just couldn't let the marshal take him in.

He clutched the marshal about the legs.

"Have mercy on a poor sinner, man. I know I did wrong, but I'm not a criminal. I just got talked into it. My woman wanted a new winter coat, we want to get a place of our own, maybe buy a car. I just yielded to temptation. You're a colored man like me, you ought to understand that. Where are we poor colored people goin' to get any money from?"

The marshal yanked Jackson to his feet.

"God damn it, get yourself together, man. Go take a drink of water. You act as if you think I'm Jesus Christ."

Jackson went to the sink and drank a glass of water. He was crying like a baby.

"You could have a little mercy," he said. "Just a little of the milk of human mercy. I've done lost all my money in this deal already. Ain't that punishment enough? Do I have to go to jail too?"

"Jackson, you're not the first man I've arrested for a crime. Suppose I'd let off everybody. Where would I be then? Out of a job. Broke and hungry. Soon I'd be on the other side of the law, a criminal myself."

Jackson looked at the marshal's hard brown face and mean, dirty eyes. He knew there was no mercy in the man. As soon as colored folks got on the side of the law, they lost all Christian charity, he was thinking.

"Marshal, I'll pay you two hundred dollars if you let me off," he offered.

The marshal looked at Jackson's wet face.

"Jackson, I shouldn't do this. But I can see that you're an honest man, just led astray by a woman. And being as you're a colored man like myself, I'm going to let you off this time. You give me the two hundred bucks, and you're a free man."

The only way Jackson could get two hundred dollars this side of the grave was to steal it from his boss. Mr. Clay always kept two or three thousand dollars in his safe. There was nothing Jackson hated worse than having to steal from Mr. Clay. Jackson had never stolen any money in his life. He was an honest man. But there was no other way out of this hole.

"I ain't got it here. I got it at the funeral parlor where I work."

"Well, that being the case, I'll drive you there in my car, Jackson. But you'll have to give me your word of honor you won't try to escape."

"I ain't no criminal," Jackson protested. "I won't try to escape, I swear to God. I'll just go inside and get the money and bring it out to you."

The marshal unlocked Jackson's handcuffs and motioned him ahead. They went down the four flights of stairs and came out on Eighth Avenue, where the apartment house fronted.

The marshal gestured toward a battered black Ford.

"You can see that I'm a poor man myself, Jackson."

"Yes, sir, but you ain't as poor as me, because I've not only got nothing but I've got minus nothing."

"Too late to cry now, Jackson."

They climbed into the car, drove south on 134th Street, east to the corner of Lenox Avenue, and parked in front of the *H. Exodus Clay Funeral Parlor.*

Jackson got out and went silently up the red rubber treads of the high stone steps; entered through the curtained glass doors of the old stone house, and peered into the dimly lit chapel where three bodies were on display in the open caskets.

Smitty, the other chauffeur and handyman, was silently embracing a woman on one of the red, velvet-covered benches similar to the ones on which the caskets stood. He hadn't heard Jackson enter.

Jackson tiptoed past them silently and went down the hall to
the broom closet. He got a dust mop and cloth and tiptoed back
to the office at the front.

At that time of afternoon, when they didn't have a funeral,
Mr. Clay took a nap on the couch in his office. Marcus, the
embalmer, was left in charge. But Marcus always slipped out to
Small's bar, over on 135th Street and Seventh Avenue.

Silently Jackson opened the door of Mr. Clay's office, tiptoed inside, stood the dust mop against the wall and began
dusting the small black safe that sat in the corner beside an
old-fashioned roll-top desk. The door of the safe was closed but
not locked.

Mr. Clay lay on his side, facing the wall. He looked like a
refugee from a museum, in the dim light from the floor-lamp
that burned continuously in the front window.

He was a small, elderly man with skin like parchment, faded
brown eyes, and long gray bushy hair. His standard dress was a
tail coat, double-breasted dove-gray vest, striped trousers, wing
collar, black Ascot tie adorned with a gray pearl stickpin, and
rimless nose-glasses attached to a long black ribbon pinned to
his vest.

"That you, Marcus?" he asked suddenly without turning
over.

Jackson started. "No sir, it's me, Jackson."

"What are you doing in here, Jackson?"

"I'm just dusting, Mr. Clay," Jackson said, as he eased open
the door of the safe.

"I thought you took the afternoon off."

"Yes sir. But I recalled that Mr. Williams' family will be
coming tonight to view Mr. Williams' remains, and I knew
you'd want everything spic and span when they got here."

"Don't overdo it, Jackson," Mr. Clay said sleepily. "I ain't
intending to give you a raise."

Jackson forced himself to laugh.

"Aw, you're just joking, Mr. Clay. Anyway, my woman ain't
home. She's gone visiting."

While he was speaking, Jackson opened the inner safe door.

"Thought that was the trouble," Mr. Clay mumbled.

In the money drawer was a stack of twenty-dollar bills, pinned together in bundles of hundreds.

"Ha ha, you're just joking, Mr. Clay," Jackson said as he took out five bundles and stuck them into his side pants pocket.

He rattled the handle of the dust mop while closing the safe's two doors.

"Lord, you just have to forgive me in this emergency," he said silently, then spoke in a loud voice, "Got to clean the steps now."

Mr. Clay didn't answer.

Jackson tiptoed back to the broom closet, put away the cloth and mop, tiptoed silently back toward the front door. Smitty and the woman were still enjoying life.

Jackson let himself out silently and went down the stairs to the marshal's car. He palmed two of the hundred-dollar bundles and slipped them through the open window to the marshal.

The marshal held them down between his legs while he counted them. Then he nodded and stuck them into his inside coat pocket.

"Let this be a lesson to you, Jackson," he said. "Crime doesn't pay."

II

AS SOON AS the marshal drove off, Jackson started running. He knew that Mr. Clay would count his money the first thing on awakening. Not because he suspected anybody would steal it. There was always someone on duty. It was just a habit. Mr. Clay counted his money when he went to sleep and when he woke up, when he unlocked his safe and when he locked it. If he wasn't busy, he counted it fifteen to twenty times a day.

Jackson knew that Mr. Clay would begin questioning the help when he missed the five hundred. He wouldn't call in the police until he was dead certain who had stolen his money. That was because Mr. Clay believed in ghosts. Mr. Clay knew damn well if ever the ghosts started collecting the money he'd cheated their relatives out of, he'd be headed for the poor house.

Jackson knew that next Mr. Clay would go to his room searching for him.

He was pressed but not panicked. If the Lord would just give him time enough to locate Hank and get him to raise the three hundred into three thousand, he might be able to slip the money back into the safe before Mr. Clay began suspecting him.

But first he had to get the twenty-dollar bills changed into ten-dollar bills. Hank couldn't raise twenties because there was no such thing as a two-hundred-dollar bill.

He ran down to Seventh Avenue and turned into Small's bar. Marcus spotted him. He didn't want Marcus to see him changing the money. He came in by one door and went out by the other; ran up the street to the Red Rooster. They only had sixteen tens in the cash register. Jackson took those and started out. A customer stopped him and changed the rest.

Jackson came out on Seventh Avenue and ran down 142nd Street toward home. It came to him, as he was slipping and sliding on the wet icy sidewalks, that he didn't know where to look for Hank. Imabelle had met Jodie at her sister's apartment in the Bronx.

Imabelle's sister, Margie, had told Imabelle that Jodie knew a man who could make money. Imabelle had brought Jodie to talk to Jackson about it. When Jackson said he'd give it a trial, it had been Jodie who'd gotten in touch with Hank.

Jackson felt certain that Imabelle would know where to find Jodie if not Hank. The only thing was, he didn't know where Imabelle was.

He stopped across the street and looked up at the kitchen window to see if the light was on. It was dark. He tried to remember if it was himself or the marshal who'd turned off the light. It didn't make any difference anyway. If the landlady had returned from work she was sure to be in the kitchen raising fifteen million dollars' worth of hell.

Jackson went around to the front of the apartment house and climbed the four flights of stairs. He listened at the front door of the apartment. He didn't hear a sound from inside. He unlocked the door, slipped quietly within. He didn't hear anyone moving about. He tiptoed down to his room and closed himself in. Imabelle hadn't returned.

He wasn't worried about her. Imabelle could take care of herself. But time was pressing him.

While trying to decide whether to wait there or go out and look for her, he heard the front door being unlocked. Someone entered the front hall, closed and locked the door. Footsteps approached. The first hall door was opened.

"Claude," an irritable woman's voice called.

There was no reply. The footsteps crossed the hall. The opposite door was opened.

"Mr. Canefield."

The landlady was calling the roll.

"As evil a woman as God ever made," Jackson muttered. "He must have made her by mistake."

More footsteps sounded. Jackson crawled quickly underneath the bed, keeping his overcoat and hat on. He heard the door being opened.

"Jackson."

Jackson could feel her examining the room. He heard her try to open Imabelle's big steamer trunk.

"They keeps this trunk locked all the time," she complained to herself. "Him and that woman. Living in sin. And him calls himself a Christian. If Christ knew what kind of Christians He got here in Harlem He'd climb back up on the cross and start over."

Jackson heard her walk back toward the kitchen. He rolled from underneath the bed and got to his feet.

"Merciful Lawd!" he heard her exclaim. "Somebody done blowed up my brand-new stove."

Jackson flung open the door to his room and ran down the hall. He got out of the front door before she saw him. He went upstairs instead of down, taking the stairs two at a time. He had scarcely turned at the landing when he heard the landlady run out into the corridor, chasing him.

"Who you be, you dirty bastard!" she yelled. "It you, Jackson, or Claude? Blew up my stove!"

He came out on the roof and ran to the roof of the adjoining building, past a pigeon cage, and found the door to the stairway unlocked. He went down the stairs like a bouncing ball but stopped at the street doorway to reconnoiter.

The landlady was peering from her doorway in the other building. He drew back his head before she saw him, and watched the sidewalk from an angle.

He saw Mr. Clay's personal Cadillac sedan turn the corner and pull in at the curb. Smitty, the other chauffeur, was driving. Mr. Clay got out and went inside.

Jackson knew they were looking for him. He turned, running, and went through the hallway and out of the back door. There was a small concrete courtyard filled with garbage cans and trash, closed in by high concrete walls. He put a half-filled garbage can against the wall and climbed over, tearing the middle button from his overcoat. He came out in the back courtyard of the building that faced 142nd Street. He ran through the hallway and turned towards Seventh Avenue.

A cruising taxi came in his direction. He hailed it. He'd have to break one of the ten-dollar bills, and that would cost him a hundred dollars, but there was no help for it now. It was just hurry-hurry.

A black boy was driving. Jackson gave him the address of Imabelle's sister in the Bronx. The black boy made a U-turn in the icy street as though he liked skating, and took off like a lunatic.

"I'm in a hurry," Jackson said.

"I'm hurrying, ain't I?" the black boy called over his shoulder.

"But I ain't in no hurry to get to heaven."

"We ain't going to heaven."

"That's what I'm scared of."

The black boy wasn't thinking about Jackson. Speed gave him power and made him feel as mighty as Joe Louis. He had his long arms wrapped about the steering wheel and his big foot jammed on the gas, thinking of how he could drive that goddam DeSoto taxicab straight off the mother-raping earth.

Margie lived in a flat on Franklin Avenue. It was a thirty-minute trip by rights, but the black boy made it in eighteen, Jackson biting his nails all the way.

Margie's husband hadn't come home from work. She looked like Imabelle, only more proper. She was straightening her hair when Jackson arrived and had a mean yellow look at being disturbed. The house smelled like a singed pig.

"Is Imabelle here?" Jackson asked wiping the sweat from his head and face and pulling down the crotch of his pants.

"No, she is not. Why did not you telephone?"

"I didn't know y'all had a telephone. When'd y'all get it?"

"Yesterday."

"I ain't seen you since yesterday."

"No, you have not, have you?"

She went back to the kitchen where her hair irons were on the fire. Jackson followed her, keeping his overcoat on.

"You know where she might be?"

"Do I know where who might be?"

"Imabelle?"

"Oh, her? How do I know if you do not know? You are the one who is keeping her."

"Know where I can find Jodie, then?"

"Jodie? And who might Jodie be?"

"I don't know his last name. He's the man who told you and Imabelle about the man who raises money."

"Raises money for what?"

Jackson was getting mad. "Raises it to spend, that's for what. He raises dollar bills into ten-dollar bills and ten-dollar bills into hundred-dollar bills."

She turned around from the stove and looked at Jackson.

"Is you drunk? If you is, I want you to get out of here and do not come back until you is sober."

"I ain't drunk. You sound more drunk than me. She met the man right here in your house."

"In my house? A man who raises ten-dollar bills into hundred-dollar bills? If you are not drunk, you is crazy. If I had met that man, he would still be here, chained to the floor, working his ass off every day."

"I ain't in no mood for joking."

"Do you think I am joking?"

"I mean the other one—Jodie. The one who knew the man who raises the money."

Margie picked up the straightening iron and began to run it through her kinky reddish hair. Smoke rose from the frying locks and a sound was heard like chops sizzling.

"God damn it, you have done made me burn my hair!" she raved.

"I'm sorry, but this is important."

"You mean my hair ain't important?"

"No, I don't mean that. I mean I got to find her."

She brandished the hot hair-iron like a club.

"Jackson, will you please take your ass away from here and let me alone? If Ima told you she met somebody in my house called Jodie, she is just lying. And if you do not know by this time that she is a lying bitch, you is a fool."

"That ain't no way to talk about your sister. I don't thank you for that one little bit."

"Who asked you to come here bothering me, anyway?" she shouted.

Jackson put on his hat and left in a huff. He began to feel cornered and panicky. He had to get his money raised before morning or he was jailhouse-bound, and he didn't know where else to look for Imabelle. He had met her at the Undertaker's Annual Dance in the Savoy Ballroom the year before. She'd been doing day work for the white folks downtown and didn't have a steady boyfriend. He'd started taking her out, but that had gotten to be so expensive she'd started living with him.

They didn't have any close friends. There was nowhere she could hide. She didn't like to get chummy with folks and didn't want anybody to know too much about her. He hardly knew anything about her himself. Just that she'd come from the South somewhere.

But he'd bet his life that she was true to him. Only she was scared of something and he didn't know what. That was what had him worried. She might have gotten so scared of the marshal she'd disappear for two or three days. He could telephone her white folks the next day to see if she'd shown up for work. But that would be too late. He needed her right then to get in touch with Hank to have his money raised, or they were both going to be in trouble.

He stopped in a drugstore and telephoned his landlady. But he put his handkerchief over the mouthpiece to disguise his voice.

"Is Imabelle Jackson there, ma'am?"

"I know who you is, Jackson. You ain't fooling me," his landlady yelled into the phone.

"Ain't nobody trying to fool you lady. I just asked you if Imabelle Jackson was there."

"No, she ain't, Jackson, and if she was here she'd be in jail by now where you is going to be as soon as the police get hold of you. Busting up my brand-new stove and messing up my house and stealing money from your boss put aside to bury the dead, and the Lawd knows what else, trying to make out like you is somebody else when you telephone here, figuring I ain't gonna know your voice much as I done heard it asking me to leave you pay me the next week. Bringing that yallah woman into my house and breaking it up, good as I done been to you."

"I ain't trying to hide my voice. I'm just in a little trouble, that's all."

"You tellin' me! You is in more trouble than you knows."

"I'm going to pay you for the stove."

"If you don't I'm goin' to put you underneath the jail."

"You don't have to worry about that. I'm going to pay you first thing tomorrow."

"I go to work tomorrow."

"I'll pay you first thing when you come home from work."

"If you ain't in jail by then. What'd you steal from Mr. Clay?"

"I ain't stole nothing from nobody. What I wanted to ask was if Imabelle comes home you tell her to get in touch with Hank—"

"If she comes here tonight, her or you either, and don't bring a hundred and fifty-seven dollars and ninety-five cents to pay for my stove, she ain't goin' to have no chance to get in touch with nobody, unless it be the judge she goin' to meet tomorrow morning."

"You call yourself a Christian," Jackson said angrily. "Here we are in trouble and—"

"Who's any worse Christian than you!" she shouted. "A thief and a liar! Living in sin! Busting my stove! Robbin' the dead! The Lawd don't even know you, I tell you that!"

She banged down the receiver so hard it stung Jackson's ears.

He left the booth, wiping the sweat from his round, shiny black face and head.

"Calls herself a Christian," he muttered to himself. "Couldn't be more of a devil if she had two horns."

He stood on the corner bareheaded, cooling his brain. There was nothing left now but to pray. He hailed a taxi, rode back to his minister's house on 139th Street in Sugar Hill.

Reverend Gaines was a big black man with a mighty voice, deeply religious. He believed in a fire-and-brimstone hell and had no sympathy for sinners whom he couldn't convert. If they didn't want to reform, accept the Lord, join the church, and live righteously, then burn them in hell. No two ways about it. A man couldn't be a Christian on Sunday and sin six days a week. Such a man must take God for a fool.

He was writing his sermon when Jackson arrived. But he put it aside for a good church-member.

"Welcome, Brother Jackson. What brings you to the house of the shepherd of the Lord?"

"I'm in trouble, Reverend."

Reverend Gaines fingered the satin lapel of his blue flannel smoking-jacket. The diamond on his third finger sparkled in the light.

"Woman?" he asked softly.

"No, sir. My woman's true. We're going to get married as soon as she gets her divorce."

"Don't wait too long, Brother. Adultery is a mortal sin."

"We can't do anything until she finds her husband."

"Money?"

"Yes, sir."

"Have you stolen some money, Brother Jackson?"

"Not exactly. I just need some money bad. Or it's going to look as if I stole some."

"Ah, yes, I understand," Reverend Gaines said. "Let us pray, Jackson."

"Yes, sir, that's what I want."

They knelt side by side on the carpeted floor. Reverend Gaines did the praying.

"Lord, help this brother to overcome his difficulties."

"Amen," Jackson said.

"Help him to get the money he needs by honest means."

"Amen."

"Help his woman find her husband so she can get her divorce and live righteously."

"Amen."

"Bless all the poor sinners in Harlem who find themselves having these many difficulties with women and money."

"Amen."

Reverend Gaines's housekeeper knocked at the door and stuck her head inside.

"Dinner is ready, Reverend," she said. "Mrs. Gaines has already sat down."

Reverend Gaines said, "Amen."

All Jackson could do was echo, "Amen."

"The Lord helps those who help themselves, Brother Jackson," Reverend Gaines said, hurrying off to dinner.

Jackson felt a lot better. His panic had passed and he began thinking with his head instead of his feet. The main thing was to have the Lord on his side. He had begun to think the Lord had quit him.

He caught a taxi on Seventh Avenue, rode down to 125th Street and turned over to the Last Word, a shoe-shine parlor and record shop at the corner of Eighth Avenue.

He put ninety dollars on numbers in the night house, playing five dollars on each. He played the *money row, lucky lady, happy days, true love, sun gonna shine, gold, silver, diamonds, dollars* and *whiskey*. Then to be on the safe side he also played *jail house, death row, lady come back, two-timing woman, pile of rocks, dark days* and *trouble*. He wasn't taking any chances.

While he was putting in his numbers behind blown-up pictures of Bach and Beethoven, the girl selling the real stuff played rock-and-roll records on request, and the shoe-shine boys were beating out the rhythm with their shine cloths. Jackson's feet took out with the beat, cutting out the steps, as though they didn't know about the trouble in his head.

Suddenly Jackson began feeling lucky. He gave up on the hope of finding Hank. He stopped worrying about Imabelle. He felt as though he could throw four fours in a row.

"Man, you know one thing, I feel good," he said to the shoe-shine boy.

"A good feeling is a sign of death, Daddy-o," the boy said.

Jackson put his faith in the Lord and headed for the dice game upstairs on 126th Street, around the corner.

III

JACKSON CLIMBED THREE flights of stairs and rapped on a red door in a brightly lit hall.

A metal disk moved from a round peephole. Jackson couldn't see the face, but the lookout saw him.

The door opened. Jackson went into an ordinary kitchen.

"You want to roll 'em or roll with 'em?" the lookout asked.

"Roll 'em," Jackson said.

The lookout searched him, took his fingernail knife and put it on the pantry shelf alongside several man-killing knives and hard-shooting pistols.

"How can I hurt anybody with that?" Jackson protested.

"You can jab out their eyes."

"The blade ain't long enough to go through the eyelid."

"Don't argue, man, just go down to the last door to the right," the lookout said, leaning against the door frame.

There were three loose nails in the door casing. By pressing them the lookout could blink the lights in the parlor, bed-rooms, and dice room. One blink for a new customer, two for the law.

Another lookout opened the door from the inside of the dice room, closed and locked it behind Jackson.

There was a billiard table in the center of the room, and

a rack holding billiard balls and cue sticks on one wall. The shooters were jammed about the table beneath a glare of light from a green-shaded drop-lamp. The stick man stood on one side of the table, handling the dice and bets. Across from him sat the rack man on a high stool, changing greenbacks into silver dollars and banking the cuts. He cut a quarter on all bets up to five dollars, and fifty cents on bets over five dollars.

The bookies sat at each end of the table. A squat, bald-headed, brown-skinned man called Stack of Dollars sat at one end; a gray-haired white man called Abie the Jew sat at the other. Stack of Dollars bet the dice to lose; took any bet to win. Abie the Jew bet the dice to win or lose, barring box cars and snake eyes.

It was the biggest standing crap game in Harlem.

Jackson knew all the famous shooters by sight. They were celebrities in Harlem. Red Horse, Four-Four and Coots were professional gamblers; Sweet Wine, Rock Candy, Chink and Beauty were pimps; Doc Henderson was a dentist; Mister Foot was a numbers banker.

Red Horse was shooting. He shook the number eight bird's eye dice loosely in his left hand, rolled them with his right hand. The dice rolled evenly down the green velvet cover, jumped the dog chain stretched across the middle of the table like two steeplechasers in a dead heat, came to a stop on four and three.

"Four-trey, the country way," the stick man sang, raking in the dice. "Seven! The loser!"

Rock Candy reached for the money in the pot. Stack of Dollars raked in his bets. Abie took some, paid some.

"You goin' to buck 'em?" the stick man asked.

Red Horse shook his head. He could pay a dollar for three more rolls.

"Next good shooter," the stick man sang and looked at Jackson. "What you shoot, short-black-and-fat?"

"Ten bucks."

Jackson threw a ten-dollar bill and fifty cents into the circle. Red Horse covered it. The bettors got down, win and lose, in the books. The stick man threw the dice to Jackson, who caught the dice, held them in his cupped hand close to his mouth and talked to them.

"Just get me out of this trouble and I ain't goin' to ask for no more." He crossed himself, then shook the dice to get them hot.

"Turn 'em loose, Reverend," the stick man said. "They ain't titties and you ain't no baby. Let 'em run wild in the big corral."

Jackson turned them loose. They hopped across the green like scared jackrabbits, jumped the dog chain like frisky kangaroos, romped toward Abie's field-cloth like locoed steers, got tired and rested on six and five.

"Natural eleven!" the stick man sang. "Eleven from heaven. The winner!"

Jackson let his money ride, threw another natural for the twenty; then crapped out for the forty with snake eyes. He shot ten again, threw seven, let the twenty ride, threw another seven, shot the forty, and crapped out again. He was twenty dollars loser. He wiped the sweat from his face and head, took off his overcoat, put it with his hat on the coat rack, loosened the double-breasted jacket of his black hard-finished suit, and said to the dice, "Dice, I beg you with tears in my eyes as big as water-melons."

He shot ten again, rapped three times in a row, and asked the stick man to change the dice.

"These don't know me," he said.

The stick man put in some black-eyed number eight dice that were stone cold. Jackson warmed them in his crotch, and threw four naturals in a row. He had eighty dollars in the pot. He took down the fifty dollars he had lost and shot the thirty. He caught a four and jumped it, took down another fifty, and shot ten.

"Jealous man can't gamble, scared man can't win," the stick man crooned.

The bettors got off Jackson to win and bet him to lose. He caught six and sevened out.

"Shooter for the game," the stick man sang. "The more you put down the more you pick up."

The dice went on to the next shooter.

By midnight Jackson was $180 ahead. He had $376, but he needed $657.95 to cover the $500 he had stolen from Mr. Clay and the $157.95 to pay for his landlady's stove.

He quit and went back to the Last Word to see if he had hit on the numbers. The last word for that night was 919, dead man's row.

So Jackson went back to the dice game.

He prayed to the dice; he begged them. "I got pains in my heart as sharp as razor blades, and misery in my mind as deep as the bottom of the ocean and tall as the Rocky Mountains."

He took off his coat when it came his second turn to shoot. His shirt was wet. His trousers chafed his crotch. He loosened his suspenders when his third turn came and let them hang down his legs.

Jackson threw more natural sevens and elevens than had ever been seen in that game before. But he threw more craps, twos, threes and twelves, than he did natural sevens and elevens. And as all good crapshooters know, crapping is the way you lose.

Day was breaking when the game gave out. They had Jackson. He was stone-cold broke. He borrowed fifty cents from the house and trudged slowly down to the snack bar in the Theresa Hotel. He got a cup of coffee and two doughnuts for thirty cents and stood at the counter.

His eyes were glazed. His black skin had turned putty-gray. He was as tired as though he'd been plowing rocks with a mule team.

"You look beat," the counterman said.

"I feel low enough to be buried in whalebones, and they're on the bottom of the sea," he confessed.

The counterman watched him gobble his doughnuts and gulp his coffee.

"You must have got broke in that crap game."

"I did," Jackson confessed.

"Looks like it. They say a rich man can't sleep, but a broke man can't get enough to eat."

Jackson looked up at the clock on the wall and the clock said hurry-hurry. Mr. Clay came down from his living quarters at nine o'clock sharp. Jackson knew he'd have to be there with the money and find some way to slip it back into the safe when Mr. Clay opened it if he expected to get away with it.

Imabelle could raise the money, but he hated to ask her. It meant she'd have to be dishonest. But the kind of trouble they were in now would make a rat eat red pepper.

He went into the hotel lobby next door and telephoned his apartment.

The Theresa lobby was dead at that hour save for a few working johns who had to make eight o'clock time downtown, and were hurrying into the hotel grill for their morning grits and bacon.

His landlady answered.

"Is Imabelle come home?" he asked.

"Your yallah woman is in jail where you ought to be too," she answered evilly.

"In jail? How come?"

"Right after you phoned here last night a United States marshal brought her back here under arrest. He was looking for you too, Jackson, and if I'd knowed where you was I'd have told him. He wanted you both on a counterfeiting charge."

"A United States marshal? He had her under arrest? What'd he look like?"

"He said you knew him."

"What did he do with Imabelle?"

"He took her to jail, that's what. And he confiscated her trunk and took that along in case he didn't find you."

"Her trunk?" Jackson was so stunned he could barely speak. "He confiscated her trunk? And took it with him?"

"He sure did, lover boy. And when he finds you—"

"Good God! He confiscated her trunk? What did he say his name was?"

"Don't ask me no more questions, Jackson. I ain't going to get myself in any trouble helping you to escape."

"You ain't got a Christian bone inside of you," he said, and slowly hung up the receiver.

He stood sagging against the wall of the telephone booth.

He felt as though he had stumbled into quicksand. Every time he struggled to get out, he went in deeper.

He couldn't figure out how the marshal managed to get hold of Imabelle's trunk. How had he found out what was in it—unless he had scared her enough to make her tell? And that meant she was in trouble.

What made it so bad for Jackson was he didn't know where to look for the marshal. He had no idea where the marshal had taken Imabelle. He didn't believe the marshal had taken her to the federal jail because the marshal was out for all he could get. The marshal wouldn't take her trunk down to the jail if he expected to get a cut for himself. But Jackson had no idea how to go about tracing him. And he didn't know what he could do to save her trunk if he found the marshal.

He stood on the empty sidewalk in front of the Theresa, trying to think of a way out. His face was knotted from mental effort. Finally he muttered to himself, "There ain't no help for it."

He'd have to see his twin brother Goldy. Goldy knew everybody in Harlem.

He didn't know where Goldy lived, so he'd have to wait until noon when Goldy appeared on the street. He was afraid to loiter on the street himself. He didn't have the price of a movie, although there was one in the block that opened at eight o'clock in the morning. But there was a professional building around the corner on 125th Street with a number of doctors' offices.

He went up on the second floor and sat in a doctor's waiting room. The doctor hadn't arrived, but there were already four patients waiting. He kept moving back in line, after the doctor had arrived, letting everybody go ahead of him.

The receptionist kept looking at him from time to time. Finally she asked in a hard voice, "Are you sick or aren't you?"

By then it was almost noon.

"I was, but I feel better now," he said and put his hat on and left.

IV

THE PLATE-GLASS front of Blumstein's Department Store, exhibiting eye-catching items of wearing apparel and house furnishings for the residents of Harlem, extended from the back of the Theresa Hotel a half block down 125th Street.

A Sister of Mercy sat on a campstool to one side of the entrance, shaking a round black collection box at the passersby and smiling sadly.

She was dressed in a long black gown, similar to the vestments of a nun, with a white starched bonnet atop a fringe of gray hair. A large gold cross, attached to a black ribbon, hung at her breast. She had a smooth-skinned, round black cherubic face, and two gold teeth in front which gleamed when she smiled.

No one paid her any special attention. There were many black Sisters of Mercy seen throughout Manhattan. They solicited in the big department stores downtown, on Fifth Avenue, in the railroad stations, up and down 42nd Street and throughout Times Square. Only a few persons knew the name of the organization they belonged to. Most of the Harlem folk thought they were nuns, just the same as there were black, kinky-headed, frizzly-bearded rabbis seen about the streets.

She glanced up at Jackson and whispered in a prayerful voice, "Give to the Lawd, Brother. Give to the poor."

Jackson stopped to one side of her stool and examined the nylon stockings on display in the window.

A colored drunk, staggering past, turned around and leered at the Sister of Mercy.

"Bless me, Sistah. Bless old Mose," he mumbled, trying to be funny.

"'Knowest not that thou art wretched, and miserable, and poor, and blind, and naked,' sayeth the Lawd," the Sister quoted.

The drunk blinked and staggered hurriedly away.

A little black girl with witch-plaited hair ran up to the nun and said in a breathless voice, "Sister Gabriel, Mama wants two tickets to heaven. Uncle Pone's dyin'."

She stuck two one-dollar bills into the nun's hand.

" 'Buy of me gold tried in the fire,' sayeth the Lawd," the nun whispered, tucking the bucks inside her gown. "What do she want two for, child?"

"Mama say Uncle Pone need two."

The nun slipped a black hand into the folds of her gown, drew out two white cards, and gave them to the little girl. Printed on the cards were the words:

ADMIT ONE
Sister Gabriel

"These'll take Uncle Pone to the bosom of the Lawd," she promised. " 'And I saw heaven opened, and beheld a white horse.' "

"Amen," the little girl said, and ran off with the two tickets to heaven.

"Shame on you, Goldy. Blaspheming the Lord like that," Jackson whispered. "The police are going to get you for selling those tickets."

"Ain't no law against it," Goldy whispered in reply. "They just say 'Admit One.' They don't say to where. Might be to the Savoy Ballroom."

"There's a law against impersonating a female," Jackson said disgustedly.

"You let the police take care of the law, Bruzz."

A couple approached to enter the store. Goldy rattled his coin box.

"Give to the Lawd, give to the poor," he begged prayerfully.

The woman stopped and dropped three pennies into the box.

Goldy's saintly smile went sour.

"Bless you, Mother, bless you. If three little pennies is all the Lawd is worth to you, then bless you."

The woman's dark brown skin turned purple. She dug up a dime.

"Bless you, Mother. Praise be the Lawd," Goldy whispered indifferently.

The woman went inside the store, but she could feel the eyes of the Lord pinned on her and the angels in heaven whispering among themselves, "What a cheapskate!" She was too ashamed to buy the dress she'd come for and she was unhappy all the rest of the day.

"I got to see you, Goldy," Jackson said, looking at the nylons in the window.

Two teenage girls were passing at the time and heard him. They had no idea he was speaking to the Sister of Mercy and there was no one else nearby. They began giggling.

"A stockin' freak," one said.

The other replied, "He calls them Goldy, too."

Goldy brushed imaginary dust from his lap, took another look at Jackson's face, then stood up slowly, moving like an elderly woman, and folded the campstool.

"Stay in back of me," he whispered. " 'Way back."

He put the stool under one arm, jangled the coin box in the other hand, and trudged down the slushy sidewalk toward Seventh Avenue, blessing the colored folk who fed coins into the kitty. He looked like a tired, fat, saintly black woman, slaving in the service of the Lord.

He was a familiar sight. No one gave him a second look.

Seventh Avenue and 125th Street is the center of Harlem, the crossroads of Black America. On one corner was the largest hotel. Diagonally across from it was a big credit jewelry store with its windows filled with diamonds and watches selling for so much down and so much weekly. Next door was a book store with a big red-and-yellow sign reading: *Books of 6,000,000 Colored People.* On the other corner was a mission church.

The people of Harlem take their religion seriously. If Goldy had taken off in a flaming chariot and galloped straight to heaven, they would have believed it—the godly and the sinners alike.

Goldy turned south on Seventh Avenue, past the Theresa Hotel entrance, past Sugar Ray's Tavern, past the barber shop where the sharp cats got their nappy kinks straightened with a mixture of Vaseline and potash lye. He turned east on 121st Street into the Valley, climbed over piles of frozen garbage, kicked a mangy cur in the ribs, and entered a grimy tobacco-store which fronted for a numbers drop and reefer shop. Three teenage boys had a fifteen-year-old girl inside, all blowing gage. They were trying to get her to undress.

"Go ahead, take 'em off, baby, take 'em off."

"Ain't nobody comin'. Go ahead and strip."

"Why don't you punks leave the girl alone," the proprietor said half-heartedly. "You can see she's 'shamed of her shape."

"I ain't 'shamed, neither," she said. "I got a good shape and I know it."

"Course you have," the proprietor said, winking at her lecherously.

He was a tall, dirty-looking yellow man with a lumpy pock-marked face and swimming red eyes.

"Bless the Lawd, Soldier," Goldy greeted him on entering. "Bless the Lawd, children." He gave the teenagers a confidential look and quoted, " 'By these three was the third part of men killed, by the fire and by the smoke and by the brimstone which issued out of their mouths.' "

"Amen, Sister," the owner said, winking at Goldy.

The girl snickered. The boys fidgeted indecisively and shut up for a moment.

No one who noticed it thought it strange for a Sister of Mercy to kick a cur dog in the ribs, enter a dope den, and quote enigmatic Scripture to reefer-smoking delinquents.

In silence, Goldy waited for Jackson to catch up, then took him through the rear door, down a damp dark hallway, stinking of many varieties of excrement, and opened a padlocked door. He switched on a dim, fly-specked drop-lamp, slipped warily into a damp, cold, windowless room furnished with a scarred wooden table, two wobbly straight-backed chairs, a couch covered with dirty gray blankets. Against one wall, mildewed cardboard cartons were stacked one atop the other. The other dark-gray concrete walls sweated from the chill, damp air.

After Jackson had entered, Goldy padlocked the door on the inside and lit a rusty black kerosene stove which smoked and stank. He then threw the stool onto the couch, put his money box on the table, and sat down with a long sigh. He took off his white bonnet and gray wig.

Seen without his disguise, he was the spitting image of Jackson. White people in the South, where they had come from, had called them the Gold Dust Twins because of their resemblance to the twins pictured on the yellow boxes of Gold Dust soap powder.

"I don't live here," Goldy said. "This is just my office."

"I don't see how nobody could," Jackson said as he eased his weight onto one of the wobbly chairs.

"There's people lives in worse places," Goldy said.

Jackson wouldn't argue the point. "Goldy, there's something I want to ask you."

"I got to feed my monkey first."

Jackson looked about for the monkey.

"He's on my back," Goldy explained.

Jackson watched him with silent disgust as Goldy took an alcohol lamp, teaspoon and a hypodermic needle from the table drawer. Goldy shook two small papers of crystal cocaine and morphine into the spoon and cooked a C and M speedball over the flame. He groaned as he banged himself in the arm while the mixture was still warm.

"It's the same stuff as Saint John the Divine used," Goldy said. "Did you know that, Bruzz? You're a churchgoing man."

Jackson was glad none of his acquaintances knew he had such a brother as Goldy, a dope-fiend crook impersonating a Sister of Mercy. Especially Imabelle. That'd be reason enough for her to quit him.

"I ain't never going to own you as my brother," he said.

"Well, Bruzz, that goes for me too. Now what's on your mind?"

"What I wanted to ask is do you know a colored United States marshal here in Harlem? He's a tall, slim colored man, and he's crooked too."

Goldy's ears perked up. "A colored U.S. marshal? And crooked? What you mean by crooked?"

"He's always trying to get bribes out of people."

Goldy smiled evilly. "What's the matter, Bruzz? You get shook down by some colored marshal?"

"Well, it was like this. I was having some money raised—"

"Raised?" Goldy's eyes popped.

"I was having ten-dollar bills raised into hundred-dollar bills."

"How much?"

"To tell the truth, all I had in the world. Fifteen hundred dollars."

"And you looked to get fifteen thousand?"

"Only twelve thousand, two hundred and fifty, after I paid off the commissions."

"And you got arrested?"

Jackson nodded. "During the operation the marshal broke into the kitchen and put us all under arrest. But the others got away."

Goldy burst out laughing and couldn't stop. The C and M speedball had taken hold and the pupils of his eyes had turned as black as ebony and had gotten as big as grapes. He laughed convulsively, as though he were having a fit. Tears streamed down his face. Finally he got himself under control.

"My own brother," he gasped. "Here us is, got the same mama and papa. Look just alike. And there you is, ain't got hep yet that you been beat. You has been swindled, man. You has been taken by The Blow. They take you for your money and they blow. You catch on? Changing tens into hundreds. What happened to your brains? You been drinking embalming fluid?"

Jackson looked more hurt than angry. "But I saw him do it once before," he said. "With my own eyes. I was looking right at him all the time. A man has got to believe his own eyes, ain't he?"

It hadn't been too hard for him to believe. Other people in Harlem believed that Father Divine was God.

"Sure, you saw him do it when he was sucking you in," Goldy said. "But what you didn't see was when he made the switch. That was when he turned to put the money into the stove to cook. What he put into the oven were just plain dummies along with a black-powder bomb. He put your money into a special pocket in the front of his coat."

"Then Imabelle got fooled, too. She was watching him, just the same as me. Neither of us saw him make the switch."

Goldy's eyelids dropped. "Who's Imabelle? Your old lady?"

"She's my woman. And she believed it even more than I did. It was her who first talked to Jodie, the man who told her about Hank. And Jodie looked like an honest, hardworking man, too."

It didn't surprise Goldy that Jackson had been trimmed on The Blow. Many smart men, even other con-men, had been stung by The Blow. There was something about raising the denomination of money that appealed to the larceny in men. But with women it was different. They were always suspicious of anything that was scientific. But he didn't know how Jackson felt about his woman, so all he said was,

"She's a trusting girl, she believe all that."

Jackson puffed up with indignation. "Do you think she'd let them cheat me if she didn't believe it, too?"

"What'd she do when the stove blew up? She try to help you save your money?"

"She tried all she could. But she ain't no Annie Oakley, carrying around two pistols. When that marshal bust into the kitchen waving his gun and flashing his badge, she ran like all the rest of us were trying to do. I was trying to run, too."

"They always catch the sucker. How else are they gonna blow with their sting? And you gave the marshal some more money to let you off?"

"I didn't know he was a crook. I gave him two hundred dollars."

"Where'd you get two hundred dollars, if he'd already taken all the money you had?"

"I had to take five hundred from Mr. Clay's safe."

Goldy whistled softly. "You give me the three hundred you got left, Bruzz, and I'll find those crooks and get all your money back."

"I haven't got it," Jackson confessed. "I lost it playing the numbers and shooting dice trying to get even."

Goldy pulled up the hem of his skirt and studied his fat black legs encased in black cotton stockings.

"For a man what calls himself a Christian, you've had yourself a night. Now what you goin' to do?"

"I got to find that man who posed as the marshal. After he took my two hundred dollars he arrested Imabelle so he could shake her down, too."

"You mean he worked another bribe out of your old lady after he got yours?"

"I don't know exactly what happened. I haven't seen her since she ran out of the kitchen with the rest of them. All I know is that when I telephoned my landlady she said a United States marshal brought Imabelle back into the house and that she was under arrest. Then he confiscated her trunk and took her away somewhere. And she hasn't been back since. That's what's got me so worried."

Goldy gave his brother an incredulous look. "Did you say he took her trunk?"

Jackson nodded. "She's got a big steamer trunk."

Goldy stared so long at Jackson his eyes seemed fixed.

"What has she got in her trunk?"

Jackson evaded Goldy's stare. "Nothing but clothes and things."

Goldy kept staring at his brother.

Finally he said, "Bruzz, listen to me close. If all that broad has got in her trunk is clothes, she has teamed up with that slim stud and helped him to swindle you. How long is it goin' to take you to see that?"

"She ain't done that," Jackson contradicted flatly. "She got no need to. I'd have given her all the money if she'd asked for it."

"How you know she ain't sweet on the stud? Might not be your money she's after. Might just be a change of sheets."

Jackson's wet-black face became swollen with anger.

"Don't talk like that about her," he said threateningly. "She ain't sweet on nobody but me. We're going to get married. Besides, she ain't seen nobody else."

Goldy shrugged. "You figure it out yourself then, Bruzz.

She's gone off with the man who beat you out o' your money.
If she don't want the man and if she don't want the money—"

"She ain't run off, he taken her off," Jackson interrupted.
"Besides which, if she'd wanted money she got her own money,
herself. She can put her hand on more money than either you
or me have ever seen."

Goldy's fat black body went dead still. Not an eyelash flickered, not a muscle moved in his face. He seemed not to breathe.
If she had more money than either of them had ever seen, it
was getting down to the nitty-gritty. Those were facts he understood. Money! And she had it stashed in her trunk, else why
did she and the slim stud come back for it? She couldn't have
had any clothes in there worth taking, not after living with a
low-paid flunky like his twin brother.

His huge black-pupiled eyes lingered trance-like on Jackson's wet, worried face.

"I'm goin' to help you find your gal, Bruzz," he whispered
confidentially. "After all, you is my twin brother."

He took a small bottle from his gown and handed it to Jackson. "Have a little taste."

Jackson shook his head.

"Go ahead and take a taste," Goldy urged irritably. "If the
devil ain't already got your soul after all you done last night,
you is saved. Take a good taste. We're going out and look for
that stud and your gal, and you is goin' to need all the courage
you can get."

Jackson wiped the mouth of the bottle with his dirty handkerchief and took a deep drink. The next instant he was gasping
for breath. It had tasted like musty tequila flavored with chicken
bile, and it had burned his gullet like cayenne pepper.

"Lord in Heaven!" he gasped. "What's that stuff?"

"Ain't nothing but smoke," Goldy said. "There's lots of folks
here in the Valley won't drink nothing else."

The drink numbed Jackson's brain. He forgot what he'd
come there for. He sat on the couch trying to get his thoughts
together.

Goldy sat across the table, silently staring at him. Goldy's
huge, black-pupiled eyes were hypnotic. They looked like

glinting black pools of evil. Jackson tried to tear his gaze away but couldn't.

Finally Goldy stood up and put on his wig and bonnet. He hadn't said anything yet.

Jackson tried to stand too, but the room began to spin. He suddenly suspected Goldy of poisoning him.

"I'll kill you," he said thickly, trying to spring toward his brother.

But the walls of the little room were spinning like a million buzz saws rotating about his head. He couldn't defend himself when Goldy took him beneath the armpits and laid him on the couch.

V

GOLDY LIVED WITH two other men on the Golden Ridge of Convent Avenue, north of City College and 140th Street. They had the ground floor of a brownstone private house that had been cut up into apartments.

All three impersonated females and lived by their wits. All were fat and black, which made it easy.

The biggest one, known as Big Kathy, was the land-prop of a house of prostitution in the Valley, on 131st Street east of Seventh Avenue. His house was known far and wide as The Circus.

The other had a flat on 116th Street where he worked the fortune-telling pitch, billing himself as Lady Gypsy. There was a card on his door that read:

LADY GYPSY
Fortune Telling
Prognostications
Formulations
Interpretations
Revelations
Numbers Given

An old woman known as Mother Goose cleaned and cooked
for them. At home they always acted with decorum. All of
them were on junk, but they never used it in their house. They
never entertained. At night a shaded floor-lamp shone in the
front window, but no one was ever seen. That was because no
one was ever there. They had the reputation of being the most
respectable women on a street where the colored folk were so
respectable they'd phone the sanitation department to remove
cat droppings from the sidewalk. People in the neighborhood
knew them as the Three Black Widows.

Goldy had a wife who lived in a flat in Lenox Avenue next
door to the Savoy Ballroom. But she worked in domestic service for a white family in White Plains, and was home only on
Thursdays and every other Sunday afternoon. On those days
Sister Gabriel was missing from his customary haunts.

When Goldy left Jackson he went home to have breakfast
with Big Kathy and Lady Gypsy. They were having baked ham,
lye hominy, stewed okra and corn, Southern biscuits, and finished with sweet-potato pie and muscatel wine. Mother Goose
served them silently.

"How does it look ouside?" Big Kathy asked Goldy.

"Cool and clear," Goldy said. "No one has been killed,
carved up, robbed, or run over this morning, to my knowledge.
But there's some new studs in town cooking with The Blow."

"That old hick-town pitch!" Lady Gypsy exclaimed. "Here
in Harlem? Who're they going to get with that?"

"There's fools everywhere," Goldy said. "It's the Christians
full of larceny who fall for that."

"Hush man! Don't I know it?"

"Well, if they'd made a sting I'm sure I would have seen
them," Big Kathy said.

"They made a sting all right," Goldy said. "Fifteen C's."

"That's strange," Big Kathy said. "They ain't been in my
place yet to get their ashes hauled. They must be on the lam
from somewhere."

"I hadn't thought of that angle," Goldy said.

Before leaving, Goldy telephoned Jackson's landlady.

"I'm the United States Federal Attorney, and I'd like some

information about a couple who lived in your house by the name of Jackson and Imabelle Perkins."

"You mean you is the DA?" she asked in an awed tone.

"No, I'm the FA."

"Oh, you is the FA. Lawd Almighty, they's in big trouble, ain't they?" she said happily.

She told him everything she knew about them except where to find them.

But he got the name of Imabelle's sister and telephoned her next.

"This is Rufus," he said. "You don't know me but I'm a friend of Imabelle's husband back home."

"I didn't know she had a husband back home."

"Sure you know she's got a husband back home."

"If he's the same kind of husband she got here then she got two husbands."

"I don't want to argue about that. I just want to know if she's still got the stuff in her trunk."

"What stuff?"

"You know—*the* stuff."

"I do not know what stuff you are talking about, whoever you might be. And I do not know anything about my sister's husbands, wherever they might be," she said, and hung up.

Next Goldy telephoned Imabelle's white employers, but they said she hadn't been to work for three days.

So he put on his gray wig and white bonnet and went down to the Harlem branch post-office on 125th Street to study the rogue's gallery of wanted criminals.

There were pictures of three colored men wanted in Mississippi for murder. That meant they had killed a white man because killing a colored man wasn't considered murder in Mississippi. Goldy studied the faces a long time. No one looked twice at the black-gowned Sister of Mercy studying the faces of wanted criminals.

Instead of returning to his stand beside the entrance to Blumstein's Department Store, Goldy made a round of the bars and joints where they were most likely to hang out. He went up Seventh Avenue to 145th Street, east to Lenox Avenue, south on

Lenox to 125th Street again. He jangled his coin box and murmured in his husky, prayerful voice, "Give to the Lord. Give
to the poor." Whenever anyone looked at him suspiciously he
quoted from *Revelation*, " 'That ye may eat the flesh of kings.' "

"If that's what you're goin' to buy with the money, Sister,
here's a half a dollar," a colored woman said.

There were more bars on his itinerary than on any other
comparable distance on earth. In every one the jukeboxes
blared, honeysuckle-blues voices dripped stickily through
jungle cries of wailing saxophones, screaming trumpets, and
buckdancing piano-notes; someone was either fighting, or had
just stopped fighting, or was just starting to fight, or drinking
ruckus juice and talking about fighting. Others were talking
about numbers. "Man, I had twelve bones on two twenty-
seven and two thirty-seven came out." Or talking about hits
and misses. "Man, I saw that chick and hit. Man, I struck solid
gold." Or talking about love. "That was when my love came
down, sugar, and that was the bitter end."

He stopped in the dice games, the bookie joints, the barbecue stands, the barber shops, professional offices, undertakers',
flea-heaven hotels, grocery stores, meat markets called "The
Hog Maw," "Chitterling Country," "Pig Foot Heaven." He
questioned dope pushers whom he could trust.

"Have you picked up on a new team, Jack?"

"Pitching what?"

"The Blow."

"Naw, Sister, that's for the sticks."

Some knew him as a man, others thought he was a hophead
Sister. It didn't make any difference to them either way.

He looked at all the faces everywhere he went.

When the coins dropped lightly into his box, he gave out a
number, quoting from *Revelation*, " 'Let him that hath understanding count the number of the beast . . . and his number is
six hundred threescore and six.' " Jokers dropped quarters and
half-dollars into his box and rushed to the nearest numbers
drop to play six-six-six.

He was worn-out by the time he went home to eat supper.
He hadn't got a lead.

Big Kathy and Lady Gypsy were at business. He ate alone and had Mother Goose give him what was left in the pot to take to Jackson.

VI

WHEN JACKSON WOKE up he found himself lying on the couch covered with the two dirty blankets. His joints were stiff as rigor mortis and his head ached like a jack hammer was drilling in his skull. The dim light burnt his eyes like pepper and his mouth was cotton-dry.

He twisted his neck as carefully as though it were made of glass. He saw Goldy sitting at the table in his sloppy black gown but minus his bonnet and wig. A covered pot sat before him on the table. Beside it were a loaf of sliced white bread in oiled-paper wrapping and a bottle half full of whiskey.

The air was blue with smoke and thick with kerosene fumes. The room was cold.

Goldy sat dreamily blowing on the gold cross he wore about his neck and shining it with a handkerchief gray from dirt.

Jackson threw off the blankets, staggered to his feet, grabbed Goldy's fat greasy neck between his two black hands, and began to squeeze. Sweat beaded on his black face like pox pimples. His eyes had turned fire-red and looked stark crazy.

Goldy's eyes popped and his face turned rusty gray. He dropped the cross, grabbed Jackson back of the neck with both hands, jerked down with all his strength, and butted heads with him. The momentum tipped his chair over backward and he went down on his back with Jackson on top of him, both knocked groggy by the butting. The bottle of whiskey fell to the floor without breaking, and rolled beneath the couch.

The blankets had sailed over the kerosene stove and were beginning to sizzle with the smell of burning wool and cotton.

The brothers threshed about the floor, grunting like two hungry cannibals fighting over the missing rib. Finally Goldy got his foot in Jackson's belly and gave a shove, separating them.

"What's the matter with you, man," he panted. "You done blown your top?"

"You doped me!" Jackson wheezed.

The blankets draped over the stove began to burn.

"Now look what you done," Goldy said, trying to free his left foot from the folds of his gown so he could get up.

Jackson clutched the edge of the table, knocking off the loaf of bread while clambering to his feet, then stepped on it as he lunged for the burning blankets. He snatched up the blankets to throw them outside, but the door was padlocked on the inside.

"Open the door," he coughed.

The room was black dark with smoke.

"You done made me lose the key," Goldy accused, scrabbling about the floor on his hands and knees looking for it.

"Goddammit, help me find the key," he shouted angrily.

Jackson threw the blankets to the floor, and began crawling about helping Goldy search for the key.

"What do you lock the door for all the time?" he complained.

"Here it is," Goldy said.

Getting to his feet to unlock the door he stepped on the bread also.

Jackson kicked the blankets into the hallway.

"You're going to be found dead locked up in here someday," he said.

"You ain't got the brains you were born with," Goldy said, pushing Jackson aside to get through to the store for water to throw onto the smoking blankets.

Afterwards he tore up a carton and gave Jackson a piece of cardboard to help fan the smoke from the room, bellyaching the while, "Here I is, putting myself out to help you just because you is my brother, and there you is, trying to kill me first thing."

"How are you trying to help me," Jackson grumbled while he fanned the smoke. "I come to you for help and you give me a mickey finn."

"Aw, man, eat your dinner and shet up."

Jackson picked up the squashed loaf of bread and straightened it out, then sat at the table and lifted the lid of the pot. It was half-filled with boiled pig's feet, black-eyed peas and rice.

"Ain't nothin' but hoppin' john," Goldy said.

"I like hoppin' john, all right," Jackson replied.

Goldy closed the door and padlocked it again. Jackson gave him a disapproving look. Goldy found the bottle of whiskey beneath the couch and poured Jackson a slug. Jackson looked at it suspiciously. Goldy gave him an evil look.

"You wouldn't even trust our mama, would you?" he said, taking a swallow to show it wasn't doped.

Jackson took a drink and grimaced.

"Do you make this stuff yourself?"

"Man, quit beefing. You ain't givin' me no money to buy you no good whiskey, so drink that and shet up."

Jackson began to eat with an aggrieved expression. Goldy cooked a C and M speedball and banged himself with quiet savor.

"I called your landlady," he said finally. "Imabelle ain't come back."

Jackson stopped eating in the middle of a chew. "I got to go out and find her."

"Naw, you ain't, unless you want to get arrested by the first cop you run into. Your boss has got a warrant out for you."

Sweat started forming on Jackson's face. "That don't make no difference. She might be in trouble."

"She ain't in no trouble. You the one what's in trouble."

Jackson dropped a polished foot-bone atop the pile on the table, wiped his mouth with the back of his hand, and looked at Goldy with the deadly indignation of a puritan.

"Listen, if you think I'm going to set here after being cheated out of my money and kidnapped out of my woman, you got another think coming. She's my woman. I'm going to look for her too."

"Take a drink and relax. You can't find her tonight. Let's give this business a little thought."

He poured Jackson another drink. Jackson looked at it with distaste then downed it with a gulp and gasped.

"What kind of thought?"

"That's what I want to know. Just what kind of things has your woman got in that trunk besides clothes?"

Jackson blinked. The food and the whiskey and the close air in the small tight room were making him sleepy.

"Heirlooms."

"Come again."

Jackson's thoughts were growing fuzzy and he suspected Goldy of trying to trick him.

"Copper pots and pans and bowls," he shouted angrily. "Stuff that was given to her when she got married."

"Copper pots! Pans and bowls!" Goldy looked at him incredulously. "You want me to believe that her and that slim man has gone off somewhere to cook?"

Jackson was so sleepy he could barely keep his eyes open.

"Just leave her trunk alone," he mumbled belligerently. "If you want to help, just help me find her, and leave her things alone."

"That's all I'm tryin' to do, Bruzz," Goldy protested. "Just tryin' to help you find your gal-friend. But I don't know yet what I'm looking for."

Jackson was too sleepy to reply. He stretched out on the couch and went to sleep instantly.

"The stuff was too strong," Goldy muttered to himself.

VII

BY KEEPING JACKSON doped half the time and scared the other half, Goldy held him prisoner in the room. Every day he told Jackson he was working on a lead and promised him definite news by evening. But it was three days later before he got his first real lead.

The three Black Widows were having breakfast when Big Kathy said, "There was a con-man called Morgan in my place last night. He was big-mouthing to my girls about how he was going to make a fortune by the lost-gold-mine pitch. You think he's one of them you're looking for?"

Goldy became alert. "Could be. What kind of a stud was he?"

"The con-man type, half-sized and sharp but not flashy, a smooth money-talker but stingy, cat-eyed, about forty. And he looked dangerous."

"He is dangerous."

"He's one then?"

"The front man. How're they goin' to work it?"

"He didn't say. When Teena tried to dig him he clammed up and got his ashes hauled and beat it."

"Did she find out where they're making their pitch?"

"Naw, he acted as if he'd talked too much already."

"He'll be back," Goldy said philosophically.

"Yeah, that girl plays 'em for the long haul."

That evening after Jackson had finished the pot of pig's ears, collard greens and okra Goldy had taken him, and Goldy had had his evening bang, Goldy said casually, "I heard today there's a man just come to Harlem who's found a real lost gold mine somewheres."

Suddenly Jackson began trembling and sweat popped from his head and face like showers of rain.

"A gold mine?"

"That's what I said. A real lost gold mine. And the word is out that they got a trunk full of gold ore to prove it." He peered at Jackson through narrowed eyes. "Does that mean anything to you, Bruzz?"

Jackson looked suddenly sick, as though he'd swallowed a live bullfrog and it was trying to hop back out of his throat. He wiped the sweat from his ashy face and looked at Goldy through sick eyes.

"Goldy, listen, that gold ore doesn't really belong to Imabelle. That's the only reason I haven't said anything about it. It belongs to her husband. She's got to give every ounce of it back whenever she gets her divorce or he'll send her to the penitentiary. She told me."

"So that's it, Bruzz." Goldy leaned back in his chair and regarded his brother with rapt contemplation. "So that's it. That's what she's got in her trunk. You've been holding out on me, Bruzz."

"I ain't been holding out. I just didn't want you to get no ideas because that gold ore don't belong to her. I wouldn't even touch an ounce of it myself, no matter how hard up I was."

"How much is it, Bruzz? Can't be all that much or you wouldn't be losin' all your money on The Blow trying to get it raised and then stealin' money from your boss."

"That ain't got nothing to do with it. It's just that it doesn't belong to her. Do you think I'd steal some of it for myself and risk her getting sent to the penitentiary?"

"Naw, I know you wouldn't do that, Bruzz. You is too honest. But just how much is it?"

"There's two hundred pounds and eleven ounces."

Goldy whistled and his eyes popped out like skinned bananas. "Two hundred pounds! Jumping Jesus! You've seen it, ain't you? You've really seen it?"

"Of course I've seen it. Lots of times. We used to take some of it out and put it on the table and sit there with the door locked and look at it. She never tried to hide it from me."

Goldy sat staring at his brother as though he couldn't remove his gaze.

"What does it look like, Bruzz?"

"It looks like gold ore. What do you think it looks like?"

"Can you see the pure gold?"

"Sure you can see the pure gold. There're layers of gold running through the rocks."

"What kind of layers? Thin layers or thick layers?"

"Thick layers. What do you think? There's as much gold as there is rock."

"Then there's about a hundred pounds of pure gold, you'd say?"

"About that."

"A hundred pounds of pure gold." Goldy blew on his gold cross and began polishing it dreamily.

"Bruzz, listen to me. If that gold ore is the real stuff, solid eighteen-carat gold, your gal is in real trouble. If it ain't, then she's working with 'em and done helped them to trim you. Ain't no two ways about it."

"I've been tellin' you they're holding her prisoner. Been

telling you all the time," Jackson said indignantly. "Do you think she'd be toting around a trunk full of gold ore if it wasn't real eighteen-carat solid gold?"

"I ain't thinking nothing. I'm asking you. Do you know for sure that gold ore is solid eighteen-carat?"

"I know for sure," Jackson stated solemnly. "It's real gold ore, as pure as it was dug out of the ground. That's why I'm so worried."

"That's all I want to know."

Goldy knew that his brother was a square, but he figured that even a five-cornered square ought to be able to tell pure gold that has come straight out of the ground.

"Do you know where I can get a pistol?" Jackson asked suddenly.

Goldy stiffened "A pistol? What you goin' to do with a pistol?"

"I'm going out of here and get my woman and her gold ore. I ain't going to set here no longer and wait on you."

"Man, listen to me. Those studs is wanted in Mississippi for killing a white man. Those studs is dangerous. All you'd do with a pistol is get yourself killed. What good are you goin' to be to your woman when you is dead?"

"I'm not going to fight them fair," Jackson said wildly.

"Man, you has gone raving crazy. You don't even know where they is at."

"I'll find them if I have to search every hole in Harlem."

"Man, Saint Peter himself don't know where every hole is at in Harlem. I've seen grandpappy rats get so lost in these holes they find themselves shacked up with a sewer full of eels."

"Then I'll rob somebody and get some money and hire somebody to help me."

"Take it easy, Bruzz. I'm goin' to find them for you. Where is your religion at? Where is your faith? Your time's comin', man."

Jackson wiped his stinging red eyes with his dirty handkerchief.

"It'd better hurry up and come soon," he said.

VIII

THEY WERE HAVING a big ball in the Savoy and people were lined up for a block down Lenox Avenue, waiting to buy tickets. The famous Harlem detective-team of Coffin Ed Johnson and Grave Digger Jones had been assigned to keep order.

Both were tall, loose-jointed, sloppily dressed, ordinary-looking dark-brown colored men. But there was nothing ordinary about their pistols. They carried specially made long-barreled nickel-plated .38-caliber revolvers, and at the moment they had them in their hands.

Grave Digger stood on the right side of the front end of the line, at the entrance to the Savoy. Coffin Ed stood on the left side of the line, at the rear end. Grave Digger had his pistol aimed south, in a straight line down the sidewalk. On the other side, Coffin Ed had his pistol aimed north, in a straight line. There was space enough between the two imaginary lines for two persons to stand side by side. Whenever anyone moved out of line, Grave Digger would shout, "Straighten up!" and Coffin Ed would echo, "Count off!" If the offender didn't straighten up the line immediately, one of the detectives would shoot into the air. The couples in the queue would close together as though pressed between two concrete walls. Folks in Harlem believed that Grave Digger Jones and Coffin Ed Johnson would shoot a man stone-dead for not standing straight in a line.

Grave Digger looked around and saw the black-gowned figure of Sister Gabriel trudging slowly down the street.

"What's the word, Sister?" he greeted.

" *'And I saw three unclean spirits like frogs come out of the mouth of the dragon*, the sixth angel said,' " Sister Gabriel quoted.

The couples nearby in the queue laughed.

"Listen to Sistah Gabriel," a young woman snickered.

"I hear you, Sister," Grave Digger said. "And what makes those three frogs hop?"

The listeners laughed again.

Sister Gabriel paused. " 'For they are the spirits of devils, working miracles.' "

"Do you think she's crazy?" a loud whisper was heard.

"Shut your mouth," came a cautious reply.

"And these frogs?" Grave Digger kept it up. "You mean they've got a frog pond in Harlem?"

It was a signal for the listeners to laugh again.

" 'And upon her forehead was a name written, Mystery,' " Sister Gabriel quoted and moved on.

"Everybody to their own Jesus," Grave Digger said to the audience.

Goldy continued down Lenox Avenue to 131st Street and turned the corner toward Big Kathy's whorehouse.

It was a six-room apartment on the second floor rear of a big crumbling five-story building. Big Kathy was giving her customers a show and the big living room was lit brightly for the occasion. The air was tinted blue with the smoke of incense. Five girls and a dozen men sat squeezed together on shabby over-stuffed chairs and sofas backed against the walls, leaving the center of the room clear.

A huge yellow woman, almost six feet tall and weighing almost two hundred and fifty pounds, was struggling furiously with a short, skinny, muscular black man about half her weight. Both were clad in skin-tight rubber suits that had been greased and their faces were streaming with sweat that couldn't escape through the body pores.

They were working off a bet whether he could throw her. The stake was a hundred dollars. Side bets had been made.

The big woman was clubbing the little man with her fists. The little man was trying to get hold of the big woman's greased limbs. It was rugged. The spectators were laughing and shouting obscene encouragement.

"Give him some more love licks, baby," a man kept shouting.

Goldy entered by the service door and went unnoticed down the hall to Big Kathy's private room. He entered without knocking.

The room was furnished with a bed, chiffonier, a desk for a dressing table, and two red plastic-covered chairs.

Big Kathy was standing at the foot of the bed beside a hinged panel that opened inward from the wall at the height of his face.

When closed, the panel was hidden by a lithograph of Mary and her Child. On the other side was a transparent mirror giving a clear view of the living room without the peeper's being seen.

Big Kathy turned his head and beckoned to Goldy.

"He's here," he whispered. "Over by the radio with Teena in his lap."

Goldy put his face to the peephole and Big Kathy looked over his shoulder. He spotted Hank instantly. Then he noticed a rough-skinned, broad-shouldered man with half-straightened hair, dressed in working pants and a leather jacket, sitting beside Hank in a straight-backed chair.

"That's another one," Goldy whispered. "The one beside him with the burnt hair."

"He calls himself Walker."

Goldy's gaze roved about the room but he didn't see the slim man.

"Can you get Teena in here?" he asked Big Kathy.

Big Kathy fingered a loose nail in the joist on which the panel was hinged. The radio dial lit up. All five girls in the big room looked at it covertly.

Then Teena got up and excused herself.

"I've got to go wee-wee."

"You're getting kind of old for that, ain't you?" Jodie said roughly.

"Quit picking at her," Hank ordered.

Teena slipped into Big Kathy's room without its being noticed.

"The Sister here wants you to dig your john tonight about his gold-mine pitch, and to get every angle there is," Big Kathy said.

Teena looked at the Sister of Mercy curiously. She had discovered by accident that Big Kathy was a man, but she didn't know anything definite about Goldy.

"What's her story?" she asked impudently.

"You're drinking too much," Big Kathy said. "You'd better be sober when you get to work, and you'd better not miss."

"I ain't goin' to miss," Teena said sullenly.

As soon as she'd returned to the sitting room, Big Kathy went in and stopped the wrestling match.

"Let's call it a draw."

"Let 'em finish!" Jodie shouted. "I got my money up."

"Take it down then," Big Kathy said harshly. "I said it's a draw."

The wrestlers were on the point of exhaustion and glad to quit.

Jodie took down the money from the girl who was holding the bet and pushed his way toward the outside door. Big Kathy let him out.

Teena took Hank to a room.

Goldy stretched out on Big Kathy's bed, but he was too tense to sleep. He was too worried about whether the gold ore was real. He believed Jackson, but he wanted to be sure.

Big Kathy sat in one of the plastic-covered armchairs, skirt drawn up above his big lumpy knees, reading the society page of a Negro weekly newspaper and commenting from time to time about friends of his who were mentioned.

They had a long wait. It was after midnight before Teena knocked softly.

"Come in," Big Kathy said.

"Whew!" Teena whistled, flopping into the other chair. "He talked my ear off."

Goldy sat up on the edge of the bed and leaned forward. "Did he want you to go in with them?"

"Hell, no! That stingy son of a bitch! He was tryin' to sell me some shares."

"Then you struck," Big Kathy said.

"I got everything but where they're making the pitch."

Goldy looked disappointed. "That was one of the main things."

"I did my best, but he wouldn't give."

"All right," Big Kathy said. "Let's have what you got."

"It's just the old lost-gold-mine pitch. The one they call Walker is supposed to be the prospector who accidentally discovered the lost gold mine in Mexico. It's the biggest and richest gold mine he's ever seen in all his years of prospecting, and all that bullshit."

"Let's hear it anyhow," Goldy said.

Teena threw him another calculating look.

"Well, Walker's afraid he'd be killed if he even so much as mentioned finding the mine. And naturally the only man he can trust to tell about it is Mr. Morgan, who's a big-time financier from Los Angeles. Mr. Morgan's known all over the West Coast for backing big business-deals and has got a reputation from coast to coast for being honest."

She started giggling.

"Go on," Big Kathy said roughly.

"Well, what prospector Walker needed was thousands of dollars' worth of tools and equipment and stuff and about a hundred miners to work for him. And besides that he's got to get a permit from the Mexican government to work the mine, which is going to cost a hundred thousand dollars just by itself.

"So the first thing Mr. Morgan does is engage the services—that's what he said—engage the—"

"Get on with the story," Big Kathy said.

"Engage the services of a gold assayer from the Federal Bureau of Assayers. I ain't seen that one, but they call him Goldsmith."

She began giggling again but a look from Big Kathy stopped her.

"Well, all three of them, Walker and Morgan and Goldsmith, was supposed to have gone to Mexico to investigate the mine. But when Mr. Morgan found out how big it was he knew he couldn't swing the deal alone. There were billions of dollars' worth of gold in the mine and it'd take half a million dollars to mine it right. Morgan said he could have financed it through his bank—he told me this straight to my face—but he didn't want the white folks to get control of it and take all the profits. So he decided to organize a corporation and sell stock just to colored folks. They're going all over the whole United States selling stock at fifty dollars a share; and to give themselves time to make a load they're telling everybody it'll take six months to get the mine in operation and another three or four months before it starts paying off."

She stopped and lit a cigarette, then looked from one to the other. "Well, that's it."

"How're they selling their stock if you couldn't find out where they're making their pitch?" Goldy asked intently.

"Oh, I forgot to tell you about that. They got a contact man called Gus Parsons, or Gus somebody-or-other. He's working all the plush bars, attending businessmen's conferences, even going to church festivals, Morgan said, contacting the suckers. Investors, Morgan calls them. Then he takes them to their headquarters blindfolded, in his own car."

Big Kathy's eyes narrowed as he looked at Teena.

Goldy kept his intent stare pinned on her.

"How come all that?" he asked.

Teena shrugged. "He said they're afraid of being robbed."

"Robbed?" Big Kathy echoed.

"Robbed of what?" Goldy asked.

"He say they got a trunk full of gold ore, whatever that is. He said it was taken from the lost mine, as if anybody'd believe that shit."

"Do they keep it at their headquarters?" Goldy asked.

There was something in Goldy's voice that made Big Kathy look at him sharply.

Teena didn't know what was happening and she began getting scared.

"I don't know where they keep it. He didn't say nothing to me about that. All he said to me was they had samples at headquarters to exhibit but if anybody had enough money to invest, they'd show 'em a whole trunk full of pure gold ore."

Goldy sighed so softly it sounded as though he were crying to himself.

Big Kathy kept staring at him with his eyes full of questions. "You through with Teena?"

Goldy nodded.

"Get out," Big Kathy said.

As soon as Teena had closed the door, he leaned far over and stared into Goldy's bowed face.

"Is it true?"

Goldy nodded slowly. "It's true."

"How much?"

"Enough for everybody."

"What do you want me to do?"

"Just play dead until after I have got it."

IX

GRAVE DIGGER AND Coffin Ed weren't crooked detectives, but they were tough. They had to be tough to work in Harlem. Colored folks didn't respect colored cops. But they respected big shiny pistols and sudden death. It was said in Harlem that Coffin Ed's pistol would kill a rock and that Grave Digger's would bury it.

They took their tribute, like all real cops, from the established underworld catering to the essential needs of the people —gamekeepers, madams, streetwalkers, numbers writers, numbers bankers. But they were rough on purse snatchers, muggers, burglars, con-men, and all strangers working any racket. And they didn't like rough stuff from anybody else but themselves. "Keep it cool," they warned. "Don't make graves."

When Goldy got to the Savoy they were just leaving with two studs who'd got into a knife fight about a girl. The stud who'd brought the girl had gotten jealous because she'd danced too much with another stud. What made Coffin Ed and Grave Digger mad was the girl had put these two studs to fighting so she could slip away with a third stud, and these two studs were too simple-minded to see it.

Goldy followed them to the 126th Street precinct station in a taxi.

The big booking room where the desk sergeant sat behind a fortress-like desk five feet high on the side toward the detective bureau was jampacked with the night's pick-up.

The patrol-car cops, foot patrolmen, plainclothes dicks all had their prisoners in tow, waiting to book them on the blotter at the desk. The desk sergeant was taking them in turn, writing down their names, charges, addresses, and arresting officers on the blotter, before turning them over to the jailors who hung waiting in the background.

The small-time bondsmen, white and colored, were hanging about the desk and threading among the prisoners, soliciting business. For a ten-dollar fee they went bail for misdemeanors.

The cops were angry because they'd have to appear in court the next morning during their off-hours to testify against the prisoners they'd arrested. They were impatient to get their prisoners booked so they could go to some of their hangouts and take a nap before quitting time.

A young white cop had arrested a middle-aged drunken colored woman for prostitution. The big rough brown-skinned man dressed in overalls and a leather jacket picked up with her claimed she was his mother and he was just walking her home.

"Gettin' so a woman can't even walk down the street with her own natural-born son," the woman complained.

"Shut up, can't you?" the cop said irritably.

"Don't you tell my mama to shut up," the man said.

"If this whore's your mama, I'm Santa Claus," the cop said.

"Don't you call me no whore," the woman said, and slammed the cop in the face with her pocketbook.

The cop struck back instinctively and knocked the woman down. The colored man hit the cop above the ear and knocked him down. Another cop let go his own prisoner and slapped the man about the head. The man staggered head-forward into another cop, who slapped him again. In the excitement someone stepped on the woman and she began screaming.

"Help! Help! They's tramplin' me!"

"They's killin' a colored woman!" another prisoner yelled.

Everybody began fighting.

The desk sergeant looked down from the sanctuary of his desk and said in a bored voice, "Jesus Christ."

At that moment Coffin Ed and Grave Digger entered with their two prisoners.

"Straighten up!" Grave Digger shouted in a stentorian voice.

"Count off!" Coffin Ed yelled.

Both of them drew their pistols at the same time and put a

fusillade into the ceiling, which was already filled with holes they'd shot into it before.

The sudden shooting in the jammed room scared hell out of prisoners and cops alike. Everybody froze.

"As you were!" Grave Digger shouted.

He and Coffin Ed pushed their prisoners through the silent pack toward the desk.

The Harlem hoodlums under arrest looked at them from the corners of their eyes.

"Don't make graves," Grave Digger cautioned.

The lieutenant in charge glanced out briefly from the precinct captain's office behind the desk, but everything was quiet.

Goldy slipped unobtrusively into the room and stood just inside the doorway, stopping all the bail bondsmen who passed him with a jangle of his collection box.

"Give to the Lawd, gentlemen. Give to the poor."

If there was anything strange about a black Sister of Mercy soliciting in a Harlem precinct police station at one o'clock in the morning, no one remarked it.

Coffin Ed and Grave Digger got their prisoners booked immediately and handed them over to the jailor. The captain wanted to keep them in the street, not tied up all night in the station.

When they left, Goldy climbed into the back of their small black sedan and left with them. They parked the car in the dark on 127th Street and Grave Digger turned around.

"All right, what's the tip about the frogs?"

" 'Blessed is he that watcheth—' " Goldy began quoting.

Grave Digger cut him off. "Can that Bible-quoting crap. We let you operate because you're a stooly, and that's all. And don't you forget, we know you, Bud."

"Know everything there is to know about you," Coffin Ed added. "And I hate a goddam female impersonator worse than God hates sin. So just give, Bud, give."

Goldy dropped his pose and talked straight.

"There's three con-men operating here that's wanted in Mississippi on a murder rap."

"We know that much already," Grave Digger said. "Just give us the monickers they're using and tell us where they're holed up."

"Two of them go as Morgan and Walker. I don't know the slim stud's handle. And I don't know where they're holed up. They're working the lost-gold-mine pitch and they're using a shill named Gus Parsons to bring in the suckers blindfolded."

"Where did you make them?"

"At Big Kathy's. Morgan and Walker were there tonight."

"Fill it in, fill it in," Grave Digger said harshly.

"I got a brother named Jackson, works for Exodus Clay. They took him for fifteen C's on The Blow. His old lady, Imabelle, tricked him into it, then she ran away with the slim stud."

"She's up with the gold-mine pitch?"

"Must be."

"What are they using for gold ore?"

"They got a few phony rocks."

Grave Digger turned to Coffin Ed. "We can take them at Big Kathy's."

"I got a better plan," Goldy said. "I'm goin' to load Jackson with a phony roll and let Gus Parsons contact him. Gus'll take him in to their headquarters and you-all can follow them."

Grave Digger shook his head. "You just said they took Jackson on The Blow."

"But Gus wasn't with them. Gus don't know Jackson. By the time Gus finds out his mistake you'll have the collar on them all."

Grave Digger and Coffin Ed exchanged looks. Coffin Ed nodded.

"Okay, Bud, we'll take them tomorrow night," Grave Digger said, then added grimly, "I suppose you're your brother's beneficiary."

"I'm just tryin' to help him, that's all," Goldy protested. "He wants his woman back."

"I'll bet," Coffin Ed said.

They let Goldy out of the car and drove off.

"Isn't there a warrant out for Jackson?" Coffin Ed remarked.

"Yeah, stole five hundred dollars from his boss."

"We'll take him too."

"We'll take them all."

The next afternoon when Jackson had finished eating, Goldy gave him a fill-in on the gang's setup and told him his plan to trap them.

"And here's the bait."

He made a huge roll out of stage money, encircled it with two bona fide ten-dollar bills, and bound it with an elastic band. That was the way jokers in Harlem carried their money when they wanted to big-time. He tossed it onto the table.

"Put that in your pocket, Bruzz, and you're goin' to be one big fat black piece of cheese. You're goin' to look like the biggest piece of cheese them rats ever seen."

Jackson looked at the phony roll without touching it.

He didn't like any part of Goldy's plan. Anything could go wrong. If there was a rumpus the detectives might grab him and let the real criminals go, like that phony marshal had done. Of course, these were real detectives. But they were colored detectives just the same. And from what he'd heard about them they believed in shooting first and questioning the bodies afterward.

"Course if you don't want your gal back—" Goldy prodded.

Jackson picked up the phony roll and slipped it into his side pants pocket. Then he crossed himself and knelt beside the table on the floor. Devoutly bowing his head, he whispered a prayer.

"Dear Lord in heaven, if You can't see fit to help this poor sinner in his hour of need, please don't help those dirty murderers either."

"What are you prayin' for, man?" Goldy said. "Ain't nothin' can happen to you. You goin' to be covered."

"That's what I'm worrying about," Jackson said. "I don't want to get covered too deep. . . ."

X

THE BRADDOCK BAR was on the corner of 126th Street and Eighth Avenue, next door to a Negro-owned loan and insurance company and the Harlem weekly newspaper.

It had an expensive-looking front, small English-type windows with diamond-shaped leaded panes. Once it had claimed respectability, had been patronized by the white and colored businessmen in the neighborhood and their respectable employees. But when the whorehouses, gambling clubs, dope dens had taken over 126th Street to prey on the people from 125th Street, it had gone into bad repute.

"This bar has gone from sugar to shit," Jackson muttered to himself when he arrived there at seven o'clock.

The cold snowy February night was already getting liquored up.

Jackson squeezed into a place before the long bar, ordered a shot of rye, and looked at his neighbors nervously.

The bar was jammed with the lowest Harlem types, pinched-faced petty hustlers, sneak thieves, pickpockets, muggers, dope pushers, big rough workingmen in overalls and leather jackets. Everyone looked mean or dangerous.

Three hefty bartenders patrolled the sloppy floor behind, silently filling shot glasses and collecting coins.

A jukebox at the front was blaring, a whiskey-voice was shouting, "*Rock me, daddy, eight to the beat. Rock me, daddy, from my head to my feet.*"

Goldy had instructed Jackson to flash his roll as soon as he'd ordered his first drink, but Jackson didn't have the nerve. He felt that everyone was watching him. He ordered a second drink. Then he noticed that everyone was watching everyone else, as though each one regarded his neighbor as either a potential victim or a stool pigeon for the police.

"Everybody in here lookin' for something, ain't they?" the man next to him said.

Jackson gave a start. "Looking for something?"

"See them whores, they're looking for a trick. See them

muggers ganged around the door, they looking for a drunk to roll. These jokers in here are just waiting for a man to flash his money."

"Seems like I've seen you before," Jackson said. "Your name ain't Gus Parsons, is it?"

The man looked at Jackson suspiciously and began moving away. "What you want to know my name for?"

"I just thought I knew you," Jackson said, fingering the roll in his pocket, trying to get up enough courage to flash it.

He was saved for the moment by a fight.

Two rough-looking men jumped about the floor, knocking over chairs and tables, cutting at one another with switchblade knives. The customers at the bar screwed their heads about to watch, but held on to their places and kept their hands on their drinks. The whores rolled their eyes and looked bored.

One joker slashed the other's arm. A big-lipped wound opened in the tight leather jacket, but nothing came out but old clothes—two sweaters, three shirts, a pair of winter underwear. The second joker slashed back, opened a wound in the front of his foe's canvas jacket. But all that came out of the wound was dried printer's ink from the layers of old newspapers the joker had wrapped about him to keep warm. They kept slashing away at one another like two rag dolls battling in buck-dancing fury, spilling old clothes and last week's newsprint instead of blood.

The customers laughed.

"How them studs goin' to get cut?" someone remarked. "Might as well be fightin' old ragman's bag."

"They ain't doin' nothin' but cheatin' the Salvation Army."

"They ain't tryin' to cut each other, man. Them studs know each other. They just tryin' to freeze each other to death."

One of the bartenders went out with a sawed-off baseball bat and knocked one of the fighters on the head. When that one fell the other one leaned down to cut him again and the bartender knocked him on the head also.

Two white cops strolled in lazily, as though they had smelled the fight, and took the battlers away.

Jackson thought it might be safe then to flash his roll. He

took out the phony bills, carefully peeled off a ten, threw it onto the bar.

"Take out for two rye whiskeys," he said.

A dead silence fell. Every eye in the joint looked at the roll in his hand, then looked at him, then at the bartender.

The bartender held the bill up to the light, peered through it, turned it over and snapped it between his hands, then he rang it up in the register and slammed the change onto the bar.

"What you want to do, get your throat cut?" he said angrily.

"What you want me to do, walk off without paying?" Jackson argued.

"I just don't want no trouble in here," the bartender said, but it was too late for that.

Underworld characters closed in on Jackson from all sides. But the whores got there first, pressing their wares so hard against Jackson he couldn't tell whether they were soliciting or trying to dispose of surplus merchandise. The pickpockets were trying to break through. The muggers waited at the door. Everyone else watched him, curious and attentive.

"That's my money," a big whiskey-headed ex-pug shouted, pushing through the crowd toward Jackson. "That mother— has done picked my pocket."

Someone laughed.

"Don't let that joker scare you, honey," one of the whores encouraged.

Another one said, "That raggedy stud ain't had two white quarters since Jesus was a child."

"I don't want no trouble in here," the bartender warned, reaching for his sawed-off bat.

"I know my money," the ex-pug shouted. "Can't nobody tell me I don't know my own money."

"What's the difference between your money and anybody else's money?" the bartender said.

A medium-sized, brown-skinned man, dressed in a camel's-hair coat, brown beaver hat, hard-finished brown-and-white striped suit, brown suede shoes, brown silk tie decorated with hand-painted yellow horses, wearing a diamond ring on his left ring finger and a gold signet ring on his right hand, carrying gloves in his left hand, swinging his right hand free, pushed open the street door and came into the bar fast. He stopped short on seeing the ex-pug grab Jackson by the shoulder. He heard the ex-pug say in a threatening voice, "Leave me see that mother-rapin' roll." He noticed the two bartenders close in for action. He saw the whores backing away. He cased the situation instantly. Pushing his way through the jam, he walked up behind the ex-pug, took hold of his arm, spun him about and kicked him solidly in the groin.

The big ex-pug doubled forward, blowing spit in a loud grunt. The man stepped back and kicked him in the solar plexus. The ex-pug's face ballooned as he gasped for breath, folding head-downward toward the floor. The man stepped back another pace and kicked him in the face with the curve of his instep, hard enough to close one eye without breaking any bones, and timed so that the ex-pug fell on his chest instead of his face. Then the man daintily inserted the tip of his brown suede shoe underneath the ex-pug's shoulder and flipped him over onto his back. Slowly he stuck his right hand into the side pocket of his overcoat and pulled out a short-barreled .38 police special revolver.

The customers scattered, getting out of range.

"You're the son of a bitch who robbed me last night," the man said to the half-conscious ex-pug on the floor. "I've got a good notion to blow out your guts."

He had a good voice and spoke in a soft, slow manner that made him sound like an educated man, to the customers in that joint.

"Don't shoot him in here, Mister," one of the bartenders said.

At sight of the gun the ex-pug's eyeballs rolled back in his head so that only the whites showed. He kept swallowing his tongue as he tried to talk.

"Twarn't me, Boss," he finally managed to blubber. "I swear 'fore the cross it warn't me. I ain't never tried to rob you, Boss."

"The hell it wasn't you. I'd know you anywhere. You jumped me on 129th Street right after midnight last night."

"I swear it warn't me, Boss. I been right here in this bar all

last night. Joe the bartender'll tell you. I been right here all last
night. Didn't leave no time."

"That's right," the bartender said. "He was here all last
night. I seen him."

The ex-pug wallowed about the floor, feeling his eye and
groaning as though half dead, trying to win sympathy.

The man put away his gun and said evenly, "Well, you son
of a bitch, I might be mistaken this time. But you've sure as hell
robbed somebody in your lifetime, so you just got what was
due you."

The ex-pug got to his feet and backed away a distance.

"I wouldn't rob you, Boss, no suh, not with what you got."

No one thought it was funny but they all laughed.

"Not you, Boss, not a man of your position," the ex-pug
kept clowning for laughs. "Anybody here will tell you I ain't
had no real money in my pockets for weeks." Suddenly he recalled that he'd just accused Jackson of picking his pocket, and
added, "Maybe it was that man at the bar what robbed you,
boss, he's sportin' a big roll he got from somewheres."

The man looked at Jackson for the first time.

"Listen, don't get me into that," Jackson said. "I hit the numbers for my money. I can prove it."

The man went over and stood beside Jackson at the bar and
ordered a drink.

"Don't worry, friend, I know it wasn't you," he said in a
friendly voice. "It was some big ragged mugger like that bastard
there. But I'll find him."

"How much did you lose?"

"Seven hundred dollars," the man said, turning the shot
glass between his fingers. "If that had happened to me a week
ago, I'd have tracked the bastard to hell. But now it don't make
too much difference. I've lucked up on a good thing since then,
something that's solid gold. Eight or nine months from now I'll
be able to give a bastard that much money just to keep from
having to kill him."

At the word *gold*, Jackson looked up quickly at the reflection
of the man in the mirror behind the bar. He ordered another
drink, pulled out his roll and peeled off a bill to pay for it.

The man eyed Jackson's roll.

"Friend, if I was you I wouldn't flash my money in this joint. That's just asking for trouble."

"I don't usually come in here," Jackson said. "But my woman's not at home right now."

The man gave Jackson a poker-faced look. He'd gotten a tip from one of the cheap hustlers he employed as lookouts that a square loaded with a big roll was in the joint. But Jackson looked too much like a square to be a real square. The man wondered if Jackson was trying to rook him with a confidence game of his own. He decided to go slow.

"I figured that," he said noncommittally.

The whores began closing in on Jackson again and the man beckoned to the bartender.

"Give these whores what they're drinking and get them off my back."

The bartender took a bottle of gin and a tray of shot glasses to one of the booths. The whores melted away from the bar, looking hostile but as though they couldn't be so much bothered as to be offended.

"You shouldn't talk that way to women," Jackson protested.

The man looked at Jackson queerly. "What can you call a two-bit whore but a whore, friend?"

"They were good enough for Jesus to save," Jackson said.

The man grinned with relief. Jackson was his boy.

"You're right, friend. I'm upset a little, don't usually talk like that. My name's Gus Parsons." He stuck out his hand. "I'm in the real-estate business."

Jackson shook hands, also relieved.

"Glad to meet you, Gus. They call me Jackson."

"What business are you in, Jackson?"

"I'm in the undertaking business."

Gus laughed. "Business must be good, considering that roll you're carrying around. How much are you carrying there, anyway?"

"It didn't come from my business. I just work for an undertaker. I hit the numbers."

"That's right. You did say you'd had a hit."

"Had twenty dollars on four eleven. I drew down ten thousand dollars."

Gus whistled softly and looked suddenly serious.

"You take my advice, Jackson, keep that roll in your pocket and go straight home. The streets of Harlem are not safe for a man with that kind of money. You'd better let me go along with you until you see a policeman."

He turned and called to the bartender. "How much do I owe?"

"Let me buy you a drink before we leave," Jackson said.

"You can buy me a drink somewhere else if you want, Jackson," Gus said, paying for his drink and the bottle of gin. "Some place that's clean and where a man can feel safe. Let's get away from these hoodlums and thieves. I tell you, let's walk down to the Palm Café."

"That's fine," Jackson said.

XI

THEY TURNED ON 125th Street and walked toward Seventh Avenue. Neon lights from the bars and stores threw multicolored rays on the multicolored people trudging down the sloppy walk, turning their complexions into strange metallic shades. Colored men passed, bundled against the cold, some in new checked overcoats, others in GI rubber slickers, gabardines, coats that looked as though they'd been made from blankets. Colored women switched by, sporting coats of such unlikely fur as horse, bear, buffalo, cow, dog, cat and even bat. Other colored people were dressed in cashmere, melton, mink and muskrat. They drove past in big new cars, looking prosperous.

A Sister of Mercy emerged from the shadows.

"Give to the Lawd. Give to the poor."

Jackson reached for his roll, but Gus stopped him.

"Keep you money hidden, Jackson. I have some change."

He dropped a half-dollar into the box.

" 'Ye have found the Spirit,' " the Sister of Mercy misquoted. " 'He that hath an ear, let him hear what the Spirit sayeth.' "

"Amen," Jackson said.

Near the intersection of Seventh Avenue they turned into the Palm Café. The bartenders wore starched white jackets, and the high-yellow waitresses plying between the tables and booths were dressed in green-and-yellow uniforms. A three-piece combo beat out hot rhythms on the raised bandstand.

The customers were the hepped-cats who lived by their wits—smooth Harlem hustlers with shiny straightened hair, dressed in lurid elegance, along with their tightly draped queens, chorus girls and models—which meant anything—sparkling with iridescent glass jewelry, rolling dark mascaraed eyes, flashing crimson fingernails, smiling with pearl-white teeth encircled by purple-red lips, exhibiting the hot excitement that money could buy.

Gus pushed to the bar and drew Jackson in beside him.

"This is the kind of place I like," he said. "I like culture. Good food. Fine wine. Prosperous men. Beautiful women. Cosmopolitan atmosphere. Only trouble is, it takes money, Jackson, money."

"Well, I got the money," Jackson said, beckoning to the bartender. "What are you drinking?"

Both ordered Scotch.

Then Gus said, "Not your kind of money, Jackson. You haven't got enough money to keep up this kind of life. I mean real money. You take your little money. If you're not careful it'll be gone inside of six months. What I mean is money that don't have any end."

"I know what you mean," Jackson said. "As soon as my woman buys herself a fur coat and I get myself some new clothes and we get ourselves a car, a Buick or something like that, we'll be stone broke. But where's a man going to get money that don't have any end?"

"Jackson, you impress me as being an honest man."

"I try to be, but honesty don't always pay."

"Yes, it does, Jackson. You've just got to know how to make it pay."

"I sure wish I knew."

"Jackson, I've a good mind to let you in on something good.

A deal that will make you some real money. The kind of money I'm talking about. The only thing is, I've got to be sure I can trust you to keep quiet about it."

"Oh, I can keep quiet. If there's any way I can make some real money I can keep so quiet they'll call me oyster-mouth."

"Come on, Jackson, let's go back here where we can talk privately," Gus said suddenly, taking Jackson by the arm and steering him to a table in the rear. "I'm going to buy you a dinner and as soon as this girl takes our order I'm going to show you something."

The waitress came over and stood beside their table, looking off in another direction.

"Are you waiting on us or just waiting on us to get up and leave?" Gus asked.

She gave him a scornful look. "Just state your order and we'll fill it."

Gus looked her over, beginning at her feet. "Bring us some steaks, girlie, and be sure they're not as tough as you are, and take the lip away."

"Two steak dinners," she said angrily, switching away.

"Lean this way," Gus said to Jackson, and drew a sheaf of stock certificates decorated with gold seals and Latin scripts from his inside coat pocket. He spread them out beneath the edge of the table for Jackson to get a better view.

"You see these, Jackson? They're shares in a Mexican gold mine. They're going to make me rich."

Jackson stretched his eyes as wide as possible. "A gold mine, you say?"

"A real eighteen-carat gold mine, Jackson. And the richest mine in this half of the world. A colored man discovered it, and a colored man has formed a corporation to operate it, and they're selling stock just to us colored people like you and me. It's a closed corporation. You can't beat that."

The waitress brought the steak dinners, but Jackson couldn't eat very much. He had eaten not long before, but Gus thought it was due to excitement.

"Don't get so excited you can't eat, Jackson. You can't enjoy your money if you're dead."

"I know that's true, but I was just thinking. I sure would like to invest my money in some of those shares, Mr. Parsons."

"Just call me Gus, Jackson," Gus said. "You don't have to shine up to me. I can't sell you any shares. You have to see Mr. Morgan, the financier who's organizing the corporation. He's the man who sells the stock. All I can do is recommend you. If they don't think you're worthy to own stock in the corporation, he won't sell you any. You can bet on that. He only wants respectable people to own shares in his corporation."

"Will you recommend me, Gus? If you have any doubts about me, I can get a letter from my minister."

"That won't be necessary, Jackson. I can tell that you are an honest upright citizen. I pride myself on being a good judge of character. A man in my business—the real-estate business—has got to be a good judge of character or he won't be in business long. How much do you want to invest, Jackson?"

"All of it," Jackson said. "The whole ten thousand."

"In that case I'll take you to see Mr. Morgan right now. They'll be working all night tonight, clearing up business here so tomorrow they can go on to Philadelphia and let a few good citizens there buy shares too. They want to give worthy colored people from all over the country a chance to share in the profits that will come from this mine."

"I can understand that," Jackson said.

When they left the Palm Café the same Sister of Mercy who had accosted them before was shuffling past, and turned to give them a saintly smile.

"Give to the Lawd. Give to the poor. Pave your way to heaven with charitable coins. Think of the unfortunate."

Gus fished out another half-dollar. "I got it, Jackson."

"Sister Gabriel blesses you, brother. 'And the Lord of the spirits of the prophets sent his angel to show unto his servants the things which must shortly come to pass. And behold, we come quickly. Blessed is he that keepeth the word of the prophecy.'"

Gus turned away impatiently.

Goldy winked at Jackson and formed words with his lips. "You dig me, Bruzz?"

"Amen," Jackson said.

"I'm suspicious about those nuns," Gus said as he led Jackson toward his car. "Has it ever occurred to you that they might be working a racket?"

"How can you think that about Sisters of Mercy?" Jackson protested quickly. He didn't want Gus to start suspecting Goldy before the trap was sprung. "They're the most holy people in Harlem."

Gus laughed apologetically. "In my business—the real-estate business—so many people try crooked dealings a man gets to be suspicious. Then I'm naturally a skeptic to begin with. I don't believe in anything until I know it's for sure. That's the way I felt about this gold mine. I had to be sure about it before I invested my money. But I can see that you're a church man, Jackson."

"Member of the First Baptist Church," Jackson said.

"You don't have to tell me, Jackson, I could see right from the start that you were a church member. That's how I knew you were an honest man."

He stopped beside a lavender-colored Cadillac. "Here's my car."

"The real-estate business must be good," Jackson said, climbing into the front seat beside Gus.

"You can't always tell by a Cadillac, Jackson," Gus said as he pushed the starter button and shifted the hydromatic clutch. "All you need these days to buy a Cadillac is a jalopy to turn in for a down payment, and then dodge the installment collector."

Jackson laughed and glanced into the rear-view mirror. He noticed a small black sedan turn the corner and fall in behind them. Then after a moment a taxi drew suddenly to the curb where they had left Goldy.

"When I get the first payment from my mine shares I'm going to buy me one of these."

"Don't count your chickens before they hatch, Jackson. Mr. Morgan hasn't sold you any shares yet."

Suddenly, when they had rounded the corner at St. Nicholas Avenue, heading north, Gus drew to the curb and stopped.

Jackson noticed the black sedan turn the corner, slow down, then drive on. It was followed at a short distance by a taxi. Gus didn't notice. He had taken a black hood from the glove compartment.

"Sorry, Jackson, but I've got to blindfold you," he said. "You just slip this over your head. You understand, Mr. Morgan and the prospector have got a hundred thousand dollars' worth of gold ore in their office and they can't take any chances of being robbed."

Jackson hesitated. "It's not that, Mr. Parsons. It's just that, well, you see, I got all this money on me—"

Gus laughed. "Call me Gus, Jackson. And don't hesitate to say what you mean."

"It's not that I don't trust you, Gus, but—"

"I understand, Jackson. You just met me and you don't know me from the man in the moon. Here, take my gun if it makes you feel any safer."

"Well, it's not that I don't feel safe with you, Gus—" Jackson said, taking the gun and slipping it into his right-hand overcoat pocket. "It's just that—"

"Say no more about it, Jackson," Gus said as he pulled the hood down over Jackson's head. "I know just how an honest man like you feels in this situation. But it can't be helped."

With the hood over his head, Jackson was suddenly scared. He put his hand on the gun for reassurance and silently prayed that Goldy knew what he was doing.

He heard the motor purr and the car move. It turned corner after corner. He tried to estimate their direction, but they turned so many corners he became confused.

Half an hour later the car slowed down and stopped. Jackson had no idea where he was.

"Well, here we are, Jackson, safe and sound," Gus said. "Nothing has happened to you. You just keep your mask on a little while longer and we'll be inside of the office, face to face with Mr. Morgan. You just give me my pistol now; you won't need it any more."

Jackson felt the sweat break out on his head and face beneath the mask. The street was silent. There were no sounds of approaching cars. If Gus had lost the detectives and Goldy, who were supposed to be following, then he was in trouble.

He reached for the pistol with his right hand and with his left hand jerked off the mask. All he had time to see was the quick movement of Gus's hand that had been resting on the steering wheel, before Gus's fist exploded on his nose, filling his vision with dripping wet stars. He put his head down and rammed toward Gus like a fat bull, trying to pin Gus down with his bulk and draw the pistol at the same time. But Gus jabbed him in the windpipe with the point of his right elbow and clutched his wrist in a steel grip before he could get the pistol from his pocket. The dripping wet stars in Jackson's vision turned into blood-red balloons the size of watermelons.

XII

THE BLACK SEDAN came up so fast it skidded to a stop slant-wise, and the two big loose-jointed colored detectives wearing shabby gray overcoats and misshapen snap-brim hats hit the pavement on each side in a flat-footed lope.

At the same moment Goldy's taxi pulled to the curb and parked a block down the street, but Goldy didn't get out.

When the two detectives converged on the flashy Cadillac they had their long-barreled nickel-plated pistols in their hands. Coffin Ed opened the door and Grave Digger hauled Gus to the pavement.

"Get your God-damned hands off me," Gus snarled, throwing a looping right-hand punch at Grave Digger's face.

Grave Digger pulled back from the punch and said, "Just slap him, Ed."

Coffin Ed slapped Gus on the cheek with his open palm. Gus's tight-fitting hat sailed off and he spun toward Grave Digger, who slapped him on the other cheek and spun him back toward Coffin Ed. They slapped him fast, from one to another, like batting a ping-pong ball. Gus's head began ringing. He lost his sense of balance and his legs began to buckle. They slapped him until he fell to his knees, deaf to the world.

Coffin Ed grabbed the collar of his overcoat to keep him from falling on his face. He knelt limply between them with his bare head lolling forward. Grave Digger lifted his chin with the barrel of his pistol. Coffin Ed looked at Grave Digger over Gus's head.

"Tender?"

"Any more tender and he'd be chopped meat," Grave Digger said.

"This boy wasn't educated right."

Jackson hadn't moved from his seat while the detectives were working on Gus, but suddenly he opened the far door and got out on the sidewalk, hoping he could get away unnoticed.

"Hold on, Bud, we're not finished with you yet," Grave Digger called.

"Yes, sir," Jackson said meekly. "I was just getting ready to see what you wanted me to do."

"We still have to get inside the joint."

"Yes, sir."

"Let's get this boy together, Ed."

Coffin Ed lifted Gus to his feet and put a pint bottle of bourbon into his hand. Gus took a drink and choked, but his ears popped and he could hear again. His legs were still wobbly, as though he were punch-drunk.

Coffin Ed took the bottle and slipped it back into his overcoat pocket. "Do you want to cooperate now?" he asked Gus.

"I ain't got no choice," Gus said.

"That's not the right attitude."

"Easy, Ed," Grave Digger cautioned. "We're not through with this boy yet. He's got to get us inside."

"That's what I mean," Coffin Ed said, looking about at his surroundings. "It's a hell of a place to make a pitch on a con game."

"They picked it for the getaway. They figure it's hard to get them cornered here."

"We'll see."

Overhead was the 155th Street Bridge, crossing the Harlem River from Coogan's Bluff on Manhattan Island to that flat section of the Bronx where the Yankee Stadium is located. The

Polo Grounds loomed in the dark on a flat strip between the sheer bluff and the Harlem River. The iron stanchions beneath the bridge were like ghostly sentinels in the impenetrable gloom. A spur of the Bronx elevated line crossed the river in the distance connecting with the station near the Stadium gates.

It was a dark, deserted, dismal section of Manhattan, eerie, shunned and unpatrolled at night, where a man could get his throat cut in perfect isolation with no one to hear his cries and no one brave enough to answer them if he did.

Gus's Cadillac was parked directly in front of a huge warehouse that had been converted into a Peace Heaven by Father Divine. The word PEACE appeared in huge white letters on each side of the gabled roof, and could be seen only by looking down from the bridge. It had later been abandoned and was now sealed in darkness.

"I'd sure hate to be here alone," Jackson said.

"Don't worry, son, we got you covered," Grave Digger reassured him. He locked Gus's Cadillac and put the key into his pocket.

"Okay, Bud, get your hat and let's get going," Coffin Ed said to Gus.

Gus picked up his hat, straightened it out and put it on. His face had already swollen so much that his eyes were almost closed.

"Just act as if nothing happened," Grave Digger ordered.

"That ain't going to be easy to do," Gus complained.

"Bud, you'd better make it good, easy or not."

"Well, coppers, here we go," Gus said.

He led them down a narrow dark alleyway beside the abandoned Heaven to a small wooden shack on the bank of the river. It was painted a dark, dull green but looked black at night. There were two shuttered windows on the side visible from the walk, and a heavy wooden door at the front. No light showed from within; no sound was heard but the distant chug-chug of tug boats towing garbage scows down the river and out to the sea.

Coffin Ed motioned to Gus with his pistol.

Gus rapped a signal on the door. He rapped at such length that Coffin Ed tensed. The slight click of his pistol being cocked shattered the silence like a giant firecracker exploding, causing Jackson to jump halfway out of his skin.

Suddenly a Judas window opened in the black door. Jackson's heart tried to fly out of his mouth. Then he found himself looking directly into an eye staring from the Judas window. He couldn't see the eye well enough to recognize it, but it seemed to speak to him.

There was a turning of locks and a drawing of bolts, and the door opened outward.

Now Jackson could see the eye and its mate plainly. A high-yellow sensual face was framed in the light of the door. It was Imabelle's face. She was looking steadily into Jackson's eyes. Her lips formed the words, "Come on in and kill him, Daddy. I'm all yours." Then she stepped back, making space for him to enter.

Her words shocked Jackson. He crossed himself involuntarily. He wanted to speak to her but he couldn't get the handle to his voice. He looked at her pleadingly, tried to swallow and couldn't make it, then stepped into the room.

It was a single room, about the size of a two-car garage. There were two shuttered windows on each side and another door at the rear, which was locked and bolted. It might have been a foreman's office or a timekeeper's bureau for some firm operating on the river.

To one side of the rear door were a large flat-topped desk and a swivel chair. Two cheap overstuffed chairs, three straight-backed wooden chairs, ashstands, a glass-topped cocktail table, a tin filing-cabinet, and a phony cardboard safe covered with black canvas so that only the bottom half of the dial could be distinguished in the dim light in the corner, had obviously been added as props by the confidence gang. This was to create an atmosphere of luxuriousness and comfort to impress the suckers while they were being trimmed. Light came from a floor-lamp between the armchairs, a ceiling lamp in a glass globe, and a green-shaded desk-lamp.

Looking past Imabelle, Jackson saw Hank sitting behind the

desk, his yellow face looking corpse-like in the green upper glow from the desk-lamp.

Jodie sat on a campstool beside the back door, dressed in high laced boots and dungarees. His straightened hair was gray with dust. All he needed was a scabby burro to give the illusion of coming down a mountain trail loaded with gold nuggets.

Slim sat in a straight-backed chair against the wall beside the desk, wearing over his suit a long khaki duster like those worn by mad scientists in low-budget horror motion pictures. The legend *U.S. Assayer* was embroidered on the chest.

At sight of Jackson all three sat bolt upright and stared.

Before anyone could move, Grave Digger put his foot against Gus's back and shoved him into the room with such force that he catapulted across the floor and rammed headfirst into Jackson's back. Jackson was knocked forward into Jodie just as Jodie was rising from his campstool. Jodie was pinned against the wall.

Following close behind, Grave Digger shouted, "Straighten up!"

Coffin Ed sealed up the open doorway with his cocked .38 and echoed, "Count off!"

Slim jumped to his feet with his hands elevated. Hank sat frozen with his hands on the desk top. Momentarily shielded from the detectives' guns by Jackson's body, Jodie punched Jackson twice, hard, in the belly.

Jackson grunted and grabbed Jodie by the throat. Jodie kneed Jackson in the groin. Jackson backed painfully into Gus. Gus grabbed Jackson by the shoulder to keep from falling, but Jackson thought Gus was trying to hold him and twisted violently from his grip.

In a blind rage, Jodie whipped out his switchblade knife and slashed open the sleeve of Jackson's overcoat.

"Drop it!" Grave Digger shouted.

Red-eyed with pain and fury, Jackson kicked Jodie on the shin as Jodie drew back the knife to stab at him again.

Imabelle saw the poised knife and screamed, "Look out, Daddy!"

Her scream was so piercing that everyone except the two

detectives ducked involuntarily. It even scratched the case-hardened nerves of Grave Digger. His finger tightened spasmodically on the hair trigger of his pistol and the explosion of the shot in the small room deafened everyone.

Gus had ducked into the line of fire and the .38 bullet penetrated his skull back of the left ear and came out over the right eye. As he fell dying, Gus made one more grab at Jackson, but Jackson leaped aside like a shying horse, and Jodie grappled with him.

Jackson clutched Jodie's wrist and tried to swing him about into Grave Digger's reach, but Jodie outpowered him and backed Jackson toward Grave Digger instead.

Taking advantage of the commotion, Hank snatched up a glass of acid sitting on the desk. The acid had been used to demonstrate the purity of the gold ore, and Hank saw his chance to throw it into Coffin Ed's eyes.

Imabelle saw him and screamed again, "Look out!"

Everybody ducked again. Jackson and Jodie butted heads accidentally. By dodging, Slim came between Coffin Ed and Hank just as Hank threw the acid and Coffin Ed shot. Some of the acid splashed on Slim's ear and neck; the rest splashed into Coffin Ed's face. Coffin Ed's shot went wild and shattered the desk-lamp.

Slim jumped backward so violently he slammed against the wall.

Hank dropped behind the desk a fraction of a second before Coffin Ed, blinded with the burning acid and a white-hot rage, emptied his pistol, spraying the top of the desk and the wall behind it with .38 slugs.

One of the bullets hit a hidden light switch and plunged the room into darkness.

"Easy does it," Grave Digger shouted in warning, and backed toward the door to cut off escape.

Coffin Ed didn't know the lights were out. He was a tough man. He had to be a tough man to be a colored detective in Harlem. He closed his eyes against the burning pain, but he was so consumed with rage that he began clubbing right and left in the dark with the butt of his pistol.

He didn't know it was Grave Digger who backed into him. He just felt somebody within reach and he clubbed Grave Digger over the head with such savage fury that he knocked him unconscious. Grave Digger crumpled to the floor at the same instant that Coffin Ed was asking in the dark, "Where are you, Digger? Where are you, man?"

For a moment the speechless dark was filled with violent commotion. Bodies collided in a desperate race for the door. There was the sound of crashing objects and shattering glass as the floor-lamp and cocktail table were overturned and trampled.

Then Imabelle screamed again, "Don't you cut me!"

A rage-thickened voice spluttered, "I'll kill you, you double-crossing bitch."

Jackson lunged toward the sound of Imabelle's voice to protect her.

"Where are you, Digger? Speak up, man," Coffin Ed yelled, groping in the dark. Despite the unendurable pain, his first duty was to his partner.

"Let her alone, she ain't done it," another voice said.

A furious struggle broke out between Jodie and Slim. Jackson realized that one of them thought Imabelle had ratted to the cops and was trying to kill her. The other one objected. He couldn't tell which was which.

He plunged toward the sound of the scuffling, prepared to fight both. Instead he landed in the arms of Coffin Ed. The next moment he was knocked unconscious by a pistol butt laid against his skull.

"Are you hurt, Digger?" Coffin Ed asked anxiously, stumbling over Grave Digger's unconscious body in the dark.

"Are you hurt, man?"

"Come on, let's go!" Hank yelled and made a running leap through the doorway.

Imabelle ran out behind him.

Suddenly, by unspoken accord, Slim and Jodie stopped fighting to chase Imabelle. But outside, where they could see better, they squared off again. Both had open knives and began slashing furiously at each other, but cutting only the cold night air.

Behind the house, an outboard motor coughed and coughed again. The third time it coughed the motor caught. Jodie broke away from Slim and ran around the side of the shack. A moment later a boat with an outboard motor roared out into the Harlem River.

Slim clutched Imabelle by the arm.

"Come on, let's scram, they done left us," he said, pulling her up the alley toward the street.

Suddenly the night was filled with the screaming of sirens as four patrol cars began converging on the spot. A motorist passing over the 155th Street Bridge had reported hearing shooting on the Harlem River and the cops were coming on like General Sherman tanks.

Coffin Ed heard them like an answer to a prayer. The furiously burning pain had become almost more than he could bear. He hadn't reloaded his gun for fear of blowing out his brains. Now he began blowing on his police whistle as though he had gone mad. He blew it so long and loud it brought Jackson back to consciousness.

Grave Digger was still out.

Coffin Ed heard Jackson clambering to his feet and quickly reloaded his pistol. Jackson heard bullets clicking into the cylinder slots and felt his flesh crawl.

"Who's there?" Coffin Ed challenged.

His voice sounded so loud and harsh Jackson gave a start and lost his voice.

"Speak up, God damn it, or I'll blow you in two," Coffin Ed threatened.

"It's just me, Jackson, Mr. Johnson," Jackson managed to say.

"Jackson! Where the hell is everybody, Jackson?"

"They all done got away 'cept me."

"Where's my buddy? Where's Digger Jones?"

"I don't know, sir. I ain't seen him."

"Maybe he's gone after them. But you stay right where you are, Jackson. Don't you move a goddam step."

"No, sir. Is there any kind of way I can help you, sir?"

"No, God damn it, just don't move. You're under arrest."

"Yes, sir."

I might have known it, Jackson was thinking. The real criminals had gotten away again and he was the only one caught.

He began inching silently toward the doorway.

"Is that you I hear moving, Jackson?"

"No, sir. It ain't me." Jackson moved a little closer. "I swear 'fore God." He inched a little closer. "Must be rats underneath the floor."

"Rats, all right, God damn it," Coffin Ed grated. "And they're going to be underneath the God damn ground before it's done with."

Through the open doorway Jackson could see alongside the abandoned Heaven of Father Divine the lights of the patrol cars moving back and forth, searching the street. He listened to the motors whining, the sirens screaming. He felt the presence of Coffin Ed behind him waving the cocked .38 in the pitch darkness of his blind eyes. The shrill, insistent blast of Coffin Ed's police whistle scraped layer after layer from Jackson's nerves. It sounded as if all hell had broken loose everywhere, top and bottom, on this side and that, and he was standing there between the devil and the deep blue sea.

Better to get shot running than standing, he decided. He crouched.

Coffin Ed sensed his movement.

"Are you still there, Jackson?" he barked.

Jackson sprang through the open doorway, landed on his hands and knees, and came up running.

"Jackson, you bastard!" he heard Coffin Ed screaming. "Holy jumping Moses, I can't take this much longer. Can't the sons of bitches hear? Jackson!" he yelled at the top of his voice.

Three shots blasted the night, the long red flame bursting the black darkness from the barrel of Coffin Ed's pistol. Jackson heard the bullets crashing through the wooden walls.

Jackson churned his knees in a froth of panic, trying to get greater speed from his short black legs. It pumped sweat from his pores, steam cooked him in his own juice, squandered his strength, upset his gait, but didn't increase his speed. In Harlem they say a lean man can't sit and a fat man can't run. He was trying to get to the other side of the old brick warehouse that had been converted into Heaven but it seemed as far off as the resurrection of the dead.

Behind him three more shots blasted the enclosing din, inspiring him like a burning rag on a dog's tail. He couldn't think of anything but an old folk song he'd learned in his youth:

> Run, nigger, run; de patter-roller catch you;
> Run, nigger, run; and try to get away . . .

His foot slipped on a muddy spot and he sailed head-on into the old wooden loading-dock at the back of the reconverted Heaven, invisible in the dark. His fat-cushioned mouth smacked into the edge of a heavy floorboard with the sound of meat slapping on a chopping block. Tears of pain flew from his eyes.

As he jumped back, licking his bruised lips, he heard the clatter of policemen's feet coming around the other side of the Heaven.

He crawled up over the edge of the dock like a clumsy crab escaping a snapping turtle. A ladder was within reach to his right, but he didn't see it.

Overhead the 155th Street Bridge hung across the dark night, strung with lighted cars slowing to a stop as passengers craned their necks to see the cause of the commotion.

A lone tug boat towing two empty garbage scows chugged down the Harlem River to pick up garbage bound for the sea. Its green and red riding lights were reflected in shimmering double-takers on the black river.

Jackson felt hemmed in on both sides; if the cops didn't get him the river would. He jumped to his feet and started to run again. His footsteps boomed like thunder in his ears on the rotten floorboards. A loose board gave beneath his foot and he plunged face forward on his belly.

A policeman rounding the other side of the Heaven, coming in from the street, flashed his light in a wide searching arc. It passed over Jackson's prone figure, black against the black boards, and moved along the water's edge.

Jackson jumped up and began to run again. The old folk song kept beating in his head:

> Dis nigger run, he run his best,
> Stuck his head in a hornet's nest.

The tricky echo of the river and the buildings made his footsteps sound to the cops as coming from the opposite direction. Their lights flashed downriver as they converged in front of the wooden shack.

"God damn it, in here," Jackson heard Coffin Ed's roar.

"Coming," he heard the quick reply.

"Somebody's getting away," Jackson heard another voice shout. He put his feet down and picked them up as fast as he could, but it took him so long to get to the end of the dock he felt as if he'd turned stark white from old age and had withered half away.

From the corners of his white-walled eyes he saw the policemen's lights swinging back up the river, slowly closing in. And he didn't have anywhere to hide.

Suddenly he went off the edge of the dock without seeing it. He was running on wooden boards and the next thing he knew he was running on the cool night air. The next moment he was skidding into a puddle of muck. His feet went out from underneath him so fast he turned a complete somersault.

The lights passed along the platform overhead and swung back along the river's edge. He was shielded by the dock, safe for the moment in the shadows.

A passageway loomed to his left, a narrow opening between the brick walls of the Heaven and the corrugated zinc walls of an adjoining warehouse. Far down, another lifetime away, was a narrow rectangle of light where it came out into the street. He made for it, slipped in the muck, caught himself on his hands, and ran the first ten yards bear-fashion.

He straightened up when he felt the ground harden under his feet. He was in a narrow passageway; he had entered it so fast he was stuck before he knew it. He thrashed and wriggled in a blind panic, like a black Don Quixote fighting two big warehouses single-handed; he got himself turned sideways, and ran crab-like toward the street.

The alley was clogged with tin cans, beer bottles, water-soaked cardboard cartons, pieces of wooden crates, and all other manner of trash. Jackson's shins took a beating; his overcoat was scraped by both walls as he propelled his fat body through the narrow opening, running in a strange sidewise motion, right foot leaping ahead, left foot dragging up behind.

He couldn't get that damn' song out of his mind. It was like a ghost haunting him:

> Dat nigger run, dat nigger flew
> Dat nigger tore his shirt in two.

XIII

WHEN SLIM AND Imabelle came out on the sidewalk, the first of the police cars was screaming up Eighth Avenue at ninety miles an hour, its red light blinking in the black night like a demon escaped from hell.

Slim's car was parked too far away to reach. He tried Gus's Cadillac and found it locked. Luckily there was a taxi parked at the curb, ahead of the Cadillac.

Slim looked at the Sister of Mercy sitting on the back seat and recognized her as the black nun who had been pointed out to him in front of Blumstein's Department Store as a stool pigeon. He jerked open the door, jumped inside first and pulled Imabelle in afterwards.

"This is an emergency," he shouted at the driver. "Knicker-bocker Hospital, and goose it."

He turned to the nun and explained, "My wife drank some poison. Got to get her to the hospital."

The burns on Slim's cheek and neck were on the far side, but Goldy had already noticed the acid burns on the shoulder of his khaki duster and knew there had been acid throwing too. He had heard the shooting, and he figured with so much shooting by those crack shots Grave Digger and Coffin Ed, somebody had to be dead. He just hoped it wasn't Jackson, or he was going to have to figure out some way of getting the trunk by himself. And that was going to be tough, because Imabelle didn't know he was Jackson's brother.

The main thing at the moment was not to arouse their suspicions.

"Put your faith in the Lord," he whispered huskily, trying to give the impression of being simple-minded. "Let not your heart be troubled."

Slim shot him a suspicious look, and for an instant Goldy was afraid he'd overplayed it. But Slim only muttered, "Gonna be troubled if we don't get going."

Imabelle had run out without her coat and she shivered suddenly from cold.

Before the taxi had gotten into second gear, a patrol car cut in front of it. Slim cursed. Imabelle put her arm about Slim's shoulder and leaned her head against his cheek to hide the acid burns. Two cops leaped out, stalked back to the taxi and flashed their lights over the occupants. On seeing the Sister of Mercy, they saluted respectfully.

"Did you see anyone run past here, Sister?" one of them asked.

"No one has run past us," Goldy replied truthfully, and turned to his companions. "Did you see anybody pass us?"

"I ain't seen nobody," Slim corroborated quickly, shooting Goldy another calculating look. "Not a soul."

Two more patrol cars pulled to a stop in the middle of the street, behind and ahead of them. Four cops hit the pavement running, but the cops questioning the occupants of the taxi waved them off. They turned, undecided, ran back to their patrol cars, roared off toward the dark parking lot beside the Polo Grounds.

"Where are you folks going?" the cop asked Goldy.

Goldy crossed his index fingers over the gold cross at his bosom and said piously, "To heaven, bless the Lord, have mercy on our souls."

The cops thought he was performing some cabalistic ritual and hesitated. But Goldy had seen the young colored driver look half around, then turn back and look rigidly ahead. He could feel Slim trembling in the seat beside him. He was trying desperately to stall the cops and at the same time prevent Slim from repeating the lie about taking Imabelle to the hospital, because even one look at Imabelle was enough to tell she was healthy as a breeding mare.

"Maybe they went that way," he added before the cops could repeat the question, and made two circles with the gold cross.

The cops stared in fascination. They'd seen many strange religious sects in Harlem, and they respected the colored folks' religion on orders from the commissioner. But this nun looked as though she might be worshipping the devil.

Finally one of the cops replied seriously, "What way?"

"The way of the transgressor is hard," Goldy said.

The cops exchanged glances.

"Let's get on," the first cop said.

The second cop gave Slim and Imabelle another scrutinizing look. "Are these folks disciples of yours, Sister?" he asked.

Suddenly Goldy put the gold cross into his mouth, then spat it out.

" 'And I took the little book out of the angel's hand, and ate it up,' " he quoted enigmatically. He knew the best way to confuse a white cop in Harlem was to quote foolishly from the Bible.

The cops' eyes stretched. Their cheeks puffed and their faces reddened as they tried to control their laughter. They touched their caps respectfully and turned quickly away. They were confused, but not suspicious.

"You think she's drunk?" one asked, loud enough for them to hear.

The other shrugged. "Either that or hopped."

They went back to their patrol car, made a screaming U-turn, and roared off toward the jungle of piers beneath the bridge.

Already people were collecting, emerging from the darkness like half-dressed phantoms.

The taxi started up again. The driver eased it cautiously past the patrol cars.

"Mother-raper, step on it!" Slim snarled.

The driver didn't relax the rigid set of his head but the taxi picked up speed and went fast down Eighth Avenue. Even the back of the driver's head looked scared.

"God damn it, get off me," Slim cursed, pushing Imabelle aside. "I'm burning up."

"Don't talk to me like that," she said, fumbling in her pocketbook.

"If you draw a knife on me—" Slim began, but she cut him off. "Shut up." She handed him a jar of face cream. "Here, put some of this on your burn."

He unscrewed the cap and smeared the white cream thickly over his acid burns.

"Hank shouldn't have done that," Imabelle said.

"Shut up yourself!" Slim grated. "Don't you know this old nun's a stool pigeon?"

Goldy felt Imabelle looking at him curiously, and bowed his head over the gold cross as though absorbed in devout meditation.

"You suspect everybody," Imabelle said to Slim. "How is she going to know what we talking about?"

"If you keep on talking you gonna make me have to cut her throat."

"All of you is knife-happy."

"Woe is past," Goldy said prayerfully.

"It's a good thing she's hopped," Slim muttered.

An ambulance came screaming up the street.

No one spoke again until they reached Knickerbocker Hospital. Slim stopped the taxi in front of the main entrance instead of having it circle the ramp to the emergency entrance. He followed Imabelle out and took her by the arm and hurried her up the stairs without stopping to pay the fare.

Goldy ordered the driver to circle the block. When they came back Slim and Imabelle were getting into a taxi ahead.

Goldy ordered his driver to follow them. The driver grumbled.

"I hope us ain't getting in no trouble, ma'am."

"'There were four and twenty elders,'" Goldy quoted, giving the driver a prediction for the day's number.

He knew that most folks in Harlem believed that holy people could look straight up into heaven and find the number coming out that day any time they wished.

The driver got the idea. He twisted his head and gave the nun a toothy grin. "Yas'm, four and twenty olders. Which one of them olders going to get here first, you reckon?"

"Four of the elders will lead the twenty," Goldy said.

"Yas'm."

The driver resolved to put five bucks on four twenty in each of Harlem's four big books before noon that day as sure as his name was Beau Diddley.

They followed the taxi of Slim and Imabelle until it stopped before a dark cold-water tenement on Upper Park Avenue. But they'd stuck so close they had to go on past when the taxi stopped. Goldy crouched out of sight in the back seat. He knew they hadn't got hep to his trailing them because they hadn't tried to lose him, but he wasn't sure whether they had recognized the taxi when it passed or not. It was a chance he had to take.

By the time they'd circled the block again, the other taxi was gone. Goldy watched the front of the tenement building, wondering whether he'd have to go inside and search for the flat.

But after a moment a light showed briefly in a front window on the third floor before the curtain was pulled. He was satisfied with that. He had the driver take him to the tobacco-store on 121st Street.

Jackson was nowhere in sight. Goldy began to worry. He let himself into the store, went back to his room, lit the kerosene stove and cooked a C and M speedball over his alcohol lamp.

He had told Jackson to return there in case there was a rumble. But he had no way of knowing whether Jackson was dead or alive. And it was too early to ask at the precinct station. If anything had happened to either Grave Digger or Coffin Ed, the white cops might get suspicious and dig him too.

When the dope started working on his imagination, he

could see everybody dead. He banged himself again to calm
his fears.

XIV

WHEN JACKSON EMERGED from the narrow passageway, a
crowd had already collected in the street. He looked like something the Harlem River had spewed up. His overcoat was torn,
the buttons missing, the sleeve slashed, he was covered with
black muck, dripping dirty slime; his mouth was swollen, his
eyes were red, and he looked half dead.

But the other people didn't look much better. The sound
of pistol shooting and the screaming of the patrol car sirens
had brought them rushing from their beds to see the cause of
the excitement. It sounded like a battle royal taking place, and
shootings and cuttings and folks dead and dying were a big
show in Harlem.

Men, women and children had piled into the street,
wrapped in blankets, two and three overcoats, pyjama legs
showing over the tops of rubber overshoes, towels tied about
their heads, draped with dusty rugs snatched hastily from the
floor. Alongside some of the apparitions, Jackson looked like a
man of elegance.

Most of them were milling about the police cordon that
blocked the entrance to the alleyway on the other side of the
Heaven, leading back to the shack where the shooting had
taken place. Necks were craned, people stood on tiptoe, some
sat astride others' backs trying to see what was happening.

Only one man wrapped up in a dirty yellow blanket like a
black cocoon saw Jackson slip from the hole. Two cops were
approaching, so all he did was wink.

The cops were looking at Jackson suspiciously and preparing
to question him when a fist fight broke out among the crowd
on the other side. They hurried to join the group of harness
cops converging on the fighters.

Jackson followed quickly, squeezed into the crowd.

"Let them niggers fight," he heard somebody say.

"Start one fight and everybody wanna fight," someone else said.

"Everybody in Harlem's a two-gun badman anyway. All they need is some horses and some cows and they'd all be rustlers."

Jackson couldn't see the fighters, but he kept worming toward the center of the crowd, trying to get lost.

A man looked at him and said, "This joker's been fighting too. Who you been fighting, shorty, yo' old lady?"

Somebody laughed.

Jackson noticed a cop looking at him. He started moving in another direction.

"They done croaked a copper," a voice said. "That's what they done."

The mob rolled back toward the cordon. The fist fight seemed to have been quelled.

"White copper?"

"Yeah, man."

"They gonna be some ass flying every whichway in Harlem 'fore this night's over."

"You ain't just saying it."

Jackson had wormed to the edge of the crowd and found himself face to face with the two cops who'd first noticed him.

"Hey, you!" one of them called.

He ducked back into the crowd. The cops started plowing after him.

Suddenly the attention of the crowd was attracted by the sound of enraged dogs growling. It sounded like a pack of wolves battling over a carcass.

"Hey, man, look at dis!" someone yelled.

The mob surged in a solid mass toward the sound of fighting dogs, sweeping Jackson away from the pursuing cops.

On the other side of the Heaven, directly in front of the passage where Jackson had escaped, two huge dogs were rolling, snapping, growling, and slavering in a furious fight. One was a Doberman Pinscher the size of a grandfather wolf; the other a Great Dane as big as a Shetland pony. They belonged to two pimps who had been walking them at the time the shooting broke out. The pimps had to walk them two or three times every night because the flats they lived in were so small they had to keep the dogs chained up all the time, and the dogs howled and kept them awake. They'd taken them off the chains to let them run. The dogs were so vicious they'd started fighting on sight.

They rolled back and forth across the sidewalk, into the gutter and out again, fangs flashing in the dim light like mouths full of knives. The pimps were flailing the fighting dogs with their iron chains. Others scattered when the dogs rolled near.

"I got five bones says the black dog wins by a knockout," a man said.

"Who you kidding?" another man replied. "I takes a black dog any day in the year."

The cops neglected Jackson momentarily to separate the dogs. They approached cautiously with drawn pistols.

"Don't shoot my dog, mister," one of the pimps pleaded.

"They ain't gonna hurt nobody," the other pimp added.

The cops hesitated.

"Why aren't those dogs muzzled?" one of the cops asked.

"They was muzzled," the pimp lied. "They lost their muzzles fighting."

"Only way you can separate them is with fire," an onlooker said.

"Them dogs needs shooting," someone replied.

"Who's got some newspaper?" the first pimp asked.

Someone ran to get some newspaper from a junk cart parked at the curb up the street. It was a dilapidated wagon with cardboard sides and bow-legged wheels pulled by a mangy, purblind, splay-legged horse that would never eat grass again. The junkman who owned it had joined the crowd around the fighting dogs.

A man grabbed a piece of newspaper from the stack the junkman had collected, brought it back on the run. He rumpled it into a torch and someone set it on fire and threw it beneath the fighting dogs. In the brief light supplied by the blaze the Doberman's bared fangs could be seen sinking into the Great Dane's throat.

The policeman leaned over and clubbed the Doberman on the head with the butt of his pistol.

"Don't kill my dog," the pimp whined.

Jackson saw the cart and headed toward it, climbed up into the seat, took the frayed rope reins and said, "Giddap."

The horse stretched its scabby neck and twisted its head about to look at Jackson. The horse didn't know the voice. But he couldn't see as far as Jackson.

"Giddap," Jackson said again and lashed the horse's flanks with the rope reins.

The horse straightened out its neck and started moving. But it moved in slow motion, like a motion picture slowed down, its legs moving with each step as though floating slowly through the air.

A cop Jackson hadn't seen before appeared suddenly and stopped him.

"Have you been here all the time?"

"Nawsuh. Ah just driv up," Jackson said, speaking in dialect to impress the cop that he was the rightful junkman.

The cop had no doubts about Jackson being a junkman. He just wanted information.

"And you didn't see anyone running past you who looked suspicious?"

"He just driv up," the man said who had seen Jackson emerging from between the buildings. "Ah seed him."

It was the code of Harlem for one brother to help another lie to white cops.

"I didn't ask you," the cop said.

"Ah ain't seed nobody," Jackson said. "Ah just setting here minding my own business and ain't seed nobody."

"Who hit you in the mouth?"

"Two young boys tried to rob me. But dat was right after dark."

The cop was irritated. Questioning colored people always irritated that cop.

"Let's see your license," he demanded.

"Yassuh." Jackson began fumbling in his coat pockets, going from one to another. "Ah got it right heah."

A police sergeant shouted to the cop.

"What are you doing with that man?"

"Just questioning him."

The sergeant looked briefly at Jackson.

"Let him go. Come here and help block this entrance." He pointed to the passage through which Jackson had escaped. "We have a man cornered back there somewhere and he might try to come through here."

"Yes, sir." The cop went to block the exit.

Jackson's colored friend winked at him.

"De hoss is gone, ain't he?"

Jackson exchanged looks. He couldn't take a chance on winking.

"Giddap," he said to the nag, beating its flanks with the reins.

The nag moved off in slow motion, impervious to Jackson's blows. At that moment the junkman looked from the crowd to see if his property was safe and saw Jackson driving off in his cart. He looked at Jackson as though he didn't believe it.

"Man, dass my wagon."

He was an old man dressed in cast-off rags and a horse blanket worn like a shawl. He had a black woolen cloth wrapped about his head like a turban, over which was pulled a floppy, stained hat. Kinky white hair sprouting from beneath the turban joined a kinky white beard, grimy with dirt and stained with tobacco juice, from which peered a wrinkled black face and watery old eyes. His shoes were wrapped in gunny sacks tied with string. He looked like Uncle Tom, down and out in Harlem.

"Hey!" he yelled at Jackson in a high, whining voice. "You stealin' mah wagon."

Jackson lashed the nag's rump, trying to get away. The junkman ran after him in a shuffling gait. Both horse and man moved so slowly it seemed to Jackson as though the whole world had slowed down to a crawl.

"Hey, he stealin' mah wagon."

A cop looked around at Jackson.

"Are you stealing this man's wagon?"

"Nawsuh, dat's mah pa. He can't see well."

The junkman clutched the cop's sleeve.

"Ah ain't you pa and Ah sees enough to see that you is stealing my wagon."

"Pa, you drunk," Jackson said.

The cop bent down and smelled the junkman's breath. He drew back quickly, blowing. "Whew."

"Come on and git in, Pa," Jackson said, winking at the junkman over the cop's head.

The junkman knew the code. Jackson was trying to get away and he wasn't going to be the one to rat on him to a white cop.

"Ah din see dat was you, son," he said, climbing up onto the seat beside Jackson.

The cop shrugged and turned away disgustedly.

The junkman fished a dirty plug of chewing tobacco from his coat pocket, blew the trash from it, bit off a chew, and offered it to Jackson. Jackson declined. The junkman stuck the plug back into his pocket, picked up the rope reins, shook them gently and whined, "Giddyap, Jebusite."

Jebusite drifted off as though coasting through space. The junkman reined him between the score of patrol cars parked at all angles in the street like tanks stalled in a desert.

Farther down the street civilian cars were parked, others were coming, curious people were converging from every direction. The word that a white cop had been killed had hit the neighborhood like a stroke of lightning.

The junkman didn't say anything until they were five blocks away. Then he asked, "Did you done it?"

"Done what?"

"Croaked dat cop?"

"I ain't done nothing."

"Den what you runnin' for?"

"I just don't want to get caught."

The junkman understood. Colored folks in Harlem didn't want to get caught by the police whether they had done anything or not.

"Me neither," he said.

He spat a stream of tobacco juice into the street and wiped his mouth with the back of his dirty cotton glove.

"You got a bone?"

Jackson started to take out his roll, thought better of it, skinned off a dollar bill and handed it to the junkman.

The junkman looked at it carefully and then tucked it out of sight beneath his rags. At 142nd Street, directly in front of the house where Jackson and Imabelle had formerly roomed, he stopped the horse, got out and started picking over the pile of garbage.

Jackson thought of Imabelle for the first time since he'd begun his escape. His heart came up and spread out in his mouth.

"Hey," he called. "You want to take me down to 121st Street?"

The junkman looked up with an armful of trash.

"You got another bone?"

Jackson skinned off another dollar bill. The junkman threw the trash into the back of the wagon, climbed back to his seat, stashed the dollar and shook the reins. The nag floated off.

They rode in silence.

Jackson felt as though he were at the bottom of the pit. He'd been clubbed, cut at, shot at, skinned up, chased, and humiliated. The knot on his head sent pain shooting down through his skull like John Henry driving steel, and his puffed, bruised lips throbbed like tom-toms.

He didn't know whether Goldy had found Imabelle's address, whether she'd been arrested, whether she was dead or alive. He hardly knew how he'd gotten out alive himself, but that didn't matter. He was sitting there riding in a junk wagon and he didn't know anything. For all he knew, right at that moment, his woman might be in deadly danger. What was more, now that the gang knew the police were on to them, they might run away with Imabelle's gold ore. But just so long as they didn't hurt Imabelle, he didn't care.

His clothes were wet on the outside from the puddle he'd fallen into, and wet on the inside from his own pure sweat. And all of it was icy cold. He sat trembling from cold and worry, and couldn't do a thing.

Colored people passed along the dark sidewalks, slinking

cautiously past the dark, dangerous doorways, heads bowed, every mother's child of them looking as though they had trouble.

Colored folks and trouble, Jackson thought, like two mules hitched to the same wagon.

"You cold?" the junkman asked.

"I ain't warm."

"Wanna drink?"

"Where's it at?"

The junkman fished a bottle of smoke from his ragged garments.

"You got another bone?"

Jackson skinned off another dollar bill, handed it to the junkman, took the bottle and tilted it to his lips. His teeth chattered on the bottle neck. The smoke burnt his gullet and simmered in his belly, but it didn't make him feel any better.

He handed the half-emptied bottle back.

"You got a woman?" the junkman asked.

"I got one," Jackson said mournfully. "But I don't know where she's at."

The junkman looked at Jackson, looked at the bottle of smoke, handed it back to Jackson.

"You keep it," he said. "You need it more'n me."

XV

GOLDY WAS STANDING in the dark, watching through the glass front door of the tobacco shop, when Jackson got down from the junk wagon. He opened the door for Jackson to enter, and locked it behind him.

"Did you find out where she's at?" Jackson asked immediately.

"Come on back to my room where we can talk."

"Talk? What for?"

"Be quiet, man."

They groped through the black dark like two ghosts, invisible to each other. Jackson begrudged every second wasted.

Goldy was trying to figure out where to hide the gold ore when he'd finally gotten it.

Goldy turned on the light in his room and padlocked the door on the inside.

"What you locking the door for?" Jackson complained. "Ain't you found out where she's at?"

Before replying, Goldy went around the table and sat down. His wig and bonnet lay on the table beside a half-empty bottle of whiskey. With his round black head poking from the bulging black gown, he looked like an African sculpture. He was so high he kept brushing imaginary specks from his gown.

"I found out where she's at all right, but first I got to know what happened."

Jackson stood just inside the door. He began swelling with rage. "Goldy, unlock this door. I feel like I'm just two feet away from jail as it is."

Goldy got up to unlock the door, shoulders twitching from the gage.

"Aw, God damn it, set down and cool off," he muttered. "Drink some of that whiskey there. You're making me nervous."

Jackson drank from the bottle. His teeth chattered so loudly on the bottle neck that Goldy jumped.

"Man, quit making those sudden noises. You sound like a rattlesnake."

Jackson banged the bottle on the table and gave Goldy a look of blue violence.

"Be careful, Brother, be careful. I've taken all I'm going to take this night from anybody. You just tell me where my woman is and I'll go get her."

Goldy sat down again and began shining his cross with quick, jerky motions. "You tell me first what happened."

"You ought to know what happened if you found out where she's at."

"Listen, man, we're just wasting time like this. I wasn't back there when the rumble happened. I was setting in a taxi out front when she and Slim came out and got in and he said she was his wife and had taken poison and he had to get her to Knickerbocker Hospital. They rode with me to the hospital then got out and switched taxis and rode over to the place on Park Avenue where they stay. I followed them and that's all I know. Now you tell me what happened back there in the shack so we can figure out what to do."

Jackson began to worry again.

"Do they know you followed them?"

"How do I know? Slim don't know, anyway, unless Imabelle told him. He was in too much pain to notice anything."

"Did some get in his eyes too?"

"Naw, just on his neck and face."

"Did they act suspicious of you?"

"I don't know. Quit asking so many questions and just tell me what you know."

"What I know don't matter if they know you followed them. Because by this time Slim will be long gone from wherever he's at, if he's still got his sight."

"Listen, Bruzz," Goldy said, trying to remain patient. "That woman is sharp. Chances are that she knows I followed her. But that don't mean she tells Slim. That depends on how she's playing it. One thing is sure, she has turned you in for a new model. That's for sure."

"I know she ain't done that," Jackson insisted doggedly.

"No you don't neither, Bruzz. But whether she's ready to turn Slim in now for another new model, nobody can say."

"That just ain't so."

"All right, square. Have it whatever way you wish. We're going to find out soon enough if you ever get around to telling me what happened back there."

"Well, Grave Digger shot Gus through the head, and Hank threw acid into Coffin Ed's eyes—that's when it got on Slim. Then the lights went out and there was a lot of shooting and fighting in the dark. Somebody was trying to cut Imabelle. I got knocked out trying to get to her to help her. And by the time I came to everybody was gone."

"Holy jumping Joseph! Did Grave Digger get killed too?"

"I don't know. When I came to he was lying on the floor—leastways I think it was him—and there weren't anybody left but me and Coffin Ed. And he was going crazy with pain, in there blind, with a loaded pistol, ready to shoot anything that moved. Only the Lord in Heaven knows how I got out of there alive."

Goldy got up abruptly and put on his wig and bonnet. Suddenly he was consumed with haste.

"Listen, we got to work fast now because those studs is hotter here in Harlem than a down-home coke oven."

"That's what I've been saying all along. Let's go."

Goldy paused long enough to give him an angry look.

"Man, wait a minute, God damn it. We can't go in our bare asses."

He raised the mattress of the couch and took out a big blued-steel Frontier Colt's .45 six-shooter.

"Great day alive! You had that thing in here all along!" Jackson exclaimed.

"You just look over there in that corner and get that piece of pipe and don't ask so many questions."

Jackson felt in behind the stack of cardboard cartons and hauled out a three-foot length of one-inch iron pipe. One end was wrapped with black machinist's tape to form a hand hold. He hoisted it once to get the feel but didn't say anything.

Goldy slipped the .45 revolver into the folds of his Sister of Mercy gown. Jackson stuck the homemade bludgeon beneath his wet, tattered overcoat. Goldy turned out the light and padlocked the door. They moved through the blackness of the store toward the front door, like two ghosts armed for mayhem.

It was snowing slightly when they got outside. The white snowflakes turned a dirty gray when they hit the black street.

"We got to get some way to move her trunk," Goldy said.

A black cat slunk from beneath a wet crate filled with garbage. Goldy kicked at it viciously.

Jackson looked disapproving.

"Let's get one of those big DeSoto taxicabs."

"Man, quit thinking with your feet. That gold ore is hot enough by now to burn a hole through the Harlem River."

"Maybe we can find that junk wagon I came home in."

"That ain't the lick either. What you got to do is steal your boss's hearse."

Jackson stopped dead still to look at Goldy.

"Steal his hearse! She ain't dead, is she?"

"Jesus Christ, man, you going to be a square all your life. Naw, she ain't dead. But we gotta have some way to move the trunk."

"You want me to steal Mr. Clay's hearse to move the trunk in?"

"You done stole everything else by now, so what are you gagging on a hearse for? You already got the keys."

Jackson felt his pants pocket. Attached to an iron chain from his belt were the keys to both the pickup hearse and the garage where it was kept.

"You've been searching my pockets while I was asleep."

"What difference does it make? You ain't got nothing for nobody to steal. Come on, let's go."

Silently they trudged up Seventh Avenue.

Most of the bars were closed. But people were still in the street, heads drawn down into turned-up collars beneath pulled-down hats, like headless people. They came and went from the apartment houses where the after-hours joints were jumping and the house-rent parties swimming and the whores plying their trade and the gamblers clipping chumps.

Traffic still rolled along the avenue, trucks and buses headed north, across the 155th Street Bridge and on up the Saw Mill River Parkway to Westchester County and beyond. Cars and taxis rushed past, stopped short, people got in and out, the cars stayed put and the taxis went on again.

Red-eyed patrol cars darted about like angry bugs, screaming to a stop, cops hitting flat-footed on the pavement, picking up every suspicious-looking character for the lineup. A black hoodlum had thrown acid in a black detective's eyes and black asses were going to pay for it as long as black asses lasted.

Masquerading as Sister Gabriel, Goldy trudged along the slushy street like a tired saint, holding the gold cross before him like a shield, scrunching to one side to hide the bulging bulk of the Western .45.

Jackson walked beside him, hugging the length of pipe beneath his dirty coat.

A half-high miss coming from an after-hours joint looked at them and said to her tall, dark escort, "He look just like her brother, don't he?"

"Short, black and squatty," the tall man said.

"Hush! Don't talk such way 'bout a nun."

No police stopped them, nobody molested them. Goldy's black gown and gold cross covered them with safety.

The garage was on the same street as the funeral parlor, half a block distant. When they came to 133rd Street they turned over to Lenox Avenue and came back on 134th Street to keep from being seen.

Jackson unlocked the door and led the way inside. "Shut the door," he said to Goldy as he groped for the light switch.

"What for, man? You don't need no light. Just get in the wagon and back it out."

"I got to change clothes. I'm freezing to death in these."

"Man, you got more excuses than Lazarus," Goldy complained, closing the door. "We ain't got all night."

"It ain't you that's freezing," Jackson said angrily as he stripped to his long damp drawers, stained black from the dye of his suit, put on an old dark gray uniform and overcoat that hung on a nail, and his new chauffeur's cap he took from a tool chest.

When he turned to climb into the driver's seat he noticed that the back of the hearse was loaded with funeral paraphernalia. It was a 1947 Cadillac that had first seen service as an ambulance. Now it was used mainly to pick up the bodies for embalming, and to do double duty as a truck. The coffin rack was half hidden beneath a pile of black bunting used to drape the rostrum during a funeral, plaster pedestals for lights and flowers, wreaths of artificial flowers, and a bucket half-filled with dirty motor-oil changed from one of the limousines.

Jackson opened the back double-doors, took out the motor-oil, and started to unload the other things.

"Leave that junk be," Goldy said. "All the time you're taking a man would think you don't care what happens to your old lady."

"I want to hurry more than you," Jackson defended himself. "I was just trying to make space for the trunk."

"We'll put it where they put the coffins. Come on, man, let's hurry."

Jackson slammed shut the back doors, went around to the front and got behind the wheel. He turned on the switch, read the gauges from habit, told Goldy to turn out the light and open the door. He started the motor and backed into the street, straight into the path of a patrol car.

The cop driving stopped the car. They looked from the nun to the driver, and alighted very deliberately, one from one side, one from the other. Moving with the same deliberation, Goldy closed and locked the garage door, thinking fast. He decided they were just meddling; he had to chance it, anyway. He walked back to meet the cops, touching his gold cross.

Jackson looked at the cops and felt the sweat dripping from his face onto his hands, running down his neck.

"Are you riding with this hearse, Sister?" one of the cops asked, touching his cap respectfully.

"Yes, sir, in the service of the Lord," Goldy said slowly in his most prayerful-sounding voice. "To take that which is left of him who hath been taken in the first death, praise the Lord, to wait in the endless river until he shall be taken in the second death."

Both cops looked at Goldy uncomprehendingly.

"You mean to pick up a dead body."

"Yes, sir, to gather in the remains of him who hath been taken in the first death."

The cops exchanged glances. The other one walked up to Jackson and flashed his light into Jackson's face. Jackson's wet face glistened like a smooth wet lump of coal. The cop bent down to smell his breath.

"This driver looks drunk. I can smell the whiskey on him."

"No sir, I'm not drunk," Jackson denied. He merely looked scared, but the cop didn't know it. "I had a drink but I ain't drunk."

"Get out," the cop ordered.

Jackson got out, moving as carefully with the pipe hidden beneath his coat as though his bones were made of sugar candy.

"Walk in a straight line to that post," the cop ordered, pointing to a lamp post on the other side of the street.

To distract the cops' attention, Goldy quoted huskily, " 'And he laid hold on the dragon—' "

The cops turned to look at him.

"What's that, Sister?"

" 'That old serpent,' " Goldy quoted, " 'which is the Devil, and Satan, and bound him a thousand years.' "

By that time Jackson had gotten to the post. But Goldy's dodge had been unnecessary. In order to keep the pipe from slipping from beneath his coat, Jackson had walked as rigidly as a zombie and as straight as the path of a bullet. But sweat was running down his legs.

"He looks sober enough," the first cop said.

"Yeah, he seems steady enough," the second cop agreed.

Neither one of them had watched him walking.

"Get back in, boy, and take this nun on her errand of mercy."

"It's mighty late to be picking up a body at this hour," the second cop remarked.

"Nobody can choose their time to go to the first death," Goldy replied. "They go when the wagon of the Lord calls for them, early or late."

The cop smiled. "We all got to go when the wagon comes. Isn't that what they say here in Harlem?"

"Yes, sir, the wagon of the Lord."

"Whose body is it?"

"Nobody can claim it now," Goldy said. "We just take it and bury it."

The cops were tired of trying to get any sense out of the nun. They shrugged and got back into their patrol car and drove away.

XVI

LOOKING EASTWARD FROM the towers of Riverside Church, perched among the university buildings on the high banks of the Hudson River, in a valley far below, waves of gray roof-tops distort the perspective like the surface of a sea. Below the surface, in the murky waters of fetid tenements, a city of black people who are convulsed in desperate living, like the voracious churning of millions of hungry cannibal fish. Blind mouths eating their own guts. Stick in a hand and draw back a nub.

That is Harlem.

The farther east it goes, the blacker it gets.

East of Seventh Avenue to the Harlem River is called the Valley. Tenements thick with teeming life spread in dismal squalor. Rats and cockroaches compete with the mangy dogs and cats for the man-gnawed bones.

The apartment where Slim and Imabelle lived was on Upper Park Avenue, between 129th and 130th Streets. That part of the Valley was called the Dusty Bottom of the Coal Bin.

The trestle of the New York Central railroad, coming from Grand Central out of ground at 95th Street and crossing over-top at the 125th Street Station, runs down the center of the street in place of the park in the downtown section from which the avenue derives its name.

It converges onto the trestle of the Third Avenue Elevated line, then curves across the Harlem River into the Bronx and the big wide world beyond.

Up there in Harlem, Park Avenue is flanked by cold-water, dingy tenement buildings, brooding between junk yards, dingy warehouses, factories, garages, trash-dumps where smart young punks raise marijuana weed.

It is a truck-rutted street of violence and danger, known in the underworld as the Bucket-of-Blood. See a man lying in the gutter, leave him lay, he might be dead.

The fat black men in their black garments in the creeping black hearse were part of the eerie night. The old Cadillac

motor, in excellent repair, purred softly as a kitten. Snow
floated vaguely through the dim lights.

"That's it," Goldy pointed out.

Jackson looked at a doorway to one side of the dirty broken
plate-glass windows of a hide shop. A moth-eaten steer's head
stared back at him through mismatched glass eyes. His skin
sprouted goose pimples. He had come to the end of the trail and
he was so scared he didn't know whether to be glad or sorry.

"Just park right here," Goldy said. "Makes no difference."

Jackson brought the hearse to a stop and doused the lights.

A truck rumbled past, headed downtown toward the Harlem
Market beyond 116th Street, leaving a darker gloom in its wake.

He and Goldy peered up and down the deserted street. Jackson felt his flesh crawl.

"Can they see us?" he asked.

"Not if they ain't looking."

That wasn't what Jackson meant, but he didn't argue. He
reached beneath his overcoat for his iron pipe.

"It ain't time for your club yet," Goldy cautioned.

Jackson was reluctant to get out of the hearse.

"I'm going to leave the motor running," he said.

"What for? You want to get it stolen?"

"Nobody'd steal a hearse."

"What you talking about? These folks over here'll steal a
blind man's eyes."

Goldy alighted to the sidewalk noiselessly. Jackson took a
deep breath and followed. They went across the sidewalk, entered a long, narrow hall lit by a dim fly-specked bulb. Graffiti
decorated the whitewashed walls. Huge genitals hung from
crude dwarfed torsos like a harvest of strange fruit. Someone
had drawn a nude couple in a sex embrace. Others had added
to it. Now it was a mural.

It was a long hall, diminishing into shadow. At the far end
stairs climbed steeply into pitch darkness.

Goldy led the way, tiptoeing, the hem of his long black
gown sweeping the dirty floor. He went noiselessly up the
wooden stairs, disappeared so suddenly in the overhead dark
that Jackson's scalp twitched. Jackson followed, his fat flesh

running with ice-cold sweat. He took out his pipe again and gripped the taped handle.

The dark hallways above smelled of stale urine and neglected dirt.

Goldy climbed to the third floor, went down the hall to the door at the front. When Jackson caught up he saw the dull blue gleam of Goldy's revolver in the dark.

Goldy knocked softly on the scabby brown door, once, then three times rapidly, once more, then twice rapidly.

"Is that the signal?" Jackson asked in a whisper.

"How the hell do I know?" Goldy whispered in reply.

Silence greeted them.

"Maybe they've left," Jackson whispered.

"We'll soon find out."

"Then what we going to do?"

Goldy gestured for silence, knocked again, softly, changing the signal.

"What are you doing that for if you don't know the signal?"

"I'm crossing 'em up."

"You think more than just Slim is here?"

"What the hell do I care? As long as the gold is here."

"Maybe they've taken it."

Goldy waited and knocked again, softly, giving another signal.

From behind the door a cautious voice asked, "Who there?" It sounded like the voice of a woman with her mouth held close to the panel.

Goldy poked Jackson in the ribs with the muzzle of his revolver, signaling him to answer the voice. But it gave Jackson such a scare he bolted like a wild horse and his pipe flew out and hit the door with a bang that sounded like a gunshot in the pitch-black, silent hall.

"Who there?" a high feminine voice asked in panic.

"It's me, Jackson. Is that you, Imabelle?"

"Jackson!" the voice said in amazement. It sounded as though it had never heard of Jackson.

Silence reigned.

"It's me, honey. Your Jackson."

After a moment the voice asked suspiciously, "If you is Jackson what is the first name of your boss?"

"Hosea. Hosea Exodus Clay. You know that as well as me, honey."

"What a square," Goldy muttered to himself.

A lock was turned, then another, then a bolt was slipped back. The door opened a crack, held by an iron chain.

A dim droplight was burning in a squalid bedroom. Jackson stuck his shiny black face into the crack of light.

"Oh, sugar!" The chain was unhooked and the door flung open. "Lawd, is I glad to see you!"

Jackson had just time to see that she was dressed in a red dress and a black coat before she fell into his arms. She smelled like burnt hair-grease, hot-bodied woman, and dime-store perfume. Jackson embraced her, holding the iron pipe clutched against her spine. She wriggled against the curve of his fat stomach and welded her rouge-greasy mouth against his dry, puckered lips.

Then she drew back.

"Lawd, Daddy, I thought you'd never come."

"I came as soon as I could get here, honey."

She held him at arms' length, looked at the pipe still gripped in his hand, then looked at his face and read him like a book. She ran the tip of her red tongue slowly across her full, cushiony, sensuous lips, making them wet-red, and looked him straight in the eyes with her own glassy, speckled bedroom eyes.

The man drowned.

When he came up, he stared back, passion cocked, his whole black being on a live-wire edge. Ready! Solid ready to cut throats, crack skulls, dodge police, steal hearses, drink muddy water, live in a hollow log, and take any rape-fiend chance to be once more in the arms of his high-yellow heart.

"Where's Slim? I'm going to bash that bastard's brains to a raspberry pulp, may the Lord forgive me," he said.

"He's gone. He just left. Come on inside, quick. He's coming back in a minute."

When Jackson stepped into the room, Goldy followed.

There was a battered white-painted iron double bed against

one wall, with the covers turned back, exposing dirty stained sheets and two pillows with slimy gray circles from hair-grease. Against the other wall was an overstuffed sofa with the heads of two springs poking from the rotten faded green seat-covering. At the back a rusty potbellied stove squatted on a square of rusty tin. To one side was a wooden box serving as a coalbin, to the other a doorway leading into the kitchen. A round table with a knife-scarred top and a three-legged straight-backed chair commanded the center of the bare wooden floor. The room was filled to the brim. When the three people entered, it overflowed.

"What's she doing here?" Imabelle asked, throwing a startled look at Goldy.

"He's my brother. He's come to help me get you away."

She looked at the big .45 in Goldy's hand. Her eyes stretched and her lips twitched. But she didn't look surprised.

"You-all has sure come leaded for bear."

"Can't come as boys to do a man's job," Goldy said.

She peered at Goldy.

"He sure looks like that Sister me and Slim rode with."

"I is." Goldy grinned, showing his two gold teeth. "That's how I found out where you is at. I trailed you."

"Well, how 'bout that! Impersonating a nun. Everybody got their racket, ain't they?"

Goldy saw the trunk first. It was at the end of the sofa, hidden from Jackson's view by the table.

"What they been doing to you, honey?" Jackson asked anxiously.

Suddenly Imabelle got into a lather of haste.

"Daddy, we ain't got time to talk. Slim has gone after Hank and Jodie. They're coming back to take my gold ore. You got to save my gold ore, Daddy."

"What else am I here for, honey? Just tell me where it's at."

He was looking through the doorway into the kitchen. The only clean thing in that flat was the kitchen floor. It was still wet from a recent scrubbing.

"It ain't in there," Goldy said, pointing toward the trunk.

"Daddy, is I glad you come!" Imabelle repeated in a loud

voice, and went around the table to get her pocketbook from beneath a pillow.

"Don't you worry, I'll save your gold, honey. I brought the hearse."

"The hearse! Mr. Clay's hearse?"

She went to the front window and peeked through the drawn shades. When she turned back she was giggling.

"Well, how 'bout that!"

"Only thing we could get to move it with," Jackson said defensively.

"Let's just take it and go, Daddy. I'll tell you everything on the way."

"Those bastards haven't hurt you, have they?"

"No, Daddy, but we ain't got time to talk about it now. We got to think of some place to hide the trunk at. They'll be looking for it everywhere."

"We can't take it home," Jackson said. "The landlady has put us out."

"We'll keep it in my room," Goldy said. "I got a room where nobody can find it. Bruzz'll tell you. It'll be safe there, won't it, Bruzz?"

"I'll think of some place," Jackson said evasively.

He had no intention of letting Goldy get his hands on that trunk full of gold ore.

"What's the matter with my place?"

"We ain't got no time to argue," Imabelle said. "Slim'll be back any minute with Hank and Jodie."

"Ain't no argument," Goldy argued. "I has already got the best place."

"We'll check it at the station," Imabelle said as the thought struck her. "But for God's sake hurry up. We ain't got no time to lose."

Jackson stuck his pipe underneath his arm and circled the table to get to the trunk.

Goldy stuck his big .45 inside of his rusty black gown and gave Jackson a regretful look.

"The older you gets the more squared you becomes, Bruzz," he said sorrowfully.

Imabelle looked from one to another and came to a sudden decision. "Take it to your brother's place, Daddy. It'll be safe there."

Goldy and Imabelle exchanged glances.

"I'll wait for you-all in the hearse," she said.

"We're coming right after you," Jackson said, hoisting his end of the trunk.

Goldy hoisted the other end. They staggered beneath its weight, squeezed between the table and sofa, pushing the table aside, angled it through the narrow doorway.

They heard Imabelle's high heels tapping quickly down the wooden stairs.

"You go first," Goldy said.

Jackson turned his back to the trunk, took the bottom corners in each hand, let the weight rest on his back, led down the steep stairs, his legs buckling at every step.

He had sweated through the back of his coat by the time they came out onto the sidewalk. Sweat was running into his eyes, blinding him. He felt his way across the sidewalk to the back of the hearse, balanced the trunk with one hand, opened the double-doors with the other, moved some of the junk out of the way, and hoisted his end onto the coffin rack. Then he got back and helped Goldy push the trunk inside.

The trunk sat between the two side windows in clear view, like a sawed-off casket fitted to a legless man.

Jackson closed the doors and went around one side of the hearse to the driver's seat. Goldy went around the other. They looked at each other across the empty seat.

"Where'd she go?" Jackson asked.

"How the hell do I know where she went? She's your woman, she ain't mine."

Jackson peered up and down the dismal street. Far down on the other side, almost to the station, he saw some people running. It didn't attract his attention. Somebody was always running in Harlem.

"She must be somewheres."

Goldy climbed into the front seat, trying to be patient.

"Leave us take the trunk on home and come back for her."

"I can't leave her here. You know that. It was her I came after in the first place."

Goldy began losing his patience. "Man, let's go. That woman can find her way."

"You leave me to run my own business," Jackson said, starting back into the tenement.

"She's not in the house, God damn it. Are you going to be a square all your life? She's gone."

"If she's gone I'm going to wait right here until she comes back."

Goldy was fingering the handle of his revolver as he struggled to control his fury.

"Man, all that bitch wants is to save her gold. She's going to find you. She don't care nothing 'bout nobody."

"I'm getting good and sick and tired of you talking about her like that," Jackson flared, approaching Goldy belligerently.

Goldy drew his revolver halfway out. It was all he could do to stop himself.

"God damn, you black son of a bitch, if you wasn't my brother I'd kill you," he said, twitching all over in a doped rage.

Jackson took a new grip on his length of iron pipe, crossed the sidewalk, climbed the tenement stairs back to the flat.

"Imabelle. You here, Imabelle?"

He searched the apartment, looking underneath the bed, behind the sofa, in the kitchen, holding the club gripped firmly in his hand, as though he were searching for someone as small as a puppy dog and dangerous as a male gorilla.

A corner of the kitchen was closed off with a faded green cotton curtain suspended from a line of sagging twine. Jackson pulled the curtain aside and looked inside.

"She left all her clothes," he said aloud.

Suddenly he felt beat, tired to the bone.

He sat down in the one kitchen chair, laid his head in the cushion of his folded arms on the kitchen table, closed his eyes in weariness, and the next instant he was asleep.

XVII

A BLACK DELIVERY truck made a fast turn into Park Avenue from 130th Street, heading south opposite the tenement building, and suddenly slackened speed.

From the driver's seat Jodie peered intently at the parked hearse. "There's a hearse out front," he said needlessly.

"I see it," Hank said, leaning forward to peer around his shoulder.

"What's it doing there, you reckon?"

"I ain't no fortuneteller."

"You reckon the cops are with it?"

"I don't reckon nothing. Let's find out."

Both of them had changed clothes since their escape from the shack on the Harlem River.

Jodie now wore a blue overcoat, black snap-brim hat parked on the back of his head, a blue suit, brown suede gloves, and black oxfords. He could have passed for a dining-car waiter, a job at which he'd been employed for four years.

Hank wore a dark brown overcoat, brown hat, and a blue suit. He had his hat pulled low over his eyes and both hands dug into his overcoat pockets.

They were dressed for a getaway.

From where he sat on the front seat of the hearse, Goldy saw the lights of the truck when it first turned into Park Avenue. When it turned so that he could see what type of truck it was, he was instantly suspicious. He knew that a delivery truck of that type had no business on that kind of street at that time of night. He bent over on the seat so that he couldn't be seen, cocking his ears to listen. He heard the truck going slowly down the opposite side of the street. It occurred to him suddenly that it might be Hank and Jodie returning to get the trunk of gold ore. He took the revolver from the folds of his gown, held it against his chest, and twisted about on the seat so that he could see into the rear-view mirror.

When the panel truck was directly opposite the hearse, Jodie said, "It's empty."

"Looks empty."

"But there's something in the back. Reckon it's a coffin?"

"You do your own reckoning."

Suddenly Jodie could see past the end of the trunk through the opposite window.

"It ain't no coffin."

Hank took a .38 automatic from his right overcoat pocket and jacked a shell into the breech.

Jodie made a U-turn before reaching the end of the block, came back on the side of the hearse, then turned inside the iron stanchions of the trestle to pass it.

Goldy watched the lights in the rear-view mirror until they had passed out of range, but he heard the truck going slowly ahead.

Now Hank was on the inside of the truck, next to the hearse.

"There's a trunk in it," he said.

Jodie peered around Hank's shoulder.

"You reckon it's her trunk?"

"We're going to see."

Jodie steered the truck to the curb ahead of the hearse, parked, and doused the lights. He took off his gloves, put them into his left overcoat pocket, stuck his hand into his right pocket, and gripped the cold bone handle of his knife.

He got out on the street side, while Hank alighted on the sidewalk. Both stood poised for an instant, casing the silent street. Then both turned in unison and walked back quietly to the silent hearse. Both glanced casually into the front seat as they passed, but didn't notice Goldy. His black gown made him invisible in the dark.

At the sides of the hearse they stopped and peered through the glass windows, examining the trunk on the coffin rack. Their gazes met over the top. They went to the back of the hearse, tried the doors, found them open, and looked inside.

"It's it, all right," Jodie said.

"I can see it."

Goldy had raised his head slightly to watch them in the rear-view mirror. He recognized them instantly. From the way

Hank stood with his right hand always in his pocket, Goldy knew he had a gun. He wasn't sure about Jodie, but he figured Hank was the one to watch.

He saw them turn and look up at the window of the third-floor flat.

"I don't see no light," Jodie said.

"That don't mean nothing."

"I'm gonna look."

"Wait a minute."

"I don't want to stand out here and get my ass blown off."

"If anybody's in there they've already seen us."

"What do you mean, if anybody's in there? You think spooks brought down this heavy trunk?"

"The way I figure it, she got Jackson to help her."

"Jackson. That mother-raping tarball. How the hell could he find out where she's at?"

"How the hell did he find out where our river hideaway was at? An eight-ball like him sweet on a high-yaller gal will find out where Hitler is buried at."

"Then it must be his boss's hearse."

"That's the way I figure it."

Jodie laughed softly.

"Let's take the mother-raping hearse too."

"Let's see if he left the keys in it."

When they turned back toward the front seat, Jodie on the street side and Hank on the sidewalk, Goldy felt along the sill of the street-side window and pushed down the button that locked the door. He figured that all Jodie had was a knife, and he could concentrate on Hank.

His body tensed as he watched their reflections vanish from the opposite edges of the rear-view mirror, his right arm stiffened, fingers tightened on the butt of the big .45. But he waited until Hank turned the handle of the front door before cocking the revolver in order to synchronize the sound with the clicking of the door lock.

Hank wasn't expecting danger from that source. When he pulled open the door, Goldy straightened up on the seat, looking like the mother of all the evil ghosts, and said, "Freeze!"

Hank looked into the muzzle of the .45 and froze. His heart stopped beating, his lungs stopped breathing, his blood stopped flowing. That big hole at the end of Goldy's .45 looked as big as a cannon bore.

Goldy figured he was protected from behind by the locked door. But the door locks on the old Cadillac hearse were out of order.

At the first sight of motion Jodie snatched open the door at Goldy's back with his left hand, snatched Goldy bodily from the seat into the street with his right hand before Goldy could squeeze the trigger, kicked the gun out of his hand while he was still in the air, kicked him again in the back of the neck the instant Goldy's fat black-gowned figure hit the pavement.

He didn't care whether it was a man, woman, or child he was kicking. He was riding a lightning bolt of maniacal violence, and all he could see was a red ball of murder.

As the revolver skidded down the street, he kicked Goldy in the ribs, and when the revolver bumped to a stop in the gutter against the curb and vanished in the black slush, he kicked Goldy in the back above the kidneys.

Hank was running around the front of the hearse with the cocked .38 automatic in his hand when Jodie kicked Goldy in the solar plexus.

"Leave off," Hank said, leveling the .38 on Jodie's heart. "You'll kill her."

Goldy writhed on the dirty wet bricks like a fish on a hook, gasping for breath. White froth had collected at the corners of his mouth before he could speak.

Jodie stood poised, anchored by Hank's gun, panting out his violence.

"One more kick and I'd a' killed her."

"Lawd, have mercy on an old lady," Goldy finally managed to wail.

The whistle of a train approaching the station sounded as it turned across the Harlem River like an echo to Goldy's wailing plea.

Hank stepped close to Goldy, suddenly reached down with his left hand and lifted Goldy's face by the chin.

Goldy was groping desperately for his gold cross that had got entangled in the folds of his gown.

"I'm a Sister of Mercy," he said in a moaning wail. "I'm in the service of the Lord."

"Don't hand us that crap, we know who you are," Hank said.

"She's that nun who stools for them two darky dicks ain't she? How you reckon she got in this deal?"

"How the hell do I know? Ask her."

Jodie looked down into Goldy's ash-gray face. There was no mercy in Jodie's muddy brown eyes.

"Talk fast," he said. " 'Cause you ain't got much time."

The sound of the approaching train, transmitted by the iron tracks on the iron trestle, slowly grew louder.

"Listen—" Goldy whined.

A short sharp blast of the train whistle, signaling that it had crossed the river into Harlem, cut him off.

"Listen, I can help you get away with it. You're strangers here, but I know this town in and out."

Hank's eyes narrowed. He was listening intently.

Jodie pulled his hand from his overcoat pocket, gripping the handle of his switch-blade knife. It had a push-button on the top of the handle, worked by the thumb, and when he pressed it a six-inch blade leaped forward with a soft click, gleaming dully in the dim light.

Goldy saw the blade from the corners of his eyes and scrambled to his knees.

"Listen, I can hide it for you."

His instinctive fear of cold steel made his eyes run tears.

"Listen, I can cover for you—"

Jodie showed his hatred for a stooly by slapping off Goldy's cap. The gray wig came off with it, leaving the round head exposed.

"This black mother-raper is a man," he said, moving around behind Goldy.

"Listen to him," Hank said.

"I got a hideout can't nobody find. Listen, I can take care of you-all. I can cover with the cops. I got ins at the precinct. You know my secret now. You know you can trust me. Listen, I can hide all of you, and there's enough for—" His voice was lost in the thunder of the approaching train.

Hank bent down to hear him better, staring into his face.

"Who else is with you?"

"Ain't nobody, I swear—"

The diesel locomotive of the train was rumbling overhead. The trestle shook, shaking the stanchions. The street shook, the building shook, the whole black night was quaking.

Goldy knelt as though in prayer, knees planted on the wet, dirty-black shaking street, his fat body shaking beneath the flowing folds of the robe, shaking as though praying in a void of pure terror.

Jodie leaned forward quickly behind him. He was shaking too.

"Lying mother—," he said in a voice of rage.

Goldy realized instantly his mistake. Somebody had had to help him bring down the trunk, it was too heavy to handle alone.

"Ain't nobody but—"

Jodie reached down with a violent motion, clutched him over the face with the palm of his left hand, put his right knee in Goldy's back between the shoulder blades, jerked Goldy's head back against the pressure of his knee, and cut Goldy's taut black throat from ear to ear, straight down to the bone.

Goldy's scream mingled with the scream of the locomotive as the train thundered past overhead, shaking the entire tenement city. Shaking the sleeping black people in their lice-ridden beds. Shaking the ancient bones and the aching muscles and the t.b. lungs and the uneasy foetuses of unwed girls. Shaking plaster from the ceilings, mortar from between the bricks of the building walls. Shaking the rats between the walls, the cockroaches crawling over kitchen sinks and leftover food; shaking the sleeping flies hibernating in lumps like bees behind the casings of the windows. Shaking the fat, blood-filled bedbugs crawling over black skin. Shaking the fleas, making them hop. Shaking the sleeping dogs in their filthy pallets, the sleeping cats, the clogged toilets, loosening the filth.

Hank jumped aside just in time.

The blood spurted from Goldy's cut throat in a shower, spraying the black street, the front fender and front wheel of the hearse. It gleamed for an instant with a luminous red sheen on the black pavement. It dulled the next instant, turning dark, fading into deep purple. The first gushing stream slackened to a slow pumping fountain as the heart pumped out its last beats. The flesh of the wide bloody wound turned back like bleeding lips, frothing blood.

The sweet sickish perfume of fresh blood came up from the crap-smelling street, mingled with the foul tenement smell of Harlem.

Jodie stepped back and let the dying body flop on its back to the pavement, jerking and twisting inside the black gown in death convulsions as though having a frantic sex culmination with an unseen mate.

The thunder of the train diminished into the brackish sound of metal grinding on metal as the train braked for a stop at the 125th Street Station.

Jodie bent down and wiped his knife blade on the hem of Goldy's black gown. The stroke had been executed so quickly there was blood only on the knife blade.

He straightened up, pressed the button releasing the catch. The blade dangled loose. With a twist of his wrist he snapped the knife shut. The lock clicked. He put it back into his coat pocket.

"I bled that mother-raper like a boar hog," he said proudly.

"Talked himself into the grave."

As though by speechless accord, Hank and Jodie looked up and down the street, up at the window of the third-story flat, into the dimly lit hall, examined the windows of the surrounding tenements.

Nothing was moving.

XVIII

THE SHORT, SHARP blast of a train whistle when it had crossed the river into Harlem awakened Jackson in a pool of terror.

He jumped to his feet, overturning the chair. He sensed someone striking at him from behind, ducked, and knocked the table aside. Wheeling about, he snatched the pipe from the table to knock Slim's brains out.

But there wasn't anybody.

"I must have been dreaming," he said to himself.

He realized then that he'd been asleep.

"There's a train coming," he said.

His wits were still fuddled.

He noticed his chauffeur's cap had fallen to the floor. He picked it up and brushed it off. But there was no dirt on it. The floor was spotlessly clean and still damp.

The scrubbed floor made him think of Imabelle. He wondered where she could have gone. To her sister's in the Bronx, maybe. But they were sure to find her there. The police were looking for her too. He'd have to phone her sister as soon as he got the gold ore checked in the baggage room at the station. He wasn't going to leave it at Goldy's, no matter what anyone said.

Suddenly he was filled with a sense of haste.

He searched his pockets for some paper to write Imabelle a note in case she came back there looking for him and didn't know where to find him. In his inside uniform pocket was a soiled sheet of stationery with Mr. Clay's letterhead containing a list of funeral items. He found a stub of pencil in his side overcoat pocket and unfolded the paper onto the kitchen table. He scribbled hurriedly:

"Honey, look for my brother, Sister Gabriel, in front of Blumstein's. He'll tell you where I am at . . ."

He was about to sign his name when it occurred to him that Slim was coming back with Hank and Jodie.

"I ain't thinking at all," he muttered to himself, balled up the sheet of stationery and threw it into the corner.

The rising thunder of the approaching train brought back

his nameless terror. He thought of a blues song his mother used
to sing,

> I flag de train an' it keep on easing by
> I fold my arms; I hang my head an' cry.

Suddenly he was running without moving. He was running
on the inside. He didn't have any time left to wonder where
Imabelle had gone. Just time left to worry. Anyway, he'd gotten
her away from Slim.

He picked up his club from the table. His eyes had turned
red. His face was gray and dry, lips chapped.

An old gray rat poked his head from underneath the grease-
covered rusty woodburning stove. The rat had red eyes also.
The rat looked at Jackson and he looked at the rat.

The house began to shake. The floor was shaking, shaking
the rat. Jackson felt himself begin to shake. His brains felt as
though they were shaking up and down in his head, about to
explode. The thunder of the train filled the room, froze the
shaking man and shaking rat in a death-like trance.

At that moment the whistle screamed. It screamed like a
stuck pig running through the corn patch with the knife still
in it.

The rat vanished.

Jackson's feet began to run.

He ran blindly from the kitchen, through the bedroom,
stumbling over the three-legged chair, jumped up and ran into
the pitch-dark hall and started down the stairs.

Then he remembered Imabelle's clothes. He turned around,
ran back to the kitchen, laid his pipe on the table, gathered the
clothes in his arms, turned around again and ran out of the flat,
forgetting his club.

He ran through the dark hall, down the steep, dark stairs,
trying to be as quiet as possible. Sweat started to pour from
his dry skin. He could feel it trickling down his neck, from
underneath his arms, down his sides, like crawling worms.

The hems of the dresses trailed on the dirty stairs. At the
bottom of the first staircase he tripped over the skirts, fell

belly-forward, holding the dresses clutched in his arms, and landed with a dull thud.

"Lord, my Savior," he muttered getting up. "Looks like I ain't got long to stay here."

He was hugging the dresses as though Imabelle were inside them, just able to see over the top of the pile, when he passed underneath the dim light in the ground-floor hall and came to the outside doorway.

He expected to see Goldy waiting impatiently on the front seat of the hearse. Instead he saw Hank and Jodie, standing on the far side of the hearse, facing each other and talking. He was petrified. He stood there with his mouth open in his wet black face, white teeth shining from purple-blue gums.

Hank and Jodie had just that instant withdrawn their gazes from the lighted hallway.

Hank was saying to Jodie, "Let's move him out the street."

"Move him where?"

"Inside the hearse."

"What for? Why don't we let the mother-raper lay where he's at?"

"He's a stooly. If the cops find him here they're on our trail like white on rice."

"If it was up to me, I'd leave him lay, and frig the cops. We're lamming, ain't we?"

Hank went back and opened the double-doors of the hearse. If he had turned his head he would have seen Jackson standing petrified in the doorway. But he was looking at the body as he walked back.

"Grab his shoulders," he said, stooping to pick up the feet.

Jodie began putting on his gloves. He was looking at the body also.

"What the hell, you scared to touch him with your hands?"

"The mother-raper's dead. That's what I'm scared of."

Jackson thought they were preparing to move the trunk. The thought released his petrified muscles. Through the rim of his vision he saw the panel truck. He thought they were going to take the trunk and put it into the truck. He didn't have any way of stopping them. He didn't even have his club.

For the first time he realized that Goldy was nowhere in sight. Maybe Goldy had seen them coming and had hidden. Goldy had the revolver. Jackson felt like damning Goldy to everlasting hell, but didn't want to commit blasphemy on top of all the other sins he'd committed.

He backed quietly down the hall, half-stumbling at each step, turned at the foot of the stairs and started to run back upstairs to the flat. Then he thought better of it. After they'd moved the trunk into their truck, they might go up to the flat for something or other.

He looked about for a place to hide.

The space underneath the stairs had been walled in to form a closet with the door facing a small dark corner at the back of the hall. He backed into the corner, tried the door of the closet, found it opened.

Garbage cans were crammed helter-skelter among dirty mops and pails. Folding the dresses to keep them from dangling into the cans, he squeezed inside, silently closed the door, and stood in the stinking dark, scarcely breathing.

Jodie took the body beneath the armpits, Hank the feet. They rammed it feet first into the funeral paraphernalia underneath the trunk. It was a tight squeeze and they had to lay it on its back and push it, with their feet against the shoulders. Finally they got the head in far enough to close the doors.

Hank went back and picked up the white bonnet and gray wig and stuck it back on the head. Then he pulled down some of the black bunting and artificial wreaths to cover the head before shutting the door.

"What you doing that for?" Jodie asked.

"In case anybody looks."

"Who's going to look?"

"How the hell do I know? We can't lock it."

They turned and looked up at the window of the third-story flat again.

Jodie took off his gloves, stuck his bare hand into his pocket and gripped the handle of his knife.

"Who helped him, you reckon?"

"I don't figure it. I had it cased as her and Jackson, but this stooly makes it different."

"You reckon Jackson's in it too?"

"Got to be, I figure. It's his hearse."

"You reckon they're still upstairs?"

"We're going to see right soon."

They turned, crossed the sidewalk, and entered the hall. Both had their hands in their overcoat pockets, Hank's gripping his .38 automatic pistol, Jodie's gripping his bone-handled knife. Their eyes searched the shadows.

As they approached the stairs they were talking loudly enough for Jackson to hear from the stinking closet underneath.

"Double-crossing bitch, I should have killed her—"

"Shut up."

Jackson could hear each footstep touching lightly on the wooden floor. He held his breath.

"I don't care if she does hear me, she ain't got no place to hide."

"Shut up. Other people are in here who can hear."

Jackson heard the footsteps as they started to ascend the stairs. Suddenly one pair stopped.

"What you mean, shut up? I'm getting good-and-goddam tired of you telling me to shut up all the time."

The second pair of footsteps stopped just as abruptly.

"I mean shut up. Just that."

Jackson held his breath so long in the dangerous silence his lungs ached before the footsteps began ascending again.

No further words were spoken.

Jackson breathed softly, listening to the steps going higher and higher, becoming fainter. He gripped the doorknob, pulled it inward with all his strength, turned it slowly so as not to make a sound, and opened the door a crack with infinite caution.

He heard the footsteps start up the second staircase, barely hearing them when they moved along the third-story hall.

He waited a moment longer, then came out of the closet running. An empty garbage can turned over with a shattering clang. The sound kicked him down the hall with his arms full of dresses, like a pointed-toe shoe in his rump.

He heard feet pounding on the wooden floor of the upper hallway, hitting the wooden steps like a booted centipede. As he crossed the sidewalk he heard a window being opened overhead.

He grabbed at the handle of the hearse door, threw it open, tossed the dresses onto the seat, jumped inside, fumbled in his pocket for the ignition key, turned on the ignition, and pressed the starter button.

"Catch, you God-damned son of a bitch, Lord forgive me," he raved at the reluctant motor. "Catch, you mother-raping bastard son of a bitch of a God-damned car—Jesus Christ, I didn't mean it."

He saw Jodie coming down the dimly lit hall, growing bigger and bigger in the rectangular perspective.

"Lord, have mercy," Jackson prayed.

Jodie came out of the doorway in a long flying leap, the knife blade flashing in the gloom. He hit the pavement, skidded toward the curb, bent forward and flailing the air with both hands as if trying to halt his charge on the edge of a prec-ipice, got his balance and turned as the old Cadillac motor roared.

Jackson shifted into drive and put weight on the treadle; the old hearse took off with a heavy whoomping sound, so fast the right edge of the front bumper hit the left rear fender of the pickup truck before Jackson got control, bent the fender into a mangled fin that scratched a river of scars on the black side of the hearse as it roared past, barely missing an iron stanchion of the overhead trestle as it turned west into 130th Street.

"One more shave that close, Lord, and this brother ain't going to be here long," Jackson muttered as he wrapped his short fat arms about the wheel and watched the street come up over the hood.

XIX

WHEN IMABELLE CAME downstairs and left Goldy and her man, Jackson, struggling with her trunk of gold ore, she glanced briefly at the parked hearse, giggled again, and started running down Park Avenue toward the 125th Street Station.

She didn't know the train schedule, but there would be a train leaving for Chicago.

"This sweet girl is going to be on it," she said to herself.

The 125th Street Station sat beneath the trestle like an artificial island, facing 125th Street. The double-track line widened into four tracks as it passed overhead on the gloomy, dimly lit wooden platform. Passengers alighting there for the first time had the impulse to turn about and climb back into the train. The platform shook like palsy and the loose boards rattled like dry bones every time a train passed.

From the platform could be seen the lighted strip of 125th Street running across the island from the Triborough Bridge, connecting the Bronx and Brooklyn, to the 125th Street ferry across the Hudson River into New Jersey.

At street level the hot, brightly lit waiting room was crammed with wooden benches, news-stands, lunch counters, slot machines, ticket windows, and aimless people. At the rear a double stairway ascended to the loading platform, with toilets underneath. Behind, out of sight, difficult to locate, impossible to get to, was the baggage room.

The surrounding area was choked with bars, flea-ridden flophouses called hotels, all-night cafeterias, hop dens, whorehouses, gambling joints, catering to all the whims of nature.

Black and white folks rubbed shoulders day and night, over the beer-wet bars, getting red-eyed and rambunctious from the ruckus juice and fist-fighting in the street between the passing cars. They sat side by side in the neon glare of the food factories, eating things from the steam tables that had no resemblance to food.

Whores buzzed about the area like green flies over stewing chitterlings.

The whining voices of blues singers, coming from the nightmare-lighted jukeboxes, floated in noisome air:

> My mama told me when I was a chile
> Dat mens and whiskey would kill me after a while.

Muggers with scarred faces cased the lone pedestrians like hyenas watching lions feast.

Purse snatchers grabbed a poke and ran toward the dark beneath the trestle, trying to dodge the cops' bullets pinging against the iron stanchions. Sometimes they did, sometimes they didn't.

White gangsters, four and six together in the bullet-proof limousines, coming and going from the syndicate headquarters down the street, passed the harness cops in the patrol cars, giving them look for look.

Inside the station plainclothes detectives were on twenty-four-hour duty. Outside on the street a patrol car was always in sight.

But Imabelle was more scared of Hank and Jodie than she was of the cops. She had never been mugged or fingerprinted. All the cops had ever wanted from her was a piece. Imabelle was a girl who believed that a fair exchange was no robbery.

She had her black coat buttoned tight, but running made the skirt flare, exposing a teasing strip of red dress.

A middle-aged church-going man, good husband and father of three school-age daughters, on his way to work, dressed in clean, starched overalls and an army jumper, heard the tapping of her heels on the pavement when he stepped from his ground-floor tenement.

"A mighty light-footed whore," he mumbled to himself.

When he came out onto the sidewalk he looked around and saw the flash of her high-yellow face and the tantalizing strip of red skirt in the spill of street light. He caught a sudden live-wire edge. He couldn't help it. His wife had been ailing and he hadn't had his ashes hauled in God knows when. As he looked at that fine yaller gal tripping his way, his teeth shone in his black face like a lighthouse on the sea.

"You is for me, baby," he said in a big bass voice, grabbing her by the arm. He was willing to put out five bucks.

Without breaking the flow of her motion she smacked him in his face with her black pocketbook.

The blow startled him more than it hurt. He hadn't meant her any harm; he just wanted to give the girl a play. But when he thought about a whore hitting a church man like himself, he became enraged. He closed in and clutched her.

"Don't you hit me, whore."

"Turn me loose, you black mother-raper," she fumed, struggling furiously in his grip.

He was a garbage collector and strong as a horse. She couldn't break free.

"Don't cuss me, whore, 'cause I'm going to get some of you whether you like it or not," he mouthed in a red raving passion of rage and lust, aiming to throw her to the pavement and rape her then and there.

"You goin' to get some of your mama, you big mother-raper," she cursed, digging a switch-blade knife, similar to Jodie's, from her coat pocket. She slashed him across the cheek.

He jumped back, clinging to her with one hand, and felt his cheek with the other. He took away his bloody hand and looked at the blood on it. He looked surprised. It was his own blood.

"You cut me, you whore," he said in a surprised voice.

"I'll cut you again, you mother-raper," she said, and began slashing at him in a feminine fury.

He released her and backed away, striking at the knife with his bare hands as though trying to beat off a wasp.

"What's the matter with you, whore?" he was saying, but his voice was drowned by the thunder of a train approaching the station. Suddenly the whistle blew like a human scream.

It scared her so much she jumped back and stared at the slashed man as though it had been he who had screamed.

"I'll kill you, you whore," he said, preparing to charge her knife.

She knew she couldn't make him run, couldn't cut him

down, and if he overpowered her he'd kill her. She turned and ran toward the station, swinging the open knife.

He ran after her, trailing blood from his face and hands.

"Don't let 'im catch you, baby," someone called encouragement from the dark.

The train overtook them, thundered by overhead, shaking the earth, shaking her running ass, shaking the blood from his wounds like scattered rain drops. It started grinding to a stop. The thunder terrified her; the brackish sound filled her mouth with acid.

She threw the knife into the gutter and ran past the line of waiting taxicabs, the cruising whores, the colored loiterers; turned, without stopping, through the side entrance into the waiting room, ran back to the women's toilet underneath the stairs, and locked herself inside.

The motley group of people standing about, sitting on the wooden benches, scarcely paid any attention. It wasn't unusual to see a woman running in that area.

But when the man hit the door, bleeding like a stuck bull, everybody sat up.

"I'm going to kill dat whore," he raved as he burst into the waiting room.

A colored brother looked at him and said, "She sho gave him some love-licks."

The man was halfway to the toilet when the white detective ran up and clutched him by both arms.

"Hold on, Brother Jones, hold on. What's the trouble?"

The man twisted in the detective's grip, but didn't break free.

"Listen, white folks, I don't want no trouble. That whore cut me and I'm going to get some of her."

"Hold on, hold on, brother. If she cut you we'll get her. But you're not going to get anybody. Understand?"

The colored detective sauntered up, looked indifferently at the bleeding man.

"Who cut him?"

"He said some woman did."

"Where'd she go?"

"She ran into the women's toilet."

The colored detective asked the cut man, "What does she look like?"

"Bright woman in a black coat and a red dress."

The colored detective laughed.

"Better let those bright whores alone, Daddy-o."

He turned, laughing, and went back toward the women's toilet.

Two uniformed cops from a patrol car came in quickly, as if expecting trouble. They looked disappointed when they didn't find any.

"Call the ambulance, will you?" the white detective said to one of them.

The cop hastened out to the patrol car to call the police ambulance on the two-way radio. The other cop just stood.

People gathered in a circle to stare at the big cut black man dripping red blood on the brown tiled floor. A porter came up with a wet mop and looked disapprovingly at the bloody floor.

Nobody thought it was unusual. It happened once or twice every night in that station. The only thing missing was that no one was dead.

"What did she cut you for?" the white detective asked.

"Just mean, that's why. She's just a mean whore."

The detective looked as though he agreed.

The colored detective found the toilet door locked. He knocked. "Open up, Bright-eyes."

No one answered. He knocked again.

"It's the law, honey. Don't make me have to get the station-master to get this door open or papa's going to be rough."

The inside bolt was slipped back. He pushed and the door opened.

Imabelle faced him from the mirror. She had washed and powdered her face, straightened her hair, rouged her lips, wiped off her high-heeled black suede shoes, and looked as though she'd just stepped from a band box.

He flashed his badge and grinned at her.

She said complainingly, "Can't a lady clean up a little in this joint without you cops busting in?"

He looked around. The only other occupants were two white women of middle age, who were cowering in a far corner.

"Are you the woman who's having trouble with that man?" he asked Imabelle, trying to trick a confession from her.

She didn't go for it. "Having trouble with what man?" She screwed up her face and looked indignant. "I came in here to clean up. I don't know what you're talking about."

"Come on, Baby, don't give papa any trouble," he said, looking her over as though he might consider laying her.

She gave him a look from her big brown bedroom eyes and flashed her pearly smile as though it might be a good consideration.

"If any man says he's having trouble with me, you can just say that's his own fault."

"I know just what you mean, Baby, but you shouldn't have cut him."

"I ain't cut nobody," she said, switching out into the waiting room.

"That's the whore who cut me," the man said, pointing a finger dripping with blood.

The morbid crowd turned to stare at her.

"Man, I'd have cut her first," some joker said. "If you know what I mean."

Imabelle ignored the crowd as she pushed her way forward. She walked up and faced the cut man and looked him straight in the face.

"This the man you mean?" she asked the colored detective.

"That's the one who's cut."

"I ain't never seen this man before in my life."

"You lying whore!" the man shouted.

"Take it easy, Daddy-o," the colored detective warned.

"What'd I cut you for, if I cut you?" Imabelle challenged.

The onlookers laughed.

One colored brother quoted:

> Black gal make a freight train jump de track.
> But a yaller gal make a preacher Ball de Jack.

"Come on, where's the knife?" the white detective said to Imabelle. "I'm getting tired of this horseplay."

"I'd better search the washroom," the colored detective said.

"She throwed it away outside," the cut man said, "I seen her throw it into the street, before she ran inside."

"Why didn't you pick it up?" the detective asked.

"Who for?" the cut man asked in surprise. "I don't need no knife to kill that whore. I can kill her with my hands."

The detective stared at him.

"For evidence. You say she cut you."

"Let's get it," one of the patrol cops said to the other and they went outside to look for the knife.

"Course she cut me. You can see for yourself," the cut man said.

The crowd laughed and started drifting away.

"Do you want to make a charge against this woman?"

"Charge? I'm charging her now. You can see for yourself she cut me."

Some joker said, "If she didn't cut you, you better see a doctor about those leaky veins."

"What are you holding me for?" Imabelle said to the white detective. "I tell you I ain't never seen this man before. He's got me mistaken for somebody else."

Another team of patrol-car cops came on the scene, looking at the cut black man with the curiosity of whites as they drew off their heavy gloves.

"You are to take these people to the precinct," the white detective said. "The man wants to enter a charge of assault against this woman."

"Jesus, I don't want him bleeding all over the car," one of the cops complained.

The whine of an ambulance sounded from the distance.

"Here comes the ambulance now," the colored detective said.

"Why they going to take me in when I haven't done any-thing?" Imabelle appealed to him.

He looked at her sympathetically. "I feel for you but I can't reach you, Baby," he said.

"If you prove your innocence you can sue him for false arrest," the white detective said.

"Well, ain't that something?" she said angrily.

Outside, the two uniformed cops searched in the gutter for the missing knife. Two colored men standing on the sidewalk watched them silently.

Finally one of the cops thought to ask them, "Did either of you men see anyone pick up a knife around here?"

"I seen a colored boy pick it up," one of the men admitted.

The cops reddened.

"God damn it, didn't you see us looking for it?" one asked angrily.

"You didn't say what you was looking for, Boss."

"By this time the bastard is probably blocks away," the second cop complained.

"Where'd he go?" the first cop asked.

The man pointed up Park Avenue.

Both cops gave him a hard threatening look.

"What did he look like?"

The colored man turned to his companion.

"What he look like, you think?"

The second colored man disapproved of his companion's volunteering information to white cops about a colored boy.

"I didn't see him," he said, showing his disapproval.

Both cops turned to stare at him in rage.

"You didn't seen him," one mimicked. "Well, God damn it, you're both under arrest."

The cops escorted the two colored men around to the front of the station and put them on the back seat of their patrol car while they got into the front seat. Passersby glanced at them with brief curiosity, and passed on.

The cops turned the car up Park Avenue on the wrong side to show their power. The red light beamed like an evil eye. They drove slowly, flashing the adjustable spotlights along the sidewalks, into the faces of pedestrians, into doorways, cracks, corners, vacant lots, searching for a colored boy who had picked up a bloodstained knife among the half-million colored people in Harlem.

They were just in time to see a panel delivery truck with a mangled rear fender turn the corner into 130th Street, but they weren't interested in it.

"What shall we do with these black sons of bitches?" one of the cops asked the other.

"Let 'em go."

The driver stopped the car and said, "Get out."

The two colored men got out and walked back toward the station.

When they arrived the ambulance was driving off, taking the cut man to Harlem Hospital so his wounds could be stitched before sending him on to the precinct station to prefer charges against Imabelle.

At the same time the patrol car carrying Imabelle to the precinct station was going east on 125th Street. It passed a hearse that turned slowly from Madison Avenue. But there was nothing suspicious about a hearse traveling about the streets in the early hours of morning. Folks were dying in Harlem at all hours.

The patrol cops turned Imabelle over to the desk sergeant to be held until the cut man came to prefer charges.

"You mean I've got to stay here until—"

"Shut up and sit down." The desk sergeant cut her off in a bored voice.

She started to act indignant, thought better of it, crossed the room to one of the wooden benches against the wall, and sat quietly with crossed legs showing six inches of creamy yellow thighs, as she contemplated her red-lacquered fingernails.

While she was sitting there, Grave Digger came out of the captain's office. He wore a white patch of bandage beneath his pushed-back hat and an expression of unadulterated danger. He looked at Imabelle casually, then did a double-take, recognizing her. He walked slowly across the room and looked down at her.

She gave him her bedroom look, hitched her red skirt higher, exposing more of her creamy yellow thighs.

"Well, bless my big flat feet," he said. "Baby-o, I got news for you."

She gave him her pearly smile of promise of pleasant things to come.

He slapped her with such savage violence it spun her out of the chair to land in a grotesque splay-legged posture on her belly on the floor, the red dress hiked so high it showed the black nylon panties she wore.

"And that ain't all," he said.

XX

WHEN JACKSON TURNED into 125th Street from Madison Avenue, headed toward the station baggage room, he was driving as cautiously as if the street were paved with eggs.

He was in a slow sweat from the crown of his burr head to the white soles of his black feet. Worrying about Imabelle, wondering if that woman of his was safe, worrying about her trunk full of gold ore, hoping nothing would go wrong now that he had rescued it from those thugs.

He was steering with one hand, crossing himself with the other.

One moment he was praying, "Lord, don't quit me now."

The next he was moaning the lowdown blues:

> If trouble was money
> I'd be a millionaire. . . .

A patrol car passed him, headed toward the precinct station, going like a bat out of hell. It went by so fast he didn't see Imabelle in the back seat. He thought they were taking some thug to jail. He hoped it was that bastard Slim.

An ambulance shot past. He skinned his eyes, his sweat turning cold, trying to see who was riding in it, and almost rammed into a taxi ahead. He caught a glimpse of the silhouette of a man and was relieved. Weren't Imabelle, whoever it was.

He wondered where that woman of his could be. He was worrying so hard about her that he almost ran down a big fat

black man doing the locomotive shuffle diagonally across the
street.

> Stood on the corner with her feets soaking wet
> Begging each and every man she met . . .

Jackson eased the hearse past Big Fats as though he were
picking his way through a brier patch. He didn't open his
mouth again. Couldn't tell what a drunk might do next. He
didn't want any trouble until he got the trunk checked and safe
from Goldy.

He had to drive past the front of the station, circle it on Park
Avenue, and come down beside the baggage room entrance
from the rear.

By the time he had pulled to the curb before the baggage-
room door, behind the line of loading taxicabs, Big Fats had
navigated the dangerous rapids of 125th Street traffic and was
shuffling up the crowded sidewalk beside the lighted windows
of the waiting room, heading up Park Avenue toward the
Harlem River.

None of them said anything to Big Fats. No need to borrow
trouble with an able-bodied colored drunk the size of Big Fats.
Especially if his eyes were red. That's the way race riots were
started.

But it made Jackson nervous to have the police congregating
in the vicinity while he was checking the trunk of gold ore. He
was so nervous as it was he was jumping from his shadow.
He left the motor running from habit. When he got out to go
to the baggage room, Big Fats spied him.

"Little brother!" Big Fats shouted, shuffling up to Jackson
and putting his big fat arm about Jackson's short fat shoulders

"Short-black-and-fat like me. You tell 'em, short and fatty.
Can't trust no fat man, can they?"

Jackson threw the arm off angrily and said, "Why don't you
behave yourself. You're a disgrace to the race."

Big Fats put the locomotive in reverse, let it idle on the track,
building up steam.

"What race, Little Brother. You want to race?"

"I mean our race. You know what I mean."

Big Fats bucked his red-veined eyes at Jackson in amazement.

"You mean to say you'd let 'em trust you with they women?" he shouted.

"Go get sober," Jackson shouted back with uncontrollable irritation, went around Big Fats like skirting a mountain, hurried into the baggage room without looking back.

Big Fats forgot him instantly, began shuffling up the street again.

Jackson found a colored porter.

"I got a trunk I want to check."

The porter looked at Jackson and became angry just because Jackson had spoken to him.

"Where you going to?" he asked gruffly.

"Chicago."

"Where's your ticket at?"

"I ain't got my ticket yet. I just want to check my trunk until I get my ticket."

The porter went into a raving fury.

"Can't check no trunk nowhere if you ain't got no ticket," he shouted at the top of his voice. "Don't you know that?"

"What are you getting so mad about? You act like we're God's angry people."

The porter hunched his shoulders as though he were going to take a punch at Jackson.

"I ain't mad. Does I look mad?"

Jackson backed away.

"Listen, I don't want to check it nowhere. I just want to check it here until I come down tonight to get my ticket."

"You don't want to check it nowhere. Man, what's the matter with you?"

"If you don't want to check it I'll go see the man," Jackson threatened.

The man was the white baggage-master.

The porter didn't want any trouble with the man.

"You means you want to check it," he said, giving in grudgingly. "Why didn't you say you just wanted to check it instead of coming in here talking 'bout going to Chicago?"

He snatched up a hand truck as though he'd take it and beat Jackson's brains out with it.

"Where's it at?"

"Outside."

The porter wheeled the hand truck onto the sidewalk and looked up and down the street.

"I don't see no trunk."

"It's in the hearse there."

He looked through the windows of the hearse and saw the trunk on the coffin rack.

"What you doing carrying a trunk around in a hearse for?" he asked suspiciously.

"We use it to carry everything."

"Well, get it out then," the porter said, still suspicious. "I ain't checking no trunk in no hearse where dead folks has been."

"Aw, man, Lord in heaven. Don't be so evil. The trunk's heavy. Ain't you going to help me lift it down?"

"I don't get paid for unloading no trunks from no hearses. I checks 'em when they is on the street."

"I'll help you git it out," a colored loiterer offered.

Jackson and the loiterer walked to the back of the hearse. The porter followed. Two white taxi drivers, taking a break, looked on curiously. From down the sidewalk a white cop eyed the group absently.

Big Fats came shuffling back down the street just as Jackson swung open the double-doors of the hearse.

"Watch out!" he shouted. "Can't trust no fat man!"

Jackson, the porter, and the third colored man stepped back from the hearse in unison as though they had suddenly looked upon the naked face of the devil.

Big Fats shuffled closer, looked over Jackson's shoulder. The locomotive stopped dead on the tracks.

All four black men had turned putty-gray.

"Great Gawdamighty!" Big Fats shouted. "Look at that!"

Underneath the trunk black cloth was piled high. Artificial flowers were scattered about in garish disarray. A horseshoe wreath of artificial lilies had slipped to the back. Looking out from the arch of white lilies was a black face. The face was looking backward from a head-down position, resting on the back of the skull. A white bonnet sat atop a gray wig which had fallen askew. The face wore a horrible grimace of pure evil. White-walled eyes stared at the four gray men with a fixed, unblinking stare. Beneath the face was the huge purple-lipped wound of a cut throat.

Jackson felt his scalp ripple as he recognized the face of his brother Goldy. His mouth came half open and caught. His eyes stretched until he felt as though the eyeballs were hanging from the sockets. His jaws began to ache. A warm wet stream flowed suddenly down his pants leg.

"That's a dead body, ain't it?" the porter said in a cracked voice, as though his suspicions had suddenly come true. His own eyes were as white-walled and fixed as the eyes of the corpse.

"Where?" Jackson said.

His brain had gone numb with panic and fear. His whole fat body began to shake as though he had the ague.

"Where?" the porter shrilled in a high whining voice that sounded like a file scraping across a saw. "Right there, that's where!"

The third colored man was still backing up the street.

"Cut sidewise to the bone," Big Fats said in a hushed, awed voice.

The taxi drivers sauntered over and looked down at the gory black head.

"Jesus Christ!" one exclaimed.

"It's a wig," the other one said.

"What is?"

"See, there's short hair underneath. By God, it's a man."

The uniformed cop approached slowly like a forerunner of doom, nonchalantly twirling his white nightstick. He looked down into the hearse with the air of a man who had been washed with all waters. The next instant he drew back in pallid shock and sucked in his breath. This was the water he'd never seen.

"How did this get there? Who did this? Whose hearse is this?" he asked stupidly, trying to collect his wits and looking quickly about for help.

He caught the eye of one of the plainclothes detectives at the waiting-room entrance and beckoned to him.

The third colored man had kept backing up Park Avenue toward the dark until he considered it safe to turn around. Now he was running up the dark street as fast as his feet would carry him.

Big Fats had turned cold sober and was trying to inch away too when the cop said sharply, "Don't anybody leave here."

"I ain't leaving," Big Fats denied. "Just stretching my feet a little."

The white taxicab drivers backed away and stood shoulder to shoulder against the baggage-room wall.

The white plainclothes detective pushed the porter aside, saying, "What's this?"

He took a look into the hearse, turned pale. "What the hell is this?"

"A body," the cop said.

"Who's the driver?"

"Me boss," Jackson quavered.

The harness cop blew out his breath in a sighing sound, glad to let the plainclothes detective take over. A crowd had begun to gather and he was glad to find something he could do.

"Get back!" he ordered. "Stand back!"

The detective took out his notebook and pencil.

"What's your name?" he asked Jackson.

"Jackson."

"Who's your boss?"

"Mr. H. Exodus Clay, on 134th Street."

"Where'd you pick up this corpse?"

"I don't know, boss. It was in there when I got in. I swear 'fore God."

The detective suddenly stopped writing and stared at Jackson incredulously.

Everyone stared at him.

"He say he done found a stiff and don't know where it come from," someone in the crowd exclaimed.

Jackson was trembling so that his teeth were chattering like ratchets. He wasn't scared now of losing his woman or losing

her gold ore. He wasn't thinking about his woman or her gold.
He was thinking only of his brother lying there in death with
his throat cut. This was the instinctive fear of the violently
dead. Fear of the dead themselves. He hadn't started yet thinking about what was going to happen to him. But the detective's
next question made him think about it.

"Do you mean to say you didn't know this corpse was in the
hearse when you took it out?"

"No sir. I swear 'fore God."

The colored detective came up at that moment and said casually, "What's the beef about?"

A patrol car turned in from 125th Street, driving on the
wrong side, plowed a path through the crowd that was spreading across the street.

"He's got a corpse in there and he says he doesn't know how
it got there," the white detective replied.

"Couldn't have walked, that's for sure," the colored detective said, pushing between Jackson and the porter to look at the
corpse.

"I'll be a mother-for-you!" he exclaimed, half choking,
more repulsed by sight of the cut throat than shocked.

Then he looked more closely.

"That's Sister Gabriel. And that son of a bitch was a man all
this time!"

The white detective continued to question Jackson as though
he were uninterested in the corpse's sex.

"How did it happen that you took the hearse out without
knowing there was a corpse in it?"

"Boss told me to bring this trunk to the station and check
it." He talked in gasps, scarcely able to breathe. "Swear 'fore
God. I just brought the trunk down like he told me to do and
put it there on the rack and drove on here to the station, like he
told me to. Lord be my judge."

"Check the trunk for what?"

Behind them the patrol-car cops were pushing back the
crowd.

"Get back, get back!"

The gray had left Jackson's face and he had begun to sweat

again. He wiped the sweat from his face, dabbing at his red-veined eyes with the dirty handkerchief.

"I didn't understand you, boss."

Bums and prostitutes and working johns and loiterers and the night thieves and bindle stiffs and blind beggars and all the flotsam that floated on the edges of the station like dirty scum on bog water were jostling each other, drawn by the word of a cut-throat corpse, trying to get a look to see what they were missing.

"I said what does he want to check the trunk for?"

"For Chicago. He's going to Chicago tonight and he wanted to check his trunk now so when he got his ticket he wouldn't be bothered with it," Jackson said gaspingly.

The white detective snapped shut his notebook.

"I don't believe a God-damned word of that bullshit."

"It could be true," the colored detective said. "One driver might have brought in the corpse and left it in the hearse for a moment and this driver—"

"But God damnit, who's checking a trunk at this time of night?"

The colored detective laughed. "This is Harlem. His boss might have the trunk stuffed with hundred-dollar bills."

"Well, I'll soon find out. You hold him. If he got the corpse legitimately, it was released by the homicide bureau." He looked about, over the heads of the crowd. "Where the hell's that patrol car? I'm going to contact the precinct station."

Suddenly Jackson could see the electric chair and himself sitting in it. If they took him to the precinct station they'd find out about Slim and his gang. And they'd find out about Coffin Ed getting blinded and Grave Digger getting hurt, maybe killed. They'd find out about the gold ore and about Goldy, and about him stealing the five hundred dollars and stealing the hearse too. They'd find out that Goldy was his brother and they'd figure that Goldy was trying to steal his woman's gold ore. And they'd figure he'd cut Goldy's throat. And they'd burn his black ass to a cinder.

"I've seen the order," he said, inching toward the sidewalk. "It was on the front seat, but I didn't know who it was for."

"Order?" the white detective snapped. "Order for what?"

"Order for the body. We get an order from the police to take the body. I saw it right there on the front seat."

"Well, God damnit, why didn't you say so? Let's see it."

Jackson went to the front of the hearse and opened the door. He looked on the bare seat.

"It was right here," he said.

He crawled halfway into the driver's compartment on his hands and knees, groping behind the seat, looking on the floor. He heard the old Cadillac motor turning over softly. He inched half of his rump onto the seat to lean over and look into the glove compartment. His elbow touched the gear lever and knocked it over to drive, but the motor purred softly and the car didn't move.

"It was right here just a minute ago," he repeated.

Now both detectives stood on the sidewalk by the door, eying him skeptically.

"Contact precinct and inquire about a recent homicide," the white detective called to a patrol-car cop. "Colored man impersonating a nun got his throat slashed. See if the body was released. Get the name of the undertaker."

"Right-o," the cop said, hurrying off to his two-way radio.

Jackson got all of his rump onto the seat in order to search on top of the sunshades where a stack of papers were shelved.

"It was right here, I saw it."

He put his right hand on the wheel to steady himself to get a better look. Suddenly, with his left hand he slammed the door shut; he put his whole weight down on the gas treadle.

The old Cadillac motor was the last of the '47 models with the big cylinder-bore and had enough power to pull a loaded freight train.

The deep-throated roar of the big-bored cylinders sounded like a four-motor stratocruiser gaining altitude as the big black hearse took off.

Pedestrians were scattered in grotesque flight. A blind man jumped over a bicycle trying to get out of the way.

There was a nine-foot gap between a big trailer truck going east toward the bridge and a taxi going west on 125th Street.

Jackson put the hearse in a straight line across the street and it went through that nine-foot hole so fast it didn't touch, straight down the narrow lane of Park Avenue beside the iron stanchions of the overhead trestle. The gearshift was clumping as it climbed into second, third, and hit the supercharger.

Pistols went off around the station like firecrackers on a Chinese New Year's day.

The soft mewling yowl of the patrol car sounded and swelled swiftly into a raving scream as the first of the patrol cars leaped into pursuit. It headed straight toward the side of the big trailer-truck as the cop tried to calculate the speed; he calculated wrong and skidded as he tried to turn. The patrol car went into the big, high, corrugated-steel trailer broadside, tried to go underneath it, was flipped back into the street, and spun to a stop with the front wheels bent out of use.

The two other patrol cars were just beginning to whine. Over and above the din of noise was the big jubilant crowing of Big Fats.

"What did I tell you? Can't trust no fat man! That little fat mother-raper done cut his own mama's throat from ear to ear!"

XXI

GRAVE DIGGER STOOD over the prone figure of Imabelle in a blind rage. That acid-throwing bastard's woman, trying to play cute with him. And his partner, Coffin Ed, was in the hospital, maybe blinded for life. The air was electric with his rage.

He was wearing Coffin Ed's pistol along with his own. He had it in his hand without knowing he had drawn it. He had his finger on the hair trigger, and it was all he could do to keep from blowing off some chunks of her fancy yellow prat.

Two harness cops, passing through the booking room, turned tentatively in his direction to restrain him, saw the pistol trembling in his hand, then drew up in silent amazement.

Two patrol cops bringing in three drunken prostitutes stopped, staring wide-eyed. The loud cursing voices of the prostitutes were cut off in mid-sentence. They seemed to shrink bodily, stood suspended in cowed postures, became sober on the spot.

Everyone in the room thought Grave Digger was going to kill Imabelle.

The silence lasted until Imabelle scrambled hastily to her feet and glared at Grave Digger with a rage equal to his own.

"What the hell's the matter with you, cop?" she shouted.

She was in such a fury she forgot to pull down her skirt and brush the dust from her clothes.

"If you open your mouth once more—" Grave Digger began.

"Easy does it," the desk sergeant said, cutting him off.

Imabelle's left cheek was bright red and swelling. Her hair was disarranged. Her eyes were cat-yellow, her mouth a mangled scar in a face gone bulldog ugly.

The harness cops looked at her sympathetically.

Grave Digger controlled himself with an effort. His motions were jerky as he holstered the pistol. His tall, lank frame moved erratically, like a puppet on strings. He couldn't trust himself to look at her again. He turned toward the desk sergeant.

"What's the rap on this woman?" His voice was thick.

"Cuttin' up a man over at the 125th Street Station."

"Bad?"

"Naw. A colored worker who lives back of the station in the bucket says she slashed him."

Grave Digger finally turned back and looked at Imabelle as if to question her, then changed his mind.

"They took him to Harlem Hospital to get stitched," the desk sergeant added. "They'll bring him in shortly to prefer charges."

"I want her," Grave Digger said in a flat voice.

The desk sergeant looked at Grave Digger's face.

"Take her," he said.

At the same time he buzzed the captain's office from the row of button signals on his desk. He didn't want to argue with Grave Digger, but he couldn't let him take the prisoner out of the station without orders.

The lieutenant who was on night duty came from the captain's office and asked, "Yeah?"

The desk sergeant nodded toward Grave Digger and Imabelle.

"Jones wants this pickup."

"She was at the whing-ding up on the river tonight," Grave Digger said thickly.

"What do you want her for?"

"She going to show me where to find them."

The lieutenant looked as though he didn't like the idea too well.

"What's on her in the book?" he asked the desk sergeant.

"A colored man says she cut him. Over on Park Avenue, in the bucket. Haven't brought him in yet."

The lieutenant turned back to Grave Digger.

"Any connection?"

"She's going to tell me," Grave Digger said in his thick, cottony voice.

"I ain't cut nobody," Imabelle said, "I ain't never seen that man before in my life."

"Shut up," the desk sergeant said.

The lieutenant looked her over carefully.

"Strictly penitentiary bait," he muttered angrily, thinking, It's these high-yellow bitches like her that cause these black boys to commit so many crimes.

"It's getting late," Grave Digger said.

The lieutenant frowned. It was irregular, and he didn't like any irregularities on his shift. But hoodlums had thrown acid in a cop's eyes. This was one of the hoodlums' women. And this was the cop's partner.

"Take her," he said. "Take somebody with you. Take O'Malley."

"I don't want anybody with me," Grave Digger said. "I got Ed's pistol with me, and that's enough."

The lieutenant turned without saying another word and went back into the captain's office.

None of the other cops said anything. They stared from Grave Digger to Imabelle.

Grave Digger walked up to her. She stood her ground defiantly. He snapped handcuffs on her wrists so quickly she didn't know what was happening. When he took her by the arm and began steering her toward the door, she turned and appealed to the desk sergeant.

"Are you going to let this crazy man take me away from here?"

The desk sergeant looked away without replying.

"I got my rights—" she shouted.

Grave Digger jerked her through the door so violently that her feet flew out from under her. He dragged her down the concrete steps.

His car was parked half a block down the street.

"Turn me loose. I can walk," she said, and he freed her arm.

The car was the same black sedan in which he had followed Gus's Cadillac to the gang's hideaway on the river. He opened the front door. She got in awkwardly, hindered by the handcuffs. He went around and got into the driver's seat.

"All right, where are they?"

"I don't know where they're at," she said sulkily.

He turned on the seat to face her.

"Don't play cute with me, woman. I want those acid-throwing bastards and you're going to take me to them or I'll pistol-whip your face until no man ever looks at you again." His voice was so thick she could barely understand him.

She felt the danger emanating from him. She might have still defied him if he had threatened to kill her. She wanted to get away herself before Hank and Jodie were caught and made to talk. Nothing could be done to her without their testimony. But she knew he meant what he said about destroying her face.

"I'll take you where they live. I want 'em caught. But I don't know whether they're still there. They might have lammed already."

He started the motor, tuned in the short-wave radio to the police signal.

"Where is it?"

"In a rooming house up on St. Nicholas Avenue, over a

doctor's. He lives in the first two floors and rents out the top two to roomers."

"I know where it is and you'd better pray that they're still there."

She had nothing to say to that.

As they turned north on St. Nicholas Avenue, a metallic voice from the radio said,

". . . pick up a black open-face hearse; 1947 Cadillac; M-series license, number unknown, driven by short, black-skinned Negro wearing chauffeur's uniform. . . . Dark green steamer trunk riding on coffin carrier visible through side windows, containing corpse of male Negro dressed in nun's habit. Known as Sister Gabriel. Slashed throat. . . . Hearse heading south on Park Avenue. . . . Over. . . . Repeat. . . . Pick up—"

"That complicates matters." Grave Digger knew immediately that Jackson was driving the hearse. It had to be one of Clay's hearses. Somehow the gang had gotten to Goldy. But why was Jackson running from the police?

Imabelle shuddered, thinking of how close she'd come to getting her own throat cut.

Grave Digger took a shot in the dark. "Where did you contact Jackson?"

"I haven't seen Jackson."

"What's in the trunk?"

"Gold ore."

He didn't look around.

They were going fast up the wet black pavement of St. Nicholas Avenue. On the east side of the street were rows of apartment buildings, becoming larger, more spacious, better kept; facing the steep cliff of the rocky park across the street. Above was the university plateau, overlooking the Hudson River.

"I haven't got time to put it together now. I'm going to get the bastards first and put it together afterward."

"I hope you kill 'em," she said viciously.

"You're going to have a lot to talk to me about later, Little Sister."

Day was breaking. The buildings high up on the plateau stood out in the morning light.

They passed the intersection of 145th Street with the subway kiosks on each corner. The car made a sickening dip and rose sharply into the section where the elite of the underworld lived among the working strivers.

A delivery truck was dumping stacks of the *Daily News* onto the wet sidewalk. Next to the drugstore was an all-night barbecue joint, the counter stools filled with early workers in the glaring neon light, eating barbecued ribs for breakfast. The hot pork ribs turned on four automatic spits before a huge electric grill built into the wall near the plate-glass front window, tended by a tall black man in a white chef's uniform.

Two doors beyond Eddie's Cellar Restaurant she pointed toward a yellow hardtop Roadmaster Buick, parked beneath a street light in front of a four-storied stone-fronted house.

"There's their car."

Grave Digger pulled in ahead, skidded to a stop, got out and looked at the dark front windows of the house. At street level was a black lacquered door with a shiny brass knocker. Three white enamel door bells were placed in a vertical row on the red door frame beneath a black-and-white plaque bearing the name of Dr. J.P. Robinson.

The house was asleep.

Grave Digger walked quickly back to the car, casing the street as he went and memorizing the number on the yellow California license plate. First he opened the engine hood, disconnected the wires from the distributor head and put it into his coat pocket, and slammed the hood down with a bang. Then he tried the doors, found them locked, and peered inside. There was a tan cowhide suitcase in back on the floor. He went around to the luggage compartment, sprung the lock with the screwdriver blade from his heavy jackknife, glanced briefly at the luggage stacked inside, pushed the lid down and walked back to his car. The operation hadn't taken more than a minute.

"Where are they?"

"At Billie's."

"All three of them?"

She nodded. "If they haven't left."

He got into his seat behind the wheel, looked up the black macadam surface of St. Nicholas rising in a wide black stripe between rows of fashionable apartment buildings on both sides, taking gray shape in the morning light.

Early workers were trudging in from the side streets, hurrying toward the subway. Later the downtown office-porters would pour from the crowded flats in a steady stream, carrying polished leather briefcases stuffed with overalls to look like businessmen, and buy the *Daily News* to read on the subway.

The men he was looking for were not in sight.

"Who has the habit?" he asked.

"Both of 'em. Hank and Jodie, I mean. Hank's on hop and Jodie on heroin."

"How about the slim one?"

"He just drinks."

"What monickers are they using with Billie?"

"Hank calls himself Morgan; Jodie—Walker; Slim—Goldsmith."

"Then Billie knows about their gold-mine pitch?"

"I don't think so."

"Woman, there are a thousand questions you're going to have to answer," he said as he shifted into gear and got the car to moving again.

They went past Lucky's Cabaret, King-of-the-Chicken restaurant, Elite Barbershop, the big stone private mansion known as Harlem's Castle, made a U-turn at 155th Street between the subway kiosks, came back past The Fat Man's Bar and Grill, and drew up before the entrance to a large swank six-storied graystone apartment building. Big expensive cars lined the curbs in that area.

From there, going down the steep descent of 155th Street to the bridge, it was less than a five-minute walk to that dark, dismal section along the Harlem River where the shooting fracas had taken place.

XXII

WHEN JACKSON TOOK off in the big old Cadillac hearse down Park Avenue, he didn't know where he was going. He was just running. He clung to the wheel with both hands. His bulging eyes were set in a fixed stare on the narrow strip of wet brick pavement as it curled over the hood like an apple-peeling from a knife blade, as though he were driving underneath it. On one side the iron stanchions of the trestle flew past like close-set fence pickets, on the other the store-fronted sidewalk made one long rushing somber kaleidoscope in the gray light before dawn.

The deep, steady thunder of the supercharger spilled out behind. The open back doors swung crazily on the bumpy road, battering the head of the corpse as it jolted up and down beneath the bouncing trunk.

He headed into the red traffic-light at 116th Street doing eighty-five miles an hour. He didn't see it. A sleepy taxi driver saw something black go past in front of him and thought he was seeing automobile ghosts.

The stalls of the Harlem Market underneath the railroad trestle begin at 115th Street and extend down to 101st Street. Delivery trucks filled with meat, vegetables, fruit, fish, canned goods, dried beans, cotton goods, clothing, were jockeying back and forth in the narrow lane between the stanchions and the sidewalk. Laborers, stall-keepers, truck jumpers and drivers were milling about, unloading the provisions, setting up the stalls, getting prepared for the Saturday rush.

Jackson bore down on the congested scene without slackening speed. Behind him were yowling sirens and the red eyes of pursuing patrol cars.

"Look out!" a big colored man yelled.

Panicked people jumped for cover. A truck did the shimmy as the driver frantically steered one way and then the other trying to dodge the hearse.

When Jackson first noticed the congested market area, it was too late to stop. All he could do was try to put the hearse through whatever opening he saw. It was like trying to thread a fine needle with a heavy piece of string.

He bent to the right to avoid the truck, hit a stack of egg crates, saw a molten stream of yellow yolks filled with splinters splash past his far window.

The right wheels of the hearse had gone up over the curb and plowed through crates of vegetables, showering the fleeing men and the store fronts with smashed cabbages, flakes of spinach, squashed potatoes and bananas. Onions peppered the air like cannon shot.

"Runaway hearse! Runaway hearse!" voices screamed.

The hearse ran into crates of iced fish spread out on the sidewalk, skidded with a heavy lurch, and veered against the side of the refrigerator truck. The back doors were flung wide and the throat-cut corpse came one-third out. The gory head hung down from the cut throat to stare at the scene of devastation from its unblinking white-walled eyes.

Exclamations in seven languages were heard.

Caroming from the refrigerator truck, the hearse wobbled wildly to the other side of the street, climbed over a side of beef a delivery man had dropped to the street to run, and tore, staggering, down the street.

He was through the market area so fast a colored laborer exclaimed in a happy voice, "God damn, that was sudden!"

"But did you see what I seen?"

"You reckon he stole it?"

"Must have, man. What else the cops chasing him for?"

"What's he gonna do with it?"

"Sell it, man, sell it. You can sell anything in Harlem."

When the hearse came into the open at 100th Street, it was splattered with eggs, stained with vegetables, spotted with blood. Chunks of raw meat, fish scales, fruit skins clung to the dented fenders. The back doors swung open and shut.

It had gained on the patrol cars, which had had to slow down in the market area. Jackson had the feeling of sitting in the middle of a nightmare. He was sealed in panic and he couldn't get out. He couldn't think. He didn't know where he was going, didn't know what he was doing. Just driving, that's all. He had forgotten why he was running. Just running. He felt like just sitting there behind the wheel and driving that hearse off the edge of the world.

He went through Puerto Rican Harlem at ninety miles an hour. An old Puerto Rican woman watched the hearse pass, saw the back doors swing open, and fainted dead away.

A patrol car screaming north on Park Avenue spotted the hearse coming south as it approached the intersection of 95th Street. The patrol car made a crying left turn. Jackson saw it and bent the big hearse in a long right turn. The back doors flew open and the corpse slid out slowly, like a body being lowered into the sea, thumped gently onto the pavement and rolled onto its side.

The patrol car swerved, trying to keep from running over it, went out of control and spun like a top on the wet street, bounced over the curb, knocked over a mailbox, and shattered the plate-glass window of a beauty shop.

Jackson went along 95th Street to Fifth Avenue. When he saw the stone wall surrounding Central Park he realized he was out of Harlem. He was down in the white world with no place to go, no place to hide his woman's gold ore, no place to hide himself. He was going at seventy miles an hour and there was a stone wall ahead.

His mind began to think. Thought rolled back on the lines of a spiritual:

> Sometimes I feel like a motherless child,
> Sometimes I feel like I'm almost gone . . .

Nothing left now but to pray.

He was going so fast that when he turned sharply north on Fifth Avenue, heading back toward Harlem, the trunk slid back, went off the end of the coffin rack, bounced on the floor of the hearse, somersaulted into the street, landed on the bottom edge and burst wide open.

Jackson was so deep in prayer he didn't notice it.

He drove straight up Fifth Avenue to 110th Street, turned

over to Seventh Avenue, kept north to 139th Street, and drew up in front of his minister's house.

He passed three patrol cars on the way. The cops gave the battered, dirty, meat-smeared, egg-stained hearse a cursory look and let it pass. No steamer trunks and dead bodies in that wreck. Jackson didn't even notice the patrol cars.

He parked in front of his minister's house, got out and went around to the back to lock the doors. When he found the hearse empty, that was the bitter end. Nothing even left to pray for. His girl was gone. Her gold ore was gone. His brother was dead, and gone too. He just wanted to throw himself on the mercy of the Lord. It was all he could do to keep from weeping.

Reverend Gaines was in the middle of a big religious dream when his housekeeper awakened him.

"Brother Jackson is downstairs in the study and says he wants to see you on something very important."

"Jackson?' Reverend Gaines exclaimed in extreme irritation, rubbing the sleep from his eyes. "You mean our brother Jackson?"

"Yes, sir," that patient colored woman said. "Your Jackson."

"Lord save us from squares," Reverend Gaines muttered to himself as he got up to slip his black silk brocaded robe over his purple silk pyjamas, and descend to the study.

"Brother Jackson, what brings you to the house of the shepherd of the Lord at this ungodly hour, when all the other Lord's sheep are sleeping peacefully in the meadows?" he asked pointedly.

"I've sinned, Reverend Gaines."

Reverend Gaines stiffened as though someone had uttered blasphemy in his presence.

"Sinned! Good Lord, Brother Jackson, is that sufficient reason to awaken me at this hour of night? Who hasn't sinned? I was just standing on the banks of the River Jordan, dressed in a flowing white robe, converting sinners by the thousands."

Jackson stared at him. "Here in the house?"

"In a dream, Brother Jackson, in a dream," the minister explained, unbending enough to smile.

"Oh, I'm sorry I woke you up, but it's an emergency."

"That's all right, Brother Jackson, sit down." He sat down himself and poured a glass of liqueur from a cut-glass decanter on his mahogany desk. "Just a little elderberry cordial to awaken my spirit. Will you have a glass?"

"No sir, thank you," Jackson declined as he sat down facing Reverend Gaines across the desk. "My spirit is already wide awake as it is."

"You're in trouble again? Or is it the same trouble? Woman trouble, wasn't it?"

"No sir, it was about money the last time. I was trying to keep it from looking as if I had stolen some money. But this time it's worse. It's about my woman too. I'm in deep trouble this time."

"Has your woman left you? At last? Because you didn't steal the money? Or because you did?"

"No sir, it's nothing like that. She's gone but she hasn't left me."

Reverend Gaines took another sip of cordial. He enjoyed solving domestic mysteries.

"Let us kneel and pray for her safe return."

Jackson was on his knees before the minister was.

"Yes sir, but I want to confess first."

"Confess!" Reverend Gaines had started to kneel but he straightened up suddenly like a Jack-in-the-box. "You haven't killed the woman, Brother Jackson?"

"No sir, it's nothing like that."

Reverend Gaines gave a sigh of relief and relaxed.

"But I've lost her trunk full of gold ore."

"What?" Reverend Gaines's eyebrows shot upward. "Her trunk full of gold ore? Do you mean to say she had a trunk full of gold ore and never told me, her minister? Brother Jackson, you had better make a full confession."

"Yes sir, that's what I want to do."

At first, as Jackson unfolded the story of being swindled on The Blow and stealing five hundred dollars from Mr. Clay's to bribe the bogus marshal and trying to get even by gambling, Reverend Gaines was filled with compassion.

"The Lord is merciful, Brother Jackson," he said consolingly.

"And if Mr. Clay is half as merciful, you will be able to work off that account. I will telephone to him about the matter. But what about this trunk full of gold ore?"

But when Jackson described the trunk and related how the gang had kidnapped his woman to get possession of it, Reverend Gaines's eyes began to widen with curiosity.

"You mean to say that that big green steamer trunk in that little room where you and she lived was filled with gold ore?"

"Yes sir. Pure eighteen-carat gold ore. But it didn't belong to her. It belonged to her husband and she had to give it back. So I had to get my brother, Goldy, to help me find them."

Revulsion replaced the curiosity in Reverend Gaines's eyes as Jackson described Goldy.

"You mean to say that Sister Gabriel was a man? Your twin brother? And he swindled our poor gullible people with tickets to heaven?"

"Yes sir, lots of people believed in them. But the only reason I went to him was because he was a crook and I needed him to help me."

As Jackson related the events of the night, Reverend Gaines's eyes got wider and wider, and horror began replacing the expression of revulsion. By the time Jackson got to his escape from the police at the 125th Street Station, Reverend Gaines was sitting forward on the edge of his seat with his mouth hanging open and his eyes bulging. But Jackson had related the story as he had seen it happen, and Reverend Gaines did not understand why he had fled from the police.

"Was it because of your brother?" he asked. "Did they discover he was impersonating a nun?"

"No sir, it wasn't that. It was because he was dead."

"Dead!" Reverend Gaines jumped as though a wasp had stung him in the rear. "Great God above!"

"Hank and Jodie had cut his throat when I went upstairs to look for Imabelle."

"Good God, man, why didn't you call for help? Didn't you hear his cries?"

"No sir. I had sat down to rest for a minute and I had fell asleep."

"Merciful heavens, man! You fell asleep while you were looking for your woman who was in grave danger. While her fortune was sitting unprotected in that street—that street too, the most dangerous street in Harlem—protected only by your brother, a foul sinner who was scarcely better than a murderer himself." Reverend Gaines's rich black skin was turning gray at the very thought of what had happened. "And they cut his throat? And put his body in the hearse?"

Jackson mopped the sweat from his eyes and face.

"Yes sir. But I didn't mean to go to sleep."

"And what did you do with the hearse? Drive it off into the Harlem River?"

"No sir, it's parked out front."

"Out front! In front of my house?"

Forgetting his ecclesiastical dignity, Reverend Gaines jumped to his feet and shambled hastily across the room to peer through the front window at the battered hearse parked at the curb in the gray dawn. When he turned back to face Jackson he looked as if he had aged twenty years. His implacable self-confidence was shaken to the core. As he shuffled slowly back to his seat, his silk brocade robe flopped open and the pants of his purple silk pyjamas began slipping down. But he paid no attention.

"Do you mean to sit there, Brother Jackson, and tell me that your brother's body with its throat cut and your woman's trunk full of gold ore are in that hearse out there, parked in front of my house?" he asked in horror.

"No sir. I lost them. They fell out somewhere, I don't know where."

"They fell out of the hearse? Into the street?"

"It must have been in the street. I didn't drive anywhere else."

"Just why did you come here, Brother Jackson? Why did you come to me?"

"I just wanted to kneel here beside you, Reverend Gaines, and give myself up to the Lord."

"What!" Reverend Gaines started as though Jackson had uttered blasphemy. "Give yourself up to the Lord? Jesus Christ, man, what do you take the Lord for? You have to go and give yourself up to the police. The Lord won't get you out of that kind of mess."

XXIII

THE RAYS OF the rising sun over the Harlem River shone blood-red on the top floor of the building where Billie ran her after-hours joint.

"Can't I just wait in the car?" Imabelle asked. She was having trouble with her breathing.

"Get out," Grave Digger said flatly.

"What do you need me for? They're up there, I tell you. You know I can't run anywhere with these handcuffs on."

He saw that she was scared. She was trembling all over.

"Well, Little Sister, if it's your grave, just remember that you dug it," he said without mercy. "If Ed was here to see you I'd let you stay."

She got out, stumbling as her legs buckled. Grave Digger came around from the other side, took her by the arm, steered her up a flight of concrete stairs, through the glass double-doors, into a small immaculate foyer furnished with a long table, polished chairs and parchment-shaded lights flanking wall mirrors.

Not a sound could be heard.

"These slick hustlers live high on the hog," he muttered. "But at least they're quiet."

They rode in a push-button elevator to the sixth floor, and turned toward the jade-green door at the left of a square hall.

"I beg you," Imabelle pleaded, trembling.

"Go ahead and buzz her," Grave Digger ordered, flattening himself against the wall beside the door and drawing his long-barreled nickel-plated pistol.

She pushed the button. After a time the Judas window clicked open.

"Oh, it's you, honey," said a deep feminine voice, strangely pleasant.

The door was unlocked.

Grave Digger held his .38 in his right hand, put his left hand on the doorknob, and rode it in.

A vague shape in the almost pitch-dark hall moved slowly to one side to let him enter, and the deep voice said to Imabelle, not so pleasantly, "Well, come on inside and shut the door."

Imabelle pushed in behind Grave Digger, and the front of the dark hall was crowded. The faint sound of her teeth chattering could be heard in the silence.

The woman closed the door and locked it without speaking.

"You got some friends I want, Billie," Grave Digger said.

"Come into my office a moment, Digger."

She unlocked the first door to the left with a Yale key attached to a chain about her neck. A copper-shaded lamp spilled a soft glow on a blond-oak writing desk. When she switched on the bright overhead light, a luxurious bedroom suite, planted in the deep pile of a vermilion rug, sprang into view. She quickly closed the door behind them.

Grave Digger searched the room with one quick glance, looked an instant longer at the knobs of the doors to the closet and bathroom, then moved out into the room so that Billie was a target against the hall door.

"Talk fast," he said. "It's getting late."

She was a brown-skinned woman in her middle forties, with a compact husky body filling a red gabardine dress. With a man's haircut and a smooth, thick, silky moustache, her face resembled that of a handsome man. But her body was a cross. The top two buttons of the dress were open, and between her two immense uplifted breasts was a thick growth of satiny black hair. When she talked a diamond flashed between her two front teeth.

She flicked a glance at Imabelle's swollen, purple-tinted cheek, across Imabelle's scared-sick eyes, and then gave her whole attention to Grave Digger.

"Don't take them in the house, Digger. I'll send them out."

"Are they all together?"

"All? There's only two here now. Hank and Jodie."

"Slim ought to be here too," Imabelle said in a breathless

voice. Both Grave Digger and Billie turned to stare at her.

"Maybe he's out looking for me."

Billie looked away from her first. Grave Digger stared an instant longer. Then both turned back toward each other.

"I'll take those two," Grave Digger said.

"Not in the house, Digger. They're hopped to the gills and kill-happy. I've got two of my best girls with them."

"That's the chance you take running this kind of joint."

"I don't run it for free, you know. I pay like hell. And the captain promised me there wouldn't be any rumbles in here."

"Where are they?"

"The captain won't like it, Digger."

Grave Digger looked at her thoughtfully.

"Billie, they threw acid in Ed's eyes."

Billie shuddered.

"Listen, Digger, I'll set them up. I'll take them down to the foyer myself and hand them over to you with their hands full of air."

"You know goddamn well they don't intend to leave that way. They're planning on going over the roof and coming out of the house next door."

"All right. Listen. I'll trade you. I'll give you three purse-snatchers, a prowler you've been wanting for a long time—"

"It's getting late, Billie."

"—and the Wilson murderer. The one who killed the liquor-store man during that stickup last month."

"I'm going to come back for them. But I'll take these two now."

She turned quickly and pulled open a top bureau-drawer.

Grave Digger drew a bead on the middle of her spine.

She pulled the drawer clear out, threw it on the bed. It was filled evenly with stacks of brand-new twenty-dollar bills.

"There's five grand. It's yours."

He didn't look at the money.

"Where are they, Billie? There isn't much time."

"They're in the pad. But they've got themselves locked in and they won't open even for me."

"They'll open for her," Grave Digger said, nodding toward Imabelle.

Billie turned to stare at Imabelle.

Imabelle had turned a sour-cream yellow with blue-black half-moons beneath her dog-sick eyes. She was trembling like a leaf.

"Don't make me do it. Please don't make me do it."

Tears streamed down her face. She knelt on the floor, clutched Grave Digger about the legs.

"I'll do anything. I'll be your woman, or a circus girl—"

"Get up," Grave Digger said without mercy. "Get up, or I'll blast open the door, holding you in front of me as a shield."

She got to her feet like an old woman.

Billie looked at her without pity.

"You know Hank when you see him?" Imabelle asked Grave Digger, talking in gasps. "The one who threw the acid?"

"I'd know that bastard in hell."

"He's the one who's got the gun."

"Digger, for God's sake be careful," Billie pleaded. "They got two of my best young girls in there. Jeanie's only sixteen and she's with Jodie—"

"You're talking yourself out of business."

"—and Jodie's on a kill-crazy edge with that knife. And Carol's only nineteen herself."

"Let's just hope neither of their numbers comes up," Grave Digger said.

He turned to Imabelle. "Go down and knock on the door."

When they came out of the room, a white man came from the bathroom next door, buttoning his fly, gave them a drunken look, and staggered quietly back to the sitting room.

Imabelle went down the hall as to her death.

There were six rooms and a bath in the flat, the four bedrooms facing across the long center-hall, the bath between Billie's office and the small bedroom called the pad. The hall ran into a big front combination dining-sitting room with shaded windows overlooking both 155th Street and St. Nicholas Avenue; a small electrically equipped kitchen was to the right.

There was a jukebox playing softly at one end of the sitting room; two white men sat on divans with three colored girls. At the other end, toward the kitchen, two colored men and a colored woman sat at a large mahogany dining table eating fried chicken and potato salad. The lights were low, the air faintly tinted with incense.

In one of the bedrooms a white man and a colored girl lay embraced between sky-blue sheets. In another, five colored men played a nearly wordless game of stud poker in the smoke-filled air, drinking cold beer from bottles and eating sandwiches.

The pad had a door opening into the hall, and another on the side at the back which opened into one end of the kitchen. Both doors were locked, with the keys in the locks. There was a single window opening onto the landing of the fire escape, but it was hidden behind heavy drapes drawn over Venetian blinds.

Hank lay on a couch, dressed in his blue suit, his head propped on two sofa pillows. He was slowly puffing opium through a water pipe. The shallow bowl with the bubbling opium pill rested on a brazier on a glass-covered cocktail table. The smoke passed through a short curved stem, bubbled in a glass decanter half-filled with tepid water, was drawn through a long transparent plastic tube into the amber mouthpiece which Hank held loosely between slack lips.

His .38 automatic lay beside him, out of sight against the wall.

A young girl wearing a white blouse over full, ripened breasts and tight-fitting slacks sat on the green carpet, her knees drawn up and her head resting back against the sofa. She had a smooth seal-brown face, big staring eyes, and a wide-lipped, flower-like mouth.

Jodie sat across the room, on a green leather ottoman. His head was bent over almost inside of the speaker of a console combination as he listened to a Hot Lips Page recording of *Bottom Blues*, playing it over and over so low that the notes were heard distinctly only by his drug-sharpened sense of hearing.

A girl sat on the floor between his outstretched legs. She wore a lemon-yellow blouse over budding breasts, and Paisley slacks. She had an olive-skinned, heart-shaped face, long black lashes concealing dark-brown eyes, and a mouth too small for the thickness of the lips. Her head rested on Jodie's knee.

Jodie was staring over her head, lost in the blue music. He ran his left hand slowly back and forth over her crisp brown curls as though he liked the sensation. His right arm rested on his thigh and in his right hand he held the bone-handled switch-blade knife, snapping it open and shut.

"Don't you have another record?" Hank asked, as if from a great distance.

"I like this record."

"Doesn't it have another side?"

"I like this side."

Jodie started the record again. Hank looked dreamily at the ceiling.

"When are we going?" Jodie asked.

"As soon as it gets daylight."

Jodie stared at the dial of his wrist watch.

"It ought to be daylight now."

"Give it some time. Ain't no hurry."

"I want to be on the road. I'm getting nervous sitting around here."

"Wait a while. Give it some time. Let some traffic get on the road. We don't want to be the only car leaving town with California plates."

"How the hell you know there's going to be any others?"

"Ohio plates, then. Illinois plates. Give it some time."

"I'm giving it some mother— time."

The record came to a stop. Jodie started it over again, bent his ear to the speaker, and clicked the knife open and shut.

"Stop clicking that knife," Hank said indifferently.

"I didn't know I was clicking it."

A hesitant knock sounded above the low-playing blues.

Hank stared dreamily at the locked door. Jodie stared tensely. The girls didn't look up.

"See who's there, Carol," Hank said to the girl beside him. She started to get up. "Just ask."

"Who is it?" she asked in a harsh, startling voice.

"Me. Imabelle."

Hank and Jodie kept staring at the locked door. The girls turned and stared at it also. No one answered.

"It's me, Imabelle. Let me in."

Hank reached down along his side and wrapped his fingers about the butt of the automatic. Jodie's knife clicked open.

"Who's with you?" Hank asked in a lazy voice.

"Nobody."

"Where's Billie?"

"She's here."

"Call her."

"Billie, Hank wants to talk to you."

"Hank?" Hank said. "Who's Hank?"

"Don't use that name," Billie said, then to Hank, "I'm here. What do you want?"

"Who's with Imabelle?"

"Nobody."

"Open the door a crack," Hank said to Carol.

She got up and crossed the room in a hip-swinging walk, unlocked the door and opened it a crack. Hank had his automatic aimed at the crack.

Imabelle put her face in view.

"It's Imabelle," Carol said.

Billie pushed the door open wider and looked past Imabelle at Hank. "Do you want to see her?"

"Sure, let her come in," Hank said, putting the gun out of sight beside him.

Carol opened the door wide and Imabelle stepped into the room. She was so scared she was biting down vomit.

Hank and Jodie stared at her tear-streaked face and swollen, purple-tinted cheek.

"Close the door," Hank said dreamily.

Imabelle stepped to one side, and Grave Digger came out of the dark hall like an apparition coming up from the sea. He had a nickel-plated pistol in each hand.

"Straighten up," he said thickly.

"It's a mother— plant," Jodie grated.

Jodie had his left hand resting on Jeanie's curly head, his right hand extended, the knife open. With a sudden tight grip his left hand closed and he lifted the girl up from the floor by her hair, holding her in front of him as a shield, and put the sharp naked blade tight against her throat as he came violently to his feet.

The girl didn't cry out, didn't utter a sound, didn't faint. Her body went flaccid beneath Jodie's grip. Her face was stretched into distortion, a drop of blood trickled slowly down her taut neck. Her eyes were huge black pools of animal terror, slanting upwards at the edges, overwhelming her small distorted face. She didn't breathe.

Grave Digger caught a look at her face from the corner of his eye, and didn't move for fear of starting that knife across her throat.

Hank stared at Grave Digger dreamily without moving, his fingers still curled about the butt of the hidden .38. Grave Digger stared back. They were watching the flicker of each other's eyes, paying no attention to Jodie and the paralyzed girl. Nobody spoke. Carol stood frozen with one hand on the doorknob. Imabelle stood trembling, out of range on the other side. Everything was in pantomime.

Jodie backed toward the door that opened into the kitchen. The girl backed with him, followed his every motion with a corresponding motion, as if performing some macabre dance. Her eyes were fixed straight ahead in pools of undripping tears.

Jodie brought up against the door. "Reach around me and open it," he ordered the girl.

The girl reached her left hand carefully around his body, felt for the key, turned it, and opened the door.

Jodie backed into the kitchen, still holding the girl in front of him.

Billie stood silently beside the white enamel electric range with a double-bladed wood-chopper's axe held poised over her right shoulder, waiting for Jodie to come into reach. He took another step backward, his eyes on Grave Digger's guns. Billie chopped his upper forearm in a forward-moving strike to knock the knife blade forward from the girl's throat. Jodie wheeled in violent reflex, his knife-arm flopping like an empty sleeve, as the knife clattered on the tiled floor, struck out backwards with the edge of his left hand. Billie took the blow across the mouth as she chopped him in the center of the back between the shoulder blades, like splitting a log, knocking him forward to his knees.

His head flew about to look at her as he cried, "Mother-raping—"

She put her whole weight in a down-chopping blow and sank the sharp blade of the axe into the side of his neck with such force it hewed through the spinal column and left his head dangling over his left shoulder on a thin strip of flesh, the epithet still on his lips.

Blood geysered from red stump of neck over the fainting girl as Billie dropped the axe, picked her up bodily in her arms, and showered her with kisses.

As if it were a signal Hank was waiting for, he swung up the black snout of his .38 automatic, knowing that he didn't have a chance.

Before it had cleared his hip, Grave Digger shot him through the right eye with his own pistol held in his right hand. While Hank's body was jerking from the bullet in the brain, Grave Digger said, "For you, Ed," took dead aim with Coffin Ed's pistol held in his left hand, and shot the dying killer through the staring left eye.

Pandemonium broke loose in the house. Imabelle slipped beneath Grave Digger's arm and bolted toward the door. Guests poured from the rooms into the narrow hall in a panic-stricken stampede.

But Grave Digger had already wheeled into the hall after Imabelle, pushed her into the corner, and blocked the door. He flicked on the bright overhead lights with the barrel of one gun and stood with his back against the door with a gun in each hand.

"Straighten up," he shouted in a big loud voice. And then, as if echoing his own voice, he mimicked Coffin Ed, "Count off."

"And now, Little Sister," he said to the cowering woman in the corner. "Where's Slim?"

Her teeth were chattering so she could scarcely speak.

"In the—in the trunk," she stammered.

XXIV

IT WAS HOT in the small room high up on the twenty-second floor of the granite-faced county building far downtown in City Center. Pink-shirted young Assistant DA John Lawrence, who had been assigned to conduct the interrogation, sat behind a large flat-topped green steel desk, his blond crew-cut hair shining with cleanliness in the slanting rays of the afternoon sun.

Jackson sat on the edge of a green leather chair across from him, dirty and disheveled and shades blacker than he ever looked in Harlem. Grave Digger sat sidewise on the wide window ledge, looking across Manhattan Island at an ocean liner going down the Hudson River, headed for the Narrows and Le Havre. A court stenographer sat at the end of the desk with a stylo poised over his notebook.

For a moment motion was suspended.

Lawrence had just finished questioning Jackson. Suddenly he stirred. He wiped the sweat from his freckled face, combed his manicured fingernails through his hair, and shifted his athletic shoulders in the Brooks Brothers gray flannel suit.

He had read Grave Digger's report over twice before he had begun his interrogation. He had read the report from the 95th Street precinct. The trunk containing Slim's body had been reported by a Fifth Avenue bus driver who had noticed it lying open in the street. The police had found Slim's body, bearing twenty stab-wounds, wrapped in a blanket weighted with rocks, and had taken it to the morgue.

The bodies of Hank and Jodie had also been taken to the morgue. They had been identified by fingerprints as the men wanted in Mississippi for murder.

The apartment on Upper Park Avenue had been investigated. All it had revealed as evidence had been a quantity of fool's gold piled on the coal in the coalbin.

He had listened for two hours to the unfolding of the saga of the high-yellow woman and the trunk full of solid gold ore with increasing stupefaction. Still he did not believe he had heard it all correctly.

He stared at Jackson with a look of awed incredulity.

"Whew!" he whistled softly.

He and the court stenographer exchanged glances.

Grave Digger didn't look around.

"Any questions you want to ask, Jones?" Lawrence asked with a note of appeal.

Grave Digger turned his head.

"What for?"

Lawrence looked back at Jackson and said helplessly, "And you insist, to the best of your knowledge, that the trunk contained gold ore and nothing else?"

Jackson mopped his own shining black face with a handkerchief almost the same color.

"Yes, sir, I'd swear to it on a stack of Bibles. As many times as I have seen it."

"You also state, to the best of your knowledge, that the Perkins woman had already left the scene—the area—when your brother—" He consulted his notes. "—er, Sister Gabriel, was murdered."

"Yes sir, I'd swear to it. I had looked all over for her and she was gone."

Lawrence cleared his throat.

"Had gone, yes. And you still contend that she—the Perkins woman, was held by this gang—this man Slim—against her will."

"I know she was," Jackson declared.

"How can you be so certain about that, Jackson? Did she tell you that?"

"She didn't have to tell me, Mr. Lawrence. I know she was. I know Imabelle. I know she wouldn't have taken up with those people without their making her. I know my Imabelle. She wouldn't do anything like that. I'd swear to it."

Grave Digger kept looking at the river.

Lawrence studied Jackson covertly, pretending he was reading his notes. He had heard of gullible colored people like Jackson, but he had never seen one in the flesh before.

"Ahem! And you insist that she had nothing to do with the gang's cheating you out of your money?"

"No sir. Why would she do that? It was as much her money as it was mine."

Lawrence sighed. "I don't suppose there's any need of asking, but it's a matter of form. You don't want to prefer charges against her, do you?"

"Prefer charges against her? Against Imabelle? What for, Mr. Lawrence? What's she done?"

Lawrence closed his notebook decisively and looked over at Grave Digger. "What's city got on him, Jones?"

Grave Digger turned back, but still didn't look at Jackson.

"Reckless driving. Destruction of property. Some of it is covered by the automobile insurance. And resisting arrest."

"Are you going to take him?"

Grave Digger shook his head. "His boss has already gone his bail."

Lawrence stared at Grave Digger.

"He has!" Jackson exclaimed involuntarily. "Mr. Clay? He's gone my bail? He hasn't got any warrant out for my arrest?"

Lawrence turned to stare at Jackson.

"He stole five hundred dollars from his boss," Grave Digger said. "Clay swore out a warrant for his arrest but late this morning he withdrew the charge."

Lawrence ran his fingers through his clipped hair again.

"All of these people sound as though they're raving crazy," he muttered, but when he noticed the stenographer taking down his words he said, "Never mind that." He looked at Grave Digger again. "What do you make of it?"

Grave Digger shrugged slightly. "Who knows?"

Lawrence stared at Jackson. "What have you got on your boss?"

Jackson fidgeted beneath the stare and mopped his face to hide his confusion. "I ain't got nothing on him."

"Shall I hold him as a material witness?" Lawrence appealed again to Grave Digger.

"What for? Witness against whom? He's told all he knows, and he's not going anywhere."

Lawrence let out his breath. "Well, you're free to go, Jackson. The county has nothing on you. But I advise you to contact all those claimants immediately—those people whose property you destroyed. Get them squared up before they press charges."

"Yes sir, I'm going to do that right away."

He stood up, then hesitated, fiddling with his chauffeur's cap.

"Have any of you-all heard anything from my woman—where she's at or anything?"

All three of them turned again to stare at him. Finally Lawrence said, "She's being held."

"She is? In jail? What for?"

They stared at him in an unbelieving manner. "We're holding her for questioning," Lawrence finally said.

"Can I see her? Talk to her, I mean?"

"Not now, Jackson. We haven't talked to her yet ourselves."

"When do you think I'll be able to see her?"

"Pretty soon, perhaps. You don't have to worry about her. She's safe. I advise you to get about squaring up those claimants as soon as you can."

"Yes sir. I'm going to see Mr. Clay right now."

When Jackson had left, Lawrence said to Grave Digger, "It's pretty well established that Jackson is as innocent as a lamb, don't you think?"

"Sheared lamb," the court stenographer put in.

Grave Digger grunted.

"Have you had any news on your partner, Jones?" Lawrence asked.

"I was by the hospital."

"How is he?"

"They said he would see, but he'd never look the same."

Lawrence sighed again, squared his shoulders and assumed a look of grim determination. He pressed a button on his desk, and when a cop poked his head in from the corridor, he said, "Bring in the Perkins woman."

Imabelle wore the same red dress, but now it looked bedraggled. The side of her face where Grave Digger had slapped her had flowered into deep purple streaked with orange.

She gave Grave Digger a quick look and shied away from

his calculating stare. Then she took the seat facing Lawrence, started to cross her legs but thought better of it and sat with her knees pressed together, her back held rigid, on the very edge of the seat.

Lawrence looked at her briefly, then studied the notes in front of him. He took his time and reread all the reports.

"Jesus Christ, all this cutting and shooting," he muttered. "This room is swimming in blood. No, no, don't take that," he added to the court stenographer.

He looked up at Imabelle again, slowly stroking his chin, wondering where to begin questioning her.

"Who was Slim?" he finally asked. "What was his real name? We have him down here as Goldsmith. In Mississippi he was known as Skinner."

"Jimson."

"Jimson! Is that a name? Christian name or family name?"

"Clefus Jimson. That was his real name."

"And the other two. What were their real names?"

"I don't know. They used a lot of names. I don't know what their real names were."

"This Jimson." The name felt unpleasant in his mouth. "We'll just call him Slim. Who was Slim? What was your connection with him?"

"He was my husband."

"I thought as much. Where were you married?"

"We weren't exactly married. He was my common-law husband."

"Oh! Were you—did you keep in touch with him? That is, while you were living with Jackson?"

"No sir. I hadn't seen him or heard anything about him for almost a year."

"Then how did he get in touch with you—or you in touch with him, however it worked?"

"I ran into him at Billie's by accident."

"Billie's?" Lawrence consulted his notes again. "Oh yes, that's where the other two were killed." My God, the blood, he was thinking. "What were you doing at Billie's?"

"Just visiting. I'd go up there afternoons when Jackson was

at work, just to sit around and visit. I didn't like to hang around in bars where it might cast reflections on him."

"Ah. I see. And when you met Slim you and he connived to-gether to cheat Jackson on the confidence game—" He glanced at his notes. "The Blow."

"I didn't want to. They made me do it."

"How could they force you to do it if you didn't want to?"

"I was scared to death of him. All three of them. They had it in for me and I was scared they'd kill me."

"You mean they had a grudge against you. Why?"

"I'd taken the trunk full of gold ore they used to work their lost-gold-mine racket with."

"You mean the fool's gold that was found in the coalbin where you and Slim lived?"

"Yes sir."

"You took it when?"

"When I left him in Mississippi. He was playing around with another woman and when I left I just up and took it and brought it to New York. I knew they couldn't work the racket without it."

"I see. And when he found you at Billie's he threatened you."

"He didn't have to. He just said, 'I'm gonna take you back and we're gonna rook that nigger you been living with.' Hank and Jodie was there too. Hank was all hopped up and in that mean dreamy way he has when he's hopped and Jodie was gaged on heroin and kept snapping that knife open and shut and looking at me as if he'd like to cut my throat. And Slim, he was half-drunk. And Hank said they were going to take the gold ore and start operating right here in New York. There wasn't nothing for me to say. I had to do it."

"All right. Then you contend that you participated under duress. That they forced you on threat of death to work with them in their racket?"

"Yes sir. It was either that or get my throat cut. There was no two ways about it."

"Why didn't you go to the police?"

"What could I say to the police? They hadn't done nothing

then. And I didn't know they were wanted in Mississippi for murder. That happened after I'd gone."

"Why didn't you go to the police after they had cheated Jackson out of fifteen hundred dollars?"

"It was the same thing. I didn't know then that Jackson had got hep that he'd been beat. If I'd gone to the police then and Jackson hadn't preferred charges, the cops would have just let them go. And they'd have killed me then for sure. I didn't know then about Jackson's brother. I just knew that Jackson himself was a square and he couldn't help me none."

"All right. But why didn't you go to the police after they'd thrown acid into Detective Johnson's face?"

She glanced fleetingly in the direction of Grave Digger, and drew into herself. Grave Digger was staring at her with a fixed expression of hate.

"I didn't have any chance," she said in a pleading tone of voice. "I would have, but I couldn't. Slim was with me all the time until we got home. Then after Hank and Jodie came down the river in that motorboat they rented, they got out underneath the railroad bridge and came straight to the place where Slim and me was at. Then there wasn't any use of thinking about going."

"What happened there?"

Sweat filmed her bruised face beneath their concentrated stares.

"Well, you see, Jodie thought I'd ratted to the police, until Slim showed him where I couldn't have ratted. I hadn't never had no chance. Jodie was gaged and evil and if it hadn't been for Hank, Jodie and Slim would have got to fighting again. Hank was the only one carried a gun, and he put his gun on Jodie and stopped him. Then Jodie wanted him and Hank to take the gold ore and lam and leave me and Slim there. Slim said they couldn't take the gold ore without taking him and me too. Then Hank said he agreed with Jodie. They couldn't take Slim on account of the acid burns on his neck and face. The cops could identify him too easy. They'd put two and two together and know just who he was. Hank said for Slim to hole up somewhere until his face got healed and they'd send for him, but meantime they'd take the gold ore. Slim said nobody was taking his gold ore, he didn't give a damn what they did. Then before Hank could stop him Jodie had stuck him in the heart and kept sticking him until Hank said, 'Let up, God damn it, or I'll kill you.' But by then Slim was dead."

"Where were you when all this was happening?"

"I was there, but I couldn't do nothing. I was scared to death that Jodie was going to start sticking me too. He would have if Hank hadn't stopped him. He was like a crazy man."

"But why did they put the body in the trunk?"

"They wanted to get rid of it to keep from having another murder rap hanging on them in New York. Hank said he knew where they could get some more fool's gold in California. So they just left enough in the trunk to weight it down and threw the rest in the coalbin. They were planning to drop the trunk into the Harlem River. Hank said he was going to get a truck to move it and Jodie was supposed to stand downstairs and keep on the lookout. I was supposed to scrub the blood off the floor. I was too scared to think about leaving with Jodie standing downstairs. I didn't know he had gone with Hank until Jackson and his brother came to take the trunk."

Lawrence rubbed his chin angrily, trying to get the picture into focus. His eyes seemed out of focus too.

"Just where did you fit into their plans?"

"They were going to take me with them. I was scared they were going to take me out and kill me on the road somewhere."

"But you had already gotten away by the time they returned and killed Goldy?"

"Yes sir. I didn't know anything about that."

"Why didn't you notify the police then?"

"I was planning to. I was going down to the police station and tell the first policeman I saw. But that man attacked me before I had even gotten there, and before I had a chance to say anything the police had rushed me off to jail for just trying to protect myself."

Lawrence paused to study the report again.

"I told Detective Jones where to find Hank and Jodie just as soon as I got a chance," she added.

Lawrence blew out a sighing breath. "But you induced your boy-friend, Jackson, and his brother—er, Sister Gabriel—to move the trunk containing Slim's body without telling them what was in it?"

"No sir, I didn't induce them. They had their minds made up to take it and I was afraid if I told them they'd stay there trying to get the gold ore and let Hank and Jodie come back and find them and there'd be more killing. I knew Jackson believed it was real gold ore and I could see his brother believed it too. I figured the best thing was to let them take the trunk and get away as fast as they could. Then they'd be gone before Hank and Jodie got back."

"You said that Jodie was standing downstairs as a lookout."

"That's what I thought at first, but when Jackson and his brother came upstairs I knew Jodie must have gone with Hank. I figured that after they'd gotten away safe I could tell the police about everything and wouldn't anybody else get hurt."

Lawrence looked over at Grave Digger. "Do you believe that?"

"No. She saddled Jackson and Goldy with the body and planned to lam on the first train leaving town. She didn't give a damn what happened to any of them."

"I just didn't want to see anybody else get hurt," Imabelle protested. "There was enough people killed already."

"All right, all right," Lawrence said. "That's your story."

"It ain't no story. It's the truth. I was going to tell the police everything. But that big black mother—that man attacked me before I had a chance."

"All right, all right, you've told your story."

Lawrence turned to Grave Digger. "I'll hold her for complicity."

"What for? You can't convict her. She claims they forced her to do it. Jackson will support her contention. He believes it and she knows he believes it. It's proven they were dangerous men. Who's left to deny her story? All the witnesses against her are dead, and any jury you find will believe her."

Lawrence mopped his hot red face.

"How about yours and Johnson's testimony?"

"Let her go, let her go," Grave Digger said harshly. He looked as if he were riding the crest of a rage. "Ed and I will square accounts. We'll catch her uptown some day with her pants down."

"No, I can't have that," Lawrence said. "I'll hold her in five thousand dollars' bail."

XXV

MR. CLAY WAS having his afternoon nap when Jackson arrived. Jackson found the front door open and walked in without knocking. Smitty, the other chauffeur, was whispering with a woman in the dimly lit chapel.

Jackson opened the door to Mr. Clay's office softly and entered quietly. Mr. Clay lay on the couch, facing the wall. Dressed in his tailcoat attire, his long bushy gray hair floating on the coverlet, parchment-like skin framed by the dark wall, he looked like a refugee from a museum, in the dim light from the floor-lamp that burned continuously in the front window.

"That you, Marcus?" he asked suddenly without turning.

"No sir, it's me, Jackson."

"Have you got my money, Jackson?"

"No sir—"

"I didn't think so."

"But I'm going to pay you back every cent, Mr. Clay—that five hundred dollars I borrowed and that two hundred you advanced me on my salary. Don't you worry about that, Mr. Clay."

"I'm not worrying, Jackson. You can put in a claim against the county for the money those hoodlums swindled you out of."

"I can? Against the county?"

"Yes. They had eight thousand dollars in their possession. But just keep it to yourself, Jackson, just keep it to yourself."

"Yes sir, I'll certainly do that."

"And Jackson—"

"Yes sir?"

"Did you bring back my hearse?"

"No sir. I didn't know whether I could. I left it parked in front of the station house."

"Then go get it, Jackson. And hurry back, because there's work for you to do."

"You're going to take me back, Mr. Clay?"

"I haven't never let you go, Jackson. A good man like you is hard to find."

"Yes sirree. Will you bury my brother for me, Mr. Clay?"

"I'm in the business, Jackson. I'm in the business. How much insurance did he have?"

"I don't know yet."

"Find out then, Jackson, and we'll talk business."

"Yes sir."

"How's that yellow woman of yours, Jackson?"

"She's fine, Mr. Clay. But she's in jail right now."

"That's too bad, Jackson. But anyway, you know she ain't cheating on you."

Jackson forced a laugh. "You're always joking, Mr. Clay. You know she wouldn't do anything like that."

"Not as long as she's in jail, anyway," Mr. Clay said sleepily.

"I'm going down to try to see her now."

"All right, Jackson. See Joe Simpson and have him go her bail—if it's not too much."

"Yes sir. Thank you, Mr. Clay."

Joe Simpson had his office on Lenox Avenue, around the corner. Jackson rode with him back downtown to the county building.

When Assistant DA Lawrence learned that Imabelle was making bail, he sent for Joe Simpson. Grave Digger and the court stenographer had gone, and Lawrence was alone in his office.

"Joe, I want to know who's going that woman's bail?" he asked.

Simpson looked at him in surprise.

"Why, Mr. Clay is."

"Jesus Christ!" Lawrence exclaimed. "What is this? What's going on here? What have they got on him? They steal his money, wreck his hearse, take advantage of him in every way that's possible, and he hastens to go their bail to get them out of jail. I want to know why."

"Two of those fellows had eight thousand dollars on them when they were killed."

"What's that got to do with it?"

"Why, I thought you knew how that worked, Mr. Lawrence. The money goes for their burials. And Mr. Clay got their funerals. It's just like they've been drumming up business for him."

Jackson was in the other wing of the building, waiting in the vestibule, when the jailor brought Imabelle from her cell. He gave a long sighing laugh and took her in his arms. She wriggled closely against the curve of his fat stomach and welded her bruised lips against his sweaty kiss.

Then she drew back and said, "Daddy, we got to hurry and see that old buzzard and get our room back so we'll have somewhere to sleep tonight."

"It's going to be all right," he told her. "I got my job back. And it was Mr. Clay who went your bail."

She held him at arms' length and looked into his eyes.

"And you got your job back too, Daddy. Well ain't that fine?"

"Imabelle," he said sheepishly. "I just want to tell you, I'm sorry I lost your trunk full of gold ore. I did the best I could to save it."

She laughed out loud and squeezed his strong, fat arms.

"Daddy, don't you worry. Who cares about an old trunk full of gold ore, as long as I got you?"

The Real Cool Killers

I

"I'm gwine down to de river,
Set down on de ground.
If de blues overtake me,
I'll jump overboard and drown . . ."

BIG JOE TURNER was singing a rock-and-roll adaptation of *Dink's Blues*. The loud licking rhythm blasted from the jukebox with enough heat to melt bones.

A woman leapt from her seat in a booth as though the music had struck her full of tacks. She was a lean black woman clad in a pink jersey dress and red silk stockings. She pulled up her skirt and began doing a shake dance as though trying to throw off the tacks one by one.

Her mood was contagious. Other women jumped down from their high stools and shook themselves into the act. The customers laughed and shouted and began shaking too. The aisle between the bar and the booths became stormy with shaking bodies.

Big Smiley, the giant-sized bartender, began doing a flat-footed locomotive shuffle up and down behind the bar.

The colored patrons of Harlem's Dew Drop Inn on 129th Street and Lenox Avenue were having the time of their lives that crisp October night.

A white man standing near the middle of the bar watched them with cynical amusement. He was the only white person present.

He was a big man, over six feet tall, dressed in a dark gray flannel suit, white shirt and blood-red tie. He had a big-featured, sallow face with the blotched skin of dissipation. His thick black hair was shot with gray. He held a dead cigar butt between the first two fingers of his left hand. On the third finger was a signet ring. He looked about forty.

The colored women seemed to be dancing for his exclusive

entertainment. A slight flush spread over his sallow face.

The music stopped.

A loud grating voice said dangerously above the panting laughter: "Ah feels like cutting me some white mother-raper's throat."

The laughter stopped. The room became suddenly silent.

The man who had spoken was a scrawny little chicken-necked bantamweight, twenty years past his fist-fighting days, with gray stubble tingeing his rough black skin. He wore a battered black derby green with age, a ragged plaid mackinaw and blue denim overalls.

His small enraged eyes were as red as live coals. He stalked stiff-legged toward the big white man, holding an open spring-blade knife in his right hand, the blade pressed flat against his overalled leg.

The big white man turned to face him, looking as though he didn't know whether to laugh or get angry. His hand strayed casually to the heavy glass ashtray on the bar.

"Take it easy, little man, and no one will get hurt," he said.

The little knifeman stopped two paces in front of him and said, "Efn' Ah finds me some white mother-raper up here on my side of town trying to diddle my little gals Ah'm gonna cut his throat."

"What an idea," the white man said. "I'm a salesman. I sell that fine King Cola you folks like so much up here. I just dropped in here to patronize my customers."

Big Smiley came down and leaned his ham-sized fists on the bar.

"Looka here, big, bad, and burly," he said to the little knife-man. "Don't try to scare my customers just 'cause you're bigger than they is."

"He doesn't want to hurt anyone," the big white man said. "He just wants some King Cola to soothe his mind. Give him a bottle of King Cola."

The little knifeman slashed at his throat and severed his red tie neatly just below the knot.

The big white man jumped back. His elbow struck the edge of the bar and the ashtray he'd been gripping flew from his hand and crashed into the shelf of ornamental wine glasses behind the bar.

The crashing sound caused him to jump back again. His second reflex action followed so closely on the first that he avoided the second slashing of the knife blade without even seeing it. The knot of his tie that had remained was split through the middle and blossomed like a bloody wound over his white collar.

". . . throat cut!" a voice shouted excitedly as though yelling Home Run!

Big Smiley leaned across the bar and grabbed the red-eyed knifeman by the lapels of his mackinaw and lifted him from the floor.

"Gimme that chiv, shorty, 'fore I makes you eat it," he said lazily, smiling as though it were a joke.

The knifeman twisted in his grip and slashed him across the arm. The white fabric of his jacket sleeve parted like a burst balloon and his black-skinned muscles opened like the Red Sea.

Blood spurted.

Big Smiley looked at his cut arm. He was still holding the knifeman off the floor by the mackinaw collar. His eyes had a surprised look. His nostrils flared.

"You cut me, didn't you?" he said. His voice sounding unbelieving.

"Ah'll cut you again," the little knifeman said, wriggling in his grip.

Big Smiley dropped him as though he'd turned hot.

The little knifeman bounced on his feet and slashed at Big Smiley's face.

Big Smiley drew back and reached beneath the bar counter with his right hand. He came up with a short-handled fireman's axe. It had a red handle and a honed, razor-sharp blade.

The little knifeman jumped into the air and slashed at Big Smiley again, matching his knife against Big Smiley's axe.

Big Smiley countered with a right cross with the red-handled axe. The blade met the knifeman's arm in the middle of its stroke and cut it off just below the elbow as though it had been guillotined.

The severed arm in its coat sleeve, still clutching the knife, sailed through the air, sprinkling the nearby spectators with drops of blood, landed on the linoleum tile floor, and skidded beneath the table of a booth.

The little knifeman landed on his feet, still making cutting motions with his half arm. He was too drunk to realize the full impact. He saw that the lower part of his arm had been chopped off; he saw Big Smiley drawing back the red-handled axe. He thought Big Smiley was going to chop at him again.

"Wait a minute, you big mother-raper, till Ah finds my arm!" he yelled. "It got my knife in his hand."

He dropped to his knees and began scrambling about the floor with his one hand, searching for his severed arm. Blood spouted from his jerking stub as though from the nozzle of a hose.

Then he lost consciousness and flopped on his face.

Two customers turned him over; one tied a necktie as a tourniquet about the bleeding arm, the other inserted a chair leg to tighten it.

A waitress and another customer were twisting a knotted towel about Big Smiley's arm. He was still holding the fire-man's axe in his right hand, a look of surprise on his face.

The white manager stood on top of the bar and shouted, "Please remain seated, folks. Everybody go back to his seat and pay his bill. The police have been called and everything will be taken care of."

As though he'd fired a starting gun, there was a race for the door.

When Sonny Pickens came out on the sidewalk he saw the big white man looking inside through one of the small front windows.

Sonny had been smoking marijuana cigarettes and he was tree-top high. Seen from his drugged eyes, the dark night sky looked bright purple and the dingy smoke-blackened tene-ments looked like brand-new skyscrapers made of strawberry-colored bricks. The neon signs of the bars and pool rooms and greasy spoons burned like phosphorescent fires.

He drew a blue steel revolver from his inside coat pocket,

spun the cylinder and aimed it at the big white man.

His two friends, Rubberlips Wilson and Lowtop Brown, looked at him in pop-eyed amazement. But before either could restrain him, Sonny advanced on the white man, walking on the balls of his feet.

"You there!" he shouted. "You the man what's been messing around with my wife."

The big white man jerked his head about and saw a pistol. His eyes stretched and the blood drained from his sallow face.

"My God, wait a minute!" he cried. "You're making a mistake. All of you folks are confusing me with someone else."

"Ain't going to be no waiting now," Sonny said and pulled the trigger.

Orange flame lanced toward the big white man's chest. Sound shattered the night.

Sonny and the white man leapt simultaneously straight up into the air. Both began running before their feet touched the ground. Both ran straight ahead. They ran head on into one another at full speed. The white man's superior weight knocked Sonny down and he ran over him.

He plowed through the crowd of colored spectators, scattering them like ninepins, and cut across the street through the traffic, running in front of cars as though he didn't see them.

Sonny jumped up to his feet and took out after him. He ran over the people the big white man had knocked down. Muscles rolled on bones beneath his feet. He staggered drunkenly. Screams followed him and car lights came down on him like shooting stars.

The big white man was moving between parked cars across the street when Sonny shot at him again. He gained the sidewalk safely and began running south along the inner edge.

Sonny followed between the cars and kept after him.

People in the line of fire did acrobatic dives for safety. People up ahead crowded into the doorways to see what was happening. They saw a big white man with wild blue eyes and a stubble of red tie which made him look as though his throat were cut, being chased by a slim black man with a big blue pistol. They drew back out of range.

But the people behind, who were safely out of range, joined the chase.

The white man was in front. Sonny was next, Rubberlips and Lowtop were running at Sonny's heels. Behind them the spectators stretched out in a ragged line.

The white man ran past a group of eight Arabs at the corner of 127th Street. All of the Arabs had heavy, grizzly black beards. All wore bright green turbans, smoke-colored glasses, and ankle-length white robes. Their complexions ranged from stovepipe black to mustard. They were jabbering and gesticulating like a frenzied group of caged monkeys. The air was redolent with the pungent scent of marijuana.

"An infidel!' one yelled.

The jabbering stopped abruptly. They wheeled in a group after the white man.

The white man heard the shout. He saw the sudden movement through the corners of his eyes. He leaped forward from the curb.

A car coming fast down 127th Street burnt rubber in an ear-splitting shriek to keep from running him down.

Seen in the car's headlights, his sweating face was bright red and muscle-ridged; his blue eyes black with panic; his gray-shot hair in wild disorder.

Instinctively he leaped high and sideways, away from the oncoming car. His arms and legs flew out in grotesque silhouette.

At that instant Sonny came abreast of the Arabs and shot at the leaping white man while he was still in the air.

The orange blast lit up Sonny's distorted face and the roar of the gunshot sounded like a fusillade.

The big white man shuddered and came down limp. He landed face down and in a spread-eagled posture. He didn't get up.

Sonny ran up to him with the smoking pistol dangling from his hand. He was starkly spotlighted by the car's headlights. He looked at the white man lying face down in the middle of the street and started laughing. He doubled over laughing, his arms jerking and his body rocking.   .

Lowtop and Rubberlips caught up. The eight Arabs joined them in the beams of light.

"Man, what happened?" Lowtop asked.

The Arabs looked at him and began to laugh.

Rubberlips began to laugh too, then Lowtop.

All of them stood in the stark white light, swaying and rocking and doubling up with laughter.

Sonny was trying to say something but he was laughing so hard he couldn't get it out.

A police siren sounded nearby.

II

THE TELEPHONE RANG in the captain's office at the 126th Street precinct station. The uniformed officer behind the desk reached for the outside phone without looking up from behind the record sheet he was filling out.

"Harlem precinct, Lieutenant Anderson," he said.

A high-pitched correct voice said, "Are you the man in charge?"

"Yes, lady," Lieutenant Anderson said patiently and went on writing with his free hand.

"I want to report that a white man is being chased down Lenox Avenue by a colored man with a gun," the voice said with the smug sanctimoniousness of a saved sister.

Lieutenant Anderson pushed aside the record sheet and pulled forward a report pad.

When he'd finished taking down the essential details of her incoherent account, he said, "Thank you, Mrs. Collins," hung up and reached for the closed line to central police on Centre Street.

"Give me the radio dispatcher," he said.

Two colored men were driving east on 135th Street in the wake of a crosstown bus. Shapeless dark hats sat squarely on their clipped kinky hair and their big frames filled up the front seat of a small, battered black sedan.

Static crackled from the shortwave radio and a metallic voice said: "Calling all cars. Riot threatens in Harlem. White man running south on Lenox Avenue at 128th Street. Chased by drunken Negro with gun. Danger of murder."

"Better goose it," the one on the inside said in a grating voice.

"I reckon so," the driver replied laconically.

He gave a short sharp blast on the siren and gunned the small sedan in a crying U-turn in the middle of the block, cutting in front of a taxi coming fast from the direction of the Bronx.

The taxi tore its brakes to keep from ramming into the sedan. Seeing the private license plates, the taxi driver thought they were two small-time hustlers trying to play big shots with the siren on their car. He was an Italian from the Bronx who had grown up with bigtime-gangsters and Harlem hoodlums didn't scare him.

He leaned out of his window and yelled, "You ain't plowing cotton in Mississippi, you black son of a bitch. This is New York City, the Big Apple, where people drive—"

The colored man riding with his girlfriend in the back seat leaned quickly forward and yanked at his sleeve. "Man, come back in here and shut yo' mouth," he warned anxiously. "Them is Grave Digger Jones and Coffin Ed Johnson you is talking to. Can't you see that police antenna stuck up from their tail."

"Oh, that's them," the driver said, cooling off as quickly as a showgirl on a broke stud. "I didn't recognize 'em."

Grave Digger had heard him but he mashed the gas without looking around.

Coffin Ed drew his pistol from its shoulder sling and spun the cylinder. Passing street light glinted from the long nickel-plated barrel of the special .38 revolver, and the five brass-jacketed bullets looked deadly in the six chambers. The one beneath the trigger was empty. But he kept an extra box of shells along with his report book and handcuffs in his greased-leather-lined right coat pocket.

"Lieutenant Anderson asked me last night why we stick to these old-fashioned rods when the new ones are so much better. He was trying to sell me on the idea of one of those new hydraulic automatics that shoot fifteen times; said they were faster, lighter and just as accurate. But I told him we'd stick to these."

"Did you tell him how fast you could reload?" Grave Digger carried its mate beneath his left arm.

"Naw, I told him he didn't know how hard these Harlem Negroes' heads are," Coffin Ed said.

His acid-scarred face looked sinister in the dim panel light.

Grave Digger chuckled. "You should have told him that these people don't have any respect for a gun that doesn't have a shiny barrel half a mile long. They want to see what they're being shot with."

"Or else hear it, otherwise they figure it can't do any more damage than their knives."

When they came onto Lenox, Grave Digger wheeled south through the red light with the siren open, passing in front of an eastbound trailer truck, and slowed down behind a sky-blue Cadillac Coupe de Ville trimmed in yellow metal, hogging the southbound lane between a bus and a fleet of northbound refrigerator trucks. It had a New York State license plate numbered B-H-21. It belonged to Big Henry who ran the "21" numbers house. Big Henry was driving. His bodyguard, Cousin Cuts, was sitting beside him on the front seat. Two other rugged-looking men occupied the back seat.

Big Henry took the cigar from his thick-lipped mouth with his right hand, tapped ash in the tray sticking out of the instrument panel, and kept on talking to Cuts as though he hadn't heard the siren. The flash of a diamond in his cigar hand lit up the rear window.

"Get him over," Grave Digger said in a flat voice.

Coffin Ed leaned out of the right side window and shot the rear-view mirror off the door hinge of the big Cadillac.

The cigar hand of Big Henry became rigid and the back of his fat neck began to swell as he looked at his shattered mirror. Cuts rose up in his seat, twisting about threateningly, and reached for his pistol. But when he saw Coffin Ed's sinister face staring at him from behind the long nickel-plated barrel of the .38 he ducked like an artful dodger from a hard thrown ball.

Coffin Ed planted a hole in the Cadillac's front fender.

Grave Digger chuckled. "That'll hurt Big Henry more than a hole in Cousin Cut's head."

Big Henry turned about with a look of pop-eyed indignation on his puffed black face, but it sank in like a burst balloon when he recognized the detectives. He wheeled the car frantically toward the curb and crumpled his right front fender into the side of the bus.

Grave Digger had space enough to squeeze through. As they passed, Coffin Ed lowered his aim and shot Big Henry's gold lettered initials from the Cadillac's door.

"And stay over!" he yelled in a grating voice.

They left Big Henry giving them a how-could-you-do-this-to-me-look with tears in his eyes.

When they came abreast the Dew Drop Inn they saw the deserted ambulance and the crowd running on ahead. Without slowing down, they wormed between the cars parked haphazardly in the street and pushed through the dense jam of people, the sirens shrieking. They dragged to a stop when their headlights focused on the macabre scene.

"Split!" one of the Arabs hissed. "Here's the things."

"The monsters," another chimed.

"Keep cool, fool," the third admonished. "They got nothing on us."

The two tall, lanky, loose-jointed detectives hit the pavement in unison, their nickel-plated .38 specials gripped in their hands. They looked like big-shouldered plowhands in Sunday suits at a Saturday-night jamboree.

"Straighten up!" Grave Digger yelled at the top of his voice.

"Count off!" Coffin Ed echoed.

There was movement in the crowd. The morbid and the innocent moved in closer. Suspicious characters began to blow.

Sonny and his two friends turned startled, pop-eyed faces.

"Where they come from?" Sonny mumbled in a daze.

"I'll take him," Grave Digger said.

"Covered," Coffin Ed replied.

Their big flat feet made slapping sounds as they converged

on Sonny and the Arabs. Coffin Ed halted at an angle that put
them all in line of fire.

Without a break in motion, Grave Digger closed on Sonny
and slapped him on the elbow with the barrel of his pistol. With
his free hand he caught Sonny's pistol when it flew from his
nerveless fingers.

"Got it," he said as Sonny yelped in pain and grabbed his
numb arm.

"I ain't—" Sonny tried to finish but Grave Digger shouted,
"Shut up!"

"Line up and reach!" Coffin Ed ordered in a threatening
voice, menacing them with his pistol. He sounded as though
his teeth were on edge.

"Tell the man, Sonny," Lowtop urged in a trembling voice,
but it was drowned by Grave Digger's thundering at the crowd:
"Back up!" He lined a shot overhead.

They backed up.

Sonny's good arm shot up and his two friends reached. He
was still trying to say something. His Adam's apple bobbed
helplessly in his dry wordless throat.

But the Arabs were defiant. They dangled their arms and
shuffled about.

"Reach where, man?" one of them said in a husky voice.

Coffin Ed grabbed him by the neck, lifted him off his feet.

"Easy, Ed," Grave Digger cautioned in a strangely anxious
voice. "Easy does it."

Coffin Ed halted, his pistol ready to shatter the Arab's teeth,
and shook his head like a dog coming out of water. Releasing
the Arab's neck, he backed up one step and said in his grating
voice: "One for the money . . . and two for the show . . ."

It was the first line of a jingle chanted in the game of hide-
and-seek as a warning from the "seeker" to the "hiders" that he
was going after them.

Grave Digger took the next line, "Three to get ready . . ."

But before he could finish it with "And here we go," the
Arabs had fallen into line with Sonny and had raised their
hands high into the air.

"Now keep them up," Coffin Ed said.

"Or you'll be the next ones lying on the ground," Grave Digger added.

Sonny finally got out the words, "He ain't dead. He's just fainted."

"That's right," Rubberlips confirmed. "He ain't been hit. It just scared him so he fell unconscious."

"Just shake him and he'll come to," Sonny added.

The Arabs started to laugh again, but Coffin Ed's sinister face silenced them.

Grave Digger stuck Sonny's revolver into his own belt, holstered his own revolver, and bent down and lifted the white man's face. Blue eyes stared fixedly at nothing. He lowered the head gently and picked up a limp, warm hand, feeling for a pulse.

"He ain't dead," Sonny repeated. But his voice had grown weaker. "He's just fainted, that's all."

He and his two friends watched Grave Digger as though he were Jesus Christ bending over the body of Lazarus.

Grave Digger's eyes explored the white man's back. Coffin Ed stood without moving, his scarred face like a bronze mask cast with trembling hands. Grave Digger saw a black wet spot in the white man's thick gray-shot black hair, low down at the base of the skull. He put his fingertips to it and they came off stained. He straightened up slowly, held his wet fingertips in the white headlights; they showed red. He said nothing.

The spectators crowded nearer. Coffin Ed didn't notice; he was looking at Grave Digger's bloody fingertips.

"Is that blood?" Sonny asked in a breaking whisper. His body began to tremble, coming slowly upward from his grasshopper legs.

Grave Digger and Coffin Ed stared at him, saying nothing.

"Is he dead?" Sonny asked in a terror-stricken whisper. His trembling lips were dust dry and his eyes were turning white in a black face gone gray.

"Dead as he'll ever be," Grave Digger said in a flat toneless voice.

"I didn't do it," Sonny whispered. "I swear 'fore God in heaven."

"He didn't do it," Rubberlips and Lowtop echoed in unison.

"How does it figure?" Coffin Ed asked.

"It figures for itself," Grave Digger said.

"So help me God, boss. I couldn't have done it," Sonny said in a terrified whisper.

Grave Digger stared at him from agate hard eyes and said nothing.

"You gotta believe him, boss, he couldn't have done it," Rubberlips vouched.

"Naw, suh," Lowtops echoed.

"I wasn't trying to hurt him, I just wanted to scare him," Sonny said. Tears were trickling from his eyes.

"It were that crazy drunk man with the knife that started it," Rubberlips said. "Back there in the Dew Drop Inn."

"Then afterwards the big white man kept looking in the window," Lowtop said. "That made Sonny mad."

The detectives stared at him with blank eyes. The Arabs were motionless.

"He's a comedian," Coffin Ed said finally.

"How could I be mad about my old lady," Sonny argued. "I ain't even got any old lady."

"Don't tell me," Grave Digger said in an unrelenting voice, and handcuffed Sonny. "Save it for the judge."

"Boss, listen, I beg you, I swear 'fore God—"

"Shut up, you're under arrest," Coffin Ed said.

III

A POLICE CAR siren sounded from the distance. It was coming from the east; it started like the wail of an anguished banshee and grew into a scream. Another sounded from the west; it was joined by others from the north and south, one sounding after another like jets taking off from an aircraft carrier.

"Let's see what these real cool Moslems are carrying," Grave Digger said.

"Count off, you sheiks," Coffin Ed said.

They had the case wrapped up before the prowl cars arrived. The pressure was off. They felt cocky.

"Praise Allah," the tallest of the Arabs said.

As though performing a ritual, the others said, "Mecca," and all bowed low with outstretched arms.

"Cut the comedy and straighten up," Grave Digger said. "We're holding you as witnesses."

"Who's got the prayer?" the leader asked with bowed head.

"I've got the prayer," another replied.

"Pray to the great monster," the leader commanded.

The one who had the prayer turned slowly and presented his white-robed backside to Coffin Ed. A sound like a hound dog baying issued from his rear end.

"Allah be praised," the leader said, and the loose white sleeves of their robes fluttered in response.

Coffin Ed didn't get it until Sonny and his friends laughed in amazement. Then his face contorted in black rage.

"Punks!" he grated harshly, somersaulted the bowed Arab with one kick, and leveled on him with his pistol as if to shoot him.

"Easy man, easy," Grave Digger said, trying to keep a straight face. "You can't shoot a man for aiming a fart at you."

"Hold it, monster," a third Arab cried, and flung liquid from a glass bottle toward Coffin Ed's face. "Sweeten thyself."

Coffin Ed saw the flash of the bottle and the liquid flying and ducked as he swung his pistol barrel.

"It's just perfume," the Arab cried in alarm.

But Coffin Ed didn't hear him through the roar of blood in his head. All he could think of was a con-man called Hank throwing a glass of acid into his face. And this looked like another acid thrower. Quick scalding rage turned his acid-burnt face into a hideous mask and his scarred lips drew back from his clenched teeth.

He fired two shots together and the Arab holding the half-filled perfume bottle said, "Oh," softly and folded slowly to the pavement. Behind, in the crowd, a woman screamed as her leg gave beneath her.

The other Arabs broke into wild flight. Sonny broke with

them. A split second later his friends took off in his wake.

"God damn it, Ed!" Grave Digger shouted and lunged for the gun.

He made a grab for the barrel, deflecting the aim as it went off again. The bullet cut a telephone cable in two overhead. It fell into the crowd, setting off a cacophony of screams.

Everybody ran.

The panic-stricken crowd stampeded for the nearest doorways, trampling the woman who was shot and two others who fell.

Grave Digger grappled with Coffin Ed and they crashed down on top of the dead white man. Grave Digger had Coffin Ed's pistol by the barrel and was trying to wrest it from his grip.

"It's me, Digger, Ed," he kept saying. "Let go the gun."

"Turn me loose, Digger, turn me loose. Let me kill 'im," Coffin Ed mouthed insanely, tears streaming from his hideous face. "They tried it again, Digger."

They rolled over the corpse and rolled back.

"That wasn't acid, that was perfume," Grave Digger said, gasping for breath.

"Turn me loose, Digger, I'm warning you," Coffin Ed mumbled.

While they threshed back and forth over the corpse, two of the Arabs followed Sonny into the doorway of a tenement. The other people crowding into the doorway stepped aside and let them pass. Sonny saw the stairs were crowded and kept on going through, looking for a back exit. He came out onto a small back courtyard, enclosed with stone walls. The Arabs followed him. One put a noose over his head, knocking off his hat, and drew it tight. The other pulled a switch-blade knife and pressed the point against his side.

"If you holler you're dead," the first one said.

The Arab leader joined them.

"Let's get him away from here," he said.

At that moment the patrol cars began to unload. Two harness cops and Detective Haggerty hit the deck and were the first on the murder scene.

"Holy mother!" Haggerty exclaimed.

The cops stared aghast.

It looked to them as though the two colored detectives had the big white man locked in a death struggle.

"Don't just stand there," Grave Digger panted. "Give me a hand."

"They'll kill him," Haggerty said, wrapping his arms about Grave Digger and trying to pull him away. "You grab the other one," he said to the cops.

"To hell with that," the cop said, swinging his black-jack across Coffin Ed's head, knocking him unconscious.

The other cop drew his pistol and took aim at the corpse. "One move out of you and I'll shoot," he said.

"He won't move; he's dead," Grave Digger said to Haggerty.

"Well, Hell," Haggerty said indignantly, releasing him. "You asked me to help. How in hell do I know what's going on?"

Grave Digger shook himself and looked at the third cop. "You didn't have to slug him," he said.

"I wasn't taking no chances," the cop said.

"Shut up and watch the Arab," Haggerty said.

The cop moved over and looked at the Arab. "He's dead, too."

"Holy Mary, the plague," Haggerty said. "Look after that woman then."

Four more cops came running. At Haggerty's order, two turned toward the woman who'd been shot. She was lying in the street, deserted.

"She's alive, just unconscious," the cop said.

"Leave her for the ambulance," Haggerty said.

"Who're you ordering about?" the cop said. "We know our business."

"To hell with you," Haggerty said.

Grave Digger bent over Coffin Ed, lifted his head and put an open bottle of ammonia to his nose. Coffin Ed groaned.

A red-faced uniformed sergeant built like a General Sherman tank loomed above him.

"What happened here?" he asked.

Grave Digger looked up. "A rumpus broke and we lost our prisoner."

"Who shot your partner?"

"He's not shot, he's just knocked out."

"That's all right then. What's your prisoner look like?"

"Black man, about five eleven, twenty-five to thirty years, one-seventy to one-eighty pounds, narrow face sloping down to chin, wearing light gray hat, dark gray hickory-striped suit, white tab collar, red striped tie, beige chukker boots. He's handcuffed."

The sergeant's small china-blue eyes went from the big white corpse to the bearded Arab corpse.

"Which one did he kill?" he asked.

"The white man," Grave Digger said.

"That's all right, we'll get him," he said. Raising his voice, he called, "Professor!"

The corporal who'd stopped to light a cigarette said, "Yeah."

"Rope off this whole goddamned area," the sergeant said. "Don't let anybody out. We want a Harlem-dressed Zulu. Killed a white man. Can't have gotten far 'cause he's handcuffed."

"We'll get 'im," the corporal said.

"Pick up all suspicious persons," the sergeant said.

"Right," the corporal said, hurrying off towards the cops that were just arriving.

"Who shot the Arab?" the sergeant asked.

"Ed shot him," Grave Digger said.

"That's all right then," the sergeant said. "We'll get your prisoner. I'm sending for the lieutenant and the medical examiner. Save the rest for them."

He turned and followed the corporal.

Coffin Ed stood up shakily. "You should have let me killed that son of a bitch, Digger," he said.

"Look at him," Grave Digger said, nodding toward the Arab's corpse.

Coffin Ed stared.

"I didn't even know I hit him," he said as though coming out of a daze. After a moment he added, "I can't feel sorry for him. I tell you, Digger, death is on any son of a bitch who tries to throw acid into my eyes again."

"Smell yourself, man," Grave Digger said.

Coffin Ed bent his head. The front of his dark wrinkled suit reeked with the scent of dime-store perfume.

"That's what he threw. Just perfume," Grave Digger said. "I tried to warn you."

"I must not have heard you."

Grave Digger took a deep breath. "God damn it, man, you got to control yourself."

"Well, Digger, a burnt child fears fire. Anybody who tries to throw anything at me when they're under arrest is apt to get shot."

Grave Digger said nothing.

"What happened to our prisoner?" Coffin Ed asked.

"He got away," Grave Digger said.

They turned in unison and surveyed the scene.

Patrol cars were arriving by the minute, erupting cops as though for an invasion. Others had formed blockades across Lenox Avenue at 128th and 126th Streets, and had blocked off 127th Street on both sides.

Most of the people had gotten off the street. Those that stayed were being arrested as suspicious persons. Several drivers trying to move their cars were protesting their innocence loudly.

The packed bars in the area were being rapidly sealed by the police. The windows of tenements were jammed with black faces and the exits blocked by police.

"They'll have to go through this jungle with a fine-toothed comb," Grave Digger said. "With all these white cops about, any colored family might hide him."

"I'll want those gangster punks too," Coffin Ed said.

"Well, we'll just have to wait now for the men from homicide."

But Lieutenant Anderson arrived first, with the harness sergeant and Detective Haggerty latched on to him. The five of them stood in a circle in the car's headlights between the two corpses.

"All right, just give me the essential points first," Anderson said. "I put out the flash so I know the start. The man hadn't been killed when I got the first report."

"He was dead when we got here," Grave Digger said in a flat, toneless voice. "We were the first here. The suspect was standing over the victim with the pistol in his hand—"

"Hold it," a new voice said.

A plain-clothes lieutenant and a sergeant from downtown homicide bureau came into the circle.

"These are the arresting officers," Anderson said.

"Where's the prisoner?" the homicide lieutenant asked.

"He got away," Grave Digger said.

"Okay, start over," the homicide lieutenant said.

Grave Digger gave him the first part then, went on:

"There were two friends with him and a group of teenage gangsters around the corpse. We disarmed the suspect and handcuffed him. When we started to frisk the gangster punks we had a rumble. Coffin Ed shot one. In the rumble the suspect got away."

"Now let's get this straight," the homicide lieutenant said. "Were the teenagers implicated too?"

"No, we just wanted them as witnesses," Grave Digger said. "There's no doubt about the suspect."

"Right."

"When I got here Jones and Johnson were fighting, rolling all over the corpse," Haggerty said. "Jones was trying to disarm Johnson."

Lieutenant Anderson and the men from homicide looked at him, then turned to look at Grave Digger and Coffin Ed in turn.

"It was like this," Coffin Ed said. "One of the punks turned up his ass and farted toward me and—"

Anderson said, "Huh!" and the homicide lieutenant said incredulously, "You killed a man for farting?"

"No, it was another punk he shot," Grave Digger said in his toneless voice. "One who threw perfume on him from a bottle. He thought it was acid the punk was throwing."

They looked at Coffin Ed's acid-burnt face and looked away embarrassedly.

"The fellow who was killed is an Arab," the sergeant said.

"That's just a disguise," Grave Digger said. "They belong to a group of teenage gangsters who call themselves Real Cool Moslems."

"Hah!" the homicide lieutenant said.

"Mostly they fight a teenage gang of Jews from the Bronx," Grave Digger elaborated. "We leave that to the welfare people."

The homicide sergeant stepped over to the Arab corpse and removed the turban and peeled off the artificial beard. The face of a colored youth with slick conked hair and beardless cheeks stared up. He dropped the disguises beside the corpse and sighed.

"Just a baby," he said.

For a moment no one spoke.

Then the homicide lieutenant asked, "You have the homicide gun?"

Grave Digger took it from his pocket, holding the barrel by the thumb and first finger, and gave it to him.

The lieutenant examined it curiously for some moments. Then he wrapped it in his handkerchief and slipped it into his coat pocket.

"Had you questioned the suspect?" he asked.

"We hadn't gotten to it," Grave Digger said. "All we know is the homicide grew out of a rumpus at the Dew Drop Inn."

"That's a bistro a couple of blocks up the street," Anderson said. "They had a cutting there a short time earlier."

"It's been a hot time in the old town tonight," Haggerty said.

The homicide lieutenant raised his brows enquiringly at Lieutenant Anderson.

"Suppose you go to work on that angle, Haggerty," Anderson said. "Look into that cutting. Find out how it ties in."

"We figure on doing that ourselves," Grave Digger said.

"Let him go on and get started," Anderson said.

"Right-o," Haggerty said. "I'm the man for the cutting."

Everybody looked at him. He left.

The homicide lieutenant said, "Well, let's take a look at the stiffs."

He gave each a cursory examination. The teenager had been shot once, in the heart.

"Nothing to do but wait for the coroner," he said.

They looked at the unconscious woman.

"Shot in the thigh, high up," the homicide sergeant said. "Loss of blood but not fatal—I don't think."

"The ambulance will be here any minute," Anderson said.

"Ed shot at the gangster twice," Grave Digger said. "It must have been then."

"Right."

No one looked at Coffin Ed. Instead, they made a pretense of examining the area.

Anderson shook his head. "It's going to be a hell of a job finding your prisoner in this dense slum," he said.

"There isn't any need," the homicide lieutenant said. "If this was the pistol he had, he's as innocent as you and me. This pistol won't kill anyone." He took the pistol from his pocket and unwrapped it. "This is a thirty-seven caliber blank pistol. The only bullets made to fit it are blanks and they can't be tampered with enough to kill a man. And it hasn't been made over into a zip gun."

"Well," Lieutenant Anderson said at last. "That tears it."

IV

THERE WAS A rusty sheet-iron gate in the concrete wall between the small back courts. The gang leader unlocked it with his own key. The gate opened silently on oiled hinges.

He went ahead.

"March!" the henchman with the knife ordered, prodding Sonny.

Sonny marched.

The other henchman kept the noose around his neck like a dog chain.

When they'd passed through, the leader closed and locked the gate.

One of the henchman said, "You reckon Caleb is bad hurt?"

"Shut up talking in front of the captive," the leader said. "Ain't you got no better sense than that."

The broken concrete paving was strewn with broken glass bottles, rags and diverse objects thrown from the back windows: a rusty bed spring, a cotton mattress with a big hole burnt in the middle, several worn-out automobile tires, the half-dried carcass of a black cat with its left foot missing and its eyes eaten out by rats.

They picked their way through the debris carefully.

Sonny bumped into a loose stack of garbage cans. One fell with a loud clatter. A sudden putrid stink arose.

"God damn it, look out!" the leader said. "Watch where you're going."

"Aw, man, ain't nobody thinking about us back here," Choo-Choo said.

"Don't call me man," the leader said.

"Sheik, then."

"What you jokers gonna do with me?" Sonny asked.

His weed jag was gone; he felt weak-kneed and hungry; his mouth tasted brackish and his stomach was knotted with fear.

"We're going to sell you to the Jews," Choo-Choo said.

"You ain't fooling me, I know you ain't no Arabs," Sonny said.

"We're going to hide you from the police," Sheik said.

"I ain't done nothing," Sonny said.

Sheik halted and they all turned and looked at Sonny. His eyes were white half-moons in the dark.

"All right then, if you ain't done nothing we'll turn you back to the cops," Sheik said.

"Naw, wait a minute, I just want to know where you're taking me."

"We're taking you home with us."

"Well, that's all right then."

There was no back door to the hall as in the other tenement. Decayed concrete stairs led down to a basement door. Sheik produced a key on his ring for that one also. They entered a dark passage. Foul water stood on the broken pavement. The air smelled like molded rags and stale sewer pipes. They had to remove their smoked glasses in order to see.

Halfway along, feeble yellow light slanted from an open door. They entered a small, filthy room.

A sick man clad in long cotton drawers lay beneath a ragged horse blanket on a filthy pallet of burlap sacks.

"You got anything for old Bad-eye," he said in a whining voice.

"We got you a fine black gal," Choo-Choo said.

The old man raised up on his elbows. "Whar she at?"

"Don't tease him," Inky said.

"Lie down and shut," Sheik said. "I told you before we wouldn't have nothing for you tonight." Then to his henchmen, "Come on, you jokers, hurry up."

They began stripping off their disguises. Beneath their white robes they wore sweat shirts and black slacks. The beards were put on with make-up gum.

Without their disguises they looked like three high-school students.

Sheik was a tall yellow boy with strange yellow eyes and reddish kinky hair. He had the broad-shouldered, trim-waisted figure of an athlete. His face was broad, his nose flat with wide, flaring nostrils, and his skin freckled. He looked disagreeable.

Choo-Choo was shorter, thicker and darker, with the egg-shaped head and flat, mobile face of the born joker. He was bowlegged and pigeon-toed but fast on his feet.

Inky was an inconspicuous boy of medium size, with a mild, submissive manner, and black as the ace of spades.

"Where's the gun?" Choo-Choo asked when he didn't see it stuck in Sheik's belt.

"I slipped it to Bones."

"What's he going to do with it?"

"Shut up and quit questioning what I do."

"Where you reckon they all went to, Sheik?" Inky asked, trying to be peacemaker.

"They went home if they got sense," Sheik said.

The old man on the pallet watched them fold their disguises into small packages.

"Not even a little taste of King Kong," he whined.

"Naw, nothing!" Sheik said.

The old man raised up on his elbows. "What do you mean, naw? I'll throw you out of here. I'se the janitor. I'll take my keys away from you. I'll—"

"Shut your mouth before I shut it and if any cops come messing around, down here you'd better keep it shut too. I'll have something for you tomorrow."

"Tomorrow? A bottle?"

The old man lay back mollified.

"Come on," Sheik said to the others.

As they were leaving he snatched a ragged army overcoat from a nail on the door without the janitor noticing. He stopped Sonny in the passage and took the noose from about his neck, then looped the overcoat over the handcuffs. It looked as though Sonny were merely carrying an overcoat with both hands.

"Now nobody'll see those cuffs," Sheik said. Turning to Inky, he said, "You go up first and see how it looks. If you think we can get by the cops without being stopped, give us the high sign."

Inky went up the rotten wooden stairs and through the doorway to the ground-floor hall. After a minute he opened the door and beckoned.

They went up in single file.

Strangers who'd ducked into the building to escape the shooting were held there by two uniformed cops blocking the outside doorway. No one paid any attention to Sonny and the three gangsters. They kept on going to the top floor.

Sheik unlocked a door with another key on his ring, and led the way into a kitchen.

An old colored woman clad in a faded blue Mother Hubbard with darker blue patches sat in a rocking chair by a coal-burning kitchen stove, darning a threadbare man's woolen sock on a wooden egg, and smoking a corn-cob pipe.

"Is that you, Caleb?" she asked, looking over a pair of ancient steel-rimmed spectacles.

"It's just me and Choo-Choo and Inky," Sheik said.

"Oh, it's you, Samson." The very note of expectancy in her voice died in disappointment. "Whar's Caleb?"

"He went to work downtown in a bowling alley, Granny. Setting up pins," Sheik said.

"Lord, that chile is always out working at night," she said with a sigh. "I sho hope God he ain't getting into no trouble with all this night work, 'cause his old Granny is too old to watch over him as a mammy would."

She was so old the color had faded in spots from her dark brown skin so that it looked like the skin of a dried speckled pea, and once-brown eyes had turned milky blue. Her bony cranium was bald at the front and the speckled skin was taut against the skull. What remained of her short gray hair was gathered into a small tight ball at the back of her head. The outline of each finger bone plying the darning needle was plainly visible through the transparent parchment-like skin.

"He ain't getting into no trouble," Sheik said.

Inky and Choo-Choo pushed Sonny into the kitchen and closed the door.

Granny peered over her spectacles at Sonny. "I don't know this boy. Is he a friend of Caleb's too?"

"He's the fellow Caleb is taking his place," Sheik said. "He hurt his hands."

She pursed her lips. "There's so many of you boys coming and going in here all the time I sho hope you ain't getting into no mischief. And this new boy looks older than you others is."

"You worry too much," Sheik said harshly.

"Hannh?"

"We're going on to our room," Sheik said. "Don't wait up for Caleb. He's going to be late."

"Hannh?"

"Come on," Sheik said. "She ain't hearing no more."

It was a shotgun flat, one room opening into the other. The next room contained two small white enameled iron beds where Caleb and his grandmother slept, and a small pot-bellied stove on a tin mat in one corner. A table held a pitcher and washbowl; there was a small dime-store mirror on top of a chest of drawers. As in the kitchen, everything was spotlessly clean.

"Give me your things and watch out for Granny," Sheik said, taking their bundled-up disguises.

Choo-Choo bent his head to the keyhole.

Sheik unlocked a large old cedar chest with another key from his ring and stored their bundles beneath layers of old blankets and house furnishings. It was Granny's hope chest; there she stored things given her by the white folks she worked for to give Caleb when he got married. Sheik locked the chest and unlocked the door to the next room. They followed him and he locked the door behind them.

It was the room he and Choo-Choo rented. There was a double bed where he and Choo-Choo slept, chest of drawers and mirror, pitcher and bowl on the table, as in the other room. The corner was curtained off with calico for a closet. But a lot of junk lay around and it wasn't as clean.

A narrow window opened to the platform of the red-painted iron fire escape that ran down the front of the building. It was protected by an iron grille closed by a padlock.

Sheik unlocked the grille and stepped out onto the fire escape.

"Look at this," he said.

Choo-Choo joined him; Inky and Sonny squeezed into the window.

"Watch the captive, Inky," Sheik said.

"I ain't no captive," Sonny said.

"Just look," Sheik said, pointing toward the street.

Below, on the broad avenue, red-eyed prowl cars were scattered thickly, like monster ants about an ant-hill. Three ambulances were threading through the maze, two police hearses, and cars from the police commissioner's office and the medical examiner's office. Uniformed cops and men in plain clothes were coming and going in every direction.

"The men from Mars," Sheik said. "The big dragnet. What you think about that, Choo-Choo?"

Choo-Choo was busy counting.

The lower landings and stairs of the fire escape were packed with other people watching the show. Every front window as far as the eye could see on both sides of the street was jammed with black heads.

"I counted thirty-one prowl cars," Choo-Choo said. "That's more than was up on Eighth Avenue when Coffin Ed got that acid throwed in his eyes."

"They're shaking down the buildings one by one," Sheik said.

"What we're going to do with our captive?" Choo-Choo asked.

"We got to get the cuffs off first. Maybe we can hide him up in the pigeon's roost."

"Leave the cuffs on him."

"Can't do that. We got to get ready for the shakedown."

He and Choo-Choo stepped back into the room. He took Sonny by the arm, and pointed toward the street.

"They're looking for you, man."

Sonny's black face began graying again.

"I ain't done nothing. That wasn't a real pistol I had. That was a blank gun."

The three of them stared at him disbelievingly.

"Yeah, that ain't what they think," Choo-Choo said.

Sheik was staring at Sonny with a strange expression. "You sure, man?" he asked tensely.

"Sure I'm sure. It wouldn't shoot nothing but thirty-seven caliber blanks."

"Then it wasn't you who shot the big white stud?"

"That's what I been telling you. I couldn't have shot him."

A change came over Sheik. His flat, freckled yellow face took on a brutal look. He hunched his shoulders, trying to look dangerous and important.

"The cops are trying to frame you, man," he said. "We got to hide you now for sure."

"What you doing with a gun that don't shoot bullets?" Choo-Choo asked.

"I keep it in my shine parlor as a gag, is all," Sonny said.

Choo-Choo snapped his fingers. "I know you. You're the joker what works in that shoe shine parlor beside the Savoy."

"It's my own shoe shine parlor."

"How much marijuana you got stashed there?"

"I don't handle it."

"Sheik, this joker's a square."

"Cut the gab," Sheik said. "Let's get these handcuffs off this captive."

He tried keys and lockpicks but he couldn't get them open. So he gave Inky a triangle file and said, "Try filing the chain in two. You and him set on the bed." Then to Sonny, "What's your name, man?"

"Aesop Pickens, but people mostly call me Sonny."

"All right then, Sonny."

They heard a girl's voice talking to Granny and listened silently to rubber-soled shoes crossing the other room.

A single rap, then three quick ones, then another single rap sounded on the door.

"Gaza," Sheik said with his mouth against the panel.

"Suez," a girl's voice replied.

Sheik unlocked the door.

A girl entered and he locked the door behind her.

She was a tall sepia-colored girl with short black curls, wearing a turtle-necked sweater, plaid skirt, bobby socks, and white buckskin shoes. She had a snub nose, wide mouth, full lips, even white teeth, and wide-set brown eyes fringed with long black lashes.

She looked about sixteen years old, and was breathless with excitement.

Sonny stared at her and muttered to himself, "If this ain't it, it'll have to do."

"Hell, it's just Sissie. I thought it was Bones with the gun," Choo-Choo said.

"Stop beefing about the gun. It's safe with Bones. The cops ain't going to shake down no garbage collector's house. His old man works for the city same as they do."

"What's this about Bones and the gun?" Sissie asked.

"Sheik's got—"

"It's none of Sissie's business," Sheik cut him off.

"Somebody said an Arab had been shot and at first I thought it was you," Sissie said.

"You hoped it was me," Sheik said.

She turned away, blushing.

"Don't look at me," Choo-Choo said to Sheik. "You tell her. She's your girl."

"It was Caleb," Sheik said.

"Caleb! Jesus!" Sissie dropped onto the bed beside Sonny. She looked stunned. "Jesus! Poor little Caleb. What will Granny do?"

"What the hell can she do?" Sheik said brutally. "Raise him from the dead?"

"Does she know?"

"Does it look like she knows?"

"Jesus! Poor little Caleb. What did he do?"

"I gave old Coffin Ed the stink gun and—" Choo-Choo began.

"You didn't!" she exclaimed.

"The hell I didn't."

"What did Caleb do?"

"He threw perfume over the monster. It's the Moslem salute for cops. I told you about it before. But the monster must have thought Cal was throwing some more acid into his eyes. He blasted so fast we couldn't tell him any better."

"Jesus!"

"Where's Sugartit?" Sheik asked.

"At home. She didn't come into town tonight. I phoned her and she said she was sick."

"Yeah. Did you have any trouble getting in here?"

"No. I told the cops at the door that I live here."

They heard the signal rapped on the door.

Sissie gasped.

Sheik looked at her suspiciously. "What the hell's the matter with you?" he asked.

"Nothing."

He hesitated before opening the door. "You ain't expecting nobody?"

"Me? No. Who could I expect?"

"You're acting mighty funny."

"I'm just nervous."

The signal was rapped again.

Sheik stepped to the door and said, "Gaza."

"Suez," a girl's lilting voice replied.

Sheik gave Sissie a threatening look as he unlocked the door.

A small-boned chocolate-brown girl dressed like Sissie slipped hurriedly into the room.

At sight of Sissie she stopped and said, "Oh!" in a guilty tone of voice.

Sheik looked from one to the other. "I thought you said she was at home," he accused Sissie.

"I thought she was," Sissie said.

He turned his gaze on Sugartit. "What the hell's the matter with you? What the hell's going on here?"

"A Moslem's been killed and I thought it was you," she said.

"All you little bitches were hoping it was me," he said.

She had sloe eyes with long black lashes that looked secretive. She threw a quick defiant look at Sissie and said, "Don't include me in that."

"Did you tell Granny?" Sheik asked.

"Of course not."

"It was your lover, Caleb," Sheik said brutally.

She gave a shriek and charged at Sheik, clawing and kicking.

"You dirty bastard!" she cried. "You're always picking at me."

Sissie pulled her off. "Shut up and keep your mouth shut," she said tightly.

"You tell her," Sheik said.

"It was Caleb, all right," Sissie said.

"Caleb!" Sugartit screamed and flung herself face down across the bed. She was up in a flash, hurling accusations at Sheik. "You did it. You got him killed. On account of me. 'Cause he had the best go and you couldn't get me to do what you made Sissie do."

"That's a lie," Sissie said.

"Caleb!" Sugartit screamed at the top of her voice.

"Shut up, Granny will hear you," Choo-Choo said.

"Granny! Caleb's dead! Sheik killed him!" she screamed again.

"Stop her," Sheik commanded Sissie. "She's getting hysterical and I don't want to have to hurt her."

Sissie clutched her from behind, put one hand over her mouth and twisted her arm behind her back with the other.

Sugartit looked furiously at Sheik over the top of Sissie's hand.

"Granny can't hear," Inky said.

"The hell she can't," Choo-Choo said. "She can hear when she wants to."

"Let me go!" Sugartit mumbled and bit Sissie's hand.

"Stop that!" Sissie said.

"I'm going to him," Sugartit mumbled. "I love him. You can't stop me. I'm going to find out who shot him."

"Your old man shot him," Sheik said brutally. "The monster, Coffin Ed."

"Did I hear someone calling Caleb?" Granny asked from the other side of the door.

Sheik closed his hands quickly about Sugartit's throat and choked her into silence.

"Naw, Granny," he called. "It's just these silly girls arguing about their cubebs."

"Hannh?"

"Cubebs!" Sheik shouted.

"You chillen make so much racket a body can't hear herself think," she muttered.

They heard her shuffling back to the kitchen.

"Jesus, she's sitting up waiting for him," Sissie said.

Sheik and Choo-Choo exchanged glances.

"She don't even know what's happening in the street," Choo-Choo said.

Sheik took his hands away from Sugartit's throat.

V

"HOW SOON CAN you find out what he was killed with?" the chief of police asked.

"He was killed with a bullet, naturally," the assistant medical examiner said.

"You're not funny," the chief said. "I mean what caliber bullet."

His brogue had begun thickening and the cops who knew him best began getting nervous.

The deputy coroner snapped his bag shut with a gesture of coyness and peered at the chief through magnified eyeballs encircled by black gutta-percha.

"That can't be known until after the autopsy. The bullet will have to be removed from the corpse's brain and subjected to tests—"

The chief listened in red-faced silence.

"I don't perform the autopsy. I'm the night man. I just pass on whether they're dead. I marked this one as D.O.A. That means dead on arrival—my arrival, not his. You know more about whether he was dead on his arrival than I do, and more about how he was killed, too."

"I asked you a civil question."

"I'm giving you a civil answer. Or, I should say, a civil service answer. The men who do the autopsy come on duty at nine o'clock. You ought to get your report by ten."

"That's all I asked you. Thanks. And damn little good that'll do me tonight. And by ten o'clock tomorrow morning the killer ought to be hell and gone to another part of the United States if he's got any sense."

"That's your affair, not mine. You can send the stiffs to the morgue when you've finished with them. I'm finished with them now. Good night, everyone."

No one answered. He left.

"I never knew why we needed a goddamned doctor to tell us whether a stiff was dead or not," the chief grumbled.

He was a big weather-beaten man dressed in a lot of gold

braid. He'd come up from the ranks. Everything about him from the armful of gold hash stripes to the box-toed custom-made shoes said "flatfoot." Behind his back the cops on Centre Street called him Spark Plug, after the tender-footed nag in the comic strip "Barney Google."

The group near the white man's corpse, of which he was the hub, had grown by then, to include, in addition to the principals, two deputy police commissioners, an inspector from homicide, and nameless uniformed lieutenants from adjoining precincts.

The deputy commissioners kept quiet. Only the commissioner himself had any authority over the chief, and he was at home in bed.

"This thing's hot as hell," the chief said at large. "Have we got our stories synchronized?"

Heads nodded.

"Come on then, Anderson, we'll meet the press," he said to the lieutenant in charge of the 126th Street precinct station.

They walked across the street to join a group of newsmen who were being held in leash.

"Okay, men, you can get your pictures," he said.

Flash bulbs exploded in his face. Then the photographers converged on the corpses and left him facing the reporters.

"Here it is, men. The dead man has been identified by his paper as Ulysses Galen of New York City. He lives alone in a two-room suite at Hotel Lexington. We've checked that. They think his wife is dead. He's a sales manager for the King Cola Company. We've contacted their main office in Jersey City and learned that Harlem is in his district."

His thick brogue dripped like milk and honey through the noisy night. Stylos scratched on pads. Flash bulbs went off around the corpses like an anti-aircraft barrage.

"A letter in his pocket from a Mrs. Helen Kruger, Wading River, Long Island, begins with Dear Dad. There's an unposted letter addressed to Homer Galen in the sixteen hundred block on Michigan Avenue in Chicago. That's a business district. We don't know whether Homer Galen is his son or another relation—"

"What about how he was killed?" a reporter interrupted.

"We know that he was shot in the back of the head by a Negro man named Sonny Pickens who operates a shoe shine parlor at 134th Street and Lenox Avenue. Several Negroes resented the victim drinking in a bar at 129th Street and Lenox—"

"What was he doing at a crummy bar up here in Harlem?"

"We haven't found that out yet. Probably just slumming. We know that the barman was cut trying to protect him from another colored assailant—"

"How did the shine assail him?"

"This is not funny, men. The first Negro attacked him with a knife—tried to attack him; the bartender saved him. After he left the bar Pickens followed him down the street and shot him in the back."

"You expect him to shoot a white man in the front."

"Two colored detectives from the 126th Street precinct station arrived on the scene in time to arrest Pickens virtually in the act of homicide. He still had the gun in his hand," the chief continued. "They handcuffed the prisoner and were in the act of bringing him in when he was snatched by a teenage Harlem gang that calls itself Real Cool Moslems."

Laughter burst from the reporters.

"What, no Mau-Maus?"

"It's not funny, men," the chief said again. "One of them tried to throw acid in one of the detective's eyes."

The reporters were silenced.

"Another gangster threw acid in an officer's face up here about a year ago, wasn't it?" a reporter said. "He was a colored cop, too. Johnson, Coffin Ed Johnson, they called him."

"It's the same officer," Anderson said, speaking for the first time.

"He must be a magnet," the reporters said.

"He's just tough and they're scared of him," Anderson said. "You've got to be tough to be a colored cop in Harlem. Unfortunately, colored people don't respect colored cops unless they're tough."

"He shot and killed the acid thrower," the chief said.

"You mean the first one or this one?" the reporter asked.

"This one, the Moslem," Anderson said.

"During the excitement, Pickens and the others escaped into the crowd," the chief said.

He turned and pointed toward a tenement building across the street. It looked indescribably ugly in the glare of a dozen powerful spotlights. Uniformed police stood on the roof, others were coming and going through the entrance; still others stuck their heads out of front windows to shout to other cops in the street. The other front windows were jammed with colored faces, looking like clusters of strange purple fruit in the stark white light.

"You can see for yourselves we're looking for the killer," the chief said. "We're going through those buildings with a fine-toothed comb, one by one, flat by flat, room by room. We have the killer's description. He's wearing toolproof handcuffs. We should have him in custody before morning. He'll never get out of that dragnet."

"If he isn't already out," a reporter said.

"He's not out. We got here too fast for that."

The reporters then began to question him.

"Is Pickens one of the Real Cool Moslems?"

"We know he was rescued by seven of them. The eighth was killed."

"Was there any indication of robbery?"

"Not unless the victim had valuables we don't know about. His wallet, watch and rings are intact."

"Then what was the motive? A woman?"

"Well, hardly. He was an important man, well off financially. He didn't have to chase up here."

"It's been done before."

The chief spread his hands. "That's right. But in this case both Negroes who attacked him did so because they resented his presence in a colored bar. They expressed their resentment in so many words. We have colored witnesses who heard them. Both Negroes were intoxicated. The first had been drinking all evening. And Pickens had been smoking marijuana also."

"Okay, chief, it's your story," the dean of the police reporters said, calling a halt.

The chief and Anderson recrossed the street to the silent group.

"Did you get away with it?" one of the deputy commissioners asked.

"God damn it, I had to tell them something," the chief said defensively. "Did you want me to tell them that a fifteen-thousand-dollar-a-year white executive was shot to death on a Harlem street by a weedhead Negro with a blank pistol who was immediately rescued by a gang of Harlem juvenile delinquents while all we got to show for the efforts of the whole god-damned police force is a dead adolescent who's called a Real Cool Moslem?"

"Sho' 'nuff cool now," Haggerty slipped in *sotto voce*.

"You want us to become the laughing stock of the whole goddamned world," the chief continued, warming up to the subject. "You want it said the New York City police stood by helpless while a white man got himself killed in the middle of a crowded nigger street?"

"Well, didn't he?" the homicide lieutenant said.

"I wasn't accusing you," the deputy commissioner said apologetically.

"Pickens is the one it's rough on," Anderson said. "We've got him branded as a killer when we know he didn't do it."

"We don't know any such goddamned thing," the chief said, turning purple with rage. "He might have rigged the blanks with bullets. It's been done, God damn it. And even if he didn't kill him, he hadn't ought to've been chasing him with a god-damned pistol that sounded as if it was firing bullets. We haven't got anybody to work on but him and it's just his black ass."

"Somebody shot him, and it wasn't with any blank gun," the homicide lieutenant said.

"Well, God damn it, go ahead and find out who did it!" the chief roared. "You're on homicide; that's your job."

"Why not one of the Moslems," the deputy commissioner offered helpfully. "They were on the scene, and these teenage gangsters always carry guns."

There was a moment of silence while they considered this.

"What do you think, Jones?" the chief asked Grave Digger.

"Do you think there was any connection between Pickens and the Moslems?"

"It's like I said before," Grave Digger said. "It didn't look to me like it. The way I figure it, those teenagers gathered around the corpse directly after the shooting, like everybody else was doing. And when Ed began shooting, they all ran together, like everybody else. I see no reason to believe that Pickens even knows them."

"That's what I gathered too," the chief said disappointedly.

"But this is Harlem," Grave Digger amended. "Nobody knows all the connections here."

"Furthermore, we don't have but one of them and that one isn't carrying a gun," Anderson said. "And you've heard Haggerty's report on the statement he took from the bartender and the manager of the Dew Drop Inn. Both Pickens and the other man resented Galen making passes at the colored women. And none of the Moslem gang were even there at the time."

"It could have been some other man feeling the same way," Grave Digger said. "He might have seen Pickens shooting at Galen and thought he'd get in a shot, too."

"These people!" the chief said. "Okay, Jones, you begin to work on that angle and see what you can dig up. But keep it from the press."

As Grave Digger started to walk away, Coffin Ed fell in beside him.

"Not you, Johnson," the chief said. "You go home."

Both Grave Digger and Coffin Ed turned and faced the silence.

"Am I under suspension?" Coffin Ed asked in a grating voice.

"For the rest of the night," the chief said. "I want you both to report to the commissioner's office at nine o'clock tomorrow morning. Jones, you go ahead with your investigation. You know Harlem, you know where you have to go, who to see." He turned to Anderson. "Have you got a man to work with him?"

"Haggerty," Anderson offered.

"I'll work alone," Grave Digger said.

"Don't take any chances," the chief said. "If you need help, just holler. Bear down hard. I don't give a goddamn how many heads you crack; I'll back you up. Just don't kill any more juveniles."

Grave Digger turned and walked with Coffin Ed to their car.

"Drop me at the Independent Subway," Coffin Ed said.

Both of them lived in Jamaica and rode the E train when they didn't use the car.

"I saw it coming," Grave Digger said.

"If it had happened earlier I could have taken my daughter to a movie," Coffin Ed said. "I see so little of her it's getting so I hardly know her."

VI

"LET HER LOOSE now," Sheik said.

Sissie let her go.

"I'll kill him!" Sugartit raved in a choked voice. "I'll kill him for that!"

"Kill who?" Sheik asked, scowling at her.

"My father. I hate him. The ugly bastard. I'll steal his pistol and shoot him."

"Don't talk like that," Sissie said. "That's no way to talk about your father."

"I hate him, the dirty cop!"

Inky looked up from the handcuffs he was filing. Sonny stared at her.

"Shut up," Sissie said.

"Let her go ahead and croak him," Sheik said.

"Stop picking on her," Sissie said.

Choo-Choo said, "They won't do nothing to her for it. All she got to say is her old man beat her all the time and they'll start crying and talking 'bout what a poor mistreated girl she is. They'll take one look at Coffin Ed and believe her."

"They'll give her a medal," Sheik said.

"Those old welfare biddies will find her a fine family to live with. She'll have everything she wants. She won't have to do nothing but eat and sleep and go to the movies and ride around in a big car," Choo-Choo elaborated.

Sugartit flung herself across the foot of the bed and burst into loud sobs.

"It'll save us the trouble," Sheik said.

Sissie's eyes widened. "You wouldn't!" she said.

"You want to bet we wouldn't?"

"If you keep talking like that I'm going to quit."

Sheik gave her a threatening look. "Quit what?"

"Quit the Moslems."

"The only way you can quit the Moslems is like Caleb quit," Sheik said.

"If I'd ever thought that poor little Caleb—"

Sheik cut her off. "I'll kill you myself."

"Aw, Sheik, she don't mean nothing," Choo-Choo said nervously. "Why don't you light up a couple of sticks and let us Islamites fly to Mecca."

"And let the cops smell it when they shake us down and take us all in. Where are your brains at?"

"We can go up on the roof."

"There're cops on the roof, too."

"On the fire escape then. We can close the window."

Sheik gave it grave consideration. "Okay, on the fire escape. I ain't got but two left and we got to get rid of them anyway."

"I'm going to look and see where the cops is at by now," Choo-Choo said, putting on his smoked glasses.

"Take those cheaters off," Sheik said. "You want the cops to identify you?"

"Aw hell, Sheik, they couldn't tell me from nobody else. Half the cats in Harlem wear their smoke cheaters all night long."

"Go 'head and take a gander at the avenue. We ain't got all night," Sheik said.

Choo-Choo started climbing out the window.

At that moment the links joining the handcuffs separated with a small clinking sound beneath Inky's file.

"Sheik, I've got 'em filed in two," Inky said triumphantly.

"Let's see."

Sonny stood up and stretched his arms.

"Who's he?" Sissie asked as though she'd noticed him for the first time.

"He's our captive," Sheik said.

"I ain't no captive," Sonny said. "I just come with you 'cause you said you was gonna hide me."

Sissie looked round-eyed at the severed handcuffs dangling from the wrists. "What did he do?" she asked.

"He's the gangster who killed the syndicate boss," Sheik said.

Sugartit stopped sobbing abruptly and rolled over and looked up at Sonny through wide wet eyes.

"Was that who he is?" Sissie asked in an awed tone. "The man who was killed, I mean."

"Sure. Didn't you know?" Sheik said.

"I done told you I didn't kill him," Sonny said.

"He claims he had a blank gun," Sheik said. "He's just trying to build up his defense. But the cops know better."

"It was a blank gun," Sonny said.

"What did he kill him for?" Sissie asked.

"They're having a gang war and he got assigned by the Brooklyn mob to make the hit."

"Oh, go to hell," Sissie said.

"I ain't killed nobody," Sonny said.

"Shut up," Sheik said. "Captives ain't allowed to talk."

"I'm getting tired of that stuff," Sonny said.

Sheik looked at him threateningly. "You want us to turn you over to the cops?"

Sonny backtracked quickly. "Naw, Sheik, but hell, ain't no need of taking advantage of me—"

Choo-Choo stuck his head in the window and cut him off: "Cops is out here like white on rice. Ain't nothing but cops."

"Where they at now?" Sheik asked.

"They're everywhere, but right now they's taking the house two doors down. They got all kinds of spotlights turned on the front of the house and cops is walking around down the street with machine guns. We better hurry if we're going to move the prisoner."

"Keep cool, fool," Sheik said. "Take a look at the roof."

"Praise Allah," Choo-Choo said, backing away on his hands and knees.

"Get out of that coat and shirt," Sheik ordered Sonny.

When Sonny had stripped to his underwear shirt, Sheik looked at him and said, "Nigger, you sure are black. When you was a baby your mama must'a had to chalk your mouth to tell where to stick it."

"I ain't no blacker than Inky," Sonny said defensively.

"I ain't in that," Inky said.

Sheik grinned at him derisively. "You didn't have no trouble, did you, Inky? Your mama used luminous paint on you."

"Come on, man, I'm getting cold," Sonny said.

"Keep your pants on," Sheik said. "Ladies present."

He hung Sonny's coat with his own clothes on the wire line behind the curtain and threw the shirt in the corner. Then he tossed Sonny an old faded red turtle-necked sweater.

"Pull the sleeves down over the irons and put on that there overcoat," he directed, indicating the old army coat he'd taken from the janitor.

"It's too hot," Sonny protested.

"You gonna do what I say, or do I have to slug you?"

Sonny put on the coat.

Sheik then took a pair of leather driving gauntlets from his pasteboard suitcase beneath the bed and handed them to Sonny, too.

"What am I gonna do with these?" Sonny asked.

"Just put them on and shut up, fool," Sheik said.

He then took a long bamboo pole from behind the bed and began passing it through the window. On one end was attached a frayed felt New York Giants pennant.

Choo-Choo came down the fire escape in time to take the pole and lean it against the ladder.

"Ain't no cops on this roof yet but the roof down where they's shaking down is lousy with 'em," he reported.

His face was shiny with sweat and the whites of his eyes had begun to glow.

"Don't chicken out on me now," Sheik said.

"I just needs some pot to steady my nerves."

"Okay, we're going to blow two now." Sheik turned to Sonny and said, "Outside, boy."

Sonny gave him a look, hesitated, then climbed out on the fire-escape landing.

"Let me come, too," Sissie said.

Sugartit sat up with sudden interest.

"I want both you little jailbaits to stay right here in this room and don't move," Sheik ordered in a hard voice, then turned to Inky, "You come on, Inky, I'm gonna need you."

Inky joined the others on the fire escape. Sheik came last and closed the window. They squatted in a circle. The landing was crowded.

Sheik took two limp cigarettes from the roll of his sweatshirt and stuck them into his mouth.

"Bombers!" Choo-Choo exclaimed. "You've been holding out on us."

"Give me some fire and less of your lip," Sheik said.

Choo-Choo flipped a dollar lighter and lit both cigarettes. Sheik sucked the smoke deep into his lungs, then passed one of the sticks to Inky.

"You and Choo-Choo take halvers and me and the captive will split this one."

Sonny raised both gloved hands in a pushing gesture. "Pass me. That gage done got me into more trouble now than I can get out of."

"You're chicken," Sheik said contemptuously, sucking another puff. He swallowed back the smoke each time it started up from his lungs. His face swelled and began darkening with blood as the drug took hold. His eyes became dilated and his nostrils flared.

"Man, if I had my heater I bet I could shoot that sergeant down there dead between the eyes," he said. The cigarette was stuck to his bottom lip and dangled up and down when he talked.

"What I'd rather have me is one of those hard-shooting long-barreled thirty-eights like Grave Digger and Coffin Ed have got," Choo-Choo said. "Them heaters can kill a rock. Only I'd want me a silencer on it and I could sit here and pick off any mother-raper I wanted. But I wouldn't shoot nobody unless he was a big shot or the chief of police or somebody like that."

"You're talking about rathers, what you'd rather have; me, I'm talking about facts," Sheik said, the cigarette bobbing up and down.

"What you're talking about will get you burnt up in Sing-Sing if you don't watch out," Choo-Choo said.

"What you mean!" Sheik said, jumping to his feet threateningly. "You're going to make me throw your ass off this fire escape."

Choo-Choo jumped to his feet, too, and backed against the rail. "Throw whose ass off where? This ain't Inky you're talking to. My ass ain't made of chicken feathers."

Inky scrambled to his feet and stepped between them. "What about the captive, Sheik?" he asked in alarm.

"Damn the captive!" Sheik raved and whipped out a bone-handled knife, shaking open the six-inch blade with the same motion.

"Don't cut 'em!" Inky cried.

He knocked Inky into the iron steps with a back-handed slap and grabbed a handful of Choo-Choo's sweat shirt collar.

"You blab and I'll cut your mother-raping throat," he said.

Violence surged through him like runaway blood.

Choo-Choo's eyes turned three-quarters white and a feverish sweat popped out on his dark brown skin.

"I didn't mean nothing, Sheik," he whined desperately, talking low. "You know I didn't mean nothing. A man can talk 'bout his rathers, can't he?"

The violence receded but Sheik was still gripped in a murderous compulsion.

"If I thought you'd pigeon I'd kill you."

"You know I ain't gonna pigeon, Sheik. You know me better than that."

Sheik let go of his collar. Choo-Choo took a deep sighing breath.

Inky straightened up and rubbed his bruised shin. "You done made me lose the stick," he complained.

"Hell with the stick," Sheik said.

"That's what I mean," Sonny said. "This here gage they sells now will make you cut your own mamma's throat. They must be mixing it with loco weed or somethin'."

"Shut up!" Sheik said, still holding the open knife in his hand. "I ain't gonna tell you no more."

Sonny cast a look at the knife and said, "I ain't saying nothing."

"You better not," Sheik said. Then he turned to Inky. "Inky, you take the captive up on the roof and you and him start flying Caleb's pigeons. You, Sonny, when the cops come you tell them your name is Caleb Bowee and you're just trying to teach your pigeons how to fly at night. You got that?"

"Yeah," Sonny said skeptically.

"You know how to make pigeons fly?"

Sonny hesitated. "Chunk rocks at 'em?"

"Hell, nigger, your brain ain't big as a mustard seed. You can't chunk no rocks up there with all those cops about. What you got to do is take this pole and wave the end with the flag at 'em every time they try to light."

Sonny looked at the bamboo pole skeptically. "S'posin' they fly away and don't come back."

"They ain't going nowhere. They just fly in circles trying all the time to get back into the coop." Sheik doubled over suddenly and started laughing. "Pigeons ain't got no sense, man."

The rest of them just looked at him.

Finally Inky asked, "What you want me to do?"

Sheik straightened up quickly and stopped laughing. "You guard the captive and see that he don't escape."

"Oh!" Inky said. After a moment he asked, "What I'm gonna tell the cops when they ask me what I'm doin'?"

"Hell, you tell the cops Caleb is teaching you how to train pigeons."

Inky bent over and started rubbing his shins again. Without

looking up he said, "You reckon the cops gonna fall for that, Sheik? You reckon they gonna be crazy enough to believe anybody's gonna be flying pigeons with all this going on all around here?"

"Hell, these is white cops," Sheik said contemptuously. "They believe spooks are crazy anyway. You and Sonny just act kind of simpleminded. They gonna swallow it like it's chocolate ice cream. They ain't going to do nothing but kick you in the ass and laugh like hell about how crazy spooks are. They gonna go home and tell their old ladies and everybody they see about two simpleminded spooks up on the roof teaching pigeons how to fly at night all during the biggest dragnet they ever had in Harlem. You see if they don't."

Inky kept on rubbing his shin. "It ain't that I doubt you, Sheik, but s'posin' they don't believe it."

"God damn it, go ahead and do what I told you and don't stand there arguing with me," Sheik said, hit by another squall of fury. "I'd take me one look at you and this nigger here and I'd believe it myself, and I ain't even no gray cop."

Inky turned reluctantly and started up the stairs toward the roof. Sonny gave another sidelong look at Sheik's open knife and started to follow.

"Wait a minute, simple, don't forget the pole," Sheik said. "I've told you not to try chunking rocks at those pigeons. You might kill one and then you'd have to eat it." He doubled over laughing at his joke.

Sonny picked up the pole with a sober face and climbed slowly after Inky.

"Come on," Sheik said to Choo-Choo, "open the window and let's get back inside."

Before turning his back and bending to open the window, Choo-Choo said, "Listen, Sheik, I didn't mean nothing by that."

"Forget it," Sheik said.

Sissie and Sugartit were sitting silently side by side on the bed, looking frightened and dejected. Sugartit had stopped crying but her eyes were red and her cheeks stained.

"Jesus Christ, you'd think this is a funeral," Sheik said.

No one replied. Choo-Choo fidgeted from one foot to the other.

"I want you chicks to wipe those sad looks off your faces," Sheik said. "We got to look like we're balling and ain't got a thing to worry about when the cops get here."

"*You* go ahead and ball by yourself," Sissie said.

Sheik lunged forward and slapped her over on her side.

She got up without a word and walked to the window.

"If you go out that window I'll throw you down on the street," Sheik threatened.

She stood looking out the window with her back turned and didn't answer.

Sugartit sat quietly on the edge of the bed and trembled.

"Hell," Sheik said disgustedly and flopped lengthwise behind Sugartit on the bed.

She got up and went to stand in the window beside Sissie.

"Come on, Choo-Choo, to hell with those bitches," Sheik said. "Let's decide what to do with the captive."

"Now you're getting down to the gritty," Choo-Choo said enthusiastically, straddling a chair. "You got any plans?"

"Sure. Give me a butt."

Choo-Choo fished two Camels from a squashed package in his sweat shirt roll and lit them, passing one to Sheik.

"This square weed on top of gage makes you crazy," he said.

"Man, my head already feels like it's going to pop open, it's so full of ideas," Sheik said. "If I had me a real mob like Dutch Schultz's I could take over Harlem with the ideas I got. All I need is just the mob."

"Hell, you and me could do it alone," Choo-Choo said.

"We'd need some arms and stuff, some real factory-made heaters and a couple of machine guns and maybe some pineapples."

"If we croaked Grave Digger and the Monster we'd have two real cool heaters to start off with," Choo-Choo suggested.

"We ain't going to mess with those studs until after we're organized," Sheik said. "Then maybe we can import some talent to make the hit. But we'd need some dough."

"Hell, we can hold the prisoner for ransom," Choo-Choo said.

"Who'd ransom that nigger," Sheik said. "I bet even his own mamma wouldn't pay to get him back."

"He can ransom hisself," Choo-Choo said. "He got a shine parlor, ain't he? Shine parlors make good dough. Maybe he's got a chariot too."

"Hell, I knew all along he was valuable," Sheik said. "That's why I had us snatch him."

"We can take over his shine parlor," Choo-Choo said.

"I got some other plans too," Sheik said. "Maybe we can sell him to the Stars of David for some zip guns. They got lots of zip guns and they're scared to use them."

"We could do that or we could swap him to the Puerto Rican Bandits for Burrhead. We promised Burrhead we'd pay his ransom and they been saying if we don't hurry up and get 'im they're gonna cut his throat."

"Let 'em cut the black mother-raper's throat," Sheik said. "That chicken-hearted bastard ain't no good to us."

"I tell you what, Sheik," Choo-Choo said exuberantly. "We could put him in a sack like them ancient cats like the Dutchman and them used to do and throw him into the Harlem River. I've always wanted to put some bastard into a sack."

"You know how to put a mother-raper into a sack?" Sheik asked.

"Sure, you—"

"Shut up, I'm gonna to tell you how. You knock the mother-raper unconscious first; that's to keep him from jumping about. Then you put a noose with a slip-knot 'round his neck. Then you double him up into a Z and tie the other end of the wire around his knees. Then when you put him in the gunny sack you got to be sure it's big enough to give him some space to move around in. When the mother-raper wakes up and tries to straighten out he chokes hisself to death. Ain't nobody killed 'im. The mother-raper has just committed suicide." Sheik rolled with laughter.

"You got to tie his hands behind his back first," Choo-Choo said.

Sheik stopped laughing and his face became livid with fury. "Who don't know that, fool!" he shouted. " 'Course you got to tie his hands behind his back. You trying to tell me I don't know how to put a mother-raper into a sack. I'll put *you* into a sack."

"I know you know how, Sheik," Choo-Choo said hastily. "I just didn't want you to forget nothing when we put the captive in a sack."

"I ain't going to forget nothing," Sheik said.

"When we gonna put him in a sack?" Choo-Choo asked. "I know where to find a sack."

"Okay, we'll put him in a sack just soon as the police finish here; then we take him down and leave him in the basement," Sheik said.

VII

GRAVE DIGGER FLASHED his badge at the two harness bulls guarding the door and pushed inside the Dew Drop Inn.

The joint was jammed with colored people who'd seen the big white man die, but nobody seemed to be worrying about it.

The jukebox was giving out with a stomp version of "Big-Legged Woman." Saxophones were pleading; the horns were teasing; the bass was patting; the drums were chatting; the piano was catting, laying and playing the jive, and a husky female voice was shouting:

> ". . . you can feel my thigh
> But don't you feel up high."

Happy-tail women were bouncing out of their dresses on the high bar stools.

Grave Digger trod on the sawdust sprinkled over the blood-stains that wouldn't wash off and parked on the stool at the end of the bar.

Big Smiley was serving drinks with his left arm in a sling.

The white manager, the sleeves of his tan silk shirt rolled up, was helping.

Big Smiley shuffled down the wet footing and showed Grave Digger most of his big yellow teeth.

"Is you drinking, Chief, or just sitting and thinking?"

"How's the wing?" Grave Digger asked.

"Favorable. It wasn't cut deep enough to do no real damage."

The manager came down and said, "If I'd thought there was going to be any trouble I'd have called the police right away."

"What do you calculate as trouble in this joint?" Grave Digger asked.

The manager reddened. "I meant about the white man getting killed."

"Just what started all the trouble in here?"

"It wasn't exactly what you'd call trouble, Chief," Big Smiley said. "It was only a drunk attacked one of my white customers with his shiv and naturally I had to protect my customer."

"What did he have against the white man?"

"Nothing, Chief. Not a single thing. He was sitting over there drinking one shot of rye after another and looking at the white man standing here tending to his own business. Then he gets red-eyed drunk and his evil tells him to get up and cut the man. That's all. And naturally I couldn't let him do that."

"He must have had some reason. You're not trying to tell me he got up and attacked the man without any reason whatever."

"Naw suh, Chief, I'll bet my life he ain't had no reason at all to wanta cut the man. You know how our folks is, Chief; he was just one of those evil niggers that when they get drunk they start hating white folks and get to remembering all the bad things white folks ever done to them. That's all. More than likely he was mad at some white man that done something bad to him twenty years ago down South and he just wanted to take it out on this white man in here. It's like I told that white detective who was in here, this white man was standing here at the bar by hisself and that nigger just figgered with all those colored folk in here he could cut him and get away with it."

"Maybe. What's his name?"

"I ain't ever seen that nigger before tonight, Chief; I don't know what is his name."

A customer called from up the bar, "Hey, boss, how about a little service up here?"

"If you want me, Jones, just holler," the manager said, moving off to serve the customer.

"Yeah," Grave Digger said, then asked Big Smiley, "Who was the woman?"

"There she is," Big Smiley said, nodding toward a booth.

Grave Digger turned his head and scanned her.

The black lady in the pink jersey dress and red silk stockings was back in her original seat in a booth surrounded by three workers.

"It wasn't on account of her," Big Smiley added.

Grave Digger slid from his stool, went over to her booth and flashed his badge. "I want to talk to you."

She looked at the gold badge and complained, "Why don't you folks leave me alone? I done already told a white cop everything I know about that shooting, which ain't nothing."

"Come on, I'll buy you a drink," Grave Digger said.

"Well, in that case . . ." she said and went with him to the bar.

At Grave Digger's order Big Smiley grudgingly poured her a shot of gin and Grave Digger said, "Fill it up."

Big Smiley filled the glass and stayed there to listen.

"How well did you know the white man?" Grave Digger asked the lady.

"I didn't know him at all. I'd just seen him around here once or twice."

"Doing what—"

"Just chasing."

"Alone?"

"Yeah."

"Did you see him pick up anyone?"

"Naw, he was one of those particular kind. He never saw nothing he liked."

"Who was the colored man who tried to cut him?"

"How the hell should I know?"

"He wasn't a relative of yours?"

"A relation of mine. I should hope not."

"Just exactly what did he say to the white man when he started to attack him?"

"I don't remember exactly; he just said something 'bout him messing about with his gal."

"That's the same thing the other man, Sonny Pickens, accused him of."

"I don't know nothing about that."

He thanked her and wrote down her name and address.

She went back to her seat.

He returned back to Big Smiley. "What did Pickens and the man argue about?"

"They ain't had no argument, Chief. Not in here. It wasn't on account of nothing that happened in here that he was shot."

"It was on account of something," Grave Digger said. "Robbery doesn't figure, and people in Harlem don't kill for revenge."

"Naw suh, leastwise they don't shoot."

"More than likely they'll throw acid or hot lye," Grave Digger said.

"Naw, suh, not on no white gennelman."

"So what else is there left but a woman," Grave Digger said.

"Naw suh," Big Smiley contradicted flatly. "You know better'n that, Chief. A colored woman don't consider diddling with a white man as being unfaithful. They don't consider it no more than just working in service, only they is getting better paid and the work is less straining. 'Sides which, the hours is shorter. And they old men don't neither. Both she and her old man figger it's like finding money in the street. And I don't mean no cruisers neither; I means church people and Christians and all the rest."

"How old are you, Smiley?" Grave Digger asked.

"I be forty-nine come December seventh."

"You're talking about old times, son. These young colored men don't go in for that slavery-time deal anymore."

"Shucks, Chief, you just kidding. This is old Smiley. I got dirt on these women in Harlem ain't never been plowed. Shucks, you and me both can put our finger on high society colored ladies here who got their whole rep just by going with some big important white man. And their old men is cashing in on it, too; makes them important, too, to have their old ladies going with some big-shot gray. Shucks, even a hard-working nigger wouldn't shoot a white man if he come home and found him in bed with his old lady with his pants down. He might whup his old lady just to show her who was boss, after he done took the money 'way from her, but he wouldn't sure 'nough hurt her like he'd do if he caught her screwing some other nigger."

"I wouldn't bet on it," Grave Digger said.

"Have it your own way, Chief, but I still think you're barking up the wrong tree. Lissen, the only way I figger a colored man in Harlem gonna kill a white man is in a fight. He'll draw his shiv if he getting his ass whupped and maybe stab him to death. But I'll bet my life ain't no nigger up here gonna shoot down no white man in cold blood—no important white gennelman like him."

"Would the killer have to know he was important?"

"He'd know it," Big Smiley said positively.

"You knew him?" Grave Digger said.

"Naw suh, not to say knew him. He come in here two, three times before but I didn't know his name."

"You expect me to believe he came in here two or three times and you didn't find out who he was?"

"I didn't mean exactly I didn't know his name," Big Smiley hemmed. "But I'se telling you, Chief, ain't no leads 'round here, that's for sure."

"You're going to have to tell me more than that, son," Grave Digger said in a flat, toneless voice.

Big Smiley looked at him; then suddenly he leaned across the bar and said in a low voice, "Try at Bucky's, Chief."

"Why Bucky's?"

"I seen him come in here once with a pimp what hangs 'round in Bucky's."

"What's his name?"

"I don't recollect his name, Chief. They driv up in his car and just stopped for a minute like they was looking for somebody and went out and drive away."

"Don't play with me," Grave Digger said with a sudden show of anger. "This ain't the movies; this is real. A white man has been killed in Harlem and Harlem is my beat. I'll take you down to the station and turn a dozen white cops loose on you and they'll work you over until the black comes off."

"Name's Ready Belcher, Chief, but I don't want nobody to know I told you," Big Smiley said in a whisper. "I don't want no trouble with that starker."

"Ready," Grave Digger said and got down from his stool.

He didn't know much about Ready; just that he operated up-town on the swank side of Harlem, above 145th Street in Washington Heights.

He drove up to the 154th Street precinct station at the corner of Amsterdam Avenue and asked for his friend, Bill Cresus. Bill was a colored detective on the vice squad. No one knew where Bill was at the time. He left word for Bill to contact him at Bucky's if he called within the hour. Then he got into his car and coasted down the sharp incline to St. Nicholas Avenue and turned south down the lesser incline past 149th Street.

Outwardly it was a quiet neighborhood of private houses and five- and six-story apartment buildings flanking the wide black-paved street. But the houses had been split up into bed-sized one-room kitchenettes, renting for $25 weekly, at the disposal of frantic couples who wished to shack up for a season. And behind the respectable-looking facades of the apartment buildings were the plush flesh cribs and poppy pads and circus tents of Harlem.

The excitement of the dragnet hadn't reached this far and the street was comparatively empty.

He coasted to a stop before a sedate basement entrance. Four steps below street level was a black door with a shiny brass knocker in the shape of three musical notes. Above it red neon lights spelled out the word *BUCKY'S*.

It felt strange to be alone. The last time had been when Coffin Ed was in the hospital after the acid throwing. The memory of it made his head tight with anger and it took a special effort to keep his temper under wraps.

He pushed and the door opened.

People sat at white-clothed tables beneath pink-shaded wall lights in a long narrow room, eating fried chicken daintily with their fingers. There was a white party of six, several colored couples, and two colored men with white women. They looked well-dressed and reasonably clean.

The walls behind them were covered with innumerable small pink-stained pencil portraits of all the great and the near-great who had ever lived in Harlem. Musicians led nine to one.

The hat-check girl stationed in a cubicle beside the entrance stuck out her hand with a supercilious look.

Grave Digger kept his hat on and strode down the narrow aisle between the tables.

A chubby pianist with shining black skin and a golden smile who was dressed in a tan tweed sport jacket and white silk sport shirt open at the throat sat at a baby grand piano wedged between the last table and the circular bar. Soft white light spilled on his partly bald head while he played nocturnes with a bedroom touch.

He gave Grave Digger an apprehensive look, got up and followed him to the semi-darkness of the bar.

"I hope you're not on business, Digger. I pay to keep this place off-limits for cops," he said in a fluttery voice.

Grave Digger's gaze circled the bar. Its high stools were inhabited by a varied crew: a big dark-haired white man, two slim young colored men, a short heavy-set white man with blond crew-cut hair, two dark women dressed in white silk evening gowns, a chocolate dandy in a box-backed double-breasted tuxedo sporting a shoestring dubonnet bow. A high-yellow waitress waited nearby with a serving tray. Another tall, slim ebony young man presided over the bar.

"I'm just looking around, Bucky," Grave Digger said. "Just looking for a break."

"Many folks have found a break in here," Bucky said suggestively.

"I don't doubt it."

"But that's not the kind of break you're looking for."

"I'm looking for a break on a case. An important white man was shot to death over on Lenox Avenue a short time ago."

Bucky gestured with lotioned hands. His manicured nails flashed in the dim light. "What has that to do with us here? Nobody ever gets hurt in here. Everything is smooth and quiet. You can see for yourself. Genteel people dining in leisure. Fine food. Soft music. Low lights and laughter. Doesn't look like business for the police in this respectable atmosphere."

In the pause that followed, one of the marcelled ebonies was heard saying in a lilting voice, "I positively did not even look at her man, and she upped and knocked me over the head with a whiskey bottle."

"These black bitches are so violent," his companion said.

"And strong, honey."

Grave Digger smiled sourly.

"The man who was killed was a patron of yours," he said. "Name of Ulysses Galen."

"My God, Digger, I don't know the names of all the ofays who come into my place," Bucky said. "I just play for them and try to make them happy."

"I believe you," Grave Digger said. "Galen was seen about town with Ready. Does that stir your memory?"

"Ready?" Bucky exclaimed innocently. "He hardly ever comes in here. Who gave you that notion?"

"The hell he doesn't," Grave Digger said. "He panders out of here."

"You hear that!" Bucky appealed to the barman in a shrill horrified voice, then caught himself as the silence from the diners reached his sensitive ears. With hushed indignation he added, "This flatfoot comes in here and accuses me of harboring panderers."

"A little bit of that goes a long way, son," Grave Digger said in his flat voice.

"Oh, that man's an ogre, Bucky," the barman said. "You go back to your entertaining and I'll see what he wants." He switched over to the bar, put his hands on his hips and looked down at Grave Digger with a haughty air. "And just what can we do for you, you mean rude grumpy man?"

The white men at the bar laughed.

Bucky turned and started off.

Grave Digger caught him by the arm and pulled him back. "Don't make me get rough, son," he muttered.

"Don't you dare manhandle me," Bucky said in a low tense whisper, his whole chubby body quivering with indignation. "I don't have to take that from you. I'm covered."

The bartender backed away, shaking himself. "Don't let him hurt Bucky," he appealed to the white men in a frightened voice.

"Maybe I can help you," the white man with the blond crew cut said to Grave Digger. "You're a detective, aren't you?"

"Yeah," Grave Digger said, holding on to Bucky. "A white man was killed in Harlem tonight and I'm looking for the killer."

The white man's eyebrows went up an inch.

"Do you expect to find him here?"

"I'm following a lead, is all. The man has been seen with a pimp called Ready Belcher who hangs out here."

The white man's eyebrows subsided.

"Oh, Ready; I know him. But he's merely—"

Bucky cut him off: "You don't have to tell him anything; you're protected in here."

"Sure," the white man said. "That's what the officer is trying to do, protect us all."

"He's right," one of the evening-gowned colored women said. "If Ready has killed some trick he was steering to Reba's the chair's too good for him."

"Shut your mouth, woman," the barman whispered fiercely.

The muscles in Grave Digger's face began to jump as he let go of Bucky. He stood up with his heels hooked into the rungs of the barstool and leaned over the bar. He caught the barman by the front of his red silk shirt as he was trying to dance away. The shirt ripped down the seam with a ragged sound but enough held for him to jerk the barman close to the bar.

"You got too goddamned much to say, Tarbelle," he said in a thick cottony voice, and slapped the barman spinning across the circular enclosure with the palm of his open hand.

"He didn't have to do that," the first woman said.

Grave Digger turned on her and said thickly, "And you, little sister, you and me are going to see Reba."

"Reba!" her companion replied. "Do I know anybody named Reba. Lord no!"

Grave Digger stepped down from his high stool.

"Cut that Aunt Jemima routine and get up off your ass," he said thickly, "or I'll take my pistol and break off your teeth."

The two white men stared at him as though at a dangerous animal escaped from the zoo.

"You mean that?" the woman said.

"I mean it," he said.

She scrunched out of the stool and said, "Gimme my coat, Jule."

The chocolate dandy took a coat from the top of the jukebox behind them.

"That's putting it on rather thick," the blond white man protested in a reasonable voice.

"I'm just a cop," Grave Digger said thickly. "If you white people insist on coming up to Harlem where you force colored people to live in vice-and-crime-ridden slums, it's my job to see that you are safe."

The white man turned bright red.

VIII

THE SERGEANT KNOCKED at the door. He was flanked by two uniformed cops and a corporal.

Another search party led by another sergeant was at the door across the hall.

Other cops were working all the corridors starting at the bottom and sealing off the area they'd covered.

"Come in," Granny called in a querulous voice. "The door ain't locked." She bit the stem of her corn-cob pipe with tooth-less gums.

The sergeant and his party entered the small kitchen. It was crowded.

At the sight of the very old woman working innocently at

her darning, the sergeant started to remove his cap, then re-membered he was on duty and kept it on.

"You don't lock your door, Grandma?" he observed.

Granny looked at the cops over the rims of her ancient spec-tacles and her old fingers went lax on the darning egg.

"Naw suh, Ah ain't got nuthin' for nobody to steal and ain't nobody want nuthin' else from an old 'oman like me."

The sergeant's beady blue eyes scanned the kitchen. "You keep this place mighty clean, Grandma," he remarked in surprise.

"Yes suh, it don't kill a body to keep clean and my old missy used to always say de cleaness is next to the goddess."

Her old milky eyes held a terrified question she couldn't ask and her thin old body began to tremble.

"You mean goodness," the sergeant said.

"Naw suh, Ah means goddess; Ah knows what she said."

"She means cleanliness is next to godliness," the corporal interposed.

"The professor," one of the cops said.

Granny pursed her lips. "Ah know what my missy said; god-dess, she said."

"Were you in slavery?" the sergeant asked as though struck suddenly by the thought.

The others stared at her with sudden interest.

"Ah don't rightly know, suh. Ah 'spect so though."

"How old are you?"

Her lips moved soundlessly; she seemed to be trying to remember.

"She must be all of a hundred," the professor said.

She couldn't stop her body from trembling and slowly it got worse.

"What for you white 'licemen wants with me, suh?" she finally asked.

The sergeant noticed that she was trembling and said reas-suringly, "We ain't after you, Grandma; we're looking for an escaped prisoner and some teenage gangsters."

"Gangsters!"

Her spectacles slipped down on her nose and her hands shook as though she had the palsy.

"They belong to a neighborhood gang that calls itself Real Cool Moslems."

She went from terrified to scandalized. "We ain't no heathen in here, suh," she said indignantly. "We be God-fearing Christians."

The cops laughed.

"They're not real Moslems," the sergeant said. "They just call themselves that. One of them, named Sonny Pickens, is older than the rest. He killed a white man outside on the street."

The darning dropped unnoticed from Granny's nerveless fingers. The corn-cob pipe wobbled in her puckered mouth; the professor looked at it with morbid fascination.

"A white man! Merciful hebens!" she exclaimed in a quavering voice. "What's this wicked world coming to?"

"Nobody knows," the sergeant said, then changed his manner abruptly. "Well, let's get down to business, Grandma. What's your name?"

"Bowee, suh, but e'body calls me Granny."

"Bowee. How do you spell that, Grandma?"

"Ah don't rightly know, suh. Hit's just short for boll weevil. My old missy name me that. They say the boll weevil was mighty bad the year Ah was born."

"What about your husband, didn't he have a name?"

"Ah neber had no regular 'usban', suh. Just whosoever was thar."

"You got any children?"

"Jesus Christ, sarge," the professor said. "Her youngest child would be sixty years old."

The two cops laughed; the sergeant reddened sheepishly.

"Who lives here with you, Granny?" the sergeant continued.

Her bony frame stiffened beneath her faded Mother Hubbard. The corn-cob pipe fell into her lap and rolled unnoticed to the floor.

"Just me and mah grandchile, Caleb, suh," she said in a forced voice. "And Ah rents a room to two workin' boys; but they be good boys and don't neber bother nobody."

The cops grew suddenly speculative.

"Now this grandchild, Caleb, Grandma—" the sergeant began cunningly.

"He might be mah great-grandchile, suh," she interrupted.

He frowned, "Great, then. Where is he now?"

"You mean right now, suh?"

"Yeah, Grandma, right this minute."

"He at work in a bowling alley downtown, suh."

"How long has he been at work?"

"He left right after supper, suh. We gennally eats supper at six o'clock."

"And he has a regular job in this bowling alley?"

"Naw suh, hit's just for t'night, suh. He goes to school—Ah don't rightly 'member the number of his new P.S."

"Where is this bowling alley he's working at tonight?"

"Ah don't know, suh. Ah guess you all'll have to ast Samson. He is one of mah roomers."

"Samson, yeah." The sergeant stored it in his memory. "And you haven't seen Caleb since supper—about seven o'clock, say?"

"Ah don't know what time it was but it war right after supper."

"And when he left here he went directly to work?"

"Yas suh, you find him right dar on de job. He a good boy and always mind me what Ah say."

"And your roomers, where are they?"

"They is in they room, suh. Hit's in the front. They got visitors with 'em."

"Visitors?"

"Gals."

"Oh!" Then to his assistants he said, "Come on."

They went through the middle room like hounds on a hot scent. The sergeant tried the handle to the front-room door without knocking, found it locked and hammered angrily.

"Who's that?" Sheik asked.

"The police."

Sheik unlocked the door. The cops rushed in. Sheik's eyes glittered.

"What the hell do you keep your door locked for?" the sergeant asked.

"We didn't want to be disturbed."

Four pairs of eyes quickly scanned the room.

Two teenaged colored girls sat side by side on the bed, leaf-ing through a colored picture magazine. Another youth stood looking out the open window at the excitement on the street.

"Who the hell you think you're kidding with this phony stage setting?" the sergeant roared.

"Not you, ace," Sheik said flippantly.

The sergeant's hand flicked out like a whip, passing inches in front of Sheik's eyes.

Sheik jumped back as though he'd been scalded.

"Jagged to the gills," the sergeant said, looking minutely about the room. His eyes lit on Choo-Choo's half-smoked package of Camels on the table. "Dump out those fags," he ordered a cop, watching Sheik's reaction. "Never mind," he added. "The bastard's got rid of them."

He closed in on Sheik like a prizefighter and shoved his red sweaty face within a few inches of Sheik's. His veined blue eyes bored into Sheik's pale yellow eyes.

"Where's that A-rab costume?" he asked in a brow-beating voice.

"What Arab costume? Do I look like an A-rab to you?"

"You look like a two-bit punk to me. You got the eyes of a yellow cur."

"You ain't got no prize-winning eyes yourself."

"Don't give me none of your lip, punk; I'll knock out your teeth."

"I could knock out your teeth too if I had on a sergeant's uniform and three big flatfeet backing me up."

The cops stared at him from blank shuttered faces.

"What do they call you, Mo-hammed or Nasser?" the ser-geant hammered.

"They call me by my name, Samson."

"Samson what?"

"Samson Hyers."

"Don't give me that crap; we know you're one of those Moslems."

"I ain't no Moslem; I'm a cannibal."

"Oh, so you think you're a comedian."

"You the one asking the funny questions."

"What's that other punk's name?"

"Ask him."

The sergeant slapped him with such force it sounded like a .22-caliber shot.

Sheik reeled back from the impact of the slap but kept his feet. Blood darkened his face to the color of beef liver; the imprint of the sergeant's hand glowed purple-red. His pale yellow eyes looked wildcat crazy. But he kept his lip buttoned.

"When I ask you a question I want you to answer it," the sergeant said.

He didn't answer.

"You hear me?"

He still didn't answer.

The sergeant loomed in front of him with both fists cocked like red meat axes.

"I want an answer."

"Yeah, I hear you," Sheik muttered sullenly.

"Frisk him," the sergeant ordered the professor, then to the other two cops said, "You and Price start shaking down this room."

The professor set to work on Sheik methodically, as though searching for lice, while the other cops started dumping dresser drawers onto the table.

The sergeant left them and turned his attention to Choo-Choo.

"What kind of Moslem are you?"

Choo-Choo started grinning and fawning like the original Uncle Tom.

"I ain't no Moslem, boss, I'se just a plain old unholy roller."

"I guess your name is Delilah."

"He-he, naw suh boss, but you're warm. It's Justice Broome."

All three cops looked about and grinned, and the sergeant had to clamp his jaws to keep from grinning too.

"You know these Moslems?"

"What Moslems, boss?"

"The Harlem Moslems in this neighborhood."

"Naw suh, boss, I don't know no Moslems in Harlem."

"You think I was born yesterday? They a neighborhood gang. Every black son of a bitch in this neighborhood knows who they are."

"Everybody 'cept me, boss."

The sergeant's palm flew out and caught Choo-Choo un-expectedly on the mouth while it was still open in a grin. It didn't rock his short thick body, but his eyes rolled back in their sockets. He spit blood on the floor.

"Boss, suh, please be careful with my chops—they're tender."

"I'm getting damn tired of your lying."

"Boss, I swear 'fore God, if I knowed anything 'bout them Moslems you'd be the first one I'd tell it to."

"What do you do?"

"I works, boss, yes suh."

"Doing what?"

"I helps out."

"Helps out with what? You want to lose some of your pearly teeth?"

"I helps out a man who writes numbers."

"What's his name?"

"His name?"

The sergeant cocked his fists.

"Oh, you mean his name, boss. Hit's Four-Four Row."

"You call that a name?"

"Yas suh, that's what they calls him."

"What does your buddy do?"

"The same thing," Sheik said.

The sergeant wheeled on him. "You keep quiet; when I want you I'll call you." Then he said to the professor, "Can't you keep that punk quiet?"

The professor unhooked his sap. "I'll quiet him."

"I don't want you to quiet him; just keep him quiet. I got some more questions for him." Then he turned back to Choo-Choo. "When do you punks work?"

"In the morning, boss. We got to get the numbers in by noon."

"What do you do the rest of the day?"

"Go 'round and pay off."

"What if there isn't any payoff?"

"Just go 'round."

"Where's your beat?"

" 'Round here."

"God damn it, you mean to tell me you write numbers in this neighborhood and you don't know anything about the Moslems?"

"I swear on my mother's grave, boss, I ain't never heard of no Moslems 'round here. They must not be in this neighborhood, boss."

"What time did you leave the house tonight?"

"I ain't never left it, boss. We come here right after we et supper and ain't been out since."

"Stop lying; I saw you both when you slipped back in here a half-hour ago."

"Naw suh, boss, you musta seen somebody what looks like us 'cause we been here all the time."

The sergeant crossed to the door and flung it open. "Hey, Grandma!" he called.

"Hannh?" she answered querulously from the kitchen.

"How long have these boys been in their room?"

"Hannh?"

"You have to talk louder; she can't hear you," Sissie volunteered.

Sheik and Choo-Choo gave her threatening looks.

The sergeant crossed the middle room to the kitchen door. "How long have your roomers been back from supper?" he roared.

She looked at him from uncomprehending eyes.

"Hannh?"

"She can't hear no more," Sissie called. "She gets that way sometime."

"Hell," the sergeant said disgustedly and stormed back to Choo-Choo. "Where'd you pick up these girls?"

"We didn't pick 'em up, boss; they come here by themselves."

"You're too goddam innocent to be alive." The sergeant was

frustrated. He turned to the professor: "What did you find on that punk?"

"This knife."

"Hell," the sergeant said. He took it and dropped it into his pocket without a glance. "Okay, fan this other punk—Justice."

"I'll do Justice," the professor punned.

The two cops crossed glances suggestively.

They had dumped out all the drawers and turned out all the boxes and pasteboard suitcases and now they were ready for the bed.

"You gals rise and shine," one said.

The girls got up and stood uncomfortably in the center of the room.

"Find anything?" the sergeant asked.

"Nothing that I'd even care to have in my dog house," the cop said.

The sergeant began on the girls. "What's your name?" he asked Sissie.

"Sissieratta Hamilton."

"Sissie what?"

"Sissieratta."

"Where do you live, Sissie?"

"At 2702 Seventh Avenue with my aunt and uncle, Mr. and Mrs. Coolie Dunbar."

"Ummm," he said. "And yours?" he asked Sugartit.

"Evelyn Johnson."

"Where do you live, Eve?"

"In Jamaica with my parents, Mr. and Mrs. Edward Johnson."

"It's mighty late for you to be so far from home."

"I'm going to spend the night with Sissieratta."

"How long have you girls been here?" he asked of both.

"About half an hour, more or less," Sissie replied.

"Then you saw the shooting down on the street?"

"It was over when we got here."

"Where did you come from?"

"From my house."

"You don't know if these punks have been in all evening or not."

"They were here when we got here and they said they'd been waiting here since supper. We promised to come at eight but we had to stay help my aunty and we got here late."

"Sounds too good to be true," the sergeant commented.

The girls didn't reply.

The cops finished with the bed and the talkative one said, "Nothing but stink."

"Can that talk," the sergeant said. "Grandma's clean."

"These punks aren't."

The sergeant turned to the professor. "What's on Justice besides the blindfold?"

His joke laid an egg.

"Nothing but his black," the professor said.

His joke drew a laugh.

"What do you say, shall we run 'em in?" the sergeant asked.

"Why not," the professor said. "If we haven't got space in the bullpen for everybody we can put up tents."

The sergeant wheeled suddenly on Sheik as though he'd forgotten something.

"Where's Caleb?"

"Up on the roof tending his pigeons."

All four cops froze. They stared at Sheik with those blank shuttered looks.

Finally the sergeant said carefully, "His grandma said you told her he was working in a bowling alley downtown."

"We just told her that to keep her from worrying. She don't like for him to go up on the roof at night."

"If I find you punks are holding out on me, God help you," the sergeant said in a slow sincere voice.

"Go look then," Sheik said.

The sergeant nodded to the professor. The professor climbed out of the window into the bright glare of the spotlights and began ascending the fire escape.

"What's he doing with them at night?" the sergeant asked Sheik.

"I don't know. Trying to make them lay black eggs, I suppose."

"I'm going to take you down to the station and have a private talk with you, punk," the sergeant said. "You're one punk who needs talking to privately."

The professor came down from the roof and called through the window, "They're holding two coons up here beside a pigeon loft. They're waiting on you."

"Okay, I'm coming. You and Price hold these punks on ice," he directed the other cops and climbed out of the window behind the professor.

IX

"GET IN," Grave Digger said.

She pulled up the skirt of her evening gown, drew the black coat tight, and eased her jumbo hams into the seat usually occupied by Coffin Ed.

Grave Digger went around on the other side and climbed beneath the wheel and waited.

"Does I just have to go along, honey," the woman said in a wheedling voice. "I can just as well tell you where she's at."

"That's what I'm waiting for."

"Well, why didn't you say so? She's in the Knickerbocker Apartments on 45th Street—the old Knickerbocker, I mean. She on the six story, 669."

"Who is she?" Grave Digger asked, probing a little.

"Who she is? Just a landprop is all."

"That ain't what I mean."

"Oh, I know what you means. You means who is she. You means you don't know who Reba is, Digger?" She tried to sound jocular but wasn't successful. "She the landprop what used to be old cap Murphy's go-between 'fore he got sent up for taking all them bribes. It was in all the papers."

"That was ten years ago and they called her Sheba then," he said.

"Yare, that's right, but she changed her name after she got into that last shooting scrape. You musta 'member that. She caught the nigger with some chippie or 'nother and made him jump buck naked out the third-story window. That wouldn't 'ave been so bad but she shot 'im through the head as he was going down. That was when she lived in the valley. Since then she done come up here on the hill. 'Course it warn't nobody but her husband and she didn't get a day. But Reba always has been lucky that way."

He took a shot in the dark. "What would anybody shoot Galen for?"

She grew stiff with caution. "Who he?"

"You know damn well who he was. He's the man who was shot tonight."

"Naw suh, I didn't know nothing 'bout that gennelman. I don't know why nobody would want to shoot him."

"You people give me a pain in the seat with all that ducking and dodging every time someone asks you a question. You act like you belong to a race of artful dodgers."

"You is asking me something I don't know nothing 'bout."

"Okay, get out."

She got out faster than she got in.

He drove down the hill of St. Nicholas Avenue and turned up the hill of 145th Street toward Convent Avenue.

On the left-hand corner, next to a new fourteen-story apartment building erected by a white insurance company, was the Brown Bomber Bar; across from it Big Crip's Bar; on the right-hand corner Cohen's Drug Store with its iron-grilled windows crammed with electric hair straightening irons, Hi-Life hair cream, Black and White bleaching cream, SSS and 666 blood tonics, Dr. Scholl's corn pads, men's and women's nylon head caps with chin straps to press hair while sleeping, a bowl of blue stone good for body lice, tins of Sterno canned heat good for burning or drinking, Halloween postcards and all the latest in enamelware hygiene utensils; across from it Zazully's Delicatessen with a white-lettered announcement on the plate-glass window: *We Have Frozen Chitterlings and Other Hard-to-find Delicacies.*

Grave Digger parked in front of a big frame house with peeling yellow paint which had been converted into offices, got out and walked next door to a six-story rotten-brick tenement long overdue at the wreckers.

Three cars were parked at the curb in front; two with up-state New York plates and the other from mid-Manhattan.

He pushed open a scaly door beneath the arch of a concrete block on which the word *KNICKER-BOCKER* was embossed.

An old gray-haired man with a splotched brown face sat in a chair just inside the doorway to the semi-dark corridor. He cautiously drew back gnarled feet in felt bedroom slippers and looked Grave Digger over with dull, satiated eyes.

"Evenin'," he said.

Grave Digger glanced at him. "Evenin'."

"Fourth story on de right. Number 421," the old man informed him.

Grave Digger stopped. "That Reba's?"

"You don't want Reba's. You want Topsy's. Dat's 421."

"What's happening at Topsy's?"

"What always happen. Dat's where the trouble is."

"What kind of trouble?"

"Just general trouble. Fightin' and cuttin'."

"I'm not looking for trouble. I'm looking for Reba."

"You're the man, ain't you?"

"Yeah, I'm the man."

"Then you wants 421. I'se de janitor."

"If you're the janitor then you know Mr. Galen."

A veil fell over the old man's face. "Who he?"

"He's the big Greek man who goes up to Reba's."

"I don't know no Greeks, boss. Don't no white folks come in here. Nothin' but cullud folks. You'll find 'em all at Topsy's."

"He was killed over on Lenox tonight."

"Sho nuff?"

Grave Digger started off.

The old man called to him, "I guess you wonderin' why we got them big numbers on de doors."

Grave Digger paused. "All right, why?"

"They sounds good." The old man cackled.

Grave Digger walked up five flights of shaky wooden stairs and knocked on a red-painted door with a round glass peephole in the upper panel.

After an interval a heavy woman's voice asked, "Who's you?"

"I'm the Digger."

Bolts clicked and the door cracked a few inches on the chain. A big dark silhouette loomed in the crack, outlined by blue light from behind.

"I didn't recognize you, Digger," a pleasant bass voice said. "Your hat shades your face. Long time no see."

"Unchain the door, Reba, before I shoot it off."

A deep bass laugh accompanied chain rattling and the door swung inward.

"Same old Digger, shoot first and talk later. Come on in; we're all colored folks here."

He stepped into a blue-lit carpeted hall reeking of incense.

"You're sure?"

She laughed again as she closed and bolted the door. "Those are not folks, those are clients." Then she turned casually to face him. "What's on your mind, honey?"

She was as tall as his six feet two, with snow-white hair cut short as a man's and brushed straight back from her forehead. Her lips were painted carnation red and her eyelids silver but her smooth unlined jet-black skin was untouched. She wore a black sequined evening gown with a red rose in the V of her mammoth bosom, which was a lighter brown than her face. She looked like the last of the Amazons blackened by time.

"Where can we talk?" Grave Digger said. "I don't want to strain you."

"You don't strain me, honey," she said, opening the first door to the right. "Come into the kitchen."

She put a bottle of bourbon and a siphon beside two tall glasses on the table and sat in a kitchen chair.

"Say when," she said as she started to pour.

"By me," Grave Digger said, pushing his hat to the back of his head and planting a foot on the adjoining chair.

She stopped pouring and put down the bottle.

"You go ahead," he said.

"I don't drink no more," she said. "I quit after I killed Sam."

He crossed his arms on his raised knee and leaned forward on them, looking at her.

"You used to wear a rosary," he said.

She smiled, showing gold crowns on her outside incisors.

"When I got real religion I quit that too," she said.

"What religion did you get?"

"Just the faith, Digger, just the spirit."

"It lets you run this joint?"

"Why not. It's nature, just like eating. Nothing in my faith 'gainst eating. I just make it convenient and charge 'em for it."

"You'd better get a new steerer; the one downstairs is simple-minded."

Her big bass laugh rang out again. "He don't work for us; he does that on his own."

"Don't make it hard on yourself," he said. "This can be easy for us both."

She looked at him calmly. "I ain't got nothing to fear."

"When was the last time you saw Galen?"

"The big Greek? Been some time now, Digger. Three or four months. He don't come here no more."

"Why?"

"I don't let him."

"How come?"

"Be your age, Digger. This is a sporting house. If I don't let a white john with money come here, I must have good reasons. And if I want to keep my other white clients I'd better not say what they are. You can't close me up and you can't make me talk, so why don't you let it go at that?"

"The Greek was shot to death tonight over on Lenox."

"I just heard it over the radio," she said.

"I'm trying to find out who did it."

She looked at him in surprise. "It said on the radio the killer was known. A Sonny Pickens. Said a teenage gang called the something-or-'nother Moslems snatched him."

"He didn't do it. That's why I'm here."

"Well, if he didn't do it, you got your job cut out," she said. "I wish I could help you but I can't."

"Maybe," he said. "Maybe not."

She raised her eyebrows slightly. "By the way, where's your sidekick, Coffin Ed? The radio said he shot one of the gang."

"Yeah, he got suspended."

She became still, like an animal alert to danger. "Don't take it out on me, Digger."

"I just want to know why you stopped the Greek from coming here."

She stared into his eyes. She had dark brown eyes with clear whites and long black lashes.

"I'll let you talk to Ready. He knows."

"Is he here now?"

"He got a little chippie here he can't stay 'way from for five minutes. I'm going to throw 'em both out soon. Would have before now but my clients like her."

"Was the Greek her client?"

She got up slowly, sighing slightly from the effort.

"I'll send him out here."

"Bring him out."

"All right. But take him away, Digger. I don't want him talking in here. I don't want no more trouble. I've had trouble all my days."

"I'll take him away," he said.

She went out and Grave Digger heard doors being discreetly opened and shut and then her controlled bass voice saying, "How do I know? He said he was a friend."

A tall man with pockmarked skin a dirty shade of black stepped into the kitchen. An old razor scar cut a purple ridge from the lobe of his ear to the tip of his chin. There was a cast in one eye, the other was reddish brown. Thin corked hair stuck to a double-jointed head shaped like a peanut. He was flashily dressed in a light tan suit. Glass glittered from two gold-plated rings. His pointed tan shoes were shined to mirror brilliance.

At sight of Grave Digger he drew up short and turned a murderous look on Reba.

"You tole me hit was a friend," he accused in a rough voice.

She didn't let it bother her. She pushed him into the kitchen and closed the door.

"Well, ain't he?" she asked.

"What's this, some kind of frame-up?" he shouted.

Grave Digger chuckled at the look of outrage on his face. "How can a buck as ugly as you be a pimp?" he asked.

"You're gonna make me talk about you mamma," Ready said, digging his right hand into his pants pocket.

With nothing moving but his arm, Grave Digger back-handed him in the solar plexus, knocking out his wind, then pivoted on his left foot and followed with a right cross to the same spot, and with the same motion raised his knee and sunk it into Ready's belly as the pimp's slim frame jack-knifed forward. Spit showered from Ready's fishlike mouth, and the sense was already gone from his eyes when Grave Digger grabbed him by the back of the coat collar, jerked him erect, and started to slap him in the face with his open palm.

Reba grabbed his arm, saying. "Not in here, Digger, I beg you; don't make him bleed. You said you'd take him out."

"I'm taking him out now," he said in a cottony voice, shaking off her hold.

"Then finish him without bleeding him; I don't want nobody coming in here finding blood on the floor."

Grave Digger grunted and eased off. He propped Ready against the wall, holding him up on his rubbery legs with one hand while he took the knife and frisked him quickly with the other.

The sense came back into Ready's good eye and Grave Digger stepped back and said, "All right, let's go quietly, son."

Ready fussed about without looking at him, straightening his coat and tie, then fished a greasy comb from his pocket and combed his rumpled conk. He was bent over in the middle from pain and breathing in gasps. A white froth had collected in both corners of his mouth.

Finally he mumbled, "You can't take me outa here without no warrant."

"Go ahead with the man and shut up," Reba said quickly.

He gave her a pleading look. "You gonna let him take me outa here?"

"If he don't I'm going to throw you out myself," she said.

"I don't want any hollering and screaming in here scaring my white clients."

"That's gonna cost you," Ready threatened.

"Don't threaten me, nigger," she said dangerously. "And don't set your foot in my door again."

"Okay, Reba, that's the lick that killed Dick," Ready said slowly. "You and him got me outnumbered." He gave her a last sullen look and turned to go.

Reba walked to the door and let them out.

"I hope I get what I want," Grave Digger said. "If I don't I'll be back."

"If you don't it's your own fault," she said.

He marched Ready ahead of him down the shaky stairs.

The old man in the ragged red chair looked up in surprise.

"You got the wrong nigger," he said. "Hit ain't him what's makin' all the trouble."

"Who is it?" Grave Digger asked.

"Hit's Cocky. He the one what's always pulling his shiv."

Grave Digger filed the information for future reference.

"I'll keep this one since he's the one I've got," he said.

"Balls," the old man said disgustedly. "He's just a halfass pimp."

X

WHITE LIGHT COMING from the street slanted upward past the edge of the roof and made a milky wall in the dark.

Beyond the wall of light the flat tar roof was shrouded in semi-darkness.

The sergeant emerged from the edge of light like a hammer-head turtle rising from the deep. In one glance he saw Sonny frantically beating a flock of panic-stricken pigeons with a long bamboo pole, and Inky standing motionless as though he'd sprouted from the tar.

"By God, now I know why they're called tarbabies!" he exclaimed.

Gripping the pole for dear life with both gauntleted hands,

Sonny speared desperately at the pigeons. His eyes were white as they rolled toward the red-faced sergeant. His ragged over-coat flapped in the wind. The pigeons ducked and dodged and flew in lopsided circles. Their heads were cocked on one side as they observed Sonny's gymnastics with beady apprehension.

Inky stood like a silhouette cut from black paper, looking at nothing. The whites of his eyes gleamed in the dark.

The pigeon loft was a rickety coop about six feet high, made of scraps of chicken wire, discarded screen windows and as-sorted rags tacked to a frame of rotten boards propped against the low brick wall separating the roofs. It had a tarpaulin top and was equipped with precarious roosts, tin cans of rusty water, and a rusty tin feeding pan.

Blue-uniformed white cops formed a jagged semi-circle in front of it, staring at Sonny in silent and bemused amazement.

The sergeant climbed onto the roof, puffing, and paused for a moment to mop his brow.

"What's he doing, voodoo?" he asked.

"It's only Don Quixote in blackface dueling a windmill," the professor said.

"That ain't funny," the sergeant said. "I like Don Quixote."

The professor let it go.

"Is he a halfwit?" the sergeant said.

"If he's got that much," the professor said.

The sergeant pushed to the center of the stage, but once there hesitated as though he didn't know how to begin.

Sonny looked at him through the corners of his eyes and kept working the pole. Inky stared at nothing with silent intensity.

"All right, all right, so your feet don't stink," the sergeant said. "Which one of you is Caleb?"

"Dass me," Sonny said, without an instant neglecting the pigeons.

"What the hell you call yourself doing?"

"I'se teaching my pigeons how to fly."

The sergeant's jowls began to swell. "You trying to be funny?"

"Naw suh, I didn' mean they didn' know how to fly. They can fly all right at day but they don't know how to night fly."

The sergeant looked at the professor. "Don't pigeons fly at night?"

"Search me," the professor said.

"Naw suh, not unless you makes 'em," Inky said.

Everybody looked at him.

"Hell, he can talk," the professor said.

"They sleeps," Sonny added.

"Roosts," Inky corrected.

"We're going to make some pigeons fly, too," the sergeant said. "Stool pigeons."

"If they don't fly, they'll fry," the professor said.

The sergeant turned to Inky. "What do they call you, boy?"

"Inky," Inky said. "But my name's Rufus Tree."

"So you're Inky," the sergeant said.

"They're both Inky," the professor said.

The cops laughed.

The sergeant smiled into his hand. Then he wheeled abruptly on Sonny and shouted, "Sonny! Drop that pole!"

Sonny gave a violent start and speared a pigeon in the craw, but he hung on to the pole. The pigeon flew crazily into the light and kept on going. Sonny watched it until he got control of himself, then he turned slowly and looked at the sergeant with big innocent white eyes.

"You talking to me, boss?" His black face shone with sweat.

"Yeah, I'm talking to you, Sonny."

"They don't calls me Sonny, boss; they calls me Cal."

"You look like a boy called Sonny."

"Lots of folks is called Sonny, boss."

"What did you jump for if your name isn't Sonny? You jumped halfway out of your skin."

"Most anybody'd jump with you hollerin' at 'em like that, boss."

The sergeant wiped off another smile. "You told your grandma you were going downtown to work."

"She don't want me messin' 'round these pigeons at night. She thinks I might fall off'n the roof."

"Where have you been since supper?"

"Right up here, boss."

"He's just been up here about a half an hour," one of the cops volunteered.

"Naw suh, I been here all the time," Sonny contradicted. "I been inside the coop."

"Ain't nobody in heah but us pigeons, boss," the professor cracked.

"Did you look in the coop?" the sergeant asked the cop.

The cop reddened. "No, I didn't; I wasn't looking for a screwball."

The sergeant glanced at the coop. "By God, boy, your pigeons lead a hard life," he said. Then turning suddenly to the other cops, he asked, "Have these punks been frisked?"

"We were waiting for you," another cop replied.

The sergeant sighed theatrically. "Well, who are you waiting for now?"

Two cops converged on Inky with alacrity; the professor and a third cop took on Sonny.

"Put that damn pole down!" the sergeant shouted at Sonny.

"No, let him hold it," the professor said. "It keeps his hands up."

"What the hell are you wearing that heavy overcoat for?" The sergeant kept on picking at Sonny. He was frustrated.

"I'se cold," Sonny said. Sweat was running down his face in rivers.

"You look it," the sergeant said.

"Jesus Christ, this coat stinks," the professor complained, working Sonny over fast to get away from it.

"Nothing?" the sergeant asked when he'd finished.

"Nothing," the professor said. In his haste he hadn't thought to make Sonny put down the pole and take off his gauntlets.

The sergeant looked at the cops frisking Inky. They shook their heads.

"What's Harlem coming to?" the sergeant complained. "All right, you punks, get downstairs," the sergeant ordered.

"I got to get my pigeons in," Sonny said.

The sergeant looked at him.

Sonny leaned the pole against the coop and began moving. Inky opened the door of the coop and began moving too. The pigeons took one look at the open door and began rushing to get inside.

"IRT subway at Times Square," the professor remarked.

The cops laughed and moved on to the next roof.

The sergeant and the professor followed Inky and Sonny through the window and into the room below.

Sissie and Sugartit sat side by side on the bed again. Choo-Choo sat in the straight-backed chair. Sheik stood in the center of the floor with his feet wide apart, looking defiant. The two cops stood with their buttocks propped against the edge of the table, looking bored.

With the addition of the four others, the room was crowded.

Everybody looked at the sergeant, waiting his next move.

"Get Grandma in here," he said.

The professor went after her.

They heard him saying, "Grandma, you're needed."

There was no reply.

"Grandma!" they heard him shout.

"She's asleep," Sissie called to him. "She's hard to wake once she gets to sleep."

"She's not asleep," the professor called back in an angry tone of voice.

"All right, let her alone," the sergeant said.

The professor returned, red-faced with vexation. "She sat there looking at me without saying a word," he said.

"She gets like that," Sissie said. "She just sort of shuts out the world and quits seeing and hearing anything."

"No wonder her grandson's a halfwit," the professor said, giving Sonny a malicious look.

"Well, what the hell are we going to do with them?" the sergeant said in a frustrated tone of voice.

The cops had no suggestions.

"Let's run them all in," the professor said.

The sergeant looked at him reflectively. "If we take in all the punks who look like them in this block, we'll have a thousand prisoners," he said.

"So what," the professor said. "We can't afford to risk losing Pickens because of a few hundred shines."

"Well, maybe we'd better," the sergeant said.

"Are you going to take her in too?" Sheik said, nodding toward Sugartit on the bed. "She's Coffin Ed's daughter."

The sergeant wheeled on him. "What! What's that about Coffin Ed?"

"Evelyn Johnson there is his daughter," Sheik said evenly.

The cops turned as though their heads were synchronized and stared at her. No one spoke.

"Ask her," Sheik said.

The sergeant's face turned bright red.

It was the professor who spoke. "Well, girl? Are you Detective Johnson's daughter?"

Sugartit hesitated.

"Go on and tell 'em," Sheik said.

The red started crawling up the back of the sergeant's neck and engulfed his ears. "I don't like you," he said to Sheik, his voice constricted.

Sheik threw him a careless look, started to say something, then bit it off.

"Yes, I am," Sugartit said finally.

"We can soon check on that," the professor said, moving toward the window. "He and his partner must be in the vicinity."

"No, Jones might be, but Johnson was sent home," the sergeant said.

"What! Suspended?" the professor asked in surprise.

Sugartit looked startled; Sheik grinned smugly; the others remained impassive.

"Yeah, for killing the Moslem punk."

"For that?" the professor exclaimed indignantly. "Since when did they start penalizing policemen for shooting in self-defense?"

"I don't blame the chief," the sergeant said. "He's protecting himself. The punk was under age and the newspapers are sure to put up a squawk."

"Anyway, Jones ought to know her," the professor said, going out on the fire escape and shouting to the cops below.

He couldn't make himself understood so he started down.

The sergeant asked Sugartit, "Have you got any identification?"

She drew a red leather card case from her skirt pocket and handed it to him without speaking.

It held a black, white-lettered identification card with her photograph and thumbprint, similar to the one issued to policemen. It had been given to her as a souvenir for her sixteenth birthday and was signed by the chief of police.

The sergeant studied it for a moment and handed it back. He had seen others like it, his own daughter had one.

"Does your father know you're here visiting these hoodlums?" he asked.

"Certainly," Sugartit said. "They're friends of mine."

"You're lying," the sergeant said wearily.

"He doesn't know she's over here," Sissie put in.

"I know damn well he doesn't," the sergeant said.

"She's supposed to be visiting me."

"Well, do your folks know you're here?"

She dropped her gaze. "No."

"Eve and I are engaged," Sheik said with a smirk.

The sergeant wheeled toward him with his right cocked high. Sheik ducked automatically, his guard coming up. The sergeant hooked a left to his stomach underneath his guard, and when Sheik's guard dropped, he crossed his right to the side of Sheik's head, knocking him into a spinning stagger. Then he kicked him in the side of the stomach as he spun and, when he doubled over, the sergeant chopped him across the back of the neck with the meaty edge of his right hand. Sheik shuddered as though poleaxed and crashed to the floor. The sergeant took dead aim and kicked him in the valley of the buttocks with all his force.

The professor returned just in time to see the sergeant spit on him.

"Hey, what's happened to him?" he asked, climbing hastily through the window.

The sergeant took off his hat and wiped his perspiring forehead with a soiled white handkerchief. "His mouth did it," he said.

Sheik was groaning feebly, although unconscious.

The professor chuckled. "He's still trying to talk." Then he said, "They couldn't find Jones. Lieutenant Anderson says he's working on another angle."

"It's okay, she's got an ID card," the sergeant said. Then asked, "Is the chief still there?"

"Yeah, he's still hanging around."

"Well, that's his job."

The professor looked about at the silent group. "What's the verdict?"

"Let's get on to the next house," the sergeant said. "If I'm here when this punk comes to I'll probably be the next one to get suspended."

"Can we leave the building now?" Sissie asked.

"You two girls can come with us," the sergeant offered.

Sheik groaned and rolled over.

"We can't leave him like that," she said.

The sergeant shrugged. The cops passed into the next room. The sergeant started to follow, then hesitated.

"All right, I'll fix it," he said.

He took the girls out on the fire escape and got the attention of the cops guarding the entrance below.

"Let these two girls pass!" he shouted.

The cops looked at the girls standing in the spotlight glare. "Okay."

The sergeant followed them back into the room.

"If I were you I'd get the hell away from this punk fast," he advised, prodding Sheik with his toe. "He's headed straight for trouble, big trouble."

Neither replied.

He followed the professor out of the flat.

Granny sat unmoving in the rocking chair where they'd left her, tightly gripping the arms. She stared at them with an expression of fierce disapproval on her puckered old face and in her dim milky eyes.

"It's our job, Grandma," the sergeant said apologetically.

She didn't reply.

They passed on sheepishly.

Back in the front room, Sheik groaned and sat up.

Everyone moved at once. The girls moved away from him. Sonny began taking off the heavy overcoat. Inky and Choo-Choo bent over Sheik and, each taking an arm, began helping him to his feet.

"How you feel, Sheik?" Choo-Choo asked.

Sheik looked dazed. "Can't no copper hurt me," he muttered thickly, wobbling on his legs.

"Does it hurt?"

"Naw, it don't hurt," he said with a grimace of pain. Then he looked about stupidly. "They gone?"

"Yeah," Choo-Choo said jubilantly and cut a jig step. "We done beat 'em, Sheik. We done fooled 'em two ways sides and flat."

Sheik's confidence came back in a rush. "I told you we was going to do it."

Sonny grinned and raised his clasped hands in the prizefight salute. "They had me sweating in the crotch," he confessed.

A look of crazed triumph distorted Sheik's flat, freckled face. "I'm the Sheik, Jack," he said. His yellow eyes were getting wild again.

Sissie looked at him and said apprehensively, "Me and Sugartit got to go. We were just waiting to see if you were all right."

"You can't go now—we got to celebrate," Sheik said.

"We ain't got nothing to celebrate with," Choo-Choo said.

"The hell we ain't," Sheik said. "Cops ain't so smart. You go up on the roof and get the pole."

"Who, me, Sheik?"

"Sonny then."

"Me!" Sonny said. "I done got enough of that roof."

"Go on," Sheik said. "You're a Moslem now and I command you in the name of Allah."

"Praise Allah," Choo-Choo said.

"I don't want to be no Moslem," Sonny said.

"All right, you're still our captive then," Sheik decreed. "You go get the pole, Inky. I got five sticks stashed in the end."

"Hell, I'll go," Choo-Choo said.

"No, let Inky go, he's been up there before and they won't think it's funny."

When Inky left for the pole, Sheik said to Choo-Choo, "Our captive's getting biggety since we saved him from the cops."

"I ain't gettin' biggety," Sonny declared. "I just want to get the hell outen here and get these cuffs off'n me without havin' to become no Moslem."

"You know too much for us to let you go now," Sheik said, exchanging a look with Choo-Choo.

Inky returned with the pole and, pulling the plug out of the end joint, he shook five cigarettes onto the table top.

"A feast!" Choo-Choo exclaimed. He grabbed one, opened the end with his thumb, and lit up.

Sheik lit another.

"Take one, Inky," he said.

Inky took one.

Everybody put on smoked glasses.

"Granny will smell it if you smoke in here," Sissie said.

"She thinks they're cubebs." Choo-Choo mimicked Granny: "Ah wish you chillens would stop smokin' them coo-bebs 'cause they make a body feel moughty funny in de head."

He and Sheik doubled over with laughter.

The room stank with the pungent smoke.

Sugartit picked up a stick, sat on the bed and lit it.

"Come on, baby, strip," Sheik urged her. "Celebrate your old man's flop by getting up off of some of it."

Sugartit stood up and undid her skirt zipper and began going into a slow striptease routine.

Sissie clutched her by the arms. "You stop that," she said. "You'd better go on home before your old man gets there first and comes out looking for you."

In a sudden rage, Sheik snatched Sissie's hands away from Sugartit and flung her across the bed.

"Leave her alone," he raved. "She's going to entertain the Sheik."

"If her old man's really Coffin Ed you oughta let her go

on home," Sonny said soberly. "You just beggin' for trouble messin' round with his kinfolks."

"Choo-Choo, go to the kitchen and get Granny's wire clothesline," Sheik ordered.

Choo-Choo went out grinning.

When he saw Granny staring at him with such fierce disapproval, he said guiltily, "Pay no 'tention to me, Granny," and began clowning.

She didn't answer.

He tiptoed with elaborate pantomime to the closet and took out her coil of clothesline.

"Just wanna hang out the wash," he said.

Still she didn't answer.

He tiptoed close to the chair and passed his hand slowly in front of her face. She didn't bat an eyelash. His grin widened. Returning to the front room, he said, "Granny's dead asleep with her eyes wide open."

"Leave her to Gabriel," Sheik said, taking the line and beginning to uncoil it.

"What you gonna do with that?" Sonny asked apprehensively.

Sheik made a running loop in one end. "We going to play cowboy," he said. "Look."

Suddenly he threw the loop over Sonny's head and pulled on the line with all his strength. The loop tightened about Sonny's neck and jerked him off his feet.

Sissie ran toward Sheik and tried to pull the wire from his hands. "You're choking him," she said.

Sheik knocked her down with a backhanded blow.

"You can let up on him now," Choo-Choo said. "We got 'im."

"Now I'm gonna show you how to tie up a mother-raper to put him in a sack," Sheik said.

XI

GRAVE DIGGER HALTED on the sidewalk in front of the yellow frame house next door to the Knickerbocker. It had been partitioned into offices and all of the front windows were lettered with business announcements.

"Can you read that writing on those windows?" Grave Digger asked Ready Belcher.

Ready glanced at him suspiciously. "Course I can read that writing."

"Read it then," Grave Digger said.

Ready stole another look. "Read what one?"

"Take your choice."

Ready squinted his good eye against the dark and read aloud, *"Joseph C. Clapp, Real Estate and Notary Public."* He looked at Grave Digger like a dog who has retrieved a stick. "That one?"

"Try another."

He hesitated. Passing car lights played on his pockmarked black face, brought out the white cast in his bad eye and lit up his flashy tan suit.

"I haven't got much time," Grave Digger warned.

He read, *"Amazing 100-year-old Gypsy Bait Oil—Makes Catfish Go Crazy."* He looked at Grave Digger again like the same dog with another stick.

"Not that one," Grave Digger said.

"What the hell is this, a gag?" he muttered.

"Just read!"

"JOSEPH, The Only and Original Skin Lightener. I guarantee to lighten the darkest skin by twelve shades in six months."

"You don't want your skin lightened?"

"My skin suit me," he said sullenly.

"Then read on."

"Magic Formula For Successful PRAYER . . . That it?"

"Yeah, that's it. Read what it says underneath."

"Here are some of the amazing things it tells you about: When to pray; Where to pray; How to pray; The Magic Formulas for Health and Success through prayer; for conquering fear through prayer; for obtaining work through prayer; for money through prayer; for influencing others through prayer; and—"

"That's enough." Grave Digger took a deep breath and said in a voice gone thick and cottony again, "Ready, if you don't tell me what I want to know, you'd better get yourself one of those prayers. Because I'm going to take you over to 129th Street near the Harlem River. You know where that is? It's a deserted jungle of warehouses and junk yards beneath the New York Central bridge."

"Yare, I know where it's at."

"And I'm going to pistol-whip you until your own whore won't recognize you again. And if you try to run, I'm going to let you run fifty feet and then shoot you through the head for attempting to escape. You understand me?"

"Yare, I understand you."

"You believe me?"

Ready took a quick look at Grave Digger's rage-swollen face and said quickly, "Yare, I believes you."

"My partner got suspended tonight for killing a criminal rat like you and I'd just as soon they suspended me too."

"You ain't asted me yet what you want to know."

"Get into the car."

The car was parked at the curb. Ready got into Coffin Ed's seat. Grave Digger went around and climbed beneath the wheel.

"This is as good a spot as any," he said. "Start talking."

" 'Bout what?"

"About the Big Greek. I want to know who killed him."

Ready jumped as though he'd been stung. "Digger, I swear 'fore God—"

"Don't call me Digger, you lousy pimp."

"Mista Jones, lissen—"

"I'm listening."

"Lots of folks mighta killed him if they'd knowed—"

He broke off. The pockmarks in his skin began filling with sweat.

"Known what? I haven't got all night."

Ready gulped and said, "He was a whipper."

"What?"

"He liked to whip 'em."

"Whores?"

"Not 'specially. If they was regular whores he wanted them to be big black mannish-looking bitches like what might cut a mother-raper's throat. But what he liked most was little colored school gals."

"That's it? That's why Reba barred him?"

"Yas suh. He proposition her once. She got so mad she drew her pistol on him."

"Did she shoot him?"

"Naw, suh, she just scared him."

"I mean tonight. Was she the one?"

Ready's eyes started rolling in their sockets and the sweat began to trickle down his mean black face.

"You mean the one what killed him? Naw suh, she was home all evening."

"Where were you?"

"I was there, too."

"Do you live there?"

"Naw, suh, I just drops by for a visit now and then."

"Where did he find the girls?"

"You mean the school girls?"

"What other girls would I mean?"

"He picked 'em up in his car. He had a little Mexican bull whip with nine tails he kept in his car. He whipped 'em with that."

"Where did he take them?"

"He brung 'em to Reba's till she got suspicious 'bout all the screaming and carrying on. She didn't think nothing of it at first; these little chippies likes to make lots of noise for a white man. But they was making more noise than seemed natural and she went in and caught 'im. That's when he proposition her."

"How did he get 'em to take it?"

"Get 'em to take what?"

"The whipping."

"Oh, he paid 'em a hundred bucks. They was glad to take it for that."

"You're certain of that, that he paid them a hundred dollars?"

"Yas suh. Not only me but lots of chippies all over Harlem knew about him. A hundred bucks didn't mean nothing to him. They boyfriends knew too. Lots of times they boyfriends made 'em. There was chippies all over town on the lookout for him. 'Course one time was enough for most of 'em."

"He hurt them?"

"He got his money's worth. Sometime he whale hell out of 'em. I s'pect he hurt more'n one of 'em bad. 'Member that kid they picked up in Broadhurst Park. It were all in the paper. She was in the hospital three, four days. She said she'd been attacked but the police thought she was beat up by a gang. I believes she was one of 'em."

"What was her name?"

"I don't recollect."

"Where'd he take them after Reba barred him from her place?"

"I don't know."

"Do you know the names of any of them?"

"Naw suh, he brung 'em and took 'em away by hisself. I never even seen any of 'em."

"You're lying."

"Naw suh, I swear 'fore God."

"How did you know they were school girls if you never saw any of them?"

"He tole me."

"What else he tell you?"

"Nuthin' else. He just talk to me 'bout gals."

"How old is your girl?"

"My gal?"

"The one you have at Reba's?"

"Oh, she twenty-five or more."

"One more lie and off we go."

"She sixteen, boss."

"She had him, too?"

"Yas suh. Once."

The sweat was streaming down Ready's face.

"Once. Why only once?"

"She got scared."

"You tried to fix it up for another time?"

"Naw suh, boss, she didn't need to. Hit cost her more'n it was worth."

"What were you doing with him in the Dew Drop Inn?"

"He was looking for a little gal he knew and he ast me to come 'long, that's all, boss."

"When was that?"

" 'Bout a month ago."

"You said you didn't know where he took them after he was barred from Reba's."

"I don't, boss, I swear 'fore—"

"Can that Uncle Tom crap. Reba said she barred him three or four months ago."

"Yas suh, but I didn't say I hadn't seed him since."

"Did Reba know you were seeing him?"

"I only seed him that once, boss. I was in the Alabama-Georgia bar and he just happen in."

Grave Digger nodded towards the three alien cars parked ahead, in front of the Knickerbocker.

"One of those cars his?"

"Them struggle buggies!" Scorn pushed the fear from Ready's voice. "Naw suh, he had a dream boat, a big green Caddy Coupe de Ville."

"Who was the girl he and you were looking for?"

"I wasn't looking for her; I just went 'long with him to look for her."

"Who was she, I asked."

"I didn't know her. Some little chippie what hung 'round in that section."

"How did he come to know her?"

"He said he'd done whipped her girlfriend once. That's how come he knew her. Said Sissie's boyfriend brought her to 'im."

"Sissie! You said you didn't know the name of any of them."

"I'd forgotten her, boss. He didn't bring her to Reba's. I didn't know nuthin' 'bout her but just what he said."

"What did he say exactly?"

"He just say Sissie's boyfriend, some boy they call Sheik, arrange it for him and he pay Sheik. Then he wanted Sheik to arrange for the other one but Sheik couldn't do it."

"What was the other one called? The one he and you were looking for?"

"He call her Sugartit. She was Sissie's girlfriend. He'd seen 'em walking together down Seventh Avenue one time after he'd whipped Sissie."

"Where did you find her?"

"We didn't find her, I swear 'fore—"

"Does your girl know them?"

"I didn' hear you."

"Your girl, does she know them?"

"Know who, boss?"

"Either Sissie or Sugartit."

"Naw suh. My gal's a pro and them is just chippies. I recollect him saying one time they all belonged to a kid gang over in that section. I means them two chippies and Sheik. He say Sheik was the chief."

"What's the name of the gang?"

"He say they call themselves the Real Cool Moslems. He thought it were funny."

"Did you listen to the news on the radio tonight?"

"You mean what it say 'bout him getting croaked? Naw suh, I was lissening to the Twelve-Eighty Club. Reba tole me 'bout it. She were lissening. That were just 'fore you come. She were telling me when the doorbell rang. She say the big Greek's croaked over on Lenox Avenue and I say so what."

"You said before that lots of people might have killed him if they'd known about him. Who?"

"All I meant was some of those gals' pas. Like Sissie's or some of 'em. He might have been hanging 'round over there looking for Sugartit again and her pa might have got hep to it some kind of way and been layin' for him and when he seed him coming down the street might have lowered the boom on 'im."

"You mean slipped up behind him?"

"He were in his car, warn't he?"

"How about the Moslems—the kid gang?"

"Them! What they'd wanta do it for? He was money in the street for them."

"Who's Sugartit's father?"

"You mean her old man?"

"I mean her father."

"How am I gonna know that, boss? I ain't never heard of her 'fore he talk 'bout her."

"What did he say about her?"

"Just say she was the gal for him."

"Did he say where she lived?"

"Naw, suh, he just say what I say he say, boss, I swear 'fore God."

"You stink. What are you sweating so much for?"

"I'se just nervous, that's all."

"You stink with fear. What are you scared of?"

"Just naturally scared, boss. You got that big pistol and you mad at everybody and talkin' 'bout killin' me and all that. Enough to make anybody scared."

"You're scared of something else, something in particular. What are you holding out?"

"I ain't holding nothing out. I done tole you everything I know, I swear boss, I swears on everything that's holy in this whole green world."

"I know you're lying. I can hear it in your voice. What are you lying about?"

"I ain't lying, boss. If I'm lying I hope God'll strike me dead on the spot."

"You know who her father is, don't you?"

"Naw suh, boss. I swear. I done tole you everything I know. You could whup me till my head is soft as clabber but I couldn't tell you no more than I'se already tole you."

"You know who her father is and you're scared to tell me."

"Naw suh, I swear—"

"Is he a politician?"

"Boss, I—"

"A numbers banker?"

"I swear, boss—"

"Shut up before I knock out your goddamned teeth."

He mashed the starter as though tromping on Ready's head. The motor purred into life. But he didn't slip in the clutch. He sat there listening to the softly purring motor in the small black nondescript car, trying to get his temper under control.

Finally he said, "If I find out that you're lying I'm going to kill you like a dog. I'm not going to shoot you, I'm going to break all your bones. I'm going to try to find out who killed Galen because that's what I'm paid for and that was my oath when I took this job. But if I had my way I'd pin a medal on him and I'd string up every goddamned one of you who were up with Galen. You've turned my stomach and it's all I can do right now to keep from beating out your brains."

XII

THE RECEPTION ROOM of the Harlem Hospital, on Lenox Avenue ten blocks south from the scene of the murder, was wrapped in a midnight hush.

It was called an interracial hospital; more than half of its staff of doctors and nurses were colored people.

A graduate nurse sat behind the reception desk. A bronze-shaded desk-lamp spilled light on the hospital register before her while her brown-skinned face remained in shadow. She looked up inquiringly as Grave Digger and Ready Belcher approached, walking side by side.

"May I help you," she said in a trained courteous voice.

"I'm Detective Jones," Grave Digger said, exhibiting his badge.

She looked at it but didn't touch it.

"You received an emergency patient here about two hours ago; a man with his right arm cut off."

"Yes?"

"I would like to question him."

"I will call Dr. Banks. You may talk to him. Please be seated."

Grave Digger prodded Ready in the direction of chairs surrounding a table with magazines. They sat silently, like relatives of a critical case.

Dr. Banks came in silently, crossing the linoleum-tiled floor on rubber-soled shoes. He was a tall, athletic-looking young colored man dressed in white.

"I'm sorry to have kept you waiting, Mr. Jones," he said to

Grave Digger whom he knew by sight. "You want to know about the case with the severed arm." He had a quick smile and a pleasant voice.

"I want to talk to him," Grave Digger said.

Dr. Banks pulled up a chair and sat down. "He's dead. I've just come from him. He had a rare type of blood—Type O—which we don't have in our blood bank. You realize transfusions were imperative. We had to contact the Red Cross blood bank. They located the type in Brooklyn, but it arrived too late. Is there anything I can tell you?"

"I want to know who he was."

"So do we. He died without revealing his identity."

"Didn't he make a statement of any kind before he died?"

"There was another detective here earlier, but the patient was unconscious at the time. The patient regained consciousness later, but the detective had left. Before leaving, he examined the patient's effects, however, but found nothing to establish his identity."

"He didn't talk at all, didn't say anything?"

"Oh yes. He cried a great deal. One moment he was cursing and the next he was praying. Most of what he said was incoherent. I gathered he regretted not killing the man whom he had attacked—the white man who was killed later."

"He didn't mention any names?"

"No. Once he said 'the little one' but mostly he used the word *mother-raper* which Harlemites apply to everybody, enemies, friends and strangers."

"Well, that's that," Grave Digger said. "Whatever he knew he took with him. Still I'd like to examine his effects too, whatever they are."

"Certainly; they're just the clothes he wore and the contents of his pockets when he arrived here." He stood up. "Come this way."

Grave Digger got to his feet and motioned his head for Ready to walk ahead of him.

"Are you an officer too?" Dr. Banks asked Ready.

"No, he's my prisoner," Grave Digger said. "We're not that hard up for cops as yet."

Dr. Banks smiled. He led them down a corridor smelling strongly of ether to a room at the far end where the clothes and personal effects of the emergency and ward patients were stored in neatly wrapped bundles on shelves against the walls. He took down a bundle bearing a metal tag and placed it on the bare wooden table.

"Here you are."

From the adjoining room an anguished male voice was heard reciting the Lord's Prayer.

Ready stared as though fascinated at the number 219 on the metal tag fastened to the bundle of clothes and whispered, "Death row."

Dr. Banks flicked a glance at him and said to Grave Digger, "Most of the attendants play the numbers. When an emergency patient arrives they put this tag with the death number on his bundle and if he dies they play it."

Grave Digger grunted and began untying the bundle.

"If you discover anything leading to his identity, let us know," Dr. Banks said. "We'd like to notify his relatives." He left them.

Grave Digger spread the blood-caked mackinaw and overalls on the table. It contained two incredibly filthy one-dollar bills, some loose change, a small brown paper sack of dried roots, two Yale keys and a skeleton key on a rusty key ring, a dried rabbit's foot, a dirty piece of resin, a cheese cloth rag that had served as a handkerchief, a putty knife, a small piece of pumice stone, and a scrap of dirty writing paper folded into a small square. The putty knife and pumice stone indicated that the man had worked somewhere as a porter, using the putty to scrape chewing gum from the floor and the pumice stone for cleaning his hands. That didn't help much.

He unfolded the square of paper and found a note on cheap school paper written in a childish hand.

GB, you want to know something. The Big John hangs out in the Inn. How about that. Just like those old Romans.
Bee.

Grave Digger folded it again and slipped it into his pocket.

"Is your girl called Bee?" he asked Ready.

"Naw, suh, she called Doe."

"Do you know any girl called Bee—a school girl?"

"Naw suh."

"GB?"

"Naw suh."

Grave Digger turned out the pockets of the clothes but found nothing more. He wrapped the bundle and attached the tag. He noticed Ready staring at the number on the tag again.

"Don't let that number catch up with you," he said. "Don't you end up with that tag on your fine clothes."

Ready licked his dry lips.

They didn't see Dr. Banks on their way out. Grave Digger stopped at the reception desk to tell the nurse he hadn't found anything to identify the corpse.

"Now we're going to look for the Greek's car," he said to Ready.

They found the big green Cadillac beneath a street lamp in the middle of the block on 130th Street between Lenox and Seventh Avenues. It had an Empire State license number—UG-16—and it was parked beside a fire hydrant. It was as conspicuous as a fire truck.

He pulled up behind it and parked.

"Who covered for him in Harlem?" he asked Ready.

"I don't know, Mista Jones."

"Was it the precinct captain?"

"Mista Jones, I—"

"One of our councilmen?"

"Honest to God, Mista Jones—"

Grave Digger got out and walked toward the big car.

The doors were locked. He broke the glass of the left-side windscreen with the butt of his pistol, reached inside past the wheel and unlocked the door. The interior lights came on.

A quick search revealed the usual paraphernalia of a motorist: gloves, handkerchiefs, Kleenex, half-used packages of differ-ent brands of cigarettes, insurance papers, a woman's plastic overshoes and compact. A felt monkey dangled from the rear-view mirror and two medium-sized dolls, a black-faced Topsy and a blonde Little Eva, sat in opposite corners on the back seat.

He found the miniature bull whip and a manila envelope of postcard-sized photos in the right-hand glove compartment. He studied the photos in the light. They were pictures of nude colored girls in various postures, each photo revealing another developed technique of the sadist. On most of the pictures the faces of the girls were distinct although distorted by pain and shame.

He put the whip in his leather-lined coat pocket, kept the photos in his hand, slammed the door, walked back to his own car and climbed beneath the wheel.

"Was he a photographer?" he asked Ready.

"Yas suh, sometime he carry a camera."

"Did he show you the pictures he took?"

"Naw suh, he never said nothing 'bout any pictures. I just seen him with the camera."

Grave Digger snapped on the top light and showed Ready the photos.

"Do you recognize any of them?"

Ready whistled softly and his eyes popped as he turned over one photo after another.

"Naw suh, I don't know none of them," he said, handing them back.

"Your girl's not one of them?"

"Naw suh."

Grave Digger pocketed the envelope and mashed the starter.

"Ready, don't let me catch you in a lie," he said again, letting out the clutch.

XIII

HE PARKED DIRECTLY in front of the Dew Drop Inn and pushed Ready through the door. On first sight it looked just as he had left it; the two white cops guarding the door and the colored patrons celebrating noisily. He ushered Ready between the bar and the booths, toward the rear. The vari-colored faces turned toward them curiously as they passed.

But in the last booth he noticed an addition. It was crowded with teenagers, three school boys and four school girls, who hadn't been there before. They stopped talking and looked at him intently as he and Ready approached. Then at sight of the bull whip all four girls gave a start and their young dark faces tightened with sudden fear. He wondered how they'd got past the white cops on the door.

All the places at the bar were taken.

Big Smiley came down and asked two men to move.

One of them began to complain. "What for I got to give up my seat for some other niggers."

Big Smiley thumbed toward Grave Digger. "He's the man."

"Oh, one of them two."

Both rose with alacrity, picked up their glasses and vacated the stools, grinning at Grave Digger obsequiously.

"Don't show me your teeth," Grave Digger snarled. "I'm no dentist. I don't fix teeth. I'm a cop. I'll knock your teeth out."

The men doused their grins and slunk away.

Grave Digger threw the bull whip on top of the bar and sat on the high bar stool.

"Sit down," he ordered Ready, who stood by hesitantly. "Sit down, Goddamn it."

Ready sat down as though the stool were covered with cake icing.

Big Smiley looked from one to another, smiling warily.

"You held out on me," Grave Digger said in his thick cot-tony voice of smoldering rage. "And I don't like that."

Big Smiley's smile got a sudden case of constipation. He threw a quick look at Ready's impassive face, found nothing there to reassure him, then fell back on his cut arm which he carried in a sling.

"Guess I must be runnin' some fever, Chief, 'cause I don't remember what I told you."

"You told me you didn't know who Galen was looking for in here," Grave Digger said thickly.

Big Smiley stole another look at Ready, but all he got was a blank. He sighed heavily.

"Who he were looking for? Is dat what you ast me?" he stalled, trying to meet Grave Digger's smoldering hot gaze. "I dunno who he were looking for, Chief."

Grave Digger rose up on the bar stool rungs as though his feet were in stirrups, snatched the bull whip from the bar and slashed Big Smiley across one cheek after another before Big Smiley could get his good hand moving.

Big Smiley stopped smiling. Talk stopped suddenly along the length of the bar, petered out in the booths. In the vacuum that followed, Lil Green's voice whined from the jukebox:

> *"Why don't you do right*
> *Like other mens do . . ."*

Grave Digger sat back on the stool, breathing hard, struggling to control his rage. Veins stood out in his temples, growing out of his short-cropped kinky hair like strange roots climbing toward the brim of his misshapen hat. His brown eyes laced with red veins generated a steady white heat.

The white manager, who'd been working the front end of the bar, hastened down toward them with a face full of outrage.

"Get back," Grave Digger said thickly.

The manager got back.

Grave Digger stabbed at Big Smiley with his left forefinger and said in a voice so thick it was hard to understand, "Smiley, all I want from you is the truth. And I ain't got long to get it."

Big Smiley didn't look at Ready any more. He didn't smile. He didn't whine.

He said, "Just ask the questions, Chief, and I'll answer 'em the best of my knowledge."

Grave Digger looked around at the teenagers in the booth. They were listening with open mouths, staring at him with popping eyes. His breath burned from his flaring nostrils. He turned back to Big Smiley. But he sat quietly for a moment to give the blood time to recede from his head.

"Who killed him?" he finally asked.

"I don't know, Chief."

"He was killed on your street."

"Yas suh, but I don't know who done it."

"Do Sissie and Sugartit come in here?"

"Yas suh, sometimes."

Out of the corners of his eyes Grave Digger noticed Ready's shoulders begin to sag as though his spine were melting.

"Sit up straight, God damn it," he said. "You'll have plenty of time to lie down if I find out you've been lying."

Ready sat up straight.

Grave Digger addressed Big Smiley. "Galen met them in here?"

"Naw suh, he met Sissie in here once but I never seen him with Sugartit."

"What was she doing in here then?"

"She come in here twice with Sissie."

"How'd you know her name?"

"I heard Sissie call her that."

"Was Sheik with her when Galen met her?"

"You mean with Sissie, when she met the big man? Yas suh."

"He paid Sheik the money?"

"I couldn't be sure, Chief, but I seen money being passed. I don't know who got it."

"He got it. Did they both leave with him?"

"You mean both Sheik and Sissie?"

"That's what I mean."

Big Smiley took out a blue bandanna handkerchief and mopped his sweating black face.

The four school girls in the booth began going through the motions of leaving. Grave Digger wheeled toward them.

"Sit down! I want to talk to you later," he ordered.

They began a shrill protest: "We got to get home . . . Got to be at school tomorrow at nine o'clock . . . Haven't finished homework . . . Can't stay out this late . . . Get into trouble . . .".

He got up and went over to show them his gold badge. "You're already in trouble. Now I want you to sit down and keep quiet."

He took hold of the two girls who were standing and forced them back into their seats.

"He can't hold you 'less he's got a warrant," the boy in the aisle seat said.

Grave Digger slapped him out of his seat, reached down and lifted him from the floor by his coat lapels and slammed him back into his seat.

"Now say that again," he suggested.

The boy didn't speak.

Grave Digger waited for a moment until they had settled down and were quiet, then he returned to his bar stool.

Neither Big Smiley nor Ready had moved; neither had looked at the other.

"You didn't answer my question," Grave Digger said.

"When he took Sissie off Sheik stayed in his seat," Big Smiley said.

"What kind of a goddamned answer is that?"

"That's the way it was, Chief."

"Where did he take her?"

Rivers of sweat poured from Big Smiley's face. He sighed.

"Downstairs," he said.

"Downstairs! In here?"

"Yas suh. They's stairs in the back room."

"What's downstairs?"

"Just a cellar like any other bar's got. It's full of bottles an' old bar fixtures and beer barrels. The compression unit for the draught beer is down there and the refrigeration unit for the ice boxes. That's all. Some rats and we keeps a cat."

"No bed or bedroom?"

"Naw suh."

"He whipped them down there in that kind of place?"

"I don't know what he done."

"Couldn't you hear them?"

"Naw suh. You can't hear nothin' through this floor. You could shoot off your pistol down there and you couldn't hear it up here."

Grave Digger looked at Ready. "Did you know that?"

Ready began to wilt again. "Naw suh, I swear 'fore—"

"Sit up straight, God damn it! I don't want to have to tell you again."

He turned back to Big Smiley. "Did he know it?"

"Not so far as I know, unless he told him."

"Is Sissie or Sugartit among those girls over there?"

"Naw suh," Big Smiley said without looking.

Grave Digger showed him the pornographic photos.

"Know any of them?"

Big Smiley leafed through them slowly without a change of expression. He pulled out three photos. "I've seen them," he said.

"What're their names?"

"I don't know only two of 'em." He separated them gingerly with his fingertips as though they were coated with external poison. "Them two. This here one is called Good Booty, t'other one is called Honey Bee. This one here, I never heard her name called."

"What are their family names?"

"I don't know none of 'em's square monickers."

"He took these downstairs?"

"Just them two."

"Who came here with them?"

"They came by theyself, most of 'em did."

"Did he have appointments with them?"

"Naw suh, not with most of 'em, anyway. They just come in here and laid for him."

"Did they come together?"

"Sometime, sometime not."

"You just said they came by themselves."

"I meant they didn't bring no boyfriends."

"Had he known them before?"

"I couldn't say. When he come in if he seed any of 'em he just made his choice."

"He knew they hung around here looking for him?"

"Yas suh. When he started comin' here he was already known."

"When was that?"

"Three or four months ago. I don't remember 'zactly."

"When did he start taking them downstairs?"

" 'Bout two months ago."

"Did you suggest it?"

"Naw suh, he propositioned me."

"How much did he pay you?"

"Twenty-five bucks."

"You're talking yourself into Sing Sing."

"Maybe."

Grave Digger examined the note addressed to GB and signed Bee that he'd taken from the dead man's effects, then passed it over to Big Smiley.

"That came from the pocket of the man you cut," he said.

Big Smiley read the note carefully, his lips spelling out each word. His breath came out in a sighing sound.

"Then he must be a relation of her," he said.

"You didn't know that?"

"Naw suh, I swear 'fore God. If I knowed that I wouldn't 'ave chopped him with the axe."

"What exactly did he say to Galen when he started toward him with the knife?"

Big Smiley wrinkled his forehead. "I don't 'member 'zactly. Something 'bout if he found a white mother-raper trying to diddle his little gals he'd cut his throat. But I just took that to mean colored women in general. You know how our folks talk. I didn't figure he meant his own kin."

"Maybe some other girl's father had the same idea with a pistol," Grave Digger suggested.

"Could be," Big Smiley said cautiously.

"So evidently he's the father and he's got more girls than one."

"Looks like it."

"He's dead."

Big Smiley's expression didn't change. "I'm sorry to hear it."

"You look like it. Who went your bail?"

"My boss."

Grave Digger looked at him soberly. "Who's covering for you?" he asked.

"Nobody."

"I know that's a lie but I'm going to pass it. Who was covering for Galen?"

"I don't know."

"I'm going to pass that lie too. What was he doing here tonight?"

"He was looking for Sugartit."

"Did he have a date with her?"

"I don't know. He said she was coming by with Sissie."

"Did they come by after he'd left?"

"Naw suh."

"Okay, Smiley, this one is for keeps. Who is Sugartit's father?"

"I don't know none of 'em's kinfolks nor neither where they lives, Chief, like I told you before. It didn't make no difference."

"You must have some idea."

"Naw suh, it's just like I say, I never thought about it. You don't never think about where a gal lives in Harlem, 'less you goin' home with her. What do anybody's address mean up here?"

"Don't let me catch you in a lie, Smiley."

"I ain't lying, Chief. I went with a woman for a whole year once and never did know where she lived. Didn't care neither."

"Who are the Real Cool Moslems?"

"Them punks! Just a kid gang around here."

"Where do they hang out?"

"I don't know 'zactly. Somewhere down the street."

"Do they come in here?"

"Only three of 'em sometime. Sheik—I think he's they leader—and a boy called Choo-Choo and the one they call Bones."

"Where do they live?"

"Somewhere near here, but I don't know 'zactly. The boy what keeps the pigeons oughtta know. He lives a coupla blocks down the street on t'other side. I don't know his name but he got a pigeon coop on the roof."

"Is he one of 'em?"

"I don't know for sure but you can see a gang of boys on the roof when he's flying his pigeons."

"I'll find him. Do you know the ages of those girls in the booth?"

"Naw suh, when I ask 'em they say they're eighteen."

"You know they're under age."

"I s'pect so but all I can do is ast 'em."

"Did he have any of them?"

"Only one I knows of."

Grave Digger turned and looked at the girls again.

"Which one?" he asked.

"The one in the green tam." Big Smiley pushed forward one of the three photos. "She's this one here, the one called Good Booty."

"Okay, son, that's all for the moment," Grave Digger said.

He got down from the stool and walked forward to talk to the manager.

As soon as he left, without saying a word or giving a warning Big Smiley leaned forward and hit Ready in the face with his big ham-sized fist. Ready sailed off the stool, crashed into the wall and crumpled to the floor.

Grave Digger looked down in time to see his head disappearing beneath the edge of the bar, then turned his attention to the white manager across from him.

"Collect your tabs and shut the bar; I'm closing up this joint and you're under arrest," he said.

"For what?" the manager challenged hotly.

"For contributing to the delinquency of minors."

The manager sputtered, "I'll be open again by tomorrow night."

"Don't say another God damned word," Grave Digger said and kept looking at him until the manager closed his mouth and turned away.

Then he beckoned to one of the white cops on the door and told him, "I'm putting the manager and the bartender under arrest and closing the joint. I want you to hold the manager and some teenagers I'll turn over to you. I'm going to leave in a minute and I'll send back the wagon. I'll take the bartender with me."

"Right, Jones," the cop said, as happy as a kid with a new toy.

Grave Digger walked back to the rear.

Ready was down on the floor on his hands and knees, spitting out blood and teeth.

Grave Digger looked at him and smiled grimly. Then he looked up at Big Smiley who was licking his bruised knuckles with a big red tongue.

"You're under arrest, Smiley," he said. "If you try to escape, I'm going to shoot you through the back of the head."

"Yas suh," Big Smiley said.

Grave Digger shook a customer loose from a plastic-covered chair and sat astride it at the end of the table in the booth, facing the scared, silent teenagers. He took out his notebook and stylo and wrote down their names, addresses, numbers of the public schools they attended, and their ages. The oldest was a boy of seventeen.

None of them admitted knowing either Sissie, Sugartit, the big white man Galen, or anyone connected with the Real Cool Moslems.

He called the second cop away from the door and said, "Hold these kids for the wagon."

Then he said to the girl in the green tam who'd given her name as Gertrude B. Richardson. "Gertrude, I want you to come with me."

One of the girls tittered. "You might have known he'd take Good Booty," she said.

"My name is Beauty," Good Booty said, tossing her head disdainfully.

On sudden impulse Grave Digger stopped her as she was about to get up.

"What's your father's name, Gertrude?"

"Charlie."

"What does he do?"

"He's a porter."

"Is that so? Do you have any sisters?"

"One. She's a year younger than me."

"What does your mother do?"

"I don't know. She don't live with us."

"I see. You two girls live with your father."

"Where else we going to live?"

"That's a good question, Gertrude, but I can't answer it. Did you know a man got his arm cut off in here earlier tonight?"

"I heard about it. So what? People are always getting cut around here."

"This man tried to knife the white man because of his daughters."

"He did?" She giggled. "He was a square."

"No doubt. The bartender chopped off his arm with an axe to protect the white man. What do you think about that?"

She giggled again, nervously. "Maybe he figured the white man was more important than some colored drunk."

"He must have. The man died in Harlem Hospital less than an hour ago."

Her eyes got big and frightened. "What are you trying to say, mister?"

"I'm trying to tell you that he was your father."

Grave Digger hadn't anticipated her reaction. She came up out of her seat so fast that she was past him before he could grab her.

"Stop her!" he shouted.

A customer wheeled from his bar stool into her path and she stuck her fingers into his eye. The man yelped and tried to hold her. She wrenched from his grip and sprang towards the door. The white cop headed her off and wrapped his arms about her. She twisted in his grip like a panic-stricken cat and clawed at his pistol. She had gotten it out the holster when a colored man rushed in and wrenched it from her grip. The white cop threw her onto the floor on her back and straddled her, pinning down her arms. The colored man grabbed her by the feet. She writhed on her back and spat into the cop's face.

Grave Digger came up and looked down at her from sad brown eyes. "It's too late now, Gertrude," he said. "They're both dead."

Suddenly she began to cry. "What did he have to mess in it for?" she sobbed. "Oh, Pa, what did you have to mess in it for?"

XIV

TWO UNIFORMED WHITE cops standing guard on a dark roof-top were talking.

"Do you think we'll find him?"

"Do I think we'll find him? Do you know who we're looking for? Have you stopped to think for a moment that we're looking for one colored man who supposedly is handcuffed and seven other colored men who were wearing green turbans and false beards when last seen. Have you turned that over in your mind? By this time they've got rid of those phony disguises and maybe Pickens has got rid of his handcuffs too. And then what does that make them, I ask you? That makes them just like eighteen thousand or one hundred and eighty thousand other colored men, all looking alike. Have you ever stopped to think there are five hundred thousand colored people in Harlem— one half of a million people with black skin. All looking alike. And we're trying to pick eight out of them. It's like trying to find a cinder in a coal bin. It ain't possible."

"Do you think all these colored people in this neighborhood know who Pickens and the Moslems are?"

"Sure they know. Every last one of them. Unless some other colored person turns Pickens in he'll never be found. They're laughing at us."

"As much as the chief wants that coon, whoever finds him is sure to get a promotion," the first cop said.

"Yeah, I know, but it ain't possible," the second cop said. "If that coon's got any sense at all he would have filed those cuffs in two a long time ago."

"What good would that do him if he couldn't get them off?"

"Hell, he could wear heavy gloves with gauntlets like—Hey! Didn't we see some coon wearing driving gauntlets?"

"Yeah, that halfwit coon with the pigeons."

"Wearing gauntlets and a ragged old overcoat. And a coal black coon at that. He certainly fits the description."

"That halfwitted coon. You think it's possible he's the one?"

"Come on! What are we waiting for?"

* * *

Sheik said, "Now all we've got to do is get this mother-raper past the police lines and throw him into the river."

"Doan do that to me, please, Sheik," Sonny's muffled voice pleaded from inside the sack.

"Shhhh," Choo-Choo cautioned. "Chalk the walking Jeffs."

The two cops leaned over and peered in through the open window.

"Where's that boy who was wearing gloves?" the first cop asked.

"Gloves!" Choo-Choo echoed, going into his clowning act like a chameleon changing color. "You means boxing gloves?"

The second cop sniffed. "A weed pad!" he exclaimed.

They climbed inside. Their gazes swept quickly over the room.

The room reeked of marijuana smoke. Everyone was high. The ones who hadn't smoked were high from inhaling the smoke and watching the eccentric motions of the ones who had smoked.

"Who's got the sticks?" the first cop demanded.

"Come on, come on, who's got the sticks?" the second cop echoed, looking from one to the other. He passed over Sheik who stood in the center of the floor where he'd been arrested in motion by Choo-Choo's warning and stared at them as though trying to make out what they were; then over Inky who was caught in the act of ducking behind the curtains in the corner and stood there half in and half out, like a billboard advertisement for a movie about bad girls; and landed on Choo-Choo who seemed the most vulnerable because he was grinning like an idiot. "You got the sticks, boy?"

"Sticks! You mean that there pigeon stick," Choo-Choo said, pointing at the bamboo pole on the floor beside the bed.

"Don't get funny with me, boy!"

"I just don't know what you means, boss."

"Forget the sticks," the first cop said. "Let's find the boy with the gloves."

He looked about. His gaze lit on Sugartit who was sitting in the straight-backed chair and staring with a fixed expression at what appeared to be a gunny sack filled with huge lumps of coal lying in the middle of the bed.

"What's in that sack?" he asked suspiciously.

For an instant no one replied.

Then Choo-Choo said, "Just some coal."

"On the bed?"

"It's clean coal."

The cop pinned a threatening look on him.

"It's my bed," Sheik said. "I can put what I want on it."

Both cops turned to stare at him.

"You're a kind of lippy bastard," the first cop said. "What's your name?"

"Samson."

"You live here?"

"Right here."

"Then you're the boy we're looking for. That's your pigeon loft on the roof."

"No, that's not him," the second cop said. "The boy we want is blacker than he is and has another name."

"What's a name to these coons?" the first cop said. "They're always changing about."

"No, the one we want is called Inky. He was the one wearing the gloves."

"Now I remember. He was called Caleb. He was the one wearing the gloves. The other one was Inky, the one who couldn't talk."

The second cop wheeled on Sheik. "Where's Caleb?"

"I don't know anybody named Caleb."

"The hell you don't! He lives here with you."

"Naw suh, you means that boy what lives down on the first floor," Choo-Choo said.

"Don't tell me what I mean. I mean the boy who lives here on this floor. He's the boy who's got the pigeon loft."

"Naw suh, boss, if you means the Caleb what's got the pigeon roost, he lives on the first floor."

"Don't lie to me, boy. I saw the sergeant bring him down the fire escape to this floor."

"Naw suh, boss, the sergeant taken him on by this floor and

carried him down on the fire escape to the first floor. We seen
'em when they come by the window. Didn't we, Amos?" he
called to Inky.

"That's right, suh," Inky said. "They went right past that
window there."

"What other window could they go by?"

"None other window, suh."

"They had another boy with 'em called Inky," Choo-Choo
said. "It looked like they had 'em both arrested."

The second cop was staring at Inky. "This boy here looks
like Inky to me," he said. "Aren't you Inky, boy?"

"Naw suh—" Inky began, but Choo-Choo quickly cut him
off: "They calls him Smokey. Inky is the other one."

"Let him talk for himself," the first said.

The second cop pinned another threatening look on Choo-
Choo. "Are you trying to make a fool out of me, boy!"

"Naw suh, boss, I'se just tryin' a help."

"Let up on him," the first cop said. "These coons are jagged
on weed; they're not strictly responsible."

"Responsible or not, they'd better be careful before they get
some lumps on their heads."

The first cop noticed Sissie standing quietly in the corner,
holding her hand to her bruised cheek.

"You know them, Caleb and Inky, don't you girl?" he
asked her.

"No sir, I just know Smokey," she said.

Suddenly Sonny sneezed.

Sugartit giggled.

The cop wheeled toward the bed, looked at the sack and
then looked at her.

"Who was that sneezed?"

She put her hand to her mouth and tried to stop laughing.

The cop turned slightly pinkish and drew his pistol.

"Someone's underneath the bed," he said. "Keep the other
covered while I look."

The second cop drew his pistol.

"Just relax and no one will get hurt," he said calmly.

The first cop got down on his hands and knees, holding his

cocked pistol ready to shoot, and looked underneath the bed.

Sugartit put both hands over her mouth and bit into her palm. Her face swelled with suppressed laughter and tears flowed down her cheeks.

The cop straightened to his knees and braced himself on the edge of the bed. There was a perplexed look on his red face.

"There's something funny going on here," he said. "There's someone else in this room."

"Ain't nobody here but us ghosts, boss," Choo-Choo said.

The cop threw him a look of frustrated fury, and started to his feet.

"By God, I'll—" His voice dried up when he heard the choking sounds issuing from inside the sack.

He jumped upward and backward as though one of the ghosts had sure enough groaned. Leveling his pistol, he said in a quaking voice, "What's in that sack?"

Sugartit burst into hysterical laughter.

For an instant no one spoke.

Then Choo-Choo said hastily, "Hit's just Joe."

"What!"

"Hit's just Joe in the sack."

"Joe!"

Gingerly, the cop leaned over, holding his cocked pistol in his right hand, and with his left untied the cord closing the sack. He drew the top of the sack open.

Popping eyes in a gray-black face stared up at him.

The cop drew back in horror. His face turned white and a shudder passed over his big solid frame.

"It's a body," he said in a choked voice. "All trussed up."

"Hit ain't no body, hit's just Joe," Choo-Choo said, not intending to play the comic.

The second cop hastened over to look. "It's still alive," he said.

"He's choking!" Sissie cried and ran over and began loosening the noose about Sonny's neck.

Sonny sucked in breath with a gasp.

"My God, what's he doing in there?" the first cop asked in amazement.

"He's just studying magic," Choo-Choo said. He was beginning to sweat from the strain.

"Magic!"

The second cop noticed Sheik inching toward the window and aimed his pistol at him.

"Oh no, you don't," he said. "You come over here."

Sheik turned and came closer.

"Studying magic!" the first cop said. "In a sack?"

"Yas suh, he's trying to learn how to get out, like Houdini."

Color flooded back into the cop's face. "I ought to take him in for indecent exposure," he said.

"Hell, he's wearing a sack, ain't he," the second cop said, amused by his own wit.

Both of them grinned at Sonny as though he were a harmless halfwit.

Then the second cop said suddenly, "It ain't possible! There can't be two such halfwits in the whole world."

The first cop looked closely at Sonny and said slowly, "I believe you're right." Then to the others at large, "Get that boy out of that sack."

Sheik didn't move, but Choo-Choo and Inky hastened over and pulled Sonny out while Sissie held the bottom of the sack.

The cops stared at Sonny in awe.

"Looks like barbecued coon, don't he?" the first cop said.

Sugartit burst into laughter again.

Sonny's black skin had a gray pallor as though he'd been dusted over lightly with wood ash. He was shaking like a leaf.

The second cop reached out and turned him around.

Everyone stared at the handcuff bracelets clamped about each wrist.

"That's our boy," the first cop said.

"Lawd, suh, I wish I'd gone home and gone to bed," Sonny said in a moaning voice.

"I'll bet you do," the cop said.

Sugartit couldn't stop laughing.

XV

THE BODIES HAD been taken to the morgue. All that remained were chalk outlines on the pavement where they had lain.

The street had been cleared of private cars. Police tow trucks had carried away those that had been abandoned in the middle of the street. Most of the patrol cars had returned to duty; those remaining blocked the area.

The chief of police's car occupied the center of the stage. It was parked in the middle of the intersection of 127th Street and Lenox Avenue.

To one side of it, the chief, Lieutenant Anderson, the lieutenant from homicide and the precinct sergeant who'd led one of the search parties were grouped about the boy called Bones.

The lieutenant from homicide had a zip gun in his hand.

"All right then, it isn't yours," he said to Bones in a voice of tried patience. "Whose is it then? Who were you hiding it for?"

Bones stole a glance at the lieutenant's face and his gaze dropped quickly to the street. It crawled over the four pairs of big black copper's boots. They looked like the Sixth Fleet at anchor. He didn't answer.

He was a slim black boy of medium height with girlish features and short hair almost straight at the roots and parted on one side. He wore a natty topcoat over his sweat shirt and tight-fitting black pants above shiny tan pointed-toed shoes.

An elderly man, a head taller, with a face grizzled from hard outdoor work, stood beside him. Kinky hair grew like burdock weeds on his shiny black dome, and worried brown eyes looked down at Bones from behind steel-rimmed spectacles.

"Go 'head, tell 'em, so, don't be no fool," he said; then he looked up and saw Grave Digger approaching with his prisoners. "Here comes Digger Jones," he said. "You can tell him, cain't you?"

Everybody looked about.

Grave Digger held Good Booty by the arm and Big Smiley and Ready Belcher, handcuffed together, were walking in front of him.

He looked at Anderson and said, "I closed up the Dew Drop Inn. The manager and some juvenile delinquents are being held by the officers on duty. You'd better send a wagon up there."

Anderson whistled for a patrol car team and gave them the order.

"What did you find out on Galen?" the chief asked.

"I found out he was a pervert," Grave Digger said.

"It figures," the homicide lieutenant said.

The chief turned red. "I don't give a goddamn what he was," he said. "Have you found out who killed him?"

"No, right now I'm still guessing at it," Grave Digger said.

"Well, guess fast then. I'm getting goddamned tired of standing up here watching this comedy of errors."

"I'll give you a quick fill-in and let you guess too," Grave Digger said.

"Well, make it short and sweet and I damn sure ain't going to guess," the chief said.

"Listen, Digger," the colored civilian interposed. "You and me is both city workers. Tell 'em my boy ain't done no harm."

"He's broken the Sullivan law concerning concealed weapons by having this gun in his possession," the homicide lieutenant said.

"That little thing," Bones's father said scornfully. "I don't b'lieve that'll even shoot."

"Get these people away from here and let Jones report," the chief said testily.

"Well, do something with them, Sergeant," Lieutenant Anderson said.

"Come on, both of you," the sergeant said, taking the man by the arm.

"Digger—" the man appealed.

"It'll keep," Grave Digger said harshly. "Your boy belonged to the Moslem gang."

"Naw-naw, Digger—"

"Do I have to slug you," the sergeant said.

The man allowed himself to be taken along with his son across the street.

The sergeant turned them over to a corporal and hurried

back. Before he'd gone three steps the corporal was summon-
ing two cops to take charge of them.

"What kind of city work does he do?" the chief asked.

"He's in the sanitation department," the sergeant said. "He's
a garbage collector."

"All right, get on Jones," the chief ordered.

"Galen picked up colored school girls, teenagers, and took
them to a crib on 145th Street," Grave Digger said in a flat
toneless voice.

"Did you close it?" the Chief asked.

"It'll keep; I'm looking for a murderer now," Grave Digger
said. Taking the miniature bull whip from his pocket, he went
on, "He whipped them with this."

The chief reached out silently and took it from his hand.

"Have you got a list of the girls, Jones?" he asked.

"What for?"

"There might be a connection."

"I'm coming to that—"

"Well, get to it then."

"The landprop, a woman named Reba—used to call herself
Sheba—the one who testified against Captain Murphy—"

"Ah, that one," the chief said softly. "She won't slip out of
this."

"She'll take somebody with her," Grave Digger warned.
"She's covered and Galen was, too."

The chief looked at Lieutenant Anderson reflectively.

The silence ran on until the sergeant blurted, "That's not in
this precinct."

Anderson looked at the sergeant. "No one's charging you
with it."

"Get on, Jones," the chief said.

"Reba got scared of the deal and barred him. Her story will
be that she barred him when she found out what he was doing.
But that's neither here nor there. After she barred him Galen
started meeting them in the Dew Drop Inn. He arranged with
the bartender so he could whip them in the cellar."

Everyone except Grave Digger seemed embarrassed.

"He ran into a girl named Sissie," Grave Digger said. "How

doesn't matter at the moment. She's the girlfriend of a boy called Sheik, who is the leader of the Real Cool Moslems."

Sudden tension took hold of the group.

"Sheik sold Sissie to him. Then Galen wanted Sissie's girl-friend Sugartit. Sheik couldn't get Sugartit, but Galen kept looking for her in the neighborhood. I have the bartender here and a two-bit pimp who has a girl at Reba's. He steered for Galen. I got this much from them."

The officers stared appraisingly at the two handcuffed prisoners.

"If they know that much, they know who killed him," the chief said.

"It's going to be their asses if they do," Grave Digger said. "But I think they're leveling. The way I figure it, the whole thing hinges on Sugartit. I think he was killed because of her."

"By who?"

"That's the jackpot question."

The chief looked at Good Booty. "Is this girl Sugartit?"

The others stared at her, too.

"No, she's another one."

"Who is Sugartit then?"

"I haven't found out yet. This girl knows but she doesn't want to tell."

"Make her tell."

"How?"

The chief appeared to be embarrassed by the question. "Well, what the hell do you want with her if you can't make her talk?" he growled.

"I think she'll talk when we get close enough. The Moslem gang hangs out somewhere near here. The bartender here thinks it might be in the flat of a boy who has a pigeon loft."

"I know where that is!" the sergeant exclaimed. "I searched there."

Everyone, including the prisoners, stared at him. His face reddened. "Now I remember," he said. "There were several boys in the flat. The boy who kept pigeons, Caleb Bowee is his name, lives there with his Grandma; and two of the others roomed there."

"Why the hell didn't you bring them in?" the chief asked.

"I didn't find anything on them to connect them with the Moslem gang or the escaped prisoner," the sergeant said, defending himself. "The boy with the pigeons is a halfwit—he's harmless, and I'm sure the grandma wouldn't put up with a gang in there."

"How in the hell do you know he's harmless?" the chief stormed. "Half the murderers in Sing Sing look like you and me."

The homicide lieutenant and Anderson exchanged smiles.

"They had two girls with them and—" the sergeant began to explain but the chief wouldn't let him.

"Why in the hell didn't you bring them in, too?"

"What were the girls' names?" Grave Digger asked.

"One was called Sissieratta and—"

"That must be Sissie," Grave Digger said. "It fits. One was Sissie and the other was Sugartit. And one of the boys was Sheik." Turning to Big Smiley, he asked, "What does Sheik look like?"

"Freckle-faced boy the color of a bay horse, with yellow cat eyes," Big Smiley said impassively.

"You're right," the sergeant admitted sheepishly. "He was one of them. I should have trusted my instinct; I started to haul that punk in."

"Well, for God's sake, get the lead out of your ass now," the chief roared. "If you still want to work for the police department."

"Well, Jesus Christ, the other girl, the one Jones calls Sugartit, was Ed Johnson's daughter," the sergeant exploded. "She had one of those souvenir police ID cards signed by yourself and I thought—"

He was interrupted by the flat whacking sound of metal striking against a human skull.

No one had seen Grave Digger move.

What they saw now was Ready Belcher sagging forward with his eyes rolled back into his head and a white cut—not yet beginning to bleed—two inches wide in the black pockmarked skin of his forehead. Big Smiley reared back on the other end of the handcuffs like a dray horse shying from a rattlesnake.

Grave Digger gripped his nickel-plated thirty-eight by the long barrel, making a club out of the butt. The muscles were corded in his rage-swollen neck and his face was distorted with violence. Looking at him, the others were suspended in motion as though turned to stone.

"Stop him, God damn it!" the chief roared. "He'll kill them."

The sculptured figures of the police officers came to life. The sergeant grabbed Grave Digger from behind in a bear hug. Grave Digger doubled over and sent the sergeant flying over his head toward the chief, who ducked in turn and let the sergeant sail on by.

Lieutenant Anderson and the homicide lieutenant converged on Grave Digger from opposite directions. Each grabbed an arm while he was still in a crouch and lifted upward and backward.

Ready was lying prone on the pavement, blood trickling from the dent in his skull, a slack arm drawn tight by the handcuffs attached to Big Smiley's wrist. He looked dead already.

Big Smiley gave the appearance of a terrified blind beggar caught in a bombing raid; his giant frame trembled from head to foot.

Grave Digger had just time enough to kick Ready in the face before the officers jerked him out of range.

"Get him to the hospital, quick!" the chief shouted; and in the next breath added, "Rap him on the head!"

Grave Digger had carried the lieutenants to the ground and it was more than either could do to follow the chief's command.

The sergeant had already picked himself up and at the chief's order set off at a gallop.

"God damn it, phone for it, don't run after it!" the chief yelled. "Where the hell is my chauffeur, anyway?"

Cops came running from all directions.

"Give the lieutenants a hand," the chief said. "They've got a wild man."

Four cops jumped into the fray. Finally they pinned Grave Digger to the ground.

The sergeant climbed into the chief's car and began talking into the telephone.

Coffin Ed appeared suddenly. No one had noticed him approaching from his parked car down the street.

"Great God, what's happening, Digger?" he exclaimed.

Everybody was quiet, their embarrassment noticeable.

"What the hell!" he said, looking from one to the other. "What the hell's going on."

Grave Digger's muscles relaxed as though he'd lost consciousness.

"It's just me, Ed," he said, looking up from the ground at his friend. "I just lost my head, is all."

"Let him go," Anderson ordered his helpers. "He's back to normal now."

The cops released Grave Digger and he got to his feet.

"Cooled off now?" the homicide lieutenant asked.

"Yeah. Give me my gun," Grave Digger said.

Coffin Ed looked down at Ready Belcher's bloody head.

"You too, eh, partner," he said. "What did this rebel do?"

"I told him if I caught him holding out on me I'd kill him."

"You told him no lie," Coffin Ed said. Then asked, "Is it that bad?"

"It's dirty, Ed. Galen was a rotten son of a bitch."

"That doesn't surprise me. Have you got anything on it so far?"

"A little, not much."

"What the hell do you want here?" the chief said testily. "I suppose you want to help your buddy beat up some more of your folks."

Grave Digger knew the chief was trying to steer the conversation away from Coffin Ed's daughter, but he didn't know how to help him.

"You two men act as if you want to kill off the whole population of Harlem," the chief kept on.

"You told me to crack down," Grave Digger reminded him.

"Yeah, but I didn't mean in front of my eyes where I would have to be a witness to it."

"It's our beat," Coffin Ed spoke up for his friend. "If you don't like the way we handle it why don't you take us off."

"You're already off," the chief said. "What in the hell did you come back for, anyway?"

"Strictly on private business."

The chief snorted.

"My little daughter hasn't come home and I'm worried about her," Coffin Ed explained. "It's not like her to stay out this late and not let us know where she is."

The chief looked away to hide his embarrassment.

Grave Digger swallowed audibly.

"Hell, Ed, you don't have to worry about Eve," he said in what he hoped was a reassuring tone of voice. "She'll be home soon. You know nothing can happen to her. She's got that police ID card you got for her on her last birthday, hasn't she?"

"I know, but she always phones her mother if she's going to stay out."

"While you're out here looking for her she's probably gone home. Why don't you go back home and go to bed? She'll be all right."

"Jones is telling you right, Ed," the chief said brusquely. "Go home and relax. You're off duty and you're in our way here. Nothing is going to happen to your daughter. You're just having nightmares."

A siren sounded in the distance.

"Here comes the ambulance," Lieutenant Anderson said.

"I'll go and phone home again," Coffin Ed said. "Take it easy, Digger. Don't get yourself docked, too."

As he turned and started off a fusillade of shots sounded from the upper floor of some nearby tenement. Ten shots from regulation .38 police specials were fired so fast that by the time the sounds had reached the street they were chained together.

Every cop within earshot froze to alert attention. They strained their ears in almost superhuman effort to place the direction from which the shots had come. Their eyes scanned the fronts of the tenements until not a spot escaped their observation.

But no more shots were fired.

The only signs of life left were the lights going out. With the rapidity of gun shots, one light after another went out until only one lighted window remained in the whole block of darkened dingy buildings. It was behind a fire-escape landing on the top floor of the tenement half a block up the street.

All eyes focused on that spot.

The grotesque silhouette of something crawling over the window sill appeared in the glare of light. Slowly it straightened and took the shape of a short, husky man. It staggered slowly along the three feet of grilled iron footing and leaned against the low outer rail. For a moment it swayed back and forth in a macabre pantomime and then, slowly, like a roulette ball climbing the last hurdle before the final slot, it fell over the railing, turned in the air, missed the second landing by a breath. The body turned again and struck the third railing and started to spin faster. It landed with a resounding thud on top of a parked car and lay there with one hand hanging down beside the driver's window as though signaling for a stop.

"Well, God damn it, get going!" the chief shouted in stentorian tone. Then, on second thought, he added, "Not you, Jones. Not you!" and ran toward his car to get his megaphone.

Already motion had broken out. Cops were heading toward the tenement like the Marines landing.

The two cops guarding the entrance ran out into the street to locate the scene of the disturbance.

The chief grabbed his megaphone and shouted, "Get the lights on that building."

Two spotlights that had been extinguished were turned back on immediately and beamed on the tenement's top floor.

A patrolman stepped from the window onto the fire-escape landing and raised his hands in the light.

"Hold it, everybody!" he shouted. "I want the chief! Is the chief there?"

"Lower the lights," the chief megaphoned. "I'm here. What is it?"

"Send for an ambulance. Petersen is shot—"

"An ambulance is coming."

"Yes sir, but don't let anybody in here yet—"

Grave Digger took hold of Coffin Ed's arm.

"Hang on tight, Ed," he said. "Your daughter's up there."

He felt Coffin Ed's muscles tighten beneath his grip as the cop went on, "We found Pickens but one of the Moslem gangsters grabbed Pete's pistol and shot him. He used his buddy as a shield and I got his buddy but he snatched one of the girls here and escaped into the back room. He's locked himself in there and there's no other way out of this shotgun shack. He says the girl is Detective Ed Johnson's daughter. He threatened to cut her throat if he can't talk to you and Grave Digger Jones. Whatcha want me to do?"

The ambulance approached and the chief had to wait until the siren had died away to make himself heard.

"Has he still got Petersen's pistol?"

"Yes, sir, but he emptied it."

"All right, Officer, sit pat," the chief megaphoned. "We'll get Petersen down the fire escape and I'll go up and see what it's all about."

Coffin Ed's acid-burnt face was hideous with fear.

XVI

"YOU STAY DOWN here, Johnson," the chief ordered. "I'll take Anderson and Jones."

"Not unless you shoot me," Coffin Ed said.

The chief looked at him.

"Let him come," Grave Digger said.

"I ought to come too; I know the flat," the sergeant said.

"It's my job to come," the lieutenant from homicide said.

"Who the hell's running this police department," the chief said.

"We haven't got any time," Grave Digger replied.

All of them went quickly and quietly as possible. No one spoke again until the chief said through the kitchen door, "All right, I'm the chief. Come out and give yourself up and you won't get hurt."

"How do I know you're the chief?" asked a fuzzy voice from within.

"If you open the door and come out you'll see."

"Don't get so mother-raping smart. You're the chief, but I'm the Sheik."

"Well, all right, you're a big-shot gang boss. What do you want?"

"Keep him talking," Coffin Ed whispered. "I'm going up on the roof."

"Who's that with you?" Sheik asked sharply.

Grave Digger pointed to the sergeant and Lieutenant Anderson.

"The precinct lieutenant and a sergeant," the chief said.

"Where's Grave Digger?"

"He's not here yet. I had to send for him."

"Send those other mother-rapers away. Let's you and me settle this, the Sheik and the Chief."

"How will you know if they're gone if you're scared to come out and look?"

"Let 'em stay then. I don't give a good goddam. And don't think I'm scared. I don't need to take any chances. I got Coffin Ed's daughter by the hair with my left hand and I'm holding a razor-edged butcher knife against her throat with my right hand. If you try to take me I'll cut her mother-raping head off before you can get through the door."

"All right, Sheik, you got us by the short hair, but you know you can't get away. Why don't you come out peaceably and give yourself up like a man. I give you my word that no one will abuse you. The officer you shot ain't seriously hurt. There's no other charge against you. You ought to get off with five years. With time off for good behavior, you'll be back in the big town in three years. Why risk sudden death or the hot seat just for a moment of playing the big shot?"

"Don't hand me that mother-raping crap. You'll hang a kid-napping charge on me for snatching your prisoner."

"What the hell! You can keep him. We don't want him any-more. We found out he didn't kill the man. All he had was a blank pistol."

"So he didn't kill the man?"

"No."

"Who killed him?"

"We don't know yet."

"So you don't know who killed the big Greek, do you?"

"All right, all right, what's that to you? What do you want to get mixed up in something that doesn't concern you?"

"You're one of those smart mother-rapers, ain't you? You're going to be so smart you're going to make me cut her mother-raping throat just to show you."

"Please don't argue with him, Mr. Chief, please," said a small scared voice from within. "He'll kill me. I know he will."

"Shut up!" Sheik said roughly. "I don't need you to tell 'im I'm going to kill you."

Beads of sweat formed on the ridge of the chief's red nose and about the blue bags beneath his eyes.

"Why don't you be a man," he urged, filling his voice with contempt. "Don't be a mad dog like Vincent Coll. Be a man like Dillinger was. You won't get much. Three years and no more. Don't hide behind an innocent little girl."

"Who the hell do you think you're kidding with that stale crap. This is the Sheik. Can't no dumb cop like you make a fool out of the Sheik. You got the chair waiting for me and you think you're going to kid me into walking out there and sitting in it."

"Don't play yourself too big, punk," the chief said, losing his temper for a moment. "You shot an officer but you didn't kill him. You snatched a prisoner but we don't want him. Now you want to take it out on a little girl who can't defend herself. And you call yourself the Sheik, the big gang leader. You're just a cheap tinhorn punk, yellow to the core."

"Keep on, just keep on. You ain't kidding me with that mother-raping sucker bait. You know it was me who killed him. You've had me tabbed ever since you found out that nigger was shooting blanks."

"What!" The chief was startled. Forgetting himself, he asked Grave Digger, "What the hell's he talking about?"

"Galen." Grave Digger formed the word with his lips.

"Galen!" the chief exclaimed. "You're trying to tell me you killed the white man, you chicken-livered punk?" he roared.

"Keep on, just keep on. You know damn well it was me lowered the boom on the big Greek." He sounded as though he bitterly resented an oversight. "Who do you think you're kidding? You're talking to the Sheik. You think 'cause I'm colored I'm dumb enough to fall for that rock-a-bye-baby crap you're putting down."

The chief had to readjust his train of thought.

"So it was you who killed Galen?"

"He was just the Greek to me," Sheik said scornfully. "Just another gray sucker up here trying to get his kicks. Yeah, I killed him." There was pride in his voice.

"Yeah, it figures," the chief said thoughtfully. "You saw him running down the street and you took advantage of that and shot him in the back. Just what a yellow son of a bitch like you would do. You were probably laying for him and were scared to go out and face him like a man."

"I wasn't laying for the mother-raper no such goddam thing," Sheik said. "I didn't even know he was anywhere about."

"You were nursing a grudge against him."

"I didn't have nothing against the mother-raper. You must be having pipedreams. He was just another gray sucker to me."

"Then why the hell did you shoot him?"

"I was just trying out my new zip gun. I saw the mother-raper running by where I was standing so I just blasted at him to see how good my gun would shoot."

"You God damned little rat," the chief said, but there was more sorrow in his voice than anger. "You sick little bastard. What the God damned hell can be done with somebody like you?"

"I just want you to quit trying to kid me, 'cause I'd just as soon cut this girl's throat right now as not."

"All right, *Mister* Sheik," the chief said in a cold, quiet voice. "What do you want me to do?"

"Is Grave Digger come yet?"

Grave Digger nodded.

"Yeah, he's here, *Mister* Sheik."

"Let him say something then, and you better can that mister crap."

"Eve, this is me, Digger Jones," Grave Digger said, spurning Sheik.

"Answer him," Sheik said.

"Yes, Mr. Jones," she said in a voice so weightless it floated out to the tense group listening like quivering eiderdown.

"Is Sissie in there with you?"

"No, sir, just Granny Bowee and she's sitting in her chair asleep."

"Where's Sissie?"

"She and Inky are in the front room."

"Has he hurt you?"

"Quit stalling," Sheik said dangerously. "I'm going to give you until I count to three."

"Please, Mr. Jones, do what he says. He's going to kill me if you don't."

"Don't worry child, we're going to do what he says," he reassured her and then said, "What do you want, boy?"

"These are my terms: I want the street cleared of cops; all the police blockades moved—"

"What the hell!" the chief exploded.

"We'll do it," Grave Digger said.

"I want to hear the chief say it," Sheik demanded.

"I'll be damned if I will," the chief said.

"Please," came a tiny voice no bigger than a prayer.

"What if she was your daughter," Grave Digger said.

"I'm going to give you until I count three," Sheik said.

"All right, I'll do it," the chief said, sweating blood.

"On your word of honor as a great white man," Sheik persisted.

The chief's red sweating face drained of color.

"All right, all right, on my word of honor," he said.

"Then I want an ambulance driven up to the door downstairs. I want all its doors left open so I can see inside, the back doors and both the side doors, and I want the motor left running."

"All right, all right, what else? The Statue of Liberty?"

"I want this house cleared—"

"All right, all right, I said I'd do that."

"I don't want any mother-raping alarm put out. I don't want anybody to try to stop me. If anybody messes with me before I get away you're going to have a dead girl to bury. I'll put her out somewhere safe when I get clear away, clear out of the state."

"Don't cross him," Grave Digger whispered tensely. "He's teaed to the eyes."

"All right, all right," the chief said. "We'll give you safe passage. If you don't hurt the girl. If you hurt her we won't kill you, but you'll beg us to. Now take five minutes and come out and we'll let you drive away."

"Who do you think you're kidding?" Sheik said. "I ain't that big a fool. I want Grave Digger to come inside of here and put his pistol down on the table, then I'm going to come out."

"You're crazy if you think we're going to give you a pistol," the chief roared.

"Then I'm going to kill her now."

"I'll give it to you," Grave Digger said.

"You're under suspension as of now," the chief said.

"All right," Grave Digger said: then to Sheik, "What do you want me to do?"

"I want you to stand outside the door with the pistol held by the barrel. When I open the door I want you to stick it forward and walk into the room so's the first thing I see is the butt. Then I want you to walk straight ahead and put it on the kitchen table. You got that?"

"Yeah, I got it."

"The rest of you mother-rapers get downstairs," Sheik said.

The two lieutenants and the sergeant looked at the chief for orders.

"All right, Jones, it's your show," the chief said, adding on second thought, "I wish you luck."

He turned and started down the stairs.

The others hesitated. Grave Digger motioned violently for them to leave too. Reluctantly they followed the chief.

It was silent in the kitchen until the sound of the officers' receding footsteps diminished into silence below.

Grave Digger stood facing the kitchen door, holding the pistol as instructed. Sweat poured down his lumpy cordovan-colored face and collected in the collar about his neck.

Finally the sound of movement came from the kitchen. The bolt of the Yale lock clicked open, a hand bolt was pulled back with a grating snap, a chain was unfastened. The door swung slowly inward.

Only Granny was visible from the doorway. She sat bolt upright in the immobile rocking chair with her hands gripping the arms and her old milky eyes wide open and staring at Grave Digger with a fixed look of fierce disapproval.

Sheik spoke from behind the door, "Turn the butt this way so I can see if it's loaded."

Without looking around, Grave Digger turned the pistol so that Sheik could see the shells in the chambers of the cylinder.

"Go ahead, keep walking," Sheik ordered.

Still without looking around, Grave Digger moved slowly across the room. When he came to the table he looked swiftly toward the small window at the far end of the back wall. It was on the other side of an old-fashioned homemade cupboard which partially blocked the view of the kitchen from the outside, so that only the section between the table and the side wall was visible.

He saw what he was looking for. He leaned slowly forward and placed the pistol on the far side of the table.

"There," he said.

Raising his hands high above his head, he turned slowly away from the table and faced the back wall. He stood so that Sheik had to either pass in front of him to reach the pistol or go around on the other side of the table.

Sheik kicked the door shut, revealing himself and Sugartit, but Grave Digger didn't turn his head or even move his eyes to look at them.

Sheik gripped Sugartit's pony tail tightly in his left hand, pulling her head back hard to make her slender brown throat taut beneath the blade of the butcher knife. They began a slow shuffling walk, like a weird Apache dance in a Montmartre night club.

Sugartit's eyes had the huge liquid look of a dying doe's, and her small brown face looked as fragile as toasted meringue. Her upper lip was sweating copiously.

Sheik kept his gaze pinned on Grave Digger's back while slowly skirting the opposite walls of the room and approaching the table from the far side. When he came within reach of the pistol he released his hold on Sugartit's pony tail, pressed the knife blade tighter against her throat and reached out with his left hand for the pistol.

Coffin Ed was hanging head-downward from the roof, only his head and shoulders visible below the top edge of the kitchen window. He had been hanging there for twenty minutes waiting for Sheik to come into view. He took careful aim at a spot just above Sheik's left ear.

Some sixth sense caused Sheik to jerk his head around at the exact instant Coffin Ed fired.

A third eye, small and black and sightless, appeared suddenly in the exact center of Sheik's forehead between his two startled yellow cat's eyes.

The high-powered bullet had cut only a small round hole in the window glass, but the sound of the shot shattered the whole pane and blasted a shower of glass into the room.

Grave Digger wheeled to catch the fainting girl as the knife clattered harmlessly onto the table top.

Sheik was dead when he started going down. He landed crumpled up beside Granny's immobile rocking chair.

The room was full of cops.

"That was too much of a risk, too much of a risk," Lieutenant Anderson said, shaking his head, a dazed expression on his face.

"What isn't risky on this job?" the chief said authoritatively. "We cops got to take risks."

No one disputed him.

"This is a violent city," he added belligerently.

"There wasn't that much risk," Coffin Ed said. He had his arm about his daughter's trembling shoulders. "They don't have any reflexes when you shoot them in the head."

Sugartit winced.

"Take Eve and go home," Grave Digger said harshly.

"I guess I'd better," Coffin Ed said, limping painfully as he guided Sugartit gently toward the door.

"Geez," a young patrol-car rookie was saying. "Geez. He hung there all that time on just some wire tied around his ankles. I don't know how he stood the pain."

"You'd've stood it too if she was your daughter," Grave Digger said.

"Forget what I said to you about being under suspension, Jones," the chief said.

"I didn't hear you," Grave Digger said.

"Jesus Christ, look at that!" the sergeant exclaimed in amazement. "All that noise and Grandma's still sleeping."

Everybody turned and looked at him. They were solemn for a moment.

"Nothing's ever going to wake her up again," the lieutenant from homicide said. "She must have been dead for hours."

"All right, all right, all right," the chief shouted. "Let's clean up here and get away. We've got this case tied up tighter than Dick's hatband." Then he added in a pleased tone of voice, "That wasn't too difficult, was it?"

XVII

IT WAS ELEVEN o'clock the next morning.

Inky and Bones had spilled their guts.

It had gone hard for them and when the cops got through with them they were as knotty as fat pine.

The remaining members of the Real Cool Moslems—Camel Mouth, Beau Baby, Punkin Head and Slow Motion—had been rounded up, questioned and were now being held along with Inky and Bones.

Their statements had been practically identical:

They had been standing on the corner of 127th Street and Lenox Avenue.

Q. What for?

A. Just having a dress rehearsal.

Q. What? Dress rehearsal?

A. Yas suh. Like they do on Broadway. We was practicing wearing our new A-rab costumes.

Q. And you saw Mr. Galen when he ran past?

A. Yas suh, that's when we seed him.

Q. Did you recognize him?

A. Naw suh, we didn't know him.

Q. Sheik knew him.

A. Yas suh, but he didn't say he knew 'im and we'd never seen him before.

Q. Choo-Choo must have known him, too.

A. Yas suh, must'ave. Him and Sheik usta room together.

Q. But you saw Sheik shoot him?

A. Yas suh. He said, "Watch this," and pulled out his new zip gun and shot at him.

Q. How many times did he shoot?

A. Just once. That's all a zip gun will shoot.

Q. Yes, these zip guns are single shots. But you knew he had the gun?

A. Yas suh. He'd been working on it for 'most a week.

Q. He made it himself?

A. Yas suh.

Q. Had you ever seen him shoot it previously?

A. Naw suh. It were just finished. He hadn't tried it out.

Q. But you knew he had it on his person?

A. Yas suh. He were going to try it out that night.

Q. And after he shot the white man, what did you do?

A. The man fell down and we went up to see if he'd hit him.

Q. Were you acquainted with the first suspect, Sonny Pickens?

A. Naw suh, we seed him for the first time too when he come past there shootin'.

Q. When you saw the white man had been killed, did you know Sheik had shot him?

A. Naw suh, we thought the other fellow had did it.

Q. Which one of you, er, passed the wind?

A. Suh?

Q. Which one of you broke wind?

A. Oh, that were Choo-Choo, suh, he the one farted.

Q. Was there any special significance in that?

A. Suh?

Q. Why did he do it?

A. That were just a salute we give to the cops.

Q. Oh! Was the perfume throwing part of it?

A. Yas suh, when they got mad Caleb threw the perfume on them.

Q. To allay their anger, er, ah, make them jolly?

A. Naw suh, to make them madder.

Q. Oh! Well, why did Sheik kidnap Pickens, the other suspect?

A. Just to put something over on the cops. He hated cops.

Q. Why?

A. Suh?

Q. Why did he hate cops? Did he have any special reason to hate cops?

A. Special reason? To hate cops? Naw suh. He didn't need none. Just they was cops, is all.

Q. Ah, yes, just they was cops. Is this the zip gun Sheik had?

A. Yas suh. Leastwise it looks like it.

Q. How did Bones come to be in possession of it?

A. He gave it to Bones when he was running off. Bones's old man work for the city and he figgered it was safe with Bones.

Q. That's all for you, boy. You had better be scared.

A. Ah is.

That was the case. Open and shut.

Sonny Pickens could not be implicated in the murder. He

was being held temporarily on a charge of disturbing the peace while a district attorney's assistant was studying the New York State criminal code to see what other charge could be lodged against him for shooting a citizen with a blank gun.

His friends, Lowtop Brown and Rubberlips Wilson had been hauled in as suspicious persons.

The cases of the two girls had been referred to the probation officers, but as yet nothing had been done. Both were supposedly at their respective homes, suffering from shock.

The bullet had been removed from the victim's brain and given to the ballistics bureau. No further autopsy was required. Mr. Galen's daughter, Mrs. Helen Kruger of Wading River, Long Island, had claimed the body for burial.

The bodies of the others, Granny and Caleb, Choo-Choo and Sheik, lay unclaimed in the morgue. Perhaps the Baptist church in Harlem, of which Granny was a member, would give her a decent Christian burial. She had no life insurance and it would be financially inconvenient for the church, unless the members contributed to defray the costs.

Caleb would be buried along with Sheik and Choo-Choo in potters field, unless the medical college of one of the universities obtained their bodies for dissection. No college would want Choo-Choo's, however, because it had been too badly damaged.

Ready Belcher was in Harlem Hospital, in the same ward where Charlie Richardson, whose arm had been chopped off, had died earlier. His condition was serious, but he would live. He would never look the same, however, and should his teenage whore ever see him again she wouldn't recognize him.

Big Smiley and Reba were being held for contributing to the delinquency of minors, manslaughter, operating a house of prostitution, and sundry other charges.

The woman who was shot in the leg by Coffin Ed was in Knickerbocker Hospital. Two ambulance-chasing shysters were vying with each other for her consent to sue Coffin Ed and the New York police department on a fifty-fifty split of the judgement, but her husband was holding out for a sixty-percent cut.

That was the story; the second and corrected story. The

late editions of the morning newspapers had gone hog wild with it:

The prominent New York Citizen hadn't been shot, as first reported, by a drunken Negro who had resented his presence in a Harlem bar. No, not at all. He had been shot to death by a teenage Harlem gangster called Sheik, who was the leader of a teenage gang called the Real Cool Moslems. Why? Well, Sheik had wanted to find out if his zip gun would actually shoot.

The copy writers used a book of adjectives to describe the bizarre aspects of the three-ring Harlem murder; meanwhile they tossed a bone of commendation to the brave policemen who had worked through the small hours of the morning, tracking down the killer in the Harlem jungle and shooting him to death in his lair less than six hours after the fatal shot had been fired.

The headlines read:

POLICE PUT HEAT ON REAL COOL MOSLEMS
DEATH IS THE KISS-OFF FOR THRILL KILL
HARLEM MANIAC RUNS AMUCK

But already the story was a thing of the past, as dead as the four main characters.

"Kill it," ordered the city editor of an afternoon paper. "Someone else has already been murdered somewhere else."

Uptown in Harlem, the sun was shining on the same drab scene it illuminated every other morning at eleven o'clock. No one missed the few expendable colored people being held on various charges in the big new granite skyscraper jail on Centre Street that had replaced the old New York City tombs.

In the same building, in a room high up on the southwest corner, with a fine clear view of the Battery and North River, all that remained of the case was being polished off.

Earlier the police commissioner and the chief of police had had a heart-to-heart talk about possible corruption in the Harlem branch of the police department.

"There are strong indications that Galen was protected by some influential person up there, either the police department or in the city government," the police commissioner said.

"Not in the department," the chief maintained. "In the first place, that low license number of his—UG-Sixteen—tells me he had friends higher up than a precinct captain, because that kind of license number is issued only to the specially privileged, and that don't even include me."

"Did you find any connections with politicians in that area?"

"Not connecting Galen; but the woman, Reba, telephoned a colored councilman this morning and ordered him to get down here and get her out on bail."

The commissioner sighed. "Perhaps we'll never know the extent of Galen's activities up there."

"Maybe not, but one thing we do know," the chief said. "The son of a bitch is dead, and his money won't corrupt anybody else."

Afterward the police commissioner reviewed the suspension of Coffin Ed. Grave Digger and Lieutenant Anderson were present along with the chief at this conference. Coffin Ed had exercised his privilege to be absent.

"In the light of subsequent developments in this case, I am inclined to be lenient toward Detective Johnson," the commissioner said. "His compulsion to fire at the youth is understandable, if not justifiable, in view of his previous unfortunate experience with an acid thrower." The commissioner had come into office by way of a law practice and could handle those jaw-breaking words with much greater ease than the cops, who'd learned their trade pounding beats.

"What's your opinion, Jones?" he asked.

Grave Digger turned from his customary seat, one ham propped on the window ledge and one foot planted on the floor, and said, "Yes sir, he's been touchy and on edge ever since that con-man threw the acid in his eyes, but he was never rough on anybody in the right."

"Hell, I wasn't disciplining Johnson so much as I was just taking the weight off the whole God damned police department," the chief said in defense of his action. "We'd have caught holy hell from all the sob sisters, male and female, in this town if those punks had turned out to be innocent pranksters."

"So you are in favor of his reinstatement?" the commissioner asked.

"Why not?" the chief said. "If he's got the jumps let him work them off on those hoodlums up in Harlem who gave them to him."

"Right ho," the commissioner said, then turned to Grave Digger again: "Perhaps you can tell me, Jones; one aspect of the case has me puzzled. All of the reports state that there was a huge crowd of people present at the victim's death, and witnessed the actual shooting. One report states—" he fumbled among the papers on his desk until he found the page he wanted. " 'The street was packed with people for a distance of two blocks when deceased met death by gunfire.' Why is this? Why do the people up in Harlem congregate at the scene of a killing as though it were a three-ring circus?"

"It is," Grave Digger said tersely. "It's the greatest show on earth."

"That happens everywhere," Anderson said. "People will congregate at a killing wherever it takes place."

"Yes, of course, out of morbid curiosity. But I don't mean that exactly. According to reports, not only the reports on this case, but all reports that have come into my office, this, er, phenomenon, let us say, is more evident in Harlem that any place else. What do you think, Jones?"

"Well, it's like this, Commissioner," Grave Digger said. "Every day in Harlem, two and three times a day, the colored people see some colored man being chased by another colored man with a knife or an axe or a club. Or else being chased by a white cop with a gun, or by a white man with his fists. But it's only once in a blue moon they get to see a white man being chased by one of them. A big white man at that. That was an event. A chance to see some white blood spilled for a change, and spilled by a black man, at that. That was greater than Emancipation Day. As they say up in Harlem, that was the greatest. That's what Ed and I are always up against when we try to make Harlem safe for white people."

"Perhaps I can explain it," the commissioner said.

"Not to me," the chief said drily. "I ain't got the time to

listen. If the folks up there want to see blood, they're going to see all the blood they want if they kill another white man."

"Jones is right," Anderson said. "But it makes for trouble."

"Trouble!" Grave Digger echoed. "All they know up there is trouble. If trouble was money, everybody in Harlem would be a millionaire."

The telephone rang. The commissioner picked up the receiver.

"Yes . . .? Yes, send him up." He replaced the receiver and said, "It's the ballistics report. It's coming up."

"Fine," the chief said. "Let's write it in the record and close this case up. It was a dirty business from start to finish and I'm sick and God damned tired of it."

"Right ho," the commissioner said.

Someone knocked.

"Come in," he said.

The lieutenant from homicide who had worked on the case came in and placed the zip gun and the battered lead pellet taken from the murdered man's brain on the commissioner's desk.

The commissioner picked up the gun and examined it curiously.

"So this is a zip gun?"

"Yes sir. It's made from an ordinary toy cap pistol. The barrel of the toy pistol is sawed off and this four-inch section of heavy brass pipe is fitted in in its place. See, it's soldered to the frame, then for greater stability it's bound with adjustable cables in place. The shell goes directly into the barrel, then this clip is inserted to prevent it from backfiring. The firing pin is soldered to the original hammer. On this one it's made from the head and a quarter-inch section of an ordinary Number Six nail, filed down to a point."

"It is more primitive than I had imagined, but it is certainly ingenious."

The others looked at it with bored indifference; they had seen zip guns before.

"And this will project a bullet with sufficient force to kill a man, to penetrate his skull?"

"Yes sir."

"Well, well, so this is the gun which killed Galen and led the boy who made it to be killed in turn."

"No sir, not this gun."

"What!"

Everybody sat bolt upright, eyes popping and mouths open. Had the lieutenant said the Empire State Building had been stolen and smuggled out of town, he couldn't have caused a greater sensation.

"What do you mean, not that gun!" the chief roared.

"That's what I came to tell you," the lieutenant said. "This gun fires a twenty-two caliber bullet. It contained the case of a twenty-two shell when the sergeant found it. Galen was killed with a thirty-two caliber fired from a more powerful pistol."

"This is where we came in," Anderson said.

"I'll be God damned if it is!" the chief bellowed like an enraged bull. "The papers have already gotten the story that he was killed with this gun and they've gone crazy with it. We'll be the laughing stock of the world."

"No," the commissioner said quietly but firmly. "We have made a mistake, that is all."

"I'll be God damned if we have," the chief said, his face turning blood-red with passion. "I say the son of a bitch was killed with that gun and that punk lying in the morgue killed him, and I don't give a God damn what ballistics show."

The commissioner looked solemnly from face to face. There was no question in his eyes, but he waited for someone else to speak.

"I don't think it's worth re-opening the case," Lieutenant Anderson said. "Galen wasn't a particularly lovable character."

"Lovable or not, we got the killer and that's the gun and that's that," the chief said.

"Can we afford to let a murderer go free?" the chief said.

The commissioner looked again from face to face.

"This one," Grave Digger said harshly. "He did a public service."

"That's not for us to determine, is it?" the commissioner said.

"You'll have to decide that, sir," Grave Digger said. "But if you assign me to look for the killer, I resign."

"Er, what? Resign from the force?"

"Yes sir. I say the killer will never kill again and I'm not going to track him down to pay for this killing even if it costs me my job."

"Who killed him, Jones?"

"I couldn't say, sir."

The commissioner looked grave. "Was he as bad as that?"

"Yes sir."

The commissioner looked at the lieutenant from homicide.

"But this zip gun was fired, wasn't it?"

"Yes sir. But I've checked with all the hospitals and the precinct station in Harlem and there has been no gunshot injury reported."

"Someone could have been injured who was afraid to report it."

"Yes sir. Or the bullet might have landed harmlessly against a building or an automobile."

"Yes. But there are the other boys who are involved. They might be indicted for complicity. If it is proved that they were his accomplices, they face the maximum penalty for murder."

"Yes sir," Anderson said. "But it's been pretty well established that the murder—or rather the action of the boy firing the zip gun—was not premeditated. And the others knew nothing of his intention to fire at Galen until it was too late to prevent him."

"According to their statements."

"Well, yes sir. But it's up to us to accept their statements or have them bound over to the grand jury for indictment. If we don't charge complicity when they go up for arraignment the court will only fine them for disturbing the peace."

The commissioner looked back at the lieutenant from homicide. "Who else knows about this?"

"No one outside of this office, sir. They never had the gun in ballistics; they only had the bullet."

"Shall we put it to a vote?" the commissioner asked.

No one said anything.

"The ayes have it," the commissioner said. He picked up the small lead pellet that had murdered a man. "Jones, there is a flat roof on a building across the park. Do you think you can throw this so it will land there?"

"If I can't sir, my name ain't Don Newcombe," Grave Digger said.

XVIII

THE OLD STONE apartment house at 2702 Seventh Avenue was heavy with pseudo-Greek trimmings left over from the days when Harlem was a fashionable white neighborhood and the Negro slums were centered around San Juan Hill on West 42nd Street.

Grave Digger pushed open the cracked glass door and searched for the name of Coolie Dunbar among the row of mail boxes nailed to the front hall wall. He found the name on a fly-specked card, followed by the apartment number 3-B.

The automatic elevator, one of the first made, was out of order.

He climbed the dark ancient stairs to the third floor and knocked on the left-hand door at the front.

A middle-aged brown-skinned woman with a worried expression opened the door and said, "Coolie's at work and we've told the people already we'll come in and pay our rent in the office when—"

"I'm not the rent collector, I'm a detective," Grave Digger said, flashing his badge.

"Oh!" The worried expression turned to one of apprehension. "You're Mr. Johnson's partner. I thought you were finished with her."

"Almost. May I talk to her?"

"I don't see why you got to keep on bothering her if you ain't got nothing on Mr. Johnson's daughter," she complained as she guarded the entrance. "They were both in it together."

"I'm not going to arrest her. I would just like to ask her a few questions to clear up the last details."

"She's in bed now."

"I don't mind."

"All right," she consented grudgingly. "Come on in. But if you've got to arrest her, then keep her. Me and Coolie have been disgraced enough by that girl. We're respectable church people—"

"I'm sure of it," he cut her off. "But she's your niece, isn't she?"

"She's Coolie's niece. I haven't got any wild ones in my family."

"You're lucky," he said.

She pursed her lips and opened a door next to the kitchen.

"Here's a policeman to see you, Sissie," she said.

Grave Digger entered the small bedroom and closed the door behind him.

Sissie lay on a narrow single bed with the covers pulled up to her chin. At sight of Grave Digger her red, tear-swollen eyes grew wide with terror.

He drew up the single hard-backed chair and sat down.

"You're a very lucky little girl," he said. "You have just missed being a murderer."

"I don't know what you mean," she said in a terrified whisper.

"Listen," he said. "Don't lie to me. I'm dog-tired and you children have already made me as depressed as I've ever been. You don't know what kind of hell it is sometimes to be a cop."

She watched him like a half-wild kitten poised for flight.

"I didn't kill him. Sheik killed him," she whispered.

"We know Sheik killed him," he said in a flat voice. He looked weary beyond words. "Listen, I'm not here as a cop. I'm here as a friend. Ed Johnson is my closest friend and his daughter is your closest friend. That ought to make us friends too. As a friend I tell you we've got to get rid of the gun."

She hesitated, debating with herself, then said quickly before she could change her mind, "I threw it down a water drain on 128th Street near Fifth Avenue."

He sighed. "That's good enough. What kind of gun was it?"

"It was a thirty-two. It had the picture of an owl's head on the handle and Uncle Coolie called it an Owl's Head."

"Has he missed it?"

"He missed it out of the drawer this morning when he started for work and asked Aunt Cora if she'd moved it. But he ain't said nothing to me yet. He was late for work and I think he wanted to give me all day to put it back."

"Does he need it in his work?"

"Oh no, he works for a garage in the Bronx."

"Good. Does he have a permit for it?"

"No, sir. That's what he's so worried about."

"Okay. Now listen. When he asks you about it tonight, you tell him you took it to protect yourself against Mr. Galen and that during the excitement you left it in Sheik's room. Tell him that I found it there but I don't know to whom it belongs. He won't say any more about it."

"Yes sir. But he's going to be awfully mad."

"Well, Sissie, you can't escape all punishment."

"No, sir."

"Why did you shoot at Mr. Galen anyway? You can tell me now since it doesn't matter."

"It wasn't account of myself," she said. "It was on account of Sugartit—Evelyn Johnson. He was after her all the time and I was afraid he was going to get her. She tries to be wild and does crazy things sometimes and I was afraid he was going to get her and do to her what he did to me. That would ruin her. She ain't an orphan like me with nobody to really care what happens to her; she's from a good family with a father and a mother and a good home and I wasn't going to let him ruin her."

He sat there listening to her, a big, tough lumpy-faced cop, looking as though he might cry.

"How'd you plan to do it?" he asked.

"Oh, I was just going to shoot him. I'd made a date with him at the Inn for me and Sugartit, but I wasn't going to take her. I was going to make him drive me out somewhere in his car by telling him we were going to pick her up; and then I was going to shoot him and run away. I took Uncle Coolie's pistol and hid it downstairs in the hall in a hole in the plaster so

I could get it when I went out. But before time came for me to go, Sugartit came by here. I wasn't expecting her and I couldn't tell her I wanted to go out, so it was late before I could get rid of her. I left her at the subway at 125th Street, thinking she was going home, then I ran all the way over to Lenox to meet Mr. Galen; but when I got over on Lenox I saw all the commotion going on. Then I saw him come running down the street and Sonny chasing him and shooting at him with a gun. It looked like half the people in Harlem were running after him. I got in the crowd and followed and when I caught up with him at 127th Street I saw that Sonny was going to shoot at him again, so I shot at him, too. I don't think anyone even saw me shoot; everybody was looking at Sonny. But when I saw him fall and all the Moslems in their costumes run up and ganged up around him I was scared one of them was going to see me, so I ran around the block and threw the gun in a drain, then came back to Caleb's from the other way and made out like I didn't know what had happened. I didn't know then that Caleb had been shot."

"Have you told anyone else about this?"

"No sir. When I saw Sugartit come sneaking into Caleb's, I was going to tell her I'd shot him because I knew she'd come back looking for him. But Choo-Choo had let it slip out that Sheik was carrying his zip gun, and then after Sonny said his gun wouldn't shoot anything but blanks I knew right away it was Sheik who'd shot him; and I was scared to say anything."

"Good. Now listen to me. Don't tell anybody else. I won't tell anybody either. We'll just keep it to ourselves, our own private secret. Okay?"

"Yes sir. You can bet I won't tell anybody else. I just want to forget it—if I ever can."

"Good. I don't suppose there's any need to tell you to keep away from bad company; you ought to have learned your lesson by now."

"I'm going to do that, I promise."

"Good. Well, Sissie," Grave Digger said, getting slowly to his feet, "you made your bed hard; if it hurts lying on it, don't complain."

* * *

It was visiting hour next day in the Centre Street jail.

Sissie said, "I brought you some cigarettes, Sonny. I didn't know whether you had a girl to bring you any."

"Thanks," Sonny said. "I ain't got no girl."

"How long do you think they'll give you?"

"Six months, I suppose."

"That much. Just for what you did."

"They don't like for people to shoot at anybody, even if you don't hit them, or even if they ain't shooting nothing but blanks like what I did."

"I know," she said sympathetically. "Maybe you're getting off easy at that."

"I ain't complaining," Sonny said.

"What are you going to do when you get out?"

"Go back to shining shoes, I suppose."

"What's going to happen to your shine parlor?"

"Oh, I'll lose that one, but I'll get me another one."

"You got a car?"

"I had one but I couldn't keep up the payments and the man took it back."

"You need a girl to look after you."

"Yeah, who don't? What you going to do yourself, now that your boyfriend's dead?"

"I don't know. I just want to get married."

"That shouldn't be hard for you."

"I don't know anybody who'll have me."

"Why not?"

"I've done a lot of bad things."

"Like what?"

"I'd be ashamed to tell you everything I've done."

"Listen, to show you I ain't scared of nothing you might have done, I want you to be my girl."

"I don't want to play around any more."

"Who's talking about playing around. I'm talking about for keeps."

"I don't mind. But there's something I've got to tell you first. It's about me and Sheik."

"What about you and Sheik?"

"I'm going to have a baby by the time you get out of jail."

"Well, that makes it different," he said. "We'd better get married right away. I'll talk to the man and ask him to see if he can't arrange it."

The Crazy Kill

I

IT WAS FOUR o'clock, Wednesday morning, July 14th, in Harlem, U.S.A. Seventh Avenue was as dark and lonely as haunted graves.

A colored man was stealing a bag of money.

It was a small white canvas bag, the top tied with a cord. It lay on the front seat of a Plymouth sedan that was double-parked on Seventh Avenue, in front of an A&P grocery store in the middle of the block between 131st and 132nd Streets.

The Plymouth belonged to the manager of the A&P store. The bag contained silver money to be used for making change. The curb was lined with big shiny cars, and the manager had double-parked until he'd unlocked the store and put the money in the safe. The manager didn't want to risk walking a block down a Harlem street at that time of morning with a bag of money in his hand.

There was always a colored patrolman on duty in front of the store when the manager arrived. The patrolman stood guard over the cartons and crates of canned goods, groceries and vegetables, which the A&P delivery truck unloaded on the sidewalk, until the manager arrived.

But the manager was a white man. He didn't trust the streets of Harlem, even with a cop on guard.

The manager's distrust was being justified.

As he stood in front of the door, taking the key from his pocket, with the colored cop standing by his side, the thief sneaked along the other side of the parked cars, stuck his long bare black arm through the open window of the Plymouth and noiselessly lifted the bag of silver money.

The manager looked casually over his shoulder at just the in-stant the stooping figure of the thief, creeping along the street, was disappearing behind another parked car.

"Stop, thief!" he shouted, assuming the man was a thief on general principles.

Before the words had got clear of his mouth the thief was high-balling for all he was worth. He was wearing a ragged dark green cotton T-shirt, faded blue jeans and dirt-blackened canvas sneakers, which, along with his color, blended with the black asphalt, making him hard to distinguish.

"Where's he at?" the cop asked.

"There he goes!" a voice said from above.

Both the cop and the manager heard the voice, but neither looked up. They had seen a dark blur turning on a sharp curve into 132nd Street, and both had taken off in pursuit simultaneously.

The voice had come from a man standing in a lighted third-story window, the only lighted window in the block of five- and six-story buildings.

From behind the man's silhouetted figure came the faint sounds of a jam session holding forth in the unseen rooms. The hot licks on a tenor sax kept time with the feet pounding on the sidewalk pavement, and the bass notes from a big piano were echoing the light dry thunder of a kettledrum.

The silhouette shortened as the man leaned farther and farther out the window to watch the chase. What had first appeared to be a tall thin man slowly became a short squat midget. And still the man leaned farther out. When the cop and the store manager turned the corner, the man was leaning so far out his silhouette was less than two feet high. He was leaning out of the window from his waist up.

Slowly his hips leaned out. His buttocks rose into the light like a slow-rolling wave, then dropped below the window ledge as his legs and feet slowly rose into the air. For a long moment the silhouette of two feet sitting upside down on top of two legs was suspended in the yellow lighted rectangle. Then it sank slowly from view, like a body going head-down into water.

The man fell in slow motion, leaning all the way, so that he turned slowly in the air.

He fell past the window underneath, which bore the black-lettered message:

STRAIGHTEN UP AND FLY RIGHT
Anoint the Love Apples
With Father Cupid's Original
ADAM OINTMENT
A Cure For All Love Troubles

To one side of the cartons and crates was a long wicker basket of fresh bread. The large soft spongy loaves, wrapped in wax paper, were stacked side by side like cotton pads.

The man landed at full length on his back exactly on top of the mattress of soft bread. Loaves flew up about him like the splash of freshly packaged waves as his body sank into the warm bed of bread.

Nothing moved. Not even the tepid morning air.

Above, the lighted window was empty. The street was deserted. The thief and his pursuers had disappeared into the Harlem night.

Time passed.

Slowly the surface of the bread began to stir. A loaf rose and dropped over the side of the basket to the sidewalk as though the bread had begun to boil. Another squashed loaf followed.

Slowly, the man began erupting from the basket like a zombie rising from the grave. His head and shoulders came up first. He gripped the edges of the basket, and his torso straightened. He put a leg over the side and felt for the sidewalk with his foot. The sidewalk was still there. He put a little weight on his foot to test the sidewalk. The sidewalk was steady.

He put his other foot over the edge to the sidewalk and stood up.

The first thing he did was to adjust his gold-rimmed spectacles on his nose. Next he felt his pants pockets to see if he'd lost anything. Everything seemed to be there—keys, Bible, knife, handkerchief, wallet and the bottle of herb medicine he took for nervous indigestion.

Then he brushed his clothes vigorously, as though loaves of bread might be sticking to him. After that he took a big swig of his nerve medicine. It tasted bittersweet and strongly alcoholic. He wiped his lips with the back of his hand.

Finally he looked up. The lighted window was still there, but somehow it looked strangely like the pearly gates.

II

DEEP SOUTH WAS shouting in a hoarse bass voice: "*Steal away, daddy-o, steal away to Jesus . . .*"

His meaty black fingers were skipping the light fantastic on the keys of the big grand piano.

Susie Q. was beating out the rhythm on his kettledrum.

Pigmeat was jamming on his tenor sax.

The big luxurious sitting room of the Seventh Avenue apartment was jam-packed with friends and relatives of Big Joe Pullen, mourning his passing.

His black-clad widow, Mamie Pullen, was supervising the serving of refreshments.

Dulcy, the present wife of Big Joe's godson, Johnny Perry, was wandering about, being strictly ornamental, while Alamena, Johnny's former wife, was trying to be helpful.

Doll Baby, a chorus chick who was carrying a torch for Dulcy's brother, Val, was there to see and be seen.

Chink Charlie Dawson, who was carrying a torch for Dulcy herself, shouldn't have been there at all.

The others were grieving out of the kindness of their hearts and the alcohol in their blood, and because grieving was easy in the stifling heat.

Holy Roller church sisters were crying and wailing and daubing at their red-rimmed eyes with black-bordered handkerchiefs.

Dining-car waiters were extolling the virtues of their former chef.

Whorehouse madams were exchanging reminiscences about their former client.

Gambler friends were laying odds that he'd make heaven on his first try.

Ice cubes tinkled in eight-ounce glasses of bourbon whis-key and ginger ale, black rum and Coca Cola, clear gin and tonic water. Everybody was drinking and eating. The food and liquor were free.

The blue-gray air was thick as split-pea soup with tobacco smoke, pungent with the scent of cheap perfume and hothouse lilies, the stink of sweating bodies, the fumes of alcohol, hot fried food and bad breath.

The big bronze-painted coffin lay on a rack against the wall between the piano and the console radio-television-record set. Flowers were banked about a horseshoe wreath of lilies as though about a horse in the winner's circle at the Kentucky Derby.

Mamie Pullen said to Johnny Perry's young wife, "Dulcy, I want to talk to you."

Her usually placid brown face, framed by straightened gray hair pulled into a tight knot atop her head, was heavily seamed with grief and fear.

Dulcy looked resentful. "For Chrissake, Aunt Mamie, can't you let me alone?"

Mamie's tall, thin, work-hardened old body, clad in a black satin Mother Hubbard gown that dragged the floor, stiffened with resolve. She looked as though she had been washed with all waters and had come out still clean.

On sudden impulse, she took Dulcy by the arm, steered her into the bathroom and closed and locked the door.

Doll Baby had been watching them intently from across the room. She moved away from Chink Charlie and pulled Alamena to one side.

"Did you see that?"

"See what?" Alamena asked.

"Mamie took Dulcy into the crapper and locked the door."

Alamena studied her with sudden curiosity.

"What about it?"

"What they go so secretive to talk about?"

"How the hell would I know?"

Doll Baby frowned. It relieved the set stupidity of her expression. She was a brownskin model type, slim, tan and cute. She wore a tight-fitting flaming orange silk dress and was adorned with enough heavy costume jewelry to sink her rapidly to the bottom of the sea. She worked in the chorus line at Small's Paradise Inn, and she looked strictly on the make.

"It looks mighty funny at a time like this," she persisted, then asked slyly, "Will Johnny inherit anything?"

Alamena raised her eyebrows. She wondered if Doll Baby was shooting at Johnny Perry. "Why don't you ask him, sugar?"

"I don't have to. I can find out from Val."

Alamena smiled evilly. "Be careful, girl. Dulcy's damn particular 'bout her brother's women."

"That bitch! She'd better mind her own business. She's so hot after Chink it's a scandal."

"It's likely to be more than that now Big Joe is dead," Alamena said seriously. A shadow passed over her face.

Once she had been the same type as Doll Baby, but ten years had made a difference. She still cut a figure in the deep purple turtle-neck silk jersey dress she was wearing, but her eyes were the eyes of a woman who didn't care any more.

"Val ain't big enough to handle Johnny, and Chink keeps pressing Dulcy as if he ain't going to be satisfied until he gets himself killed."

"That's what I can't see," Doll Baby said in a puzzled tone of voice. "What's he giving such a big performance for? Unless he's just trying to get Johnny's goat?"

Alamena sighed, involuntarily fingering the collar covering her throat.

"Somebody better tell him that Johnny's got a silver plate in his head and it's sitting too heavy on his brain."

"Who can tell that yellow nigger anything?" Doll Baby said. "Look at him now."

They turned and watched the big yellow man push his way through the crowded room to the door as though enraged about something, then go out and slam the door behind him.

"He's gotta make out like he's mad just because Dulcy went into the crapper to talk to Mamie, when all he's really tryin' to do is get the hell away from her before Johnny comes."

"Why don't you go too and take his temperature, sugar," Alamena said maliciously. "You been holding his hand all evening."

"I ain't interested in that whiskey jockey," Doll Baby said.

Chink worked as a bartender in the University Club downtown on East 48th Street. He made good money, ran with the Harlem dandies and could have girls like Doll Baby by the dozen.

"Since when ain't you interested?" Alamena asked sarcastically. "Since he just went out the door?"

"Anyway, I gotta go find Val," Doll Baby said defensively, moving off. She left immediately afterward.

Sitting on the lid of the toilet seat inside of the locked bathroom, Mamie Pullen was saying, "Dulcy, honey, I wish you'd keep away from Chink Charlie. You're making me awfully nervous, child."

Dulcy grimaced at her own reflection in the mirror. She was standing with her thighs pressed against the edge of the washbowl, causing the rose-colored skin-tight dress to crease inside the valley of her round, seductive buttocks.

"I'm trying to, Aunt Mamie," she said, nervously patting her short-cut orange-yellow curls framing the olive-brown complexion of her heart-shaped face. "But you know how Chink is. He keeps putting himself in my face no matter how hard I try to show him I ain't interested."

Mamie grunted skeptically. She didn't approve of the latest Harlem fad of brownskin blondes. Her worried old eyes surveyed Dulcy's flamboyant decor—the rainbow-hued whore-shoes with the four-inch lucite heels; the choker of cultured pink pearls; the diamond-studded watch; the emerald bracelet; the heavy gold charm bracelet; the two diamond rings on her left hand and the ruby ring on her right; the pink pearl earrings shaped like globules of petrified caviar.

Finally she commented, "All I can say is, honey, you ain't dressed for the part."

Dulcy turned angrily, but her hot long-lashed eyes dropped quickly from Mamie's critical stare to Mamie's man-fashioned straight-last shoes protruding from beneath the skirt of Mamie's long black satin dress.

"What's the matter with the way I dress?" she argued belligerently.

"It ain't designed to hide you," Mamie said drily, then, before Dulcy could frame a comment, she asked quickly, "What really happened between Johnny and Chink at Dickie Wells's last Saturday night?"

Dulcy's upper lip began to sweat.

"Just the same old thing. Johnny's so jealous of me sometimes I think he's crazy."

"Why do you egg him on then? Do you just have to switch your ass at every man that passes by?"

Dulcy looked indignant.

"Me and Chink was friends before I even knew Johnny, and I don't see why I can't say hello to him if I want to. Johnny don't take no trouble to ignore his old flames, and Chink never was even that."

"Child, you're not trying to tell all that rumpus come just from you saying hello to Chink."

"You don't have to believe it unless you want to. Me and Val and Johnny was sitting at a ringside table when Chink came by and said, 'Hello, honey, how's the vein holding out?' I laughed. Everybody in Harlem knows that Chink calls Johnny my gold vein, and if Johnny had any sense he'd just laugh, too. But instead of that he jumped up before anybody knew what was happening and pulled his frog-sticker and began shouting about how he was going to teach the mother-raper some respect. So naturally Chink drew his own knife. If it hadn't been for Val and Joe Turner and Big Caesar keeping them apart Johnny would have started chivving on him right there. Didn't nothing really happen though 'cepting they knocked over some tables and chairs. What made it seem like such a big rumpus was some of those hysterical chicks began screaming and carrying on, trying to impress their niggers that they was scared of a little cutting."

She giggled suddenly. Mamie gave a start.

"It ain't nothing to laugh about," Mamie said sternly.

Dulcy's face fell. "I ain't laughing," she said. "I'm scared. Johnny's going to kill him."

Mamie went rigid. Moments passed before she spoke. Her voice was hushed from fear.

"Did he tell you that?"

"He ain't had to. But I know it. I can feel it."

Mamie stood up and put her arm about Dulcy. Both of them were trembling.

"We got to stop him somehow, child."

Dulcy twisted about to face the mirror again, as though seeking courage from her looks. She opened her pink straw handbag and began repairing her make-up. Her hand trembled as she painted her mouth.

"I don't know how to stop him," she said when she'd finished. "Without my dropping dead."

Mamie took her arm from about Dulcy's waist and wrung her hands involuntarily.

"Lord, I wish Val would hurry up and get here."

Dulcy glanced at her wrist watch.

"It's already four-twenty-five. Johnny ought to be here now himself." After a moment she added, "I don't know what's keeping Val."

III

SOMEONE BEGAN hammering loudly on the door.

The sound was scarcely heard above the din inside the room.

"*Open the door!*" a voice screamed.

It was so loud that even Dulcy and Mamie heard it through the locked bathroom door.

"Wonder who that can be," Mamie said.

"It sure ain't neither Johnny or Val making all that fuss," Dulcy replied.

"Probably some drunk."

One of the drunks already on the inside said in a minstrel man's voice, "Open de do', Richard."

That was the title of a popular song in Harlem that had orig-inated with two blackface comedians on the Apollo Theatre stage doing a skit about a colored brother coming home drunk and trying to get Richard to let him into the house.

The other drunks on the inside laughed.

Alamena had just stepped into the kitchen. "See who's at the door," she said to Baby Sis.

Baby Sis looked up from her chore of washing dishes and said sulkily, "All these drunks make me sick."

Alamena froze. Baby Sis was just a girl whom Mamie had taken in to help about the house, and had no right to criticize the guests.

"Girl, you're getting beside yourself," she said. "You'd better mind how you talk. Go open the door and then get this mess cleaned up in here."

Baby Sis looked sidewise about the disordered kitchen, her slant eyes looking evil in her greasy black face.

The table, sink, sidestands and most of the available floor space were strewn with empty and half-filled bottles—gin, whiskey and rum bottles, pop bottles, condiment bottles; pots, pans and platters of food, a dishpan containing leftover potato salad, deep iron pots with soggy pieces of fried chicken, fried fish, fried pork chops; baking pans with mashed and mangled biscuits, pie pans with single slices of runny pies; a washtub containing bits of ice floating about in trashy water; slices of cake and spongy white-bread sandwiches, half eaten, lying everywhere—on the tables, sink and floor.

"Ain't never gonna get this mess cleaned up nohow," she complained.

"Git, girl," Alamena said harshly.

Baby Sis shoved her way through the mob of crying drunks in the packed sitting room.

"Somebody open this door!" the voice yelled desperately from outside.

"I'm coming!" Baby Sis shouted from inside. "Keep your pants on."

"Hurry up then!" the voice shouted back.

"Baby, it's cold outside," one of the drunks inside cracked.

Baby Sis stopped in front of the locked door and shouted,

"Who is you who been beating on this door like you tryna bust it down?"

"I'm Reverend Short," the voice replied.

"I'm the Queen of Sheba," Baby Sis said, doubling over laughing and beating her big strong thighs. She turned to the guests to let them share the joke. "He say he's Reverend Short."

Several of the guests laughed as though they were stone, raving crazy.

Baby Sis turned around toward the closed door again and shouted, "Try again, Buster, and don't tell me you is Saint Peter coming for Big Joe."

The three musicians kept riffing away in dead-pan trances, their fixed eyes staring from petrified faces into the Promised Land across the river Jordan.

"I tell you I am Reverend Short," the voice said.

Baby Sis's laughing expression went abruptly evil and malevolent.

"You want to know how I know you ain't Reverend Short?"

"That's exactly what I would like to know," the voice said exasperatedly.

"Cause Reverend Short is already inside of here," Baby Sis replied triumphantly. "And you can't be Reverend Short, 'cause you is out there."

"Merciful God in heaven," the voice said moaningly. "Give me patience."

But instead of being patient, the hammering commenced again.

Mamie Pullen unlocked the bathroom door and stuck out her head.

"What's happening out there?" she asked, then, seeing Baby Sis standing before the door, she called, "Who's that at the door?"

"Some drunk what claim's he's Reverend Short," Baby Sis replied.

"I'm Reverend Short!" the voice outside screamed.

"It can't be Reverend Short," Baby Sis argued.

"What's the matter with you, girl, you drunk?" Mamie said angrily, advancing across the room.

From the kitchen doorway Alamena said, "It's probably Johnny, pulling one of his gags."

Mamie reached the door, pushed Baby Sis aside and flung it inward.

Reverent Short stepped across the threshold, tottering as though barely able to stand. His parchment-colored bony face was knotted with an expression of extreme outrage, and his reddish eyes glinted furiously behind the polished, gold-rimmed spectacles.

"Hush my mouth!" Baby Sis exclaimed in an awed voice, her black greasy face graying and her bulging eyes whitening as though she'd seen a ghost. "It is Reverend Short."

Reverend Short's thin, black-clad body shook with fury like a sapling in a gale.

"I told you I was Reverend Short," he sputtered.

He had a mouth shaped like that of a catfish, and when he talked he sprayed spit over Dulcy, who had come over to stand with her arm about Mamie's shoulder.

She drew back angrily and wiped her face with the tiny black silk handkerchief that she held in her hand and that represented her dress of mourning.

"Quit spitting on me," she said harshly.

"He didn't mean to spit on you, honey," Mamie said soothingly.

"*Po' sinner stands a-trembling . . .*" Deep South shouted.

Reverend Short's body twitched convulsively, as though he were having a fit. Everyone stared at him curiously.

"*. . . stands a-trembling, Daddy Joe,*" Susie Q. echoed.

"Mamie Pullen, if you don't stop those devils from jamming that sweet old spiritual, *Steal Away*, I swear before God I won't preach Big Joe's funeral," Reverend Short threatened in a rage-croaking voice.

"They're just trying to show their gratitude." Mamie shouted to make herself heard. "It was Big Joe who started them on their way to fame when they was just hustling tips in Eddy Price's joint, and now they're just trying to send him on his way to heaven."

"That ain't no way to send a body to heaven," he said

hoarsely, his voice giving out from shouting. "They're making enough noise to wake up the dead who're already there."

"Oh, all right, I'll stop 'em," Mamie said, and went over and put her black wrinkled hand on Deep South's dripping wet shoulder. "That's been fine, boys, but you can rest a while now."

The music stopped so suddenly it caught Dulcy whispering angrily—"Why do you let that store-front preacher run your business, Aunt Mamie—" in a sudden pool of silence.

Reverent Short turned a look on her that glinted with malevolence.

"You'd better dust off your own skirts before criticizing me, Sister Perry," he croaked.

The silence became weighted.

Baby Sis chose that moment to say in a loud drunken voice, "What I want to know, Reverend Short, is how in the world did you get outside that door?"

The tension broke. Everyone laughed.

"I was pushed out of the bedroom window," Reverend Short said in a voice that was sticky with evil.

Baby Sis doubled over, started to laugh, caught sight of Reverend Short's face and chopped it off in the middle of the first guffaw.

The others who had started to laugh stopped abruptly. Dead silence dropped like a shroud over the revelry. The guests stared at the Reverend Short in pop-eyed wonder. Their faces wanted to continue laughing, but their minds pulled the reins. On the one hand, the expression of suppressed vindictiveness on Reverend Short's face could easily be that of a man who'd been pushed out of a window. But on the other hand, his body didn't show the effects of a three-story fall to the concrete sidewalk.

"Chink Charlie did it," Reverend Short croaked.

Mamie gasped. "What!"

"You kidding or joking?" Alamena said harshly.

Baby Sis was the first to recover. She laughed experimentally and gave Reverend Short an appreciative push.

"You takes the cake, Reverend," she said.

Reverend Short clutched her arm to keep from falling.

She grinned the imbecilic admiration of one practical joker for another.

Mamie turned in a squall of fury and slapped her face.

"You get yourself right straight back to that kitchen," she said sternly. "And don't you dast drink another drop of likker tonight."

Baby Sis's face puckered up like a dried prune and she began blubbering. She was a big strong-bodied mule-like young woman, and crying gave her an expression of pure idiocy. She turned to run back to the kitchen but stumbled over a foot and fell drunkenly to the floor. No one paid her any attention because, with her support withdrawn, Reverend Short began to fall.

Mamie clutched him by the arm and helped him into an armchair. "You just set right there, Reverend, and tell me what happened," she said.

He clutched his left side as though in great pain and croaked in a breathless voice, "I went into the bedroom to get a breath of fresh air, and while I was standing in the window watching a policeman chasing a thief, Chink Charlie sneaked up behind me and pushed me out of the window."

"My God!" Mamie exclaimed. "Then he was trying to kill you."

"Of course he was."

Alamena looked down at the twitching bony face of Reverend Short and said in a reassuring tone, "Mamie, he's just drunk."

"I'm not the least bit drunk," he denied. "I've never drunk a drop of intoxicating liquor in my life."

"Where's Chink?" Mamie asked, looking about. "Chink!" she called. "Somebody get Chink in here."

"He's gone," Alamena said. "He left while you and Dulcy were in the crapper."

"Your preacher's just making that up, Aunt Mamie," Dulcy said. "Just 'cause him and Chink had an argument 'bout the guests you got here."

Mamie looked from her to Reverend Short. "What's wrong with 'em?"

She intended the question for Reverend Short, but Dulcy answered. "He said there shouldn't be nobody here but church members and Big Joe's lodge brothers, and Chink told him he was forgetting that Big Joe was a gambler himself."

"I'm not saying that Big Joe didn't sin," Reverend Short said in his loud pulpit voice, forgetting for the moment he was an invalid. "But Big Joe was a dining-car cook on the Pennsylvania Railroad for more than twenty years, and he was a member of the First Holy Roller Church of Harlem, and that's how God sees him."

"But these folks here is all his friends," Mamie protested with a look of bewilderment. "Folks who worked with him and saw him all the time."

Reverend Short pursed his lips. "That ain't the point. You can't surround his poor soul with all manner of sin and adultery and expect God to take it to his bosom."

"Jus' what do you mean by that?" Dulcy challenged hotly.

"Let him alone," Mamie said. "Everything has done gone bad enough without all this argument."

"If he don't stop picking at me with his dirty hints all the time I'm gonna have Johnny whip his ass," Dulcy said in a low grating voice intended only for Mamie, but everyone heard her.

Reverend Short gave her a look of triumphant malevolence.

"Threaten all you want, you Jezebel, but you can't hide it from the Lord that it was your own devilishness that drove Joe Pullen to an early death."

"That just ain't so," Mamie Pullen contradicted. "It was just his time. He's been taking naps like that, with his cigar in his mouth, for years, and it was just his time that he happened to swallow it and choke to death."

"If you want to put up with this chicken-season preacher's lying, you can," Dulcy said to Mamie. "But I'm going home, and you can just tell Johnny why when he gets here."

Silence followed her as she turned and walked from the apartment. She slammed the door behind her.

Mamie sighed. "Lord, I wish Val was here."

"This house is full of murderers!" Reverend Short exclaimed.

"You shouldn't say that just because you've got a grudge against Chink Charlie," Mamie said.

"For Christ's sake, Mamie!" Alamena exploded. "If he'd fallen from your bedroom window he'd be lying out there on the sidewalk dead."

Reverend Short stared at her through glazed eyes. A white froth had collected in the corners of his mouth.

"I see a terrible vision," he muttered.

"That ain't no lie," Alamena said disgustedly. "All you is seeing is visions."

"I see a dead man stabbed in the heart," he said.

"Let me fix you a toddy and put you to bed," Mamie said soothingly. "And, Alamena—"

"He don't need no more to drink," Alamena cut her off.

"For Jesus Christ's sake, Alamena, stop it. Go phone Doctor Ramsey and tell him to come over here."

"He's not sick," Alamena said.

"I didn't say I was sick," Reverend Short said.

"He's just trying to stir up trouble for some reason."

"I'm hurt," Reverend Short stated. "You'd be hurt, too, if somebody had pushed you out of a window."

Mamie took Alamena by the arm and tried to pull her away. "Go now and telephone the doctor."

But Alamena pulled back. "Listen, Mamie Pullen, for God's sake be your age. If he fell out of that window it's a cinch he couldn't have walked back upstairs. I suppose he's going to tell you next that he fell into the lap of God."

"I fell into a basket of bread," Reverend Short declared.

At last the guests laughed with relief. Now they knew the good reverend was joking. Even Mamie couldn't restrain herself.

"See what I mean?" Alamena said.

"Reverend Short, shame on you, pulling our leg like that," Mamie said indulgently.

"If you don't believe me, go look at the bread," Reverend Short challenged.

"What bread?"

"The basket of bread I fell into. It's on the sidewalk in front of the A&P store. God put it there to break my fall."

Mamie and Alamena exchanged glances.

"I'll go look, you go call the doctor," Mamie said.

"I want to look, too."

Everybody wanted to look.

Sighing loudly, as though indulging the whims of a lunatic against her better judgement, Mamie led the way.

The bedroom door was closed. When she opened it, she exclaimed, "Why, the light's on!"

With growing trepidation she crossed the lighted bedroom and leaned out of the open window. Alamena leaned out beside her. The others squeezed into the medium-sized room. As many as could peered over the two women's shoulders.

"Is it there?" someone in back asked.

"Does they see it?"

"There's a basket of some kind, sure enough," Alamena said.

"But it don't look like it's no bread in it," the man peering over her shoulder said.

"It don't even look like a bread basket," Mamie said, trying to penetrate the early morning shadows with her near-sighted gaze. "It looks like one of them wicker baskets they take away dead bodies in."

By then Alamena's sharp vision had become accustomed to the dark.

"It's a bread basket, all right. But there's a man already lying in it."

"A drunk," Mamie said in a voice of relief. "No doubt that's what Reverend Short saw that gave him the idea of fooling us."

"He don't look drunk to me," said the man who was leaning over her shoulder. "He's lying too straight, and drunks always lay crooked."

"My God!" Alamena exclaimed in a fear-stricken voice. "He's got a knife sticking in him."

Mamie let out a long moaning keen. "Lord, protect us, can you see his face, child? I'm getting so old I can't see a lick. Is it Chink?"

Alamena put her arm about Mamie's waist and slowly pulled her from the window.

"No, it ain't Chink," she said. "It looks to me like Val."

IV

EVERYONE RUSHED TOWARD the outside door to be the first downstairs. But before Mamie and Alamena could get out the telephone began to ring.

"Who in the hell could that be at this hour?" Alamena said roughly.

"You go ahead, I'll answer it," Mamie said.

Alamena went on without replying.

Mamie went back into the bedroom and lifted the receiver of the telephone on the nightstand beside the bed.

"Hello."

"Are you Mrs. Pullen?" a muffled voice asked. It was so blurred she could scarcely distinguish the words.

"Yes."

"There's a dead man out in front of your house."

She could have sworn the voice held a note of laughter.

"Who are you?" she asked suspiciously.

"I ain't nobody."

"It ain't so goddam funny that you got to make a joke about it," she said roughly.

"I ain't joking. If you don't believe me, go to the window and take a look."

"Why the hell didn't you call the police?"

"I reckoned that maybe you wouldn't want them to know."

Suddenly the whole conversation stopped making sense to Mamie. She tried to collect her thoughts, but she was so tired her head buzzed. And all this monkey business of Reverend Short's, and then Val's getting stabbed to death with Big Joe lying dead there in the coffin, left her feeling as though she had stepped off the edge of sanity.

"Why the hell wouldn't I want the police to know?" she asked savagely.

"Because he came from your apartment."

"How do you know he came from my apartment? I ain't seen him in my house tonight."

"I did. I saw him fall out of your window."

"What? Oh, you're talking about Reverend Short. And you sure enough seen him fall?"

"That's what I'm telling you. And he's lying down on the sidewalk in the A&P bread basket, dead as all hell."

"That ain't Reverend Short. He didn't even get hurt. He come back upstairs."

The voice didn't say anything, so she went on. "It's Val. Valentine Haines. And he was stabbed to death."

She waited for an answer, but the voice still didn't speak.

"Hello," she said. "Hello! You still there! You're so goddam smart how come you didn't see that?"

She heard a very soft click.

"The bastard hung up," she mumbled to herself, then added, "Now if that ain't almighty strange—"

She stood still for a moment, trying to think, but her mind wouldn't work. Then she crossed to the dressing table and picked up a can of snuff. Using a cotton dauber, she dipped a lipful, leaving the dauber in the pocket of her lip with the stick protruding. It quieted her growing sense of panic. Out of respect for her guests, she hadn't taken a dip all night, and as a rule she lived with a dip in her lip.

"Lord, if Big Joe was alive, he'd know what to do," she said to herself as she went with slow, dragging steps back into the sitting room.

It was littered with dirty glasses and plates containing scraps of food, ashtrays overflowing with smoldering cigarette and cigar butts. The maroon-carpeted floor was a mess. Burning cigarettes had left holes in the upholstery, burned scars on the tabletops. The ashy skeleton of a cigarette lay intact atop the grand piano. There was a resemblance to a fairground after a circus has gone, and the smell of death and lilies of the valley and man-made stink was overpowering in the hot, close room.

Mamie dragged herself across the room and looked down into the bronze-painted coffin at the body of her late husband.

Big Joe was dressed in a cream-colored Palm Beach suit, pale green crepe de Chine shirt, brown silk tie with hand-painted angels held in place by a diamond horse-shoe stickpin. His big square dark-brown face was clean-shaven, with deep creases encircling the wide mouth. It looked freshly massaged. His eyes were closed. His stiff gray kinky hair had been cut short after death and had been painstakingly combed and brushed. She had done it herself, and she had dressed him, too. His hands were folded across his chest, exhibiting a diamond ring on his left hand and his lodge signet ring on his right.

She removed all of the jewelry and put it down into the deep front pocket of her long black satin Mother Hubbard dress that swept the floor. Then she closed the coffin.

"One hell of a wake this turned out to be," she said.

"He's dead," Reverend Short said suddenly in his new croaking voice.

Mamie gave a start. She hadn't seen Reverend Short.

He sat slouched on the end of his spine in an overstuffed armchair, staring with a fixed expression toward the opposite wall.

"What the hell do you think," she said roughly. All her social affections had left since the discovery of Val's body. "You think I'd bury him if he was alive?"

"I saw it happen," Reverend Short continued as though she hadn't spoken.

She stared at him in perplexity. "Oh, you mean Val."

"A woman filled with the sin of lust and adultery came from the pit of hell and stabbed him in the heart."

His words sunk slowly into Mamie's clogged thoughts.

"A woman?"

"*And I gave her space to repent of her fornication, and she repented not.*"

"You saw her do it?"

"*For her sins have reached unto heaven, and God hath remembered her iniquities.*"

Mamie saw the room tilt.

"May the Lord have mercy," she said.

She saw Big Joe in his coffin, the grand piano and the

console radio-television set begin a slow ascent toward heaven. Then the dark maroon carpet rose slowly until it spread out before her eyes like a sea of dark, congealed blood into which she buried her face.

"Sin and lust and abomination in the sight of the Lord," Reverend Short croaked, then added in a small dry whisper, "She ain't nothing but a whore, O Lord."

V

THE AUTOMATIC ELEVATOR was on the ground floor, and most of the curious mourners chose to run down the stairs rather than wait for it. But they were not the first to arrive.

Dulcy and Chink stood facing each other across the basket of bread containing the body. He was a big yellow man, young but going to fat, dressed in a beige summer suit. He leaned over tensely.

The first to approach heard Dulcy exclaiming, "Jesus Christ, you didn't have to kill him!" and Chink replying in a voice choked with sudden passion, "Not even for you—" Then he broke off and cautioned in a tense whisper, speaking between set lips, "Shut up and play it dumb."

She didn't speak again until all the mourners from the wake had gathered and had their look and said their say.

"It's Val, and he's dead all right."

"If he ain't, Saint Peter's going to be mighty surprised."

Alamena had wormed close enough to get a clear view of the body. She heard a dining-car waiter say, "You reckon he was stabbed where he's at?"

A voice behind her replied, "Must have been—there ain't no blood nowhere else."

The body lay at full length on the mattress of soft wrapped loaves of bread as though the basket had been fitted to its measure. The left hand, exhibiting the band of a single gold ring, lay palm upward across a heavy, black silk knitted tie knotted about the collar of a soft sand-colored linen silk shirt; the right hand lay palm downward across the center button of the jacket of an olive drab sheen gabardine suit. The feet pointed straight up, exposing the slightly worn crepe-rubber soles of lightweight Cordovan English-made shoes.

The knife protruded from the jacket just beneath the breast pocket, which was adorned with a quarter-inch stripe of white handkerchief. It was a stag-handle knife with a push-button opener and handguard, such as used by hunters to skin game.

Blood made irregular patterns over the jacket, shirt and tie. Splotches were on the waxed-paper wrappings of the loaves of bread, and on one side of the woven rattan basket. There was none on the sidewalk.

The face was set in a fixed expression of utter disbelief; the eyes, widened into protruding white-rimmed balls, stared fixedly at some point above and beyond the feet.

It was a handsome face, with smooth brown skin and features bearing a close resemblance to Dulcy's. The head was bare, revealing curly black hair, thickly plastered with pomade.

An odd moment of silence followed the last speaker's statement as the fact sunk in that the murder had been committed on the spot.

Dulcy said into the silence, "He looks so surprised."

"You'd look surprised, too, if someone stuck a knife in your heart," Alamena said grimly.

With a startling abruptness, Dulcy became hysterical.

"Val!" she screamed. "I'll get him, Val, sugar, oh God—"

She would have thrown herself atop Val's body, but Alamena quickly wrenched her away, and several of the mourners closed in and held her.

She struggled furiously and screamed, "Turn me loose, you mother-rapers! He's my brother and some mother-raper's going to pay—"

"For Jesus sake, shut up!" Alamena shouted.

Chink stared at her, his big yellow face distorted with rage. She shut up and got herself under control.

A colored patrolman came from the doorway of the adjoining building. When he saw the crowd he drew himself up and began adjusting his uniform.

"What's happened here?" he asked in a loud self-conscious voice. "Somebody get hurt?"

"You can call it that," someone replied.

The patrolman pushed in close and looked down at the body. The collar of his blue uniform was open, and he smelled like sweat.

"Who stabbed him?" he asked.

Pigmeat replied in a high falsetto voice, "Don't you wish you knew."

The patrolman blinked his eyes, then suddenly grinned, showing rows of big yellow teeth.

"What minstrel you with, sonny-o?"

Everyone stared at him, waiting to see what he would do. Their faces took dark shape in the graying light of dawn.

He stood there grinning, doing nothing. He didn't know what to do, but he wasn't perturbed by it.

The distant sound of a siren floated in the humid air. The crowd began to scatter.

"Don't nobody leave the scene," the patrolman ordered.

The red eye of a patrol car came north up Seventh Avenue. The patrol car made a screaming U-turn around the park dividing the traffic lanes and dragged to a stop, double-parking beside the cars at the curb. Another red eye was coming south down the dark street in a screaming fury. A third turned the corner of 132nd Street, almost colliding with it. A fourth turned in from 129th Street and screamed north on the wrong side of the avenue.

The white precinct sergeant arrived in the fifth patrol car.

"Keep everybody here," he ordered in a loud voice.

By then half-clad people were hanging from every front window in the block, and others began collecting in the street.

The sergeant noticed a white man clad in a short-sleeved white sport shirt and khaki trousers standing apart, and asked him, "Do you work in this A&P store?"

"I'm the manager."

"Open it up. We're going to put these suspects inside."

"I object," the white man said. "I've been robbed once

tonight by a shine, right under my eyes, and the cop hasn't even caught the thief."

The sergeant looked at the colored cop.

"It was his buddy," the A&P manager said.

"Where is he now?" the sergeant asked.

"How in the hell do I know?" the store manager replied. "I had to leave and come back to open the store."

"Well, go ahead and open it," the colored cop said.

"I'll be responsible if anything is stolen," the sergeant said.

The manager went to unlock the door without replying.

An inconspicuous black sedan pulled to the curb and parked at the end of the block unnoticed, and two tall, lanky colored men dressed in black mohair suits that looked as though they'd been slept in got out and walked back toward the scene. Their wrinkled coats bulged beneath their left shoulders. The shiny straps of their shoulder holsters showed across the fronts of their blue cotton shirts.

The one with the burnt face went to the far side of the crowd; the other remained on the near side.

Suddenly a loud voice shouted, "Straighten up!"

An equally loud voice echoed, "Count off!"

"Detectives Grave Digger Jones and Coffin Ed Johnson reporting for duty, General," Pigmeat muttered.

"Jesus Christ!" Chink fumed. "Now we've got those damned Wild West gunmen here to mess up everything."

The sergeant said, winking at a white cop, "Herd 'em into the store, Jones, you and Johnson. You fellows know how to handle 'em."

Grave Digger gave him a hard look. "They all look alike to us, Commissioner—white, blue, black and merino." Then turning to the crowd he shouted, "Inside, cousins."

"They're going to hold prayer meeting," Coffin Ed said.

As the cops were closing the door on the corralled suspects, a big cream-colored, made-to-order Cadillac convertible with the top down stopped in the street, double-parking behind the row of patrol cars.

A small white-faced playing card was embossed on each door. In the corners of each card were an inlaid spade, heart, diamond and club. Each door was the size of a barn gate.

One of the doors swung open. A man got out. He was a big man but, standing, his six-foot height lost impressiveness in his slanting shoulders and long arms. He was wearing a powder blue suit of shantung silk; a pale yellow crepe silk shirt; a hand-painted tie depicting an orange sun rising on a dark blue morning; highly glossed light tan rubber-soled shoes; a miniature ten-of-hearts tie pin with opal hearts; three rings, including a heavy gold signet ring of his lodge, a yellow diamond set in a heavy gold band and a big mottled stone of a nameless variety, also set in a heavy gold band. His cuff links were heavy gold squares with diamond eyes. It wasn't from vanity he wore so much gold. He was a gambler, and it was his bank account in any emergency.

He was bareheaded. His kinky hair, powdered with gray, was cut as short as a three-days' growth of whiskers, with a part shaved on one side. In the dim light of morning his big-featured, knotty face showed it had taken its lumps. In the center of his forehead was a puffed, bluish scar with ridges pronging off like immobilized octopus tentacles. It gave him an expression of perpetual rage, which was accentuated by the smoldering fire that lay always just beneath the surface of his muddy brown eyes, ready to flame into a blaze.

He looked hard, strong, tough and unafraid.

"Johnny Perry!"

The name came involuntarily to the lips of everyone who lived in Harlem. "He's the greatest," they said.

Dulcy waved to him from inside the store.

He walked toward the cops who were congregated about the door. His step was springy, and he walked on the balls of his feet like a prize fighter. A wave of nervous motion stirred among the cops.

"What's the rumble?" he asked the sergeant.

For an instant no one spoke.

Then the sergeant said, nodding toward the bread basket on the sidewalk, "Man's been killed," as though the words had been forced from him by the quick hot flame that began to flicker in Johnny's eyes.

Johnny turned his head to look, then walked over and stared down at Val's body. He stood as though frozen for almost a minute. When he walked back his dark face had taken on a deep purple tint, and the tentacles of the scar on his forehead seemed to have come alive. His eyes had the hot steamy glow of water-logged wood beginning to burn.

But his voice had the same slow, deep, gambler's pitch that never changed.

"Do you know who stuck him?"

The sergeant gave him back look for look. "Not yet. Do you?"

Johnny put his left hand forward, fingers stiff and splayed, then drew it in and stuck it into his coat pocket, the same as his other hand. He did not reply.

Dulcy had wormed between the displays close enough to the plate-glass to rap on it.

Johnny threw her a look, then said to the sergeant, "You got my old lady in there. Let her out."

"She's a suspect," the sergeant said tonelessly.

"It's her brother," Johnny said.

"You can see her at the station. The wagons will be here soon," the sergeant replied indifferently.

The flames leaped up in Johnny's muddy eyes.

"Let her out," Grave Digger said. "He'll bring her in."

"Who in the God-damned hell's going to bring him in?" the sergeant raved.

"We'll bring him in," Grave Digger said. "Me and Ed."

The first of the wagons turned the corner into Seventh Avenue. The sergeant opened the door and said, "All right, let's start getting them out."

Dulcy was the third in line. She had to wait until the cops shook down the two men in front of her. One of the cops asked her to hand over her pocketbook, but she ran past him and flew into Johnny's arms.

"Oh Johnny," she sobbed, staining the front of his powder blue silk suit with lipstick, mascara and tears as she buried her face in his chest.

He embraced her with a tenderness that seemed startling in a man of his appearance.

"Don't cry, baby," he said in his changeless voice, "I'll get the mother-raper."

"You'd better get into the wagon," a white patrol cop said, approaching Dulcy. Grave Digger gestured him back.

Johnny escorted Dulcy toward his parked Cadillac convertible as though she were an invalid.

When Alamena came out, she stepped from line, walked quickly to the Cadillac and got in beside Dulcy.

No one said anything to her.

Johnny started the motor, but was held up for a moment by a car from the coroner's office that had stopped in front of him. The assistant coroner got out with his black bag and walked toward the body. Two cops came from the apartment entrance with Mamie Pullen and Reverend Short.

"Over here," Alamena called.

"Thank God," Mamie said. She made her way slowly between the parked cars and climbed into the back seat.

"There's room for you too, Reverend Short," Alamena called.

"I'll not ride with a murderer," he replied in his croaking voice, and went tottering toward the second of the wagons that had just pulled up.

The eyes of every cop went quickly from his face toward the occupants of the cream-colored Cadillac.

"Take your curse off me!" Dulcy screamed, becoming hysterical again.

"Shut up!" Alamena said harshly.

Johnny shifted into drive without looking around, and the big shiny car moved slowly off. The small black battered sedan bearing Coffin Ed and Grave Digger followed close behind.

VI

THE PRELIMINARY QUESTIONING was made by another sergeant, Detective Sergeant Brody from downtown Homicide, with the precinct detectives, Grave Digger Jones and Coffin Ed Johnson, assisting.

The questioning was conducted in a soundproof room without windows on the first floor. This room was known to the Harlem underworld as the "Pigeon Nest." It was said that no matter how tough an egg was, if they kept him in there long enough he would hatch out a pigeon.

The room was lit by the hot bright glare of a three-hundred-watt spotlight focused on a low wooden stool bolted to the boards in the center of the bare wooden floor. The seat of the stool was shiny from the squirming of countless suspects who had sat on it.

Sergeant Brody sat with his elbows propped atop a big battered flat-topped desk that stood along the inner wall beside the door. The desk was beyond the edge of shadow that screened the interrogator from the suspects sizzling in the glaring light.

At one end of the desk, a police reporter sat in a straight-backed chair with his notebook on the desk in front of him.

Coffin Ed made a tall indistinct shadow in the corner behind.

Grave Digger stood at the other end of the desk, his foot propped on the one remaining chair. Both had kept on their hats.

The principals—Val's friends and intimates, Johnny and Dulcy Perry, Mamie Pullen, Reverend Short and Chink Charlie—were being held upstairs in the detective bureau for the last.

The others had been herded into the bull pen downstairs and were brought out four at a time and lined abreast in the circle of light.

The sight of the corpse and the subsequent ride in the wagon had sobered them too suddenly. They were sweaty and evil, men and women alike, their haggard, vari-colored faces looking like African war masks in the dead white light.

After their names, addresses and occupations had been taken, Sergeant Brody asked them routine questions in a passionless copper's voice:

"Were there any arguments at the wake? Fights? Did any of you hear anyone mention Valentine Haines's name? Did any of you see Chink Charlie Dawson leave the room? What time? Was he alone? Did Doll Baby leave with him? Before? After?

"Did any of you see Reverend Short leave the house? Leave the sitting room? Go into the bedroom? Did you notice whether the bedroom door was open or closed most of the evening? How much time elapsed between the time he disappeared until his return?

"Did any of you notice Dulcy Perry leave the house? Before or after Reverend Short returned?

"How much time elapsed between Reverend Short's return and when all of you went to the window to look for the bread basket? Five minutes? More? Less? Did anyone else leave during that time? Do any of you know if Val had any enemies? Anyone who might have had a grudge against him? Was he in any kind of trouble?"

There were seven men in the pickup who hadn't been at the wake. Brody asked if they'd seen anyone fall from the third-story-front window; if they'd seen anyone passing along the street, walking or in a car. None admitted seeing anything. All swore that they'd been inside of their homes, in bed, and had gone out on the street after the patrol cars arrived.

"Did any of you hear anyone cry out?" Brody asked. "Hear the sound of a car passing? Any strange sound of any kind?"

His questions all drew negatives.

"All right, all right," he growled. "All of you were in bed, sleeping the sleep of the righteous, dreaming about the angels in heaven—you didn't see anything, didn't hear anything, and you don't know anything. All right . . ."

All were asked to identify the murder knife, which Brody exhibited to each group. None did.

In between the questions and the answers, the stylo of the police reporter was heard scratching on sheet after sheet of foolscap paper.

The contents of each person's pockets had been dumped on top of the desk as each group was ushered in. The sergeant examined only the knives. When the blades exceeded the two inches allowed by law, he inserted them into the crevice between the top of the center drawer and the desk top and broke them with a slight downward pressure. As time went on broken blades piled up inside the drawer.

When he'd finished with the last group, Brody looked at his watch.

"Two hours and seventeen minutes," he said. "And all I've learned so far is that the folks here in Harlem are so respectable their fingers don't stink."

"What did you expect?" Coffin Ed asked. "For somebody to say they did it?"

"Do you want me to read the transcript?" the police reporter asked.

"Hell no. The coroner's report says the victim was killed where he lay. But nobody saw him arrive. Nobody remembers exactly when Chink Charlie left the flat. Nobody knows when Dulcy Perry left. Nobody knows for certain whether Reverend Short even fell out of the God-damned window. Do you believe that, Digger?"

"Why not? This is Harlem, where anything can happen."

"We people here in Harlem will believe anything," Coffin Ed said.

"You're not trying to pull my leg, are you, pal?" Brody said dryly.

"I'm just trying to tell you that these people are not so simple as you think," Coffin Ed replied. "You're trying to find the murderer. All right, I'll believe anybody did it if we get enough proof."

"Okay, fine," Brody said. "Bring in Mamie Pullen."

When Grave Digger escorted Mamie into the room, he placed the chair he'd been using for a footrest in a comfortable position so she could lean an arm on the desk if she wished, then went over and adjusted the light so it wouldn't bother her.

Sergeant Brody's first glance had taken in the black satin dress with its skirt that dragged the floor, reminiscent of the rigid uniform of whorehouse madams in the 1920's. He'd gotten a peep at the toes of the men's straight-last shoes protruding from beneath. His gaze remained longer on the two-carat diamond in the platinum band encircling her gnarled brown ring finger, and rested for an appreciable time on the white jade necklace that dropped to her waist like a greatly cherished rosary with a black onyx cross attached to the end. Then he looked at the old brown face, lined with grief and worry, sagging in loose folds beneath the tight knot of short, straightened, gray-streaked hair.

"This is Sergeant Brody, Aunt Mamie," Grave Digger said. "He must ask you a few questions."

"How do you do, Mr. Brody," she said, sticking her gnarled unadorned right hand across the desk.

"It's a bad business, Mrs. Pullen," the sergeant said, shaking her hand.

"It looks like one death always calls for another," she said. "Been that way ever since I could remember. One person dies and then there ain't no end. I guess that's the way God planned it."

Then she looked up to see the face of the cop who had been so gentle with her, and exclaimed, "Lord bless my soul, you're little Digger Jones. I've known you ever since you were a little shavetail kid on 116th Street. I didn't know you were the one they called Grave Digger."

Grave Digger grinned sheepishly, like a little boy caught stealing apples.

"I've grown up now, Aunt Mamie."

"Doesn't time fly. As Big Joe always used to say; *Tempers fugits*. You must be all of thirty-five years old now."

"Thirty-six. And here's Eddy Johnson, too. He's my partner."

Coffin Ed stepped forward into the light. Mamie was stunned at sight of his face.

"God in heaven!" she exclaimed involuntarily. "What hap—" then caught herself.

"A hoodlum threw a glass of acid in my face." He shrugged. "Occupational hazard, Aunt Mamie. I'm a cop. I take my chances."

She apologized. "Now I remember reading about it, but I didn't know it was you. I hardly ever go anywhere, but just out with Big Joe, when he was alive." Then she added with sincerity, "I hope they put whoever did it in the jail and throw away the key."

"He's already buried, Aunt Mamie," Coffin Ed said.

Then Grave Digger said, "Ed's having skin grafted on his face from his thigh, but it takes time. It'll take about a year altogether before it's finished."

"Now, Mrs. Pullen," the sergeant inserted firmly, "suppose you just tell me in your own words what happened in your place last night, or rather this morning."

She sighed. "I'll tell you what I know."

When she'd finished her account, the sergeant said, "Well, at least that gives us a pretty clear picture of what actually happened inside of your house from the time Reverend Short returned upstairs until the body was discovered.

"Do you believe that Reverend Short fell from your bedroom window?"

"Oh, I believe that. There wasn't reason for him to say he'd fallen if he hadn't. 'Sides which, he was outside and nobody had seen him leave by the door."

"You don't think that's extraordinary? For him to fall out of a third-story window?"

"Well, sir, he's a frail man and given to having trances. He might have had a trance."

"Epilepsy?"

"No, sir, just religious trances. He sees visions."

"What kind of visions?"

"Oh, all kinds of visions. He preaches about them. He's a prophet, like Saint John the Divine."

Sergeant Brody was a Catholic and he looked bewildered.

Grave Digger explained, "Saint John the Divine is the prophet who saw the seven veils and the four horsemen of the apocalypse. The people here in Harlem have a great regard for Saint John. He was the only prophet who ever saw any winning numbers in his visions."

"The *Revelation* is the fortune teller's Bible," Coffin Ed added.

"It's not only just that," Mamie said. "Saint John saw how wonderful it was in heaven and how terrible it was in hell."

"Well now, to get back to this murder, would Chink Charlie have any reason to try to kill Reverend Short?" Brody questioned. "Other than the fact the Reverend was a prophet."

"No, sir, absolutely not. It was just that Reverend Short had the sense knocked out of him by his fall and didn't know what he was saying."

"But he and Chink had been arguing earlier."

"Not really arguing. Reverend Short and him was just disagreeing about the kind of people I had to the wake. But it weren't neither one of them's business."

"Is there bad blood between Dulcy and Reverend Short?"

"Bad blood? No, sir. It's just that Reverend Short thinks Dulcy needs saving and she just takes every chance to bitch him off. But I suspects he's carrying a secret torch for her, only he's shamed of it 'cause of him being a preacher and she being a married woman."

"How was the Reverend with Johnny and Val?"

"They all three respected one another's intentions and that's as far as it went."

"How long was it between the time Dulcy left the house and you went to the window and discovered the body?"

"It wasn't no time at all," she declared positively. "She hadn't even had time to get downstairs."

He asked a few questions about the other mourners, but found no connection with Val.

Then he came in from another angle.

"Did you recognize the voice of the man who telephoned you after the body was discovered?"

"No, sir. It just sounded distant and fuzzy."

"But whoever it was knew there was a dead body there in that bread basket?"

"No, sir, it was just like I told you before. Whoever it was wasn't talking about Val. He was talking about Reverend Short. He'd seen the reverend fall and thought he was lying there dead, and that's why he called. I'm sure of that."

"How could he know he was dead unless he had come close enough to examine him?"

"I don't know, sir. I suppose he just thought he was dead. You'd think anybody was dead who'd fallen out a third-story window, and then lay there without getting up."

"But according to testimony, Reverend Short did get

up and come all the way back upstairs on his own power."

"Well, I couldn't say how it was. All I know is someone telephoned and when I said he'd been stabbed—Val, I mean—they
just hung up as if they might have been surprised."

"Could it have been Johnny Perry?"

"No, sir, I'm dead certain it wasn't him. And I sure ought to
know his voice if anybody does, as long as I've been hearing it."

"He's your stepson? Or is it your godson?"

"Well, he ain't rightly neither, but we thought of him as a
son because when he came out of stir—"

"What stir? Where?"

"In Georgia. He did a stretch on the chain gang."

"For what?"

"He killed a man for beating his mother—his stepfather.
At least she was his common-law wife, his ma, but she was no
good and Johnny was always a good boy. They gave him a year
on the road."

"When was that?"

"It was twenty-six years ago when he got out. While he was
inside his ma ran off with another man and me and Big Joe
was coming North. So we just brought him along with us.
He was just twenty years old."

"That makes him forty-six now."

"Yes, sir. And Big Joe got him a job on the road."

"Waiting tables?"

"No, sir, helping in the kitchen. He couldn't wait tables on
account of that scar."

"How'd he get that?"

"On the chain gang. He and another con got to fighting with
pickaxes over a card game. Johnny was always hot-headed, and
that con had accused him of cheating him out of a nickel. And
Johnny was always as honest as the day is long."

"When did he open his gambling club here?"

"The Tia Juana club? He opened that about ten years ago.
Big Joe staked him. But he had another little house-rent game
he used to run before that."

"Is that when he married Dulcy—Mrs. Perry—when he
opened the Tia Juana club?"

"Oh no-no-no, he just married her a year and a half ago—January second last year, the day after New Year's day. Before then he was married to Alamena."

"Is he married to Dulcy or just living with her?" The sergeant gave her a confidential look.

Her back stiffened. "Their marriage is as legal as whiskey. Me and Big Joe were the witnesses. They were married in City Hall."

The sergeant turned a bright fiery red.

Grave Digger said softly, "Couples do get married in Harlem."

Sergeant Brody felt himself on bumpy water and took another tack.

"Does Johnny keep much cash on hand?"

"I don't know, sir."

"In the bank then, or in property? Do you know what property he owns?"

"No, sir. Maybe Big Joe knew, but he never told me."

He dropped it.

"Do you mind telling me what you and Dulcy—Mrs. Perry—were talking about that was so important you had to lock yourself in the bathroom?"

She hesitated and looked appealingly toward Grave Digger.

He said, "We're not after Johnny, Aunt Mamie. This has nothing to do with his gambling club or income taxes or anything concerning the federal government. We're just trying to find out who killed Val."

"Lord, it's a mystery who'd want to hurt Val. He didn't have an enemy in the world."

The sergeant let that pass. "Then it wasn't Val you and Dulcy were talking about?"

"No, sir. I'd just asked her about a run-in Johnny and Chink had at Dickie Wells's last Saturday night."

"About what? Money? Gambling debts?"

"No, sir. Johnny's crazy jealous of Dulcy—he's going to kill somebody about that gal some day. And Chink imagines he's God's gift to women. He keeps shooting at Dulcy. Folks say he don't mean nothing by it, but—"

"What folks?"

"Well, Val and Alamena and even Dulcy herself. But there ain't no telling what any man means when he keeps after a woman unless it's to get her. And Johnny's so jealous and hot-headed I'm scared to death there's going to be blood trouble."

"What part did Val play in that?"

"Val. He was always just a peacemaker. 'Course, he was on Johnny's side. He spent most of his time, it looked like, just trying to keep Johnny out of trouble. But he didn't have nothing against Chink, either."

"Then Johnny's enemies are his enemies, too?"

"No, sir, I wouldn't say that. Val wasn't the kind of person who had enemies. He and Chink always got along fine."

"Who's Val's woman?"

"He's never had a steady. Not to my knowledge. He just plays the field. I think his latest was Doll Baby. But he wasn't intending to get corralled by no gal."

"Tell me one thing, Mrs. Pullen—didn't you notice anything strange about the body?"

"Well—" She knitted her brows. "Not as I recollect. I didn't get to see him close up, of course. I just saw him from my window. But I didn't notice nothing strange."

The sergeant stared at her.

"Wouldn't you call a knife sticking in his heart strange?"

"Oh, you mean him being stabbed. Yes, sir, I thought that was strange. I couldn't imagine nobody wanting to kill Val."

The sergeant kept staring at her as though he didn't quite know what to make of that statement.

"If it had been Johnny there instead of Val it wouldn't have struck you as strange."

"No, sir."

"But didn't it strike you as strange how he came to be lying there in that bread basket just a few minutes after Reverend Short had fallen from your window into the same bread basket?"

For the first time her face took on a look of fear.

"Yes, sir," she replied in a whisper, leaning on the desk for support. "Powerful strange. Only the Lord knows how he came there."

"No, the murderer knows, too."

"Yes, sir. But there's one thing, Mr. Brody. Johnny didn't do it. He might not have had no burning love for his brother-in-law, but he tolerated him on account of Dulcy, and he wouldn't have let nobody hurt a hair on his head, much less have done it hisself."

Brody took the murder knife from a drawer and laid it on the desk top. "Have you ever seen this before?"

She stared at it, more out of curiosity than horror. "No, sir."

He let it drop. "When is the funeral to be held?"

"This afternoon at two o'clock."

"All right, you may go now. You've been a great help to us."

She arose slowly, bracing her hands on the desk top, and extended her hand to Sergeant Brody with Southern-bred courtesy.

Sergeant Brody wasn't used to it. He was the law. People on the other side of this desk were generally on the other side of the law. He found himself so confused that he clambered to his feet, knocking over his chair, and pumped her hand up and down, his face glowing like a freshly boiled lobster.

"I hope your funeral goes well, Mrs. Pullen—that is, I mean, your husband's funeral."

"Thank you, sir. All we can do is put him in the ground and hope."

Grave Digger and Coffin Ed stepped forward and escorted her with deference to the door, holding it open for her to pass through. Her black satin dress dragged on the floor, sweeping dust over her straight-last shoes.

Sergeant Brody didn't sigh. He prided himself on the fact that he never sighed. But, as he glanced at his watch again, he looked as though he would have loved to.

"It's ten-twenty. Think we can finish before lunch?"

"Let's get it over with," Coffin Ed said harshly. "I haven't had any sleep and I'm hungry enough to eat dog."

"Let's have the preacher, then."

On catching sight of the shiny wooden stool sitting in the spill of glaring light, Reverend Short drew up just inside the door and shuddered like a stuck sheep.

"No!" he croaked, trying to back out into the corridor. "I won't go in there."

The two uniformed cops who'd brought him from the detention block gripped his arms and forced him inside.

He struggled in their grip, performing exercises like an adagio dancer. Veins roped in his bony temples. His eyes protruded behind his gold-rimmed spectacles like a bug's under a microscope, and his Adam's apple bobbed like a float on a fishing line.

"No! No! It's haunted with the souls of tortured Christians," he screamed.

"Come on, buddy boy, quit performing," one of the cops said, handling him rough. "Ain't no Christians been in here."

"Yes! Yes!" he screamed in his croaking voice. "I hear their cries. It's the chamber of the Inquisition. I smell the blood of the martyred."

"You must be having a nosebleed," the other cop said, trying to be funny.

They lifted him bodily, feet and legs dangling grotesquely like a puppet's from a gibbet, carried him across the floor and deposited him on the stool.

The three inquisitors stared at him without moving. The chair in which Mamie Pullen had sat once more served Grave Digger as a footstool. Coffin Ed had retired to his dark corner.

"Caesars!" he croaked.

The cops stood flanking him, a hand on each shoulder.

"Cardinals!" he screamed. "The Lord is my shepherd, I shall not fear."

His eyes glinted insanely.

Sergeant Brody's face remained impassive, but he said, "Ain't nobody here but us chickens, Reverend."

Reverend Short leaned forward and peered into the shadow as though trying to make out a blurred figure in a thick fog.

"If you're a police officer then I want to report that Chink Charlie pushed me out of the window to my death, but God placed the body of Christ on the ground to break my fall."

"It was a basket of bread," the sergeant corrected.

"The body of Christ," Reverend Short maintained.

"All right, Reverend, let's cut the comedy," Brody said. "If you're trying to build a plea of insanity, you're jumping the gun. No one is accusing you of anything."

"It was that Jezebel Dulcy Perry who stabbed him with the knife Chink Charlie gave her to commit the murder." Brody leaned forward slightly.

"You saw him give her the knife?"

"Yes."

"When?"

"The day after Christmas. She was sitting in her car outside my church and thought there wasn't nobody looking. He came up and got into the seat beside her, gave her the knife and showed her how to use it."

"Where were you?"

"I was watching through a crack in the window. I knew there was something fishy about her coming to my church to give me some old clothes for charity."

"Were she and Johnny members of your church?"

"They called themselves members just 'cause Big Joe Pullen was a member, but they never come 'cause they don't like to roll."

Grave Digger saw that Brody didn't get it, so he explained. "It's a Holy Roller church. When the members get happy they roll about on the floor."

"With one another's wives," Coffin Ed added.

Brody's face went sort of slack, and the police reporter stopped writing to stare open-mouthed.

"They keep their clothes on," Grave Digger amended. "They just roll about on the floor and have convulsions, singly and in pairs."

The reporter looked disappointed.

"Ahem," Brody said, clearing his throat. "So when you first looked out of the window you saw Val's body lying in the bread basket with the knife sticking in it. And you recognized the knife as the same knife you had seen Chink Charlie give to Dulcy Perry?"

"There wasn't any bread there then," Reverend Short stated.

Sergeant Brody blinked. "What was there if there wasn't any bread?"

"There was a colored cop and a white man chasing a thief."

"Ah, so you saw that," Brody said, finally getting something tangible to put his teeth into. "Then you must have actually seen the murder being committed."

"I saw her stab him," Reverend Short declared.

"You couldn't have seen her because she hadn't left the flat then," Brody said.

"I didn't see it then. I was pushed out of the window then. I didn't see it until after I had returned to the room."

"Returned to what room?"

"The room where the casket was."

Brody stared at him and slowly began to redden. "Listen, Reverend," he warned. "This is serious. This is a murder investigation. This is no place to joke."

"I'm not joking," Reverend Short said.

"All right, then, you mean you imagined all of this?"

Reverend Short straightened his back and stared at Brody indignantly.

"I saw it in a vision."

"And it was in this vision you saw yourself pushed out of the window?"

"It was after I was pushed out of the window that I had the vision."

"Do you have these visions often?"

"Regularly, and they're always true."

"All right, then how did she kill him—in your vision, that is?"

"She went downstairs on the elevator, and when she went outside there was Valentine Haines lying in the basket where I had fallen—"

"I thought you said there wasn't any basket?"

"There wasn't at the time, but the body of Christ had turned into a basket of bread, and it was in this bread that he was lying when she took the knife from her pocketbook and went up to him and stabbed him."

"What was Val doing there?"

"He was lying there, waiting for her to come out."

"And stab him, I suppose."

"He didn't expect her to stab him. He didn't even know she had a knife."

"All right. I don't buy any of that. Did you see anyone actually leave the house—that is actually see them—while you were downstairs?"

"My eyes were veiled. I knew a vision was coming on."

"All right, Reverend, I'm going to let you go," Brody said, looking over the contents of Reverend Short's pockets lying on the desk before him. "But for a man who calls himself a minister of the Gospel you haven't been very cooperative."

Reverend Short didn't move.

Brody pushed the pocket Bible, handkerchief, bunch of keys and wallet across the desk, hesitated over the bottle of medicine and on sudden impulse drew the cork and smelled it. He looked startled. He tilted it to his lips and tasted it, spat it out on the floor.

"Jesus Christ!" he exclaimed. "Peach brandy and laudanum. You drink this stuff?"

"It's for my nerves," Reverend Short said.

"For your visions, you mean. If I drank this stuff I'd have visions, too." To the cops Brody said disgustedly, "Take him away."

Suddenly Reverend Short began to scream, "Don't let her get away! Arrest her! Burn her! She's a witch! She's in collusion with the devil! And Chink's her accomplice!"

"We'll take care of her," one of the cops cajoled as they lifted him from the stool. "We've got just the place for witches—and wizards, too, so you'd better look out."

Reverend Short broke from their grasp and fell to the floor. He rolled and threshed about convulsively, frothing at the mouth as though having a fit.

"I see what you mean by Holy Roller," Brody said.

The police reporter snickered.

"No, this is probably a vision coming on," Grave Digger said with a straight face.

Brody looked at him sharply.

The cops picked Reverend Short up by the feet and shoulders and carried him off bodily. After a moment one of them came back for the reverend's possessions.

"Is he crazy or just acting?" Brody asked.

"Maybe both," Grave Digger replied.

"After all, there might be something in what he said," Coffin Ed ventured. "As I recall my Bible, all the prophets were either crazy or epileptic."

"I like some of what he said, all right," Brody admitted. "I just don't like the way he said it."

"Who's next?" Grave Digger asked.

"Let's see Johnny's former wife," Brody said.

Alamena came in docilely, fingering the high-necked collar about her throat, like a girl who might have been in there before and knew what to expect.

She sat down in the circle of light and folded her hands in her lap. She wore no jewelry of any kind.

"What do I call you?" Brody asked.

"Just Alamena," she said.

"Fine. Now just give me a quick fill-in on Val and Dulcy."

"There ain't much to it. Dulcy came here to sing in Small's Cabaret a couple of years ago, and after six months she'd hooked Johnny and landed on easy street. Val came for the wedding and stayed."

"Who were Dulcy's boyfriends before she married?"

"She played the field, prospecting."

"How about Val? Was he prospecting, too?"

"Why should he? He had a claim staked out for him before he got here."

"He just helped out in the club?" Brody suggested.

"Not so you could notice," she said. "Anyway, Johnny wouldn't have never trusted Val to gamble his money."

"Just what was going on between Dulcy and Chink and Val and Johnny?"

"Nothing, as I know of."

"All right, all right. Who were Val's enemies?"

"He didn't have any enemies. He wasn't the type."

Blood mottled Brody's face.

"God damn it, he didn't stab himself in the heart."

"It's been done before," she said.

"But he didn't. We know that. On the other hand, there were no superficial signs of his being either drugged or drunk. Of course, the coroner can't be absolutely certain until after the autopsy. But let's just imagine he was lying there, at that time of morning, in that basket of bread. Why?"

"Maybe he was standing up and just fell there after he was stabbed."

"No, he was stabbed while he was lying there. And from the condition of the bread he knew absolutely that someone or something had already lain in it. Perhaps he had even seen Reverend Short fall from the window. Now I want to ask you just one simple question. Why would he lie there of his own free will, let someone lean over him with a knife and stab him to death without his even putting up any kind of defense?"

"Nobody expects to be stabbed to death by a friend they think is just playing," she said.

All three detectives tensed imperceptibly.

"You think a friend did it?"

She shrugged, gesturing slightly with her hands. "Don't you?"

Brody took the knife out of the drawer. She looked at it indifferently, as though she'd seen a lot of knives.

"Is this it?"

"It looks like it."

"Have you ever seen it before?"

"Not that I know of."

"You'd know of it if you'd seen it?"

"Everybody in Harlem carries a knife. Do you think I know everybody's knife by sight?"

"Everybody in Harlem don't carry this kind of knife," Brody said. "This is a hand-tooled, imported English knife with a blade of Sheffield steel. The only place we've found so far where it can be bought in New York City is at Abercrombie and Fitch's, downtown on Madison Avenue. It costs twenty bucks. Can you imagine a Harlem punk going downtown and paying twenty bucks for an imported hunter's knife, then leaving it sticking in his victim?"

Her face turned a strange shade of dirty yellow, and her dark brown eyes looked haunted.

"Why not? It's a free country," she whispered. "So they say."

"You're free to go now," Brody said.

No one moved as she got up and went across the floor, in the stiff, blind manner of a sleepwalker, and left the room.

Brody fumbled in his coat pockets for his pipe and plastic tobacco pouch. He took his time stuffing the battered brier pipe, then struck a kitchen match on the edge of the desk and got his pipe going.

"Who cut her throat?" he asked through a cloud of smoke, holding the pipe in his teeth.

Grave Digger and Coffin Ed avoided each other's gazes, and both appeared strangely embarrassed.

"Johnny," Grave Digger said finally.

Brody froze, but relaxed so quickly it was scarcely perceptible.

"Did she charge him?"

"No. It went as an accident."

The police reporter stopped fiddling with his notes and stared.

"How the hell can you get your throat cut accidentally?" Brody asked.

"She said he didn't intend to do it—that he was just playing."

"Playing kind of rough," the police reporter commented.

"Why?" Brody asked. "Why did he do it?"

"She hung on too long," Grave Digger said. "He wanted Dulcy and she wouldn't let go."

"And she still hangs on to him."

"Why not? He cut her throat, and now she's got him for life."

"It's a funny way to keep a man, is all I can say."

"Maybe. But don't forget this is Harlem. Folks here are happy just to be alive."

VII

THEY CALLED CHINK next.

He said he'd started the night with a little friendly stud poker session in his room. It had broke up at one-thirty and he'd arrived at the wake at two A.M. He had left the wake at five minutes to four to keep a tête-à-tête with Doll Baby in her kitchenette apartment in the building next door.

"Did you look at your watch when you left?" Brody asked.

"No, when I went down in the elevator."

"Exactly where was Reverend Short when you left?"

"Reverend Short? Hell, I didn't pay no attention." He paused briefly, as though trying to remember, and said, "I think he was standing beside the coffin, but I can't be sure."

"What was happening outside when you got down to the street?"

"Nothing. A colored cop was standing there guarding the A&P store groceries on the sidewalk. He might remember seeing me."

"Was there anyone with him?"

"No, not unless it was a ghost."

"All right, son, let's have the facts without the comedy," Brody said with irritation.

Chink said he'd waited for Doll Baby in the front hall and they had walked up to her apartment on the second-floor rear. But she hadn't been in the mood, so he'd gone out to pick up a few sticks of marijuana weed from a friend who lived down the street.

"Where?" Brody asked.

"Make a guess," Chink said defiantly.

Brody let it pass.

"Were there any people on the street that time?" he asked.

"Just as I stepped out on the sidewalk Dulcy Perry came from next door, and we saw Val's body in the bread basket at the same time."

"Had you noticed the bread basket before?"

"Sure. It was full of plain bread."

"There was no one else in sight when you and Dulcy met?"

"No one."

"How did she react when she saw her brother's body?"

"She just started going crazy."

"What did she say?"

"I don't remember."

Brody showed him the knife.

Chink admitted that it looked like the knife that had been stuck in Val's body, but denied ever having seen it before.

"Reverend Short testified that he saw you give this knife to Dulcy Perry in front of his church the day after Christmas, and that you showed her how to use it," Brody said.

Chink's sweaty yellow face paled to the color of a dirty sheet.

"That mother-raping preacher's blowing his top drinking that opium extract and cherry brandy," he raved. "I ain't given Dulcy any mother-raping knife and ain't never seen it before."

"But you've been after her like a dog after a bitch in heat," Brody charged. "Everybody says that."

"You can't hang a man for trying," Chink argued.

"No, but you can kill a woman's brother if he gets in the way," Brody said.

"Val wasn't no trouble," Chink muttered. "He'd have set it up for me if he hadn't been scared of Johnny."

Brody called in the harness cops.

"Hold him," he ordered.

"I want to call my lawyer," Chink demanded.

"Let him call his lawyer," Brody said. Then he asked if they'd picked up Doll Baby Grieves.

"Long time ago," one replied.

"Send her in."

Doll Baby had changed into a day dress that still looked like a nightgown in disguise. She sat on the stool in the circle of light and crossed her legs as though she liked being spotlighted in the same room with three men, even though they were cops.

She confirmed Chink's testimony, only she said he'd gone out for sandwiches instead of marijuana.

"Didn't you get enough to eat at the wake?" Brody asked.

"Well, we were just talking and that always makes me hungry," she said.

Brody asked about her relationship with Val, and she said they were engaged.

"And you were entertaining another man in your rooms at that hour of morning?"

"Well, after all, I had waited for Val 'til four o'clock, and I just figured he was out chasing." She giggled. "And what's good for the goose is good for the gander."

"He's dead now, or did you forget?" Brody reminded her.

She sobered suddenly and looked appropriately sad.

Brody asked her if she'd seen anyone when she left the wake. She said she'd seen a colored cop with the A&P store manager who'd just driven up. She recognized the manager because she shopped in the store, and she knew the cop personally. Both had greeted her.

"When did you last see Val?" Brody asked.

"He came to see me at about ten-thirty."

"Had he been to the wake?"

"No, he said he'd just come from home. I phoned Mr. Small and got the night off to attend Big Joe's wake—I generally work from eleven till four—and then me and Val sat there talking until one-thirty."

"Are you certain about the time?"

"Yeah, he looked at his watch and said it was one-thirty, and he'd have to leave in a hour because he wanted to stop by Johnny's club before he went to the wake, and I said I wanted some fried chicken."

"You don't like Mamie Pullen's cooking," Brody suggested.

"Oh, sure, I like it fine, but I was hungry."

"You're a hungry girl."

She giggled. "Talking always makes me hungry."

"Where did you go for your fried chicken?"

"We got a taxi and went over to the College Inn at 151st Street and Broadway. We just stayed there for an hour, and then he looked at his watch and said it was two-thirty and he was going by Johnny's and would meet me at the Wake in about an hour. We got a taxi and he dropped me off at Mamie's and kept on downtown to Johnny's."

"What was his racket?" Brody shot at her.

"Racket? He didn't have any. He was a gentleman."

"Who were his enemies?"

"He didn't have any, unless it was Johnny."

"Why Johnny?"

"Johnny might have got tired of having him around all the time. Johnny's funny and awfully hot-headed."

"How about Chink? Didn't Val resent Chink's familiarity with his fiancée?"

"He didn't know about it."

Brody showed her the knife. She denied ever having seen it at any time.

He released her.

Dulcy was brought in next. She was accompanied by Johnny's attorney, Ben Williams.

Ben was a brown-skinned man of about forty, slightly on the fat side, with neatly barbered hair, and a heavy moustache. He was wearing the double-breasted gray flannel suit, horn-rimmed spectacles and conservative black shoes of the Harlem professional man.

Brody skipped the routine questions and asked Dulcy, "Were you the first one to discover the body?"

"You don't have to answer that," the attorney said quickly.

"Why the hell doesn't she?" Brody flared.

"The Fifth Amendment," the attorney stated.

"This isn't any Communist investigation," Brody said disgustedly. "I can hold her as a material witness and let her talk to the grand jury, if that's what you want."

The attorney appeared to meditate. "Okay, you can answer," he said to Dulcy. After that he kept quiet; he had earned his money.

She said that Chink was standing beside the bread basket when she came out of the door.

"Are you certain of that?" Brody asked.

"I ain't blind," she retorted. "That's what made me look down to see what he was looking at, and then I saw Val."

Brody left it for a moment and started at the beginning of her career in Harlem. The gist of what he got had already been given.

"Did your husband give him an allowance?" Brody asked.

"Naw, he just slipped him money from his pocket whenever Val asked for a loan, and sometimes he'd let him win in the game. Then I gave him what I could."

"How long had he been engaged to Doll Baby?"

She laughed sarcastically. "Engaged! He was just keeping himself regular with that slut."

Brody dropped it and repeated the questions about Val's racket, enemies, whether he was carrying a large sum of money when he was killed, and asked her to describe the jewelry he was wearing. The wrist watch, gold ring and cuff links checked with what had been found on the body. She said the thirty-seven dollars found in his wallet would be about right.

Then Brody worked on the time element.

She said Val had left home about ten o'clock. He had said he was going to see a show at the Apollo Theatre—Billy Eckstine's band was doubling with the Nicholas Brothers—and had asked to come with him, but she had an appointment with her hairdresser. So he'd decided to drop by the club and come with Johnny to the wake, and said they'd pick her up there.

She'd left home at twelve midnight with Alamena, who lived in a rented room downstairs in the same building.

"How long were you and Mamie locked in the bathroom?" Brody asked.

"Oh, a half-hour, more or less. I can't be sure. When I looked at my watch it was four-twenty-five, and Reverend Short began knocking on the door right then."

Brody showed her the knife and repeated what Reverend Short had said.

"Did Chink Charlie give you this knife?" he asked.

The attorney broke in to say she didn't have to answer that.

She began laughing hysterically, and it was five minutes before she had calmed down sufficiently to say, "He ought to get married, watching them Holy Rollers every Sunday and wanting to roll himself."

Brody turned red.

Grave Digger grunted. "I thought a Holy Roller preacher got the call to roll with all the sisters," he said.

"Most of 'em is," Dulcy said. "But Reverend Short's too full of visions to roll with anyone, unless it be a ghost."

"Well, that's all for now," Brody said. "I'm going to have you held in five-thousand-dollar bail."

"Don't worry about that," the attorney said to her.

"I ain't," she said.

Johnny was fifteen minutes late in appearing. His attorney had to telephone the bail-bondsman to arrange for Dulcy's bail, and he refused to be questioned without him.

Before Brody could fire his first question, the attorney produced affidavits given by Johnny's two helpers, Kid Nickels and Pony Boy, to the effect that Johnny had left his Tia Juana Club at the corner of 124th Street and Madison Avenue at 4:45 A.M., alone, and that Val had not been inside of the club all evening.

Without waiting to be questioned, Johnny volunteered the information that he hadn't seen Val since leaving his flat at nine the night before.

"How did you feel about supporting a brother-in-law who did nothing to deserve it?" Brody asked.

"It didn't bother me," Johnny said. "If I hadn't taken him in she'd have been slipping him money, and I didn't want to put her in the middle."

"You didn't resent it?" Brody persisted.

"It's just like I already said," Johnny stated in his toneless voice. "It didn't bother me. He wasn't a square, but he wasn't sharp, neither. He didn't have any racket, he couldn't gamble, he couldn't even be a pimp. But I liked to have him around. He was funny, always ready for a gag."

Brody showed him the knife.

Johnny picked it up, opened and closed it, turned it over in his hand and put it back.

"You could turn a mother-raper every way but loose with that chiv," he said.

"You never saw it before?" Brody asked.

"If I had I'd have gotten me one like it," Johnny said.

Brody told him what Reverend Short had said about Chink Charlie giving Dulcy the knife.

When Brody had finished talking, there was no expression of any kind on Johnny's face.

"You know that preacher's off his nut," he said. His voice was toneless and indifferent.

They exchanged stares for a moment, both poker-faced and unmoving.

Then Brody said, "Okay, boy, you can go now."

"Fine," Johnny said, getting to his feet. "Just don't call me boy."

Brody reddened. "What the hell do you want me to call you—Mr. Perry?"

"Everybody else calls me Johnny—ain't that enough of a handle for you?" Johnny said.

Brody didn't answer.

Johnny left with his attorney at his heels.

Brody stood up and looked from Grave Digger to Coffin Ed. "Have we got any candidates?"

"You might try to find out who bought the knife," Grave Digger said.

"That was done the first thing this morning. Abercrombie and Fitch put six knives in stock a year ago, and so far they haven't sold any."

"Well, they're not the only store that sells hunting equipment in New York," Grave Digger argued.

"That won't get us nothing anyway," Coffin Ed said. "There's no way of telling who did it until we find out why it was done."

"That's going to be the lick that killed Nick," Grave Digger said. "That's the hard one."

"I don't agree," Brody said. "One thing is certain. He wasn't stabbed for money, so he must have been stabbed about a woman. *Churchy lay dame*, as the French say. But that don't mean another woman didn't do it."

Grave Digger took off his hat and rubbed his short kinky hair.

"This is Harlem," he said. "Ain't no other place like it in

the world. You've got to start from scratch here, because these folks in Harlem do things for reasons nobody else in the world would think of. Listen, there were two hard-working colored jokers, both with families, got to fighting in a bar over on Fifth Avenue near a hundred-eighteenth Street and cut each other to death about whether Paris was in France or France was in Paris."

"That ain't nothing," Brody laughed: "Two Irishmen over in Hell's Kitchen got to arguing and shot each other to death over whether the Irish were descended from the gods or the gods descended from the Irish."

VIII

ALAMENA WAS WAITING for them in the back seat of the car. Johnny and Dulcy got in the front, and the attorney got in the back beside Alamena.

A few doors down the street, Johnny pulled to the curb and turned about to bring both Dulcy and Alamena into vision.

"Listen, I want you women to keep buttoned up about this business. We're going to Fats's, and I don't want either one of you to start making waves. We don't know who did it."

"Chink did it," Dulcy said positively.

"You don't know that."

"The hell I don't."

He looked at her so long she began fidgeting.

"If you know it, then you know why."

She bit off a manicured nail and said with sullen defiance, "I don't know why."

"Did you see him do it?"

"No," she admitted.

"Then keep your goddam mouth shut and let the cops find out who did it," he said. "That's what they get paid for."

Dulcy began to cry. "You don't even care 'bout him being dead," she accused.

"I got my own ways about caring, and I don't want to see nobody framed if he didn't do it."

"You're always trying to play little Jesus Christ," Dulcy blubbered. "Why do all of us have to take the cop's gaff if I know Chink did it?"

"Because anybody might have done it. He's been asking for it all his mother-raping life. Him and you both."

No one said anything. Johnny kept looking at Dulcy. She bit off another manicured nail and looked away. The attorney squirmed about in his seat as if ants were stinging him. Alamena stared at Johnny's profile without expression.

Johnny turned about in his seat, eased the car from the curb and drove slowly off.

Fats's Down Home Restaurant had a narrow front, with a curtained plate-glass window beneath a neon sign depicting the outline of a man shaped like a bull hippopotamus.

Before the big Cad had pulled to a full stop, it was surrounded by skinny black children, clad in scant cotton clothes, crying, "Four Ace Johnny Perry . . . Fishtail Johnny Perry . . ."

They touched the sides of the car and the gleaming fishtails with bright-eyed awe, as though it were an altar.

Dulcy jumped out quickly, pushing the children aside, and hastened across the narrow sidewalk, her high heels tapping angrily, toward the curtained glass door.

Alamena and the attorney followed at a more leisurely pace, but neither bothered to smile at the children.

Johnny took his time, turned off the ignition and pocketed the keys, watching the kids caress his car. His face was deadpan, but his eyes were amused. He stepped out to the sidewalk, leaving the top down with the sun beating on the black leather upholstery, and was mobbed by the kids, who pulled at his clothes and stepped on his feet as he crossed the sidewalk toward the door.

He patted the Topsy-plaited heads of the skinny black girls, the burred heads of the skinny black boys. Just before entering he dug into his pockets and turned to scatter the contents of change over the street. He left the kids scrambling.

Inside it was cool, and so dark he had to take off his sun

glasses on entering. The unforgettable scent of whiskey, whores and perfume filled his nostrils, making him feel relaxed.

Wall light spilled soft stain over shelves of bottles and a small mahogany bar that was presided over by a giant black man in a white sport shirt. At sight of Johnny, he stood silently without moving, holding the glass he'd been polishing.

Three men and two women turned on their high bar stools to greet Johnny. Everything about them said gamblers and their women, whorehouse madams.

"Death always doubles off," one of the madams said sympathetically.

Johnny stood loosely, his big sloping-shouldered frame at perfect ease.

"We all gotta fall when we're on the turn," he said.

Their voices were low-pitched and without inflection, with the flat toneless quality of Johnny's. They talked in the casual manner of their trade.

"Too bad about Big Joe," one of the hustlers said. "I'm going to miss him."

"Big Joe was a real man," a madam said.

"You ain't just saying it," the others confirmed.

Johnny stuck his hand across the bar and shook the giant bartender's hand.

"What say, Pee Wee."

"Just standing here and moaning low, pops." He made a small gesture with the hand holding the half polished glass. "It's on the house."

"Bring us a pitcher of lemonade."

Johnny turned toward the arch leading toward the dining room at the rear.

"See you at the funeral, pops," a voice said behind him.

He didn't reply, because a man living up to his notices had stopped him with his belly. He resembled the balloon that had discovered stratosphere, but hundreds of degrees hotter. He wore an old-fashioned white silk shirt without the collar, fastened about the neck with a diamond-studded collar button, and black alpaca pants; but his legs were so large they seemed joined together, and his pants resembled a funnel-shaped skirt.

His round brown head, which could have passed for a safety balloon in case his stomach burst, was clean-shaven. Not a hair showed above his chest—either on his face, nostrils, ears, eyebrows or eyelashes—giving the impression that his whole head had been scalded and scraped like the carcass of a pork.

"How's it going to chafe us, pops?" he asked, sticking out a huge, spongy hand. His voice was a wheezing whisper.

"Nobody knows 'til the deal goes down," Johnny said. "Everybody's just peeping at their hole cards now."

"The betting comes next." He looked down, but his felt-slippered feet, planted on the sawdust-covered floor, were hidden from his view by his belly. "I sure hate to see Big Joe go."

"Lost your best customer," Johnny said, rejecting the consolation.

"You know, Big Joe never ate nothing here. He just come in to gape at the chippies and beef about the cooking." Fats paused, then added, "But he was a man."

"Hurry up, Johnny, for God's sake," Dulcy called from across the room. "The funeral starts at two, and it's almost near one o'clock." She had kept on her sun glasses and looked strictly Hollywoodish in her pink silk dress.

The room was small, its eight square kitchen tables covered with white-and-red checked oilcloth planted in the inch of fresh, slightly damp sawdust covering the floor.

Dulcy sat at the table in the far corner, flanked by Alamena and the attorney.

"I'll let you go eat," Fats said. "You must be hungry."

"Ain't I always?"

The sawdust felt good beneath Johnny's rubber-soled shoes, and he thought fleetingly of how good life had been when he was a simple plow boy in Georgia, before he'd killed a man.

The cook stuck his head through the opening from the kitchen where the orders were filled and called, "Hiyuh, pops."

Johnny waved a hand.

Three other tables were occupied by men and women in

the trade. It was strictly a hangout for the upper-class Harlem hustlers, those in the gambling and prostitution professions, and none others were allowed. Everybody knew everybody else, and all the diners greeted Johnny as he passed.

"Sad about Big Joe, pops."

"You can't stop the deal when the dealer falls."

Nobody mentioned Val. He'd been murdered, and nobody knew who did it. It was nobody's business but Johnny's, Dulcy's and the cops'; and everybody was letting it strictly alone.

When Johnny sat down the waitress came with the menu, and Pee Wee brought in a big glass pitcher of lemonade, with slices of lemons and limes and big chunks of ice floating about in it.

"I want a Singapore Sling," Dulcy said.

Johnny gave her a look.

"Well, brandy and soda then. You know good and well that ice-cold drinks give me indigestion."

"I'll have iced tea," the attorney said.

"You get that from the waitress," Pee Wee said.

"Gin and tonic for me," Alamena said.

The waitress came with the silver, glasses and napkins, and Alamena gave the attorney the menu.

He started to grin as he read the list of dinners:

Today's Special — Alligator tail & rice
Baked Ham — sweet potatoes & succotash
Chitterlings & collard greens & okra
Chicken and drop dumplings — with rice or sweet potatoes
Barbecued ribs
Pig's feet à la mode
Neck bones and lye hominy

(*Choice of hot biscuits or corn bread*)

Side Dishes

Collard greens — okra — black-eyed peas & rice — corn on the cob — succotash — sliced tomatoes and cucumbers

DESSERTS
Homemade ice cream — deep-dish sweet potatoe pie — peach cobbler — watermelon — blackberry pie

BEVERAGES
Iced tea — buttermilk — sassafras-root tea — coffee

But he looked up and saw the solemn expressions on the faces of the others and broke off.

"I haven't had breakfast as yet," he said, then to the waitress, "Can I have an order of brains and eggs, with biscuits?"

"Yes, sir."

"I want some fried oysters," Dulcy said.

"We ain't got no oysters. It ain't the month for 'em." She gave Dulcy a sly, sidewise look.

"Then I'll take the chicken and dumplings, but I don't want nothing but the legs," Dulcy said haughtily.

"Yes'm."

"Baked ham for me," Alamena said.

"Yes'm." She looked at Johnny with calf-eyed love. "The same as always, Mr. Johnny?"

He nodded. Johnny's breakfast, which never varied, consisted of a heaping plate of rice, four thick slices of fried salt pork, the fat poured over the rice, and a pitcher of blackstrap sorghum molasses to pour over that. With this came a plate of eight Southern-style biscuits an inch and a half thick.

He ate noisily without talk. Dulcy had drunk three brandy-and-sodas and said she wasn't hungry.

Johnny stopped eating long enough to say, "Eat anyway."

She picked at her food, watching the faces of the other diners, trying to catch snatches of their conversation.

Two people got up from a far table. The waitress went over to clear their places. Chink walked in with Doll Baby.

She had changed into a fresh pink linen backless dress, and wore huge black-tinted sun glasses with pink frames.

Dulcy stared at her with liquid venom. Johnny drank two glasses of ice-cold lemonade.

The room filled with silence.

Dulcy stood up suddenly.

"Where you going?" Johnny asked.

"I want to play a record," she said defiantly. "Do you have any objections?"

"Sit down," he said tonelessly. "And don't be so mother-raping cute."

She sat down and bit off another fingernail.

Alamena fingered her throat and looked down at her plate.

"Tell the waitress," she said. "She'll play it."

"I was going to play that platter of Jelly Roll Morton's, *I Want A Little Girl To Call My Own.*"

Johnny raised his face and looked at her. Rage started leaping in his eyes.

She picked up her drink to hide her face, but her hand trembled so she spilled some on her dress.

Across the room Doll Baby said in a loud voice, "After all, Val was my fiancé."

Dulcy stiffened with fury. "You're a lying bitch!" she yelled back.

Johnny gave her a dangerous look.

"And if the truth be known, he was just knifed to keep me from having him," Doll Baby said.

"He'd already had a bellyful of you," Dulcy said.

Johnny slapped her out of her seat. She spun into the corner of the wall and crumpled to the floor.

Doll Baby let out a high shrill laugh.

Johnny spun his chair about on its hind legs.

"Keep the bitch quiet," he said.

Fats waddled over and put his bloated hand on Johnny's shoulder.

Pee Wee came from behind the bar and stood in the entrance.

Silently, Dulcy got back into her chair.

"Keep her quiet your God-damned self," Chink said.

Johnny stood up. Chairs scraped as everybody moved away from Chink's table. Doll Baby jumped up and ran into the kitchen. Pee Wee moved toward Johnny.

"Easy, pops," Pee Wee said.

Fats waddled quickly over to Chink's table and said, "Get

her out. And don't you never come in here no more neither. Taking advantage of me like that."

Chink stood up, his yellow face flushed and swollen. Doll Baby came from the kitchen and joined him. As he left, walking high-shouldered and stiff-kneed, he said to Johnny, "I'll see you, big shot."

"See me now," Johnny said tonelessly, starting after him.

The scar on his forehead had swollen and come alive.

Pee Wee blocked his path.

"That nigger ain't worth killing, pops."

Fats gave Chink a push in the back.

"Punk, you're lucky, lucky, lucky," he wheezed. "Git going before your luck runs out."

Johnny looked at his watch, giving Chink no more attention.

"We gotta go, the funeral's already started," he said.

"We all is coming," Fats said. "But you go on ahead 'cause you is the number two mourner."

IX

HEAT SHIMMERED FROM the big black shiny Cadillac hearse parked before the door to the store-front church of the Holy Rollers at the corner of Eighth Avenue and 143rd Street. A skinny little black boy with big white shining eyes touched the red-hot fender and snatched back his hand.

The black painted windows of what had been a supermarket before the Holly Rollers took it over reflected distorted images of the three black Cadillac limousines, and of the big flashy cars strung out behind the big cocky hearse like a line of laying hens.

People of many colors, clad in garb of all descriptions, their burr heads covered with straw hats of every shape, crowded about for a glimpse of the Harlem underworld celebrities attending Big Joe Pullen's funeral. Black ladies carried bright-colored parasols and wore green eyeshades to protect them from the sun.

These people ate cool slices of watermelon, spit out the black seeds and sweated in the vertical rays of the July sun. They drank quart bottles of beer and wine, and smaller bottles of pop and cola, from the flyspecked grocery stores nearby. They sucked chocolate-coated ice-cream bars from the refrigerated pushcart of the Good Humor man. They chewed succulent sections of barbecued pork-rib sandwiches, cast the polished bones to the friendly dogs and cats and the bread crusts to the flocks of molting Harlem sparrows.

Trash blew from the dirty street against their sweaty skin and into their gritty eyes.

The jumble of loud voices, strident laughter and the tinkle of the vendor's bells mingled with the sounds of mourning coming from the open church door and the loud summer thunder of automobiles passing in the street.

A picnic had never been better.

Sweating horse cops astride lathered horses, harness bulls with open collars and patrol cars with rolled-down windows rode herd.

When Johnny backed his big fishtail Cadillac into a reserved spot and climbed out behind Dulcy and Alamena, a murmur ran through the crowd and his name sprang from every lip.

Inside the church was like an airless oven. The crude wooden benches were jam-packed with friends who had come to bury Big Joe—gamblers, pimps, whores, chippies, madams, dining-car waiters and Holy Rollers—but were being cooked instead.

With his two women, Johnny pushed forward toward the mourners' bench. They found places beside Mamie Pullen, Baby Sis, and the pallbearers—who included a white dining-car steward; the Grand Wizard of Big Joe's lodge, dressed in the most impressive red-and-blue, gold-braided uniform ever seen on land or sea; a gray-haired, flat-footed waiter known as Uncle Gin; and two Holy Roller Deacons.

Big Joe's coffin, banked with hothouse roses and lilies of the valley, occupied the place of honor in front of the soapbox pulpit. Green flies buzzed above the coffin.

Behind it, Reverend Short was jumping up and down on the flimsy pulpit like some devil with the hotfoot dancing on red- and white-hot flames.

His bony face was quivering with religious fervor and streaming with rivers of sweat that overflowed his high celluloid collar and soaked into the jacket of his black woolen suit. His gold-rimmed spectacles were clouded. A band of sweat had formed about his trousers' belt and was coming through his coat.

"*And the Lord said,*" he was screaming, swatting at the green flies trying to light on his face and spraying hot spit like a garden sprinkler. "*As many as I love, I rebuke and chasten. . . . Does you hear me?*"

"We hears you," the church members chanted in response.

"*Be zealous therefore, and repent . . .*"

". . . repent . . ."

"*So I'm going to take my text from Genesis . . .*"

". . . Genesis . . ."

"*The Lord God made Adam in his image . . .*"

". . . Lord made Adam . . ."

"*Therefore I'm your preacher and I want to make a parable.*"

". . . preacher make parable . . ."

"*There lies Big Joe Pullen in his coffin, as much of a man as Adam ever was, as dead a man as Adam ever will be, made in God's image . . .*"

". . . Big Joe in God's image . . ."

"*Adam bore two sons, Cain and Abel . . .*"

". . . Cain and Abel . . ."

"*And Cain rose up against his brother in the field, and he stuck a knife in Abel's heart and he murdered him . . .*"

". . . Jesus Savior, murdered him . . ."

"*I see Jesus Christ leaving heaven with all His grandeur, clothing himself in the garments of your preacher, making his face black, pointing the finger of accusation, and saying to you unrepented sinners, 'He who lives by the sword shall die by the sword . . .'*"

". . . die by the sword, Lord, Lord . . ."

"*I see Him point his finger and say, 'If Adam was alive today he'd be laying in that coffin dead and his name would be Big Joe Pullen . . .'*"

". . . have mercy, Jesus . . ."

"*And he'd have a son named Abel . . .*"

". . . have a son, Abel . . ."

"And his son would have a wife . . ."

". . . son would have a wife . . ."

"And his wife would be the sister of Cain . . ."

". . . sister of Cain . . ."

"I can see Him step out on the rib bone of nothing . . ."

". . . rib bone of nothing . . ."

Spit drooled from the corners of his fishlike mouth as he pointed a trembling finger straight in Dulcy's direction.

"I can hear him say, 'Oh, you sister of Cain, why slayest thou thy brother?' "

A dead silence dropped like a pall over the cooking congregation. Every eye was turned on Dulcy. She cringed in her seat. Johnny stared at the preacher with a sudden alertness, and the scar in his forehead came suddenly alive.

Mamie half arose and cried, "It ain't so! You know it ain't so!"

Then a sister in the amen corner jumped to her feet, with her arms stretched upward and her splayed fingers stiffened, and screamed, "Jesus in heaven, have mercy on the poor sinner."

Pandemonium broke loose as the Holy Rollers jumped to their feet and began having convulsions.

"Murderess!" Reverend Short screamed in a frenzy.

". . . murderess . . ." the church members responded.

"It ain't so!" Mamie shouted.

"Adulteress!" Reverend Short screamed.

". . . adulteress . . ." the congregation responded.

"You lying mother-raper!" Dulcy shouted, finally finding her voice.

"Let him rave on," Johnny said, his face wooden and his voice toneless.

"Fornication!" Reverend Short screamed.

At the mention of fornication the joint went mad.

Holy Rollers fell to the floor, frothing at the mouth, rolled and threshed, screaming, "Fornication . . . fornication . . ."

Men and women wrestled and rolled. Benches were splintered. The church rocked. The coffin shook. A big stink of sweating bodies arose. "Fornication . . . fornication . . ." the religious, mad people screamed.

"I'm getting out of here," Dulcy said, getting to her feet.

"Sit down," Johnny said. "These religious folks are dangerous."

The church organist began jamming the chorus of *Roberta Lee* on the church harmonium trying to restore order, and a big fat dining-car waiter cut loose in a high tenor voice:

> "Dis world is high,
> Dis world is low,
> Dis world is deep and wide,
> But de longes' road I ever did see,
> Was de one I walked and cried . . ."

Thoughts of the long road brought the fanatics to their feet. They brushed off their clothes and sheepishly straightened up the broken benches, and the organist went into *Roll, Jordan, Roll.*

But Reverend Short had gone beyond restraint. He'd left the pulpit and come down in front of the coffin to shake his finger in Dulcy's face. The undertaker's two assistants threw him to the floor and knelt on him until he'd calmed down; then the business of the funeral proceeded.

The congregation arose to the harmonium strains of *Nearer My God To Thee* and filed past the coffin for a last look at Big Joe Pullen's mortal remains. Those on the mourners' bench were the last to pass, and when the coffin lid was finally closed Mamie flung herself across it, crying, "Don't go, Joe, don't leave me here all alone."

The undertaker pried her loose, and Johnny put his arm about her waist and started guiding her toward the exit. But the undertaker stopped him, tugging at his sleeve.

"You're the chief pallbearer, Mr. Perry, you can't go."

Johnny turned Mamie over to the care of Dulcy and Alamena.

"Go along with her," he said.

Then he took his place with the five other pallbearers, and

they lifted the coffin, bore it down the cleared aisle and between the lines of police on the sidewalk and slid it into the hearse.

Members of Big Joe's lodge were lined up in parade formation in the street, clad in their full regalia of scarlet coats with gold braid, light blue trousers with gold stripes, and headed by the lodge band.

The band broke out with *The Coming of John*, and the people in the street joined in singing with the choir.

The funeral procession, led by the hearse, fell in behind the marching lodge brothers.

Dulcy and Alamena sat flanking Mamie Pullen in the first of the black limousines.

Johnny rode alone behind the third limousine in his big open-top fishtail Cadillac.

Two cars behind him, Chink and Doll Baby followed in a blue Buick convertible.

The band was playing the old funeral chant in swingtime, and the trumpet player took a chorus and rode the staccato notes clear and high in the hot Harlem sky. The crowd was electrified. The people broke loose in mass hysteria, marching in swingtime. But they marched in all directions, forward, backward, circling, zigzagging, their bodies gyrating to the rocking syncopation. They went rocking and rolling back and forth across the street, between the parked cars, up and down the sidewalks, sometimes a boy taking a whirl with a girl, most times marching alone to the music, but not in time with the music. They were marching and dancing to the rhythm, between the beats, not on them, marching and dancing to the feeling of the swing, and still keeping up with the slowly moving procession.

The procession went down Eighth Avenue to 125th Street, east to Seventh Avenue, turned the corner by the Theresa Hotel and went north toward the 155th Street Bridge to the Bronx.

But at the bridge the band pulled up, the marchers halted, the crowd began to disperse, the procession thinned out. Harlem ended at the bridge, and only the principals crossed into the Bronx and made the long journey out Bronx Park Road, past the Bronx Park Zoo, to Woodlawn Cemetery.

The built-in record player in the hearse began playing an organ recording, the thin saccharine notes drifting back over the procession from the amplifiers.

They went through the arched gateway into the huge cemetery and stopped in a long line behind the yellow clay mouth of the open grave.

The mourners encircled the grave while the pallbearers lifted the coffin from the hearse and placed it upon a mechanical derrick that lowered it slowly into the grave.

An organ recording of *Swing Low, Sweet Chariot* began playing, and the choir sang a moaning accompaniment.

Reverend Short had gotten himself under control and stood at the head of the grave, intoning in his croaking voice:

"*. . . in the sweat of thy face shalt thou eat bread, till thou return unto the ground; for out of it was thou taken: for dust thou art, and unto dust shalt thou return . . .*"

When the coffin touched the bottom of the grave, Mamie Pullen screamed and tried to throw herself after it. While Johnny was holding her, Dulcy suddenly crumpled and swayed toward the edge of the pit. Alamena clutched her about the waist, but Chink Charlie stepped forward from behind and put his arm about Dulcy and laid her upon the grass. Johnny caught a glimpse of them out of the corner of his eye, and he pushed Mamie into the arms of a deacon and wheeled toward Chink, his eyes yellow with rage and the scar on his forehead livid and crawling with a life of its own.

Chink saw him coming, stepped back and tried to pull his knife. Johnny feinted with his left and kicked Chink on the right shin. The sharp bone pain doubled Chink forward from the head down. Before the reflex motion had ceased, Johnny hit Chink back of the ear with a clubbing right; and when Chink fell reeling to his hands and knees, Johnny kicked at his head with his left foot, but missed it and grazed Chink's left shoulder instead. His lightning glance saw a spade in a grave digger's hand, and he snatched it out and swung the edge at the back of Chink's neck. Big Tiny from Fats's restaurant had closed in to stop Johnny and grabbed at his arm as he swung the spade. He didn't get a grip but managed to turn Johnny's arm so the flat of the spade instead of the edge hit Chink in the middle of the back and knocked him head over heels into the grave, on top of the coffin.

Then Tiny and half a dozen other men disarmed Johnny and wrestled him back to the gravel drive behind the plot of graves.

Johnny was circled in by his underworld friends, with Fats wheezing, "God damn it, Johnny, let's don't have no more killings. That wasn't nothing to get that mad about."

Johnny shook off their hands and straightened his disarranged clothes. "I don't want that half-white mother-raper to touch her," he said in his toneless voice.

"Jesus Christ, she'd fainted," Fats wheezed.

"Not even if she's dropping stone-cold dead," Johnny said.

His friends shook their heads.

"You have hurt him enough for one day anyway, chief," Kid Nickels said.

"I ain't going to hurt him no more," Johnny said. "Just bring my womenfolks over to the car. I'm going to take them home."

He went over and got into his car.

A moment later the music ceased. The undertaker's equipment was removed from about the grave. The grave diggers began spading in the earth. The silent mourners slowly returned to the cars.

Mamie came between Dulcy and Alamena and got into the back of Johnny's car with Alamena. Baby Sis followed silently.

"Lord, Lord," Mamie said in a moaning voice. "They ain't nothing but trouble on this earth, but I know my time ain't long."

X

ON LEAVING THE cemetery, the procession disbanded and each car went its own way.

Just before turning into the bridge back to Harlem, Johnny got held up by a traffic jam caused by Yankee Stadium letting out after a ball game.

He and Dulcy, along with other well-heeled Harlem pimps,

madams and numbers bankers, lived on the sixth floor of the flashy Roger Morris apartment house. It stood at the corner of 157th Street and Edgecombe Drive, on Coogan's Bluff, overlooking the Polo Grounds, the Harlem River and the inclined streets of the Bronx beyond.

It was seven o'clock when Johnny pulled his fishtail Cadillac before the entrance.

"I've come a long way from an Alabama cotton chopper to lose it all now," he said.

Everybody in the car looked at him, but only Dulcy spoke. "What you talking about?" she said warily.

He didn't answer.

Mamie's joints creaked as she started to alight.

"Come on, Baby Sis, we'll get a taxi," she said.

"You're coming up and eat with us," Johnny said. "Baby Sis and Alamena can fix supper."

She shook her head. "Me and Baby Sis will just go on home. I don't want to start being no trouble to nobody."

"It won't be no trouble," Johnny said.

"I ain't hungry," Mamie said. "I just want to go home and lie down and get some sleep. I'm powerfully tired."

"It ain't good for you to be alone now," Johnny argued. "Now's when you need to be around folks."

"Baby Sis'll be there, Johnny, and I just wanna sleep."

"Okay, I'll drive you home," Johnny said. "You know you ain't gotta ride in a taxi long as I got a car that'll run."

No one moved.

He turned to Dulcy and said, "You and Alamena get the hell out. I didn't say I was taking you."

"I'm getting good and tired of you hollering at me," Dulcy said angrily, getting from the car with a flounce. "I ain't no dog."

Johnny gave her a warning look but didn't answer.

Alamena got out of the back seat, and Mamie got in front with Johnny and put a hand over her closed eyes to shut out the terrible day.

They drove to her apartment without talking.

After Baby Sis had left them and gone inside, Mamie said,

"Johnny, you're too hard on womenfolks. You expects them to act like men."

"I just expect them to do what they're told and what they're supposed to do."

She gave a long, sad sigh. "Most women does, Johnny, but they just got their own ways of doing it, and that's what you don't understand."

They were silent for a moment, watching the crowds on the sidewalk drift past in the twilight.

It was a street of paradox: unwed young mothers, suckling their infants, living on a prayer; fat black racketeers coasting past in big bright-colored convertibles with their solid gold babes, carrying huge sums of money on their person; hard-working men, holding up the buildings with their shoulders, talking in loud voices up there in Harlem where the white bosses couldn't hear them; teenage gangsters grouping for a gang fight, smoking marijuana weed to get up their courage; everybody escaping the hotbox rooms they lived in, seeking respite in a street made hotter by the automobile exhaust and the heat released by the concrete walls and walks.

Finally Mamie said, "Don't kill him, Johnny. I'm an old lady and I tell you there ain't any reason."

Johnny kept looking at the stream of cars passing in the street. "Either's he's pressing her or she's asking for it. What do you want me to believe?"

"It ain't drawn that fine, Johnny. I'm an old lady, and I tell you, it ain't drawn that fine. You're splitting snake hairs. He's just a show-off and she just likes attention, that's all."

"He's gonna look good in a shroud," Johnny said.

"Take it from an old lady, Johnny," she said. "You don't give her no attention. You got your own affairs, your gambling club and everything, which takes up all your time, and she ain't got nothing."

"Aunt Mamie, that was the same trouble with my ma," he said. "Pete worked hard for her, but she wasn't satisfied 'less she was messing 'round with other men, and I had to kill him to keep him from killing her. But it was my ma who was wrong, and I always knowed it."

"I know, Johnny, but Dulcy ain't like that," Mamie argued. "She ain't messing around with nobody, but you gotta be patient with her. She's young. You knew how young she was when you married her."

"She ain't that young," he said in his toneless voice, still without looking at Mamie. "And if she ain't messing around with him then he's messing around with her—there ain't no two ways about it."

"Give her a chance, Johnny," Mamie pleaded. "Trust her."

"You don't know how much I wanna trust that gal," Johnny confessed. "But I ain't gonna let her nor him nor nobody else make a chump out of me. I ain't gonna fatten no frogs for snakes. And that's final."

"Oh Johnny," she begged, sobbing into her black-lace bordered handkerchief. "There's already been one killing too many. Don't kill nobody else."

For the first time Johnny turned and looked at her.

"What killing too many?"

"I know you couldn't help it that time 'bout your ma," she said. "But you ain't got to kill nobody else." She was trying to dissemble, but she talked too quickly and in too strained a voice.

"That ain't what you meant," Johnny said. "You meant about Val."

"That ain't what I said," she said.

"But that's what you meant."

"I wasn't thinking about him. Not in that way," she denied again. "I just don't want to see any more blood trouble, that's all."

"You don't have to pussyfoot about what you mean," he said in his toneless voice. "You can call his name. You can say he was stabbed to death, right over there on the sidewalk. It don't bother me. Just say what you mean."

"You know what I mean," she said stubbornly. "I mean just don't let her be the cause of no more killings, Johnny."

He tried to catch her eye, but she wouldn't meet his gaze. "You think I killed him," he said.

"I didn't say no such thing," she denied.

"But that's what you think."

"I ain't said nothing like that and you know it."

"I ain't talking about what you said. What I want to know is why you think I wanted to kill him."

"Oh Johnny, I don't think no such thing that you killed him," she said in a wailing voice.

"That ain't what I'm talking about, Aunt Mamie," he said. "I want to know what reason you think I'd have for killing him. Whether you think I killed him or not don't bother me. I just want to know what reason you think I'd do it for."

She looked him straight in the eyes. "There ain't any reason for you to have killed him, Johnny," she said. "And that's the Gospel truth."

"Then why'd you start off pleading for me to trust Dulcy so much and then the next thing you're figuring she's done give me reason enough to kill Val. That's what I want to know," he persisted. "What kind of reasoning is that?"

"Johnny, in this game of life, you got to give her as much as you ask to get from her," she said. "You can't win without risking."

"I know," he admitted. "That's a gambler's rule. But I got to put in eight hours every day in my club. It's as much for her as it is for me. But that means she's got all the chances in the world to play me for a sucker."

Mamie reached her gnarled old hand over and tried to take his hard long-fingered hand, but he drew it back.

"I ain't asking for mercy," he said harshly. "I don't want to hurt nobody, either. If she wants him, all I want her to do is walk out and go to him. I ain't gonna hurt her. If she don't want him, I ain't gonna have him pressing her. I don't mind losing. Every gambler got to lose sometime. But I ain't gonna be cheated."

"I know how you feel, Johnny," Mamie said. "But you got to learn to trust her. A jealous man can't win."

"A working man can't gamble and a jealous man can't win," said Johnny, quoting the old gambler's adage. After a moment he added, "If it's like you said, ain't nobody going to get hurt."

"I'm going up and get some sleep," she said, getting slowly to the sidewalk. Then she paused with her hand on the door and added, "Somebody's got to preach his funeral. Do you know any preacher who'd do it?"

"Get your own preacher," he said. "That's what he likes best, to preach somebody's funeral."

"You talk to him," she said.

"I don't want to talk to that man," he said. "Not after what he said today."

"You got to talk to him," she insisted. "Do it for Dulcy's sake."

He didn't say anything, and she didn't say any more. When she vanished within the entrance he started the motor and drove slowly through the idling traffic up to the store-front Church of the Holy Rollers on Eighth Avenue.

Reverend Short lived in a room at the back that had once been a storeroom. The street door was unlocked. Johnny entered without knocking and walked down the aisle between the broken benches. The door leading to Reverend Short's bedroom was cracked open a couple of inches. The plate-glass windows at the front were painted black on the inside three-quarters high, but enough twilight filtered through the dingy glass overtop to glint on Reverend Short's spectacles as he peered through the narrow opening of the door.

The spectacles withdrew and the door closed as Johnny skirted the soapbox pulpit, and he heard the lock click shut as he approached.

He knocked and waited. Silence greeted him.

"It's Johnny Perry, Reverend; I want to talk to you," he said.

There was a rustling sound like rats scurrying about inside, and Reverend Short spoke abruptly in his croaking voice. "Don't think I haven't been expecting you."

"Good," Johnny said. "Then you know it's about the funeral."

"I know why you've come and I'm prepared for you," Reverend Short croaked.

Johnny had had a long hard day, and his nerves were on edge. He tried the door and found it locked.

"Open this door," he said roughly. "How the hell you expect to do business through a locked door?"

"Aha, do you think you're deceiving me," Reverend Short croaked.

Johnny rattled the doorknob. "Listen, preacher," he said. "Mamie Pullen sent me and I'm going to pay you for it, so what the hell's the matter with you."

"You expect me to believe that a holy Christian like Mamie Pullen sent you to—" Reverend Short began croaking when all of a sudden Johnny grabbed the knob in a fit of rage and started to break in the door.

As though reading his thoughts, Reverend Short warned in a thin dry voice as dangerous as the rattle of a rattlesnake, "Don't you break down that door!"

Johnny snatched his hand back as though a snake had struck at him. "What's wrong with you, preacher, you got a woman in there with you?" he asked suspiciously.

"So that's what you're after?" Reverend Short said. "You think that murderess is hiding in here."

"Jesus Christ, man, are you stone raving crazy?" Johnny said, losing control of his temper. "Just open this mother-raping door. I ain't got all night to stand out here and listen to that loony stuff."

"Drop that gun!" Reverend Short warned.

"I ain't got no gun, preacher—are you jagged?"

Johnny heard the click of some sort of weapon being cocked.

"I warn you! Drop that gun!" Reverend Short repeated.

"To hell with you," Johnny said disgustedly, and started to turn away.

But his sixth sense warned him of imminent danger, and he dropped flat to the floor just before a double blast from a twelve-gauge shotgun blew a hole the size of a dinner plate through the upper panel of the wooden door.

Johnny came up from the floor as though he were made of rubber. He hit the door with a driving shoulder-block that had so much force it broke the lock and flung the door back against the wall with a bang loud enough to be an echo to the shotgun blast.

Reverend Short dropped the gun and whipped a knife from his side pants pocket, so quick the blade was open in his hand before the shotgun clattered on the floor.

Johnny was charging head first so fast he couldn't stop, so he stuck out his left hand and grabbed the wrist of Reverend Short's knife hand and butted him in the solar plexus. Reverend Short's glasses flew from his face like a bird taking wing, and he fell backwards across an unmade bed with a white-painted iron frame. Johnny landed on top of him, muscle-free as a cat landing on four feet, and in the same instant twisted the knife from Reverend Short's grip with one hand and began throttling him with the other.

His knees were locked about Reverend Short's middle as he put the pressure on his throat. Reverend Short's near-sighted eyes began bulging like bananas being squeezed from their skins, and all they could see was the livid scar on Johnny's blood-purple forehead, puffing and wriggling like a maddened octopus.

But he showed no signs of fear.

Just short of breaking the skinny neck Johnny caught himself. He took a deep breath, and his whole body shuddered as though from an electric shock to his brain. Then he took his hands from Reverend Short's throat and straightened up, still straddling him, and looked down soberly at the blue-tinted face beneath him on the bed.

"Preacher," he said slowly. "You're going to make me kill you."

Reverend Short returned his stare as he gasped for breath. When finally he could speak, he said in a defiant voice, "Go ahead and kill me. But you can't save her. They're going to get her anyway."

Johnny backed from the bed and got to his feet, stepping on Reverend Short's spectacles. He kicked them angrily from underfoot and looked down at Reverend Short lying supine in the same position.

"Listen, I want to ask you just one question," he said in his toneless, gambler's voice. "Why would she want to kill her own brother?"

Reverend Short returned his look with malevolence.

"You know why," he said.

Johnny stood dead still, as though listening, looking down at him. Finally he said, "You've tried to kill me. I ain't going to do nothing about that. You've called her a murderess. I ain't going to do nothing about that, either. I don't think you're crazy, so we can rule that out. All I want to ask you is *why?*"

Reverend Short's near-sighted eyes filled with a look of malignant evil.

"There's only two of you who would have done it," he said in a thin dry voice no louder than a whisper. "That's you and her. And if you didn't do it, then she did. And if you don't know why, then ask her. And if you think you're going to save her by killing me, then go ahead and do it."

"I ain't got much of a hand," Johnny said. "But I'll call it."

He turned and picked his way through the church benches toward the door. Light from the street lamps came in through the unpainted upper rim of the dingy front windows, showing him the way.

XI

IT WAS EIGHT o'clock, but still light.

"Let's go for a ride," Grave Digger said to Coffin Ed, "and look at some scenery. See the brown gals blooming in pink dresses, smell the perfume of poppies and marijuana."

"And listen to the stool pigeons sing," Coffin Ed supplied.

They were cruising south on Seventh Avenue in the small battered black sedan. Grave Digger eased the little car behind a big slow-moving trailer truck, and Coffin Ed kept his eyes skinned along the sidewalk.

A numbers writer standing in front of Madame Sweetie-pie's hairdressing parlor, flashing a handful of paper slips with the day's winning numbers, looked up and saw Coffin Ed's baleful eyes pinned on him and began eating the paper slips as though they were taffy candy.

Hidden behind the big truck trailer, they sneaked up on a

group of weedheads standing in front of the bar at the corner of 126th Street. Eight young hoodlums dressed in tight black pants, fancy straw hats with mixed-colored bands, pointed shoes and loud-colored sport shirts, wearing smoked glasses, and looking like an assemblage of exotic grasshoppers, had already finished one stick and were passing around the second one when one of them exclaimed, "Split! Here comes King Kong and Frankenstein."

The boy smoking the stick swallowed it so fast the fire burnt his gullet and he doubled over, strangling.

The one called Gigolo said, "Play it cool! Play it cool! Just clean, that's all."

They threw their switchblade knives onto the sidewalk in front of the bar. Another boy palmed the two remaining sticks and stuck them quickly in his mouth, ready to eat them if the detectives stopped.

Grave Digger smiled grimly.

"I could hit that punk in his belly and make him vomit up enough evidence to give him a year in the cooler," he said.

"We'll teach him that trick some other time," Coffin Ed said.

Two of the boys were beating the strangling boy on the back, the others began talking with big gestures as though discussing a scientific treatise on prostitution. Gigolo stared at the detectives defiantly.

Gigolo was wearing a chocolate-colored straw hat with a wide yellow band polka-dotted with blue. When Coffin Ed fingered his right coat lapel with the first two fingers of his right hand, Gigolo pushed his straw hat back on his head and said, "Nuts to them mother-rapers, they ain't got nothing on us."

Grave Digger drove on slowly without stopping, and in the rear-view mirror he saw the punk take the wet marijuana sticks from his mouth and start blowing on them to dry them.

They kept on down to 119th Street, turned back to Eighth Avenue, went uptown again and parked before a dilapidated tenement house between 126th and 127th Streets. Old people were sitting on the sidewalk in kitchen chairs propped against the front of the building.

They climbed the dark steep stairs to the fourth floor. Grave Digger knocked on a door at the rear, three single raps spaced exactly ten seconds apart.

For the space of a full minute no sound was heard.

There was no sound of locks being opened, but slowly the door swung inward five inches, held by two iron cables at top and bottom.

"It's us, Ma," Grave Digger said.

The ends of the cables were removed from the slots and the door opened all the way.

A thin old gray-haired woman with a wrinkled black face, who looked to be about ninety years old, wearing a floor-length Mother Hubbard dress of faded black cotton, stood to one side and let them pass into the pitch-dark hallway and closed the door behind them.

They followed her without further comment down to the far end of the hall. She opened a door and sudden light spilled out, showing a snuff stick in the corner of her wrinkled mouth.

"There he," she said, and Coffin Ed followed Grave Digger into a small back bedroom and closed the door behind him.

Gigolo sat on the edge of the bed with his fancy hat pushed to the back of his head, biting his dirty nails to the quick. The pupils of his eyes were big black disks in his tight, sweaty brown face.

Coffin Ed sat facing him, straddling the single straight-backed wooden chair, and Grave Digger stood glaring down at him and said, "You've had a bang of heroin."

Gigolo shrugged. His skinny shoulders jerked beneath the canary-colored sport shirt.

"Don't get him excited," Coffin Ed warned, and then asked Gigolo in a confidential tone of voice, "Who made the sting last night, sport?"

Gigolo's body began jerking as though someone had slipped a hot poker down the seat of his pants.

"Poor Boy got new money," he said in a rapid blurred voice.

"Who kind of money?" Grave Digger asked.

"Hard money."

"No green money?"

"If he is, he ain't showed it."

"Where's he likely to be at this time?"

"Acey-Deucey's poolroom. He's a pool freak."

Grave Digger asked Coffin Ed, "Do you know him?"

"This town is full of Poor Boys," Coffin Ed said, turning back to the stool pigeon. "What's he look like?"

"Slim black boy. Plays it cool. Working stiff jive. Don't never flash. Looks a little like Country Boy used to look 'fore they sent him to the pen."

"How does he dress?" Grave Digger asked.

"Like I just said. Wears old blue jeans, T-shirt, canvas sneakers, always looks raggedy as a bowl of yakamein."

"Has he got a partner?"

"Iron Jaw. You know Iron Jaw."

Grave Digger nodded.

"But he don't seem to be in on this sting. He ain't showed outside today," Gigolo added.

"Okay, sport," Coffin Ed said, standing up. "Lay off the heroin."

Gigolo's body began to jerk more violently. "What's a man going to do? You folks keeps me scared. If anybody finds out I'm stooling for you I be scared to shake my head." He was referring to a story they tell in Harlem about two jokers in a razor fight and one says, Man, you ain't cut me, and the other one says, if you don't believe I done cut you, just shake you head and it goin' to fall off.

"The heroin isn't going to keep your head on any better," Coffin Ed warned.

On the way out, he said to the old lady who'd let them in, "Cut down on Gigolo, Ma, he's getting so hopped he's going to blow his top one day."

"Lawd, I ain't no doctor," she complained. "I don't know how much they needs. I just sells it if they got the money to pay for it. You know, I don't use that junk myself."

"Well, cut down anyway," Grave Digger said harshly. "We're just letting you run because you keep our stool pigeons supplied."

"If it wasn't for these stool pigeons you'd be out of business," she argued. "The cops ain't goin' to never find out nothing if don't nobody tell 'em."

"Just put a little baking soda in that heroin, and don't give it to them straight," Grave Digger said. "We don't want these boys blind. And let us out this hole, we're in a hurry."

She shuffled down the black dark hall with hurt feelings and opened the three heavy locks on the front door without a sound.

"That old crone is getting on my nerves," Grave Digger said as they climbed into their car.

"What you need is a vacation," Coffin Ed said. "Or else a laxative."

Grave Digger chuckled.

They drove over to 137th Street and Lenox Avenue, on the other side from the Savoy Ballroom, climbed a narrow flight of stairs beside the Boll Weevil Bar to the Acey-Deucey poolroom on the second floor.

A small space at the front was closed off by a wooden counter for an office. A fat, bald-headed brown-skinned man, wearing a green eyeshade, a collarless silk shirt and a black vest adorned with a pennyweight gold chain, sat on a high stool behind the cash register on the counter and looked over the six pool tables arranged crosswise down the long, narrow room.

When Grave Digger and Coffin Ed appeared at the top of the stairs, he greeted in a low bass voice usually associated with undertakers. "Howdy do, gentlemen, how is the police business this fine summer day?"

"Booming, Acey," Coffin Ed said, his eyes roving over the lighted tables. "More folks getting robbed, slugged and stabbed to death in this hot weather than usual."

"It's the season of short tempers," Acey said.

"You ain't lying, son," Grave Digger said. "How's Deucey?"

"Resting as usual," Acey said. "Far as I heard."

Deucey was the man he had bought the business from, and he had been dead for twenty-one years.

Grave Digger had already spotted their man down at the fourth table and led the way down the cramped aisle. He took a seat at one end of the table and Coffin Ed took a seat at the other.

Poor Boy was playing a slick half-white pool shark straight pool, twenty-no-count, for fifty cents a point, and was already down forty dollars.

The balls had been racked for the start of a new game. It was Poor Boy's break and he was chalking his cue stick. He looked slantwise from one detective to the other and chalked his stick for so long the shark said testily, "Go head and break, man, you got enough chalk on that mother-raping stick to make a fifteen-cushion billiard shot."

Poor Boy put his cue ball on the marker, worked his stick back and forth through the circle of his left index finger and scratched. He didn't tear the velvet, but he made a long white stripe. His cue ball trickled down the table and tapped the racked balls so lightly as to barely loosen them.

"That boy looks nervous," Coffin Ed said.

"He ain't been sleeping well," Grave Digger replied.

"I ain't nervous," the shark said.

He broke the balls and three dropped into pockets. Then he settled down and ran a hundred without stopping, going from the break seven times, and when he reached up with his cue stick and flipped the century marker against the other ninety-nine on the line overhead, all the other games had stopped and jokers were standing on the table edges to get a look.

"You ain't nervous yet," Coffin Ed corrected.

The shark looked at Coffin Ed defiantly and crowed, "I told you I wasn't nervous."

When the rack man put the paper sack holding the stakes on the table, Coffin Ed got down from his seat and picked it up.

"That's mine," the shark said.

Grave Digger moved in behind, putting both the shark and Poor Boy between himself and Coffin Ed.

"Don't start getting nervous now, son," he said. "We just want to look at your money."

"It ain't nothing but plain United States money," the shark argued. "Ain't you wise guys never seen no money?"

Coffin Ed upended the bag and dumped the contents onto

the table. Dimes, quarters and half-dollars spilled over the green velvet, along with a roll of greenbacks.

"You ain't been in Harlem long, son," he said to the shark.

"He ain't goin' to be here long either," Grave Digger said, reaching out to flip the roll of greenbacks apart from the silver money. "There's your roll, son," he said. "Take it and find yourself another town. You're too smart for us country dicks in Harlem." When the shark opened his mouth to protest, he added roughly, "And don't say another God-damned word or I'll knock out your teeth."

The shark pocketed his roll and melted into the crowd. Poor Boy hadn't said a word.

Coffin Ed scooped up the change and put it back into the paper sack. Grave Digger touched the slim black boy on his T-shirted shoulder.

"Let's go, Poor Boy, we're going to take a ride."

Coffin Ed made an opening through the crowd. Silence followed them.

They put Poor Boy between them in the car and drove around the corner and parked.

"What would you rather have?" Grave Digger asked him. "A year in the Auburn state pen or thirty days in the city jail?"

Poor Boy looked at him slantwise through his long muddy eyes. "What you mean?" he asked in a husky Georgia voice.

"I mean you robbed that A and P store manager this morning."

"Naw suh, I ain't even seen no A and P store this morning. I made that money shining shoes down at the 125th Street Station."

Grave Digger hefted the sack of silver in his hand. "It's over a hundred dollars here," he said.

"I was lucky pitching halves and quarters," Poor Boy said. "You can ask anybody who was round there this morning."

"What I mean, son," Grave Digger explained, "is that when you steal over thirty-five dollars that makes it grand larceny, and that's a felony, and they give you one to five years in the state stir. But if you cooperate, the judge will let you take a plea to petty larceny and save the state the cost of a jury trial and appointing state lawyers, and you get off with thirty days in the workhouse. It depends on whether you want to cooperate."

"I ain't stole no money," Poor Boy said. "It's like what I done said, I made this money shining shoes and pitching halves."

"That's not what Patrolman Harris and that A and P store manager are going to say when they see you in that line-up tomorrow morning," Grave Digger said.

Poor Boy thought that over. Sweat started beading on his forehead and in the circles underneath his eyes, and oily beads formed over the surface of his smooth flat nose.

"Cooperate how?" he said finally.

"Who was riding with Johnny Perry when he drove down Seventh Avenue early this morning, just a few minutes before you made your sting?" Grave Digger asked.

Poor Boy blew air from his nose as though he'd been holding his breath. "I ain't seen Johnny Perry's car," he said with relief.

Grave Digger reached down and turned on the ignition and started the motor.

Coffin Ed said, "Too bad, son, you ought to have better eyes. That's going to cost you eleven months."

"I swear to God I ain't seen Johnny's big Cad in nearmost two days," Poor Boy said.

Grave Digger pulled out into the street and began driving toward the 126th Street precinct station.

"Y'all gotta believe me," Poor Boy said. "I ain't seen nobody on all of Seventh Avenue."

Coffin Ed looked at the people standing on the sidewalks and sitting on the stoops uninterestedly. Grave Digger concentrated on driving.

"There warn't a car moving on the avenue, I swear to God," Poor Boy whined. " 'Ceptin' that store manager when he drove up and that cop what's always there."

Grave Digger pulled to the curb and parked just before turning into 126th Street.

"Who was with you?" he asked.

"Nobody," Poor Boy said. "I swear to God."

"That's just too bad," Grave Digger said, reaching toward the ignition key.

"Listen," Poor Boy said. "Wait a minute. You say all I'm goin' to get is thirty days."

"That depends on how good your eyes were at four-thirty this morning, and how good your memory is now."

"I didn't see nothing," Poor Boy said. "And that's the God's truth. And after I grabbed that poke I was running so fast I didn't have time to see nothing. But Iron Jaw might of seen something. He was hiding in a doorway on 132nd Street."

"Where were you?"

"I was on 131st Street, and when the man drove up Iron Jaw was supposed to start yelling bloody murder and draw the cop. But he ain't let out a peep, and there I was, had already done sneaked up beside the car, and I just had to grab the poke and run."

"Where's Iron Jaw now?" Coffin Ed asked.

"I don't know. I ain't seen him all day."

"Where does he usually hang out?"

"At Acey-Deucey's like me most times, else downstairs in the Boll Weevil."

"Where does he live?"

"He got a room at the Lighthouse Hotel at 123rd and Third Avenue, and if'n he ain't there he might be at work. He pick chickens at Goldstein's Poultry Store on 116th Street and sometimes they stay open 'til twelve o'clock."

Grave Digger started the motor again and turned into 126th Street toward the precinct station.

When they drew up before the entrance, Poor Boy asked, "It's gonna be like you say, ain't it? If I cop a plea I don't get but thirty days?"

"That depends on how much your pal Iron Jaw saw," Grave Digger said.

XII

"I DON'T LIKE these mother-raping mysteries," Johnny said.

His thick brown muscles knotted beneath his sweat-wet

yellow crepe shirt as he banged the lemonade glass on the glass top of the cocktail table.

"And that's for sure," he added.

He sat leaning forward in the center of a long green plush davenport, his silk-stockinged, sweaty feet planted on the bright red carpet. The veins coming from his temples were swollen like exposed tree roots, and the scar on his forehead wriggled like a knot of live snakes. His dark brown lumpy face was taut and sweaty. His eyes were hot, vein-laced and smoldering.

"I done told you a dozen times or more I don't know why that nigger preacher's been telling all those lies about me," Dulcy said in a whining defensive voice.

Johnny looked at her dangerously and said, "Yeah, and I'm good and God-damned tired of hearing you tell me."

Her gaze touched fleetingly on his tight-drawn face and ran off to look for something more serene.

But there wasn't anything serene in that violently colored room. The overstuffed pea green furniture garnished with pieces of blonde wood fought it out with the bright red carpet, but the eyes that had to look at it were the losers.

It was a big front corner room with two windows on Edgecombe drive and one window on 159th Street.

"I'm just as tired of hearing you ask me all those goddam questions as you is tired of hearing me tell you I don't know the answers," she muttered.

The lemonade glass shattered in his hand. He threw the fragments across the floor and filled another one.

She sat on a yellow leather ottoman on the red carpet, facing the blond television-radio-record set that was placed in front of the closed-off fireplace beneath the mantelpiece.

"What the hell are you shivering for?" he asked.

"It's cold as hell in here," she complained.

She had shed down to her slip, and her legs and feet were bare. Her toenails were painted the same shade of crimson as her fingernails. Her smooth brown skin was sandy with goose pimples, but her upper lip was sweating, accentuating the downy black hairs of her faint moustache.

The big air conditioner unit in the side window behind her was going full blast, and a twelve-inch revolving fan beside it on the radiator cover sprayed her with cold air.

Johnny drank his glass of lemonade and put the glass down carefully, like a man who prided himself on self-control under any circumstances.

"No wonder," he said. "Why don't you get up and put some clothes on?"

"For Christsake, it's too hot to wear clothes," she said.

Johnny poured and gulped another glass of lemonade to keep his brain from overheating.

"Listen, baby, I ain't being unreasonable," he said. "All I'm asking you is three simple things—"

"What's simple to you ain't simple to nobody else," she complained.

His hot glance struck her like a slap.

She said with quick apology, "I don't know why that preacher's got it in for me."

"Listen to me, baby," Johnny went on reasonably. "I just want to know why Mamie all of a sudden begins pleading your case when I ain't even suspected you of doing nothing. Is that unreasonable?"

"How the hell do I know what goes on in Aunt Mamie's head?" she flared.

Then, on seeing rage pass across his face like summer lightning, she gulped a big swallow of the brandy highball she was drinking and strangled.

Spookie, her black cocker spaniel bitch, who had been resting at her feet, jumped up and tried to climb into her lap.

"And quit drinking so God-damned much," Johnny said. "You don't know what you're saying when you're drunk."

She looked about guiltily for a place to put the glass, started to put it on the television set, caught his warning look, then put it on the floor beside her feet.

"And stop that damn dog from lapping you all the time," he said. "You think I want you always covered with dog spit?"

"Get down, Spookie," she said, pushing the dog from her lap.

The dog stuck his hind leg into the highball glass and turned it over.

Johnny looked at the stain spreading over the red carpet and his jaw muscles roped like ox tendons.

"Everybody knows I'm a reasonable man," he said. "All I'm asking you is three simple things. First, how come that preacher tells the police a story about Chink Charlie giving you that knife?"

"For God's sake, Johnny," she cried, and buried her face in her hands.

"Get me straight," he said. "I ain't said I believed that. But even if the mother-raper had it in for you—"

At that moment the commercial appeared on the television screen, and four cute blonde girls wearing sweaters and shorts began singing a commercial in a loud cheerful voice.

"Cut off that mother-raping noise," Johnny said.

Dulcy reached up quickly and toned down the voice, but the quartet of beautiful-legged pygmies continued to hop about in happy, zippy pantomime.

The veins started swelling in Johnny's forehead.

Suddenly the dog began to bark like a hound treeing a coon.

"Shut up, Spookie," Dulcy said quickly, but it was too late.

Johnny leaped up from his seat like a raving maniac, over-turning the cocktail table and pitcher of lemonade, sprang across the floor and kicked the bitch in the ribs with his stockinged foot. The bitch sailed through the air and knocked over a red glass vase filled with imitation yellow roses sitting on a green lacquered end table. The vase shattered against the radiator, spilling paper yellow roses over the red carpet, and the bitch stuck its tail between its legs and ran yelping toward the kitchen.

The glass cover of the cocktail table had shattered against the overturned pitcher, and fragments of glass mingled with lumps of ice on the big wet splotch made by the spilt lemonade.

Johnny turned around, stepped over the debris and returned to his seat, like a man who prided himself on his self-control under all circumstances.

"Listen, baby," he said. "I'm a patient man. I'm the most reasonable man in the world. All I'm asking you is—"

"Three simple things," she muttered under her breath.

He took a long deep breath and ignored it.

"Listen, baby, all I want to know is how in the hell could that preacher make that up?"

"You always want to believe everybody but me," she said.

"And how come he keep on saying it was you who did it?" he kept on, ignoring her remark.

"God damn it, do you think I did it?" she flared.

"That ain't what's bothering me," he said, brushing that off. "What's bothering me is why in the hell *he* thinks you did it? What reason has he got to think you had for doing it?"

"You keep talking about mysteries," she said, showing signs of hysteria. "How come it was you didn't see Val all last night. He told me for sure he was going by the club and coming with you to the wake. He ain't had no reason to tell me he was if he wasn't. That's a mystery to me."

He looked at her long and thoughtfully. "If you keep popping off on that idea, that will get us all into trouble," he said.

"Then what you keep blowing off at me with all those crazy ideas you got about me, as if you think I kilt him," she said defiantly.

"It don't bother me who kilt him," he said. "He's dead and that's it. What bother me is all these mother-raping mysteries about you. You're alive and you're my woman, and I want to know why in the goddam hell all these people keep thinking things about you that I ain't never even thought of, and I'm your man."

Alamena came in from the hall and looked indifferently at the debris scattered about the room. She hadn't changed clothes but had put on a red plastic apron. The dog peeped out from behind her legs to see if the coast was clear, but decided that it wasn't.

"You all going to sit here and argue all night or do you want to come and get something to eat?" Alamena said indifferently, as though she didn't give a damn whether they ate or not.

For a moment both of them stared at her blankly, without replying. Then Johnny got to his feet.

Thinking Johnny didn't see her, with quick furtive motions

Dulcy snatched up the glass the dog had stepped into and poured it half full of brandy from a bottle she had cached behind the television set.

Johnny was walking toward the hallway, but he turned suddenly without a break of motion and slapped the glass from her hand. Brandy splashed in her face as the glass sailed through the air and went spinning across the floor.

She hit him in the face with her balled right fist as fast as a cat catching fish. It was a solid pop with fury in it, and it knocked tears from his eyes.

He turned in blind rage and clutched her by the shoulders and shook her until her teeth rattled.

"Woman!" he said, and for the first time she heard his voice change tone. It was deep, throaty and came out of his guts, and it worked on her like an aphrodisiac. "Woman!"

She shuddered and went candy. Her eyes got limpid and her mouth suddenly wet, and her body just folded into his.

He went as soft as drugstore cotton and pulled her to his chest. He kissed her eyes, her nose and throat, and bent over and kissed her neck and the curve of her shoulder.

Alamena turned quickly and went back to the kitchen.

"Why don't you believe me," Dulcy said against his biceps.

"I'm trying to, baby," he said. "But you got to admit it's hard."

She dropped her arms to her sides and he took his arms from around her and put his hands in his pockets. They went down the hall to the kitchen.

The two bedrooms, separated by the bathroom, were on the left side of the hall which opened onto the outside corridor. The dining room and the kitchen were on the right side. There was a back door in the kitchen, and a small alcove opening to the service staircase at the end of the corridor.

The three of them sat on the plastic-covered, foam-rubber cushioned chairs about an enamel-topped table covered with a red-and-white checked cloth and helped themselves from a steaming dish of boiled collard greens, okra, and pig's feet, a warmed-over bowl of black-eyed peas and a platter of cornbread.

There was half a bottle of bourbon whiskey on the table, but the two women avoided it and Johnny asked, "Ain't there no lemonade left?"

Alamena got a gallon jar from the refrigerator and filled a glass pitcher without comment. They ate without talking.

Johnny doused his food with red-hot sauce from a bottle with a label depicting two bright red, long-horned devils dancing in knee-deep bright red flames, and ate two heaping platefuls, six pieces of cornbread, and drank a half pitcher of ice-cold lemonade.

"It's hot as hell in here," he complained and got up and switched on a ten-inch revolving fan attached to the wall; then he sat down again and began picking his teeth with a wooden toothpick selected from the glass of toothpicks that remained on the table with the salt, pepper and other condiments.

"That fan ain't goin' to help you none with all that red devil sauce you've eaten," Dulcy said. "Some day your guts are going to catch on fire, and you ain't goin' to be able to get enough lemonade down inside of you to put it out."

"Who's going to preach Val's funeral?" Alamena asked.

Johnny and Dulcy stared at her.

Then Johnny started again. "If I hadn't just felt that mother-raper lowering the boom on me I'd be lying there right now blown half in two," he said.

Alamena's eyes stretched. "You mean Reverend Short?" she asked. "He shoot at you?"

Johnny ignored her question and kept hammering at Dulcy. "That don't bother me so much as why," he said.

Dulcy continued to eat without replying. Johnny's veins began to swell again.

"Listen, girl," he said. "I'm telling you, all I want to know is why."

"Well, for Christsake," Dulcy flared. "If I'm going to take the blame for what that opium-drinking lunatic does, I just may as well quit living."

The doorbell rang. Spookie began to bark.

"Shut up, Spookie," Dulcy said.

Alamena got up and went to the door.

She came back and took her seat without saying anything.

Doll Baby stopped in the doorway and put one hand on her hip.

"Don't bother about me," she said. "I'm practically one of the family."

"You've got the nerve of a brass monkey," Dulcy cried, starting to her feet. "And I'm going to shut your mouth right now."

"No you ain't," Johnny said without moving. "Just set down and shut up."

Dulcy hesitated for a moment, as though to defy him, but decided against it and sat down. If looks could kill, Doll Baby would have dropped stone-dead.

Johnny turned his head slightly and said to Doll Baby, "What do you want, girlie?"

"I just want what's due me," Doll Baby said. "Me and Val was engaged, and I got a right to his inheritance."

Johnny stared at her. Both Dulcy and Alamena stared at her, too.

"Come again?" Johnny said. "I didn't get that."

She waved her left hand about, flashing a brilliant stone set in a gold-colored band.

"He gave me this diamond engagement ring if you want proof," she said.

Dulcy let loose with a shrill, scornful laugh. "If you got that from Val it ain't nothing but glass," she said.

"Shut up," Johnny said to her, then to Doll Baby he said, "I don't need no proof. I believe you. So what?"

"So I got a right as his fiancée to anything he left," she argued.

"He ain't left nothing but this world," Johnny said.

Doll Baby's stupid expression gave way to a frown. "He must have left some clothes," she said.

Dulcy started to laugh again, but a look from Johnny silenced her. Alamena dropped her head to hide a smile.

"What about his jewelry? His watch and rings and things," Doll Baby persisted.

"The police are the people for you to see," Johnny said. "They got all his jewelry. Go tell them your story."

"I'm going to tell them my story, don't you worry," she said.

"I ain't worrying," Johnny said.

"What about that ten thousand dollars you were going to give him to open a liquor store?" Doll Baby said.

Johnny didn't move. His whole body became rigid, as though it were suddenly turned into bronze. He kept his unblinking gaze pinned on her so long she began to fidget.

Finally he said, "What about it?"

"Well, after all, I was his fiancée and he said you were going to put up ten grand for him to open that store, and I guess I got some kind of widow's rights," she said.

Dulcy and Alamena stared at her with a curious silence. Johnny's stare never left her face. She began to squirm beneath the concentrated scrutiny.

"When did he tell you that?" Johnny asked.

"The day after Big Joe died—day before yesterday, I guess it was," she said. "Him and me was planning on setting up housekeeping, and he said he was going to get ten grand from you for sure."

"Listen, girlie, you're sure about that?" Johnny asked. His voice hadn't changed, but he looked thoughtful and puzzled.

"As sure as I'm living," Doll Baby said. "I'd swear it on my mother's grave."

"And you believed it?" Johnny kept after her.

"Well, after all, why shouldn't I?" she countered. "He had Dulcy batting for him."

"You lying whore!" Dulcy cried, and was out of her chair and across the room and tangling with Doll Baby before Johnny could move.

He jumped up and pulled them apart, holding them by the backs of their necks.

"I'm going to get you for this," Doll Baby threatened Dulcy.

Dulcy spat in her face. Johnny hurled her across the kitchen with one hand. She snatched a razor-sharp kitchen knife from the sideboard drawer and charged back across the room. Johnny released Doll Baby and turned to meet her, spearing her wrist with his left hand and twisting the knife from her grip.

"If you don't get her out of here I'm going to kill her," she raved.

Alamena got up calmly, went out into the hall and closed the front door. When she had returned and taken her seat, she said indifferently, "She's already gone. She must have been reading your mind."

Johnny resumed his seat. The cocker spaniel bitch came out from beneath the stove and began licking Dulcy's bare feet.

"Get away, Spookie," Dulcy said, and took her own seat again.

Johnny poured himself a glass of lemonade.

Dulcy poured a water glass half full of bourbon whiskey and drank it down straight. Johnny watched her without speaking. He looked alert and wary, but puzzled. Dulcy choked and her eyes filled with tears. Alamena stared down at her dirty plate.

Johnny lifted the glass of lemonade, changed his mind and poured it back into the pitcher. He then poured the glass one-third full of whiskey. But he didn't drink it. He just stared at it for a long time. No one said anything.

He stood up without drinking the whiskey, and said, "Now I got another mother-raping mystery," and left the kitchen, walking silently on his stockinged feet.

XIII

IT WAS AFTER seven o'clock when Grave Digger and Coffin Ed parked in front of Goldstein's Poultry Store on 116th Street between Lexington and Third Avenues.

The name appeared in faded gilt letters above dingy plate-glass windows, and a wooden silhouette of what passed for a chicken hung from an angle-bar over the entrance, the word *chickens* painted on it.

Chicken coops, most of which were empty, were stacked six and seven high on the sidewalk flanking the entrance, and were chained together. The chains were padlocked to heavy iron attachments fastened to the front of the store.

"Goldstein don't trust these folks with his chickens," Coffin Ed remarked as they alighted from the car.

"Can you blame him?" Grave Digger replied.

There were more stacks of coops inside the store containing more chickens.

Mr. and Mrs. Goldstein and several younger Goldsteins were bustling about, selling chickens on the feet to a number of late customers, mostly proprietors of chicken shacks, barbecue stands, nightclubs and after-hours joints.

Mr. Goldstein approached them, washing his hands with the foul-scented air. "What can I do for you gentlemen?" he asked. He had never run afoul of the law and didn't know any detectives by sight.

Grave Digger drew his gold-plated badge from his pocket and exhibited it in the palm of his hand.

"We're the men," he said.

Mr. Goldstein paled. "Are we breaking the law?"

"No, no, you're doing a public service," Grave Digger replied. "We're looking for a boy who works for you called Iron Jaw. His straight monicker is Ibsen. Don't ask us where he got it."

"Oh, Ibsen," Mr. Goldstein said with relief. "He's a picker. He's in the back." Then he began worrying again. "You're not going to arrest him now, are you? I've got many orders to fill."

"We just want to ask him a few questions," Grave Digger assured him.

But Mr. Goldstein wasn't assured. "Please, sirs, don't ask him too many questions," he entreated. "He can't think about but one thing at a time, and I think he's been drinking a little, too."

"We're going to try not to strain him," Coffin Ed said.

They went through the door into the back room.

A muscular, broad-shouldered young man, naked to the waist, with sweat streaming from his smooth, jet-black skin, stood over the picking table beside the scalding vat, his back to the door. His arms were working like the driving rod of a speeding locomotive, and wet feathers were raining into a bushel basket at his side.

He was singing to himself in a whiskey-thick voice:

"Cap'n walkin' up an' down
Buddy layin' there dead, Lord,
On de burnin' ground,
If I'da had my weight in line,
I'da whup dat Cap'n till he went stone blind."

Chickens were lined up on one side of the big table, lying quietly on their backs with their heads tucked beneath their wings and their feet stuck up. Each one had a tag tied to a leg.

A young man wearing glasses came from behind the wrapping table, glanced at Grave Digger and Coffin Ed without curiosity, and walked over behind the picker. He pointed at one of the live chickens on the far corner of the table, a big-legged Plymouth Rock pullet, minus a tag.

"What's that chicken doing there, Ibsen?" he asked in a suspicious voice.

The picker turned to look at him. In profile his jaw stuck out from his muscle-roped neck like a pressing iron, and his flat-nosed face and sloping forehead slanted back at a thirty-degree angle.

"Oh, that there chicken," he said. "Well, suh, that there chicken belongs to Missus Klein."

"Why ain't it got a tag on it then?"

"Well, suh, she don't know whether she gonna take it or not. She ain't come back for it yet."

"All right, then," the young man said peevishly. "Get on with your work. Just don't stand there—we got these orders to fill."

The picker turned and his arms began working like locomotive driving rods. He began again to sing to himself. He hadn't seen the two detectives standing just inside the doorway.

Grave Digger gestured toward the door with his head. Coffin Ed nodded. They slipped out silently.

Mr. Goldstein deserted a customer for a moment as they passed through the front room. "I'm glad you didn't arrest Ibsen," he said, washing his hands with air. "He's a good worker and an honest man."

"Yeah, we noticed how much you trust him," Coffin Ed said.

They got in their car, drove two doors down the street, parked again and sat waiting.

"I'll bet a pint of rye he gets it," Grave Digger said.

"Hell, what kind of bet is that?" Coffin Ed replied. "That boy has stole so many chickens from those Goldsteins he's one quarter chicken himself. I'll bet he could steal a chicken out of the egg without cracking the shell."

"Anyway, we're going to soon see."

They almost missed him. The picker left by the back door and came out into the street from a narrow walk ahead of them.

He was wearing a big loose-fitting olive drab canvas army jacket with a ribbed cotton collar and a drawstring at the bottom, and his nappy head was covered with a GI fatigue cap worn backward, the visor hanging down the back of his neck. In that getup his iron jaw was more prominent. He looked as though he had tried to swallow the pressing iron and it had sunk between his bottom teeth underneath his tongue.

He went over to Lexington Avenue and started uptown, staggering slightly but careful not to bump into anyone, and whistling the rhythm of *Rock Around The Clock* in high, clear notes.

The detectives followed in their car. When he turned east on 119th Street, they pulled ahead of him, drew in to the curb and got out, blocking his path.

"What you got there, Iron Jaw?" Grave Digger asked.

Iron Jaw tried to get him into focus. His large muddy eyes slanted upward at the edges and had a tendency to look out from opposite corners. When finally they focused on Grave Digger's face they looked slightly crossed.

"Why don't you folks leave me alone," he protested in his whiskey-thick voice, swaying slightly. "I ain't done nothing."

Coffin Ed reached out quickly and pulled his jacket zipper open almost to the bottom. Smooth black shiny skin gleamed from a muscular hairless chest. But, down near the stomach, black and white feathers began.

The chicken lay cradled in the warm nest at the bottom of

the jacket, its yellow legs crossed peacefully like a corpse in a casket, and its head tucked out of sight underneath its outer wing.

"What are you doing with that chicken then?" Coffin Ed asked. "Nursing it?"

Iron Jaw looked blank. "Chicken, suh. What chicken?"

"Don't give me that cornfed Southern bull," Coffin Ed warned him. "My name ain't Goldstein."

Grave Digger reached down with his index finger and lifted the chicken's head from beneath the wing.

"This chicken, son."

The chicken cocked its head and gave the two detectives a startled look from one of its beady eyes, then it turned its head completely about and looked at them from its other eye.

"Looks like my mother-in-law whenever I have to wake her up," Grave Digger said.

All of a sudden the chicken started squawking and flapping about, trying to get out of its nest.

"Sounds like her, too," Grave Digger added.

The chicken got a footing on Iron Jaw's belly and flew toward Grave Digger, flapping its wings and squawking furiously, as though it resented the remark.

Grave Digger speared at it with his left hand and caught hold of a wing.

Iron Jaw pivoted on the balls of his feet and took off, running down the center of the street. He was wearing dirty canvas rubber-soled sneakers, similar to those worn by Poor Boy, and he was running like a black streak of light.

Coffin Ed had his long-barreled nickel-plated pistol in his hand before Iron Jaw had started to run, but he was laughing so hard he couldn't cry halt. When he finally got his voice he yelled, "Whoa, Billy-boy, or I'll blast you!" and fired three rapid shots into the sky.

Grave Digger was hampered by the chicken and was late with his pistol, which was identical with Coffin Ed's. Then he had to clip the chicken in the head to save it for evidence. When he finally looked up he was just in time to see Coffin Ed shoot the fleeing Iron Jaw in the bottom of the right foot.

The .38 caliber slug caught in the rubber sole of Iron Jaw's canvas sneaker and ripped it from his foot. His foot sailed out from underneath him, and he slid along the pavement on his rump. His flesh hadn't been touched, but he thought he'd been shot.

"They kilt me!" he cried. "The police has shot me to death!"

People began to collect.

Coffin Ed came up, swinging his pistol at his side, and looked at Iron Jaw's foot.

"Get up," he said, yanking him to his feet. "You haven't been scratched."

Iron Jaw tested his foot on the pavement and found that it didn't hurt.

"I must be shot somewhere else," he argued.

"You're not shot anywhere," Coffin Ed said, taking him by the arm and steering him back to their car.

"Let's get away from here," he said to Grave Digger.

Grave Digger looked about at the curious people crowding about. "Right," he said.

They put Iron Jaw between them on the front seat and the dead chicken on the back seat and drove east on 119th Street to a deserted pier on the East River.

"We can get you thirty days in the cooler for chicken steal-ing or we can give you back your chicken and let you go home and fry it," Grave Digger began. "It just depends on you."

Iron Jaw looked slantwise from one detective to the other.

"I don't know what y'all means, boss," he said.

"Listen, son," Coffin Ed warned. "Cut out that uncle tom-ming. Save it for the white folks. It doesn't have any effect on us. We know you're ignorant, but you're not that stupid. So just talk straight. You understand?"

"Yassuh, boss."

Coffin Ed said, "Don't say I didn't warn you."

"Who was riding with Johnny Perry when he drove down 132nd Street this morning just before Poor Boy robbed the A and P store manager?" Grave Digger asked.

Iron Jaw's eyes stretched. "I don't know what you all is

talking about, boss. I was dead asleep in bed all morning 'til I went to work."

"Okay, son," Grave Digger said. "If that's your story that'll cost you thirty days."

"Boss, I swear to God—" Iron Jaw began, but Coffin Ed cut him off, "Listen, punk, we've already got Poor Boy tagged for the job and are holding him for the morning court. He said you were standing in a doorway on 132nd Street just off of the Avenue, so we know you were there. We know that Johnny Perry drove past on 132nd Street while you were standing there. We're not trying to stick you for the robbery. We've already got you on chicken stealing. All we want to know is who was riding with Johnny Perry."

Sweat glistened on Iron Jaw's sloping, flat-featured face. "Boss men, I don't want no trouble with that Johnny Perry. I'd just as leave take my thirty days."

"There's not going to be any trouble," Grave Digger assured him. "We're not after Johnny. We're after the man who was with him."

"He stuck Johnny up and got away with two grand," Grave Digger improvised, taking a shot in the dark.

Iron Jaw whistled. "I thought there was something funny," he admitted.

"Didn't you notice that the man had a gun stuck in Johnny's side when they drove past?" Grave Digger said.

"Naw suh, I didn't see the gun. They drove up and parked just 'fore the corner, and the top was up and I couldn't see no gun. But I thought there was something funny 'bout them stopping right there as if they didn't want nobody to see 'em."

Grave Digger and Coffin Ed exchanged looks across Iron Jaw's stupid expression.

"Well, that pins that down," Grave Digger said. "He and Val had parked on 132nd Street before Poor Boy robbed the A and P store manager." He addressed his next question to Iron Jaw. "Did they get out of the car together or did Val get out alone?"

"Boss, I ain't seen no more than what I just told you, I swear to God," Iron Jaw declared. "When Poor Boy cut out with that poke, with that cop and that white man chasing him, there was a man looking out a window, and when they turned the corner it seemed like he tried to look around the corner to see where they was going, and the next thing I seed he was falling through the air. So I just naturally took off up Seventh Avenue, 'cause I didn't want to be there when the cops got there and started asking a lot of questions."

"You didn't notice how badly he was hurt?" Grave Digger persisted.

"Naw suh, I just figured he was dead and gone to Jesus," Iron Jaw said. "And it warn't like as if I was a big shot like Johnny Perry. If the cops found me there they was just liable as not to claim I pushed him out the window."

"You make me sad, son," Grave Digger said seriously. "Cops are not that bad."

"We'd like to let you take your chicken and go home and have your pleasure," Coffin Ed said. "But Valentine Haines was stabbed to death this morning, and we've got to hold you as a material witness."

"Yassuh," Iron Jaw said stoically. "That's what I mean."

XIV

IT WAS TEN-FIFTEEN at night when Grave Digger and Coffin Ed finally got around to calling on Chink Charlie.

First they'd had a foot race with a young man peddling skinned cats for rabbits. An old lady customer had asked for the feet, had become suspicious and called the police when told that they were nub-legged rabbits.

Then they'd had to interview two matronly Southern schoolteachers, living in the Theresa Hotel and taking summer courses at New York University, who had given a man posing as the house detective their money to put in the hotel safe.

They parked in front of the bar at 146th Street and St. Nicholas Avenue.

Chink had a room with a window in the fourth-floor apartment on St. Nicholas Avenue. He had chosen the black and yellow decor himself and had furnished it in modernistic style. The carpet was black, the chairs yellow, the day bed had a yellow spread, the combination television-record player was black trimmed with yellow, the small table-model refrigerator was black on the outside and yellow on the inside, the curtains were black-and-yellow striped, and the dressing table and chest of drawers were black.

The record player was stacked with swing classics, and Cootie Williams was doing a trumpet solo in Duke Ellington's *Take The A Train*. A ten-inch revolving fan on the sill of the open window blew in exhaust fumes, dust, hot air and the sound of loud voices from the congregation of whores and drunks in front of the bar down below.

Chink was standing in the glow of the table lamp in front of the window. His sweat-slick oily yellow body was clad in blue nylon boxer-type shorts. The fringe of a large purple-red scar, left by an acid burn, showed on his left hip above his blue shorts.

Stripped to her black nylon brassiere, black sheer nylon panties and high-heeled red shoes, Doll Baby was practicing her chorus routine in the center of the floor. She had her back to the window and was watching her reflection in the dressing-table mirror. A tray of dirty dishes containing leftovers from the chili bean and stewed chitterling dinners they'd ordered from the bar restaurant rested on the table top, cutting her reflection in half just below the panties, as though she might have been served without legs along with the other delicacies. The outline of three heavy embossed scars running across her buttocks were visible beneath the sheer black panties.

Chink was looking at them absently as they jiggled in front of his vision.

"I don't get it," he was saying. "If Val really thought he was going to get ten G's from Johnny and wasn't just bulling you—"

She flared up. "What the hell's got into you, nigger. You think I can't tell when a man's talking straight?"

She had told Chink about her interview with Johnny, and they were trying to think up some angle to put the squeeze on him.

"Sit down, can't you!" Chink shouted. "How the hell can I think—"

He broke off to stare at the door. Doll Baby stopped dancing in the middle of a step.

The door had opened quietly, and Grave Digger had come into the room. While they were staring, he went quickly across to the window and drew the shade. Coffin Ed stepped inside, closed the door behind him and leaned back against it. Both wore their hats pulled low over their eyes.

Grave Digger turned and sat on the edge of the window table beside the lamp.

"Well, go on, son," he said. "What's the only way to figure it?"

"What the hell do you mean by breaking into my room like this?" Chink said in a choking voice. His yellow face was diffused with rage.

The window curtain beating against the fan guard made so much noise Grave Digger reached over and turned the fan off.

"What was that, son?" he asked. "I didn't hear you."

"He's beefing because we didn't knock," Coffin Ed said.

Grave Digger spread his hands. "Your landlady said you had company, but we figured it was too hot for you to be engaged in anything embarrassing."

Chink's face began to swell. "Listen, you cops don't scare me," he raved. "When you cross that threshold without a warrant I consider it as breaking and entering like two burglars, and I can take my pistol and blow your brains out."

"That's not the right attitude for a man first on the scene of a murder," Grave Digger said, standing erect.

Coffin Ed crossed the floor, pulled open the top drawer, dug beneath a stack of handkerchiefs and brought out a Smith & Wesson .38 caliber pistol.

"And I've got a permit for it," Chink shouted.

"Sure," Coffin Ed conceded. "Your white folks down at the club where you work as a whiskey jerker got it for you."

"Yeah, and I'm going to have them take care of you two nigger cops," Chink threatened.

Coffin Ed dropped Chink's gun back into the drawer.

"Listen, punk—" he began, but Grave Digger cut him off.

"After all, Ed, be easy on the boy. You can see these two yellow people are not Negroes like you and me."

But Coffin Ed was too angry to go for the joke. He kept on talking to Chink. "You're out on bail as a material witness. We can pull you in any time we wish. We're trying to give you a break, and all we get from you is a lot of cute crap. If you don't want to talk to us here we can take you down and talk to you in the Pigeon Nest."

"You mean if I object to your pushing me around in my own house you can take me down to the precinct station and push me around there," Chink said venomously. "That's how you got to look like Frankenstein's monster, pushing people around."

Coffin Ed's acid-burned face went hideous with rage. Before Chink had finished speaking he had taken two steps and knocked him spinning across the yellow-covered bed. He had his long-barreled pistol in his hand and was moving in to pistol-whip Chink when Grave Digger grabbed him by the arms from behind.

"This is Digger," Grave Digger said in a quick pacifying voice. "This is Digger, Ed. Don't hurt the boy. Listen to Digger, Ed."

Slowly Coffin Ed's taut muscles relaxed, as the murderous rage drained out of him.

"He's a mouthy punk," Grave Digger went on. "But he's not worth killing."

Coffin Ed stuck his pistol back into the holster, turned and left the room without uttering a word, stood for a moment in the corridor and cried.

When he returned Chink was sitting on the edge of the bed, looking sullen and smoking a cigarette.

Grave Digger was saying, "If you're lying about the knife, son, we're going to crucify you."

Chink didn't reply.

Coffin Ed said thickly, "Answer."

Chink replied sullenly, "I don't know nothing about the knife."

Grave Digger didn't look at his partner, Coffin Ed. Doll Baby had backed over to the far corner of the bed and was sitting on its edge as though expecting it to explode underneath her any moment.

Coffin Ed asked her suddenly, "What racket were you and Val scheming?"

She jumped as if the bed had blown up as expected.

"Racket?" she repeated stupidly.

"You know what a racket is," Coffin Ed hammered. "As many rackets as you've been up with in your lifetime."

"Oh, you mean did he have a hype?" She swallowed. "Val didn't do nothing like that. He was a square—well, what I mean is he was straight."

"How did you two lovebirds expect to live? On your salary as a chorus girl or were you intending to do a little hustling on the side?"

She was too scared to act indignant, but she protested meekly. "Val was a gentleman. Johnny was going to stake him to ten grand to open a liquor store."

Chink turned his head about and gave her a look of pure venom. But the two detectives just stared at her, and suddenly became completely still.

"Did I say something?" she asked with a frightened look.

"No, you didn't," Grave Digger lied. "You told us that before." He flicked a glance at Coffin Ed.

Chink said quickly, "That's something she dreamed up."

Coffin Ed said flatly, "Shut up."

Grave Digger said casually, "What we're trying to find out is why. Johnny's too tight a gambler for a deal that tricky."

"After all, Val was Dulcy's brother," Doll Baby argued stupidly. "And what's tricky about opening a liquor store?"

"Well, first of all, Val couldn't get a license," Grave Digger explained. "He did a year in the Illinois state reformatory, and New York state doesn't grant liquor store licenses to ex-cons. Johnny's an ex-con himself, so he couldn't get the license in his own name. That means they'd have to bring a third party as a front to get the license and operate the business in his name.

The profits would be split too thin, and neither Johnny nor Val would have any legal way of collecting."

Doll Baby's eyes had stretched as big as saucers during this explanation. "Well, he swore to me that Dulcy was going to get the dough for him, and I know he wasn't lying," she said defensively. "I had him hooked."

For the next fifteen minutes the detectives questioned Chink and her about Val's and Dulcy's past life, but came up with nothing new. As they turned to leave, Grave Digger said, "Well, baby, we don't know what game you're playing, but if what you say is true, you've just about cleared Johnny of suspicion. Johnny's hot-headed enough to kill anybody in a rage, but Val was killed with cold-blooded premeditation. And, if he was trying to shake Johnny down for ten grand, that would be the same as if Johnny left his name on the murder. And Johnny ain't the boy for that."

"Well how about that!" Doll Baby protested. "I give you a reason for Johnny to have done it and you turn around and say that proves he didn't do it."

Grave Digger chuckled. "Just goes to show how stupid cops are."

They went out into the hall and closed the door behind them. Then, after talking briefly with the landlady, they went down the hall, left by the front door and closed that door behind them.

Neither Chink nor Doll Baby spoke until they heard the landlady locking and bolting the front door. But the detectives had merely stepped outside, then had turned quickly and re-entered the flat. By the time the landlady was bolting the front door they had stationed themselves in front of Chink's bedroom door and were listening through the thin wooden panel.

The first thing Chink said, jumping to his feet and turning on Doll Baby furiously, was, "Why in the God-damned hell did you tell 'em about the ten grand, you God-damned idiot?"

"Well for Christ's sake," Doll Baby protested loudly. "Do you think I wanted them think I was goin' to marry a mother-raping beggar?"

Chink grabbed her by the throat and yanked her from the

bed. The detectives glanced at each other when they heard her body thud against the carpeted floor. Coffin Ed raised his eyebrows interrogatingly but Grave Digger shook his head. After a moment they heard Doll Baby saying in a choked voice, "What the hell you trying to kill me for, you mother-raper?"

Chink had released her and had gone to the refrigerator for a bottle of beer.

"You've let the mother-raper out the trap," he accused.

"Well, if he didn't kill him, who did?" she said. Then she caught the expression on his face and said, "Oh."

"Whoever killed him it don't make no difference now," he said. "What I want to know is what he had on Johnny?"

"Well, I've done told you all I know," she said.

"Listen, bitch, if you're holding out on me—" he began, but she cut him off with, "You're holding out on me more than I'm holding out on you. I ain't holding out nothing."

"If you think I'm holding out anything, you had better just think it and not say it," he threatened.

"I ain't going to say nothing about you," she promised, and then complained, "Why the hell do you and me have to argue? We ain't trying to find out who killed Vall, is we? All we're trying to do is shake Johnny down for a stake." Her voice began getting confidential and loving. "I'm telling you, honey, all you've got to do is keep pressing him. I don't know what Val had on him, but if you keep pressing him he's got to give."

"I'm going to press him all right," Chink said. "I'm going to keep pressing him until I test his mother-raping nerve."

"Don't test it too hard," she warned. "Cause he's got it."

"That ugly mother-raper don't scare me," Chink said.

"Look what time it is!" Doll Baby exclaimed suddenly. "I gotta go. I'm goin' to be late as it is."

Grave Digger nodded toward the outside door, and he and Coffin Ed tiptoed down the hall. The landlady let them out quietly.

As they were going down the stairs, Grave Digger chuckled. "The pot's beginning to boil," he said.

"All I hope is that we don't overcook it," Coffin Ed replied.

"We ought to hear from Chicago by tomorrow or the

day after," Grave Digger remarked. "Find out what they've dug up."

"I just hope it ain't too late," Coffin Ed said.

"All that's missing is just one link," Grave Digger went on. "What it was that Val had on Johnny that was worth ten G's. If we had that we'd have it chained down."

"Yeah, but without it the dog's running loose," Coffin Ed replied.

"What you need is to get good and drunk one time," Grave Digger told his friend.

Coffin Ed rubbed the flat of his hand down his acid-burned face. "And that ain't no lie," he said in a muffled voice.

XV

IT WAS 11:32 O'CLOCK when Johnny parked his fishtail Cadillac on Madison Avenue near the corner and walked down 124th Street to the private staircase that led to his club on the second floor.

The name *Tia Juana* was lettered on the upper panel of the black steel door.

He touched the buzzer to the right of the doorknob once lightly, and an eye appeared immediately in the peephole within the letter *u* in the word *Juana*. The door swung open into the kitchen of a three-room flat.

A mild-mannered, skinny, bald-headed, brown-skinned man wearing starched khaki pants and a faded purple polo shirt said, "Tough, Johnny, two deaths back to back."

"Yeah," Johnny said. "How's the game going, Nubby?"

Nubby fitted the cushioned stump of his left arm, which was cut off just above the wrist, into the cup of his right hand and said, "Steady. Kid Nickels is running it."

"Who's winning?"

"I ain't seen. I been taking bets on the harness races for to-night at Yonkers."

Johnny had bathed, shaved and changed into a light green silk suit and a rose crepe shirt.

The phone rang and Nubby reached for the receiver on the paybox on the wall, but Johnny said, "I'll take it."

Mamie Pullen was calling to ask how Dulcy was.

"She's knocked herself out," Johnny said. "I left Alamena with her."

"How are you, son?" Mamie asked.

"Still kicking," Johnny said. "You get your sleep and don't worry 'bout us."

When he hung up Nubby said, "You look beat, boss. Why don't you just take a look about and cut back to the nest. Us three oughta be able to run it for one night."

Johnny turned toward his office without replying. It was located in the outer of the two bedrooms situated to the left of the kitchen. It contained an old-fashioned roll-top desk, a small round table, six chairs and a safe. The room across from it, equipped with a big deal table, was used as a spare gambling room.

Johnny hung up his green coat neatly on a hanger on the wall beside his desk, opened the safe and took out a sheaf of money tied with brown paper tape on which was written: $1,000.

Beyond the kitchen was a bathroom, and then the hallway ran into a large front room the width of the flat with a three-window bay overlooking Madison Avenue. The windows were closed and the curtains drawn.

Nine players sat about a large round-top table, padded with felt and covered with soiled tan canvas, in the center of the room. They were playing a card game called Georgia Skin.

Kid Nickels was shuffling a brand-new deck of cards. He was a short black burr-headed man with red eyes and rough pock-marked skin, wearing a red silk shirt several shades brighter than Johnny's.

Johnny walked into the room, put the sheaf of money on the table and said, "I'll take over now, Kid."

Kid Nickels got up and gave him his seat.

Johnny patted the sheaf of bank notes. "Here's fresh money that ain't got nobody's brand."

"Let's hope I latch on to some of it," Bad Eye Lewis said.

Johnny shuffled the cards. Crying Shine, the first player to his right, cut them.

"Who wants to draw?" Johnny asked.

Three players drew cards from the deck, showed them to each other to avoid duplication and put them on the table face down.

Johnny bet them ten dollars each for drawing. They had to call or turn in their cards. They called.

In Georgia Skin the suits—spades, hearts, clubs and diamonds—have no rank. The cards are played by denomination. There are thirteen denominations in the deck, the ace through the king. Therefore thirteen cards may be played.

A player selects a card. When the next card for that denomination is dealt from the deck, the first card loses. Skin players say the card has fallen. It goes into the dead, and can't be played again that deal.

Therefore a player bets that his card does not fall before his opponents' cards fall. If a player selects a seven, and the cards of all other denominations in the deck have been dealt off twice before the second seven shows, that player wins all the bets he has made.

Johnny spun the top card face upward and it dropped in front of Doc, the player who sat across the table from him. It was an eight.

"My hatred," Bad Eye Lewis said.

"I ain't got no hatred unless it be death," Doc said. "Throw down, all you pikers."

The players carried their bets to him.

Johnny edged up the deck and fitted it into the deal box, which was open on one side with a thumb-hole for dealing. He spun the three of spades from the deck for his own card.

Soft intense curses rose in the smoky light as the cards spun face upward from the box. Each time a card fell the bets were picked up by the winners and the loser played the next clean card dealt from the deck.

Johnny played the three throughout the deal without it falling. He placed twelve bets and made a hundred and thirty dollars on the deal.

Chink Charlie staggered into the room, waving a handful of money.

"Make way for a skinner from way back," he said in a whiskey-thickened voice.

Johnny was sitting with his back to the door and didn't look around. He shuffled the deck, edged it and put it down.

"Cut 'em, K.C.," he said.

The other players had looked once at Chink. Now they looked once at Johnny. Then they stopped looking.

"I don't suppose I'm barred from this mother-raping game," Chink said.

"I ain't never barred a gambler with money," Johnny said in his toneless voice without looking about. "Pony, get up and give the gambler your seat."

Pony Boy got up and Chink flopped into his seat.

"I feel lucky tonight," Chink said, slapping the money on the table in front of him. "All I want to win is ten grand. How 'bout it, Johnny boy? You got ten grand to lose?"

Once again the players looked at Chink, then back to Johnny, then at nothing.

Johnny's face didn't flicker, his voice didn't change. "I don't play to lose, buddy boy, you'd better find out that. But you can gamble here in my club as long as you got money, and walk out of here with everything you've won. Now who wants to draw?" he asked.

No one moved to draw a card from the deck.

"You don't scare me," Chink said, and drew one from the bottom.

Johnny charged him a hundred dollars. When Chink covered it he had only nineteen dollars left.

Johnny turned off the queen.

Doc played it.

Chink bet him ten dollars.

The queen of hearts doubled off.

"Some black snake is sucking my rider's tongue," somebody said.

Chink picked up the twenty dollars.

Johnny put the deck in the deal box and turned himself the three of spades again.

"Lightning never strikes twice in the same place," Bad Eye Lewis said.

"Man, don't start talking about lightning striking," Crying Shine said. "You're sitting right in the middle of a thunder storm."

Johnny turned off the deuce of clubs for Doc, who had first choice for a clean card.

Doc looked at it with distaste. "I'd rather be bit in the ass by a boa constrictor than play a mother-raping black deuce," he said.

"You want to pass it?" Johnny asked.

"Hell," Doc said, "I ain't gambling my rathers. Throw back, yellow kid," he said to Chink.

"That'll cost you twenty bucks," Chink said.

"That don't hurt the money, son," Doc said, covering it.

Johnny carried fifteen dollars to Doc, and began turning off the cards. Players reached for them, and bets were made. No one spoke. The silence grew.

Johnny spun the cards in the tight white silence.

A card fell. Hands reached for bets.

Doc fell again and looked through the dead for a clean card, but there wasn't any.

Johnny spun the cards and the cards fell. Chink's card held up. Johnny and Chink raked in the bets.

"I'll bet you some more, gambler," Johnny said to Chink.

"Throw down," Chink said.

Johnny carried him another hundred dollars. Chink covered it and had money left.

Johnny spun another card, then another. The veins roped in his forehead and the tentacles of his scar began to move. Blood left Chink's face until it looked like yellow wax.

"Some more," Johnny said.

"Throw down," Chink said. He was beginning to lose his voice.

They pressed their bet another twenty dollars.

Johnny eyed the money Chink had left. He pulled a card halfway out of the box and knocked it back.

"Some more, gambler," he said.

"Throw down," Chink whispered.

Johnny carried fifty dollars to Chink.

Chink covered twenty-nine and passed the rest back.

Johnny spun the card. The seven of diamonds flashed in the spill of light and fell on its face.

"Dead men falls on their face," Bad Eye Lewis said.

Blood rushed to Chink's face, and his jowls began to swell.

"That's you, ain't it?" Johnny said.

"How the hell you know it's me, lest you reading these cards," Chink said thickly.

"It's got to be you," Johnny said. "It's the only clean card left."

The blood left Chink's face again, and it turned ashy. Johnny reached over and turned up the card that lay in front of Chink. The seven of spades looked up.

Johnny raked in the stack of money.

"You shot me, didn't you," Chink accused. "You shot me. You saw the seven-spot on the turn when you pulled it halfway out the box."

"You ain't got but one more time to say that, gambler," Johnny said. "Then you goin' to have to prove it."

Chink didn't speak.

"If you bet fast you can't last," Doc said.

Chink got up without speaking and left the club.

Johnny began losing. He lost all his winnings and seven hundred dollars from the bank. Finally he stood up and said to Kid Nickels, "You take over, Kid."

He went back into his office, took a .38 Army Colt revolver from the safe and stuck it inside of his belt to the left of the buckle, put his green suit jacket over his rose crepe shirt. Before leaving the club he said to Nubby, "If I don't come back, tell Kid to take the money home with him."

Pony Boy came back to the kitchen to see if Johnny needed him, but Johnny was gone.

"That Chink Charlie," he said. "Death ain't two feet off him."

XVI

ALAMENA ANSWERED THE door bell.

Chink said, "I want to talk to her."

She said, "You're stark raving crazy."

The black cocker spaniel bitch stood guard behind Alamena's legs and barked furiously.

"What are you barking at, Spookie?" Dulcy called in a thick voice from the kitchen.

Spookie kept on barking.

"Don't try to stop me, Alamena, I warn you," Chink said, trying to push past her. "I've got to talk to her."

Alamena planted herself firmly in the entrance and wouldn't let him by.

"Johnny's here, you fool!" she said.

"Naw, he ain't," Chink said. "I just left him at the club."

Alamena's eyes widened. "You went to Johnny's club?" she asked incredulously.

"Why not," he said unconcernedly. "I ain't scared of Johnny."

"Who the hell is that you're talkin' to, Meeny?" Dulcy called thickly.

"Nobody," Alamena said.

"It's me, Chink," he called.

"Oh, it's you," Dulcy called. "Well, come on in then, honey, or else go 'way. You're making Spookie nervous."

"Hell with Spookie," Chink said, pushing past Alamena and entering the kitchen.

Alamena closed the entrance door and followed him. "If Johnny comes back and finds you here, he'll kill you sure as hell," she warned.

"Hell with Johnny," Chink fumed. "I got enough on Johnny to send him to the electric chair."

"If you live that long," Alamena said.

Dulcy giggled. "Meeny's scared of Johnny," she said thickly.

Both Alamena and Chink stared at her.

She was sitting on one of the rubber-cushioned kitchen chairs with her bare feet propped on the table top. She was clad only in her slip, with nothing underneath.

"Cops," she said, coyly, catching Chink's look. "You're peeping."

"If you weren't drunk I'd give you something to giggle about," Alamena said grimly.

Dulcy took her feet down and tried to sit straight.

"You're just mad 'cause I got Johnny," she said slyly.

Alamena's face went blank and she looked away.

"Why don't you get out and let me talk to her," Chink said. "It's important."

Alamena sighed. "I'll go up front and watch out the window for Johnny's car."

Chink pulled up a chair and stood in front of Dulcy with his foot on the seat. He waited until he heard Alamena enter the front room, then suddenly went and closed the kitchen door, came back and took his stance.

"Listen to me, baby, and listen well," he said, bending over and trying to hold Dulcy's gaze. "You're either going to get me those ten G's you promised to Val or I'm going to lower the boom."

"Boom!" Dulcy said drunkenly. Chink gave a violent start. She giggled. "Thought you wasn't scared?" she said.

Chink's face became mottled with red. "Listen, I ain't playing, girl," he said dangerously.

She reached up as though she'd forgotten his presence and began to scratch her hair. Suddenly she looked up and caught him glaring at her. "It's just one of Spookie's fleas," she said. He began swelling about the jowls, but she didn't notice. "Spookie," she called. "Come here, darling, and sit on Mama's lap." The dog came over and began to lick her bare legs, and she picked it up and held it in her lap. "It's just one of your little black fleas, ain't it, baby?" she said, bending over to let the dog lick her face.

Chink slapped the dog from her lap with such savage violence it crashed against the table leg and began running about the floor yelping and trying to get out.

"I want you to listen to me," Chink said, panting with rage.

Dulcy's face darkened with lightning-quick fury and she tried to stand up, but Chink put his hands on her shoulders and pinned her in the chair.

"Don't you hit my dog, you mother-raper!" she shouted. "I don't allow nobody to hit my dog but me. I'll kill you quicker for hitting my dog—"

Chink cut her off. "God damn it, I want you to listen."

Alamena entered the kitchen hurriedly, and when she saw Chink holding Dulcy pinned to her seat she said, "Let her alone, nigger. Can't you see she's drunk?"

He took away his hands but said furiously, "I want her to listen."

"Well, that's your problem," Alamena said. "You're a bar jockey. Get her sober."

"You want to get your throat cut again?" he said viciously.

She didn't let it touch her. "No damned nigger like you will ever do it. And I'm not going to watch out for more than fifteen minutes, so you'd better get your talking done in a hurry."

"You don't need to watch out for me at all," Chink said.

"I ain't doing it for you, nigger, you needn't worry 'bout that," Alamena said as she left the kitchen and went back to her post. "Come on, Spookie." The dog followed her.

Chink sat down and wiped the sweat from his face.

"Listen, baby, you're not that drunk," he said.

Dulcy giggled, but this time it sounded strained. "You're the one that's drunk if you think Johnny's going to give you ten grand," she said.

"He ain't the one who's going to give it to me," he said. "You're the one who's going to give it to me. You're going to get it from him. And you want me to tell you why you're going to do this, baby?"

"No, I just want you to give me time to brush off some of these hundred-dollar bills you see growing on me," she said, sounding more and more sober.

"There's two reasons why you're going to do this," he said.

"First, it was your knife that killed him. The same one I gave you for Christmas. And don't tell me you've lost it, because I know better. You wouldn't carry it around with you unless you intended using it, because you'd be too scared of Johnny seeing it."

"Oh no you don't, honey," she said. "You ain't going to make that stick. It was your knife. You're forgetting that you showed me both of them when you told me that man down at your club, Mr. Burns, had brought them back from London and said one was for you and one was for your girlfriend in case you got too handy with yours. I've still got the one you gave me."

"Let's see it."

"Let me see yours."

"You know damn well I don't carry that big knife around with me."

"Since when?"

"I ain't never carried it on me. It's at the club."

"That's just fine. Mine's at the seashore."

"I ain't joking with you, girl."

"If you think I'm joking with you, just try me. I can put my hand on my knife this minute. And if you keep pressing me about it I'm liable to get it and stick it into you." She didn't sound the least bit drunk any more.

Chink scowled at her. "Don't threaten me," he said.

"Don't you threaten me then."

"If you've still got yours, why didn't you tell the cops about mine?" he said.

"And have Johnny take the one I got and cut your throat and maybe mine too?" she said.

"If you're all that scared, why didn't you get rid of it?" he said. "If you think Johnny's going to find it and start chivving on you."

"And take a chance on you turning rat and saying it was my knife that killed him?" she said. "Oh no, honey, I ain't going to leave myself open for that."

His face began to swell, but he managed to keep his temper.

"All right then, let's say it wasn't your knife," he said. "I know it was but let's just say it wasn't—"

"All together now," she cut in. "Let's say bull."

"All right then," he said, "but I know you were going to shake Johnny down for ten grand. I know that for sure."

"And what I know for sure is that you and me ain't been drinking out the same bottle," she said. "You must have been drinking extract of gold or U.S. mint juleps, the way you keep talking about ten grand."

"You'd better listen to me, girl," he said.

"Don't think I ain't listening," she said. "I just keep hearing stuff that don't make any sense."

"I ain't saying it was your idea," he said. "But you were going to do it. That's for sure. And that means just one thing. You and Val had something on Johnny that was worth that much money or you'd never have gotten up the nerve to try it."

Dulcy laughed theatrically, but it didn't come off. "You remind me of that old gag where the man says to his girl, 'now let's both get on top.' That I'd like to see—just what me and Val had on Johnny that was worth ten grand."

"Well, baby, I'm going to tell you," he said. "It ain't as if I need to know what you had on him. I know you had something on him, and that's enough. When that's tied together with the knife, which you claim you've still got but ain't showing nobody, that means a murder rap for one of you. I don't know which one and I don't care. If it don't hurt you, don't holler. I'm giving you your chance. If you pass, I'm going to Johnny. If he plays tough I'm going to have a little talk with those two Harlem sheriffs, Grave Digger and Coffin Ed. And you know what that's going to mean. Johnny might be tough, but he ain't that tough."

Dulcy got up and staggered over to the sideboard and drank two fingers of brandy straight. She tried to stand, but she found herself teetering and flopped into another chair.

"Listen, Chink, Johnny's got enough trouble as it is," she said. "If you press him just a little bit now, he'll blow his top and kill you if they burn him in hell for it."

He tried to look unimpressed. "Johnny's got sense, baby. He might have a silver plate in his head but he don't want to burn any more than anybody else."

"Anyway, Johnny don't have that kind of money," she said. "You niggers in Harlem think Johnny's got a backyard full of money trees. He ain't no numbers man. All he's got is that little skin game."

"It ain't so little," Chink said. "And if he ain't got that kind of money, let him borrow it. He's got that much credit with the syndicate. And whatever he's got ain't going to do neither one of you no good if I drop the boom."

She sagged. "All right. Give me two days."

"If you can get it in two days you can get it by tomorrow," he said.

"All right, tomorrow," she conceded.

"Give me half now," he said.

"You know damn well Johnny don't have no five G's in this house," she said.

He kept pressing her. "How about you? Ain't you stole that much yet?"

She looked at him with steady scorn. "If you wasn't such a goddam nigger I'd stick you in the heart for that," she said. "But you ain't worth it."

"Don't try to kid me, baby," he kept on. "You got some dough stashed. You ain't the kind of chick to take a chance on getting kicked out on your bare ass."

She started to argue but changed her mind. "I've got about seven hundred dollars," she admitted.

"Okay, I'll take that," he said.

She got up and staggered toward the door. He stood up too, but she said, "Don't follow me, nigger."

He started to ignore her but changed his mind and sat down again.

Alamena heard her leave the kitchen and started back from the front room, but she called, "Don't bother, Meeny."

After a moment she returned to the kitchen with a handful of greenbacks. She threw them across the table and said, "There, nigger, that's all I've got."

He started to get up and pocket the money, but the sight of the green patch on the red-and-white checked cloth nauseated her, and before he could reach the money she had bent over and vomited all over it.

He grabbed her by the arms and slammed her into a chair, cursing a blue streak. Then he took the filthy money to the sink and began washing it.

Suddenly the dog came tearing into the kitchen and began barking furiously at the door that led to the service entrance, which was in the corner of the kitchen. It opened into a small alcove which led into the service stairway. The dog had heard the sound of a key being inserted quietly in the lock.

Alamena came running into the kitchen on its heels. Her brown face had turned pasty gray.

"Johnny," she whispered, pressing her finger to her lips.

Chink turned a strange shade of yellow, like a person who'd been sick for a long time with yellow jaundice. He tried to ram the half washed, dripping wet money into his side coat pocket, but his hands were trembling so violently he could scarcely find it. Then he looked wildly about as though he might jump out of the window if he weren't restrained.

Dulcy began laughing hysterically. "Who ain't scared of who?" she choked.

Alamena gave her a furiously frightened look, took Chink by the hand and led him toward the front door.

"For God's sake, shut up," she whispered toward Dulcy.

The dog kept barking furiously.

Then suddenly the sound of voices came from the back stairway.

Grave Digger and Coffin Ed had converged from the shadows the instant Johnny put his key in the lock.

In the kitchen they heard Grave Digger saying, "Just one minute, Johnny. We'd like to ask you and the missus some questions."

"You don't have to shout at me," Johnny said. "I ain't deaf."

"Occupational traits," Grave Digger said. "Cops talk louder than gamblers."

"Yeah. You got a warrant?" Johnny said.

"What for? We just want to ask you some friendly questions," Grave Digger said.

"My woman's drunk and ain't able to answer any questions, friendly or not," Johnny said. "And I ain't going to."

"You're getting kind of big for your britches, ain't you, Johnny," Coffin Ed said.

"Listen," Johnny said. "I ain't trying to be no big shot or play tough. I'm just tired. A lot of folks are pressing me. I pay a lawyer to talk for me in court. If you got a warrant for me or Dulcy, then take us. If you ain't, then let us be."

"Okay, Johnny," Coffin Ed said. "It's been a long day for everybody."

"Are you wearing your rod?" Grave Digger asked.

"Yeah. You want to see my license?" Johnny said.

"No, I know you got a license for it. I just want to tell you to take it easy, son," Grave Digger said.

"Yeah," Johnny said.

While they were talking, Alamena had let Chink out of the front door.

Chink had buzzed for the elevator and was waiting for it to come when Johnny let himself into the kitchen of his flat.

Alamena was washing the tablecloth. The dog was barking. Dulcy was still laughing hysterically.

"Why, imagine seeing you, daddy," Dulcy said in a blurred drunken voice. "I thought you were the garbage man, coming in that way."

"She's drunk," Alamena said quickly.

"Why didn't you put her to bed?" Johnny said.

"She didn't want to go to bed."

"Nobody puts Dulcy to bed when she don't want to go to bed," Dulcy said drunkenly.

The dog kept barking.

"She was sick on the tablecloth," Alamena said.

"Go home," Johnny said. "And take this little yapping dog with you."

"Come on, Spookie," Alamena said.

Johnny picked up Dulcy in his arms and carried her into the bedroom.

Outside in the corridor, Grave Digger and Coffin Ed joined Chink at the elevator doors.

"You're trembling," Grave Digger observed.

"Sweating, too," Coffin Ed added.

"I just got a chill is all," Chink said.

"Damn right," Grave Digger said. "That's the way to get chilled permanently, fooling around with another man's wife, and in his own house, too."

"I just been tending to my own business," Chink said argumentatively. "Why don't you cops try that sometime?"

"That's the thanks we get for giving you a break," Grave Digger said. "We held him up until you had time to get away."

"Don't talk to that son of a bitch," Coffin Ed said harshly. "If he says another word I'll knock out his teeth."

"Not before he talks," Grave Digger warned. "He's going to need his teeth to make himself understood."

The automatic elevator stopped on the floor. The three of them got in it.

"What is this, a pinch?" Chink asked.

Coffin Ed hit him in the solar plexus. Grave Digger had to restrain him. Chink walked out of the house between the two detectives, holding his stomach as though to keep it from falling out.

XVII

CHINK SAT ON the stool within the glaring circle of light in the Pigeon Nest, where Detective Sergeant Brody from Central Homicide had questioned him that morning.

But now he was being questioned by the Harlem precinct detectives, Grave Digger Jones and Coffin Ed Johnson, and it wasn't the same.

Sweat was streaming down his waxen face, and his beige summer suit was wringing wet. He was trembling again and he was scared. He looked at the wet money stacked on one end of the desk through sick, vein-laced eyes.

"I've got a right to have my lawyer," he said.

Grave Digger sat on the edge of the desk in front of him, and Coffin Ed stood in the shadows behind him.

Grave Digger looked at his watch and said, "It's five minutes after two o'clock, and we've got to have some answers."

"But I've got a right to have my lawyer," Chink said in a pleading tone. "Sergeant Brody said this morning I had a right to have my lawyer when I was questioned."

"Listen, boy," Coffin Ed said. "Brody is a homicide man and solving murders is his business. He goes at it in a routine way like the law prescribes, and if some more people get killed while he's going about it, that's just too bad for the victims. But me and Digger are two country Harlem dicks who live in this village and don't like to see anybody get killed. It might be a friend of ours. So we're trying to head off another killing."

"And there ain't much time," Grave Digger added.

Chink mopped his face with a wet handkerchief. "If you think anybody's going to kill me—" he began, but Coffin Ed cut him off.

"I personally wouldn't give a goddam if you were killed—"

"Take it easy, Ed," Grave Digger said, and then to Chink, "We want to ask you one question. And we want a true answer. Did you give Dulcy the knife that killed Val as Reverend Short said you did?"

Chink squeezed out a laugh. "I've already told you, I don't know anything about that knife."

"Because if you did give the knife to her," Grave Digger went on talking softly, "and Johnny got hold of it and killed Val with it, he's going to kill her, too, if we don't stop him. That's for sure. And maybe if we don't get him soon enough he's going to kill you, too."

"You cops act as if Johnny was a black Dillinger or Al Capone—" Chink was saying, but his teeth were chattering so loudly he sounded as though he were speaking pig Latin.

Grave Digger cut him off, still talking in a soft, persuasive voice. "And we know that you've got something on Dulcy, or else she wouldn't have let you in Johnny's house and taken the risk of talking to you for thirty-three minutes by the clock.

And if it wasn't something goddam serious she wouldn't have given you seven hundred and thirty bucks to keep quiet." He banged the meaty edge of his fist on the stack of squashy money, jerked it back and wiped his hand with his handkerchief. "Dirty money. Which one of you puked on it?"

Chink tried to meet his gaze defiantly but couldn't do it, and his own gaze kept dropping until it rested on Grave Digger's big flat feet.

"So there are only two possibilities," Grave Digger went on. "You either gave her the knife or else you found out what Val knew about her that he was going to use to make her dig ten grand out of Johnny. And we don't figure you found that out since we talked to you because we've been shadowing you, and we know you went straight from your room to Johnny's club and from there to see Dulcy. So you must know about the knife."

He stopped talking and they waited for Chink to answer.

Chink didn't speak.

Suddenly, without warning, Coffin Ed stepped forward from the shadows and chopped Chink across the back of his neck with the edge of his hand. It knocked Chink forward, stunning him, and Coffin Ed grabbed him beneath the arms to keep him from falling on his face.

Grave Digger slid quickly from the desk and handcuffed Chink's ankles, drawing the bracelets tight just above the ankle bones. Then Coffin Ed handcuffed Chink's hands behind his back.

Without saying another word, they opened the door, lifted Chink from the chair and hung him upside down from the top of the door by his handcuffed ankles, so that the top part of the door split his legs down to his crotch. His back lay flat against the bottom edge, with the lock bolt sticking into him.

Then Grave Digger inserted his heel into Chink's left armpit and Coffin Ed did the same with his right, and they pushed down gradually.

Chink thought about the ten thousand dollars that Dulcy was going to get for him that day and tried to stand it. He tried to scream, but he had waited too late. All that came out was his tongue and he couldn't get it back. He began choking, and his eyes began to bulge.

"Let's take him down now," Grave Digger said.

They lifted him down and stood him on his feet, but he couldn't stand. He pitched forward. Grave Digger caught him before he hit the floor and lifted him back onto the stool.

"All right, spill it," Coffin Ed said. "And it'd better be straight."

Chink swallowed. "Okay," he said in a gasping voice. "I gave her the knife."

Coffin Ed's burnt face contorted with rage. Chink ducked automatically, but Coffin Ed merely clenched and opened his fists.

"When did you give it to her?" Grave Digger asked.

"It was just like the preacher said," Chink confessed. "One of the club members, Mr. Burns, brought it back from London and gave it to me for a Christmas present, and I gave it to her."

"What for?" Coffin Ed asked.

"Just for a gag," Chink said. "She's so scared of Johnny I thought it'd be a good joke."

"Damn right," Grave Digger said sourly. "It would have been awfully funny if you'd found it stuck between your own ribs."

"I didn't figure she'd let Johnny find it," Chink said.

"How do you know he found it?" Coffin Ed asked.

"We haven't got time for guesses," Grave Digger said.

They removed the handcuffs from Chink's wrists and ankles and booked him on suspicion of murder.

Then they tried to contact the Mr. Burns whom he said had given him the knife to verify the story. But the night clerk at the University Club said, in reply to their phone call, that Mr. Burns was in Europe somewhere.

They went back to Johnny's flat, rang the bell and hammered on the door. No one answered. They tried the service door. Grave Digger listened with his ear to the panel.

"Quiet as a grave," he said.

"Something's happened to the dog," Coffin Ed said.

They looked at one another.

"If we go in without a search warrant it's going to be risky," Grave Digger said. "If he's in there and he's already killed her, we're going to have to kill him. And if he hasn't done anything to her at all and they're both in there just keeping quiet and we break in, there's going to be hell to pay. He's liable to get us busted down to harness."

"I just hate to have Johnny kill his woman and go to the chair on account of a rat-tail punk like Chink," Coffin Ed said. "For all we know she might have killed Val herself. But if Johnny finds out she got the knife from Chink, her life ain't worth a damn."

"Chink might be lying," Grave Digger suggested.

"If he is, he'd better disappear from the face of the earth," Coffin Ed said.

"We'd better go in the front way then," Grave Digger said. "If Johnny's laying in there in the dark with his heater we'll have a better chance in that straight hall."

The door was framed on both sides and at the top by heavy iron angle-bars, making it impossible to pry open, and it was secured by three separate Yale locks.

It took Coffin Ed fifteen minutes working with seven master keys before he got it open.

They stood flanking the door with drawn revolvers while Grave Digger pushed it open with his foot. No sound came from the dark tunnel of the hall.

There was a chain-bolt on the door which, when fastened, kept it from opening more than a crack, but it hadn't been fastened.

"The chain's off," Grave Digger said. "He's not here."

"Don't take any chances," Coffin Ed warned.

"What the hell! Johnny's no lunatic," Grave Digger said, and walked into the dark hall. "It's me, Digger, and Ed Johnson, if you're in here, Johnny," he said quietly, felt for the light switch and turned on the hall light.

Their eyes went straight to a hasp and staple fitted to the outside of the master-bedroom door. It was fastened with a heavy brass Yale padlock. Coffin Ed closed the outside door, and they went down the hall and listened with their ears against the panel of the bedroom door. The only sound from within came from a radio tuned to an all-night disk jockey program of swing music.

"Anyway, she ain't dead," Grave Digger said. "He wouldn't lock up a corpse."

"But he's got hold of something or else he's blowing his top," Coffin Ed replied.

"Let's see what's in the rest of the house," Grave Digger suggested.

They started with the sitting room across the front and worked back to the kitchen. None of the rooms had been cleaned or straightened. The broken glass from the overturned cocktail table lay on the sitting-room carpet.

"Looks like it got kind of rough," Coffin Ed observed.

"It could be he's beaten her up," Grave Digger conceded.

The two bedrooms were across the hall from the kitchen and were separated by the bathroom. There, doors from each opened into the bathroom, which could be bolted from both sides. The door leading into the room Val had occupied was ajar, but the one to the master bedroom was bolted. Grave Digger slipped the bolt and they went in.

The shades were drawn and the room was dark save for a faint glow from the radio dial.

Coffin Ed switched on the light.

Dulcy lay on her side with her knees drawn up and her hands between her legs. She had kicked the covers off, and her nude sepia body had the dull sheen of metal. She was breathing silently, but her face was greasy from sweat and saliva had drooled from the bottom corner of her mouth.

"Sleeping like a baby," Grave Digger said.

"A drunken baby," Coffin Ed amended.

"Smells it, too," Grave Digger admitted.

There was an empty brandy bottle on the carpet beside the bed and an overturned glass in the center of a wet stain.

Coffin Ed crossed to the single window opening onto the inside fire escape and parted the drapes. The heavy iron grille on the outside of the window was padlocked.

He turned and came back to the bed. "Do you think this

sleeping beauty knows she's been locked in?" he asked.

"Hard to say," Grave Digger admitted. "How do you figure it?"

"The way I figure it is Johnny's on to something, but he doesn't know what," Coffin Ed said. "He's out scouting about trying to find out something, and he's locked her up just in case he finds out the wrong thing."

"Do you think he knows about the knife?"

"If he does, he's out looking for Chink, and that's for sure," Coffin Ed said.

"Let's see what she's got to say," Grave Digger suggested, shaking her by the shoulder.

She awakened and brushed at her face drunkenly.

"Wake up, little sister," Grave Digger said.

"Go way," she muttered without opening her eyes. "Done give you all I got." Suddenly she giggled. "All but you-know-what. Ain't never going to give you none of that, nigger. That's all for Johnny."

Grave Digger and Coffin Ed looked at each other.

"I don't figure this at all," Grave Digger admitted.

"Maybe we'd better take her in," Coffin Ed ventured.

"We could, but if it turns out later that we're wrong and Johnny hasn't got anything against her other than just being normally jealous—"

"What do you call being normally jealous?" Coffin Ed interrupted. "You call locking up your woman being normally jealous?"

"For Johnny, anyway," Grave Digger said. "And if he comes back and finds we've broken into his house and arrested his woman—"

"On suspicion of murder," Coffin Ed interrupted again.

"Not even that would save us from a suspension. It's not as if we were picking her up off the street. We've broken into her house, and there's no evidence of a crime having been committed in here. And we'd need a warrant even if the charge were murder itself."

"Well, the only thing to do is to find him before he finds out what he's looking for," Coffin Ed acceded.

"Yeah, and we'd better get going because time is getting short," Grave Digger said.

They went back through the bathroom, leaving the door wide open, and locked the front door with only the automatic lock.

First they went to the garage on 155th Street where Johnny kept his fishtail Cadillac, but he hadn't been in. Then they went by his club. It was dark and closed.

Next they began touring the cabarets, the dice games, the after-hours joints. They dropped the word they were looking for Chink Charlie.

The bartender at Small's Paradise Inn said, "I ain't seen Chink all evening. He must be in jail. You looked for him there?"

"Hell, that's the last place cops ever look for anybody," Grave Digger said.

"Let's see if he's gone home yet," Coffin Ed suggested finally.

They went back to the flat, rang the bell. Receiving no answer they went in again. It was just as they had left it. Dulcy was sleeping in the same position. The radio station was signing off.

Coffin Ed looked at his watch. "It's four o'clock," he said. "Nothing for it now but to call it a day."

They drove back to the precinct station and made out their report. The lieutenant on charge at night sent for them and read the report before letting them off.

"Hadn't we better pick up the Perry woman?" he said.

"Not without a warrant," Grave Digger said. "We haven't been able to verify Chink Charlie Dawson's story about the knife, and if he's lying she can sue us for false arrest."

"What the hell," the lieutenant said. "You sound like she's Mrs. Vanderbilt."

"Maybe she's not Mrs. Vanderbilt, but Johnny Perry carries his weight in this town," Grave Digger said. "And that's out of our precinct, anyway."

"Okay, I'll have the 152nd Street precinct station put a couple of men in the building to arrest Johnny when he shows," the lieutenant said. "You fellows get some sleep. You've earned it."

"Anything yet from Chicago on Valentine Haines?" Grave Digger asked.

"Not a thing," the lieutenant said.

The sky was overcast when they left the station, and the air was hot and muggy.

"It looks like it's going to rain cats and dogs," Grave Digger said.

"Let it come down," Coffin Ed said.

XVIII

MAMIE PULLEN WAS having breakfast when the telephone rang. She had a plate full of fried fish and boiled rice, and was dipping hot biscuits into a mixture of melted butter and black-strap sorghum molasses.

Baby Sis had finished her breakfast an hour before, and was filling Mamie's cup from a pot of leftover coffee that had been boiling on the stove.

"Go answer it," Mamie said sharply. "Just don't stand there like a lump on a log."

"I just don't seem to be able to get myself together this mawning," Baby Sis said as she shuffled from the kitchen, through the sitting room, into the bedroom at the front.

When she returned Mamie was sipping jet-black coffee hot enough to scald a fowl.

"It's Johnny," she said.

Mamie was holding her breath as she got up from the table.

She was dressed in a faded red-flannel kimono and a pair of Big Joe's old working shoes. On her head she wore a black cotton stocking, knotted in the middle and hanging down her back.

"What you doing up so soon?" she asked into the phone. "Or has you gone to bed yet?"

"I'm in Chicago," Johnny said. "I flew here this morning."

Mamie's thin old body began trembling violently beneath the slack folds of the rusty old kimono, and the telephone shook in her hands as though she had the palsy.

"Trust her, son," she pleaded in a whining voice. "Trust her. She loves you."

"I trust her," Johnny said in his flat toneless voice. "How much trust am I supposed to have?"

"Then let it alone son," she begged. "You got her all for yourself. Ain't that enough?"

"I don't know whether I got her all for myself or not," he said. "That's what I want to find out."

"Ain't no good ever come from digging up the past," she warned.

"You tell me what it is and I'll stop digging," he said.

"Tell you what, son?"

"Whatever in the hell it is," he said. "If I knew I wouldn't be here."

"What is you want to know?"

"I just want to know what it is she thinks I'll pay ten grand for her to tell me," he said.

"You got it all wrong, Johnny," she argued in a moaning voice. "That's just Doll Baby lying to try to make herself look big. If Val was alive he'd tell you she was lying."

"Yeah. But he ain't alive," Johnny said. "And I got to find out for myself whether she's lying or not."

"But Val must have told you something," she said, sobbing deep in her thin old chest. "He must of told you something or else—" She broke off and began to swallow as though to swallow the words she'd already said.

"Or else what?" he asked in his toneless voice.

She kept swallowing until she could say finally, "Well, it's got to be something that you went all the way to Chicago for, 'cause it can't just be what a lying little bitch like Doll Baby says."

"All right then, what about you?" he said. "You ain't been lying. What you keep pleading Dulcy's case for then, if there ain't nothing to plead for?"

"I just don't want to see no more trouble, son," she moaned. "I just don't want to see no more blood spilt. Whatever it might have been, it's over with and she's all yours now, you can believe that."

"You ain't doing nothing but just adding to the mystery," he said.

"There ain't never been any mystery," she argued. "Not on her part. Not unless you made it."

"Okay, I made it," he said. "Let's drop it. What I called to tell you was I got her locked up in the bedroom—"

"Good Lord above!" she exclaimed. "What good you think that's going to do?"

"Just listen to me," he said. "The door's padlocked from the outside with a Yale lock. The key is on the kitchen shelf. I want you to go and let her out long enough to get something to eat and then lock her up again."

"Lord have mercy, son," she said. "How long do you think you can keep her locked up like that?"

"Until I straighten out some of these mysteries," he said. "That ought to be before the day's over."

"Don't forget one thing, son," she pleaded. "She loves you."

"Yeah," he said, and hung up.

Mamie dressed quickly in her black satin Mother Hubbard and her own men's shoes, dipped her bottom lip full of snuff and took the snuff stick and box of snuff along with her.

The sky was black-dark like an eclipse of the sun, and the street lights were still burning. Not a grain of dust nor a scrap of paper moved in the still close air. People walked about silently, in slow motion, like a city full of ghosts, and cats and dogs tiptoed from garbage can to garbage can as though afraid their footsteps might be heard. Before she found an empty taxi she felt herself suffocating from the exhaust fumes that didn't rise ten feet above the pavement.

"It's going to rain tadpoles and bull frogs," the colored driver said.

"It'll be a blessing," she said.

She had her own set of keys to the apartment, but it took her a long time to get in because Grave Digger and Coffin Ed had left the locks unlocked and she locked them thinking she was opening them.

When finally she got inside she had to sit for a moment in the kitchen to steady her trembling. Then she took the key from the shelf and unlocked the bedroom door from the hall. She noticed that the bathroom door was standing open but her thoughts were so confused it held no meaning for her.

Dulcy was still asleep.

Mamie covered her with a sheet and took the empty brandy bottle and glass back to the kitchen. She began cleaning the house to occupy her mind.

It was ten minutes to twelve and she was scrubbing the kitchen floor when the thunderstorm broke. She drew the shades, put away the scrub brush and pail and sat at the table with her head bowed low and began to pray.

"Lord, show them the way, show them the light, don't let him kill nobody else."

The sound of the thunder had awakened Dulcy, and she stumbled toward the kitchen, calling in a frightened voice, "Spookie. Here, Spookie."

Mamie looked up from the table. "Spookie ain't here," she said.

Dulcy gave a start at sight of her. "Oh, it's you!" she exclaimed. "Where's Johnny?"

"Didn't he tell you?" Mamie asked.

"Tell me what?"

"He flew to Chicago."

Dulcy's eyes widened with terror and her face blanched to a muddy yellow. She flopped into a chair, but got up the next instant, got a bottle of brandy and a glass from the cabinet and gulped a stiff drink to quiet her trembling. But she kept on trembling. She brought the bottle and glass back to the table and sat down again and poured herself half a glass and started to drink it. Then she caught Mamie's look and put it down on the table. Her hand was trembling so violently the glass rattled on the enameled table top.

"Put on some clothes, child," Mamie said compassionately. "You're shaking from cold."

"I ain't cold," Dulcy denied. "I'm just scared to death, Aunt Mamie."

"I am, too, child," Mamie said. "But put on some clothes anyway, you ain't decent."

Dulcy got up without replying and went into the bedroom and put on a yellow flannel robe and matching mules. When she returned she picked up the glass and gulped the brandy down. She choked and sat down, gasping for breath.

Mamie dipped another lipful of snuff.

They sat silently without looking at each other.

Then Dulcy poured another drink.

"Don't, child," Mamie begged her. "Drinking ain't going to help none."

"Well, you got your lip full of snuff," Dulcy charged.

"That ain't the same thing," Mamie said. "Snuff purifies the blood."

"Alamena must have took her with her," Dulcy said. "Spookie, I mean."

"Didn't Johnny say nothing at all to you?" Mamie asked. A sudden clap of thunder made her shudder and she moaned, "God above, the world's coming to an end."

"I don't know what he said," Dulcy confessed. "All I know is he came sneaking in the back door and that's the last thing I remember."

"Was you alone?" Mamie asked fearfully.

"Alamena was here," Dulcy said. "She must have taken Spookie home with her." Then suddenly she caught Mamie's meaning. "My God, Aunt Mamie, you must think I'm a whore!" she exclaimed.

"I'm just trying to find out why he flew to Chicago all of a sudden," Mamie said.

"To check up on me," Dulcy said, gulping her drink defiantly. "For what else? He's always trying to check up on me. That's all he ever does, just check up on me." A roll of thunder rattled the windowpanes. "My God, I can't stand all that thunder!" she cried, jumping to her feet. "I got to go to bed."

She grabbed the brandy bottle and glass and fled to the bedroom. Lifting the top of the combination radio and record player, she put on a record, got into the bed and pulled the covers up to her eyes.

Mamie followed after a moment and sat in the chair beside the bed.

The wailing voice of Bessie Smith began to pour into the room over the sound of the rain beating against the windowpanes:

When it rain five days an' de skies turned dark as night
When it rain five days an' de skies turned dark as night
Then trouble taken place in the lowland that night

"Don't you even know why he locked you up?" Mamie asked.

Dulcy reached over and turned the player down.

"Now, what'd you say?" she asked.

"Johnny had you padlocked in this room," Mamie said. "He phoned me from Chicago to come over and let you out. That's how come I knew he was in Chicago."

"That ain't nothing strange for him," Dulcy said. "He's chained me to the bed."

Mamie began to sob quietly to herself. "Child, what's happening?" she asked. "What happened here last night to send him off like that?"

"Ain't nothing happened no more than usual," Dulcy said sullenly. Then after a moment she added, "You know that knife?"

"Knife? What knife?" Mamie looked blank.

"The knife what killed Val," Dulcy whispered.

Thunder rolled and Mamie gave a start. Rain slashed at the windows.

"Chink Charlie gave me a knife just like it," Dulcy said.

Mamie held her breath while Dulcy told her about the two knives, one of which Chink had given to her and the other he'd kept for himself. Then she sighed so profoundly with relief it sounded as though she were moaning again.

"Thank God then we know it was Chink who done it," she said.

"That's what I've been saying all along," Dulcy said. "But ain't nobody wanted to listen to me."

"But you can prove it, child," Mamie said. "All you got to do is show the police your knife and then they'll know it was his that killed him."

"But I ain't got mine no more," Dulcy said. "That's what I'm so scared of. I always kept it hidden in my lingerie drawer and then about two weeks ago it come up missing. And I been scared to ask anybody about it."

Mamie's complexion turned a strange ashy gray, and her face shrank until the skin was stretched tight against the bones. Her eyes looked sick and haggard.

"It just don't have to be Johnny what took it, does it?" she asked piteously.

"No, it don't have to be for sure," Dulcy said. "But there ain't nobody else who could have took it but Alamena. I don't know why she'd have taken it unless just to keep Johnny from finding it. Or else to have something to hold over me."

"You has a woman to come in here to clean," Mamie said.

"Yes, she could have taken it too," Dulcy admitted.

"It don't sound like Meeny," Mamie said. "So it must have been her. You tell me who she is, child, and if she took it I'll get it out of her."

They looked at one another through frightened, white-circled eyes.

"We just kidding ourselves, Aunt Mamie," Dulcy said. "Ain't nobody took that knife but Johnny."

Mamie looked at her and the tears rolled down her old ashy-black cheeks.

"Child, did Johnny know any reason to kill Val?" she asked.

"What reason could he have had?" Dulcy countered.

"I didn't ask what reason he could have had," Mamie said. "I asked what reason he might have known about."

Dulcy slid down into the bed until only her eyes were showing above the covers, but still she couldn't meet Mamie's gaze. She looked away.

"He didn't know of none," she said. "He liked Val."

"Tell me truth, child," Mamie insisted.

"If he did," Dulcy whispered. "He didn't learn it from me."

The record played out and Dulcy started it over again.

"Did you ask Johnny to give you ten thousand dollars to get rid of Val?" Mamie asked.

"Jesus Christ no!" Dulcy flared. "That whore's just lying about that!"

"You're not holding anything back on me, are you, child?" Mamie asked.

"I might ask you the same thing," Dulcy said.

"About what, child?"

"How could Johnny have found out, if he did find out, if you didn't tell him?"

"I didn't tell him," Mamie said. "And I know Big Joe didn't tell him because he'd just found out himself and he up and died before he had a chance to tell anybody."

"Somebody must have told him," Dulcy said.

"Then maybe it was Chink," Mamie said.

"It wasn't Chink 'cause he don't know," Dulcy said. "All Chink knows about is the knife and he's trying to blackmail me for ten grand. He claims if I don't get it for him he's going to tell Johnny." Dulcy began laughing hysterically. "As if that'd make any difference if Johnny knows about the other."

"Stop that laughing," Mamie said sharply and reached over and slapped her.

"Johnny will kill him," she added.

"I wish Johnny would," Dulcy said viciously. "If he don't really know about the other then that would settle everything."

"There must be some other way," Mamie said. "If the Lord will just show us the light. You can't just settle everything by killing people."

"If he just doesn't already know," Dulcy said.

The recording played out and she put it on again.

"For God's sake, child, can't you play something else," Mamie said. "That tune gives me the willies."

"I like it," Dulcy said. "It's just as blue as I feel."

They listened to the wailing voice and the intermittent sound of thunder from without.

The afternoon wore on. Dulcy kept on drinking, and the level of the bottle went down and down. Mamie dipped snuff. Every now and then one of them would speak and the other would answer listlessly.

No one telephoned. No one called.

Dulcy played the one recording over and over and over. Bessie Smith sang:

Backwater blues done cause me to pack mah things an' go
Backwater blues done cause me to pack mah things an' go
Cause mah house fell down an' I cain' live there no mo'

"Jesus Christ, I wish he'd come on home and kill me and get it over with if that's what he wants to do!" Dulcy cried.

The front door was unlocked and Johnny came into the flat. He walked into the bedroom wearing the same green silk suit and rose crepe shirt he'd worn to the club the night before, but now it was wrinkled and soiled. His .38 caliber automatic pistol made a lump in his right coat pocket. His hands were empty. His eyes burned like live coals but looked tired, and the veins stood out like roots from his graying temples. The scar on his forehead was swollen but still. He needed a shave, and the gray hairs in his beard glistened whitely against his dark skin. His face was expressionless.

He grunted as his eyes took in the scene, but he didn't speak. The two women watched him with fear-stricken eyes, unmoving, as he crossed the room and turned off the record player, then parted the drapes and raised the window. The storm had stopped, and the afternoon sun was reflected from the windows across the airwell.

Finally he came around the bed, kissed Mamie on the forehead and said, "Thanks, Aunt Mamie, you can go home now." His voice was expressionless.

Mamie didn't move. Her old, bluish-tinted eyes remained terror-stricken as they searched his face, but it revealed nothing.

"No," she said. "Let's talk it over now, while I'm here."

"Talk what over?" he said.

She stared at him.

Dulcy said defiantly, "Ain't you going to kiss me?"

Johnny looked at her as though studying her under a microscope. "Let's wait until you get sober," he said in his toneless voice.

"Don't do nothing, Johnny, I beg you on bending knees," Mamie said.

"Do what?" Johnny said, without taking his gaze from Dulcy.

"For God's sake, don't look at me as though I crucified Christ," Dulcy whimpered. "Go ahead and do whatever you want to do, just quit looking at me."

"I don't want you to say I took advantage of you while you were drunk," he said. "Let's wait until you get sober."

"Son, listen to me—" Mamie began, but Johnny cut her off. "All I want to do is sleep," he said. "How long do you think I can go without sleeping?"

He took the pistol from his pocket, put it beneath his pillow and began stripping off his clothes before Mamie had got up from the chair.

"Leave these in the kitchen as you go out," he said, giving her the near-empty brandy bottle and glass.

She took them away without further comment. He piled his clothes on the chair she'd vacated. His heavy brown muscles were tattooed with scars. When he'd stripped naked he set the radio alarm for ten o'clock, rolled Dulcy over and got into bed beside her. She tried to caress him but he pushed her away.

"There's ten G's in C-notes in my inside coat pocket," he said. "If that's what you want, just don't be here when I wake up."

He was asleep before Mamie left the house.

XIX

WHEN CHINK ENTERED the flat where he roomed, the telephone was ringing. He was grimy with dirt, unshaven, and his beige summer suit showed that he'd slept in it. His yellow skin looked like a greasy paste lined with wrinkles where the witches had ridden him in his sleep. There were big black half-moons beneath his beaten muddy eyes.

His lawyer had taken all the money he'd gotten from Dulcy to get him out on bail again. He felt like a whipped cur, chagrined, deflated and humiliated. Now that he was out, he wasn't sure whether it wouldn't have been better for him to have stayed in jail. If the cops hadn't picked up Johnny he'd have to keep on the run, but no matter how much he ran there was no place in Harlem where he could hide. Everybody would be against him when they found out he'd turned rat.

"It's for you, Chink," the landlady called to him.

He went into the bedroom where she kept her telephone, with a padlock on the dial.

"Hello," he said in a mean voice and gave his landlady a mean look for lingering in the room.

She went out and closed the door.

"It's me, Dulcy," the voice from the telephone said.

"Oh!" he said and his hands began to shake.

"I've got the money," she said.

"What!" He looked as though someone had stuck a gun in his belly and asked him if he wanted to bet it wasn't loaded. "Ain't he been arrested?" he asked involuntarily before he could catch himself.

"Arrested?" Her voice sounded suddenly suspicious. "Why the hell should he be arrested? Unless you've ratted about the knife."

"You know damn well I ain't ratted," he declared. "You think I'm going to blow away ten grand?" Thinking fast, he added, "It's just I ain't seen him around all day."

"He's gone to Chicago to check up on me and Val," she said.

"Then how'd you get the ten grand?" he wanted to know.

"That's none of your business," she said.

He suspected a trap, but the thought of getting ten thousand dollars filled him with a reckless greed. He had to hold himself in. He felt as though he were going to explode with exultation. All his life he'd wanted to be a big shot, and now was his chance if he played his cards right.

"Okay," he said. "I don't give a damn how you got it, whether you stole it or cut his throat for it, just so long as you've got it."

"I've got it," she said. "But you'll have to bring me your knife before I'll give it to you."

"What the hell do you think I am?" he said. "You bring me the money here and we'll talk about the knife."

"No, you've got to come here to the house and get the money and bring me the knife," she said.

"I ain't that crazy, baby," he said. "It ain't that I'm scared of Johnny, but I don't have to take no rape-fiend chance like that. It's your little tail that's in the vise, and you're goin' to have to pay to get it out."

"Listen, honey, there ain't no chance in it," she said. "He can't get back before tomorrow night because it's going to take him all day tomorrow to find out what he's looking for, and when he gets back I got to be gone myself."

"I don't dig you," Chink said.

"You ain't so smart then, honey," she said. "What he's going to find out is what caused Val to wind up dead."

Suddenly Chink began to see the light. "Then it was you—"

She cut him off. "What difference does it make now? I got to be gone when he gets back, and that's for sure. I just want to leave him a souvenir."

An expression of triumph lit Chink's face. "You mean you want me, there in his own house?"

"In his own bed," she said. "The mother-raper always suspected me of cheating on him when I wasn't. Now I'm going to fix him."

Chink gave a low vicious laugh. "You and me, baby, we're going to fix him together."

"Well, hurry up then," she said.

"Give me half an hour," he said.

She had unhooked the extension in the bedroom and was talking from the extension in the kitchen. When she hung up she said to herself, "You asked for it."

Dulcy was watching from the peephole and opened the door before he rang. She wore her robe with nothing underneath.

"Come on in, honey," she said. "The place is ours."

"I knew I'd get you," he said, making a grab at her, but she slipped neatly out of his arms and said, "All right then, don't make me wait."

He looked into the kitchen.

"If you're scared, search the house," she said.

"Who's scared?" he said belligerently.

The bedroom which Val had used was directly across from the kitchen and the master bedroom beyond the bathroom, adjoining the sitting room.

She started to lead Chink into Val's room, but he went up to the front and looked into the sitting room, then he hesitated before the door to the master bedroom. Dulcy had padlocked it with the heavy Yale lock Johnny had used to lock her in.

"What's in there?" Chink asked.

"That was Val's room," Dulcy said.

"What's it doing locked?" he wanted to know.

"The police locked it," she said. "If you want it open, go ahead and break down the door."

He laughed, then looked into the bathroom. The water was running in the tub.

"I'm going to take a bath first," she said. "Do you mind?"

He kept on laughing to himself with a crazy sort of exultation.

"You're a real bitch," he said, taking her by the arms and pushing her into Val's bedroom and back across the bed. "I knew you were a bitch, but I didn't know how much bitch you really are."

He began kissing her.

"Let me take a bath first," she said. "I stink."

He laughed jubilantly, as though laughing to himself at his own private joke.

"A real solid-gold bitch," he said as though talking to himself. Then suddenly he sat up straight. "Where's the money?"

"Where's the knife?" she countered.

He took it from his pocket and held it in his hand.

She pointed to an envelope on the dressing table.

He picked it up, opened it with one hand while holding onto the knife with the other and shook hundred-dollar bills onto the bedspread. She eased the knife from his hand and slipped it into the pocket of her robe, but he didn't notice. He was rooting his face in the money like a hog in swill.

"Put it away and undress," she said.

He stood up, laughing crazily to himself, and began stripping off his clothes.

"I'll just leave it there and look at it," he said.

She sat at the dressing table and massaged her face with cream until he'd finished undressing.

But instead of getting beneath the covers he lay on top of the coverlet, and he kept picking up the brand-new money and letting it rain down over his naked body like falling leaves.

"Have a good time," she said, going into the bathroom. She heard him laughing crazily to himself as she closed the adjoining door.

She quickly stepped across the bathroom, opened the opposite door and stepped into the other bedroom.

Johnny slept on his back with one arm flung out across the cover and the other folded loosely across his stomach. He snored lightly.

She closed the bathroom door behind her, crossed the room quietly, and set the radio to alarm within five minutes. Then she dressed quickly in a slack suit without stopping to put on underwear, slipped into the robe again, and went back into the bathroom.

The water had been running all the while and had reached the overflow outlet. She turned off the faucet, turned on the shower and pulled the drain stopper.

Then she went quickly into the hall, turned into the kitchen, took her saddle-leather shoulder handbag from one of the cabinet shelves and went out through the service doorway.

She was crying so hard as she ran down the stairs she bumped into two uniformed white cops coming up. They stood aside to let her pass.

XX

THE RADIO CAME on with a blast.

Some big brassy band was beating out a rock and roll rhythm. Johnny came awake as though he'd been bitten by a snake, leaped out of the bed and grabbed for the pistol underneath his pillow.

Then he realized it was only the radio. He grunted sheepishly and noticed that Dulcy was out of bed. He felt his inside coat pocket with his free hand, still holding the pistol in his right hand, and discovered the ten thousand dollars were gone.

He patted the coat absently where it lay on the chair beside the bed, but he was looking at the empty bed. His breath came shallowly, but his face was expressionless.

"Sevened out," he said to himself. "You lost that bet."

The radio was playing so loudly he didn't hear the door to the bathroom open. He merely caught a flicker of movement from the corner of his eye and turned.

Chink stood naked, with his eyes dilated and his mouth wide open, in the doorway.

They stared at each other until the moment ran out.

Suddenly the veins popped out in Johnny's temples as though they were about to explode. The scar ballooned out from his forehead and the tentacles wriggled as though trying to free themselves from his head. Then a blinding flash went off inside of his skull as though his brains had been dynamited.

His brain made no record of his next actions.

He squeezed the trigger of his .38 automatic until it had pumped all its slugs into Chink's stomach, lungs, heart and head. Then he leaped across the floor and stomped Chink's dying bloody body with his bare feet until two of Chink's teeth were stuck into his calloused heel. After that he leaned over and clubbed Chink's head into a bloody pulp with his pistol butt.

But he didn't know he had done it.

The next thing he knew consciously after having first caught sight of Chink was that he was being held forcibly by two white uniformed cops and Chink's bloody corpse lay on the floor in the doorway, half in the bedroom and half in the bathroom, and the shower was pouring down into an empty tub.

"Turn me loose so I can dress," he said in his toneless voice. "You can't take me to jail buck naked."

The cops freed him and he began to dress.

"We've called precinct and they're sending over some jokers

from Homicide," one of them said. "You want to buzz your mouthpiece before they get here?"

"What for?" Johnny said, without stopping dressing.

"We heard the shots and the back door was open, so we came on in," the other cop said half apologetically. "We thought maybe it was her you'd shot."

Johnny said nothing. He was dressed before the men from Homicide arrived.

They held him there until Detective Sergeant Brody came.

"Well, you killed him," Brody said.

"There's all the evidence," Johnny said.

They took him back to the 116th Street Precinct station for questioning because Grave Digger and Coffin Ed were on the case and they worked out of that station.

Brody sat as before behind the desk in the Pigeon Nest. Grave Digger was perched on the edge of the desk, and Coffin Ed stood in the shadow in the corner.

It was 8:37 o'clock and still light outside, but it didn't make any difference to them because the room didn't have any windows.

Johnny sat in the spill of light on the stool in the center of the room, facing Brody. The vertical light made grotesque patterns of the scar on his forehead and the veins swelling from his temples, but his big muscular body was relaxed and his face was expressionless. He looked like a man who'd gotten a load from his shoulders.

"Why don't you just let me tell you what I know," he said in his toneless voice. "If you don't buy it, you can question me afterwards."

"Okay, shoot," Brody said.

"Let's begin with the knife, and get that cleared up with," Johnny said. "I found the knife in her drawer on a Tuesday afternoon a little over two weeks ago. I just thought she'd bought it to protect herself from me. I put it in my pocket and took it to the club. Then I got to thinking about it and I was going to put it back, but Big Joe seen it. If she was so scared of me she needed to keep a skinner's knife hidden in the drawer where she kept her underwear, I was going to let her keep it. But I was handling it and Big Joe said he'd like to have a knife like that, and I gave it to him. That's the last I seen it or even thought about it until you showed it to me here on that desk and said it was the knife that killed Val, and that the preacher had said he'd seen Chink when he gave it to her."

"You don't know what Big Joe did with it?" Brody asked.

"No, he never said. All he ever said was that if he carried it around he was scared he might get mad some day and cut somebody with it, and it was the kind of knife that would cut a man's head off when all you were trying to do was mark him."

"Did you ever see another knife like it?" Brody asked.

"Not exactly like it," Johnny said. "I've seen knives what look kind of like it, but none what look exactly like it."

Brody took the knife from the desk drawer as he had done the first time and pushed it across the desk.

"Is this the knife?"

Johnny leaned forward and picked it up.

"Yeah, but how it got stuck into Val, I couldn't say."

"This one wasn't stuck into Val," Brody said. "This one was found on a shelf in your kitchen cabinet less than a half-hour ago." He then put the duplicate knife on the desk top. "This was the one found stuck in Val."

Johnny looked from one knife to the other without speaking.

"How do you account for that?" Brody asked.

"I don't know," Johnny said, without expression.

"Could Big Joe have left it in the house at some time, and somebody have put it on the shelf?" Brody asked.

"If he did, I don't know about it," Johnny said.

"All right, that's your story," Brody said. "Let's get back to Val. When was the last time you saw him?"

"It was about ten minutes of four when I came down from the club," Johnny said. "I'd been winning and the players didn't want me to quit, so I was late. Val was setting in the car waiting for me."

"Wasn't that unusual?" Brody interrupted.

Johnny looked at him.

"Why didn't he come up to the club?" Brody asked.

"Wasn't nothing strange 'bout that," Johnny said. "He liked to set in my car and play the radio. He had a set of keys, him and her both, just for emergency 'cause I never let him drive. And he'd set in it by the hour. I suppose it made him feel like a big shot. I don't know how long he'd been setting there. I didn't ask him. He'd said he'd come from talking to Reverend Short and he had something to tell me. But we were late and I was afraid the wake would break up before we got there—"

"He said he'd been talking with Reverend Short?" Brody interrupted again. "At that time of night—morning, rather?"

"Yeah, but I didn't think anything about it at the time," Johnny replied. "I told him to stow it and tell me later, but just before we got to Seventh Avenue he said he didn't feel like going to the wake. He said he was going away, he was going to catch an early train to Chicago and he didn't know where he was going from there and I'd better listen to what he had to say 'cause it was important. I pulled up to the corner and parked. He said he'd been up to the preacher's church—if you call it a church; he'd met him there 'bout two o'clock that morning and they'd had a long talk. But before he'd got to say any more I saw a stud slipping along beside the parked cars across the street and I knew he was going to try to steal the A and P store manager's change poke. I said, wait a minute, let's watch this little play. There was a colored cop named Harris standing beside the manager while he unlocked the door, and there was some stud leaning out Big Joe's bedroom window watching the play, too. This stud lifted the poke from the car seat and took off, but the manager saw him, and he and the cop took off after him—"

Brody cut him off. "We know about that. What happened after Reverend Short got up?"

"I didn't know it was the preacher until he got up out of that bread basket," Johnny said. "Funniest thing you ever saw. He got up and began shaking himself like a cat what's fell in a pile of dung. When I made out who he was I figured he was full of that wild cherry brandy and opium juice he drinks, then he took another drink from his bottle and went back into the house, tiptoeing and shaking himself like a wet-footed cat. Val was laughing, too. He said you can't hurt a drunk. Then all of a sudden I thought of how we could pull a good gag. I told Val to go across the street and lie down in the bread basket where the preacher had fallen and I'd go around to Hamfat's all-night joint and telephone Mamie and tell here there was a dead man there who'd fallen out of her window. Hamfat's place is on 135th and Lenox, and it wouldn't have taken me longer than five minutes to make the call. But some chick was using the phone and I figured by the time I got the call through somebody would have already found Val and the gag would have been lost—"

"How did you go to Hamfat's?" Brody interrupted.

"I drove," Johnny said. "I turned up Seventh Avenue to 135th Street and crossed over. I didn't know he'd been stabbed until Mamie told me on the phone."

"Did you see anyone coming from the house, or anyone at all on the street when you drove up Seventh Avenue?" Brody asked.

"Not a soul."

"Did you tell Mamie who you were?"

"No, I tried to disguise my voice. I knew she'd know it was a gag if she recognized my voice."

"You don't think she recognized it?" Brody insisted.

"I don't think so," Johnny said. "But I couldn't say."

"Okay, that's your story," Brody said. "Now what did you go to Chicago for?"

"I was trying to find out what it was Val wanted to tell me before he got himself killed," Johnny admitted. "After Doll Baby came to my house that afternoon right after the funeral and claimed that Val was going to get ten grand from me to open up a liquor store, I wanted to know what it was I was going to give him ten grand for to know. He never had a chance to tell me, and I had to find out for myself."

"Did you find out?" Brody asked, leaning forward slightly.

Grave Digger bent over from the waist as though to hear better, and Coffin Ed stepped forward from the shadows.

"Yeah," Johnny said in his toneless voice, his face remaining without expression. "He was her husband. I figure he was going to ask me for ten grand so he could go away. I figure he was going to take Doll Baby with him."

The three detectives remained alert, as though listening for a sound that would presage the instant of danger.

"Would you have given it to him?" Brody asked.

"Not so you could notice," Johnny said.

"Was it his idea or hers?" Brody insisted.

"I couldn't say," Johnny said. "I ain't God."

"Would she have done it for him if he had made her, tried to make her?" Brody kept on.

"I couldn't say," Johnny said.

Brody kept hammering. "Or would she have killed him?"

"I couldn't say," Johnny said in his toneless voice.

"What was Chink Charlie doing in your house?" Brody continued. "Was he blackmailing her about the knife?"

"I couldn't say," Johnny said.

"Ten thousand dollars in hundred-dollar bills were strewn over the bed in the other bedroom," Brody said. "Did he come to collect that?"

"I couldn't say what he come for," Johnny said. "You know what he got."

"It was your money," Brody persisted.

"No, it was hers," Johnny said. "I got it for her when I came back from Chicago. If all she wanted out of me was ten grand she was welcome to it. All she had to do was take it and get out. It was easier for me to go in debt to give her ten grand than to have to kill her."

"Do you have any idea where she might have gone?" Brody asked.

"I couldn't say," Johnny said. "She's got her own car, a Chevy convertible I gave her for Christmas. She could have gone anywhere."

"Okay, Johnny, that's all for now," Brody said. "We're going to hold you on manslaughter and suspicion of murder. You can telephone your lawyer now. Maybe he can get you out on bail."

"What for?" Johnny said. "All I want to do is sleep."

"You can sleep better at home," Brody said. "Or else go to a hotel."

"I sleep fine in jail," Johnny said. "It ain't like as if it was the first time."

When the jailors had taken Johnny away, Brody said, "It looks to me as if she's our little pet. She killed her legal husband to keep from fouling up her little gravy train. Then she had to set a trap and get her illegal husband to kill Chink Charlie, trying to save herself from the electric chair."

"What about the knife?" Coffin Ed said.

"She either had both knives, or else she got this one from Chink and left it there when she went out," Brody said.

"But why did she leave it there where it was sure to be found?" Coffin Ed persisted. "If she really had the second knife, why didn't she get rid of it? Then Johnny would be tapped for killing Val, too. He'd have to prove that he gave the knife to Big Joe, and Big Joe is dead. It would be an open and shut case against Johnny if it wasn't for the second knife."

"Maybe Johnny got the second knife and put it there himself," Grave Digger said. "He's the smartest one of all."

"We should have done like I said and brought her in last night," Coffin Ed said.

"Let's quit guessing and second-guessing and go get her now," Grave Digger said.

"Right," Brody said. "In the meantime I'll go over all the reports."

"Don't take any unnecessary chances with those bad words," Coffin Ed said with a straight face.

"Yeah," Grave Digger amended with equal solemnity. "Don't let none of them sneak up behind you and stab you while you're not looking."

"What the hell!" Brody said, reddening. "You guys'll be out chasing the hottest piece of tail in Harlem. I envy you."

XXI

THEY FOUND MAMIE ironing the clothes Baby Sis had washed that morning. It was steaming in the kitchen from the pair of flatirons Mamie heated on her electric stove.

They told her Dulcy had left home, Johnny had killed Chink and was in jail.

She sat down and started moaning.

"Lord, I knowed there was goin' to be another killing," she said.

"Where would she go, now that both Chink and Val are dead and Johnny's locked up?" Grave Digger asked.

"Only the Lord knows," she said in a wailing voice. "She might have gone to see the reverend."

"Reverend Short!" Grave Digger said in a startled voice. "Why would she go to him?"

Mamie looked up in surprise. "Why, she's in deep trouble and he's a man of God. Dulcy's religious underneath. She might have gone to seek God in her misery."

Baby Sis giggled. Mamie gave her a threatening look.

"He is a man of God," Mamie said. "Only thing he drinks too much of that poison and sometimes it makes him a little crazy."

"If she's there, let's just hope he ain't too crazy," Coffin Ed said.

Five minutes later they were tiptoeing through the semi-dark of the store-front church. The shotgun hole in the door to Reverend Short's room at the rear had been closed by a piece of cardboard, shielding the light from within, but the croaking sound of Reverend Short's voice could be distinctly heard. They crept forward silently and bent toward the door to listen.

"But, Jesus Christ, why did you have to kill him?" they heard a blurred feminine voice exclaim.

"You are a harlot," they heard Reverend Short croak in reply. "I must save thy soul from hell. You are mine. I have slain thy husband. Now I must give you unto God."

"Crazy as a loon," Grave Digger said aloud.

There was a sound of sudden scurrying inside the room. "Who's there?" Reverend Short croaked in a voice as thin and dry as a rattlesnake's warning.

"The law," Grave Digger said, flattening himself against the wall beside the door. "Detectives Jones and Johnson. Come out with your hands up."

Before he'd finished speaking Coffin Ed was sprinting down

the corridor between the benches to go outside and circle to the rear windows.

"You can't have her," Reverend Short croaked. "She belongs to God now."

"We don't want her. We want you," Grave Digger said.

"I'm God's instrument," Reverend Short said.

"I don't doubt that," Grave Digger said, trying to hold his attention until Coffin Ed had time to approach the rear windows. "All we want to do is see that you get back safe and sound into God's instrument case."

The shotgun blasted from inside, without the warning sound of being cocked, and blew a hole through the center of the door.

"You didn't get me," Grave Digger called. "Try the other barrel."

There was a sound of movement inside the room, and Dulcy screamed. The sound of two shots from a .38 revolver coming from the courtyard in back followed instantly. Grave Digger turned on the balls of his big flat feet, hit the door with his left shoulder and rocketed into the room with his long-barreled nickel-plated .38 cocked and ready in his right hand. Reverend Short was sprawled face downward across the seat of the wooden chair beside the bed, trying to reach the shotgun, which lay on the floor half underneath the table. He was reaching for it with his left hand. His right hand dangled uselessly at his side.

Grave Digger leaned forward and hit him across the back of the head with his pistol barrel, just hard enough to knock him unconscious without braining him, then turned to give his attention to Dulcy before Reverend Short had rolled over and fallen to the floor.

She lay spread-eagled on the bed, her hands and feet tied to the bedposts with clothesline. Her torso and feet were bare, but she still wore the pants of a bright red slack suit. The bone handle of a knife was sticking straight up from the crevice between her breasts. She looked at Grave Digger from huge black terror-stricken eyes.

"I bad hurt?" she asked in a whisper.

"I doubt it," Grave Digger said, then looked at her closer and added, "You're too pretty to be bad hurt. Only ugly women ever get hurt bad."

Coffin Ed was tearing off the chicken-wire screen from the rear window. Grave Digger crossed the room and raised the window and finished kicking it out. Coffin Ed climbed inside.

Grave Digger said, "Let's get these beauties to the hospital."

Reverend Short was taken to the psychiatric ward of Bellevue Hospital downtown on First Avenue and 29th Street. He was given a shot of paraldehyde and was docile and rational when the detectives went in to wind up the case. He sat propped up in bed with his right arm in a sling.

Detective Sergeant Brody from Homicide had ridden downtown with Grave Digger and Coffin Ed, and he sat beside the bed and did the questioning. The police reporter sat beside him.

Coffin Ed sat on the other side of the bed and stared down at the chart hanging at the foot. Grave Digger sat on the window sill and watched the tug boats chugging up and down the East River.

"Just a few little questions, Reverend," Brody said cheerfully. "First, why did you kill him?"

"God directed me to," Reverend Short replied in a calm, quiet voice.

Brody glanced at Coffin Ed, but Coffin Ed didn't notice. Grave Digger continued to stare out at the river.

"Tell us about it," Brody said.

"Big Joe Pullen found out that he was her husband and they were still living in sin while she was supposed to be married to Johnny Perry," Reverend Short began.

"When did he find that out?" Brody asked.

"On his last trip," Reverend Short said quietly. "He was going to talk to Val and tell him to clear out, go to Chicago, get his divorce quietly and just disappear. But before Joe Pullen had a chance to talk to him he died. When I came to help Mamie arrange for the funeral she told me what Big Joe had found out, and asked me for spiritual advice. I told her to leave it to me and I'd take care of it, being as I was both her and Big Joe's spiritual advisor and Johnny and Dulcy Perry were members of my church, too, although they never attended the services. I telephoned Val and told him I wanted to talk to him, and he said he didn't have time to talk to preachers. So I had to tell him what I wanted to talk to him about. He said he'd come and see me in my church the night of the wake, and we made an appointment for two o'clock. I think he was preparing to do me injury, but I was prepared, and I put it to him straight. I told him I'd give him twenty-four hours to get out of town and leave her alone or I'd tell Johnny. He told me he'd go. I was satisfied he was telling me the truth, so I went back to the wake to comfort Mamie in her last hours with Big Joe's mortal remains. It was while I was there that God directed me to slay him."

"How did that happen, Reverend?" Brody asked gently.

Reverend Short took off his glasses, laid them aside and ran his hand down over his thin bony face. He put his glasses back on.

"I am give to receiving instructions from God, and I don't question them," he said. "While I was standing in the room where Big Joe's mortal remains lay in the casket, I felt an over-whelming urge to go into the front bedroom. I knew right away that God was sending me on some mission. I obeyed without reservation. I went into the bedroom and closed the door. Then I felt the urge to look among Big Joe's things . . ."

Coffin Ed slowly turned his head to stare at him. Grave Digger turned his gaze from the East River and stared at him, too. The police reporter glanced up quickly and down again.

"As I was looking through his things I came across the knife laying in his dresser drawer among his hairbrushes and safety razors and things. God told me to take it. I took it. I put it into my pocket. God told me to go to the window and look out. I went to the window and looked out. Then God caused me to fall—"

"As I remember it, you said before that Chink Charlie pushed you," Brody interrupted.

"That was what I thought then," Reverend Short said in his quiet voice. "But since then I've come to realize it was God who pushed me. I had the urge to fall, but I was holding back, and God had to give me a little push. Then God placed that basket of bread on the sidewalk to break my fall."

"Before you said it was the body of Christ," Brody reminded him.

"Yes," Reverend Short admitted. "But since then I've communed with God and now I know it was bread. When I got out of the bread basket and found myself unhurt, I knew right away that God had placed me in that position to accomplish some task, but I didn't know what. So I stood in the hallway downstairs, out of sight, waiting for God to direct me what to do—"

"You're sure it wasn't just to take a leak," Coffin Ed cut in.

"Well, I did that, too," Reverend Short admitted. "I have a weak bladder."

"No wonder," Grave Digger said.

"Let him go on," Brody said.

"While I was waiting for God to instruct me, I saw Valentine Haines crossing the street," Reverend Short said. "I knew right away that God wanted me to do something about him. I stood out of sight and watched him from the shadows. Then I saw him walk up to the bread basket and lie down as though to go to sleep. He lay just as though he were lying in a coffin awaiting his burial. I knew then what it was that God wanted me to do. I opened the knife and held it up my sleeve and stepped outside. Val saw me right away and said, I thought you went back upstairs to the wake, Reverend. I said, no, I've been waiting for you. He said, waiting for me for what. I said, waiting to kill you in the name of the Lord, and I leaned down and stabbed him in the heart."

Sergeant Brody exchanged glances with the two colored detectives.

"Well, that wraps it up," he said, then, turning back to Reverend Short, he remarked cynically, "I suppose you'll cop a plea of insanity."

"I'm not insane," Reverend Short said serenely. "I'm holy."

"Yeah," Brody said. He turned to the police reporter. "Get a copy of that statement typed for him to sign as soon as possible."

"Right," the police reporter said, closing his notebook and hurrying from the room.

Brody rang for the attendant and left him with Grave Digger and Coffin Ed. Outside he turned to Grave Digger and said, "You were right after all when you said that folks in Harlem do things for reasons nobody else in the world would think of."

Grave Digger grunted.

"Do you think he's really crazy?" Brody persisted.

"Who knows?" Grave Digger said.

"Depends on what you mean by crazy," Coffin Ed amended.

"He was just sexually frustrated and lusting after a married woman," Grave Digger said. "When you get to mixing sex and religion it will make anybody crazy."

"If he sticks to his story, he'll beat it," Brody said.

"Yeah," Coffin Ed said bitterly. "And if the cards had fallen just a little differently Johnny Perry would have got burned."

Dulcy had been taken to Harlem Hospital. Her wound was superficial. The knife thrust had been stopped by her sternum.

But they kept her in the hospital because she could pay for a room.

She telephoned Mamie and Mamie went to her immediately. She cried her heart out on Mamie's shoulder, while telling her the story.

"But why didn't you just get rid of Val, child?" Mamie asked her. "Why didn't you send him away?"

"I wasn't sleeping with him," Dulcy said.

"It didn't make any difference—he was still your husband and you kept him there in the house."

"I felt sorry for him, that's all," Dulcy said. "He wasn't worth a damn for nothing, but I felt sorry for him just the same."

"Well, for God's sake, child," Mamie said. "Anyway, why didn't you tell the police about Chink having another knife instead of getting Johnny to kill him?"

"I know I should have done it," Dulcy confessed. "But I didn't know what to do."

"Then why didn't you go to Johnny, child, and make a clean breast and ask him what to do?" Mamie said. "He was your man, child. He was the only one for you to go to."

"Go to Johnny!" Dulcy said, laughing with an edge of hysteria. "Imagine me going to Johnny with that story. I thought he had done it himself."

"He would have listened to you," Mamie said. "You ought to know Johnny that well by now, child."

"It wasn't that, Aunt Mamie," Dulcy sobbed. "I know he would have listened. But he would have hated me."

"There, there, don't cry," Mamie said, caressing her hair. "It's all over now."

"That's what I mean," Dulcy said. "It's all over." She buried her face in her hands and sobbed heartbrokenly. "I love the ugly bastard," she said sobbingly. "But I ain't got no way to prove it."

It was a hot morning. The neighborhood kids were playing in the street.

Johnny's lawyer, Ben Williams, had got him out on bail. The garage had sent a man down to the jail with his fishtail Cadillac. Johnny came out and got in behind the wheel and the man from the garage sat in back. The lawyer sat beside Johnny.

"We'll get that manslaughter charge nol-prossed," the lawyer said. "You ain't got a thing to worry about."

Johnny pressed the starter, shifted to drive, and the big convertible moved off slowly.

"That ain't what I'm worrying about," he said.

"What is it?" the lawyer asked.

"You wouldn't know anything about it," Johnny said.

Skinny black kids in their summer shifts ran after the big flashy Cadillac, touching it with love and awe.

"Fishtail Johnny Perry," they called after him. "Four Ace Johnny Perry."

He threw up his left hand in a sort of salute.

"Try me," the lawyer said. "I'm supposed to be your brain."

"How can a jealous man win?" Johnny said.

"By trusting his luck," the lawyer said. "You're the one who's the gambler, you ought to know that."

"Well, pal," Johnny said. "You'd better be right."

Cotton Comes to Harlem

I

THE VOICE FROM the sound truck said:

"Each family, no matter how big it is, will be asked to put up one thousand dollars. You will get your transportation free, five acres of fertile land in Africa, a mule and a plow and all the seed you need, free. Cows, pigs and chickens cost extra, but at the minimum. No profit on this deal."

A sea of dark faces wavered before the speaker's long table, rapturous and intent.

"Ain't it wonderful, honey?" said a big black woman with eyes like stars. "We're going back to Africa."

Her tall lean husband shook his head in awe. "After all these four hundred years."

"Here I is been cooking in white folk's kitchens for more than thirty years. Lord, can it be true?" A stooped old woman voiced a lingering doubt.

The smooth brown speaker with the honest eyes and earnest face heard her. "It's true all right," he said. "Just step right up and give us the particulars and deposit your thousand dollars and you'll have a place on the first boat going over."

A grumpy old man with a head of white hair shuffled forward to fill out a form and deposit his thousand dollars, muttering to himself, "It sure took long enough."

The two pretty black girls taking applications looked up with dazzling smiles.

"Look how long it took the Jews to get out of Egypt," one said.

"The hand of God is slow but sure," said the other.

It was a big night in the lives of all these assembled colored people. Now at last, after months of flaming denouncements of the injustice and hypocrisy of white people, hurled from the pulpit of his church; after months of eulogy heaped upon the holy land of Africa, young Reverend Deke O'Malley was at last putting words into action. Tonight he was signing up the people to go on his three ships back to Africa. Huge hand-drawings of the ships stood in prominent view behind the speaker's table, appearing to have the size and design of the SS *Queen Elizabeth*. Before them stood Reverend O'Malley, his tall lithe body clad in dark summer worsted, his fresh handsome face exuding benign authority and inspiring total confidence, flanked by his secretaries and the two young men most active in recruiting applicants.

A vacant lot in the "Valley" of Harlem near the railroad tracks, where slum tenements had been razed for a new housing development, had been taken over for the occasion. More than a thousand people milled about the patches of old, uneven concrete amid the baked, cindery earth littered with stones, piles of rubbish, dog droppings, broken glass, scattered rags and clusters of stinkweed.

The hot summer night was lit by flashes of sheet lightning, threatening rain, and the air was oppressive with dust, density and motor fumes. Stink drifted from the surrounding slums, now more overcrowded than ever due to the relocation of families from the site of the new buildings to be erected to relieve the overcrowding. But nothing troubled the jubilance of these dark people filled with faith and hope.

The meeting was well organized. The speaker's table stood at one end, draped with a banner reading: BACK TO AFRICA— LAST CHANCE!!! Behind it, beside the drawings of the ships, stood an armored truck, its back doors open, flanked by two black guards wearing khaki uniforms and side arms. To the other side stood the sound truck with amplifiers atop. T-shirted young men in tight-fitting jeans roamed about with solemn, unsmiling expressions, swelled with a sense of importance ready to eject any doubters.

But for many of these true-believers it was also a picnic. Bottles of wine, beer and whiskey were passed about. Here and there a soul-brother cut a dance step. White teeth flashed in black, laughing faces. Eyes spoke. Bodies promised. They were all charged with anticipation.

A pit had been dug in the center of the lot, housing a charcoal fire covered with an iron grill. Rows of pork ribs were slowly cooking on the grill, dripping fat into the hot coals with a sizzling of pungent smoke, turned from time to time by four "hook-men" with long iron hooks. A white-uniformed chef with a long-handled ladle basted the ribs with hot sauce as they cooked, supervising the turning, his tall white chef's cap bobbing over his sweating black face. Two matronly women clad in white nurses' uniforms sat at a kitchen table, placing the cooked ribs into paper plates, adding bread and potato salad, and selling them for one dollar a serving.

The tempting, tantalizing smell of barbecued ribs rose in the air above the stink. Shirt-sleeved men, thinly clad women and half-naked children jostled each other good-naturedly, eating the spicy meat and dropping the bones underfoot.

Above the din of transistor radios broadcasting the night's baseball games, and the bursts of laughter, the sudden shrieks, the other loud voices, came the blaring voice of Reverend Deke O'Malley from the sound truck: "Africa is our native land and we are going back. No more picking cotton for the white folks and living on fatback and corn pone. . . ."

"Yea, baby, yea."

"See that sign," Reverend O'Malley shouted, pointing to a large wooden sign against the wire fence which proclaimed that the low-rent housing development to be erected on that site would be completed within two and one half years, and listed the prices of the apartments, which no family among those assembled there could afford to pay. "Two years you have to wait to move into some boxes—if you can get in, and if you can pay the high rent after you get in. By that time you will be harvesting your second crop in Africa, living in warm sunny houses where the only fire you'll ever need will be for cooking, where we'll have our own governments and our own rulers—*black*, like us—"

"I hear you, baby, I hear you."

The thousand-dollar subscriptions poured in. The starry-eyed black people were putting their chips on hope. One after another they went forward solemnly and put down their thousand dollars and signed on the dotted line. The armed guards took the money and stacked it carefully into an open safe in the armored truck.

"How many?" Reverend O'Malley asked one of his secretaries in a whisper.

"Eighty-seven," she whispered in reply.

"Tonight might be your last chance," Reverend O'Malley said over the amplifiers. "Next week I must go elsewhere and give all of our brothers a chance to return to our native land. God said the meek shall inherit the earth; we have been meek long enough; now we shall come into our inheritance."

"Amen, Reverend! Amen!"

Sad-eyed Puerto Ricans from nearby Spanish Harlem and the lost and hungry black people from black Harlem who didn't have the thousand dollars to return to their native land congregated outside the high wire fence, smelling the tantalizing barbecue, dreaming of the day when they could also go back home in triumph and contentment.

"Who's that man?" one of them asked.

"Child, he's the young Communist Christian preacher who's going to take our folks back to Africa."

A police cruiser was parked at the curb. Two white cops in the front seat cast sour looks over the assemblage.

"Where you think they got a permit for this meeting?"

"Search me. Lieutenant Anderson said leave them alone."

"This country is being run by niggers."

They lit cigarettes and smoked in sullen silence.

Inside the fence, three colored cops patrolled the assemblage, swapping jokes with their soul-brothers, exchanging grins, relaxed and friendly.

During a lull in the speaker's voice, two big colored men in dark rumpled suits approached the speaker's table. Bulges from pistols in shoulder slings showed beneath their coats. The guards of the armored truck became alert. The two young recruiting agents, flanking the table, pushed back their chairs. But the two big men were polite and smiled easily.

"We're detectives from the D.A.'s office," one said to O'Malley apologetically, as both presented their identifications. "We have orders to bring you in for questioning."

The two young recruiting agents came to their feet, tense and angry.

"These white mothers can't let us alone," one said. "Now they're using our brothers against us."

Reverend O'Malley waved them down and spoke to the detectives, "Have you got a warrant?"

"No, but it would save you a lot of trouble if you came peacefully."

The second detective added, "You can take your time and finish with your people, but I'd advise you to talk to the D.A."

"All right," Reverend O'Malley said calmly. "Later."

The detectives moved to one side. Everyone relaxed. One of the recruiting agents ordered a serving of barbecue.

For a moment attention was centered on a meat delivery truck which had entered the lot. It had been passed by the zealous volunteers guarding the gate.

"You're just in time, boy," the black chef called to the white driver as the truck approached. "We're running out of ribs."

A flash of lightning spotlighted the grinning faces of the two white men on the front seat.

"Wait 'til we turn around, boss," the driver's helper called in a southern voice.

The truck went forward towards the speaker's table. Eyes watched it indifferently. The truck turned, backed, gently plowing a path through the milling mob.

Ignoring the slight commotion, Reverend O'Malley continued speaking from the amplifiers: "These damn southern white folks have worked us like dogs for four hundred years and when we ask them to pay off, they ship us up to the North. . . ."

"Ain't it the truth!" a sister shouted.

"And these damn northern white folks don't want us—" But he never finished. He broke off in mid-sentence at the sight of two masked white men stepping from the back of the meat delivery truck with two black deadly-looking submachine guns in their hands. "Unh!!!" he grunted as though someone had hit him in the stomach.

For the brief instant following, silence reigned. The scene became a tableau of suspended motion. Eyes were riveted on the black holes of death at the front ends of the machine guns. Muscles became paralyzed. Brains stopped thinking.

Then a voice that sounded as though it had come from the backwoods of Mississippi said thickly: "Everybody freeze an' nobody'll git hurt."

The black men guarding the armored truck raised their hands in reflex action. Black faces broke out with a rash of white eyes. Reverend Deke O'Malley slid quickly beneath the table. The two big colored detectives froze as ordered.

But the young recruiting agent at the left end of the table, who was taking a bite of barbecue, saw his dream vanishing and reached towards his hip pocket for his pistol.

There was a burst from a machine gun. A mixture of teeth, barbecued pork ribs, and human brains flew through the air like macabre birds. A woman screamed. The young man, with half a head gone, sank down out of sight.

The Mississippi voice said furiously: "Goddamn stupid mother-raper!"

The softer southern voice of the gunner said defensively, "He was drawing."

"Mother-rape it! Git the money, let's git going." The big heavy white man with his black mask slowly moved the black-holed muzzle of his submachine gun over the crowd like the nozzle of a fire hose, saying, "Doan git daid."

Bodies remained rigid, eyes riveted, necks frozen, heads stationary, but there was a general movement away from the gun as though the earth itself were moving. Behind, among the people at the rear, panic began exploding like Chinese firecrackers.

The driver's helper got out from the front seat, waving another submachine gun, and the black people melted away.

The two sullen cops in the police cruiser jumped out and rushed to the fence, trying to see what was happening. But all they could see was a strange milling movement of black people.

The three colored cops inside, pistols drawn, were struggling forward against a tide of human flesh, but being slowly washed away.

The second machine-gunner, who had fired the burst, slung his gun over his shoulder, rushed towards the armored truck and began scooping money into a "gunny sack."

"Merciful Jesus," a woman wailed.

The black guards backed away, arms elevated, and let the white men take the money. Deke remained unseen beneath the table. All that was seen of the dead young man were some teeth still bleeding on the table, before the horrified eyes of the two young secretaries. The colored detectives hadn't breathed.

Outside the fence the cops rushed back to their cruiser. The motor caught, roared; the siren coughed, groaned, began screaming as the car went into a U-turn in the middle of the block heading back towards the gate.

The colored cops on the inside began shooting into the air, trying to clear a path, but only increased the pandemonium. A black tidal wave went over them as from a hurricane.

The white machine-gunner got all of the money—all $87,000—and jumped into the back of the delivery truck. The motor roared. The other machine-gunner followed the first and slammed shut the back door. The driver's helper climbed in just as the car took off.

The police cruiser came in through the gate, siren screaming, as though black people were invisible. A fat black man flew through the air like an over-inflated football. A fender bumped a woman's bottom and started her spinning like a whirling dervish. People scattered, split, diving, jumping, running to get out of the cruiser's path, colliding and knocking one another down.

But a path was made for the rapidly accelerating meat delivery truck. The cops looked at the driver and his helper as they passed. The two white men looked back, exchanging white looks. The cops went ahead, looking for colored criminals. The white machine-gunners got away.

The two black guards climbed into the front seat of the armored truck. The two colored detectives jumped on the running-boards, pistols in their hands. Deke came out from underneath the table and climbed into the back, beside the empty safe. The motor came instantly to life, sounding for all the world like a big Cadillac engine with four hundred horsepower. The armored truck backed, filled, pointed towards the gate, then hesitated.

"You want I should follow them?" the driver asked.

"Get 'em, goddammit. Run 'em down!" one of the colored detectives grated.

The driver hesitated a moment longer. "They're armed for bear."

"Bear ass!" the detective shouted. "They're getting away, mother!"

There was a glimpse of gray paint as the meat delivery truck went past a taxi on Lexington Avenue, headed north.

The big engine of the armored truck roared; the truck jumped. The police cruiser wheeled to head it off. A woman wild with fright ran in front of it. The car slewed to miss her and ran head-on into the barbecue pit. Steam rose from the burst radiator pouring on to the hot coals. A sudden flash of lightning lit the wild stampede of running people, seen through the cloud of steam.

"Great Godamighty, the earth's busted open," a voice cried.

"An' let out all hell," came the reply.

"Halt or I'll shoot," a cop cried, climbing from the smoking ruins.

It was the same as talking to the lightning.

The armored truck bulldozed a path to the gate, urged on by a voice shouting, "Go get 'em, go get 'em."

It turned into Lexington on screaming tires. The off-side detective fell off to the street, but they didn't stop for him. A roll of thunder blended with the motor sound as the big engine gathered speed, and another police cruiser fell in behind.

O'Malley tapped on the window separating the front seat from the rear compartment and passed an automatic rifle and a sawed-off shotgun to the guard. The remaining detective on the inside running-board was squatting low, holding on with his left hand and gripping a Colt .45 automatic in his right.

The armored truck was going faster than any armored truck ever seen before or since. The red light showed at 125th Street and a big diesel truck was coming from the west. The armored truck went through the red and passed in front of that big truck as close as a barber's shave.

A joker standing on the corner shouted jubilantly, "Gawawwwed damn! Them mothers got it."

The police cruiser stopped for the truck to pass.

"And gone!" the joker added.

The driver urged greater speed from the big laboring motor, "Get your ass to moving." But the meat delivery truck had got out of sight. The scream of the police siren was fading in the past.

The meat delivery truck turned left on 137th Street. In turning the back door was flung open and a bale of cotton slid slowly from the clutching hands of the two white machine-gunners and fell into the street. The truck dragged to a screaming sidewise stop and began backing up. But at that moment the armored truck came roaring around the corner like destiny coming on. The meat delivery truck reversed directions without a break in motion and took off again as though it had wings.

From inside the delivery truck came a red burst of machine-gun fire and the bullet-proof windshield of the armored truck was suddenly filled with stars, partly obscuring the driver's vision. He narrowly missed the bale of cotton, thinking he must have d.t.'s.

The guard was trying to get the muzzle of his rifle through a gun slot in the windshield when another burst of machine-gun fire came from the delivery truck and its back doors were slammed shut. No one noticed the detective on the running-board of the armored truck suddenly disappear. One moment he was there, the next he was gone.

The colored people on the tenement stoops, seeking relief from the hot night, began running over one another to get indoors. Some dove into the basement entrances beneath the stairs.

One loudmouthed comic shouted from the safety below the level of the sidewalk, "Harlem Hospital straight ahead."

From across the street another loudmouth shouted back, "Morgue comes first."

The meat delivery truck was gaining on the armored truck. It must have been powered to keep meat fresh from Texas.

From far behind came the faint sound of the scream of the siren from the police cruiser, seeming to cry, "Wait for me!"

Lightning flashed. Before the sound of thunder was heard, rain came down in torrents.

II

"WELL, KISS MY foot if it isn't Jones," Lieutenant Anderson exclaimed, rising from behind the captain's desk to extend his hand to his ace detectives. Slang sounded as phony as a copper's smile coming from his lips, but the warm smile lighting his thin pale face and the twinkle in his deep-set blue eyes squared it. "Welcome home."

Grave Digger Jones squeezed the small white hand in his own big, calloused paw and grinned. "You need to get out in the sun, Lieutenant, 'fore someone takes you for a ghost," he said as though continuing a conversation from the night before instead of a six months' interim.

The lieutenant eased back into his seat and stared at Grave Digger appraisingly. The upward glow from the green-shaded desk-lamp gave his face a gangrenous hue.

"Same old Jones," he said. "We've been missing you, man."

"Can't keep a good man down," Coffin Ed Johnson said from behind.

It was Grave Digger's first night back on duty since he had been shot up by one of Benny Mason's hired guns in the caper resulting from the loss of a shipment of heroin. He had been in the hospital for three months fighting a running battle with death, and he had spent three months at home convalescing. Other than for the bullet scars hidden beneath his clothes and the finger-size scar obliterating the hairline at the base of his skull where the first bullet had burned off the hair, he looked much the same. Same dark brown lumpy face with the slowly smoldering reddish-brown eyes; same big, rugged, loosely knit frame of a day laborer in a steel mill; same dark, battered felt hat worn summer and winter perched on the back of his head; same rusty black alpaca suit showing the bulge of the long-barreled, nickel-plated, brass-lined .38 revolver on a .44 frame made to his own specifications resting in its left-side shoulder sling. As far back as Lieutenant Anderson could remember, both of them, his two ace detectives with their identical big hard-shooting, head-whipping pistols, had always looked like two hog farmers on a weekend in the Big Town.

"I just hope it hasn't left you on the quick side," Lieutenant Anderson said softly.

Coffin Ed's acid-scarred face twitched slightly, the patches of grafted skin changing shape. "I dig you, Lieutenant," he said gruffly. "You mean on the quick side like me." His jaw knotted as he paused to swallow. "Better to be quick than dead."

The lieutenant turned to stare at him, but Grave Digger looked straight ahead. Four years previous a hoodlum had thrown a glass of acid into Coffin Ed's face. Afterwards he had earned the reputation of being quick on the trigger.

"You don't have to apologize," Grave Digger said roughly. "You're not getting paid to get killed."

In the green light Lieutenant Anderson's face turned slightly purple. "Well, hell," he said defensively. "I'm on your side. I know what you're up against here in Harlem. I know your beat. It's my beat too. But the commissioner feels you've killed too many people in this area—" He held up his hand to ward off an interruption. "Hoodlums, I know—dangerous hoodlums—and you killed in self-defense. But you've been on the carpet a number of times and a short time ago you had three months' suspensions. Newspapers have been yapping about police brutality in Harlem and now various civic bodies have taken up the cry."

"It's the white men on the force who commit the pointless brutality," Coffin Ed grated. "Digger and me ain't trying to play tough."

"We are tough," Grave Digger said.

Lieutenant Anderson shifted the papers on the desk and looked down at his hands. "Yes, I know, but they're going to drop it on you two—if they can. You know that as well as I do. All I'm asking is to play it safe, from the police side. Don't take any chances, don't make any arrests until you have the evidence, don't use force unless in self-defense, and above all don't shoot anyone unless it's the last resort."

"And let the criminals go," Coffin Ed said.

"The commissioner feels there must be some other way to curtail crime besides brute force," the lieutenant said, his blush deepening.

"Well, tell him to come up here and show us," Coffin Ed said.

The arteries stood out in Grave Digger's swollen neck and his voice came out cotton-dry. "We got the highest crime rate on earth among the colored people in Harlem. And there ain't but three things to do about it: Make the criminals pay for it—you don't want to do that; pay the people enough to live decently—you ain't going to do that; so all that's left is let 'em eat one another up."

A sudden blast of noise poured in from the booking room— shouts, curses, voices lifted in anger, women screaming, whines of protest, the scuffling of many feet—as a wagon emptied its haul from a raid on a whore-house where drugs were peddled.

The intercom on the desk spoke suddenly: "Lieutenant, you're wanted out here on the desk; they've knocked over Big Liz's circus house."

The lieutenant flicked the switch. "In a few minutes, and for Christ's sake keep them quiet."

He then looked from one detective to the other. "What the hell's going on today? It's only ten o'clock in the evening and judging from the reports it's been going on like this since morning." He leafed through the reports, reading charges: "Man kills his wife with an axe for burning his breakfast pork chop . . . man shoots another man demonstrating a recent shooting he had witnessed . . . man stabs another man for spilling beer on his new suit . . . man kills self in a bar playing Russian roulette with a .32 revolver . . . woman stabs man in stomach fourteen times, no reason given . . . woman scalds neighboring woman with pot of boiling water for speaking to her husband . . . man arrested for threatening to blow up subway train because he entered wrong station and couldn't get his token back—"

"All colored citizens," Coffin Ed interrupted.

Anderson ignored it. "Man sees stranger wearing his own new suit, slashes him with a razor," he read on. "Man dressed as Cherokee Indian splits white bartender's skull with homemade tomahawk . . . man arrested on Seventh Avenue for hunting cats with hound dog and shotgun . . . twenty-five men arrested for trying to chase all the white people out of Harlem—"

"It's Independence Day, " Grave Digger interrupted.

"*Independence Day!*" Lieutenant Anderson echoed, taking a long, deep breath. He pushed away the reports and pulled a memo from the corner clip of the blotter. "Well, here's your assignment—from the captain."

Grave Digger perched a ham on the edge of the desk and cocked his head; but Coffin Ed backed against the wall into the shadow to hide his face, as was his habit when he expected the unexpected.

"You're to cover Deke O'Hara," Anderson read.

The two colored detectives stared at him, alert but unquestioning, waiting for him to go on and give the handle to the joke.

"He was released ten months ago from the federal prison in Atlanta."

"As who in Harlem doesn't know, " Grave Digger said drily.

"Many people don't know that ex-con Deke O'Hara is Reverend Deke O'Malley, leader of the new Back-to-Africa movement."

"All right, omit the squares."

"He's on the spot; the syndicate has voted to kill him," Anderson said as if imparting information.

"Bullshit," Grave Digger said bluntly. "If the syndicate had wanted to kill him, he'd be decomposed by now."

"Maybe."

"What *maybe*? You could find a dozen punks in Harlem who'd kill him for a C-note."

"O'Malley's not that easy to kill."

"Anybody's easy to kill," Coffin Ed stated. "That's why we police wear pistols."

"I don't dig this," Grave Digger said, slapping his right thigh absentmindedly. "Here's a rat who stooled on his former policy racketeer bosses, got thirteen indicted by the federal grand jury—even one of us, Lieutenant Brandon over in Brooklyn—"

"There's always one black bean," Lieutenant Anderson said unwittingly.

Grave Digger stared at him. "Damn right," he said flatly.

Anderson blushed. "I didn't mean it the way you're thinking."

"I know how you meant it, but you don't know how I'm thinking."

"Well, how are you thinking?"

"I'm thinking do you know why he did it?"

"For the reward," Anderson said.

"Yeah, that's why. This world is full of people who will do anything for enough money. He thought he was going to get a half-million bucks as the ten percent reward for exposing tax cheats. He told how they'd swindled the government out of over five million in taxes. Seven out of thirteen went to prison; even the rat himself. He was doing so much squealing he confessed he hadn't paid any taxes either. So he got sent down too. He did thirty-one months and now he's out. I don't know how much Judas money he got."

"About fifty grand," Lieutenant Anderson said. "He's put it all in his setup."

"Digger and me could use fifty G's, but we're cops. If we squeal it all goes on the old pay cheque," Coffin Ed said from the shadows.

"Let's not worry about that," Lieutenant Anderson said impatiently. "The point is to keep him alive."

"Yeah, the syndicate's out to kill him, poor little rat," Grave Digger said. "I heard all about it. They were saying, 'O'Malley may run but he can't hide.' O'Malley didn't run and all the hiding he's been doing is behind the Bible. But he isn't dead. So what I would like to know is how all of a sudden he got important enough for a police cover when the syndicate had ten months to make the hit if they had wanted to."

"Well, for one thing, the people here in Harlem, responsible people, the pastors and race leaders and politicians and such, believe he's doing a lot of good for the community. He paid off the mortgage on an old church and started this new Back-to-Africa movement—"

"The original Back-to-Africa movement denies him," Coffin Ed interrupted.

"—and people have been pestering the commissioner to give him police protection because of his following. They've convinced the commissioner that there'll be a race riot if any white gunmen from downtown come up here and kill him."

"Do you believe that, Lieutenant? Do you believe they've convinced the commissioner of that crap? That the syndicate's out to kill him after ten months?"

"Maybe it took these citizens that long to find out how useful he is to the community," Anderson said.

"That's one thing," Grave Digger conceded. "What are some other things?"

"The commissioner didn't say. He doesn't always take me and the captain into his confidence," the lieutenant said with slight sarcasm.

"Only when he's having nightmares about Digger and me shooting down all these innocent people," Coffin Ed said.

" 'Ours not to reason why, ours but to do or die,' " Anderson quoted.

"Those days are gone forever," Grave Digger said. "Wait until the next war and tell somebody that."

"Well, let's get down to business," Lieutenant Anderson said. "O'Malley is cooperating with us."

"Why shouldn't he? It's not costing him anything and it might save his life. O'Malley's a rat, but he's not a fool."

"I'm going to feel downright ashamed nursemaiding that ex-con," Coffin Ed said.

"Orders are orders," Anderson said. "And maybe it's not going to be like you think."

"I just don't want anybody to tell me that crime doesn't pay," Grave Digger said and stood up.

"You know the story about the prodigal son," Anderson said.

"Yeah, I know it. But do you know the story about the fatted calf?"

"What about the fatted calf?"

"When the prodigal son returned, they couldn't find the fatted calf. They looked high and low and finally had to give up. So they went to the prodigal son to apologize, but when they saw how fat he'd gotten to be, they killed him and ate him in the place of the fatted calf."

"Yes, but just don't let that happen to our prodigal son," Anderson warned them unsmilingly.

At that instant the telephone rang. Lieutenant Anderson picked up the receiver.

A big happy voice said, "*Captain?*"

"*Lieutenant.*"

"Well, who ever you is, I just want to tell you that the earth has busted open and all hell's got loose over here," and he gave the address where the Back-to-Africa rally had taken place.

III

"AND THEN JESUS say, 'John, the only thing worse than a two-timing woman is a two-timing man.'"

"Jesus say that? Ain't it the truth?"

They were standing in the dim light directly in front of the huge brick front of the Abyssinian Baptist Church. The man was telling the woman about a dream he'd had the night before. In this dream he'd had a long conversation with Jesus Christ.

He was a nondescript-looking man with black and white striped suspenders draped over a blue sport shirt and buttoned to old-fashioned wide-legged dark brown pants. He looked like the born victim of a cheating wife.

But one could tell she was strictly a church sister by the prissy way she kept pursing up her mouth. One could tell right off that her soul was really saved. She was wearing a big black skirt and a lavender blouse and her lips pursed and her face shone with righteous indignation when he said:

"So I just out and asked Jesus who was the biggest sinner; my wife going with this man, or this man going with my wife, and Jesus say: 'How come you ask me that, John? You ain't thinking 'bout doing nothing to them, is you?' I say, 'No, Jesus, I ain't gonna bother 'em, but this man, he's married just like my wife, and I ain't going to be responsible for what might break out between him and his wife,' and Jesus say, 'Don't you worry, John, there's always going to be some left.'"

Suddenly they were lit by a flash of lightning, which showed up a second man on his knees directly in back of the fascinated church sister. He held a safety razor blade between his right thumb and forefinger and he was cutting away the back of her skirt with such care and silence she didn't suspect a thing. First, holding the skirt firmly by the hem with his left hand, he split it in a straight line up to the point where it began to tighten over her buttocks. Then he split her slip in the same manner. After which, holding the right halves of both skirt and slip firmly but gently between the thumb and forefinger of his left hand, he cut out a wide half-circle down through the hem and carefully removed the cutout section and threw it carelessly against the wall of the church behind him. The operation revealed one black buttock encased in rose-colored rayon pants and the bare back of one thick black thigh showing above the rolled top of a beige rayon stocking. She hadn't felt a thing.

"'Anyone who commits adultery, makes no difference whether it be man or woman, breaks one of my Father's commandments,' Jesus say: 'Makes no difference how good it is,'" John said.

"Amen!" the church sister said. Her buttocks began to tremble as she contemplated this enormous sin.

Behind her, the kneeling man had begun to cut away the left side of her skirt, but the trembling of her buttocks forced him to exercise greater caution.

"I say to Jesus, 'That's the trouble with Christianity, the good things is always sinful,'" John said.

"Lawd, ain't it the truth," the church sister said, leaning forward to slap John on the shoulder in a spontaneous gesture of rising joy. The cutout left side section of the skirt and slip came off in the kneeling man's hand.

Now revealed was all the lower part of the big wide rose-encased buttocks and the backs of two thick black thighs above beige stockings. The black thighs bulged in all directions so that just below the crotch, where the torso began, there was a sort of pocket in which one could visualize the buttocks of some man gripped as in a vice. But now, in that pocket, hung a waterproof purse suspended from elastic bands passing up through the pants and encircling the waist.

With breathless delicacy but a sure touch and steady hand, as though performing a major operation on the brain, the kneeling man reached into the pocket and began cutting the elastic band which held the purse.

John leaned forward and touched her on the shoulder like a spontaneous caress. His voice thickened with suggestion. "But Jesus say, 'Commit all the 'dultry you want to, John. Just be prepared to roast in hell for it.'"

"He-he-he," laughed the church sister and slapped him again on the shoulder. "He was just kidding you. He'd forgive us for just *one* time," and she suddenly switched her trembling buttocks, no doubt to demonstrate Jesus's mercy.

In so doing she felt the hand easing the purse from between her legs. She slapped back automatically before she could begin to turn her body, and struck the kneeling man across the face.

"Mother-raper, you is trying to steal my money," she screamed, turning on the thief.

Lightning flashed, revealing the thief leaping to one side and the big broad buttocks in rose-colored pants twitching in fury. And before the sound of thunder was heard, the rain came down.

The thief leapt blindly into the street. Before the church sister could follow, a meat delivery truck coming at blinding speed hit the thief head-on and knocked the body somersaulting ten yards down the street before running over it. The driver lost control as the truck went over the body. The truck jumped the curb and knocked down a telephone pole at the corner of Seventh Avenue; it slewed across the wet asphalt and crashed against the concrete barrier enclosing the park down the middle of the avenue.

The church sister ran toward the mangled body and snatched her purse still clutched in the dead man's hand, unmindful of the bright lights of the armored truck rushing towards her like twin comets out of the night, unmindful of the rain pouring down in torrents.

The driver of the armored car saw the rose-encased buttocks of a large black woman as she bent over to snatch something from what looked like a dead man lying in the middle of the street. He was convinced he had d.t.'s. But he tried desperately to avoid them at the speed he was going on that wet street, d.t.'s or not. The armored truck skidded, then began wobbling as though doing the shimmy. The brakes meant nothing on the wet asphalt of Seventh Avenue and the car skidded straight on across the avenue and was hit broadside by a big truck going south.

The church sister hurried down the street in the opposite direction, holding the purse clutched tightly in her hand. Near Lexington Avenue, men, women and children crowded about the body of another dead colored man lying in the street, being washed for the grave by the rain. It lay in a grotesque position on its stomach at right angle to the curb, one arm outflung, the other beneath it. The side of the face turned up had been shot away. If there had been a pistol anywhere, now it was gone.

A police cruiser was parked nearby, crosswise to the street. One of the policemen was standing beside the body in the rain. The other one sat in the cruiser, phoning the precinct station.

The church sister was hurrying past on the opposite side of the street, trying to remain unnoticed. But a big colored laborer, wearing the overalls in which he had worked all day, saw her. His eyes popped and his mouth opened in his slack face.

"Lady," he called tentatively. She didn't look around. "Lady," he called again. "I just wanted to say, your ass is out."

She turned on him furiously. "Tend to your own mother-raping business."

He backed away, touching his cap politely, "I didn't mean no harm, lady. It's *your* ass."

She hurried on down the street, worrying more about her hair in the rain than about her behind showing.

At the corner of Lexington Avenue, an old junk man of the

kind who haunt the streets at night collecting old paper and discarded junk was struggling with a bale of cotton, trying to get it into his cart. Rain was pouring off his sloppy hat and wetting his ragged overalls to dark blue. His small dried face was framed with thick kinky white hair, giving him a benevolent look. No one else was in sight; everybody who was out on the street in all that rain was looking at the body of the dead man. So when he saw this big strapping lady coming towards him he stopped struggling with the wet bale of cotton and asked politely, "Ma'am, would you please help me get this bale of cotton into my cart, please, ma'am?"

He hadn't seen her from the rear so he was slightly surprised by her sudden hostility.

"What kind of trick is you playing?" she challenged, giving him an evil look.

"Ain't no trick, ma'am. I just tryna get this bale of cotton into my cart."

"Cotton!" she shouted indignantly, looking at the bale of cotton with outright suspicion. "Old and evil as you is you ought to be ashamed of yourself tryna trick me out my money with what you calls a bale of cotton. Does I look like that kinda fool?"

"No, ma'am, but if you was a Christian you wouldn't carry on like that just 'cause an old man asked you to help him lift a bale of cotton."

"I is a Christian, you wicked bastard," she shouted. "That's why all you wicked bastards is tryna steal my money. But I ain't the kind of Christian fool enough not to know there ain't no bales of cotton lying in the street in New York City. If it weren't for my hair, I'd beat your ass, you old con-man."

It had been a rough night for the old junk man. First he and a crony had found a half-filled whiskey bottle with what they thought was whiskey and had sat on a stoop to enjoy themselves, passing the bottle back and forth, when suddenly his crony had said, "Man, dis ain't whiskey; dis is piss." Then after he'd spent his last money for a bottle of "smoke" to settle his stomach, it had started to rain. And here was this evil bitch calling him a con-man, as broke as he was.

"You touch me and I'll mark you," he threatened, reaching in his pocket.

She backed away from him and he turned his back to her, muttering to himself. He didn't see her wet red buttocks above her shining black legs when she hurried down the street and disappeared into a tenement.

Four minutes later, when the first of the police cruisers sent to bottle up the street screamed around the corner from Lexington Avenue, he was still struggling with the bale of cotton in the rain.

The cruiser stopped for the white cops to put the routine question to a colored man: "Say, uncle, you didn't see any suspicious-looking person pass this way, did you?"

"Nawsuh, just an evil lady mad 'cause her hair got wet."

The driver grinned, but the cop beside him looked at the bale of cotton curiously and asked, "What you got there, uncle, a corpse bundled up?"

"Cotton, suh."

Both cops straightened up and the driver leaned over to look at it too.

"*Cotton?*"

"Yassuh, this is cotton—a bale of cotton."

"Where the hell did you get a bale of cotton in this city?"

"I found it, suh."

"Found it? What the hell kind of double-talk is that? Found it where?"

"Right here, suh."

"Right here?" the cop repeated incredulously. Slowly and deliberately he got out of the car. His attitude was threatening. He looked closely at the bale of cotton. He bent over and felt the cotton poking through the seams of the burlap wrapping. "By God, it *is* cotton," he said straightening up. "A bale of cotton! What the hell's a bale of cotton doing here in the street?"

"I dunno, boss, I just found it here is all."

"Probably fell from some truck," the driver said from within the cruiser. "Let somebody else take care of it, it ain't our business."

The cop in the street said, "Now, uncle, you take this cotton

to the precinct station and turn it in. The owner will be looking for it."

"Yassuh, boss, but I can't get it into my waggin."

"Here, I'll help you," the cop said, and together they got it
onto the cart.

The junk man set off in the direction of the precinct station,
pushing the cart in the rain, and the cop got back into the
cruiser and they went on down the street in the direction of
the dead man.

IV

WHEN GRAVE DIGGER and Coffin Ed arrived at the lot where
the Back-to-Africa rally had taken place, they found it closed
off by a police cordon and the desolate black people, surrounded
by policemen, standing helpless in the rain. The police cruiser
was still smoking in the barbecue pit and the white cops in
their wet black slickers looked mean and dangerous. Coffin
Ed's acid-burned face developed a tic and Grave Digger's neck
began swelling with rage.

The dead body of the young recruiting agent lay face up in
the rain, waiting for the medical examiner to come and pro-
nounce it dead so the men from Homicide could begin their
investigation. But the men from Homicide had not arrived, and
nothing had been done.

Grave Digger and Coffin Ed stood over the body and looked
down at all that was left of the young black face which a few
short minutes ago had been so alive with hope. At that moment
they felt the same as all the other helpless black people standing
in the rain.

"Too bad O'Malley didn't get it instead of this young boy,"
Grave Digger said, rain dripping from his black slouch hat over
his wrinkled black suit.

"This is what happens when cops get soft on hoodlums,"
Coffin Ed said.

"Yeah, we know O'Malley got him killed, but our job is to
find out who pulled the trigger."

They walked over to the herded people and Grave Digger asked, "Who's in charge here?"

The other young recruiting agent came forward. He was hatless and his solemn black face was shining in the rain. "I guess I am; the others have gone."

They walked him over to one side and got the story of what had happened as he saw it. It wasn't much help.

"We were the whole organization," the young man said. "Reverend O'Malley, the two secretaries and me and John Hill who was killed. There were volunteers but we were the staff."

"How about the guards?"

"The two guards with the armored truck? Why, they were sent with the truck from the bank."

"What bank?"

"The African Bank in Washington, D.C."

The detectives exchanged glances but didn't comment.

"What's your name, son?" Grave Digger asked.

"Bill Davis."

"How far did you get in school?"

"I went to college, sir. In Greensboro, North Carolina."

"And you still believe in the devil?" Coffin Ed asked.

"Let him alone," Grave Digger said. "He's telling us all he knows." Turning to Bill he asked, "And these two colored detectives from the D.A.'s office. Did you know them?"

"I never saw them before. I was suspicious of them from the first. But Reverend O'Malley didn't seem perturbed and he made the decisions."

"Didn't seem perturbed," Grave Digger echoed. "Did you suspect it might be a plant?"

"Sir?"

"Did it occur to you they might have been in cahoots with O'Malley to help him get away with the money?"

At first the young man didn't understand. Then he was shocked. "How could you think that, sir? Reverend O'Malley is absolutely honest. He is very dedicated, sir."

Coffin Ed sighed.

"Did you ever see the ships which were supposed to take you people back to Africa?" Grave Digger asked.

"No, but all of us have seen the correspondence with the steamship company—The Afro-Asian Line—verifying the year's lease he had negotiated."

"How much did he pay?"

"It was on a per head basis; he was going to pay one hundred dollars per person. I don't believe they are really as large as they look in these pictures, but we were going to fill them to capacity."

"How much money had you collected?"

"Eighty-seven thousand dollars from the . . . er . . . subscribers, but we had taken in quite a bit from other things, church socials and this barbecue deal, for instance."

"And these four white men in the delivery truck got all of it?"

"Well, just the eighty-seven thousand dollars we had taken in tonight. But there were five of them. One stayed inside the truck behind a barricade all the time."

The detectives became suddenly alert. "What kind of barricade?" Grave Digger asked.

"I don't know exactly. I couldn't see inside the truck very well. But it looked like some kind of a box covered with burlap."

"What provision company supplied your meat?" Coffin Ed asked.

"I don't know, sir. That wasn't part of my duties. You'll have to ask the chef."

They sent for the chef and he came wet and bedraggled, his white cap hanging over one ear like a rag. He was mad at everything—the bandits, the rain, and the police cruiser that had fallen into his barbecue pit. His eyes were bright red and he took it as a personal insult when they asked about the provision company.

"I don't know where the ribs come from after they left the hog," he said angrily. "I was just hired to superintend the cooking. I ain't had nothing to do with them white folks and I don't know how many they was—'cept too many."

"Leave this soul-brother go," Coffin Ed said. "Pretty soon he wouldn't have been here."

Grave Digger wrote down O'Malley's official address, which he already knew, then as a last question asked, "What was your connection with the original Back-to-Africa movement, the one headed by Mr. Michaux?"

"None at all. Reverend O'Malley didn't have anything at all to do with Mr. Michaux's group. In fact he didn't even like Lewis Michaux; I don't think he ever spoke to him."

"Did it ever occur to you that Mr. Michaux might not have had anything to do with Reverend O'Malley? Did you ever think that he might have known something about O'Malley that made him distrust O'Malley?"

"I don't think it was anything like that," Bill contended. "What reason could he have to distrust O'Malley? I just think he was envious, that's all. Reverend O'Malley thought he was too slow; he didn't see any reason for waiting any longer; we've waited long enough."

"And you were intending to go back to Africa too?"

"Yes, sir, still intend to—as soon as we get the money back. You'll get the money back for us, won't you?"

"Son, if we don't, we're gonna raise so much hell they're gonna send us all back to Africa."

"And for free, too," Coffin Ed added grimly.

The young man thanked them and went back to stand with the others in the rain.

"Well, Ed, what do you think about it?" Grave Digger asked.

"One thing is for sure, it wasn't the syndicate pulled this caper—not the crime syndicate, anyway."

"What other kinds of syndicates are there?"

"Don't ask me, I ain't the F.B.I."

They were silent for a moment with the rain pouring over them, thinking of these eighty-seven families who had put down their thousand-dollar grubstakes on a dream. They knew that these families had come by their money the hard way. To many, it represented the savings of a lifetime. To most it represented long hours of hard work at menial jobs. None could afford to lose it.

They didn't consider these victims as squares or suckers. They understood them. These people were seeking a home—

just the same as the Pilgrim Fathers. Harlem is a city of the homeless. These people had deserted the South because it could never be considered their home. Many had been sent north by the white southerners in revenge for the desegregation ruling. Others had fled, thinking the North was better. But they had not found a home in the North. They had not found a home in America. So they looked across the sea to Africa, where other black people were both the ruled and the rulers. Africa to them was a big free land which they could proudly call home, for there were buried the bones of their ancestors, there lay the roots of their families, and it was inhabited by the descendants of those same ancestors—which made them related by both blood and race. Everyone has to believe in something; and the white people of America had left them nothing to believe in. But that didn't make a black man any less criminal than a white; and they had to find the criminals who hijacked the money, black or white.

"Anyway, the first thing is to find Deke," Grave Digger put voice to their thoughts. "If he ain't responsible for this caper he'll sure as hell know who is."

"He had better know," Coffin Ed said grimly.

But Deke didn't know any more than they did. He had worked a long time to set up his movement and it had been expensive. At first he had turned to the church to hide from the syndicate. He had figured if he set himself up as a preacher and used his reward money for civil improvement, the syndicate would hesitate about rubbing him out.

But the syndicate hadn't shown any interest in him. That had worried him until he figured out that the syndicate simply didn't want to get involved in the race issue; he had already done all the harm he could do, so they left him to the soul-brothers.

Then he'd gotten the idea for his Back-to-Africa movement from reading a biography of Marcus Garvey, the Negro who had organized the first Back-to-Africa movement. It was said that Garvey had collected over a million dollars. He had been sent to prison, but most of his followers had contended that he was innocent and had still believed in him. Whether he had been innocent or not was not the question; what appealed to him was the fact his followers had still believed in him. That was the con-man's real genius, to keep the suckers always believing.

So he had started his own Back-to-Africa movement, the only difference being when he had got his million, he was going to cut out—he might go back to Africa, himself. He'd heard that people with money could live good in certain places there. The way he had planned it he would use two goons impersonating detectives to impound the money as he collected it; in that way he wouldn't have to bank it and could always keep it on hand.

He didn't know where these white hijackers fitted in. At the first glimpse he thought they were guns from the syndicate. That was why he had hidden beneath the table. But when he discovered they'd just come to grab the money, he had known it was something else again. So he had decided to chase them down and get the money back.

But when they had finally caught up with the meat delivery truck, the white men had disappeared. Perhaps it was just as well; by then he was outgunned anyway. Neither of his guards had been seriously hurt, but he'd lost one of his detectives. The wrecked truck hadn't told him anything and the driver of the truck that had run into them kept getting in the way.

He hadn't had much time so he had ordered them to split and assemble again every morning at 3 A.M. in the back room of a pool hall on Eighth Avenue and he would contact his other detective himself.

"I've got to see which way this mother-raping cat is jump-ing," he said.

He had enough money on him to operate, over five hundred dollars. And he had a five-grand bank account under an alias in an all-night bank in midtown for his getaway money in case of an emergency. But he didn't know yet where to start looking for his eighty-seven grand. Some kind of lead would come. This was Harlem where all black folks were against the whites, and somebody would tell him something. What worried him most was how much information the police had. He knew that in any event they'd be rough on him because of his record; and he knew he'd better keep away from them if he wanted to get his money back.

First, however, he had to get into his house. He needed his pistol; and there were certain documents hidden there—the forged leases from the steamship line and the forged credentials of the Back-to-Africa movement—that would send him back to prison.

He walked down Seventh Avenue to Small's bar, on the pretense of going to call the police, and got into a taxi without attracting any attention. He had the driver take him over to Saint Mark's Church, paid the fare and walked up the stairs. The church door was closed and locked, as he had expected, but he could stand in the shadowed recess and watch the entrance to the Dorrence Brooks apartment house across the street where he lived.

He stood there for a long time casing the building. It was a V-shaped building at the corner of 138th Street and St. Nicholas Avenue and he could see the entrance and the streets on both sides. He didn't see any strange cars parked nearby, no police cruisers, no gangster-type limousines. He didn't see any strange people, nothing and no one who looked suspicious. He could see through the glass doors into the front hall and there was not a soul about. The only thing was it was too damn empty.

He circled the church and entered the ark on the west side of St. Nicholas Avenue and approached the building from across the street. He hid in the park beside a tool shed from which he had a full view of the windows of his fourth-floor apartment. Light showed in the windows of the living room and dining room. He watched for a long time. But not once did a shadow pass before one of the lighted windows. He got dripping wet in the rain.

His sixth sense told him to telephone, and from some phone booth in the street where the call couldn't be traced. So he walked up to 145th Street and phoned from the box on the corner.

"Hellooo," she answered. He thought she sounded strange.

"Iris," he whispered.

Standing beside her, Grave Digger's hand tightened warningly on her arm. He had already briefed her what to say when O'Malley called and the pressure meant he wasn't playing.

"Oh, Betty," she cried. "The police are here looking for—"

Grave Digger slapped her with such sudden violence she caromed off the center table and went sprawling on her hands and knees; her dress hiked up showing black lace pants above the creamy yellow skin of her thighs.

Coffin Ed came up and stood over her, the skin of his face jumping like a snake's belly over fire. "You're so goddamn cute—"

Grave Digger was speaking urgently into the telephone: "O'Malley, we just want some information, that's—" but the line had gone dead.

His neck swelled as he jiggled the hook to get the precinct station.

At the same moment Iris came up from the floor with the smooth vicious motion of a cat and slapped Coffin Ed across the face, thinking he was Grave Digger in her blinding fury.

She was a hard-bodied high-yellow woman with a perfect figure. She never wore a girdle and her jiggling buttocks gave all men amorous ideas. She had a heart-shaped face with the high cheekbones, big wide red painted mouth, and long-lashed speckled brown eyes of a sexpot and she was thirty-three years old, which gave her the experience. But she was strong as an ox and it was a solid pop she laid on Coffin Ed's cheek.

With pure reflex action he reached out and caught her around the throat with his two huge hands and bent her body backward.

"Easy, man, easy!" Grave Digger shouted, realizing instantly that Coffin Ed was sealed in such a fury he couldn't hear. He dropped the telephone and wheeled, hitting Coffin Ed across the back of the neck with the edge of his hand just a fraction of a second before he'd have crushed her windpipe.

Coffin Ed slumped forward, carrying Iris down with him, beneath him, and his hands slackened from her throat. Grave Digger picked him up by the armpits and propped him on the sofa, then he picked up Iris and dropped her into a chair. Her eyes were huge and limpid with fear and her throat was going black and blue.

Grave Digger stood looking down at them, listening to the phone click frantically, thinking. *Now we're in for it*; then thinking bitterly, *These half-white bitches*. Then he turned back to the telephone and answered the precinct station and asked for the telephone call to be traced. Before he could hang up, Lieutenant Anderson was on the wire.

"Jones, you and Johnson get over to 137th Street and Seventh Avenue. Both trucks are smashed up and everyone gone, but there are two bodies DOA and there might be a lead." He paused for a moment, then asked, "How's it going?"

Grave Digger looked from the slumped figure of Coffin Ed into the now blazing eyes of Iris and said, "Cool, Lieutenant, everything's cool."

"I'm sending over a man to keep her on ice. He ought to be there any moment."

"Right."

"And remember my warning—no force. We don't want anyone hurt if we can help it."

"Don't worry, Lieutenant, we're like shepherds with new-born lambs."

The lieutenant hung up.

Coffin Ed had come around and he looked at Grave Digger with a sheepish expression. No one spoke.

Then Iris said in a thick, throat-hurting voice, "I'm going to get you coppers fired if it's the last thing I do."

Coffin Ed looked as though he was going to reply, but Grave Digger spoke first: "You weren't very smart, but neither were we. So we'd better call it quits and start all over."

"Start over shit," she flared. "You break into my house without a search warrant, hold me prisoner, attack me physically, and say let's call it quits. You must think I'm a moron. Even if I'm guilty of a murder, you can't get away with that shit."

"Eighty-seven colored families—like you and me—"

"Not like me!"

"—have lost their life's savings in this caper."

"So what? You two are going to lose your mother-raping jobs."

"So if you cooperate and help us get it back you'll get a ten percent reward—eight thousand, seven hundred dollars."

"You chickenshit cop, what can I do with that chicken feed? Deke is worth ten times that much to me."

"Not any more. His number's up and you'd better get on the winning side."

She gave a short, harsh laugh. "That ain't your side, big and ugly."

Then she got up and went and stood directly in front of Coffin Ed where he sat on the sofa. Suddenly her fist flew out and hit him squarely on the nose. His eyes filled with tears as blood spurted from his nostrils. But he didn't move.

"That makes us even," he said and reached for his handkerchief.

Someone rapped on the door and Grave Digger let in the white detective who had come to take over. Neither of them spoke; they kept the record straight.

"Come on, Ed," Grave Digger said.

Coffin Ed stood up and the two of them walked to the door, Coffin Ed holding the bloodstained handkerchief to his nose. Just before they went out, Grave Digger turned and said, "Chances go around, baby."

V

THE RAIN HAD stopped when they got outside and people were back on the wet sidewalks, strolling aimlessly and looking about as if to see what might have been washed from heaven. They walked up a couple of blocks where their little black battered sedan with the supercharged motor was parked. It had got much cleaner from the rain.

"You've got to take it easy, Ed man," Grave Digger said. "One more second and you'd have killed her."

Coffin Ed took away the handkerchief and found that his nose had stopped bleeding. He got into the car without replying. He felt guilty for fear he might have gotten Digger into trouble, but for his part he didn't care.

Grave Digger understood. Ever since the hoodlum had thrown acid into his face, Coffin Ed had had no tolerance for crooks. He was too quick to blow up and too dangerous for safety in his sudden rages. But hell, Grave Digger thought, what can one expect? These colored hoodlums had no respect for colored cops unless you beat it into them or blew them away. He just hoped these slick boys wouldn't play it too cute.

The trucks were still where they had been wrecked, guarded by harness cops and surrounded by the usual morbid crowd; but they drove on down to where the bodies lay. They found Sergeant Wiley of Homicide beside the body of the bogus detective, talking to a precinct sergeant and looking bored. He was a quiet, gray-haired, scholarly-looking man dressed in a dark summer suit.

"Everything is wrapped up," he said to them. "We're just waiting for the wagon to take them away." He pointed at the body. "Know him?"

They looked him over carefully. "He must be from out of town, eh, Ed?" Grave Digger said.

Coffin Ed nodded.

Sergeant Wiley gave them a rundown: No real identification of any kind, just a phoney ID card from the D.A.'s office and a bogus detective shield from headquarters. He had been a big man but now he looked small and forlorn on the wet street and very dead.

They went up and looked at the other body and exchanged looks.

Wiley noticed. "Run over by the delivery truck," he said. "Mean anything?"

"No, he was just a sneak thief. Must have got in the way is all. True monicker was Early Gibson but he was called Early Riser. Worked with a partner most of the time. We'll try to find his partner. He might give us a lead."

"Sure as hell ain't got no other," Coffin Ed added.

"Do that," Wiley said. "And let me know what you find out."

"We're going to take a look at the trucks."

"Right-o, there's nothing more here. We took a statement from the driver of the truck that smashed the armored job and let him go. All he knew was what the three of them looked like and we know what they look like."

"Any other witness?" Grave Digger asked.

"Hell, you know these people, Jones. All stone blind."

"What you expect from people who're invisible themselves?" Coffin Ed said roughly.

Wiley let it pass. "By the way," he said, "you'll find those heaps hopped up. The armored truck has an old Cadillac engine and the delivery truck the engine of a Chrysler 300. I've taken the numbers and put out tracers. You don't have to worry about that."

They left Sergeant Wiley to wait for the wagon and went over to examine the trucks. The tonneau of the armored truck had been built on to the chassis of a 1957 Cadillac, but it didn't tell them anything. The Chrysler engine had been installed in the delivery truck, and it might be traced. They copied the license and engine numbers on the off-chance of finding some garage that had serviced it, but they knew it was unlikely.

The curious crowd that had collected had begun to drift away. The harness cops guarding the wrecks until the police tow trucks carried them off looked extremely bored. The rain hadn't slackened the heat; it had only increased the density. The detectives could feel the sweat trickling down their bodies beneath their wet clothes.

It was getting late and they were impatient to get on to the trail of Deke, but they didn't want to overlook anything so they examined the truck inside and out with their hand torches.

The indistinct lettering: FREYBROS. INC. *Quality Meats, 173 West 116th Street*, showed faintly on the outside panels. They knew there wasn't any such thing as a meat provision firm at that address.

Then suddenly, as he was flashing his light inside, Coffin Ed said, "Look at this."

From the tone of his voice Grave Digger knew it was

something curious before he looked. "Cotton," he said. He and Coffin Ed looked at each other, swapping thoughts.

Caught on a loose screw on the side panel were several strands of cotton. Both of them climbed into the truck and examined it carefully at close range.

"Unprocessed," Grave Digger said. "It's been a long time since I've seen any cotton like that."

"Hush, man, you ain't never seen any cotton like that. You were born and raised in New York."

Grave Digger chuckled. "It was when I was in high school. We were studying the agricultural products of America."

"Now what can a meat provision company use cotton for?"

"Hell, man, the way this car is powered, you'd think meat spoiled on the way to the store—if you want to think like that."

"Cotton," Coffin Ed ruminated. "A mob of white bandits and cotton—in Harlem. Figure that one out."

"Leave it to the fingerprinters and the other experts," Grave Digger said, jumping down to the pavement. "One thing is for sure, I ain't going to spend all night looking for a mother-raping sack of cotton—or a cotton picker either."

"Let's go get Early Riser's buddy," Coffin Ed said, following him.

Grave Digger and Coffin Ed were realists. They knew they didn't have second sight. So they had stool pigeons from all walks of life: criminals, straight men and squares. They had their time and places for contacting their pigeons well organized; no pigeon knew another; and only a few of those who were really pigeons were known as pigeons. But without them most crimes would never be solved.

Now they began contacting their pigeons, but only those on the petty-larceny circuit. They knew they wouldn't find Deke through stool pigeons; not that night. But they might find a witness who saw the white men leave.

First they stopped in Big Wilt's Small's Paradise Inn at 135th Street and Seventh Avenue and stood for a moment at the front of the circular bar. They drank two whiskeys each and talked to each other about the caper.

The barstools and surrounding tables were filled with the flashily dressed people of many colors and occupations who could afford the price for air-conditioned atmosphere and the professional smiles of the light-bright chicks tending bar. The fat black manager waved the bill on the house and they accepted; they could afford to drink freebies at Small's, it was a straight joint.

Afterwards they sauntered towards the back and stood beside the bandstand, watching the white and black couples dancing the twist in the cabaret. The horns were talking and the saxes talking back.

"Listen to that," Grave Digger said when the horn took eight on a frenetic solo. "Talking under their clothes, ain't it?"

Then the two saxes started swapping fours with the rhythm always in the back. "Somewhere in that jungle is the solution to the world," Coffin Ed said. "If we could only find it."

"Yeah, it's like the sidewalks trying to speak in a language never heard. But they can't spell it either."

"Naw," Coffin Ed said. "Unless there's an alphabet for emotion."

"The emotion that comes out of experience. If we could read that language, man, we would solve all the crimes in the world."

"Let's split," Coffin Ed said. "Jazz talks too much to me."

"It ain't so much what it says," Grave Digger agreed. "It's what you can't do about it."

They left the white and black couples in their frenetic embrace, guided by the talking of the jazz, and went back to their car.

"Life could be great but there are hoodlums abroad," Grave Digger said, climbing beneath the wheel.

"You just ain't saying it, Digger; hoodlums high, and hoodlums low."

They turned off on 132nd Street beside the new housing development and parked in the darkest spot in the block, cut the motor and doused the lights and waited.

The stool pigeon came in about ten minutes. He was the shiny-haired pimp wearing a white silk shirt and green silk pants who had sat beside them at the bar, with his back turned, talking to a tan-skinned blonde. He opened the door quickly and got into the back seat in the dark.

Coffin Ed turned around to face him. "You know Early Riser?"

"Yeah. He's a snatcher but I don't know no sting he's made recently."

"Who does he work with?"

"Work with? I never heard of him working no way but alone."

"Think hard," Grave Digger said harshly without turning around.

"I dunno, boss. That's the honest truth. I swear 'fore God."

"You know about the rumble on '37th Stret?" Coffin Ed continued.

"I heard about it but I didn't go see it. I heard the syndicate robbed Deke O'Hara out of a hundred grand he'd just collected from his Back-to-Africa pitch."

That sounded straight enough so Coffin Ed just said, "Okay. Do some dreaming about Early Riser," and let him go.

"Let's try lower Eighth," Grave Digger said. "Early was on shit."

"Yeah, I saw the marks," Coffin Ed agreed.

Their next stop was a dingy bar on Eighth Avenue near the corner of 112th Street. This was the neighborhood of the cheap addicts, whiskey-heads, stumblebums, the flotsam of Harlem; the end of the line for the whores, the hard squeeze for the poor honest laborers and a breeding ground for crime. Blank-eyed whores stood on the street corners swapping obscenities with twitching junkies. Muggers and thieves slouched in dark doorways waiting for someone to rob; but there wasn't anyone but each other. Children ran down the street, the dirty street littered with rotting vegetables, uncollected garbage, battered garbage cans, broken glass, dog offal—always running, duck-ing and dodging. God help them if they got caught. Listless mothers stood in the dark entrances of tenements and swapped talk about their men, their jobs, their poverty, their hunger, their debts, their gods, their religions, their preachers, their children, their aches and pains, their bad luck with the numbers and the evilness of white people. Workingmen staggered down the sidewalks filled with aimless resentment, muttering curses, hating to go to their hotbox hovels but having nowhere else to go.

"All I wish is that I was God for just one mother-raping second," Grave Digger said, his voice cotton-dry with rage.

"I know," Coffin Ed said. "You'd concrete the face of the mother-raping earth and turn white folks into hogs."

"But I ain't God," Grave Digger said, pushing into the bar.

The barstools were filled with drunken relics, shabby men, ancient whores draped over tired laborers drinking ruckus juice to get their courage up. The tables were filled with the already drunk sleeping on folded arms.

No one recognized the two detectives. They looked prosperous and sober. A wave of vague alertness ran through the joint; everyone thought fresh money was coming in. This sudden greed was indefinably communicated to the sleeping drunks. They stirred in their sleep and awakened, waiting for the moment to get up and cadge another drink.

Grave Digger and Coffin Ed leaned against the bar at the front and waited for one of the two husky bartenders to serve them.

Coffin Ed nodded to a sign over the bar. "Do you believe that?"

Grave Digger looked up and read: NO JUNKIES SERVED HERE! He said, "Why not? Poor and raggedy as these junkies are, they ain't got no money for whiskey."

The fat bald-headed bartender with shoulders like a woodchopper came up. "What's yours, gentlemen?"

Coffin Ed said sourly, "Hell, man, you expecting any gentlemen in here?"

The bartender didn't have a sense of humor. "All my customers is gentlemen," he said.

"Two bourbons on the rocks," Grave Digger said.

"Doubles," Coffin Ed added.

The bartender served them with the elaborate courtesy he reserved for all well-paying customers. He rang up the bill and slapped down the change. His eyes flickered at the fifty-cent tip. "Thank you, gentlemen," he said, and strolled casually down the bar, winking at a buxom yellow whore at the other end clad in a tight red dress.

Casually she detached herself from the asbestos joker she was trying to kindle and strolled to the head of the bar. Without preamble she squeezed in between Grave Digger and Coffin Ed and draped a big bare yellow arm about the shoulders of each. She smelled like unwashed armpits bathed in dime-store perfume and overpowering bed odor. "You wanna see a girl?" she asked, sharing her stale whiskey breath between them.

"Where's any girl?" Coffin Ed said.

She snatched her arm from about his shoulder and gave her full attention to Grave Digger. Everyone in the joint had seen the obvious play and were waiting eagerly for the result.

"Later," Grave Digger said. "I got a word first for Early Riser's gunsel."

Her eyes flashed. "Loboy! He ain't no gunsel, he the boss."

"Gunsel or boss, I got word for him."

"See me first, honey. I'll pass him the word."

"No, business first."

"Don't be like that, honey," she said, touching his leg. "There's no time like bedtime." She fingered his ribs, promising pleasure. Her fingers touched something hard; they stiffened, paused, and then she plainly felt the big .38 revolver in the shoulder sling. Her hand came off as though it had touched something red hot; her whole body stiffened; her eyes widened and her flaccid face looked twenty years older. "You from the syndicate?" she asked in a strained whisper.

Grave Digger fished out a leather folder from his right coat pocket, opened it. His shield flashed in the light. "No, I'm the man."

Coffin Ed stared at the two bartenders.

Every eye in the room watched tensely. She backed further away; her mouth came open like a scar. "Git away from me," she almost screamed. "I'm a respectable lady."

All eyes looked down into shot glasses as though reading the answers to all the problems in the world; ears closed up like safe doors, hands froze.

"I'll believe it if you tell me where he's at," Grave Digger said.

A bartender moved and Coffin Ed's pistol came into his hand. The bartender didn't move again.

"Where who at?" the whore screamed. "I don't know where nobody at. I'm in here, tending to my own business, ain't bothering nobody, and here you come in here and start messing with me. I ain't no criminal, I'm a church lady—" she was becoming hysterical from her load of junk.

"Let's go," Coffin Ed said. One of the sleeping drunks staggered out a few minutes later. He found the detectives parked in the black dark in the middle of the slum block on 113th Street. He got quickly into the back and sat in the dark as had the other pigeon.

"I thought you were drunk, Cousin," Coffin Ed said.

Cousin was an old man with unkempt, dirty, gray-streaked, kinky hair, washed-out brown eyes slowly fading to blue, and skin the color and texture of a dried prune. His wrinkled old thrown-away summer suit smelled of urine, vomit and offal. He was strictly a wino. He looked harmless. But he was one of their ace stool pigeons because no one thought he had the sense for it.

"Nawsah, boss, jes' waitin'," he said in a whining, cowardly-sounding voice.

"Just waiting to get drunk."

"Thass it, boss, thass jes' what."

"You know Loboy?" Grave Digger said.

"Yassah, boss, knows him when I sees him."

"Know who he works with?"

"Early Riser mostly, boss. Leasewise they's together likes as if they's working."

"Stealing," Grave Digger said harshly. "Snatching purses. Robbing women."

"Yassah, boss, that's what they calls working."

"What's their pitch? Snatching and running or just mugging?"

"All I knows is what I hears, boss. Folks say they works the *holy dream*."

"*Holy dream*! What's that?"

"Folks say they worked it out themselves. They gits a church sister what carries her money twixt her legs. Loboy charms her lak a snake do a bird telling her this holy dream whilst Early Riser kneel behind her and cut out the back of her skirt and nip off de money sack. Must work, they's always flush."

"Live and learn," Coffin Ed said and Grave Digger asked: "You seen either one of them tonight?"

"Jes' Loboy. I seen him 'bout an hour ago looking wild and scairt going into Hijenks to get a shot and when he come out he stop in the bar for a glass of sweet wine and then he cut out in a hurry. Looked worried and movin' fast."

"Where does Loboy live?"

"I dunno, boss, 'round here sommers. Hijenks oughta know."

"How 'bout that whore who makes like he's hers?"

"She just big-gatin', boss, tryna run up de price. Loboy got a fay chick sommers."

"All right, where can we find Hijenks?"

"Back there on the corner, boss. Go through the bar an' you come to a door say 'Toilet.' Keep on an' you see a door say 'Closet.' Go in an' you see a nail with a cloth hangin' on it. Push the nail twice, then once, then three times an' a invisible door open in the back of the closet. Then you go up some stairs an' you come to 'nother door. Knock three times, then once, then twice."

"All that? He must be a connection."

"Got a shooting gallery's all I knows."

"All right, Cousin, take this five dollars and get drunk and forget what we asked you," Coffin Ed said, passing him a bill.

"Bless you, boss, bless you." Cousin shuffled about in the darkness, hiding the bill in his clothes, then he said in his whining cowardly voice, "Be careful, boss, be careful."

"Either that or dead," Grave Digger said.

Cousin chuckled and got out and melted in the dark.

"This is going to be a lot of trouble," Grave Digger said. "I hope it ain't for nothing."

VI

REVEREND DEKE O'MALLEY didn't know it was Grave Digger's voice over the telephone, but he knew it was the voice of a cop. He got out of the booth as though it had caught on fire. It was still raining but he was already wet and it just obscured his vision. Just the same he saw the light of the taxi coming down the hill on St. Nicholas Avenue and hailed it. He climbed in and leaned forward and said, "Penn Station and goose it."

He straightened up to wipe the rain out of his eyes and his back hit the seat with a thud. The broad-shouldered young black driver had taken off as though he were powering a rocket ship to heaven.

Deke didn't mind. Speed was what he needed. He had got so far behind everyone the speed gave him a sense of catching up. He figured he could trust Iris. Anyway, he didn't have any choice. As long as she kept his documents hidden, he was relatively safe. But he knew the police would keep her under surveillance and there'd be no way to reach her for a time. He didn't know what the police had on him and that worried him as much as the loss of the money.

He had to admit the robbery had been a cute caper, well organized, bold, even risky. Perhaps it had succeeded just because it was risky. But it had been too well organized for a crime of that dimension, for $87,000, or so it seemed to him; it couldn't have been any better organized for a million dollars. But there seemed a lot of easier ways to get $87,000. One interpretation, of course, was that the syndicate had staged it not only to break him but to frame him. But if it had been the syndicate, why hadn't they just hit him?

Penn Station came before he had finished thinking.

He found a long line of telephone booths and telephoned Mrs. John Hill, the wife of the young recruiting agent who had been killed. He didn't remember her but he knew she was a member of his church.

"Are you alone, Mrs. Hill?" he asked in a disguised voice.

"Yes," she replied tentatively, fearfully. "That is—who's speaking, please?"

"This is Reverend O'Malley," he announced in his natural voice.

He heard the relief in hers. "Oh, Reverend O'Malley, I'm so glad you called."

"I want to offer my sympathy and condolences. I cannot find the words to express my infinite sorrow for this unfortunate accident which has deprived you of your husband—" He knew he sounded like an ass but she'd understand that kind of proper talk.

"Oh, Reverend O'Malley, you are so kind."

He could tell that she was crying. *Good!* he thought. "May I be of help to you in any way whatsoever?"

"I just want you to preach his funeral."

"Of course I shall, Mrs. Hill, of course. You may set your mind at peace on that score. But, well, if you will forgive my asking, are you in need of money?"

"Oh, Reverend O'Malley, thank you, but he had life insurance and we have a little saved up—and, well we haven't any children."

"Well, if you have any need you must let me know. Tell me, have the police been bothering you?"

"Oh, they were here but they just asked questions about our life—where we worked and that kind of thing—and they asked about our Back-to-Africa movement. I was proud to tell them all I knew. . . ." Thank God that was nothing, he thought. "Then, well, they left. They were—well, they were white and I knew they were unsympathetic—I could just feel it—and I was glad when they left."

"Yes, my dear, we must be prepared for their attitude, that is why our movement was born. And I must confess I have no idea who the vicious white bandits are who murdered your fine . . . er . . . upstanding husband. But I am going to find them and God will punish them. But I have to do it alone. I can't depend on the white police."

"Oh, don't I know it."

"In fact, they will do everything to stop me."

"What makes white folks like that?"

"We must not think *why* they are like that. We must accept it as a fact and go ahead and outwit them and beat them at their own game. And I might need your help, Mrs. Hill."

"Oh, Reverend O'Malley, I'm so glad to hear you say that. I understand just what you mean and I'll do everything in my power to help you track down those foul murderers and get our money back."

Thank God for squares, O'Malley thought as he said, "I have utmost confidence in you, Mrs. Hill. We both have the same aim in view."

"Oh, Reverend O'Malley, your confidence is not misplaced."

He smiled at her stilted speech but he knew she meant it.

"The main thing is for me to stay free of the police while we conduct our own investigation. The police must not know of my whereabouts or that we are working together to bring these foul murderers to justice. They must not know that I have communicated with you or that I will see you."

"I won't mention your name," she promised solemnly.

"Do you expect them to return tonight?"

"I'm sure they're not coming back."

"In that case I will come to your house in an hour and we will make that our headquarters to launch our investigation. Will that be all right?"

"Oh, Reverend O'Malley, I'm thrilled to be doing some-thing to get revenge—I mean to see those white murderers punished—instead of just sitting here grieving."

"Yes, Mrs. Hill, we shall hunt down the killers for God to punish and perhaps you will draw your shades before I come."

"And I'll turn out the lights too so you won't have to worry about anyone seeing you."

"Turn out the lights?" For a moment he was startled. He en-visioned himself walking into a pitch-dark ambush and being seized by the cops. Then he realized he had nothing to fear from Mrs. Hill. "Yes, very good," he said. "That will be fine. I will telephone you shortly before arriving and if the police are there you must say, 'Come on up,' but if you are alone, say, 'Reverend O'Malley, it's all right.'"

"I'll do just that," she promised. He could hear the excitement in her voice. "But I'm sure they won't be here."

"Nothing in life is certain," he said. "Just remember what to say when I telephone—in about an hour."

"I will remember; and good-bye now, until then."

He hung up. Sweat was streaming down his face. He hadn't realized until then it was so hot in the booth.

He found the big men's room and ordered a shower. Then he undressed and gave his suit to the black attendant to be pressed while he was taking his shower. He luxuriated in the warm needles of water washing away the fear and panic, then he turned on cold and felt a new life and exhilaration replace the fatigue. . . . *The indestructible Deke O'Hara*, he thought gloatingly. *What do I care about eighty-seven grand as long as there are squares?*

"Your suit's ready, daddy," the attendant called, breaking off his reverie.

"Right-o, my man."

Deke dried, dressed, paid and tipped the attendant and sat on the stand for a shoeshine, reading about the robbery and himself in the morning *Daily News*. The clock on the wall read 2:21 A.M.

Mrs. Hill lived uptown in the Riverton Apartments near the Harlem River north of 135th Street. He knew she would be waiting impatiently. He was very familiar with her type: young, thought herself good-looking with the defensive conceit with which they convinced themselves they were more beautiful than all white women; ambitious to get ahead and subconsciously desired white men, hating them at the same time because they frustrated her attempts to get ahead and refused to recognize her innate superiority over white women. More than anything she wanted to escape her drab existence; if she couldn't be middle class and live in a big house in the suburbs she wanted to leave it all and go back to Africa, where she just *knew* she would be important. He didn't care for the type, but he knew for these reasons he could trust her.

He went out to the ramp to get a taxi. Two empty taxis with white drivers passed him; then a colored driver, seeing his predicament, passed some white people to pick him up. The white policeman supervising the loading saw nothing.

"You know ain't no white cabby gonna take you to Harlem, man," the colored driver said.

"Hell, they're just losing money and ain't making me mad at all," Deke said.

The colored driver chuckled.

Deke had him wait at the 125th Street Station while he phoned. The coast was clear. She buzzed the downstairs door the moment he touched the bell and he went up to the seventh floor and found her waiting in her half-open doorway. Behind her the apartment was pitch-dark.

"Oh, Reverend O'Malley, I was worried," she greeted him. "I thought the police had got you."

He smiled warmly and patted her hand as he passed to go inside. She closed the door and followed him and for a moment they stood in the pitch-dark of the small front hall, their bodies slightly touching.

"We can have some light," he said. "I'm sure it's safe enough."

She clicked switches and the rooms sprang into view. The shades were drawn and the curtains closed and the apartment was just as he had imagined it. A living room opening through a wide archway to a small dining room with the closed door of the kitchen beyond. On the other side a door opening to the bedroom and bath. The furniture was the polished oak veneer featured in the credit stores that tried to look expensive, and to one side of the living room was a long sofa that could be let out into a bed. It had already been let out and the bed made up.

She saw him looking and said apologetically, "I thought you might want to sleep first."

"That was very thoughtful of you," he said. "But first we must talk."

"Oh, yesss," she agreed jubilantly.

The only surprise was herself. She was a really beautiful woman with a smooth brown oval face topped by black curly hair that came in natural ringlets. She had sloe eyes and a petite turned-up nose with very faint black down on her upper lip. Her mouth was wide, generous, with rose-tinted lips and a sudden smile showing even white teeth. Wrapped in a bright blue silk negligee which showed all her curves, her body looked adorable.

He sat at the small round table which had been pushed to one side when the bed was made and indicated her to sit opposite. Then he began speaking to her with pontifical solemnity and seriousness.

"Have you prepared for John's funeral?"

"No, the morgue still has his body but I'm hoping to get Mr. Clay for the undertaker and have the funeral in your—our church—and for you to preach the funeral sermon."

"Of course, Mrs. Hill, and I hope by then to have our money back and turn an occasion of deep sorrow also into one of thanksgiving."

"You can call me Mabel, that's my name," she said.

"Yes, Mabel, and tomorrow I want you to go to the police and find out what they know so we can use it for our own investigation." He smiled winningly. "You're going to be my Mata Hari, Mabel—but one on the side of God."

Her face lit up with her own brilliant, trusting smile. "Yes, Reverend O'Malley, oh, I'm so thrilled," she said delightedly, involuntarily leaning towards him.

Her whole attitude portrayed such devotion he blinked. My God, he thought, this bitch has already forgotten her dead husband and he isn't even in his coffin.

"I'm so glad, Mabel." He reached across the table and took one of her hands and held it while he looked deeply into her eyes. "You don't know how much I depend on you."

"Oh, Reverend O'Malley, I'll do anything for you," she vowed.

He had to exercise great restraint. "Now we will kneel and pray to God for the salvation of the soul of your poor dead husband."

She suddenly sobered and knelt beside him on the floor.

"O Lord, our Savior and our Master, receive the soul of our dear departed brother, John Hill, who gave his life in support of our humble aspiration to return to our home in Africa."

"Amen," she said. "He was a good husband."

"You hear, O Lord, a good husband and a good, upright and honest man. Take him and keep him, O Lord, and have mercy and kindness to his poor wife who must remain longer in this vale of tears without the benefit of a husband to fulfill her desires and quench the flames of her body."

"Amen," she whispered.

"And grant her a new lease on life, and yes, O Lord, a new man, for life must go on even out of the depths of death, for life is everlasting, O Lord, and we are but human, all of us."

"Yes," she cried. "Yes."

He figured it was time to cut that shit out before he found himself in bed with her and he didn't want to confuse the issue —he just wanted his money back. So he said, "Amen."

"Amen," she repeated, disappointedly.

They arose and she asked him if she could fix him anything to eat. He said he wouldn't mind some scrambled eggs, toast and coffee, so she took him into the kitchen and made him sit on one of the padded tubular chairs to the spotless masonite tubular table while she went about preparing his snack. It was a kitchen that went along with the rest of the apartment—electric stove, refrigerator, coffee maker, eggbeater, potato whipper and the like; all electric—compactly arranged, brightly painted and superbly hygienic. But he was entranced by the curves of her body beneath the blue silk negligee as she moved about, bent over to get cream and eggs from the refrigerator, turned quickly here and there to do several things at once; and the swinging of her hips when she moved from stove to table.

But when she sat down opposite him she was too self-conscious to talk. A slow blush rose beneath her smooth brown skin, giving her a sun-kissed look. The snack was excellent, crisp bacon, soft scrambled eggs, firm brown toast with a veneer of butter. English marmalade and strong black espresso coffee with thick cream.

He kept the conversation going on the merits of her late husband and how much he would be missed by the Back-to-Africa movement; but he was slowly getting impatient for her to go to bed. It was a relief when she stacked the dishes in the

sink and retired to her bedroom with a shy good-night and a
wish that he sleep well.

He waited until he felt she was asleep and cracked her door
soundlessly. He listened to the even murmur of her breathing.
Then he turned on the light in the living room so he could see
her better. If she had awakened he would have pretended to
be searching for the bathroom, but she was sleeping soundly
with her left hand tight between her legs and her right flung
across her exposed breasts. He closed the door and went to the
telephone and dialed a number.

"Let me speak to Barry Waterfield, please," he said when he
got an answer.

A sleepy male voice said evilly, "It's too damn late to be
calling roomers. Call in the morning."

"I just got in town," Deke said. "Just passing through—I'm
leaving on the 5:45 for Atlanta. I got an important message for
him that won't keep."

"Jussa minute," the voice said.

Finally another voice came on the line, harsh and heavy
with suspicion. "Who's there?"

"Deke."

"Oh!"

"Just listen and say nothing. The police are after me. I'm
holed up with the wife of our boy, John Hill, who got croaked."
He gave the telephone number and address. "Nobody knows
I'm here but you. And don't call me unless you have to. If she
answers tell her your name is James. I'll brief her. Stay out of
sight today. Now hang up."

He listened to the click as the phone was hung up, then
waited to see if the line was still open and someone was eavesdropping. Satisfied, he hung up and went back to bed. He
turned out the light and lay on his back. A thousand thoughts
ran though his mind. He banished them all and finally went
to sleep.

He dreamed he was running through a pitch-dark forest
and he was terrified and suddenly he saw the moon through
the trees and the trees had the shapes of women with breasts
hanging like coconuts and suddenly he fell into a pit and it was

warm and engulfed him in a warm wet embrace and he felt the most exquisite ecstasy—

"Oh, Reverend O'Malley!" she cried. Light from the bedroom shone across her body, clad only in a frilly nightgown, one ripe brown breast hanging out. She was trembling violently and her face was streaked with tears.

He was so shocked seeing her like this after his dream he leapt from bed and put his arm about her trembling body, wondering if he had attacked her in his sleep. He could feel the warm firm flesh move beneath his hand as she sobbed hysterically.

"Oh, Reverend O'Malley, I've had the most terrible dream."

"There, there," he soothed, pulling her body to his. "Dreams don't mean anything."

She drew away from him and sat on his bed with her face cupped in her hands, muffling her voice. "Oh, Reverend O'Malley, I dreamed that you were hurt terribly and when I came to your rescue you looked at me as though you thought I had betrayed you."

He sat down beside her and began gently stroking her arm. "I would never think you had betrayed me," he said soothingly, counting the soft gentle strokes of his hand on the smooth bare flesh of her arm, thinking, any woman will surrender within a hundred strokes. "I believe in you utterly. You would never be the cause of hurt to me. You will always bring me joy and happiness."

"Oh, Reverend O'Malley, I feel so inadequate," she said.

Gently, still counting the strokes of his hand on her arm, he pushed her back and said, "Now lie down and try not to blame yourself for a silly dream. If I get hurt it will be God's will. We must all bow to God's will. Now repeat after me: If Reverend O'Malley gets hurt, it will be God's will."

"If Reverend O'Malley gets hurt, it will be God's will," she repeatedly dutifully in a low voice.

"We must all bow to God's will."

"We must all bow to God's will."

With his free hand he opened her legs.

"God's will must be served," he said.

"God's will must be served," she repeated.

"This is God's will," he said hypnotically.

"This is God's will," she repeated trance-like.

When he penetrated her she believed it was God's will and she cried, "Oh-oh! I think you're wonderful!"

VII

GRAVE DIGGER DROVE east on 113th Street to Seventh Avenue and Harlem showed another face. A few blocks south was the north end of Central Park and the big kidney-shaped lagoon; north of 116th Street was the "Avenue"—the lush bars and night clubs, Shalimar, Sugar Ray's, Dickie Wells's, Count Basie's, Small's, The Red Rooster; the Hotel Theresa, the National Memorial Book Store (*World History Book Outlet on 600,000,000 Colored People*); the beauty parlors (hairdressers); the hash joints (home cooking); the undertakers and the churches. But here, at 113th Street, Seventh Avenue was deserted at this late hour of the night and the old well-kept stone apartment buildings were dark.

Coffin Ed telephoned the station from the car and got Lieutenant Anderson. "Anything new?"

"Homicide got a colored taxi driver who picked up three white men and a colored woman outside of Small's and drove them to an address far out on Bedford Avenue in Brooklyn. He said the men didn't look like people who go to Small's and the woman was just a common prostitute."

"Give me his address and the firm he works for."

Anderson gave him the information but said, "That's Homicide's baby. We got nothing on O'Hara. What's your score?"

"We're going to Hijenks' shooting gallery looking for a junkie called Loboy who might know something."

"Hijenks. That's up on Edgecombe at the Roger Morris, isn't it?"

"He's moved down on Eight. Why don't the Feds knock him off? Who's he paying?"

"Don't ask me; I'm a precinct lieutenant."

"Well, look for us when we get there."

They drove down to 110th Street and turned back to Eighth Avenue and filled in the square. Near 112th Street they passed an old junk man pushing his cart piled high with the night's load.

"Old Uncle Bud," said Coffin Ed. "Shall we dig him a little?"

"What for? He won't cooperate; he wants to keep on living."

They parked the car and walked to the bar on the corner of 113th Street. A man and a woman stood at the head of the bar, drinking beer and swapping chatter with the bartender. Grave Digger kept on through to the door marked "Toilet" and went inside. Coffin Ed stopped at the middle of the bar. The bartender looked quickly towards the toilet door and hastened towards Coffin Ed and began wiping the spotless bar with his damp towel.

"What's yours, sir?" he asked. He was a thin, tall, stooped-shouldered, light-complexioned man with a narrow moustache and thinning straight hair. He looked neat in a white jacket and black tie; far too neat for that neck of the woods, Coffin Ed thought.

"Bourbon on the rocks." The bartender hesitated for an instant and Coffin Ed added, "Two." The bartender looked relieved.

Grave Digger came back from the toilet as the bartender was serving the drinks.

"You gentlemen are new around here, aren't you?" the bartender asked conversationally.

"We aren't, but you are," Grave Digger said.

The bartender smiled noncommittally.

"You see that mark down there on the bar?" Grave Digger said. "I made it ten years ago."

The bartender looked down the bar. The wooden bar was covered with marks—names, drawings, signatures. "What mark?"

"Come here, I'll show you," Grave Digger said, going down to the end of the bar.

The bartender followed slowly, curiosity overcoming caution. Coffin Ed followed him. Grave Digger pointed at the only unmarked spot on the entire bar. The bartender looked. The couple at the front of the bar had stopped talking and stared curiously.

"I don't see nothing," the bartender said.

"Look closer," Grave Digger said, reaching inside his coat.

The bartender bent over to look more closely. "I still don't see nothing."

"Look up then," Grave Digger said.

The bartender looked up into the muzzle of Grave Digger's long-barreled, nickel-plated .38. His eyes popped from their sockets and he turned yellow-green.

"Keep looking," Grave Digger said.

The bartender gulped but couldn't find his voice. The couple at the head of the bar, thinking it was a stickup, melted into the night. It was like magic, one instant they were there the next instant they were gone.

Chuckling, Coffin Ed went through the "Toilet" and opened the "Closet" and gave the signal on the nail holding a dirty rag. The nail was a switch and a light flashed in the entrance hallway upstairs where the lookout sat, reading a comic book. The lookout glanced at the red bulb which should flash the bartender's signal that strangers were downstairs. It didn't flash. He pushed a button and the back door in the closet opened with a soft buzzing sound. Coffin Ed opened the door to the bar and beckoned to Grave Digger, then jumped back to the door upstairs to keep it from closing.

"Good night," Grave Digger said to the bartender.

The bartender was about to reply but lights went on in his head and briefly he saw the Milky Way before the sky turned black. A junkie was coming from outside when he saw Grave Digger hit the bartender alongside the head and without putting down his foot turned on his heel and started to run. The bartender slumped down behind the bar, unconscious. Grave Digger had only hit him hard enough to knock him out. Without another look, he leapt towards the "Toilet" and followed Coffin Ed through the concealed door in the "Closet" up the narrow stairs.

There was no landing at the top of the stairs and the door

was the width of the stairway. There was no place to hide.

Halfway up, Grave Digger took Coffin Ed by the arm. "This is too dangerous for guns; let's play it straight," he whispered.

Coffin Ed nodded.

They walked up the stairs and Grave Digger knocked out the signal and stood in front of the peephole so he could be seen.

Inside was a small front hallway furnished with a table littered with comic books; above hung a rack containing numerous pigeonholes where weapons were placed before the addicts were allowed into the shooting gallery. A padded chair was drawn up to the table where the lookouts spent their days. On the left side of the door there were several loose nails in the doorframe. The top nail was the switch that blinked the lights in the shooting gallery in case of a raid. The lookout peered at Grave Digger with a finger poised over the blinker. He didn't recognize him.

"Who're you?" he asked.

Grave Digger flashed his shield and said, "Detectives Jones and Johnson from the precinct."

"What you want?"

"We want to talk to Hijenks."

"Beat it, coppers, there ain't nobody here by that name."

"You want me to shoot this door open?" Coffin Ed flared.

"Don't make me laugh," the lookout said. "This door is bulletproof and you can't butt it down."

"Easy, Ed," Grave Digger cautioned, then to the lookout: "All right, son, we'll wait."

"We're just having a little prayer meeting, with the Lord's consent," the lookout said, but he sounded a little worried.

"Who's the Lord in this case?" Coffin Ed asked harshly.

"Ain't you," the lookout said.

After that there was silence. Then they heard him moving around inside. Finally they heard another voice ask, "What is it, Joe?"

"Some nigger cops out there from the precinct."

"I'll see you sometime, Joe; see who's the niggermost," Coffin Ed grated.

"You can see me now—" Joe began to bluster, grown brave in the presence of his boss.

"Shut up, Joe," the voice said. Then they heard the slight sound of the peephole being opened.

"It's Jones and Johnson, Hijenks," Grave Digger said. "We just want some information."

"There's no one here by that name," Hijenks said.

"By whatever name," Grave Digger conceded. "We're looking for Loboy."

"For what?"

"He might have seen something on that caper where Deke O'Hara's Back-to-Africa group got hijacked."

"You don't think he was involved?"

"No, he's not involved," Grave Digger stated flatly. "But he was in the vicinity of 137th Street and Seventh Avenue when the trucks were wrecked."

"How do you know that?"

"His sidekick was run over and killed by the hijackers' truck."

"Well—" Hijenks began, but the lookout cut him off.

"Don't tell those coppers nothing, boss."

"Shut up, Joe; when I want your advice I'll ask it."

"We're going to find him anyway, even if we have to get the Feds to break in here to look for him. So if he's here, you'd be doing yourself a favor as well as us if you send him out."

"At this hour of the night you might find him in Sarah's crib on 105th Street in Spanish Harlem. Do you know where it is?"

"Sarah is an old friend of ours."

"I'll bet," Hijenks said. "Anyway, I don't know where he lives."

That ended the conversation. No one expected any gratitude for the information; it was strictly business.

They drove across town on 110th Street, past the well-kept old apartment houses overlooking the north end of Central Park and the lagoon where the more affluent colored people lived. It was a quiet street, renamed Cathedral Parkway in honor of the Cathedral of St. John the Divine, New York's most beautiful church, which fronted on it—a street of change. The west end, in the vicinity of the cathedral, was still inhabited by whites; but the colored people had taken over that section of Morningside which fronts on the park.

At Fifth Avenue they came to the circle where Spanish Harlem begins. Suddenly the street goes squalid, dirty, teeming with the many colors of Puerto Ricans—so many packed into the incredible slums it seems as though the rotten walls are bursting with human flesh. The English language gives way to Spanish, colored Americans give way to colored Puerto Ricans. By the time they reached Madison Avenue, they were in a Puerto Rican city with Puerto Rican customs, Puerto Rican food; with all stores, restaurants, professional offices, business establishments and such bearing signs and notices in Spanish, offering Puerto Rican services and Puerto Rican goods.

"People talk about Harlem," Grave Digger said. "These slums are many times worse."

"Yeah, but when a Puerto Rican becomes white enough he's accepted as white, but no matter how white a spook might become he's still a nigger," Coffin Ed replied.

"Hell, man, leave that for the anthropologists," Grave Digger said, turning south on Lexington towards 105th Street.

Sarah had the top flat in an old-fashioned brick apartment building that had seen better days. Directly beneath her top-floor crib lived a Puerto Rican clan of so many families the apartments on the floor could not hold them all; therefore eating, sleeping, cooking and making love was done in turns while the others stayed outside in the street until those inside were finished. Radios blared at top volume all day and night. Combined with the natural sounds of Spanish speech, laughter and quarreling, the din drowned all sounds that might come from Sarah's above. How the families below fared was of no concern.

Grave Digger and Coffin Ed parked down the street and walked. No one gave them a second look. They were men and that's all that interested Sarah: white men, black men, yellow men, brown men, straight men, crooked men and squares. Sarah said she only barred women; she didn't run a joint for "freaks." She paid for protection. Everyone knew she was a stool pigeon; but she pigeoned on the police too.

The first thing that hit the detectives when they entered the dimly lit downstairs hallway was the smell of urine.

"What American slums need is toilets," Coffin Ed said.

Smelling odors of cooking, loving, hair frying, dogs farting, cats pissing, boys masturbating and the stale fumes of stale wine and black tobacco, Grave Digger said, "That wouldn't help much."

Next they noticed the graffiti on the walls.

"Hell, no wonder they make so many babies; that's all they think about," Coffin Ed concluded.

"If you lived here, what else would you think about?"

They ascended in silence. The stink lessened as they climbed the six flights, the walls became less tattooed. The whore-house floor was practically clean.

They knocked at a red-painted door at the front. It was opened by a grinning Puerto Rican girl who didn't bother to look through the peephole. "Welcome, señors," she said. "You're at the right place."

They entered a vestibule and looked at the hooks on the walls.

"We want to talk to Sarah," Grave Digger said.

The girl waved towards a door. "Come on in. You don't have to see her."

"We want to see her. You go in like a good little girl and send her out."

The girl stopped grinning. "Who're you?"

Both detectives flashed their shields. "We're the law."

The girl sneered and turned quickly into the big front room, leaving the door ajar. They could see into what Sarah called her "reception room." The floor was covered with polished red linoleum. Chairs lined the walls: overstuffed chairs for the johns, straight-backed chairs for the girls; but most of the time the girls were either sitting in the laps of the johns or bringing them food and drink.

The girls were all dressed alike in one-piece shifts showing their shapes, and high-heeled shoes of different colors. They were all light-complexioned Puerto Rican girls with hair shades ranging from blonde to black; all were young. They looked gay and natural and picturesque flitting about the room, peddling their bodies.

Against the back wall a brilliantly lighted jukebox was playing Spanish music and two couples were dancing. The others were sitting, drinking whiskey highballs and eating, saving their energy for the real thing.

Alongside the jukebox was a long dimly lit hallway, flanked by the small bedrooms for business. The bathroom and the kitchen were at the rear. A dark brown motherly-type woman fried the chicken, dished out the potato salad and mixed the drinks, keeping a sharp eye on the money.

Two apartments had been put together to make Sarah's crib and the back apartment was her private residence.

Grave Digger said, "If our people were ever let loose they'd be a sensation in the business world, with the flair they got for crooked organizing."

"That's what the white folks is scared of," Coffin Ed said.

They watched Sarah come from the back and cross the big room. The girls treated her as though she were the queen. She was a buxom black woman with snow-white hair done in curls as tight as springs. She had a round face, broad flat nose, thick, dark, unpainted lips and a dazzling white-toothed smile. She wore a black satin gown with long sleeves and a high décolleté; on one wrist was a small platinum watch with a diamond-studded band; on the ring finger a wedding ring set with a diamond the size of an acorn. Several keys dangled on a gold chain about her neck.

She came towards them smiling only with her teeth; her dark eyes were stone cold behind rimless lenses. She closed the door behind her.

"Hello, boys," she said, shaking hands in turn. "How are you?"

"Fine, Sarah, business is booming; how's your business?" Grave Digger said.

"Booming too, Digger. Only the criminals got money, and all they do with it is buy pussy. You know how it is, runs hand in hand; girls sell when cotton and corn are a drag on the market. What do you boys want?"

"We want Loboy, Sarah," Grave Digger said harshly, souring at this landprop's philosophy.

Her smiled went out. "What's he done, Digger?" she asked in a toneless voice.

"None of your mother-raping business," Coffin Ed flared.

She looked at him. "Be careful, Edward," she warned.

"It's not what he's done this time, Sarah," Grave Digger said soothingly. "We're curious about what he's seen. We just want to talk to him."

"I know what that means. But he's kinda nervous and upset now—"

"High, you mean," Coffin Ed said.

She looked at him again. "Don't get tough with me, Edward. I'll have you thrown out here on your ass."

"Look, Sarah, let's level," Grave Digger said. "It's not like you think. You know Deke O'Hara got hijacked tonight."

"I heard it on the radio. But you ain't stupid enough to think Loboy was on that caper."

"Not that stupid, Sarah. And we don't give a damn about Deke either. But eighty-seven grand of colored people's hard-earned money got lost in the caper; and we want to get it back."

"How's Loboy fit that act?"

"Chances are he saw the hijackers. He was working in the neighborhood when their getaway truck crashed and they had to split."

She studied his face impassively; finally she said, "I dig." Suddenly her smile came on again. "I'll do anything to help our poor colored people."

"I believe you," Coffin Ed said.

She turned back into the reception room without another word and closed the door behind her. A few minutes later she brought out Loboy.

They took him to 137th Street and told him to reconstruct his activities and tell everything he saw before he got out of the vicinity.

At first Loboy protested, "I ain't done nothing and I ain't

seen nothing and you ain't got nothing against me. I been sick all day, at home and in bed." He was so high his speech was blurred and he kept dozing off in the middle of each sentence.

Coffin Ed slapped him with his open palm a half-dozen times. Tears came to his eyes.

"You ain't got no right to hit me like that. I'm gonna tell Sarah. You ain't got nothing against me."

"I'm just trying to get your attention is all," Coffin Ed said.

He got Loboy's attention, but that was all. Loboy admitted getting a glimpse of the driver of the delivery truck that hit Early Riser, but he didn't remember what he looked like. "He was white is all I remember. All white folks look alike to me," he said.

He hadn't seen the white men when they had got from the wrecked truck. He hadn't seen the armored truck at all. By the time it had passed he had jumped the iron fence beside the church and was running down the passageway to 136th Street, headed towards Lenox.

"Which way did the woman go?" Grave Digger asked.

"I didn't stop to see," Loboy confessed.

"What did she look like?"

"I don't remember; big and strong is all."

They let him go. By then it was past four in the morning. They drove to the precinct station to check out. They were frustrated and dead beat, and no nearer the solution than at the start. Lieutenant Anderson said nothing new had come in; he had put a tap on Deke's private telephone line but no one had called.

"We should have talked to the driver who took those three white men to Brooklyn, instead of wasting time on Loboy," Grave Digger said.

"There's no point in second-guessing," Anderson said. "Go home and get some sleep."

He looked white about the gills himself. It had been a hot, raw night—Independence night, he thought—filled with big and little crime. He was sick of crime and criminals; sick of both cops and robbers; sick of Harlem and colored people. He liked colored people all right; they couldn't help it because they were colored. He was quite attached to his two ace colored detectives; in fact he depended on them. They probably kept his job for him. He was second in command to the precinct captain, and had charge of the night shift. His was the sole responsibility when the captain went home, and without his two aces he might not have been able to carry it. Harlem was a mean rough city and you had to be meaner and rougher to keep any kind of order. He understood why colored people were mean and rough; he'd be mean and rough himself if he was colored. He understood all the evils of segregation. He sympathized with the colored people in his precinct, and with colored people in general. But right now he was good and goddamned sick of them. All he wanted was to go home to his quiet house in Queens in a quiet white neighborhood and kiss his white wife and look in on his two sleeping white children and crawl into bed between two white sheets and go to hell to sleep.

So when the telephone rang and a big happy colored voice sang, ". . . O where de cotton and de corn grow . . ." he turned purple with anger.

"Go on the stage, clown!" he shouted and banged down the receiver.

The detectives grinned sympathetically. They hadn't heard the voice but they knew it had been some lunatic talking in jive.

"You'll get used to it if you live long enough," Grave Digger said.

"I doubt it," Anderson muttered.

Grave Digger and Coffin Ed started home. They both lived on the same street in Astoria, Long Island, and they only used one of their private cars to travel back and forth to work. They kept their official car, the little battered black sedan with the hopped-up engine, in the precinct garage.

But tonight when they went to put it away, they found it had been stolen.

"Well, that's the bitter end," Coffin Ed said.

"One thing is for sure," Grave Digger said. "I ain't going in and report it."

"Damn right," Coffin Ed agreed.

VIII

THE NEXT MORNING, at eight o'clock, an open bed truck pulled up before a store on Seventh Avenue that was being re-modeled. Formerly, there had been a notion goods store with a shoeshine parlor serving as a numbers drop on the site. But it had been taken over by a new tenant and a high board wall cov-ering the entire front had been erected during the remodeling.

There had been much speculation in the neighborhood con-cerning the new business. Some said it would be a bar, others a night club. But Small's Paradise Inn was only a short distance away, and the cognoscenti ruled those out. Others said it was an ideal spot for a barbershop or a hairdresser, or even a bowl-ing alley; some half-wits opted for another funeral parlor, as though colored folks weren't dying fast enough as it is. Those in the know claimed they had seen office furnishings moved in during the night and they had it at first hand that it was going to be the headquarters for the Harlem political committee of the Republican Party. But those with the last word said that Big Wilt Chamberlain, the professional basketball player who had bought Small's Cabaret, was going to open a bank to store all the money he was making hand over fist.

By the time the workmen began taking down the wall, a small crowd had collected. But when they had finished, the crowd overflowed into the street. Harlemites, big and little, old and young, strong and feeble, the halt and the blind, male and female, boys and girls, stared in pop-eyed amazement.

"Great leaping Jesus!" said the fat black barber from down the street, expressing the opinion of all.

Plate-glass windows, trimmed with stainless steel, formed a glass front above a strip of shining steel along the sidewalk. Across the top, above the glass, was a big wooden sign glisten-ing with spotless white paint upon which big, bold, black letters announced:

HEADQUARTERS OF
B.T.S. BACK-TO-THE-SOUTHLAND

MOVEMENT B.T.S.
Sign Up Now!!! Be a "FIRST NEGRO!"
$1,000 Bonus to First Families Signing!

The entire glass front was plastered with bright-colored paintings of conk-haired black cotton-pickers, clad in overalls that resembled Italian-tailored suits, delicately lifting enormous snow-white balls of cotton from rose-colored cotton bolls that looked for all the world like great cones of ice cream, and grinning happily with even whiter teeth; others showed darkies, clad in the same Italian fashion, hoeing corn as though doing the cakewalk, their heads lifted in song that must surely be spirituals. One scene showed these happy darkies at the end of the day celebrating in a clearing in front of ranch-type cabins, dancing the twist, their teeth gleaming in the setting sun, their hips rolling in the playful shadows to the music of a banjo player in a candy-striped suit; while the elders looked on with approval, bobbing their nappy white heads and clapping their manicured hands. Another showed a tall white man with a white mane of hair, a white moustache and white goatee, wearing a black frock coat and shoestring tie, his pink face bubbling with brotherly love, passing out fantastic bundles of bank notes to a row of grinning darkies, above the caption: *Paid by the week.* Lodged between the larger scenes were smaller paintings identified as ALL GOOD THINGS TO EAT: grotesquely oversized animals and edibles with the accompanying captions: *Big-legged Chickens . . . Chitterling Bred Shoats . . . Yams! What Am . . . O! Possum! . . . Lasses In The Jug . . . Grits and Gravy . . . Pappy's Bar-B-Q and Mammy's Hog Maw Stew . . . Corn Whiskey . . . Buttermilk . . . Hoppin John.*

In the center of all this jubilation of good food, good times and good pay, were a blown-up photomontage beside a similarly sized drawing: one showing pictures of famine in the Congo, tribal wars, mutilations, depravities, hunger and disease, above the caption, *Unhappy Africa*; the other depicting fat, grinning colored people sitting at tables laden with food, driving about in cars as big as Pullman coaches, black children entering modernistic schools equipped with stadiums and swimming-pools, elderly people clad in Brooks Brothers suits and Saks Fifth Avenue dresses filing into a church that looked astonishingly like Saint Peter's Cathedral in Rome, with its caption: *The Happy South*.

At the bottom was another big white-painted, black-lettered banner reading:

FARE PAID . . . HIGH WAGES . . .
ACCOMMODATIONS FOR COTTON PICKERS
$1,000 Bonus for Each Family of Five Able-Bodied Persons

The small notice in one lower corner which read, *Wanted, a bale of cotton*, went unnoticed.

On the inside, the walls were decorated with more slogans and pictures of the same papier-mâché cotton plants and bamboo corn stalks were scattered about the floor, in the center of which was an artificial bale of cotton bearing the etched brass legend: *Our Front Line of Defense*.

At the front to one side was a large flat-topped desk with a nameplate stating: Colonel Robert L. Calhoun. Colonel Calhoun in the flesh sat behind the desk, smoking a long, thin cheroot and looking out the window at the crowd of Harlemites with a benign expression. He looked like the model who had posed for the portrait of the colonel in the window, paying off the happy darkies. He had the same narrow, hawklike face crowned by the same mane of snow-white hair, the same wide, drooping white moustache, the same white goatee. There the resemblance stopped. His narrow-set eyes were ice-cold blue and his back was ramrod-straight. But he was clad in a similar black frock coat and black shoestring tie, and on the ring finger of his long pale hand was a solid-gold signet ring with the letters CSA.

A young blond white man in a seersucker suit, who looked as though he might be an alumnus of Ole Miss, sat on the edge of the Colonel's desk, swinging his leg.

"Are you going to talk to them?" he asked in a college-trained voice with a slight southern accent.

The Colonel removed his cheroot and studied the ash on the

tip. His actions were deliberate; his expression impassive. He spoke in a voice that was slow and calculated, with a southern accent as thick as molasses in the winter.

"Not yet, son, let's let it simmer a bit. You can't rush these darkies; they'll come around in their own good time."

The young man peered through a clear crack in the plastered window. He looked anxious. "We haven't got all the time in the world," he said.

The Colonel looked up at him, smiling with perfect white dentures, but his eyes remained cold. "What's your hurry, son, you got a gal waiting?"

The young man blushed and looked down sullenly. "All these niggers make me nervous," he confessed.

"Now don't start feeling guilty, son," the Colonel said. "Remember it's for their own good. You got to learn to think of niggers with love and charity."

The young man smiled sardonically and remained silent.

At the back of the room were two desks side by side, bearing the legends: *Applications*. They were presided over by two neat young colored men who shuffled application forms to look occupied. From time to time the Colonel looked at them approvingly, as though to say, "See how far you've come." But they had the expressions of guilty fathers who've been caught robbing their babies' banks.

Outside, on the sidewalk and in the street, black people were expressing righteous indignation.

"Ain't it a scandal, Lord, right up here in Harlem?"

"God ought to strike 'em daid, that's whut."

"These peckerwoods don't know what they want. One day they's sending us north to get rid of us, and the next they's up here tryna con us into going back."

"Man, trust white folks and go from Cadillacs to cotton sacks."

"Ain't it the truth! I'd sooner trust a white-mouthed moccasin sucking at my tiddy."

"Man, I ought to go in there and say to that ol' colonel, 'You wants me to go back south, eh?' and he says, 'That's right, boy,' and I says, 'You gonna let me vote?' and he says, 'That's right, boy, vote all you want, just so long you don't cast no ballots,' and I says, 'You gonna let me marry yo' daughter—' "

His audience fell out laughing. But one joker didn't think it was funny; he said, "There he is, what's stopping you?"

Everyone stopped laughing.

The comedian said shamefacedly, "Hell, man, I don't do everything I oughta do, you knows that."

A big matronly woman said, "Just you wait 'til Reverend O'Malley hears 'bout all this, and then you'll see some action."

Reverend O'Malley had already heard. Barry Waterfield, the phoney detective in his employ, had telephoned him and given him the lowdown. Reverend O'Malley had sent him to see the Colonel with implicit instructions.

Barry was a big, clean-shaven man with hair cropped short and a nose flattened in the ring. His dark brown face bore other lumps it had taken during his career as bodyguard, bouncer, mugger and finally killer. He had small brown eyes partly obscured by scar tissue, and two gold teeth in front. He was easily identifiable, which limited his usefulness, but Deke didn't have any other choice.

Barry shaved, carefully brushed his hair, dressed in a dark business suit, but couldn't resist the hand-painted tie depicting an orange sunset on a green background.

When he pushed through the crowd and entered the office of the Back-to-the-Southland movement, talk stopped momentarily and people stared at him. No one knew him, but no one would forget him.

He walked straight to the Colonel's desk and said, "Colonel Calhoun, I'm Mr. Waterfield from the Back-to-Africa movement."

Colonel Calhoun looked up through cold blue eyes and appraised him from head to foot. Colonel Calhoun dug him instantly. The Colonel removed the cheroot from his white moustache and his dentures gleamed whitely.

"What can I do for you . . . er . . . what did you say your name was?"

"Barry Waterfield."

"Barry. What can I do for you, boy?"

"Well, you see, we have a group of good people we're going to send back to Africa."

"Back to Africa!" the Colonel exclaimed in horror. "My boy, you must be raving mad. Uprooting these people from their native land. Don't do it, boy, don't do it."

"Well, sir, you see, it's going to cost a lot—" He remained standing, as the Colonel had not invited him to be seated.

"A fortune, my boy, a veritable fortune," the Colonel agreed, rearing back in his chair. "And who's going to pay for this costly nonsense?"

"Well, sir, you see, that's the trouble. You see, last night we were having a big rally to sign up the families who were going to leave first, and then some bandits robbed us of their money. Eighty-seven thousand dollars."

The Colonel whistled softly.

"You must have heard about it, sir."

"No, I can't say that I have, my boy; but I've been pretty busy with this philanthropy of ours. But I'm sorry for those misguided people, even though their misfortune might turn out to be a blessing in disguise. I'm ashamed of you, my boy, an honest-looking American nigra like you, leading your people astray. If you knew what we know, you wouldn't dream of sending your poor people to Africa. Only pestilence and starvation await them there, in those foreign lands. The South is the place for them, the good old reliable Southland. We love and take care of our darkies."

"Well, you see, sir, that's what I want to talk to you about. These poor people have got ready to go somewhere, and now since they can't go back to Africa it might be best they go back south."

"Right you are, my boy. You just send them to me and we'll do right by them. The Happy Southland is the only home of your people."

The two young colored clerks who had been eavesdropping on the conversation were downright shocked to hear Barry say, "Well, sir, I'm inclined to agree with you, sir. "

The blond young man was standing at the front window, peering out at the milling black mob which he now began to see in a different light. They didn't look dangerous any longer; now they appeared innocent and gullible and he could barely suppress a smile as he thought of how easy it was going to be. Then he frowned at a sudden memory and turned back to stare at Barry with searching suspicion. This nigger sounded too good to be true, he thought.

But the Colonel didn't seem to entertain a doubt. "You just trust me, my boy," he went on, "and we'll take care of your people."

"Well, you see, sir, I trust you," Barry said. "I know you'll do the right thing by us. But our leader, Reverend O'Malley, won't like it, my giving you my confidence. You see, sir, he's a dangerous man."

A line of white dentures peeped from beneath the Colonel's white moustache, and Barry had a fleeting thought that this mother-raping white man looked too mother-raping white. But the Colonel continued unsuspectingly, "Don't worry about that nigra, my boy, we're going to take care of him and put an end to his un-American activities."

Barry leaned a little forward and lowered his voice. "You see, sir, the point is we have the eighty-seven families of able-bodied people all packed and ready to go; and I've got to tell them if you're ready to pay them their bonuses."

"My boy, their bonuses is as good as in the bank. You tell them that," the Colonel said and rolled the cheroot between his lips only to find it had gone out.

He tossed it carelessly on the floor and carefully selected another from a silver case in his breast pocket. Then he clipped the end with a cigar cutter from his vest pocket, stuck the clipped cheroot between his lips and rolled it over and over until the outer leaves of the lip-end were agreeably wet. Both Barry and the blond young man snapped their lighters to offer a light, but the Colonel preferred Barry's flame.

Barry said, "Well, that is fine of you, sir, that's all I want to know. We got more than a thousand families recruited and I'll sell you the whole list."

For an instant both the Colonel and the blond young man became immobile. Then the Colonel's dentures showed. "If I heard you correctly, my boy," he said smoothly, "you said *sell*."

"Well, sir, you see, sir, it's like this," Barry began, his voice pitched low and grown husky. "Naturally I would want a little something for myself, taking all this risk. You see, sir, the list is highly confidential and it has taken us months to select and recruit all these able-bodied people. And if they knew I was turning this list over to you, they might make trouble, sir— even though it is for their own good. And I'd want to be able to get away for a while, sir. You understand, sir."

"My boy, nothing could be plainer," the Colonel said and puffed his cheroot. "Plain talk suits me fine. Now how much do you want for your list?"

"Well, sir. I was thinking fifty dollars a family would be about fair, sir."

"You're a boy after my own heart, even though you do belong to the nigra race," the Colonel said. The blond young man frowned and opened his mouth as though to speak, but the Colonel ignored him. "Now, my boy, I understand your predicament and I don't want to jeopardize your position and usefulness by permitting you to come back here and be seen and suspected by all your people. So I'm going to tell you what I want you to do. You bring the list to me at midnight. I'll be waiting down by the Harlem River underneath the subway extension to the Polo Grounds in my cab, and I'll pay you right then and there. It will be dark and deserted at that time of night and nobody'll see you."

Barry hesitated, looking torn between fear and greed. "Well, frankly, sir, that's a good sound idea, but I'm scared of the dark, sir," he confessed.

The Colonel chuckled. "There's nothing about the dark to fear, my boy. That's just nigra superstition. The dark never hurt anyone. You'll be as safe as in the arms of Jesus. I give you my word."

Barry looked relieved at this. "Well, sir, if you give me your word I know can't nothing happen to me. I'll be there at midnight sharp."

Without further ado, the Colonel waved a hand, dismissing him.

"Are you going to trust that—" the blond young man began.

For the first time the Colonel showed displeasure in a frown. The blond young man shut up.

As he was leaving, Barry noticed the small sign in the window through the corners of his eyes: *Wanted, a bale of cotton.* What for? he wondered.

IX

NO ONE KNEW where Uncle Bud slept. He could be found any night somewhere on the streets of Harlem, pushing his cart, his eyes searching the darkness for anything valuable enough to sell. He had an exceptional divination of anything of value, because in Harlem no one ever threw anything away valuable enough to sell, if they knew it. But he managed to collect enough saleable junk to exist, and when day broke he was to be seen at one of those run-down junkyards where scrawny-necked, beady-eyed white men paid a few cents for the rags, paper, glass and iron he had collected. Actually he slept in his cart during the summer. He would wheel it to some shady spot on some slum street where no one thought it strange to find a junk man sleeping in his cart, and curl up on the burlap rags covering his load and sleep, undisturbed by the sounds of motor-cars and trucks, children screaming, men cursing and fighting, women gossiping, police sirens wailing, or even by the dead awakening. Nothing troubled his sleep.

On this night, because his cart was filled with the bale of cotton, he wheeled it towards a street beneath the 125th Street approach to the Triborough Bridge, where he would be near Mr. Goodman's junkyard when he woke up.

A police cruiser containing two white cops pulled up beside him. "What you got there, boy?" the one on the inside asked.

Uncle Bud stopped and scratched his head and ruminated. "Wal, boss, I'se got some cahdbo'd and papuh an' I'se got some bedsprings an' some bottles an' some rags an'—"

"You ain't got no money, have you?" the cop cracked. "You ain't got no eighty-seven thousand dollars?"

"Nawsuh, wish I did."

"What would you do with eighty-seven grand?"

Uncle Bud scratched his head again. "Wal, suh, I'd buy me a brand-new waggin. An' then I reckon I'd go to Africa," he said, adding underneath his breath: "Where wouldn't any white mother-rapers like you be fucking with me all the time."

Naturally the cops didn't hear the last, but they laughed at the first and drove on.

Uncle Bud found a spot beside an abandoned truck down by the river and went to sleep. When he awakened the sun was high. At about the same time Barry Waterfield was approaching Colonel Calhoun on Seventh Avenue, he was approaching the junkyard alongside the river south of the bridge.

It was a fenced-in enclosure about piles of scrap iron and dilapidated wooden sheds housing other kinds of junk. Uncle Bud stopped before a small gate at one side of the main office building, a one-story wooden box fronting on the street. A big black hairless dog the size of a Great Dane came silently to the gate and stared at him through yellow eyes.

"Nice doggie," Uncle Bud said through the wire gate.

The dog didn't blink.

A shabbily dressed, unshaven white man came from the office and led the dog away and chained it up. Then he returned and said, "All right, Uncle Bud, what you got there?"

Uncle Bud looked at the white man through the corners of his eyes. "A bale of cotton, Mr. Goodman."

Mr. Goodman was startled. "A bale of cotton?"

"Yassuh," Uncle Bud said proudly as he uncovered the bale. "Genuwine Mississippi cotton."

Mr. Goodman unlocked the gate and came outside to look at it. Most of the cotton was obscured by the burlap covering. But he pulled out a few shreds from the seams and smelled it. "How do you know it's *Mississippi* cotton?"

"I'd know Mississippi cotton anywhere I seed it," Uncle Bud stated flatly. "Much as I has picked."

"Ain't much of this to be seen," Mr. Goodman observed.

"I can smell it," Uncle Bud said. "It smell like nigger-sweat."

Mr. Goodman sniffed at the cotton again. "Anything special about that?"

"Yassuh, makes it stronger."

Two colored workmen in overalls came up. "Cotton!" one exclaimed. "Lord, lord."

"Makes you homesick, don't it?" the other one said.

"Homesick for your mama," the first one said, looking at him sidewise.

"Watch out, man, I don't play the dozens," the second one said.

Mr. Goodman knew they were just kidding. "All right, get it on the scales," he ordered.

The bale weighed four hundred and eighty-seven pounds.

"I'll give you five dollars for it," Mr. Goodman said.

"Five bones!" Uncle Bud exclaimed indignantly. "Why, dis cotton is worth thirty-nine cents a pound."

"You're thinking about the First World War," Mr. Goodman said. "Nowadays they're giving cotton away."

The two workmen exchanged glances silently.

"I ain't giving dis away," Uncle Bud said.

"Where can I sell a bale of cotton?" Mr. Goodman said. "Who wants unprocessed cotton? Not even good for bullets no more. Nowadays they shoot atoms. It ain't like as if it was drugstore cotton."

Uncle Bud was silent.

"All right, ten dollars then," Mr. Goodman said.

"Fifty dollars," Uncle Bud countered.

"*Mein Gott*, he wants fifty dollars yet!" Mr. Goodman appealed to his colored workmen. "That's more than I'd pay for brass."

The colored workmen stood with their hands in their pockets, blank-faced and silent. Uncle Bud kept a stubborn silence. All three colored men were against Mr. Goodman. He felt trapped and guilty, as though he'd been caught taking advantage of Uncle Bud.

"Since it's you, I'll give you fifteen dollars."

"Forty," Uncle Bud muttered.

Mr. Goodman gestured eloquently. "What am I, your father, to give you money for nothing?" The three colored men stared at him accusingly. "You think I am Abraham Lincoln instead of Abraham Goodman?" The colored men didn't think he was funny. "Twenty," Mr. Goodman said desperately and turned towards the office.

"Thirty," Uncle Bud said.

The colored workmen shifted the bale of cotton as though asking whether to take it in or put it back.

"Twenty-five," Mr. Goodman said angrily. "And I should have my head examined."

"Sold," Uncle Bud said.

About that time the Colonel had finished his interview with Barry and was having his breakfast. It had been sent from a "home-cooking" restaurant down the street. The Colonel seemed to be demonstrating to the colored people outside, many of whom were now peeking through the cracks between the posters covering most of the window, what they could be eating for breakfast if they signed up with him and went back south.

He had a bowl of grits, swimming with butter; four fried eggs sunny side up; six fried homemade sausages; six down-home biscuits, each an inch thick, with big slabs of butter stuck between the halves; and a pitcher of sorghum molasses. The Colonel had brought his own food with him and merely paid the restaurant to cook it. Alongside his heaping plate stood a tall bourbon whiskey highball.

The colored people, watching the Colonel shovel grits, eggs and sausage into his mouth and chomp off a hunk of biscuit, felt nostalgic. But when they saw him cover all his food with a thick layer of sorghum molasses, many felt absolutely homesick.

"I wouldn't mind going down home for dinner ever day," one joker said. "But I wouldn't want to stay overnight."

"Baby, seeing that scoff makes my stomach feel lak my throat is cut," another replied.

Bill Davis, the clean-cut young man who was Reverend O'Malley's recruiting agent, entered the Back-to-the-Southland office as Colonel Calhoun was taking an oversize mouthful of grits, eggs and sausage mixed with molasses. He paused before the Colonel's desk, erect and purposeful.

"Colonel Calhoun, I am Mister Davis," he said. "I represent the Back-to-Africa movement of Reverend O'Malley's. I want a word with you."

The Colonel looked up at Bill Davis through cold blue eyes, continuing to chew slowly and deliberately like a camel chewing its cud. But he took much longer in his appraisal than he had done with Barry Waterfield. When he had finished chewing, he washed his mouth with a sip from his bourbon highball, cleared his throat and said, "Come back in half an hour, after I've et my breakfast."

"What I have to say to you I'm going to say now," Bill Davis said.

The Colonel looked up at him again. The blond young man who had been standing in the background moved closer. The young colored men at their desks in the rear became nervous.

"Well, what can I do for you . . . er . . . what did you say your name was?" the Colonel said.

"My name is *Mister* Davis, and I'll make it short and sweet. *Get out of town!*"

The blond young man started around the desk and Bill Davis got set to hit him, but the Colonel waved him back.

"Is that all you got to say, my boy?"

"That's all, and I'm not your boy," Bill Davis said.

"Then you've said it," the Colonel said and deliberately began eating again.

When Bill emerged, the black people parted to let him pass. They didn't know what he had said to the Colonel, but whatever it was they were for him. He had stood right up to that ol' white man and tol' him something to his teeth. They respected him.

A half-hour later the pickets moved in. They marched up and down Seventh Avenue, holding aloft a Back-to-Africa banner and carrying placards reading: *Goddamn White Man GO! GO! GO! Black Man STAY! STAY! STAY!* There were twenty-five in the picket line and two or three hundred followers. The pickets formed a circle in front of the Back-to-the-Southland office and chanted as they marched, "Go, white man, go while you can. . . . Go, white man, go while you can. . . ." Bill Davis stood to one side between two elderly colored men.

Colored people poured into the vicinity from far and wide, overflowed the sidewalks and spilled into the street. Traffic was stopped. The atmosphere grew tense, pregnant with premonition. A black youth ran forward with a brick to hurl through the plate-glass window. A Back-to-Africa follower grabbed him and took it away. "None of that, son, we're peaceful," he said.

"What for?" the youth asked.

The man couldn't answer.

Suddenly the air was filled with the distant wailing of the sirens, sounding at first like the faint wailing of banshees, growing ever louder as the police cruisers roared nearer, like souls escaped from hell.

The first cruiser plowed through the mob and shrieked to a stop on the wrong side of the street. Two uniformed white cops hit the pavement with pistols drawn, shouting, "Get back! Get off the street! Clear the street!" Then another cruiser plowed through the mob and shrieked to a stop. . . . Then a third. . . . Then a fourth. . . . Then a fifth. Out came the white cops, brandishing their pistols, like trained performers in a macabre ballet entitled "If You're Black Get Back."

The mood of the mob became dangerous. A cop pushed a black man. The black man got set to hit the cop. Another cop quickly intervened.

A woman fell down and was trampled. "Help! Murder!" she screamed.

The mob moved in her direction, taking the cops with it.

"Goddamned mother-raping shit! Here it is!" a young black man shouted, whipping out his switch-blade knife.

Then the precinct captain arrived in a sound truck. "All officers back to your cars," he ordered, his voice loud and clear from the amplifiers. "Back to your cars. And, folks, let's have some order."

The cops retreated to their cars. The danger passed. Some people cheered. Slowly the people returned to the sidewalks. Passenger cars that had been lined up for more than ten blocks began to move along, curious faces peering out at the black people crowding the sidewalks.

The captain went over and talked to Bill Davis and the two men with him. "Only nine persons are permitted on a picket line by New York law," he said. "Will you thin these pickets down to nine?"

Bill looked at the elderly men. They nodded. He said, "All right," to the captain and thinned out the picket line.

Then the captain went inside the office and approached Colonel Calhoun; he asked to see his license. The Colonel's papers were in order; he had a New York City permit to recruit farm labor as the agent of the Back-to-the-Southland movement, which was registered in Birmingham, Alabama.

The captain returned to the street and stationed ten policemen in front of the office to keep order, and two police cruisers to keep the street clear. Then he shook hands with Bill Davis and got back into the sound truck and left.

The mob began to disperse.

"I knew we'd get some action from Reverend O'Malley, soon as he heard about all this," the church sister said.

Her companion looked bewildered. "What I wants to know," she asked, "is we won or lost?"

Inside, the blond young man asked Colonel Calhoun, "Aren't we pretty well finished now?"

Colonel Calhoun lit a fresh cheroot and took a puff. "It's just good publicity, son," he said.

By then it was noon, and the two young colored clerks slipped out the back door to go to lunch.

Later that afternoon one of Mr. Goodman's workmen stood in the crowd surrounding the Back-to-Africa pickets, admiring the poster art on the windows of the Back-to-the-Southland office. He had bathed and shaved and dressed up for a big Saturday night and he was just killing time until his date. Suddenly his gaze fell on the small sign in the corner reading: *Wanted, a bale of cotton.* He started inside. A Back-to-Africa sympathizer grabbed his arm.

"Don't go in there, friend. You don't believe that crap, do you?"

"Baby, I ain't thinking 'bout going south. I ain't never been south. I just wanna talk to the man."

" 'Bout what?"

"I just wanna ask the man if them chicken really got legs that big," he said, pointing to the picture of the chicken.

The man bent over laughing. "You go 'head and ast him, man, and you tell me what he say."

The workman went inside and walked up to Colonel Calhoun's desk and took off his cap. "Colonel," he said, "I'm just the man you wanna see. My name is Josh."

The Colonel gave him the customary cold-eyed appraisal, sitting reared back in his chair as though he hadn't moved. The blond young man stood beside him.

"Well, Josh, what can you do for me?" the Colonel asked, showing his dentures in a smile.

"I can get you a bale of cotton," Josh said.

The tableau froze. The Colonel was caught in the act of returning the cheroot to his lips. The blond young man was caught in the act of turning to look out towards the street. Then, deliberately, without a change of expression, the Colonel put the cheroot between his lips and puffed. The blond young man turned back to stare wordlessly at Josh, leaning slightly forward.

"You want a bale of cotton, don't you?" Josh asked.

"Where would you get a bale of cotton, my boy?" the Colonel asked casually.

"We got one in the junkyard where I work."

The blond young man let out his breath in a disappointed sigh.

"A junk man sold it to us just this morning," Josh went on, hoping to get an offer.

The blond young man tensed again.

But the Colonel continued to appear relaxed and amiable. "He didn't steal it, did he? We don't want to buy any stolen goods."

"Oh, Uncle Bud didn't steal it, I'm sure," Josh said. "He must of found it somewheres."

"Found a bale of cotton?" The Colonel sounded skeptical.

"Must have," Josh contended. "He spends every night traveling 'bout the streets, picking up junk what's been lost or thrown away. Where could he steal a bale of cotton?"

"And he sold it to you this morning?"

"Yassuh, to Mr. Goodman, that is; he owns the junkyard, I just work there. But I can get it for you."

"When?"

"Well, ain't nobody there now. We close at noon on Sat'day and Mr. Goodman go home; but I can get it for you tonight if you wants it right away."

"How?"

"Well, suh, I got a key, and we don't have to bother Mr. Goodman; I can just sell it to you myself."

"Well," the Colonel said and puffed his cheroot. "We'll pick you up in my cah at the 125th Street railroad station at ten o'clock tonight. Can you be there?"

"Oh, yassuh, I can be there!" Josh declared, then hesitated. "That's all right, but how much you going to pay me?"

"Name your own price," the Colonel said.

"A hundred dollars," Josh said, holding his breath.

"Right," the Colonel said.

X

IRIS LAY ON her sofa in the sitting room reading *Ebony* magazine and eating chocolate candy. She had been under twenty-four-hour surveillance since the hijacking. A police matron had spent the night in her bedroom while a detective had sat up in the sitting room. Now there was another detective there alone. He had orders not to let her out of his sight. He had followed her from room to room, even keeping the bathroom door in view after having removed the razor blades and all other instruments by which she might injure herself.

He sat facing her in an overstuffed chair, leafing through a book called *Sex and Race* by W. G. Rogers. The only other books in the house were the Bible and *The Life of Marcus Garvey*.

Sex and Race didn't interest him. Garvey didn't interest him either. He had read the Bible, at least all he needed to read.

He was bored. He didn't like his assignment. But the captain thought that sooner or later Deke was going to try to contact her, or she him, and he was taking every precaution. The telephone was bugged and the operators alerted to trace all incoming calls; and there was a police cruiser with a radio-telephone parked within thirty seconds' distance down the street, manned by four detectives.

The captain wanted Deke as bad as people in hell want ice water.

Iris threw down the magazine and sat up. She was wearing a silk print dress and the skirt hiked up, showing smooth yellow thighs above tan nylon stockings.

The book fell from the detective's hands.

"Why the hell don't you just arrest me and have it done with?" she flared in her vulgar husky voice.

Her voice grated on the detective's nerves. And her vulgar sensuality bothered him. He was a home-loving man with a wife and three children, and her perfumed voluptuous body with its effluvium of sex outraged his sensibilities. His puritanical soul felt affronted by this aura of sex and his perverse imagination filled him with a sense of guilt. But he had himself well under control.

"I just take orders, ma'am," he said mildly. "Any time you want to go to the station of your own accord I'll take you."

"Shit," she said, looking at him with disgust.

He was a tall, balding, redheaded, middle-aged man with a slight stoop. A small dried face between huge red ears gave him a monkeyish look and his white skin was blotched with large brown freckles. He was a plain-clothes precinct detective and he looked underpaid.

Iris examined him appraisingly. "If you weren't such an ugly mother-raper at least we could pass time making love," she said.

He was beginning to suspect that was the reason the captain had chosen him for the assignment and he felt slightly piqued. But he just grinned and said, jokingly, "I'll put a sack over my head."

She started to grin and then looked suddenly caught. Her face mirrored her thoughts. "All right," she said, getting up.

He looked alarmed. "I was just joking," he said foolishly.

"I'll go undress and you come in with nothing showing but your eyes and mouth."

He grinned shamefacedly. "You know I couldn't do that."

"Why not?" she said. "You ain't never had nobody like me."

Red came out in his face as though it had caught fire. He looked like a small boy caught in a guilty act. "Now, ma'am, you got to be sensible; this surveillance ain't going to last for ever—"

She turned quickly on her high heels and started towards the kitchen. Her walk was exaggerated, like that of a prostitute soliciting trade. But he had to follow her, cursing his instincts which kept defying his will.

She searched in the pantry, paying him no attention. He felt a slight trace of trepidation, fearing she might come out with a gun. But she found what she wanted, a brown paper sack. She turned and tried to put it over his head, but he jumped back and warded her off as though she held a live rattlesnake.

"I just wanted to try it for size," she said, trying it on her own head instead. "What are you anyway, a pansy?"

He was incensed by her allusion to his masculinity, but he consoled himself with the thought that in different circumstances he'd ride that yellow bitch until she yelled quits.

She switched past him, looking at him through the corners of her eyes and brushing him lightly with her hips. Then she deliberately shook her buttocks and waved the sack over her head like a dare and went into the bedroom.

He debated whether to follow her. This bitch was getting on his nerves, he told himself. She wasn't the only one who could make love, hell, his wife—He stopped that thought; that wasn't going to get him anywhere. Finally he gave in and followed her. Orders were orders, he told himself.

He found her with a pair of nail scissors in her hand, cutting eyeholes in the paper sack. He felt his ears burning. He looked about the room for a telephone extension, but didn't see any.

Against his will he watched her cut out a place for his mouth. Unconsciously his vision strayed to her wide luscious mouth. She licked her lips and stuck out the tip of her tongue.

"Now, ma'am, this has gone far enough," he protested.

She acted as though she hadn't heard, measuring his head with her eyes. Then she cut out a place for his ears, saying, "Big ears, big you-know-what." His ears burned as though on fire. For a moment she stood looking at her handiwork. He looked too.

"You've got to breathe, haven't you, baby?" she cooed and cut out a place for his nose.

"Now you come out of here and sit down and behave yourself," he said, trying to sound stern, but his voice was thick with tongue.

She went over to the small record player against the wall and put on a slow sexy blues number and stood for a moment weaving her body tantalizingly, snapping her fingers.

"I'll have to use force," he warned.

She swung around and threw open her arms and advanced on him. "Come on and force me, daddy," she said.

He turned his back and stood in the doorway. She stood before the mirror and took off her ear-rings and necklace and ran her fingers through her hair, whistling a low accompaniment to the music, seemingly paying him no attention. Then she took off her dress.

He turned around to see what she was doing and damn near jumped out of his skin. "Don't do that!" he shouted.

"You can't stop me from undressing in my own bedroom," she said.

He went over and snatched up the dressing-table chair and planted it in the doorway and plopped himself down with an air of determination. "All right, go ahead," he said, turning his profile towards her so he could watch her for mischief through the corners of his eyes.

She tilted the dressing-table mirror so he could see her reflection, then pulled up her slip over her head. Now her creamy yellow body was clad only in a thin black strapless bra and tiny black pants trimmed with lace, over a garter belt.

COTTON COMES TO HARLEM

"If you're scared, go home," she taunted.

He gritted his teeth and continued to look away.

She took off her bra and pants and stood facing the mirror, cupping her breasts in her hands and gently caressing her teaties. With only the garter belt and nylon stockings and high-heeled shoes, she looked more nude than were she stark-naked. She saw him peeping at her reflection in the mirror, and began doing things with her stomach and hips.

He swallowed. From the neck up he was blindly furious; but from the neck down he was on a live-wire edge. His insides were a battleground for his will and his lust, with his organs suffering the consequences. Whole areas of his body seemed on fire. The fire seemed breaking through his skin. Centipedes were crawling over his testicles and ants were attacking his phallus. He squirmed in his seat as it became more and more unbearable; his pants were too tight; his coat was too small; his head was too hot; his mouth was too dry.

With a flourish like a stripteaser removing her G-string, she took off one shoe and tossed it into his lap. He knocked it violently aside. She took off the other shoe and tossed it into his lap. He caught himself just in time to keep from grabbing it and biting it. She stripped off her stockings and garter belt and approached him to drape them about his neck.

He came to his feet like a Jack-in-the-box, saying in a squeaky voice, "This has gone far enough."

"No, it hasn't," she said and moved into him.

He tried to push her away but she clung to him with all strength, pushing her stomach into him and wrapping her legs about his body. The odor of hot-bodied woman, wet cunt and perfume came up from her and drowned him.

"Goddamned whore!" he grated, and backed her to the bed. He tore off his coat, mouthing, "I'll show you who's a pansy, you hot-ass slut."

But at the last moment he regained enough composure to go hang his holstered pistol on the outside doorknob out of her reach, then he turned back towards her.

"Come and get it, pansy," she taunted, lying on the bed with her legs open and her brown-nippled teats pointing at him like the vision of the great whore who lives in the minds of all puritanical men.

He stripped the zipper of his pants getting them off; popped the buttons from his shirt. When he was nude he tried to dive into her like into the sea, but she fought him off.

"You got to put on your sack first," she said, snatching it up from the floor and pulling it down over his head backwards by mistake. "Oop!" she cried.

Blinded momentarily, his hands flew up to tear it off, but she snatched it off first and slipped it on him the right way, so that only his eyes, mouth, nose and ears were showing.

"Now, baby, now," she cried.

At that moment the telephone rang.

He jumped out of bed as though the furies had attacked him, his lust going out like a light. In his haste he knocked over the chair in the doorway, bruising his shins, and slammed into the doorjamb. Curses spewed from his gasping mouth like geysers of profanity. His lank white body with stooped shoulders and reddish hair moved awkwardly and looked as though it had just come from the grave.

With a quick lithe motion she opened a secret compartment in the bed-table, snatched up the receiver of the telephone extension, and cried, "Help!" then quickly hung up.

In his haste he didn't hear her. He reached the telephone in the sitting room and said breathlessly, "Henderson speaking," but the connection had been broken. She could hear him jiggling the receiver as she slipped on a sport coat and snatched up a pair of shoes. "Hello, hello," he was still shouting when she went barefooted from the bedroom, locking the door behind her and taking the key, on back to the kitchen and went barefooted out of the house by the service door.

"Your party has hung up," came the cool voice of the telephone operator.

He realized instantly the call had come from the police cruiser parked down the street. Panic exploded in his head as he realized he didn't even have his pistol. He ran naked back to the bedroom, snatched his pistol from the doorknob and tried to open the door. He found it locked. He became frantic.

He couldn't risk shooting off the lock, he might hit her. The detectives from the cruiser would be there any instant and he'd catch hell. He had to get into the goddamned room. He tried breaking in, but it was a strong door with a good lock and his shoulder was taking a beating. He had forgotten the paper sack over his head.

The detectives from the cruiser had rushed there post-haste and had let themselves in with a pass-key. Over the telephone they had heard a woman cry for help. God only knew what was going on in there, but they were ready for it. They went into the apartment and spread out, their pistols in their hands. The sitting room was empty.

They started through towards the rear. They drew up as though they had run into an invisible wall.

Down the hall was a buck-naked white man with a paper sack over his head and a holstered pistol in his hand, trying to break down the bedroom door with his bare shoulder.

No one ever knew who was the first one to explode with laughter.

Iris went down the service stairway barefooted. The sport coat was a belted wraparound of tan gaberdine and no one could tell she was naked underneath it. At the service exit on St. Nicholas Avenue, she slipped into her shoes and peeped out into the street.

A car stood at the kerb in front of the apartment next door with the motor idling. A smartly dressed woman got out and ran towards the entrance. Iris cased her as an afternoon prostitute or a cheating wife. The man behind the wheel called softly, "Bye now, baby," and the woman fluttered her fingers and ducked out of sight.

Iris walked rapidly to the car, opened the door and got into the seat the other woman had just vacated. The man looked at her and said, " 'Lo, baby," as though she was the same woman he'd just told good-bye. He was a nice-looking chocolate-brown man dressed in a beautiful gray silk suit, but Iris just glanced at him.

"Drive on, daddy," she said.

He steered from the curb and climbed St. Nicholas Avenue. "Running *to* or *from*?" he asked.

"Neither," she said and when they came to the church at 142nd Street she said: "Turn left here up to Convent."

He left-turned up the steep hill past Hamilton Terrace to the quiet stretch of Convent Avenue north of City College.

"Right here," she directed.

He right-turned north on Convent and when he came opposite the big apartment house she said, "This is good, daddy."

"Could be better," he said.

"Later," she said and got out.

"Coming back?" he called but she didn't hear him.

She was already running across the street, up the steps and into the foyer of a big well-kept apartment house with two automatic elevators. One was waiting and she took it to the fourth floor and turned towards the apartment at the back of the hall. A serious-looking man wearing black suspenders, a white collarless shirt, and sagging black pants opened the door. He took himself as seriously as a deacon in a solvent church.

"And what can I do for you, young lady?"

"I want to see Barry Waterfield."

"He don't want to see you, he's already got company," he leered. "How 'bout me?"

"Stand aside, buster," she said, pushing past him. "And quit peeping through keyholes."

She went straight to Barry's room but the door was locked and she had to knock.

"Who is it?" asked a woman's voice.

"Iris. Tell Barry to let me in."

The door was unlocked and Barry stood to one side wearing only a purple silk dressing-gown. He closed the door behind her. A naked high-yellow woman lay in the bed with the sheet drawn up to her neck.

Clothes were draped over the only chair so Iris sat on the bed and ignored the naked woman. "Where's Deke?" she asked Barry.

He hesitated before replying, "He's all right, he's holed up safe."

"If you're scared of talking then write it," she said.

He looked uncomfortable. "How'd you get away?"

"None of your business," she snapped.

"You're sure you weren't tailed?"

"Don't make me laugh. If the cops wanted you they'd have had you long ago, stupid as you are. Just tell me where Deke is and let others do the thinking."

"I'll call him," he said, going towards the door.

She started to go with him but pressure on her hip stopped her, and she said only, "Tell him I'm coming to see him."

He went out and locked the door from the outside without answering.

The woman in the bed whispered quickly, "He's with Mabel Hill in the Riverton Apartments," and gave the street, number and telephone. "I heard Barry talking."

Iris looked blank. "Mabel Hill. The only Mabel Hill I know vaguely is the Mabel Hill who was married to the John Hill who got croaked."

"That's the cutie," the woman whispered.

Iris couldn't control the rage that distorted her face.

Barry came in at that moment and looked at her, "What's the matter with you?"

"Did you get Deke?" she countered.

He wasn't clever enough to dissemble and she knew he was lying when he said, "Deke's cut out but he left word he would call me. He's changing his hideout."

"Thanks for nothing," Iris said, getting up to go.

The naked woman underneath the sheet said, "Wait a minute and I'll give you a lift. I got my car downstairs."

"No, you ain't," Barry said roughly, pushing her down.

Iris unlocked the door and opened it, then turned and said, "Go to hell, you big mother-raping square," and slammed the door behind her.

XI

DEKE HADN'T LEFT Mabel's apartment but he'd had some close shaves. Two Homicide detectives had shown up at ten o'clock to question her again. He had hid in the closet, feeling defenseless and stark-naked without a gun, listening to every word with his heart in his mouth for fear he might have left something incriminating in the room, sweating blood from fear they might decide to search the house, and literally sweating in the close dusty heat. The dust had tickled his nose and he'd had to bite his lip to keep from sneezing.

Later, Mr. Clay, the undertaker, had come and caught him in the bedroom and he'd had to hide under the bed. They had talked so interminably about money he had begun to wonder whether they intended to bury John Hill or hold his body for ransom.

Then Mabel had again turned into the weeping widow and bemoaned her fate with buckets of tears and enough hysterics for a revival meeting and nothing turned them off but to console her in bed. He had consoled her in bed so many times he'd concluded that if John Hill hadn't been shot she'd have loved him to death. Or was she like that because her mother-raping husband was dead? he asked himself. Was this some kind of freakishness that came out in her? Whore complex or something? But if she had to wait for her mother-raping husband to get killed before she could get her nuts off, hadn't he better take care himself? Or was he the exception being her minister; a minister is supposed to minister. Or was it that she thought if she sinned with her minister, God would forgive her; and the more she sinned, the greater would be God's forgiveness? Or did this bitch just have a hot ass? Anyway, he was godamned tired of her everlasting urge and he was mentally damning John Hill to hell for getting himself killed.

But finally just before he'd had to holler calf-rope she'd calmed down enough to keep her appointment with the undertaker to go get John's body from the morgue.

It gave him a chance to contact Barry and his other two guns and arrange the caper with the Colonel for that night. So when she came home hysterical again he was ready for her.

Afterwards he was just lounging around in his shorts, drinking bourbon highballs, and she was in the kitchen doing he didn't know what—probably taking an aphrodisiac—when the telephone rang.

It was Barry, telling him that Iris had got loose and was looking for him. He didn't want to see Iris and he didn't want her to find him for fear she might be tailed. So he had given Barry his answer. He figured if the police picked her up it was better she didn't know where he was, then they couldn't get it out of her. Furthermore, she was too damn jealous, and one hitch at a time was enough.

To his annoyance he saw that Mabel had been listening to his conversation. She made herself a lemon Coke with ice and sat down beside him on the sofa.

"I'm glad she's not coming here," she said.

"Jealousy is one of the seven cardinal sins," he said.

For a moment he thought she was going to become hysterical again, but she just looked at him possessively and said, "Oh, Reverend O'Malley, pray with me."

"Later," he snapped and got up to get a refill.

He was in the kitchen getting ice from the tray when the doorbell rang. Ice cubes flew into the air like startled birds. He didn't have time to retrieve them. He shoved the tray back, slammed the door shut and dumped his drink into the sink. Then he rushed into the closet in the back hall opposite the bathroom where his clothes were hung, waving a signal to Mabel as he passed through the sitting room. He had found an old .32 revolver of John Hill's and he snatched it from the shelf where he had hidden it and held it in his shaking hand.

Mabel was flustered. She didn't know whether he had meant she should answer the door or not answer it.

The bell rang again, long and insistently, as though whoever it was must know she was at home. She decided to answer it. There was a chain on the door; and anyway, even if the police did catch Reverend O'Malley there, he hadn't done anything really wrong, she thought. He was just trying to get their money back.

She unlocked the door and someone tried to push it open but the chain caught it. Then through the crack she saw the face of Iris, distorted with rage.

"Open this mother-raping door," Iris grated in her throaty voice, her lips popping wetly.

"He's not here," Mabel said smugly from behind the chained door. "Reverend O'Malley, I mean."

"I'll start screaming and get the police here and then you tell them that," Iris threatened.

"If that's all he means to you . . ." Mabel began and flung wide the door. "Come in." And she chained and locked the door after her.

Iris went through the house like a gun dog looking for a game bird.

"He heard what you said," Mabel called after her.

"These mother-raping bitches!" Deke muttered to himself and came out of the closet, covered with a film of sweat, still holding the pistol in his hand. "Why don't you have some sense?" he said to Iris's back as she was looking into the bathroom.

She wheeled, and her eyes widened and went pitch-black when she saw him in his shorts. Her face convulsed with uncontrollable jealousy. All she thought of then was him in bed with this other woman.

"You chickenshit cheat," she mouthed, spittle flying from her popping lips. "You sneaking pimp. You get me out of the way and shack up with some chippy whore."

"Shut up," he said dangerously. "I had to hide out."

"Hide out? Between this slut's legs!"

From the doorway into the sitting room Mabel said, "Reverend O'Malley is just trying to get our money back; he doesn't want it all bungled by the police."

Iris turned on her. "I suppose you call him Reverend O'Malley in bed," she stormed. "If your mouth isn't too full."

"I'm not like you," Mabel said angrily. "I do it the way God intended."

Iris rushed at her and tried to scratch her face. Her coat flew open, showing her naked body. Mabel grabbed her by the wrists and shouted tauntingly, "I'm going to have his baby." Iris couldn't have a baby and it was the worst thing Mabel could have said. Iris went berserk; she spat in Mabel's face and kicked her shins and struggled to break free. But Mabel was the stronger and she spat back in Iris's face and let go her hands to grab her hair. Iris scratched her on the neck and shoulders and tore her negligee, but Mabel was pulling her hair out by the roots and pain filled her eyes with tears, blinding her.

Deke grabbed Iris by the coat collar with his left hand, still holding the revolver in his right. He hadn't had time to put it away and he was afraid to drop it on the floor. Iris's coat came off in his hand and she was naked except for shoes and there was nothing else to clutch. So he tried to break Mabel's grip on her hair. But Mabel was so infuriated she wouldn't turn loose.

"Break loose, you mother-raping whores!" Deke grated and hit at Mabel's hands with his pistol.

He mashed her fingers against Iris's skull. Iris screamed and scratched eight red lines across his ribs. He hit her in the stomach with his free left hand, then grabbed Mabel's negligee to pull her away. The negligee came off in his hand and she was naked too. Iris clawed her like a cat, streaking her body, and the blood began to flow. Mabel couldn't use her hands but she bent Iris's head down with her arms and bit her in the shoulder. Screaming in pain, with her head bent down, Iris saw the pistol in Deke's hand. She snatched it and shot Mabel in the body until it was empty.

It happened so fast it didn't register on Deke's brain. He heard the thunder of shots; he saw the surprised look of anguish on Mabel's face as she loosened her grip on Iris's head and slowly began to crumble. But it was like a horrifying nightmare before the horror comes.

Then awareness hit him like a time bomb exploding in his head. His body erupted into action as his brain went rattled with panic. He hit Iris in the breast with his left fist, rocking her back, and crossed a right to her neck, knocking her off-balance.

He kicked her in the stomach with his bare foot and, when she doubled over, hit her on the back of the head with the side of his fist, knocking her face downward to the floor.

Suddenly the panic started going off in his head like a chain of explosions, each one bigger than the ones before. He leapt over Iris's prostrate figure, started towards the closet to get his clothes, then wheeled and snatched up the pistol from the floor where Iris had dropped it. He didn't look at Mabel; his mind knew she was dead but he tried not to think of it. Somewhere in his head he knew he didn't have any more bullets for the pistol which wasn't his. He dropped it to the floor as though it was burning his hand.

Wheeling, he leapt into the hall, rushed to the closet. The knob slipped in his hand and one half of his brain began cursing, the other half praying.

In the front of all other thoughts was the sure knowledge that in a few minutes the police would come. Before the shooting, there had been enough screaming to raise the dead; and he knew in this nigger-proper house someone would have called the police. He knew his only hope was flight. To get away before the police got there. It was his life. And these mother-raping seconds were running out. But he knew he'd never get away looking half-dressed. Some meddling mother-raper in this nigger-heaven house would stop him on suspicion and he didn't have a gun.

He tried to dress fast. Quick-quick-quick, urged his brain. But his mother-raping fingers had turned to thumbs. It seemed as though it took him seven hundred mother-raping years to button up his shirt; and some more mother-raping centuries to lace his shoes.

He leapt to the mirror to tie his tie and search for tell-tale scratches. His dark face was powder gray, his stretched eyes like black eight-balls, but there were no scratches showing. He was trying to decide whether to take the elevator down five floors and walk the remaining two, or take the fire escape and try the roof. He didn't know how these buildings were made, whether the roofs were on the same level and he could get from one to another. In the back of his head he kept thinking there was something he was leaving. Then he realized it was Iris's life. Fear urged him to go back and take the pistol and beat her to death; stop her from talking forever.

He turned from the bathroom, turned towards the sitting room, and was caught in midstep by the hammering on the door. He ran on his toes to the back window in the bedroom that let onto the outside fire escape. He opened it quickly, went out and down without hesitation. He didn't have time to decide; he was committed. His feet felt nothing as they touched the iron steps of the steep ladder. His eyes searched the windows he passed.

The fire escape was on one of the private streets of the housing development. He could only be seen by people across the street or in the windows he passed. Halfway down he saw the hem of a curtain fluttering from a half-open bedroom window. He didn't hesitate. He stopped at the window, opened it and went in. The apartment was arranged the same as the one he had just quit. There was no one in the bedroom. He went through on his toes, praying the house was empty, but with no intention of stopping if it was filled with wedding guests. He came out into the back hall. He could hear a woman singing in the kitchen at the front of the sitting room. He got to the front door, found it locked and chained. He tried to open it silently; he held his breath as he turned the lock and took off the chain. Time was drowning him in a whirlpool of flying seconds. He got the door unlocked, the chain off. He heard the singing stop. He closed the door quickly behind him and ran down the hall towards the service stairway. He got onto the landing and closed the door just before he heard a faint woman's voice call, "Henry, where are you, Henry?"

He went down the stairway like a dive-bomber, didn't stop until he was in the basement. He heard footsteps coming his way. He froze behind the closed door, assembling his face, making up his story. But the footsteps went on past him into silence. Cautiously he looked out into the basement. No one was in sight. He went in the direction opposite the one the footsteps had taken and found a door. It opened onto a short flight of stairs. He went up the stairs and found a heavy iron door locked with a Yale snap lock. He unlocked it and pushed the door open a crack and looked out.

He saw 135th Street. Colored people were out in numbers, walking about in their summertime rags. Two men were eating watermelon from a wagon. In the wagon the melons were kept on ice to keep them cool. Children were gathered around a small pushcart, eating cones of shaved ice flavored with colored syrups from bottles. Others were playing stickball in the street. Women were conversing in loud voices; a drunken man weaved down the sidewalk, cursing the world; a blind beggar tapped a path with his white stick, rattling a penny in his tin cup; a dog was messing on the sidewalk; a line of men was sitting in the shade on the steps of a church, talking about the white folks and the Negro problem.

He stepped from the doorway and crossed the street, and soon he was lost in that big turbulent sea of black humanity which is Harlem.

XII

WHEN GRAVE DIGGER and Coffin Ed came on duty at 8 P.M., Lieutenant Anderson said, "Your car was found abandoned up at 163rd Street and Edgecombe Drive. Does that tell you anything?"

Coffin Ed backed against the wall in the shadows where Anderson couldn't see his expression, but Anderson heard him make some kind of sound that sounded like a snort. Grave Digger perched a ham on the edge of the desk and massaged his chin. The curve of his back concealed the bulge of the .38 revolver over his heart but made his shoulders look wider. He thought about it and chuckled.

"Tell me it was stolen," he said finally. "What you think, Ed?"

"Either that or it drove itself."

Anderson looked quizzically from one to the other. "Well, was it stolen?"

Grave Digger chuckled again. "Think we're going to admit it if it was?"

"It was them chickens, boss?" Coffin Ed said.

Lieutenant Anderson reddened slightly and shook his head. He didn't always dig the private humor of his two ace detectives and sometimes it made him feel uncomfortable. But he realized they attached no significance to the fact their car had been stolen. Whenever they got a clue of importance the air around them became electric.

It became electric now when he said, "We're holding Deke O'Hara's woman Iris on a homicide rap."

Both detectives froze in that immobility which denotes full attention. But neither spoke; they knew a story went with it. They waited.

"She was arrested in the apartment of the man killed in the Back-to-Africa hijack, John Hill. John Hill's wife Mabel had been shot five times; she was dead when the police arrived. Both women were nude and badly mauled—scratched and beaten as though they'd had a furious go with each other. Tenants had called the police before the shooting to report what sounded like a woman fight in the apartment. A gun was found on the floor—a .32 revolver. It had been recently fired and there's no doubt it is the murder gun; but it has gone to ballistics. Her fingerprints were on the stock and smeared on the trigger but are partly obliterated by a clear set of prints by a man. Homicide figures a man handled the gun afterwards; maybe Deke. They're checking against his Bertillon card and we'll soon know."

Grave Digger and Coffin Ed exchanged looks but said nothing.

"Iris contends Deke wasn't there. An hour earlier she had escaped from her own apartment. She admits going there looking for him but swears he hadn't been there. She had escaped on a ruse—you'll hear all about it. She admits that she and the Hill woman had a fight and she says she took the gun away from the Hill woman and it went off accidentally. She says it was a private fight and had nothing to do with the Back-to-Africa hijacking, but she won't give any reason for it."

Both detectives turned and looked at him as though guided by the same impulse.

"Do you want to talk to her?" Anderson asked.

The detectives exchanged looks.

"How long after the shooting before the car crew arrived?" Grave Digger asked.

"About two and a half minutes."

"What floor?"

"Seventh, but there's a fast elevator and he would have had time to get down and away before the police arrived," he said, reading their thoughts.

"Not if they were naked," Coffin Ed said.

Anderson blushed. He hadn't gotten to be a lieutenant by being a square but he was always slightly embarrassed by their bald way of stating the facts of life.

"And he'd have to dress well in that neighborhood," Grave Digger added.

"And completely," Coffin Ed concluded.

"There was an open window on the fire escape at the back," Anderson said. "But no one has been found who saw him leave." He looked through the reports on his desk. "A woman on the fourth floor directly below telephoned to report that she thought she heard her front door being opened and when she went to look found the chain off. But nothing was missing from the house. Homicide found the window open onto the fire escape but she said she had left it open. Any prints that might have been left on the doorknob were smeared by her son coming and going afterwards, and she wiped whatever prints there may have been from the windowsill when dusting."

"They believe in keeping spick and span in those apartments," Grave Digger said.

"So clean that even Deke gets away clean," Coffin Ed said.

"Who knows?" Grave Digger said. "Let's go talk to her."

They had her taken from the cell where she was held, awaiting magistrate's court Monday morning, to the interrogation room in the basement known to the Harlem underworld as the "Pigeons' Nest." It was claimed that more pigeons were hatched there than beneath all the eaves in Harlem.

It was a soundproof, windowless room with a stool in the center bolted to the floor and surrounded by floodlights bright enough to make the blackest man transparent.

But only the overhead light was on when the jailor brought her in. She saw Grave Digger standing beside the stool, waiting for her. The door was closed and locked behind her. She had a sudden feeling of being taken from the earth. Then she saw the vague outline of Coffin Ed backed against the wall in the shadows. His acid-burned face looked like a Mardi Gras masque to scare little children. She shuddered.

Grave Digger said, "Sit down, baby, and tell us how you are."

She stood defiantly. "I'm not talking in this hole. You've got it bugged."

"What for? Ed and me are going to remember anything you say."

Coffin Ed stepped forward. He looked like the dead killer in the play *Winterset*, coming up out of East River. "Sit down anyway," he said.

She sat down. He stepped towards her. Grave Digger switched on the floodlights. She blinked. Coffin Ed had intended to slap her. But now he saw her. He caught his hand. "Well, well, well," he said. "Ain't you beautiful."

Her smooth, yellow, creamed and perfumed flesh of the day before now ran through all the colors of the spectrum, from black to bright orange; her neck was swollen, one breast was twice the size of the other; red, raw scratches ran down her face, over her neck and shoulders, to disappear beneath her dress; and her hair looked like it had been doused in the river Styx.

"It could have been worse," Grave Digger said.

"How?" she asked, squinting at the bright lights. The bruises and scratches looked painted on her transparent skin.

"You could be dead."

She shrugged faintly. "You call that worse?"

"Well, hell, you're still alive," Coffin Ed said. "And you can get eight thousand and seven hundred dollars' reward money if you help us."

"How about this chickenshit rap they're holding me on?" she bargained.

"That's your baby," Grave Digger said.

She winced at the word *baby*; that was what had started it all.

"And it ain't chickenshit," Coffin Ed added.

"It's a rap," she said.

"Where's Deke?" Grave Digger asked.

"If I knew where the mother-raper was, I'd sure tell you."

"But you went there to see him."

She sat thinking for a time, then seemingly she made up her mind. "He was there," she admitted. "In his drawers. Why else would I be mad enough to shoot the chippy whore. But I don't remember him getting away. He had knocked me unconscious." After a moment she added, "I wonder why he didn't kill me."

"How did you get away from the detective guarding you?" he asked.

She laughed suddenly and her marks formed another pattern like one of those innocuous pictures revealing shocking obscenities at certain angles. "That was a beauty," she said. "It could only happen to a white man."

Grave Digger looked sardonic. "As long as it's got nothing to do with this caper, let's skip it."

"It was just between me and him."

"What we want to know, baby, is what was the set-up of Deke's Back-to-Africa pitch."

"Where have you been all your life, you don't know that?" she said.

"We know it. We just want you to confirm it."

Some of her flippancy returned. "What's in it for me?" she asked.

Coffin Ed stepped forward. "Try it on, anyway," he grated. "Just for size."

She looked towards his voice but she couldn't see him through the light and that made it sound more frightening.

"Well, you know he was going to take the money and blow," she began. "But not until he'd played other cities too. He had the armored car made. The guards were his. Only the agents and other personnel were squares. The detectives were to come in and get him off the hook by confiscating the money until an investigation could be made. Since all the suckers thought he was honest, there was nothing to fear. He borrowed the idea from the Marcus Garvey movement."

"We know all that," Grave Digger said. "We want some names and descriptions."

She gave him the name and address of Barry Waterfield, alias Baby Jack Johnson, alias Big Papa Domore. She said the two guns who had guarded the truck were known as Four-Four and Freddy; she had never heard them called by their real monickers and she didn't know where they were staying. They were Deke's men, he probably got them from prison; and he kept them out of sight. The dead man who had impersonated the other detective had been called Elmer Sanders. They were all from Chicago.

That was what they wanted and Coffin Ed relaxed.

But Grave Digger asked, "He wasn't putting the double-cross on his own men by having himself hijacked?"

She thought for a moment, then said, "No, I don't think so. I'm reckoning on the way he's acted afterwards."

"Any idea who they were?"

"I keep thinking of the Syndicate. Just because I can't think of anyone else, I guess."

"It wasn't the Syndicate," Grave Digger stated flatly.

"Then I don't know. He never seemed scared of anybody else—of course he never told me everything."

Grave Digger smiled sourly at the understatement.

"What you got on Deke?" Coffin Ed asked.

She looked towards the voice behind the lights and felt a tremor run through her body. Why did that mother-raper scare her so? she wondered. Finally she said simply, "The proof."

Both detectives froze as though listening for an echo. It didn't come.

"You want us to take him, don't you?" Grave Digger said.

"Take him," she said.

"Be ready," he said.

"I'm ready," she said.

* * *

On their way out they stopped again to see Lieutenant Anderson and have him put a tail on Barry Waterfield.

Then Grave Digger said, "We're going to put our pigeons on Deke. If they get anything they'll phone it to you and you call us in the car."

"Right," Anderson said. "I'll have a couple of cars on alert for an emergency."

"There ain't going to be any emergency," Coffin Ed said and they left.

They began contacting all the stool pigeons they could reach. They got many tips on unsolved crimes and wanted criminals but nothing on Deke O'Hara. They filed away the information for later use, but for all of their stool pigeons they had only one instruction: "Find Deke O'Hara. He's loose on the town. Telephone Lieutenant Anderson at the precinct station, drop the message and hang up. And disappear."

It was a slow, tedious process, but they had no other. There were five hundred thousand colored people in Harlem and so many holes in which to hide that sewer rats have been known to get lost.

Barry telephoned Deke at Mabel's from Bowman's Bar at the corner of St. Nicholas Place and 155th Street on the dot of 10 P.M. as he had been instructed. The phone rang once, twice, three times. Abruptly a warning sounded in his head; his sixth sense told him the police were there and were tracing the call. He hung up as though letting go a snake and headed towards the exit. The bar girl looked at him as he passed, eyebrows raised, wondering what had spurred him so suddenly. He tossed fifty cents on the bar to pay for his thirty-five-cent beer and went out fast, looking for a taxi.

He caught one headed downtown and said, "Drop me at 145th and Broadway." When they turned west on 145th he heard the faint whine of a siren headed towards Bowman's and sweat filmed his upper lip.

Broadway is a fringe street. Black Harlem has moved solidly to its east side but its west side is still mixed with Puerto Ricans and leftover whites. He got out on the northeast corner, crossed the street, walked rapidly up to 149th and went down towards the Hudson River. He turned into a small neat apartment house halfway down the block and climbed three flights of stairs.

The light-bright-damn-near-white woman who had been naked in his bed when Iris had called opened the door for him. She was talking before she closed it: "Iris killed Mabel Hill right after she left us. Ain't that something? They got her in jail. It just came over the radio." Her voice was strident with excitement.

"Deke?" he asked tensely.

"Oh, he got away. They're looking for him. Let me fix you a drink."

His gaze swept the three-room apartment, reading every sign. It was a nice place but he didn't see it. He was thinking that Deke must have tried to contact him while he was out.

"Drive me home," he said.

She began to pout but one look at his face cooled her.

Five minutes later, the young colored detective Paul Robinson, assigned with his partner Ernie Fisher to tail Barry, saw him get out of the closed convertible in front of the apartment where he lived and run quickly up the stairs. Paul was sitting in a black Ford sedan with regular Manhattan plates, parked across the street, pointed uptown. He got Lieutenant Anderson on the radio-telephone and said, "He just came in."

"Keep on him," Anderson said.

When Barry got off at the fourth floor there was a young man standing in the hall waiting to go down. He was Ernie Fisher. For two hours he had been standing there, waiting to descend every time the elevator stopped. But this time he went. When he came out on the street he got into a two-toned Chevrolet sedan parked in front of the entrance, pointed downtown.

Paul got out of the Ford sedan, crossed the street and entered the apartment without glancing at his partner. He took the stand on the fourth floor, waiting to descend.

The deacon-looking landlord told Barry he had had several urgent calls from a Mr. Bloomfield who had left a message saying if he didn't want the car he had found another buyer.

Barry went immediately to the telephone and called Mr. Bloomfield.

"Bloomfield," replied a voice having no affinity to such a name.

"Mr. Bloomfield, I want the car," Barry said. "I'm ready right now to close the deal. I've been out raising the money."

"Come to my office right away," Mr. Bloomfield said and hung up.

"Right away, Mr. Bloomfield," Barry said into the dead phone for the landlord's ears.

He stopped in his room on his way out, strapped on a shoulder holster with a .45 Colt automatic, and changed into a loose black silk sport jacket made to accommodate the gun.

When he came out into the hall he saw a young man standing by the elevator, jabbing the button impatiently. There was nothing about the young man to incur suspicion or jog his memory. He stood beside him and they rode down together. The young man walked rapidly ahead of him and ran down the stairs and across the street without looking back. Barry didn't give him another thought.

A Chevrolet sedan parked at the curb was just moving off and Barry hailed a taxi that drew up in the place vacated. The taxi went downtown, through City College, past the convent from which the street derives its name, and down the hill towards 125th Street. The Chevrolet stayed ahead. The Ford had made a U-turn and was following the taxi a block to the rear.

Convent came to an end at 125th Street. Taking a chance, Ernie turned his Chevrolet left, towards Eighth Avenue. The taxi turned sharply right. The Ford closed in behind it.

Barry had seen the Ford through the rear window. He had his driver stop suddenly in front of a bar. The Ford whizzed past, the driver looking the other way, and turned left where the street splits.

Barry had his driver make a U-turn and head back towards the east side. He didn't see anything unusual about the Chevrolet pulling out from the curb near Eighth Avenue; it looked just like any other hundreds of Chevrolets in Harlem—a poor man's Cadillac. He had the taxi turn right at the Theresa Hotel on Seventh Avenue and pull to the curb. The Chevrolet kept on down 125th Street.

Barry dismissed his taxi and entered the hotel lobby, then suddenly turned about and went outside and had the doorman hail another taxi. He didn't even notice the black Ford sedan parked near the entrance to Sugar Ray's bar. This street was always lined with parked cars. The taxi kept straight on down to 116th Street and turned sharp right. The Ford kept straight ahead. There were a number of cars coming cross town from Lenox on 116th Street, among which were several Chevrolet sedans.

The red light caught the taxi at Eighth Avenue and among the stream of cars going north was a black Ford sedan. Harlem was full of Ford sedans—the poor man's Lincoln—and Barry didn't give it a look. When the light changed he had the taxi turn right and stop in the middle of the block. The black Ford sedan was nowhere in sight. The Chevrolet sedan kept on across Eighth Avenue.

Paul double-parked the Ford around the corner on 117th Street and quickly walked back to Eighth Avenue. He saw Barry enter a poolroom down the street. He crossed Eighth Avenue, keeping the poolroom in sight, and stood on the opposite side-walk. Hundreds of Saturday-night drunks and hopheads were standing about, weaving in and out the joints, putting forth their voices. There was nothing to set him apart other than he was better dressed than most and the whores started buzzing around him.

Within a minute a Chevrolet sedan turned south on Eighth from 119th Street and double-parked near 116th Street behind two other double-parked cars.

Paul crossed the street and made as though to enter the pool-room, then seemed to think better of it and turned aimlessly towards 117th Street, collecting whores from all directions.

The Chevrolet sedan moved off, turned the corner on 116th Street and double-parked out of sight. Ernie called Lieutenant Anderson and reported, "He went into a poolroom on Eighth Avenue," and gave the name of the poolroom and number.

"Stay with him," Anderson said, and got Grave Digger and Coffin Ed on the radio-telephone.

XIII

THEY WERE TALKING to a blind man when they got the call.

The blind man was saying, "There were five white men in this tank. That in itself was enough to make me suspicious. Then when it stopped, the white man with the goatee who was sitting in the front seat leaned across the driver and beckoned to this colored boy who had been loitering around the station. I turned like I was alarmed when I heard the door click and took a picture. I think I got a clear shot."

Coffin Ed answered the radio-phone and heard Anderson say, "They got him stationed for the time being in a pool hall on Eighth Avenue," and gave the name and number.

"We're on the way," Coffin Ed said. "Just play it easy."

"It's your baby," Anderson said. "Holler if you need help."

Grave Digger said to the blind man, "Keep it until later, Henry."

"Nothing ever spoils," Henry said and got out, putting on his dark glasses at the same time.

It was five minutes by right from where they were parked on Third Avenue, but Grave Digger made it in three and one half without using the horn.

They found Paul in the Ford across the street from the poolroom. He said Barry was inside and Ernie was bottling up the back.

"You go and help him," Grave Digger said. "We'll take care of this end."

They pulled into the spot he had vacated and settled down to wait.

"You think he's contacting Deke in there?" Coffin Ed said.

"I ain't thinking," Grave Digger said.

Time passed.

"If I had a dollar an hour for all the time I've spent waiting for criminals to come and get themselves caught, I'd take some time off and go fishing," Coffin Ed said.

Grave Digger chuckled. "You're a glutton for punishment, man. That's the only thing I don't like about fishing, the waiting."

"Yeah, but there ain't any danger at the end of that kind of waiting."

"Hell, Ed, if you were scared of danger you'd have been a bill collector."

It was Coffin Ed's turn to chuckle. "Naw I wouldn't," he said. "Not in Harlem, Digger, not in Harlem. There ain't any more dangerous a job in Harlem than collecting bills."

They lapsed into silence, thinking of all the reasons folks in Harlem didn't pay bills. And they thought about the eighty-seven thousand dollars taken from those people who were already so poor they dreamed hungry. "If I had the mother-raper who got it I'd work his ass at fifty cents an hour shoveling shit until he paid it off," Coffin Ed said.

"There ain't that much shit," Grave Digger said drily. "What with all this newfangled shitless food."

Men came from the poolroom and others entered. Some they knew, others they didn't, but none they wanted.

An hour passed.

"Think they've lammed?" Coffin Ed ventured.

"How the hell would I know?" Grave Digger said. "Maybe they're waiting like us."

A car pulled up before the poolroom and double-parked. Suddenly they sat up. It was a black, chauffeur-driven Lincoln Mark IV, as out of place in that neighborhood as the Holy Virgin.

A uniformed colored chauffeur got out and hastened into the poolroom. Within a matter of seconds he came back and got behind the wheel and started the motor. Suddenly Barry came out. For a moment he stood on the sidewalk, looking up and down, casing the street. He looked across the street. Coffin Ed had ducked out of sight and Grave Digger was studiously searching for an acquaintance among the bums lounging in the doorways on their side of the street, and all Barry saw of him was the back of his head. It looked like the back of any other big black man's head. Satisfied, Barry turned and rapped on the door and another man came out and went straight to the limousine and got in beside the driver. Then Deke came out and went fast between two parked cars and got into the back of the limousine and Barry followed. The limousine took off like a streak, but had to slow for the lights at 125th Street.

Grave Digger had to make a U-turn and by the time he got straightened out, the limousine was out of sight.

"We ought to have got some help," Coffin Ed said.

"Too late now," Grave Digger said, gunning the hopped-up car past the slow-moving traffic. "We ought to've had second sight, too."

He went straight north on Eighth Avenue without pausing to reconnoiter.

"Where the hell are we going?" Coffin Ed asked.

"Damned if I know," Grave Digger confessed.

"Hell," Coffin Ed said disgustedly. "One day we lose our car and the next day we lose our man."

"Just let's don't lose our lives," Grave Digger shouted above the roar of the traffic they were passing.

"Pull down," Coffin Ed shouted back. "At this rate we'll be in Albany."

Grave Digger pulled up to the curb at 145th Street. "All right, let's give this some thought," he said.

"What kind of mother-raping thought?" Coffin Ed said.

He was near enough to the scene where the acid had been thrown into his face to evoke the memory. The tic started in his face and his nerves got on edge.

Grave Digger looked at him and looked away. He knew how he was feeling but this wasn't the time for it, he thought. "Listen," he said. "They were driving a stolen car. What does that mean?"

Coffin Ed came back. "A rendezvous or a getaway."

"Getaway for what? If they had the money they'd already be gone."

"Well, where the hell would you rendezvous, if you weren't scared?" Coffin Ed said.

"That's right," Grave Digger said. "Underneath the bridge."

"Anyway, we ain't scared," Coffin Ed said.

The two guns who had handled Deke's armored car were on the front seat, the same one driving. He was also a car thief specialist, and had stolen this one. He doused the lights when they came to the end of Bradhurst Avenue and eased the big car off the road that led to the Polo Grounds, stopping between two stanchions underneath the 155th Street Bridge.

"You two guys spot the car," Deke ordered. "We'll wait here."

The gunmen got out, careful of the rifles on the floor, and split in the darkness.

Deke took a large manila envelope from his inside coat pocket and handed it to Barry. "Here's the list," he said. He had had it made weeks before from the telephone directories of Manhattan, the Bronx and Brooklyn by a public stenographer in the Theresa Hotel. "You let him do the talking. We're going to have you covered every second."

"I don't like this," Barry confessed. He was scared and nervous and he couldn't see the Colonel giving any clues away. "He ain't going to pay no fifty grand for this," he said, taking it gingerly and sticking it into his inside pocket above his pistol.

"Naturally not," Deke said. "But don't argue with him. Answer his questions and take whatever he gives you."

"Hell, Deke, I don't dig this," Barry protested. "What's this cracker outfit got to do with our eighty-seven grand?"

"Let me do the thinking," Deke said coldly. "And give me that rod."

"Hell, you want me to go with my bare ass to see that nut? You're asking me a lot."

"What the hell can happen to you? We're all going to have you covered. Man, goddammit, you're going to be as safe as in the arms of Jesus Christ."

As Barry was handing over the gun he remembered, "That's what the Colonel said."

"He was right," Deke said, taking the pistol from the holster and sticking it into his right coat pocket. "Just his reasons are wrong."

They were silent with their thoughts until the gunmen materialized out of the darkness and took their places on the front seat. "They're over by the El," the driver said, easing the big car soundlessly through the dark as though he had eyes of infra-red.

The trucks and cars manned by the workers cleaning the stadium were moving about in the black dark area beneath the subway extensions and the bridge, which was used by day as a parking space, their bright lights lancing the darkness. Once the black limousine of the Colonel was picked up in a beam of light, but it didn't look out of place in that area where architects and bankers came at night to plan the construction of new buildings when the old stadium was razed. The Lincoln kept to the edge of the area, avoiding the lights, and stopped behind a big trailer truck parked for the night.

The gunmen picked their rifles from the floor and got out on each side and took stations at opposite ends of the truck. They had .303 automatic Savage rifles loaded with .190-point brass-nosed shells, equipped with telescopic sights.

"All right," Deke said. "Play it cool."

Barry shook his head once like shaking off a premonition. "My mama taught me more sense than this," he said and got out. Deke got out on the other side. Barry walked around the front of the truck and kept on ahead. His black coat and dark gray trousers were swallowed by the darkness. Deke stopped beside one of his gunmen.

"How does it look?" he asked.

In the telescopic sight Barry looked like the silhouette of half a man neatly quartered, the sight lines crossing in the center of his back as the gunman tracked him through the dark.

"All right," the gunman said. "Black on black, but it'll do."

"Don't let him get hurt," Deke said.

"He ain't gonna get hurt," the gunman said.

When Barry stopped walking, two other silhouettes came into the sights, close together like three wise monkeys.

The gunmen widened their sights to take in the limousine

and its occupants. Their eyes had become accustomed to the dark. In the faint glow of reflected light, the scene was clearly visible. The Colonel sat in the front seat beside the blond young man in the driver's seat. A white man stood on each side of Barry and a third, standing in front of him, shook him down and took the envelope from his inside pocket and passed it to the Colonel. The Colonel put it into his pocket without looking at it. Suddenly the two men flanking Barry seized his arms and twisted them behind him.

The third man moved up close in front of him.

Grave Digger cut off his lights when they approached the dark sinister area underneath the bridge. In the faint light reflected from the lights of the trucks and filtering down from above, the area looked like a jungle of iron stanchions, standing like giant sentinels in the eerie dark. The skin on Coffin Ed's face was jumping with a life of its own and Grave Digger felt his collar choking as his neck swelled.

He pulled the car over into the darkness and let the engine idle soundlessly. "Let's load some light," he said.

"I got light," Coffin Ed said.

Grave Digger nodded in the dark and took out his longbarreled, nickel-plated .38-caliber revolver and replaced the first three shells with tracer bullets. Coffin Ed drew his revolver, identical to the special made job of Grave Digger's, and spun the cylinder once. Then he held it in his lap. Grave Digger slipped his into his side coat pocket. Then they sat in the dark, listening for the sound that might never come.

"Where's the cotton?" the Colonel asked Barry so abruptly it hit him like a slap.

"Cotton!" he echoed with astonishment.

Then something clicked in his brain. He remembered the small sign advertising for a bale of cotton in the window of the Back-to-the-Southland office. His eyes stretched. *Good God!* he thought. Then he felt the danger of the instant squeeze him like an iron vise. His body turned ice-cold as though the blood had been squeezed out; his head exploded with terror. His mind sought an answer that would save his life, but he could only think of one that might satisfy the Colonel. "Deke's got it!" he blurted out.

Everything happened at once. The Colonel made a gesture. The white men tightened their grips on Barry's arms. The third man in front of Barry drew a hunting knife from his belt. Barry lunged to one side, throwing the man holding his right arm around behind him. And the big hard unmistakable sound of a high-powered rifle shot exploded in the night, followed so quickly by another it sounded like an echo.

The gunman beside Deke had shot the white man behind Barry dead through the heart. But the high-powered big-game bullet had gone through the white man's body and penetrated Barry just above the heart and lodged in his breastbone. The gunman at the other end of the truck had taken the white man holding Barry's left arm, the bullet going through one lung, ricocheting off a rib and ending up in his hip. All three fell together.

The third man with the knife wheeled and ran blindly. The big limousine sprang forward like a big cat, knocked him down, and ran over his body as though it were a bump in the road.

"Take the car!" Deke yelled, meaning, "Take out the car."

His gunmen thought he meant take their car and they wheeled and ran towards the Lincoln.

"Mother-rapers," Deke mouthed and followed them.

Grave Digger was coming from three hundred yards' distance, his bright lights stabbing the darkness from where he'd heard the shots. Coffin Ed was shouting into the radio-telephone: "All cars! The Polo Grounds. Seal it!"

The Lincoln was turning past the head of the trailer truck on two wheels when Grave Digger caught it in his lights. Coffin Ed leaned out the window and snapped a tracer bullet. It made a long incandescent streak, missing the rear of the disappearing Lincoln and sloping off towards the innocent earth. Then the truck was between them.

"Stop for Barry!" Deke yelled to his driver.

The driver tamped the brakes and the car skidded straight to a stop. Deke leaped out and rushed towards the grotesque pile of bodies. The white man who'd been run over was writhing in agony and Deke hit him with the .45 in passing and crushed his brain. Then he tried to pull Barry from beneath the other bodies.

"No!" Barry screamed in pain.

"For God's sake, the key!" Deke cried.

"Cotton . . ." Barry whispered, blood coming from his mouth and nose as his big body relaxed in death.

Grave Digger came around the truck so fast the little car slewed sideways and Coffin Ed's tracer bullet intended for the gasoline tank shattered the rear window of the Lincoln Mark IV and set fire to the lining of the roof. The Lincoln went off in a hard straight line like a missile being fired and began zigzagging perilously in the dark. He threw another tracer and punctured the back door. Then he was shooting at the dark and the Lincoln kept going faster.

Grave Digger dragged the little car down and was out and running towards Deke, gun leveled, before it stopped moving. Coffin Ed hit the ground flat-footed on the other side, prepared to add his one remaining bullet. But it wasn't necessary. Deke saw them coming towards him. He had seen the Lincoln drive away. He dropped the pistol and raised his hands. He wanted to live.

"Well, well, look who's here," Grave Digger said as he went forward to snap on the handcuffs.

"Ain't this a pleasant surprise?" Coffin Ed echoed.

"I want to phone my lawyer," Deke said.

"All in good time, lover boy, all in good time," Grave Digger said.

XIV

NOW IT WAS I A.M. Homicide had been there and gone. The medical examiner had pronounced all four bodies "Dead On Arrival." The bodies were on their way to the morgue. Both the Colonel's limousine and the Lincoln had gotten away. A search was being made. The seventeen police cruisers that had bottled up the area to keep them from escaping had been returned to regular duty. The workmen cleaning the Polo Grounds had returned to their work. The city lived and breathed and slept as usual. People were lying, stealing, cheating, murdering; people were praying, singing, laughing, loving and being loved; and people were being born and people were dying. Its pulse remained the same. New York City. The Big Town.

But the heads, the mothers and fathers, of those eighty-seven families who had sunk their savings on a dream of going back to Africa lay awake, worrying, wondering if they'd ever get their money back.

Deke was in the "Pigeons' Nest" in the precinct station, sitting on the wooden stool bolted to the floor, facing the barrage of spotlights. He looked fragile and translucent in the bright light; his smooth black face was more the purplish-orange color of an overpowdered whore than the normal gray of a black man terrified.

"I want to see my lawyer," he was saying for the hundredth time.

"Your lawyer is asleep at this time of night," Coffin Ed said with a straight face.

"He'd be mad if we woke him," Grave Digger added.

Lieutenant Anderson had let them have him first. They were in a jovial mood. They had Deke where they wanted him.

It wasn't funny to Deke. "Don't get your britches torn," he warned. "All you got against me is suspicion of homicide; and I have a perfect right to see my lawyer."

Coffin Ed slapped him with his cupped palm. It was a light slap but it sounded like a firecracker and rocked Deke's head.

"Who's talking about homicide?" Grave Digger said as though he hadn't noticed it.

"Hell, all we want to know is who's got the money," Coffin Ed said.

Deke straightened up and took a deep breath.

"So we can go and get it and give it back to those poor people you swindled," Grave Digger added.

"Swindled my ass," Deke said. "It was all legitimate."

Grave Digger slapped him so hard his body bent one-sided like a rubber man, and Coffin Ed slapped him back. They slapped him back and forth until his brains were addled, but left no bruises.

They let him get his breath back and gave him time for his brains to settle. Then Grave Digger said, "Let's start over."

Deke's eyes had turned bright orange in the glaring light. He closed his lids. A trickle of blood flowed from the corner of his mouth. He licked his lips and wiped his hand across his mouth.

"You're hurting me," he said. His voice sounded as though his tongue had thickened. "But you ain't killing me. And that's all that counts."

Coffin Ed drew back to hit him but Grave Digger caught his arm. "Easy, Ed," he said.

"Easy on this mother-raping scum?" Coffin Ed raved. "Easy on this incestuous sister-raping thief?"

"We're cops," Grave Digger reminded him. "Not judges."

Coffin Ed restrained himself. "The law was made to protect the innocent," he said.

Grave Digger chuckled. "You heard the man," he said to Deke.

Deke looked as though he might reply to that but thought better of it. "You're wasting your time on me," he said instead. "My Back-to-Africa movement was on the square and all I know about this shooting caper is what I saw in passing. I saw the man was dying and tried to save his life."

Coffin Ed turned and walked into the shadow. He slapped the wall with the palm of his hand so hard it sounded like a shot. It was all Grave Digger could do to keep from breaking Deke's jaw. His neck swelled and veins sprouted like ropes along his temples.

"Deke, don't try us," he said. His voice had turned light and cotton-dry. "We'll take you out of here and pistol-whip you slowly to death—and take the charge."

It showed on Deke's face he believed him. He didn't speak.

"We know the set-up of the Back-to-Africa movement. We got the FBI records on Four-Four and Freddy. We got the

Cook County Bertillon report on Barry and Elmer. We got your prison record too. We know you haven't got the money or you wouldn't still have been around. But you got the key."

"Got what key?" Deke asked.

"The key to the door that leads to the money."

Deke shook his head. "I'm clean," he said.

"Punk, listen," Grave Digger said. "You're going up any way. We got the proof."

"Got it from where?" Deke asked.

"We got it from Iris," Grave Digger said.

"If she said the Back-to-Africa movement was crooked she's a lying bitch, and I'll tell her to her teeth."

"All right," Grave Digger said.

Three minutes later they had Iris in the room. Lieutenant Anderson and two white detectives had come with her.

She stood in front of Deke and looked him dead in the eyes. "He killed Mabel Hill," she said.

Deke's face distorted with rage and he tried to leap at her but the white detectives held him.

"Mabel found out that the Back-to-Africa movement was crooked and she was going to the police. Her husband had been killed and she had lost her money and she was going to get him." She sounded as if it was good to her.

"You lying whore!" Deke screamed.

"When I stood up for him, she attacked me," Iris continued. "I was struggling to defend myself. He grabbed me from behind and put the pistol in my hand and shot her. When I tried to wrestle the pistol away from him, he knocked me down and took it."

Deke looked sick. He knew it was a good story. He knew if she took it to court, dressed in black, her eyes downcast in sorrow, and spoke in a halting manner—with his record—she could make it stick. She didn't have any kind of a criminal record. He could see the chair in Sing Sing and himself sitting in it.

He stared at her with resignation. "How much are they paying you?" he asked.

She ignored the question. "The forged documents which

prove the Back-to-Africa movement is crooked are hidden in our apartment in the binding of a book called *Sex and Race*." She smiled sweetly at Deke. "Good-bye, big shit," she said and turned towards the door.

The white detectives looked at one another, then looked at Deke. Anderson was embarrassed.

"How does that feel?" Coffin Ed asked Deke in a grating voice.

Grave Digger walked with Iris to the door. When he turned her over to the jailor he winked at her. She looked surprised for an instant, then winked back, and the jailor took her away.

Deke had wilted. He didn't look hurt, or even frightened; he looked beat, like a condemned man waiting for the electric chair. All he needed was the priest.

Anderson and the two white detectives left without looking at him again.

When the three of them were again alone, Grave Digger said, "Give us the key and we'll strike off the murder."

Deke looked up at him as though from a great distance. He looked as though he didn't care about anything any more. "Frig you," he said.

"Then give us the eighty-seven grand and we'll drop the whole thing," Grave Digger persisted.

"Frig you twice," Deke said.

They turned him over to the jailor to be taken back to his cell.

"I got a feeling we're overlooking something," Grave Digger said.

"That is for sure," Coffin Ed agreed. "But what?"

They were in Anderson's office, talking about Iris. As usual, Grave Digger sat with a ham perched on the edge of the desk and Coffin Ed was backed against the wall in the shadow.

"She'll never get away with it," Lieutenant Anderson said.

"Maybe not," Grave Digger conceded. "But she sure scared the hell out of him."

"How much did it help?"

Grave Digger looked chagrined.

"None," Coffin Ed admitted ruefully. "She put it on too thick. We didn't expect her to accuse him of the murder."

Grave Digger chuckled at that. "She didn't hold anything back. I thought for a moment she was going to accuse him of rape."

Anderson colored slightly. "Then how far have you got?"

"Nowhere," Grave Digger confessed.

Anderson sighed. "I hate to see people tearing at one another like rapacious animals."

"Hell, what do you expect?" Grave Digger said. "As long as there are jungles there'll be rapacious animals."

"Remember the colored taxi driver who picked up the three white men and the colored woman in front of Small's, right after the trucks were wrecked?" Anderson asked, changing the conversation.

"Took them to Brooklyn. Maybe we ought to talk to him."

"No use now. Homicide took him down to the morgue. On a hunch. And he identified the bodies of the three white men as the same ones."

Grave Digger shifted his weight and Coffin Ed leaned forward. For a moment they were silent, lost in thought, then Grave Digger said, "That ought to tell me something," adding, "but it don't."

"It tells me they ain't got the money either," Coffin Ed said.

"What they?"

"How the hell do I know? I didn't see the ones who got away," Coffin Ed said.

Anderson thumbed through the report sheets on his desk. "The Lincoln was found abandoned on Broadway, where the subway trestle passes over 125th Street, with the two rifles still inside," he noted. "It showed where you hit it."

"So what?"

"The gunmen haven't been found but Homicide has got leaders out. Anyway, we know who they are and they won't get far."

"Don't worry about those birds, they'll never fly," Coffin Ed said.

"Those are not the flying kind," Grave Digger added. "Those are jailbirds, headed for home."

"And we're headed for food," Coffin Ed said. "My stomach is sending up emergency calls."

"Damn right," Grave Digger agreed. "As Napoleon said, 'A woman thinks with her heart but a man with his stomach.' And we've got some heavy thinking to do."

Anderson laughed. "What Napoleon was that?"

"Napoleon Jones," Grave Digger said.

"All right, Napoleon Jones, don't forget crime," Anderson said.

"Crime is what pays us," Coffin Ed said.

They went to Mammy Louise's. She had changed her pork store with the tiny restaurant in back into a fancy all-night barbecue joint. Mr. Louise was dead and a slick young black man with shiny straightened hair and fancy clothes had taken his place. The English bulldog who used to keep Mr. Louise at home was still there, but his usefulness was gone and he looked lonely for the short fat figure of Mr. Louise, whom he delighted in scaring. The new young man didn't look like the type anything could keep home, bulldog or whatnot.

They sat at a rear table facing the front. The barbecue grill was to their right, presided over by a white-clad chef. To their left was the jukebox, blaring out a Ray Charles number.

Mammy Louise's slick young man came personally to take their orders, playing the role of Patron with mincing arrogance.

"Good evening, gentlemen, what will you gentlemen have tonight?"

Grave Digger looked up. "What have you got?"

"Barbecued ribs, barbecued feet, barbecued chicken, and we got some chitterlings and hog maws and some collard greens with ears and tails—"

"You'd go out of business if hogs had only loins," Coffin Ed interrupted.

The young man flashed his teeth. "We got some ham and succotash and some hog head and black-eyed peas—"

"What do you do with the bristles?" Grave Digger asked.

The young man was becoming irritated. "Anything you want, gentlemen," he said with a strained smile.

"Don't brag," Coffin Ed muttered.

The smile went out.

"Just bring us two double orders of ribs," Grave Digger said quickly. "With side dishes of black-eyed peas, rice, okra, collard greens with fresh tomatoes and onions, and top it off with some deep-dish apple pie and vanilla ice cream. Okay?"

The young man smiled again. "Just a light snack."

"Yeah, we want to think," Coffin Ed said.

They watched the young man walk away with a switch.

"Mr. Louise must be turning over in his grave," Coffin Ed said.

"Hell, he's more likely running after some chippy angel, now that he's got away from that bulldog."

"If he went in that direction."

"All chippies were angels to Mr. Louise," Grave Digger said.

The place was filled mostly with young people who peeped at them through the corners of their eyes when they came back to play the jukebox. Everyone knew them. They looked at these young people, thinking they didn't know what it was all about yet.

Suddenly they were listening.

"Pres," Grave Digger recognized, cocking his ear. "And Sweets."

"Roy Eldridge too," Coffin Ed added. "Who's on the bass?"

"I don't know him or the guitar either," Grave Digger confessed. "I guess I'm an old pappy."

"What's that platter?" Coffin Ed asked the youth standing by the jukebox who had played the number.

His girl looked at them through wide dark eyes, as though they'd escaped from the zoo, but the boy replied self-consciously, " 'Laughing to Keep from Crying.' It's foreign."

"No, it ain't," Coffin Ed said.

No one contradicted him. They were silent with their thoughts until a waiter brought the food. The table was loaded. Grave Digger chuckled. "Looks like a famine is coming on."

"We're going to head it off," Coffin Ed said.

The waiter brought three kinds of hot sauce—Red Devil, Little Sister's Big Brother, West Virginia Coke Oven—vinegar, a plate of yellow corn bread and a dish of country butter.

"Bone apperteet," he said.

"*Merci, m'sieu*," Coffin Ed replied.

"Black Frenchman," Grave Digger commented when the waiter had left.

"Good old war," Coffin Ed said. "It got us out of the South."

"Yeah, now the white folks want to start another war to get us back."

That was the last of that conversation. The food claimed their attention. They sloshed the succulent pork barbecue with Coke Oven hot sauce and gnawed it from the bones with noisy relish. It made the chef feel good all over to watch them eat.

When they had finished, Mammy Louise came from the kitchen. She was shaped like a weather balloon on two feet, with a pilot balloon serving as a head. The round black face beneath the bandanna which encased her head was shiny with sweat, but still she wore a heavy sweater over a black woolen dress. She claimed she had never been warm since coming north. Her ancestors were runaway slaves who had joined a tribe of southern Indians and formed a new race known as "Geechies." Her native language was a series of screeches punctuated by grunts, but she spoke American with an accent. She smelled like stewed goat.

"How's y'all, nasty 'licemen?" she greeted them jovially.

"Fine, Mammy Louise, how's yourself?"

"Cold," she confessed.

"Don't your new love keep you warm?" Coffin Ed asked.

She cast a look at the mincing dandy flashing his teeth at two women at a front table. " 'Oman lak me tikes w'ut de good Lawd send 'thout question, I'se 'fied."

"If you are satisfied, who're we to complain?" Grave Digger said.

A man poked his head in the door and said something to her fine young man and he hurried back to their table and said, "Your car's calling."

They jumped up and hurried out without paying.

XV

LIEUTENANT ANDERSON SAID, "A man was found dead in a junkyard underneath 125th Street approach to the Triborough Bridge."

"What about it?" Coffin Ed replied.

"*What about it?*" Anderson flared. "Have you guys quit the force? Go over and look at it. You might learn that killing is a crime. Just the same as robbery."

Coffin Ed felt his ears burning. "Right away," he said respectfully.

"What about it?" he heard Anderson muttering as he switched off.

Grave Digger was chuckling as he wheeled the car into the traffic. "Got your ass torn, eh, buddy?"

"Yeah, the boss man got salty."

"Let that be a lesson to you. Don't play murder cheap."

"All right, I'm outnumbered," Coffin Ed said.

They found Sergeant Wiley in charge of the crew from Homicide. His men were casting footprints, dusting for fingerprints, and taking photographs. A young pink-faced assistant medical examiner was tagging the body DOA and whistling cheerfully.

"My old friends, the lion tamers," Sergeant Wiley greeted them. "Have no fear, the dog is dead."

They looked at the dead dog, then glanced casually about.

"What've you got here?" Grave Digger asked.

"Just another corpse," Wiley said. "My fifth for the night."

"So you covered the caper at the Polo Grounds?"

"Caper! Hell, when I arrived there were only four stiffs. You men got the live one."

"You can have him."

"For what? If he wasn't any good for you what the hell I want him for?"

"Who knows? Maybe he'll like you better."

Wiley smiled. He looked more like a professor of political science at the New School than a homicide detective sergeant but Grave Digger and Coffin Ed knew him for a cool clever cop. "Let's look around," he said, leading the way into the shed where the body was found. "Here's the score. We got a social security card from his wallet which gives his name as Joshua Peavine and an address on West 121st Street. He was stabbed once in the heart. That's all we know."

The detectives looked carefully over the junk-filled shed. Three aisles, flanked by junk stacked to the corrugated-iron ceiling, branched off from the main aisle that led in from the door. All available space was filled except an empty spot at the end of the main aisle beside the back wall.

"Somebody got something," Coffin Ed remarked.

"What the hell would anybody want from here?" Wiley asked, gesturing towards the stacks of flattened cardboard, old books and magazines, rags, radios, sewing-machines, rusty tools, battered mannequins and unidentifiable scraps of metal.

"The man got killed for something, much less the dog," Coffin Ed maintained.

"Might have been a sex crime," Grave Digger ventured. "Suppose he came here with a white man. It's happened before."

"I thought of that," Wiley said. "But the dead dog contradicts it."

"He'd kill the dog if it was worth it," Coffin Ed said.

Wiley raised his eyebrows. "All that secrecy in Harlem?"

"He'd do what was necessary if the pay was right."

"Maybe," Wiley conceded. "But here's the twist. We found a ball of meat that looks as though it might be poisoned in his pocket—we'll have it analyzed of course. So the dog was already poisoned by someone else. Unless he had two balls of poisoned meat—which wouldn't seem necessary."

"This empty space bothers me," Grave Digger confessed. "This empty space in all this conglomeration of junk. Was there anything knocked off the hijack truck the other night that might identify it? Something that might wind up in a junkyard. A spare wheel?"

Wiley shook his head. "Maybe a gun could have been lost, but nothing I can think of that would be sold here. Nothing at least to fill this empty space. I think we're on the wrong track there."

"There's only one way to find out," Grave Digger said.

Wiley nodded. The door to the office had been forced by Wiley's men but nothing had been found to draw attention. The three of them went in and Wiley telephoned Mr. Goodman at his home in Brooklyn.

Mr. Goodman was horrified. "Everything happens to me," he cried. "Such a good boy, so honest. He wouldn't hurt a fly yet."

"We want you to come over and tell us what is missing."

"Missing!" Mr. Goodman screamed. "You're not thinking Josh was killed protecting my place? He wasn't a nitwit."

"We're not thinking anything. We just want you to tell us what's missing."

"You think thieves have stolen something from my junk-yard? Diamonds, maybe. Bricks of gold. Necklaces of rubies. Have you seen my junk? Only another junk man would want anything from my junkyard and he'd need a truck to take away ten dollars' worth."

"We just want you to come over and take a look, Mr. Good-man," Wiley said patiently.

"*Mein Gott*, at this hour of the morning! You say Josh is dead. Poor boy. My heart bleeds. But can I bring him back to life, at two o'clock in the morning? Can I raise the dead? If there is junk missing you can see it for yourself. Do you think I can identify my junk? How can anyone identify junk? Junk is junk; that's what makes it junk. If someone has taken some of my junk he is welcome. There will be signs where he has taken truck-loads, unless he is a lunatic. Look you for a lunatic, there is your man. And my Reba is awake and worrying should I go over in that place full of lunatic murderers at this time of night. She is a lunatic too. You just put Josh in the morgue and I will come Monday morning and identify his body."

"This is important, Mr. Goodman—" The line went dead. Wiley jiggled the hook. "Mr. Goodman, Mr. Goodman—" The voice of the operator came on. Wiley looked about and said, "He hung up," and hung up himself.

"Send for him," Coffin Ed said.

Wiley looked at him. "On what charge? I'd have to get a court order to get him out of Brooklyn."

"There's more ways than one to skin a cat," Grave Digger said.

"Don't tell me," Wiley said, leading the way back to the yard. "Let me stay ignorant."

They stood for a moment looking at the carcass of the dead dog. The ruddy-faced assistant medical examiner passed them, singing cheerfully, "*I'll be glad when you're dead, you rascal you; I'll be standing at Broad and High when they bring your dead ass by, I'll be glad when you're dead. . . .*"

Grave Digger and Coffin Ed exchanged looks.

Wiley noticed and said, "It's a living."

"More bodies, more babies," Grave Digger agreed.

The morgue wagon came and took away the body of the man and the carcass of the dog. Wiley called his men and prepared to leave. "I'm going to let you have it," he said.

"We got it," Coffin Ed said. "Sleep tight."

Left to themselves they went back over the ground in detail. "Anywhere else it would figure something was stolen," Coffin Ed said. "Here it don't make any sense."

"Let's quit guessing, let's go get Goodman."

Coffin Ed nodded. "Right."

They closed the shed and turned out the lights and went slowly through the yard to the gate. When they started to cross the street to where their car was parked, a dark shape came from beneath the bridge like a juggernaut. They couldn't see what it was but they ran because years of police work had taught them that nothing moves in the dark but danger. When they saw it was a black car moving at incredible speed they dove face downward on the pavement on the other side. A burst of flame lit the night as the silence exploded; machine-gun bullets sprayed over them as the black car passed. It was over. For a brief instant there was the diminishing whine of a high-powered engine, then silence again. The black shape had disappeared as though it had never been.

By now they had their pistols in their hands, but they still lay cautiously flat to the pavement, searching the night for a moving target. Nothing moved. Finally they crawled to the protection of their little car and stood up, still searching the shadows for movement. They eased into the car like wary shadows themselves. Their breathing was audible. They still looked around.

Car lights had slowed in the moving chain on the bridge overhead, but the deserted, off-beat street below remained dark.

"Report it," Grave Digger said as they sat in the dark.

Coffin Ed called the precinct from the car and got Lieutenant Anderson. He gave it just like it happened.

"Why, for God's sake?" Anderson said.

"I don't figure it," Coffin Ed confessed. "We got nothing, no description, no license number—and no ideas."

"I don't know what you're on to, but be careful," Anderson warned.

"How much more careful can a cop be?"

"You could use some help."

"Help to get killed," Coffin Ed grumbled and felt a warning pressure from Grave Digger's hand. "We're going to Brooklyn now to get the owner of this junkyard."

"Well, if you have to, but for God's sake go easy; you don't have any jurisdiction in Brooklyn and you can get us all in a jam."

"Easy does it," Coffin Ed said and cut off.

Grave Digger mashed the starter and they went down the dark street. He was frowning from his thoughts. "Ed, we're just missing something," he said.

"Goddamned right," Coffin Ed agreed. "Just missing getting killed."

"I mean, doesn't this tell you something?"

"Tells me to get the hell off the Force while I'm still alive."

"What I mean is, so much nonsense must make sense," Grave Digger persisted as he entered the approach to the East Side throughway.

"Do you believe that shit?" Coffin Ed said.

"I was thinking why would anyone want to rub us out because a junkyard laborer was murdered?"

"You tell me."

"What's so important about this killing? It smells like some kind of double-cross."

"I don't see it. Unless you're trying to tie this to the hijack caper. And that sure don't make any sense. People are getting killed in Harlem all the time. Why not you and me?"

"I got to think something," Grave Digger said and entered the stream of traffic on the throughway without stopping.

Mr. Goodman was still awake when they arrived. The news of Josh's murder had upset him. He was clad in bathrobe and nightgown and looked as though he'd been raiding the kitchen. But he still protested against going back to Harlem just to look over his junkyard.

"What good can it do? How can it help you? No one steals junk. I only kept the dog to keep bums from sleeping in the yard, and cart pushers like Uncle Bud from filling his cart with my junk to sell to another junk man."

"Listen, Mr. Goodman, the other night eighty-seven poor colored families lost their life savings in a robbery—"

"Yes, yes, I read in the papers. They wanted to go back to Africa. I want to get back to Israel where I've never been either. It comes to no good, this looking for bigger apples on foreign trees. Here every man is free—"

"Yes, Mr. Goodman," Grave Digger interrupted with feigned patience. "But we're cops, not philosophers. And we just want to find out what is missing from your junkyard and we can't wait until Monday morning because by then someone else might be killed. Even us. Even you."

"If I must, I must, to keep some other poor colored man from being killed, about some junk," Mr. Goodman said resignedly, adding bitterly: "What this world is coming to nobody knows, when people are killed about some junk—not to speak of a poor innocent dog."

He led them into the parlor to wait while he dressed. When he returned ready to go, he said, "My Reba don't like it."

The detectives didn't comment on his Reba's dislikes.

* * *

At first Mr. Goodman did not see where anything was missing. It looked exactly as he had left it.

"All this trouble, getting up and dressing and coming all this distance in the dark hours of morning, for nothing," he complained.

"But there must have been something in this empty space," Coffin Ed insisted. "What are you keeping this space for?"

"Is that a crime? Always I keep space for what might come in. Did poor Josh get killed for this empty space? Just who is the lunatic, I ask you?" Then he remembered. "A bale of cotton," he said.

Grave Digger and Coffin Ed froze. Their nostrils quivered like hound dogs on a scent. Thoughts churned through their heads like sheets of lightning.

"Uncle Bud brought in a bale of cotton this morning," Mr. Goodman went on. "I had it put out here. I haven't thought of it since. With income taxes and hydrogen bombs and black revolutions, who thinks of a bale of cotton? Uncle Bud is one of the cart men—"

"We know Uncle Bud," Coffin Ed said.

"Then you know he must have found this bale of cotton on his nightly rounds." Mr. Goodman shrugged and spread his hands. "I can't ask every cart man for a bill of sale."

"Mr. Goodman, that's all we want to know," Grave Digger said. "We'll drive you to a taxi and pay for your time."

"Pay I want none," Mr. Goodman said. "But curious I am. Who would kill a man about a bale of cotton? *Cotton, mein Gott.*"

"That's what we want to find out," Grave Digger said and led the way to their car.

Now it was three-thirty in the morning and they were back at the precinct station talking it over with Lieutenant Anderson. Anderson had already alerted all cars to pick up Uncle Bud for questioning and they were trying to fix the picture.

"You're certain this bale of cotton was carried by the meat delivery truck used by the jackers?" Anderson said.

"We found fibers of raw cotton in the truck. Uncle Bud finds a bale of cotton on 137th Street and sells it to the junkyard. The bale of cotton is missing. A junkyard laborer has been killed. We're certain of that much," Grave Digger said.

"But what could make this bale of cotton that important?"

"Identification. Maybe it points directly to the hijackers," Grave Digger said.

"Yes, but remember the dog was dead before Josh and his murderer arrived. Maybe the cotton was gone by then too."

"Maybe. But that doesn't change the fact that somebody wanted the cotton and didn't let him live to tell whether they got it, or somebody got it before."

"Let's quit guessing and go find the cotton," Coffin Ed said.

Grave Digger looked at him as though he felt like saying, "Go find it then."

During the silence the phone rang and Anderson picked up the receiver and said, "Yes . . . yes . . . yes, 119th Street and Lenox . . . yes . . . well, keep looking." He hung up.

"They found the junk cart," Grave Digger said more than asked.

Anderson nodded. "But Uncle Bud wasn't with it."

"It figures," Coffin Ed said. "He's probably in the river by now."

"Yeah," Grave Digger said angrily. "This mother-raping cotton punished the colored man down south and now it's killing them up north."

"Which reminds me," Anderson said. "Dan Sellers of Car 90 says he saw an old colored junk man who'd found a bale of cotton on 137th Street right after the trucks crashed the night of the hijack. The old man was trying to get it into his cart—probably Uncle Bud—and they stopped to question him. Then he got out and helped him load it and ordered him to bring it to the station. But he never came."

"Now you tell us," Grave Digger said bitterly.

Anderson colored. "I'd forgotten it until now. After all, we hadn't thought of cotton."

"You hadn't," Coffin Ed said.

"Speaking of cotton, what do you know about a Colonel Calhoun who's opened a store-front office on Seventh Avenue to recruit people to go south and pick cotton? Calls it the Back-to-the-Southland movement," Grave Digger asked.

Anderson looked at him curiously. "Lay off him," he warned, "I admit it's a stupid pitch, but it's strictly on the legitimate. The captain has questioned him and checked his license and credentials; they're all in order. And he's got influential friends."

"I don't doubt it," Grave Digger said drily. "All southern crackers got influential friends up north."

Anderson looked down.

"The Back-to-Africa members are picketing him," Coffin Ed said. "They don't want that crap in Harlem."

"The Muslims haven't bothered him," Anderson said defensively.

"Hell, they're just giving him enough rope."

"Just his timing is bad," Coffin Ed argued. "Right after this Back-to-Africa movement is hijacked he opens this go-south-and-pick-cotton pitch. If you ask me, he's looking for trouble."

Anderson thumbed through the reports on his desk. "Last night at ten P.M. he phoned and reported that his car had been stolen from in front of his office on Seventh Avenue. Gave his home address as Hotel Dixie on 42nd Street. A cruiser stopped by but the office was closed for the night. We gave it a routine check at midnight. The desk said he had come home at ten-thirty-five P.M. and hadn't left his suite. His nephew was with him."

"What kind of car?" Grave Digger asked.

"Black limousine. Special body. Ferrari chassis. Birmingham, Alabama, plates. And just lay off of him. We got enough trouble as it is."

"I'm just thinking that cotton grows in the South," Grave Digger said.

"And tobacco grows in Cuba," Anderson said. "Go home and get some sleep. Whatever's going to happen has happened by now."

"We're going, boss," Grave Digger said. "No more we can do tonight anyway. But don't hand us that crap. This caper has just begun."

XVI

EVERYTHING HAPPENS IN Harlem six days a week, but Sunday morning, people worship God. Those who are not religious stay in bed. The whores, pimps, gamblers, criminals and racketeers catch up on their sleep or their love. But the religious get up and put on their best clothes and go to church. The bars are closed. The stores are closed. The streets are deserted save for the families on their way to church. A drunk better not be caught molesting them; he'll get all the black beat off him.

All of the Sunday newspapers had carried the story of the arrest of Reverend D. O'Malley, leader of the Back-to-Africa movement, on suspicion of fraud and homicide. The accounts of the hijacking had been rehashed and pictures of O'Malley and his wife, Iris, and Mabel Hill added to the sensationalism.

As a consequence Reverend O'Malley's interdenominational church, "The Star of Ham," on 121st Street between Seventh and Lenox Avenues, was crowded with the Back-to-Africa followers and the curious. A scattering of Irish people who had read the story in *The New York Times*, which didn't carry pictures, had made their way uptown, thinking Reverend O'Malley was one of them.

Reverend T. Booker Washington (no relation to the great Negro educator), the assistant minister, led the services. At first he led the congregation in prayer. He prayed for the Back-to-Africa followers, and he prayed that their money be returned; and he prayed for sinners and for good people who had been falsely accused, and for all black people who had suffered the wages of injustice.

Then he began his sermon, speaking quietly and with dignity and understanding of the unfortunate robbery, and of the tragic deaths of young Mr. and Mrs. Hill, members of the church and active participants in the Back-to-Africa movement. The congregation sat in hushed silence. Then Reverend Washington spoke openly and frankly of the inexplicable tragedy which seemed to haunt the life of that saintly man, Reverend O'Malley, as though God were trying him.

"It is as though God was testing this man with the trials of Job to ascertain the strength of his faith and his endurance and courage for some great task ahead."

"Amen," a sister said tentatively.

Reverend Washington moved carefully, sampling the reaction of his audience before proceeding to controversial ground.

"All of his life this noble and selfless man has been subjected to the cruel and biased judgement of the white people whom he defies for you."

"Amen," the sister cried louder and with more confidence. A few timid "amens" echoed.

"I know Reverend O'Malley is innocent of any crime," Reverend Washington said loudly, letting passion creep into the solemnity of his voice. "I would trust him with my money and I would trust him with my life."

"Amen!" the sister shouted, rising from her seat. "He's a good man."

The congregation warmed up. Ripples of confirmation ran through all the women.

"He will conquer this calumny of false accusation; he will be vindicated!" Reverend Washington thundered.

"Set him free!" a woman screamed.

"Justice will set him free!" Reverend Washington roared. "And he will get back our money and lead us out of this land of oppression back to our beloved homeland in Africa."

"*Amens*" and "*hallelujas*" filled the air as the congregation was swept off its feet. In the grip of emotionalism, O'Malley appeared in their imaginations as a martyr to the injustice of whites, and a brave and noble leader.

"His chains will be broken by the Almighty God and he will come and set us free," Reverend Washington concluded in a thundering voice.

The Back-to-Africa followers believed. They wanted to believe. They didn't have any other choice.

"Now we will take up a collection to help pay for Reverend O'Malley's defense," Reverend Washington said in a quiet voice. "And we will delegate Brother Sumners to take it to him in his hour of Gethsemane."

Five hundred and ninety-seven dollars was collected and Brother Sumners was charged to go forthwith and present it to Reverend O'Malley. The precinct station where O'Malley was being held for the magistrate's court was only a few blocks distant. Brother Sumners returned with word from O'Malley before the service had adjourned. He could scarcely contain his sense of importance as he mounted the rostrum and brought them word from their beloved minister.

"Reverend O'Malley is spending the day in his cell praying for you, his beloved followers—for all of us—and for the speedy return of your money, and for our safe departure for Africa. He says he will be taken to court Monday morning at ten o'clock when he will be freed to return to you and continue his work."

"Lord, protect him and deliver him," a sister cried, and others echoed: "Amen, amen."

The congregation filed out, filled with faith in Reverend O'Malley, blended with compassion and a sense of satisfaction for their own good deed of sending him the big collection.

On many a table there was chicken and dumplings or roast pork and sweet potatoes, and crime took a rest.

Grave Digger and Coffin Ed always slept late on Sundays, rarely stirring from bed before six o'clock in the evening. Sunday and Monday were their days off unless they were working on a case, and they had decided to let the hijacking case rest until Monday.

But Grave Digger had dreamed that a blind man had told him he had seen a bale of cotton run down Seventh Avenue and turn into a doorway, but he awakened before the blind man told him what doorway. There was a memory knocking at his mind, trying to get in. He knew it was important but it had not seemed so at the time. He lay for a time going over in detail all that they had done. He didn't find it; it didn't come. But he had a strong feeling that if he could remember this one thing he would have all the answers.

He got up and slipped on a bathrobe and went to the kitchen and got two cans of beer from the refrigerator.

"Stella," he called his wife, but she had gone out.

He drank one can of beer and prowled about the house, holding the other in his hand. He was looking inward, searching his memory. A cop without a memory is like meat without potatoes, he was thinking.

His two daughters were away at camp. The house felt like a tomb. He sat in the living room and leafed through the Saturday edition of the *Sentinel*, Harlem's twice-weekly newspaper devoted to the local news. The hijacking story took up most of the front page. There were pictures of O'Malley and Iris, and of John and Mabel Hill. O'Malley's racketeer days and prison record were hammered on and the claim he had been marked for death by the syndicate. There were stories about his Back-to-Africa movement, bordering on libel, and stories of the Back-to-Africa movement of L.H. Michaux, handled with discretion; and stories of the original Back-to-Africa movement of Marcus Garvey, containing some bits of information that Garvey hadn't known himself. He turned the pages and his gaze lit on an advertisement for the Cotton Club, showing a picture of Billie Belle doing her exotic cotton dance. *I've got cotton on the brain*, he thought disgustedly and threw the paper aside.

He went to the telephone extension in the hall, from where he could look outdoors, and called the precinct station in Harlem and talked to Lieutenant Bailey, who was on Sunday duty. Bailey said, no, Colonel Calhoun's car had not been found, no, there was no trace of Uncle Bud, no, there was no trace of the two gunmen of Deke's who had escaped.

"The *noes* have it," Bailey said.

"Well, as long as the head's gone they can't bite," Grave Digger said.

Coffin Ed phoned and said his wife, Molly, had gone out with Stella, and he was coming over.

"Just don't let's talk about crime," Grave Digger said.

"Let's go down to the pistol range at headquarters and practice shooting," Coffin Ed suggested. "I've just got through cleaning the old lady."

"Hell, let's drink some highballs and get gay and take the ladies out on the town," Grave Digger said.

"Right. I won't mind being gay for a change."

The phone rang right after Coffin Ed hung up. Lieutenant Bailey said the Back-to-the-Southland people were assembling a group of colored people in front of their office for a parade down Seventh Avenue and there might be trouble.

"You and Ed better come over," he said. "The people know you."

Grave Digger called back Coffin Ed and told him to bring the car as Stella had taken his. Coffin Ed arrived before he had finished dressing, and they got into his gray Plymouth sedan and took off for Harlem. Forty-five minutes later they were rapidly threading through the Sunday afternoon traffic, heading north on Seventh Avenue.

A self-ordained preacher was standing on the sidewalk outside the Chock Full o' Nuts at 125th Street and Seventh Avenue, exhorting the passersby to take Jesus to their hearts. "Ain't no two ways about it," he was shouting. "The right one is with God and Jesus and the wrong one with the devil."

A few pious people had stopped to listen. Most of the Sunday afternoon strollers took the devil's way and passed without looking.

Diagonally across the intersection the Harlem branch of the Black Muslims was staging a mass meeting in front of the National Memorial Bookstore, headquarters of Michaux's Back-to-Africa movement. The store front was plastered with slogans: GODDAMN WHITE MAN ... WHITE PEOPLE EAT DOG ... ALLAH IS GOD ... BLACK MEN UNITE. ... At one side a platform had been erected with a public-address hook-up for the speakers. Below to one side was an open black coffin with a legend: *The Remains of Lumumba*. The coffin contained pictures of Lumumba in life and in death; a black suit said to have been worn by him when he was killed; and other mementoes said to have belonged to him in life. Bordering the sidewalk on removable flagstaffs were the flags of all the nations of black Africa.

Hundreds of people were lined up on the sidewalk in a packed mass. Three police cruisers were parked along the curb and white harness cops patrolled up and down in the street.

Muslims wearing the red fezzes they had adopted as their symbol were lined in front of the bookstore, side by side, keeping a clear path on the sidewalk demanded by the police. The shouting voice of a speaker came from the amplifiers: "White Man, you worked us for nothing for four hundred years. Now pay for it. . . ."

Grave Digger and Coffin Ed didn't stop. As they neared 130th Street they saw the parade heading in their direction on the other side of the street. They knew that within five blocks it would run head-on into the Black Muslims and there'd be hell to pay. Already some of O'Malley's Back-to-Africa group were collecting at 129th Street for an attack.

Police cruisers were parked along the avenue and cops were standing by.

The detectives noted immediately that the parade was made up of mercenary hoodlums, paid for the occasion. They were laughing belligerently and looking for trouble. They carried knives and walked tough. Colonel Calhoun led them, clad in his black frock coat and a black wide-brimmed hat. His silvery hair and white moustache and goatee shone in the rays of the afternoon sun. He was calmly smoking a cheroot. His tall thin figure was ramrod-straight and he walked with the indifference of a benevolent master. His attitude seemed that of a man dealing with children who might be unruly but never dangerous. The blond young man brought up the rear.

Coffin Ed double-parked and he and Grave Digger walked over to the raised park in the center of Seventh Avenue and assessed the situation.

"You go down to 129th Street and hold those brothers and I'll turn these soul-brothers here," Grave Digger said.

"I got you, partner," Coffin Ed said.

Grave Digger lined himself opposite a wooden telephone post and Coffin Ed crossed to the sidewalk and stood facing the concrete wall enclosing the park.

When the parade reached the intersection at 130th Street, Grave Digger drew his long-barreled .38 revolver and put two bullets into the wooden post. The nickel-plated pistol shone in the sun like a silver jet.

"Straighten up!" he shouted at the top of his voice.

The parading hoodlums hesitated.

From down the street came the booming blast of two shots as Coffin Ed fired into the concrete wall, followed by his voice, like an echo, "Count off!"

The mob preparing for the attack on the parade fell back. People in Harlem believed Coffin Ed and Grave Digger would shoot a man stone-cold dead for crossing an imaginary line. Those who didn't believe it didn't try it.

But Colonel Calhoun kept right ahead across 130th Street without looking about. When he came to the invisible line, Grave Digger shot off his hat. The Colonel slowly took the cheroot from his mouth and looked at Grave Digger coldly, then turned with slow deliberation to pick up his hat. Grave Digger shot it out of his hand. It flew on to the sidewalk and with slow deliberation, without another glance in Grave Digger's direction, the Colonel walked after it. Grave Digger shot it out into 130th Street as the Colonel was reaching for it.

The hoodlums in the parade were shuffling about, afraid to advance but taking no chances on breaking and running with those bullets flying about. The young blond man was keeping out of sight at the rear.

"Squads right!" Grave Digger shouted. Everyone turned but no one left. "March!" he added.

The hoodlums turned right on 130th Street and shuffled towards Eighth Avenue. They went straight past the Colonel, who stood in the center of the street looking at the holes in his hat before putting it on his head. Midway down the block they broke and ran. The first thing a hoodlum learns in Harlem is never run too soon.

The mob at 129th Street turned towards Eighth Avenue to head them off, but Coffin Ed drew a line with two bullets ahead of them. "As you were!" he shouted.

The Colonel stood there for a moment with three bullet holes in his hat, and residents who had come out to see the excitement began to laugh at him. The blond young man caught up with him and they turned back to Seventh Avenue and began walking towards their office, the jeers and laughter of the colored people following them. The Black Muslims had looked but hadn't moved.

Then the mob herded by Coffin Ed relaxed and started laughing too.

"Man, them mothers," a cat said admiringly in a loud jubilant voice. "Them mothers! They'll shoot off a man's ass for crossing a line can't nobody see."

"Baby, you see that old white mother-raper tryna git his hat? I bet the Digger would have taken his head off if he'da crossed that line."

"I seen old Coffin Filler shoot the fat offen a cat's stomach for stickin his belly 'cross that line."

They slapped one another on the shoulders and fell out, laughing at their own lies.

The white cops looked at Grave Digger and Coffin Ed with the envious awe usually reserved for a lion tamer with a cage of big cats.

Coffin Ed joined Grave Digger and they walked to a call box and phoned Lieutenant Bailey.

"All over for today," Grave Digger reported.

Bailey gave a sigh of relief. "Thank God! I don't want any riots up here on my tour."

"All you got to worry about now are some killings and robberies," Grave Digger said. "Nothing to worry the commissioner."

Bailey hung up without commenting. He knew of their feud with the commissioner. Both of them had been suspended at different times for what the commissioner considered unnecessary violence and brutality. He knew also that colored cops had to be tough in Harlem to get the respect of colored hoodlums. Secretly he agreed with them. But he wasn't taking any sides.

"Well, now we're back to cotton," Coffin Ed said as they walked back towards their car.

"Maybe you are; I ain't," Grave Digger said. "All I want to do is go out and break some laws. Other people have all the fun."

"Damn right. Let's put five bucks on a horse."

"Hell, man, you call that breaking the law? Let's take the ladies to some unlicensed joint run by some wanted criminal and drink some stolen whiskey."

Coffin Ed chuckled. "You're on," he said.

XVII

THE TELEPHONE RANG at 10:25 A.M. Grave Digger hid his head beneath the pillow. Stella answered it sleepily. A brisk, wide-awake and urgent voice said, "This is Captain Brice. Let me speak to Jones, please."

She pulled the pillow from over his head. "The captain," she said.

He groped for the receiver, experimentally opening his eyes. "Jones," he mumbled.

He listened to the rapid staccato voice for three minutes. "Right," he said, tense and wide-awake, and was getting out of the bed before he hung up the receiver.

"What is it?" she asked in a tiny voice, frightened and alarmed as she always was when these morning summonses came.

"Deke's escaped. Two officers killed." He had put on his shorts and undershirt and was pulling up his pants.

She was out of the bed and moving towards the kitchen. "You want coffee?"

"No time," he said, putting on a clean shirt.

"Nescafé," she said, disappearing into the kitchen.

With his shirt on he sat on the side of the bed and put on clean socks and his shoes. Then he went into the bathroom and washed his face and brushed his short kinky hair. Without a shave his dark lumpy face looked dangerous. He knew how he looked but it couldn't be helped. He didn't have time for a shave. He put on a black tie, went into the bedroom and took his holstered pistol from a hook in the closet. He laid the pistol on the dresser while he strapped on his shoulder sling and then picked it up and spun the cylinder. It always carried five shells, the hammer resting on a empty chamber. The shades were still drawn, and the long nickel-plated revolver glinting in the subdued light from three table lamps looked as dangerous as himself. He slipped it into the greased holster and began stuffing his pockets with the other tools of his trade: a leather-covered buckshot sap with a whalebone handle, a pair of handcuffs, report book, flashlight, stylo, and the leather-bound metal snap case made to hold fifteen extra shells he always carried in his leather-lined side coat pocket. They also kept an extra box or two of shells in the glove compartment of their official car.

He was standing at the kitchen table, drinking coffee, when Coffin Ed blew for him. Stella tensed. Her smooth brown face grew strained.

"Be careful," she said.

He stepped around the table and kissed her. "Ain't I always?" he said.

"Not always," she murmured.

But he was gone, a big, rough, dangerous man in need of a shave, clad in a rumpled black suit and an old black hat, the bulge of a big pistol clearly visible on the heart side of his broad-shouldered frame.

Coffin Ed looked the same; they could have been cast from the same mold with the exception of Coffin Ed's acid-burned face that was jerking with the tic that came whenever he was tense.

Yesterday, Sunday afternoon, it had taken forty-five minutes to get to Harlem. Today, Monday morning, it took twenty-two.

Coffin Ed said only, "The fat is in the fire."

"It's going to burn," Grave Digger said.

Two white officers had been killed and the precinct station looked like headquarters for the invasion of Harlem. Official cars lined the street. The commissioner's car was there, and cars of the chief inspector, the chief of Homicide, the medical examiner and a D.A.'s assistant. Police cruisers from downtown, from Homicide, from all the Harlem precincts, were scattered about. The street was closed to civilian traffic. There was no place inside for all the army of cops and the overflow stood outside, on the sidewalks, in the street, waiting for their orders.

Coffin Ed parked in the driveway of a private garage and they walked to the station house. The brass was assembled in the captain's office. The lieutenant on the desk said, "Go on in, they want to see you."

Heads turned when they entered the office. They were stared at as though they were criminals themselves.

"We want Deke O'Hara and his two gunmen, and we want them alive," the commissioner said coldly without greeting. "It's your bailiwick and I'm giving you a free hand."

They stared back at the commissioner but neither of them spoke.

"Let me give them the picture, sir," Captain Brice said.

The commissioner nodded. The captain led them into the detectives' room. A white detective got up from his desk in the corner and gave the captain a seat. Other detectives nodded to Grave Digger and Coffin Ed as they passed. No one spoke. They nodded back. They kept the record straight. There was no friendship lost between them and the other precinct detectives; but there was no open animosity. Some resented their position as the aces of the precinct and their close associations with the officers in charge; others were envious; the young colored detectives stood in awe of them. But all took care not to show anything.

Captain Brice sat behind the desk and Grave Digger perched a ham on the edge as usual. Coffin Ed drew up a straight-backed chair and sat opposite the captain.

"Deke was being taken to the magistrate's court," the captain said. "There were thirteen others going. The wagon was drawn up in the back court and we were bringing the prisoners from their cells, handcuffed together two by two as customary. Two officers were standing by, supervising the loading—the driver and his helper—and two jailors were bringing the prisoners from the bullpen through the back door and herding them downstairs to the yard and into the wagon. Deke's Back-to-Africa group had collected in the street out front, a thousand or more. They were chanting, 'We want O'Malley. . . . We want O'Malley,' and trying to break through the front door. They were getting unruly and I sent the extra officers out into the street to herd them to one side and keep order. Then they began getting noisy and started rioting. Some began throwing stones through the front windows and others began battering the gate to the driveway with garbage cans. I sent two men from out back to clear the driveway to the street. When they opened the gates to go out they were mobbed and disarmed and the mob streamed into the driveway. Deke had just come from the back door on his way down the stairs, handcuffed to a suspected murderer, one Mack Brothers, when the mob came in sight and saw him. Six prisoners had already been loaded. Then, from what I've been told by a trusty looking out a jail window—all the officers were out front trying to contain the riot—the jailors slammed and locked the door, leaving the two officers alone with the wagon. And at that moment the two gunmen came up from both sides of the high back wall and shot the two officers dead. The gunmen were dressed in officers' uniforms so at first they didn't attract much attention. Then they jumped down inside, put Deke in the wagon and closed the door and got into the front seat—and took the wagon out of the yard." He stopped and looked at them to see what they would say but they said nothing. So he went on. "Some of the mob had jumped astride the hood and onto the front bumpers and others were running along beside it. They were shouting, 'Make way for O'Malley! Make way for O'Malley!' and they rode the wagon out into the street. The rioters went wild and the officers could only use their saps and billies. They couldn't shoot into those thousand people. The wagon got through. We found it parked a block away around the corner. There must have been a car waiting. They got away. We captured the other prisoners in a matter of minutes."

"What about the one he was handcuffed to?" Coffin Ed asked.

"Him too. He was wandering in the street. He had been sapped and the cuffs were still on him."

"It was organized all right, but it needed luck," Grave Digger said.

"The mob seemed organized too," the captain said.

"Probably, but I doubt if there was a connection."

"More likely some planted agitators. They wouldn't have to know an escape was planned. They might have thought of freeing O'Malley by numbers," Coffin Ed said.

"A holy crusade," Grave Digger amended.

The captain looked sour. "We got three hundred of them in the bullpen. You want to talk to them?"

Grave Digger shook his head. "What are you holding them for?"

Captain Brice reddened with anger. "Complicity, goddammit. Assisting criminals to escape. Rioting. Accessories to murder. Two officers were killed. And I'll arrest every black son of a bitch in Harlem."

"Including me and Digger?" Coffin Ed grated, his face jumping like a live snake in a hot fire.

The captain cooled. "Hell, goddammit, don't be offended," he threw out the left-handed apology. "These goddamned lunatics help in a planned escape without knowing what they're doing and cause two officers to get killed. You ought to be mad too."

"How mad are *you*?" Grave Digger asked. He felt Coffin Ed look at him. He nodded slightly. He knew Coffin Ed read his thoughts and agreed.

"Mad enough for anything," Captain Brice said. "Shoot a few of these hoodlums. I'll cover you."

Grave Digger shook his head. "The commissioner wants them alive."

"I'm not talking about them," the captain raved. "Shoot any of these goddamn hoodlums."

"Take it easy, Captain," Coffin Ed said.

Grave Digger shook his head warningly. The room had become silent. Everyone was listening. Grave Digger leaned forward and said in a voice only for the captain's ears, "Are you mad enough to let us have Iris, Deke's woman—if she hasn't gone to county?"

The captain sobered instantly. He looked cornered and annoyed. He wouldn't meet Grave Digger's eyes. "You're asking for too much," he growled. "And you know it," he accused. Finally he said, "I couldn't if I wanted to. Her case is on the docket. I'm responsible to deliver her. If she doesn't appear it's officially an escape."

"Is she still here?" Grave Digger persisted.

"Nobody's gone out," the captain said. "All the hearings have been postponed, but that makes no difference."

Still leaning forward, Grave Digger whispered, "Let her escape."

The captain banged his fist on the desk. "No, goddammit! And that's final."

"The commissioner wants Deke and the two cop killers," Grave Digger whispered urgently. "You had two nights and a day to find those boys—you and the whole Force. And they weren't found. We're only two men. What do you expect us to do that the whole Force couldn't do?"

"Well," the captain said, expelling his breath. "Do the best you can."

"We can find them," Grave Digger kept on. "But you got to pay for it."

"I'll speak to the commissioner," the captain said, starting to rise.

"No," Grave Digger said. "He'll only say no and that will be the end of it. You've got to make the decision on your own."

The captain sat down. He thought for a moment, then looked up into Grave Digger's eyes. "How bad do you want Deke yourself?" he asked.

"Bad," Grave Digger said.

"If you can get her out of here without my knowledge, take her," the captain said. "I won't know anything about it. If you get caught, take the consequences. I won't cover for you."

Grave Digger straightened up. Veins stood out on his temples and his neck had swelled like a cobra's. His eyes had turned blood-red. He was so mad the captain's image was blurred in his vision.

"I wouldn't do this for nobody but my own black people," he said in a voice that was cotton-dry.

He wheeled from the desk and Coffin Ed fell in beside him and they walked fast out of the room and softly closed the door behind them.

They got their official car from the garage and drove up to Blumstein's Department Store on 125th Street and went into the women's department. Grave Digger bought a bright red dress, size 14, a pair of dark tan lisle stockings and a white plastic handbag. Coffin Ed bought a pair of gilt sandals, size 7, and a hand mirror. They put their packages into a shopping bag and drove up to Rose Murphy's House of Beauty on 145th Street, near Amsterdam Avenue, and bought some quick-action black skin dye and some make-up for a black woman and a dark-haired wig. They put these into their shopping bag and returned to the precinct station.

All the brass had left but the chief inspector in charge of homicide. They had nothing to say to him. Many of the police cruisers had been assigned to special detail and had gone about their business. But the street was still closed and heavily guarded and no one was permitted to enter the block or leave any of the buildings without police scrutiny.

Grave Digger parked in front of the station house and he and Coffin Ed went inside, carrying their shopping bag. They kept on through the booking room and past the captain's office and the detectives' room until they came to the head jailor's cubicle at the rear.

"Send Iris O'Malley down to the interrogation room and give us the key," Grave Digger said.

The jailor reached out languidly for the order.

"We haven't got any order," Grave Digger said. "The captain's too busy to write orders at this time."

"Can't have her 'less you got an order," the jailor insisted.

"She'll keep," Grave Digger said. "It just holds up the investigation, that's all."

"Can't do it," the jailor said stubbornly.

"Then give us the key to the bullpen," Coffin Ed said. "We'll start in the Back-to-Africa group."

"You know I can't do that either 'less you got an order," the jailor protested. "What's the matter with you fellows today?"

"Hell, where have you been, man?" Grave Digger said. "The captain's busy, can't you understand that?"

The jailor shook his head. He didn't want to be the cause of any escapes.

"Call the captain for goddamn's sake," Coffin Ed grated. "We can't just stand here and argue with you."

The jailor got the captain's office on the intercom, and asked if he should let Jones and Johnson interview the Back-to-Africa group in the bullpen.

"Let them see who they goddamn want," the captain shouted. "And don't bother me again."

The jailor looked crestfallen. Now he was anxious to co-operate to keep in their good graces. "You want to see Iris O'Malley first or afterwards?" he asked.

"Well, we'll just see her first," Grave Digger said.

The jailor gave them a key and called his underling on the tier where Iris was celled and instructed him to take her down to the "Pigeons' Nest."

They were there waiting when the jailor brought her in and left, and they locked the door behind him. They put her on the stool and turned on the battery of lights. Her scratches were healing and the swelling was almost gone from her face but her skin was still the colors of the rainbow. Without make-up her eyes were sexless and ordinary. She wore a dark blue denim uniform but without a number, since she hadn't been bound over to the grand jury.

"You look good," Coffin Ed said levelly.

"Tell it to your mother," she said.

"Deke got away," Grave Digger said.

"The lucky mother-raper," she said, squinting into the light.

Grave Digger turned down all the lights except one. It left her starkly visible but didn't blind her.

"How'd you like to escape?" Grave Digger asked.

"I'd like it fine," she said. "How'd you like to lay me? Both of you. At the same time."

"Where?" Coffin Ed asked.

"How is the question," Grave Digger said.

"Here," she said. "And let me worry about *how*."

"All joking aside—" Grave Digger began again, but she cut him off.

"I'm not joking."

"All sex aside then. Do you know Deke's hideout?"

"If I knew I wouldn't tell you," she said. "Anyway, not for nothing."

"We'll clear you," he said.

"Shit," she said. "You can't clear your own mother-raping selves, much less me. Anyway, I don't know it," she added.

"Can you find it?"

A sly look came into her eyes. "I could find it if I was out."

"I'm reading your mind," Grave Digger said.

"And it don't read good," Coffin Ed said.

The sly look went out of her eyes. "I can't find him from here, and that's for sure."

"That's for sure," Grave Digger agreed.

They stared at one another. "What's in it for me?" she asked.

"Freedom, maybe," he said. "When we get Deke we're going to drop the load on him. His two boys are going to fry for cop killing and we're going to fry him for killing Mabel Hill. And you get the ten percent reward from the eighty-seven grand if we find it."

They watched the thoughts reflected in her eyes and Coffin Ed said, "Steady, girl. If you try to cross us there won't be room enough for you in the world. We'll hunt you down and kill you."

"And don't think you'll be lucky enough to get shot," Grave Digger added. His lumpy unshaven face looked sadistic from behind the stabbing light, like the vague shadow of a monster's. "Want me to spell it out?"

She shuddered. "And if I don't find him?"

He chuckled. "We'll arrest you for escaping."

She was consumed with sudden rage. "You dirty mother-rapers," she mouthed.

"Better to be dirty than dumb," Coffin Ed said. "Are you on?"

She blushed beneath her rainbow color. "If I could only rape you, you dirty bastard."

"You can't. So are you on?"

"I'm on," she said. "You son of a bitch, you knew it all the time." After a moment she added, "Maybe if I don't find Deke you'll rape me."

"You'll have a better chance if you find him," he said.

"I'll find him," she promised.

XVIII

"MAKE YOURSELF INTO a black woman and don't ask any questions," Grave Digger said. "You'll find everything in there you'll need—make-up, clothes and some money. Don't worry about the dye; it'll come off."

He turned on the bright lights and he and Coffin Ed went out and locked the door behind them. She found the mirror and went to work. Coffin Ed stood outside the door and listened for a time; he didn't think she'd yell and try to draw attention, but he wanted to make sure. Satisfied she was tending to the business, he went upstairs and waited for Grave Digger to come with the keys to the bullpen. They went inside and interrogated the sullen prisoners until they found a young black woman about Iris's size and age, named Lotus Green. They filled out a card on Lotus, then took her down to the Pigeons' Nest for further questioning.

"What you want with me?" she protested. "I done tole you everything I know."

"We like you," Coffin Ed said.

She shocked the hell out of him by blowing coy. "You got to pay me," she said. "I don't do it with strangers for nothing."

"We ain't strangers by now," he said.

He stood outside, listening to her explain why he was still a stranger while Grave Digger went inside to get Iris. She was ready, a fly black woman in a cheap red dress.

"These shit-skin sandals are too big," she complained.

"Watch your language and act dignified," Grave Digger said. "You're a churchwoman named Lotus Green and you hope to go back to Africa."

"My God!" she exclaimed.

He took her out past the real Lotus while Coffin Ed took the real Lotus inside.

"We're going to put you in the bullpen and when the officer comes for Lotus Green you come out with him," Grave Digger instructed. "Just act sullen and don't answer any questions."

"That won't be hard," she said.

Coffin Ed locked the real Lotus in the place of Iris, assuring her that he was going to get some money, and joined Grave Digger. They went to the captain's office and asked permission to take out Lotus Green, one of the Back-to-Africa group.

"She saw where the woman went who was robbed that night, but she doesn't know the number," Grave Digger explained. "And that woman might have seen all the hijackers."

The captain suspected some kind of trick. Furthermore he wasn't interested in the hijacking, he just wanted Deke. But it put him on the spot.

"All right, all right," he snapped. "I'll send for her and you can take her from my office. Just don't forget your assignment."

"It's all the same thing," Grave Digger said. "Here's the report on her," and gave him the card.

They went back to see the head jailor. "We're going to try Iris once more and if she doesn't give we're going to leave her in the dark for a spell. We'll fix it so she can't hurt herself and don't get edgy if someone hears her screaming. She won't be hurt."

"I don't know what you fellers do down there and I don't want to know," the jailor said.

"Right," Grave Digger said and they went down and stood outside the bullpen. When they saw a jailor taking Iris, disguised as Lotus, to the captain's office, they went downstairs and got the real Lotus Green and took her back to the bullpen.

"I waited and I waited," she complained.

"What else could you do?" Coffin Ed said and they went back upstairs to the captain's office and walked out of the station with Iris between them. They got into their car and drove off.

"We're on our own now," Coffin Ed said.

"Yeah, we've jumped into the fire," Grave Digger agreed.

"Well, little sister, where do you want to get out?" Coffin Ed asked the black woman on the back seat.

"Let me out on the corner," she said.

"What corner?"

"Any corner."

They pulled to the curb on Seventh Avenue and 125th opposite the Theresa Hotel. They wanted all the stool pigeons in the neighborhood to see her getting out of their car. They knew no one would recognize her, but they were marking her for themselves—just in case.

"This is what you do," Coffin Ed said, turning about to face her. "When you contact Deke—"

"*If* I contact Deke," she cut in.

He looked at her for a moment and said, "Just don't try getting cute because we sprung you. That ain't going to make any difference if you try a double-cross."

She didn't answer.

He said, "When you contact Deke, just say you know where the bale of cotton is."

"The *what!*" she exclaimed.

"The bale of cotton. And let him take it from there. Then when you get him located, keep him waiting and contact us."

"Are you sure you mean a bale of *cotton*?" she asked incredulously.

"That's right, a bale of cotton."

"And how do I contact you?"

"Call either of these two numbers." He gave her the telephone numbers of their homes. "If we're not there, leave a number and we'll call back."

"Shit on that," she said.

"All right, then call back in half an hour and you'll be given a number where to contact us. Just say you're Abigail."

Grave Digger muttered, "Ed, you're giving us a lot of trouble."

"What do you suggest that's better?"

Grave Digger thought about it for a moment. "Nothing," he confessed.

"Bye-bye then," Iris said, adding under her breath, "Blackbirds," and got out. She walked east on 125th.

Grave Digger eased into the traffic on Seventh Avenue and drove north.

Iris stopped in front of a United Tobacco store and watched their car until it passed from sight. The store had five telephone booths ranged along one wall. Iris chose one quickly and dialed a number.

A cautious voice answered: "Holmes Radio Repair Shop."

"I want to talk to Mr. Holmes," Iris said.

"Who's calling?"

"His wife. I just got back."

After a moment another disguised voice said, "Honey, where are you?"

"I'm here," Iris said.

"How'd you get out?"

Don't you wish you knew? she thought. Aloud she said, "How would you like to buy a bale of cotton?"

There was a long pregnant silence. "Tell me where you are and I'll have my chauffeur pick you up."

"Stay put," she said. "I'm dealing in cotton."

"Just don't deal in death," the voice sounded a deadly warning.

She hung up. When she stepped outside she looked up and down the street. Cars were parked on both sides. Crosstown traffic flowed from the Triborough Bridge headed towards the West Side Highway and the 125th Street ferry and vice versa. There was nothing about the black Ford to set it apart from any other car. It was empty and looked put for some time. She didn't see the two-toned Chevrolet parked down the street. But when she started walking again, she was being tailed.

Grave Digger and Coffin Ed drove their official car, the little black car with the hopped-up engine that was so well known in Harlem, into a garage on 155th Street and left it for a tune-up. Then they walked up the hill to the subway and rode the "A" train down to Columbus Circle at 59th Street and Broadway.

They walked over to the section of pawnshops and second-hand clothing stores on Columbus Avenue and went into Katz's pawnshop and bought black sunglasses and caps. Grave Digger chose a big checkered cap called the "Sportsman" while Coffin Ed selected a red, long-billed fatigue cap modeled after those worn by the Seabees during the war. When they emerged, they looked like two Harlem cats, high off pot.

They walked up Broadway to a car rental agency and selected a black panel truck without any markings. The rental agent didn't want to trust them until they put down a large deposit. He took it and grinned, figuring them for Harlem racketeers.

"Will this jalopy run?" Grave Digger asked.

"Run!" the agent exclaimed. "Cadillacs get out of its way."

"Damn right," Coffin Ed said. "If I owned a Cadillac I'd get out of its way too."

They got in and drove it back uptown.

"Now I know why the world looks so vague to weedheads," Grave Digger said from behind the wheel.

"Too bad there isn't any make-up to disguise us as white," Coffin Ed said.

"Hell, I remember when old Canada Lee was made up as a white man, playing on Broadway in a Shakespearean play; and if Canada Lee could look like a white man, I'm damn sure we could."

The mechanic at the garage didn't recognize them until Grave Digger flashed his shield.

"I'll be a *mother*," he said, grinning. "When I saw you coming I locked the safe."

"Just as well," Grave Digger said. "You never know who's in a panel truck."

"Ain't it the truth?" the mechanic said.

They had him take their radio-telephone from their official car and install it temporarily in the truck. It took forty-five minutes and Coffin Ed called home. His wife said no one named Abigail had called either her or Stella, but the precinct station had been calling every half-hour trying to get in touch with them.

"Just tell them you don't know where we are," Coffin Ed said. "And that's the truth."

When they left the garage they were able to pick up all the police calls. All cars had been alerted to contact them and order them back to the station. Then the cars were instructed to pick up a slim black woman wearing a red dress, named Lotus Green.

Coffin Ed chuckled. "By this time that yellow gal has damn sure got that dye off, much as she hates being black."

"And she ain't wearing that cheap red dress, either," Grave Digger added.

They drove over to a White Rose bar at the corner of 125th and Park Avenue, across the street from the 125th Street railroad station, and parked behind a two-toned Chevrolet. Ernie was sitting in a shoeshine stand outside the bar, facing Park. The sign on the awning read: AMERICAN LEGION SHOE SHINE. Two elderly white men were shining colored men's shoes. Across the avenue, seen between the stanchions of the railroad trestle, was another shoeshine, its awning proclaiming: FATHER DIVINE SHOE SHINE. Two elderly colored men were shining white men's shoes.

"Democracy at work," Coffin Ed said.

"Down to the feet."

"Down *at* the feet," Coffin Ed corrected.

Ernie saw them go into the bar but gave no sign of recognition. They stood at the bar like two cats having a sip of something cold to dampen their dry jag, and ordered beer. After a while Ernie came in and squeezed to the bar beside them. He ordered a beer. The white barman put down an open bottle and a glass. Ernie wasn't looking when he poured it and some sloshed on to Grave Digger's hand. He turned and said, "Excuse me, I wasn't looking."

"That's what's on all them tombstones," Grave Digger said.

Ernie laughed. "She's at Billie's, the dancer, on 115th Street," he said under his breath.

"Don't pay no 'tention to me, son, I was just joking," Grave Digger said aloud. "Stay with it."

The bartender was passing. He looked from one to the other. *Stay with it*, he thought. Stay with what? As long as he'd been working in Harlem, he had never learned these colored folks' language.

Grave Digger and Coffin Ed finished their beers and ordered two more and Ernie finished his and went out. Coffin Ed used

the bar phone and telephoned his home. There had been no
call from Abigail, but the precinct station had been calling
regularly. The bartender was listening furtively but Coffin Ed
hadn't said a word. Then finally he said, "Stay with it." The
bartender started. Nuts, he thought looking vindicated.

They left their beers half finished and went around the
corner and sat in their truck.

"If we could tap the phone," Coffin Ed said.

"She's not going to phone from there," Grave Digger said.
"She's too smart for that."

"I just hope she don't get too mother-raping smart to live,"
Coffin Ed said.

Billie was alone when Iris knocked with the brass-hand knocker
on the black and yellow lacquered door. She opened the door
on the chain. She was wearing yellow chiffon lounging slacks
over a pair of black lace pants and a long-sleeved white chiffon
blouse fastened at the cuffs with turquoise links. She might as
well have been naked. Her slim, bare, dancer's feet had bright
red lacquered nails. As always she was made up as though to
step before the cameras. She looked like the favorite in a sultan's
harem.

Through the crack she saw a woman who looked too black
to be real, dressed like a housemaid on her afternoon off. She
blinked. "You've got the wrong door," she said.

"It's me," Iris said.

Billie's eyes widened "*Me* who? You sound like somebody
I know but you sure don't look like anybody I'd ever know."

"Me, Iris."

Billie scrutinized her for a moment, then broke into hysterical laughter. "My God, you look like the last of the Topsys.
Whatever happened to you?"

"Unchain the door and let me in," Iris snapped. "I know
how I look."

Billie unchained the door, still laughing hysterically, and
locked and chained it behind her. Then suddenly, watching Iris
hurry towards the bath, she called, "Hey, I read you were in
jail," running after her.

Iris was already at the mirror, smearing cleansing cream over her face, when Billie came in. "I'm out now, as you can see."

"Well, how 'bout you," Billie said, sitting on the edge of the bathtub. "Who sprung you? The paper said you lowered the boom on Deke and now he's escaped."

Iris snatched a clean towel and began frantically rubbing her face to see if the black would come off. Yellow skin appeared. Reassured, she became less frantic. "The monsters," she said. "They want me to help 'em find Deke."

Billie looked shocked. "You wouldn't!" she exclaimed.

Iris was slipping out of the cheap red dress. "The hell I wouldn't," she said.

Billie jumped to her feet. "I certainly won't help you," she said. "I always liked Deke."

"You can have him, sugar," Iris said sweetly, peeling off the lisle stockings. "I'll swap him for a dress."

Billie left the room, looking indignant, while Iris shed to the skin and began removing the black in earnest. After a while Billie returned and threw clothes across the side of the tub. She looked at Iris's nude body critically.

"You sure got beat up, baby. You look like you've been raped by three cannibals."

"That'd be a kick," Iris mumbled, smearing her face more thoroughly with the cleansing cream.

"Here, use Ponds," Billie said, handing her a different jar. "That's Chanel's you're wasting on that blackening and this is just as good for that."

Iris exchanged the jar without comment and went on smearing her face, neck, arms and legs.

"Did you really kill her?" Billie asked as though casually.

Iris stopped applying the cream and turned around and looked at her. "Don't ask me that question. There never was a man I'd kill for." There was a warning in her voice that frightened Billie.

But she had to know. "Were you and her—"

"Shut up," Iris snapped. "I didn't know the bitch."

"You can't stay here," Billie said bitchily, showing her disbelief. "They'd lock me up too if they found me."

"Don't be so fucking jealous," Iris said and began kneading in the cleansing cream again. "Nobody knows I'm here and not even Deke knows about us."

Billie smiled with secret pleasure. Mollified, she asked, "How do you expect to get to Deke after you've ratted on him?"

Iris laughed as at a good joke. "I'm going to cook up a good story about where to find the money he's lost and see what he'll pay me for it. Deke will forgive anything for money."

"The Back-to-Africa money? Honey, that money has gone with the wind."

"Don't think I don't know it. I just want to get something out of that two-timing mother-raper any kind of way."

Billie had her secret smile again. "Baby, how you talk," she said, adding: "You can wipe it off now," referring to the cream. "I'll make you up in tan so you'll look brand-new."

"You're a darling," Iris said absently, but in the back of her mind she was thinking furiously why Deke would want a bale of cotton.

Billie was looking at her nude body lustfully. "Don't tempt me," she said.

XIX

THE MONDAY EDITION of the Harlem *Sentinel* came out around noon. Coffin Ed picked up a copy at the newsstand by the Lexington Avenue Subway Kiosk at one-thirty for them to read with their lunch. There had been no word from Abigail, and Paul had just ridden past giving the high sign that Iris was still put.

They wanted to eat some place where it was unlikely they'd be spotted, and where they wouldn't look out of place in their black weedhead sunglasses. They decided to go to a joint on East 116th Street called Spotty's, run by a big black man with white skin spots and his albino wife.

After years of bemoaning the fact that he looked like an overgrown Dalmatian, Spotty had made a peace with life and opened a restaurant specializing in ham hocks, red beans and rice. It sat between a store-front church and a box factory and had no side windows, and the front was so heavily curtained the light of day never entered. Spotty's prices were too moderate and his helpings too big to afford bright electric lights all day. Therefore it attracted customers such as people in hiding, finicky people who couldn't bear the sight of flies in their food, poor people who wanted as much as they could get for their money, weedheads avoiding bright lights, and blind people who didn't know the difference.

They took a table in the rear across from two laborers. Spotty brought them plates of red beans, rice and ham hocks, and a stack of sliced bread. There wasn't any choice.

Coffin Ed wolfed a mouthful hungrily and gasped for breath. "This stuff will set your teeth on fire," he said.

"Take some of this hot sauce and cool it off," one of the laborers said with a straight face.

"It cools you off these hot days," the other laborer said. "Draws all the heat to the belly and leaves the rest of you cool."

"What about the belly?" Grave Digger asked.

"Hell, man, what kind of old lady you got?" the laborer said.

Grave Digger shouted for two beers. Coffin Ed took out the paper and divided it in two. He could barely see the large print through his smoked glasses. "What you want, the inside or the outside?"

"You expect to read in here?" Grave Digger said.

"Ask Spotty to give you a candle," the laborer said with a straight face.

"Never mind," Grave Digger said. "I'll read one word and guess two."

He took the inside of the paper and folded it on the table. The classified ads were up. His gaze was drawn to an ad in a box: *Bale of cotton wanted immediately. Telephone Tompkins 2— before seven p.m.* He passed the paper to Coffin Ed. Neither of them said anything. The laborers looked curious but Grave Digger turned over the page before they could see anything.

"Looking for a job?" the talkative laborer asked.

"Yeah," Grave Digger said.

"That ain't the paper for it," the laborer said.

No one replied. Finally the two laborers got tired of trying to find out their business and got up and left. Grave Digger and Coffin Ed finished eating in silence.

Spotty came to their table. "Dessert?" he asked.

"What is it?"

"Blackberry pie."

"Hell, it's too dark in here to eat blackberry pie," Grave Digger said and paid him and they got up and left.

Coffin Ed called his home from a street booth, but there was still no word from Abigail. Then he called the Tompkins number. A southern voice answered, "Back-to-the-Southland office, Colonel Calhoun speaking." He hung up.

"The Colonel," he told Grave Digger when he got back in the truck.

"Let's don't think about it here," Grave Digger said. "They might be tracing our calls home."

They drove back past the 125th Street railroad station and found the Chevrolet parked near the Fischer Cafeteria. Ernie gave them the sign that Iris was still put. They were driving on when they saw a blind man tapping his way along. They pulled around the corner of Madison Avenue and waited.

Finally the blind man came tapping along Madison. He was selling Biblical calendars. Coffin Ed leaned from the truck and said, "Hey, let me see one of those."

The blind man tapped over towards the edge of the side-walk, feeling his way cautiously. He pulled a calendar from his bag and said, "It's got all the names of the Saints and the Holy Days, and numbers straight out of the Apocalypse; and it's got the best days for births and deaths." Lowering his voice he added, "It's the photograph I told you about night before last."

Coffin Ed made as though he were leafing through it. "How'd you make us?" he whispered.

"Ernie," the blind man whispered back.

Satisfied, Coffin Ed said loudly, "Got any dream readings in here?"

Passersby hearing the question stopped to listen.

"There's a whole section on dream interpretations," the blind man said.

"I'll take this one," Coffin Ed said and gave the blind man a half-dollar.

"I'll take one too," another man said. "I dreamed last night I was white."

Grave Digger drove off, turned east on 127th Street and parked. Coffin Ed passed him the photograph. It showed distinctly the front of a big black limousine. A blond young man sat behind the wheel. Colonel Calhoun sat next to him. Three vague white men sat on the rear seat. Approaching the car was Josh, the murdered junkyard laborer, grinning with relief.

"This cooks him," Grave Digger said.

"It won't fry him," Coffin Ed said, "but it'll scorch the hell out of him."

"Anyway, he didn't get the cotton."

"What does that prove? He might already have the money and the cotton might just be evidence. He might have killed the boy just to keep from tipping his hand," Grave Digger argued.

"And advertise for the cotton today? Hell, let's take him anyway, and find the cotton later."

"Let's get Deke first," Grave Digger said. "The Colonel will keep. He's got more than eighty-seven thousand dollars behind him—the whole mother-raping white South—and he's playing a deeper game than just hijacking."

"We'll see, said the blind man," Coffin Ed said and they drove back to the White Rose bar at 125th and Park. Paul was waiting at the bar, drinking a Coke. They pushed in beside him. He spoke in a low voice but openly. "We've been assigned to another case. Captain Brice doesn't know we've been working for you and we won't tell him, but we have to report to the station now. Ernie's waiting for you to take over. She hasn't moved but that doesn't mean she hasn't phoned."

"Right," Grave Digger said. "We're on the lam, you know."

"I know."

The bartender approached with a wise, knowing look. These nuts again, he was thinking. But they left without ordering. He nodded his head wisely, as if he'd known it all the time. They drove over to 115th Street and found Ernie parked near the corner watching the entrance of the apartment house through his rear-view mirror while pretending to read a newspaper. Coffin Ed gave him a sign and he drove off.

There was a bar with a public telephone on the corner of Lenox Avenue. So they parked down towards Seventh Avenue, opposite the entrance, so they would be behind Iris if she came out to telephone. Grave Digger got out and began jacking up the right rear wheel, keeping bent over out of sight of Billie's windows. Coffin Ed walked towards the bar, shoulders hunched and red cap pulled low over his black weedhead sunglasses. He looked like one of the real-gone cats with his signifying walk. They figured she had to make her move soon.

But it had turned dark before Iris left the apartment. By now the tenements had emptied of people seeking the cool of evening, and the sidewalks were crowded. But Iris walked fast, looking straight ahead, as though the people on the street didn't exist.

Her skin was a smooth painted tan without a blemish, like the soft velvety leather of an expensive handbag. She wore silk Paisley slacks and a blue silk jersey blouse of Billie's, and one of the red-haired wigs Billie used in her act. Her hips were pitching like a rowboat on a stormy sea, but her cold, aloof face said: Your eyes may shine and your teeth may grit, but none of this fine ass will you git.

This puzzled Grave Digger as he pulled the truck out from the curb a half-block behind her. She wanted to be seen. Coffin Ed had the telephone covered but she didn't look towards the bar. Instead she turned north on Lenox, walking fast but not looking back. Grave Digger picked up Coffin Ed and they followed a block behind, careful but not cute.

She turned east on 121st Street and went directly to O'Malley's church, The Star of Ham. The front door was locked, but she had a key.

Grave Digger parked just around the corner on Lenox and they hit the pavement in a flat-footed lope. But she was already out of sight.

"Cover the back," he said, and ran up the stairs and tried the front door.

There was no time for finesse. Coffin Ed jumped the iron gate at the side and ran down the walk towards the back.

The front door was locked. Grave Digger studied the windows. Coffin Ed studied the back door and found it locked too. He hoisted himself up on to the brick wall separating the back yard of the apartment next door for a better view.

From the hideout underneath the rostrum, all three distinctly heard her key in the lock, heard the lock click, the door opening and closing, the lock clicking shut, and her footsteps on the wooden floor.

"Here she is now," Deke said with relief.

"It's a goddamn good thing for you," the oily-haired gunman said. He had a Colt .45 automatic in his right hand and he kept slapping the barrel in the palm of his left hand as he looked down at Deke.

Deke was tied to one of the two straight-backed tubular chairs and sweat was streaming down his face as though he were crying. He had been tied in that position, with his arms about the chair's back, since Iris had first telephoned, seven hours previous.

The other gunman lay on the couch, his eyes closed, seemingly asleep.

They were silent as they listened over the electronics pickup to Iris's footsteps tripping across the floor above, but their attention was alerted when they heard another sound at the front door.

"She's tailed," the gunman on the couch said, sitting up.

He was a stout, light-complexioned man with thinning straight brown hair, slitted brown eyes and a nasty-looking mouth as though he dribbled food. He spat on the floor as they listened.

The footsteps rounded the pulpit and stopped on the other side and there was no more sound from the front door.

"She's on to it," Deke said, licking the sweat trickling into his mouth. "She's going out through the wall to lose them."

The gunman on the couch said, "She better lose them good, baby."

They heard the secret door through the wall into an apartment in the building next door being opened and closed and then silence.

The gunman standing slapped the Colt against the palm of his hand as though perplexed. "How come you trust this bitch when she's ratted on you before?"

The sweat stung Deke's eyes and he blinked. "I don't trust her, but that bitch likes money; and she's always going keep this secret for her own safety," he said.

The gunman on the couch said, "It's your life, baby."

The gunman standing said, "She'd better come back soon or it's gonna be too late. It's getting hotter all the time."

"It's safe here," Deke said desperately. "You're safer here until we get the money than being on the loose. Nobody knows about this hideout."

The gunman on the couch spat. " 'Cept Iris and the people who built it."

"White men built it," Deke said. He couldn't keep the smugness out of his voice. "They didn't suspect a thing. They thought it was to be a crypt."

"What's that?" asked the standing gunman.

"A vault, for dead saints maybe."

The gunman looked at him, then looked around as though seeing the room for the first time. It was a small square room with soundproof walls, and access from above through the back of the church organ. There was a niche in one wall with a silver icon flanked by prints of Christ and the Virgin. Deke had furnished it with a couch, two tubular chairs, a small kitchen table and a refrigerator which he kept well stocked with prepared food, beer and whiskey. Soiled dishes on the table attested to the fact they had eaten there at least once.

One entire wall was taken up by the electronics system with pickup and amplifier that recorded every sound made in the church above. When turned up full volume even the footsteps of a mouse could be heard. On the opposite wall was a gun rack containing two rifles, two sawed-off shotguns and a submachine gun. Deke was proud of the place. He had had it built when reconditioning the church. He felt completely safe there. But the gunman was unimpressed.

"Let's just hope them white men don't remember," he said. "Or that she don't bring a police tail back here. This place ain't no more safe than a coffin."

"Believe me," Deke said. "I know it's safe."

"We sprang you, baby, to get the money," the sitting gunman said flatly. "We figured we'd spring you and then sell your life to you for eighty-seven grand. You get the picture, baby. You going to buy it?"

"Freddy," Deke appealed to the sitting gunman but got nothing from his eyes but a blank deadly stare. "Four-Four," he appealed to the oily-haired one standing with the Colt in his hand and drew another blank stare. "You've got to trust me," he pleaded. "I've never let you down. You've got to give me time. . . ."

"You got time," Freddy said, standing up and going to the icebox for another can of beer. He spat on the floor, slammed shut the box. "But not all of it."

From atop the brick wall in back of the church, Coffin Ed got a glimpse of Iris's face peeping from behind the curtains of the back window of a first-floor apartment. It came more from a sixth sense than actual sight. There was only a dim light in back of her, outlining a mere shadow, and the light from outside was filtered from surrounding windows. And she was visible for only a moment. It was the timing more than anything which told him. Who else in the vicinity might be peering furtively from a back window at just that moment.

He knew automatically she had got through the wall. How, he didn't care. He knew she had not only recognized him then, but had made them both from the start. A smart bitch—too smart. He debated whether to burst in on her openly, or take cover and let her make her move. Then he decided to go back and confer with Grave Digger.

"Let her go," Grave Digger said. "She can't hide for ever, she ain't invisible. And she's made us now. So let her go, let her go. Maybe she'll contact us."

They walked back to the truck and drove up to a bar, and

Coffin Ed telephoned home. His wife Molly said Abigail hadn't called but Anderson was on duty now and he wanted them to call him.

"Call him," Grave Digger said.

Anderson said, "Bring in Iris while I'm on duty and I'll try to cover for you. Otherwise you're certain to be picked up by tomorrow and you'll be finished on the Force—probably face a rap. Captain Brice is furious."

"He knows about it," Coffin Ed said. "He promised to lay off."

"That's not the way he tells it. He's reported to the commissioner that you've abducted her and he's seeing red."

"He's mad just because we tricked him; and he's covering himself at our expense."

"Be that as it may, he's mad enough to break you."

They sat silent for a moment, tense and worried.

"You figure she might try to take a powder?" Coffin Ed said.

"We got enough to worry about without that," Grave Digger said. "And we ain't got time for it."

"Let's go to Billie's."

"She's left there for good. Let's go back to the church."

"That was just to shake us," Coffin Ed argued. "She's finished with the church."

"Maybe, maybe not. Deke wouldn't put in an escape door for nothing. There must be something else there."

Coffin Ed thought about it. "Maybe you're right."

They parked on 122nd Street and cased the back of the church. The backyard was separated by the high brick wall from the garbage-strewn backyards surrounding it. They scaled the wall and examined the back door. It had an ordinary Yale snap lock with an iron grille covering its dirty panes but they didn't touch it. They peered through a window into the vestry back of the choir but it was black dark inside.

Then they went down the narrow walk alongside the church. It was a brick structure and in good condition and on that side two arched stained-glass windows flanked a stained-glass oval high in the wall. The other side of the church was built flush with the apartment house.

"If they got a hideout in there they got some kind of hearing device for protection," Grave Digger reasoned. "They can't have a lookout hiding all the time."

"What do you want to do, wait outside for her?"

"She'll return through the wall, or she might already be in there."

They looked at one another thinking.

"Listen—" Coffin Ed began and explained.

"Anyway, it beats a blank," Grave Digger said, as he stopped in the darkness to take off his shoes.

They stood behind the gate and watched the street until it was momentarily empty. Then they scaled the iron gate and hurried up the stairs to the church door, and Coffin Ed began picking the lock. If anyone had passed they would have been taken for two drunks urinating against the church door. When it was open, Grave Digger sat astride Coffin Ed's shoulders and they went inside and closed the door behind them.

The tableau in the hideout was much the same. Deke was still tied to the chair and the oily-haired gunman, Four-Four, was letting him drink from a can of beer. Beer was spilling from his mouth onto his pants and Four-Four said irritably, "Can't you swallow, goddammit?" slapping his own thigh with the barrel of the Colt. Freddy was lying on the couch again as though he were asleep.

Suddenly they froze at the sound of the front door lock being picked. Four-Four took the beer can from Deke's mouth and put it atop the table and changed the Colt to his left hand, flexing his right. Freddy swung his feet over to the floor and sat up, listening with his mouth open. They heard the door swing open and someone step inside and the door being closed.

"We got a visitor," Freddy said.

They heard the footsteps come down the center aisle.

"A dick," Four-Four said, appraising the walk.

Freddy stepped over to the gun rack and casually took down a sawed-off shotgun. They listened to the steps move around the choir and the pulpit and approach the organ. Freddy looked at the access ladder as though in a trance.

"A big boy," he said. "Big as two men. Think I ought go up and cut him down to size?"

"Let him stick his head in, ha-ha," Four-Four laughed.

"You're not going to leave me tied up!" Deke protested.

"Sure, baby, that or dead," Freddy said.

The heavy man's footsteps passed the organ, paused for a moment as though he were looking around, then moved on slowly as though he were examining everything. Through the electronics pickup they could hear his heavy breathing.

"A fat baby with a heart," Four-Four said.

"Guts too," Deke said. "Coming here alone."

"I got something for his guts," Freddy said, swinging the sawed-off shotgun.

The footsteps circled the pulpit, stopped for a moment, then went down into the auditorium and moved along the walls. They could hear knuckles sounding the walls. The footsteps moved slowly as the man encircled the walls, sounding for a false door. Ear-shattering bangs suddenly shook the small hide-out as the man began sounding the wooden floor with his pistol butt.

"Cut that damn thing down," Four-Four shouted. "The mother-raper will hear himself upstairs."

Freddy turned it down until the tapping on the floor became muted. It went on and on until seemingly every inch of the floor was covered. There was silence for a long time as though the man was listening. Then they heard the faint click of his pocket torch being turned on. Finally they heard his footsteps moving towards the door. Half-way they heard him stop and put what sounded like the palms of his hands on the floor.

"What the hell's he doing now?" Four-Four asked.

"Damn if I know," Freddy said. "Probably planting a time bomb." He laughed at his own humor.

"It wouldn't be so damn funny if you got your ass blown off," Four-Four said sourly.

They heard the imagined dick open the snap lock on the front door and pass out, closing the door behind him.

"It's time for that bitch of yours to be showing," Four-Four said disagreeably.

"She's coming," Deke said.

"She'd better come ready," Freddy said. "If she don't know where the money is, you can preach both of youse funerals." He chuckled.

"Dry up," Four-Four said.

XX

IRIS CAME IN with perfect assurance. She knew she hadn't been tailed. She had shaken Grave Digger and Coffin Ed and she wasn't afraid. She knew where the cotton was and how they could get it. She knew with this information she could handle Deke. And she had confidence that Deke could handle his gorillas.

Deke and his gunmen heard her when she entered.

"That's her now," Deke said, sighing with relief.

Freddy got up from the couch and took down the shotgun again. Four-Four jacked a shell into the chamber of his .45 automatic and slid back the safety. Both were tense but neither spoke.

Deke was listening to her walk. He could tell from the rhythm of her steps she was walking with assurance.

"She got it," he said with a confident look.

"She'd better have it," Freddy said dangerously.

"I mean the information," Deke said hurriedly for fear they might mistake his meaning.

Neither answered.

Grave Digger lay face down between two benches, breathing into a black cotton handkerchief, his hand on his pistol underneath his body. His black suit blended with the darkness and she didn't see a thing as she passed. He waited until he heard her footsteps ascending the rostrum, then scuttled down the center aisle on hands and knees to open the front door for Coffin Ed, hoping the sound of her footsteps would cover whatever sound he made.

But they heard it anyway.

"What the hell's she got with her?" Four-Four said.

"Sounds like her dog," Freddy said and started to laugh, but the look from Four-Four cut it off.

They heard the soft tap on the organ pipe that was the signal for entrance. Four-Four pushed a button and a panel in the back of the organ raised, revealing a small square space beneath the pipes. He pushed the second button and a heavy steel trapdoor opened upward. He raised the ladder and her gilt high-heeled sandals and legs encased in Paisley silk slacks came into view as she descended. He pushed the buttons closing the door behind her when her enticing buttocks showed. Then he raised the cocked .45 automatic and leveled it towards her back.

Her feet touched the floor and she turned around. She looked into the muzzle of the .45 and it looked like the head of a Gorgon. Her body turned to stone. Only the lids of her eyes moved as they continued to stretch as though her eyeballs were squeezed from her head. Slowly, without breathing, her eyes sought the face of Freddy and saw no pity; they slid off and she saw Deke tied to the chair, looking at her with raw anxiety, sweat streaming from a face contorted with terror; next they took in the shotgun in Freddy's hands and finally his nasty-mouthed sadistic face.

Nausea came up in her like the waves of the ocean and she gritted her teeth to keep from fainting. Her terror was so intense it became sexual—and she had an orgasm. All her life she had searched for kicks, but this was the kick she never wanted.

"Who was with you?" Four-Four asked.

She swallowed twice before she could find the handle to her voice, then it came in a husky whisper: "No one, I swear."

"We heard something strange."

"I wasn't tailed, I know," she whispered. Sweat beaded on her upper lip and her eyes were limpid pools of terror. "I'm clean, please listen to me," she begged. "Don't just kill me for nothing."

"Tell them, baby, tell them quick," Deke babbled in terror.

"It's in the cotton," she said.

"We know that," Four-Four said. "Where's the cotton?"

She kept swallowing as though choking. "I'm not going to tell you just to get killed," she whispered.

With a sudden movement that made her start, Freddy whipped the second straight-backed chair around behind Deke and said, "Sit down."

Four-Four stuck his pistol in his belt and took a coil of nylon clothesline from the floor beneath the gun rack. "Put your hands behind you, in back of the chair." She was slow in obeying and he slapped her across the face with the rope. She did as ordered and he began tying her methodically.

"Tell them," Deke begged piteously.

"She'll tell us," Freddy said.

Four-Four was tying her chair back to back with Deke's when they heard someone whistling in the street. They froze, listening, but the whistling stopped and there was silence. Four-Four finished tying them together on the two chairs back to back, then they all started nervously as they heard the front door of the church being opened. There was a soft sound like the padded feet of an animal and the door closed softly.

"We better look," Four-Four said. His voice stuttered slightly and his eyelids blinked rapidly as with a tic.

Freddy's nasty-looking mouth seemed breaking apart and his lips trembled. He got another .45 automatic from beneath the couch, jacked a shell in the chamber and slid off the safety. His motions were jerky but his hands were steady. He stuck the pistol in his belt and held the shotgun in his right hand. "Let's go," he said.

Grave Digger and Coffin Ed were deploying along opposite walls when Freddy came from behind the organ, searching quickly with the muzzle of the shotgun like a rabbit shooter. Coffin Ed went down out of sight but Freddy saw the moving shadow. The church exploded with the heavy thumping boom of a twelve-gauge shell of buckshot firing and the heavy charge took a section out of the back of the bench beneath which Coffin Ed had flopped. Grave Digger threw a tracer bullet and in the lightning flash from the trajectory saw the bullet burn through Freddy's sport-shirt collar as he dove towards the floor, and the outline of Four-Four coming from in back of him full speed with the .45 searching.

Grave Digger went down himself, scuttling like a crab, as

bursts from the .45 splintered benches above his head. For a moment there was stealthy movement in the dark with no one visible. Then the side of the organ began to burn where the tracer bullet had punctured it.

When Coffin Ed peeped up five rows away from where the shotgun charge had knocked a hole in the back of a bench, the rostrum was deserted and no one was in sight. But he saw the top of a head coming around the front bench on the center aisle and threw a tracer bullet at the round mop. He saw the bullet go through the bushy hair and penetrate the front of the platform supporting the rostrum and the choir. The scream was commencing as he ducked.

A figure with burning hair loomed in the flickering red light from the burning organ with a .45 searching the gloom and Grave Digger peeped. The shotgun went off and splintered the back of the bench in front of him and the church quivered from the blast. Grave Digger fell belly down and began crawling fast, shaken by his narrow escape. Forty-five bullets were breaking up the benches all around him and he didn't dare look. He lay on his belly beneath the benches, looking towards the sound, and made out the vague outline of trousered legs limned against the platform that had caught on fire. He took careful aim and shot a leg. He saw the leg break off like a wooden stick where the tracer bullet hit it dead center, and saw the trouser leg catch fire suddenly. Now the screaming slashed into the pool of silence like needles of flame and seared his nerves.

The burning shape of the body issuing these screams fell atop the broken leg, on the floor between two benches, and Grave Digger pumped two tracer bullets into it and watched the flames spring up. The dying man clawed at the book rack above him, breaking the fragile wood, and a prayer book fell on top of his burning body.

The burning-headed gunman was down beneath a bench, rubbing his oily hair with blistered hands, while Coffin Ed was peeping above the benches, searching for him with his long-barreled .38 in the red glare from the brightly burning organ.

The smoke had penetrated the hideout below, and the prisoners tied back-to-back on the two chairs had gone crazy from terror. They were spitting curses and accusations, and trying desperately to get at each other.

"You're a pimp for your mother and sister, you money-sucking snake," Iris screamed with face distorted and eyes terrified like the eyes of a burning horse.

"You two-bit stooling whore, I'll kill you," Deke grated.

Their legs were tied together like their arms but their feet touched the floor. They were straining with arched bodies and gripping feet to push each other into the wall. The chairs slid on the concrete floor, back and forth, rocking precariously. Arteries in their necks were swelled to bursting, muscles stretched like frayed cables, bodies twisting, breasts heaving, mouths gasping and drooling like two people in a maniacal sex act. Her make-up became streaked from sweat and her wig fell off. Deke doubled forward on his feet tied to the chair's legs, trying to bang Iris sideways against the gun rack. Her chair rose from the floor and bloodcurdling screams came wetly from her scar-like mouth as his chair tilted forward from his superhuman effort and they turned slowly over in a grotesque arc. He fell forward, face downward, striking his forehead on the concrete floor, as she came overtop in her chair. The momentum kept them turning until her head and forehead scraped on the concrete in turn and he was lifted from the floor. They landed up against the wall, her feet touching it, his chair on top supported only by the angle of hers on the floor. She kept trying to use her feet to push back from the wall, while he twisted violently, trying to rub her face against the concrete. The motion rocked them from side to side until both chairs fell sideways with a crash and they were left on their sides on the concrete floor between the gun rack and the table, unable to move. The thunder of the gunfight above that had shaken the room had quieted to darkening with smoke. Both were too spent to curse, they remained still, gasping for breath in the slowly suffocating smoke.

Upstairs in the church, light from the burning gunman on the floor lit up the figure of the gunman with his head on fire crouched behind the end of a bench ahead.

On the other side of the church Coffin Ed was standing with

his pistol leveled, shouting, "Come out, mother-raper, and die like a man."

Grave Digger took careful aim between the legs of the benches at the only part of the gunman that was visible and shot him through the stomach. The gunman emitted an eerie howl of pain, like a mortally wounded beast, and stood up with his .45 spewing slugs in a blind stream. The screaming had risen to an unearthly pitch, filling the mouths of the detectives with the taste of bile. Coffin Ed shot him in the vicinity of the heart and his clothes caught fire. The screaming ceased abruptly as the gunman slumped across the bench in a kneeling posture, as though praying in fire.

Now the entire platform holding the pulpit and the choir and the organ was burning brightly, lighting up the stained-glass pictures of the saints looking down from the windows. From outside came a banshee wail as the first of the cruisers came tearing into the street.

Grave Digger and Coffin Ed ran barefooted through the flame and kicked in the back of the organ with scorched feet. But they couldn't budge the steel trapdoor.

When the first of the police arrived they had reloaded and were shooting into the floor, trying to find the lock. Screams were heard coming from below and a dark cloud of smoke enveloped them. More police arrived and all worked frantically to open the door, but it wasn't until eight minutes later, when the first firemen arrived with axes and crowbars, it got opened.

Grave Digger pushed everyone aside and went down first with Coffin Ed following. He grabbed the chairs with the two figures and righted them. Iris was facing them and she was strangling in the smoke and tears were streaming down her face. Before moving to release her, he leaned down and looked into her face.

"And now, little sister, where's the cotton?"

Firemen and policemen were crowding around, coughing and crying in the dense smoke.

"Let them loose, take them out of here," a uniformed sergeant ordered. "They'll suffocate."

Iris looked down, thinking furiously, trying to figure an angle for herself.

"What cotton?" she said, to give herself time.

Grave Digger leaned forward until his face almost touched hers. His eyes were bright red and veins stood out in his temples. His neck swelled and his lumpy unshaven face contorted with rage.

"Baby, you'd have never come here if you didn't know," he said in a cotton-dry voice, gasping and coughing for breath. He raised his long-barreled .38 and aimed it at one of her eyes.

Coffin Ed drew his pistol and held back the policemen and firemen. His acid-burned face was jumping as though cooking in the heat and his eyes looked insane.

"And you'll never leave here alive unless you tell," Grave Digger finished.

Silence fell. No one moved. No one believed he would kill her, but no one dared interfere because of Coffin Ed; he looked capable of anything.

Iris looked down at Grave Digger's burned stockinged feet. Fearfully her gaze lifted to his burning red eyes. She believed it.

"Billie's doing a dance with it," she whispered.

"Take them," Grave Digger said, as he and Coffin Ed turned, hurrying off.

XXI

THE DANCE FLOOR of the Cotton Club stood on a platform level with the tops of the tables and also served as a stage for the big floor-shows presented. At the back were curtained exits into the wings which contained the dressing rooms.

When Grave Digger and Coffin Ed peered from behind the curtains to one of the wings, they saw the club was filled with well-dressed people, white and colored, sitting about small tables with cotton-white covers, their eyes shining like liquid crystals in faces made exotic by candlelight.

A piano was playing frenetically, a saxophone wailing

aphrodisiacally, the bass patting suggestively, the horn demand-
ing and the guitar begging. A blue-tinted spotlight from over
the heads of the diners bathed the almost naked tan body of
Billie in blue mist as she danced slowly about a bale of cotton,
her body writhing and her hips grinding as though making
easy-riding love. Spasms caught her from time to time and she
flung herself against the bale convulsively. She rubbed her belly
against it and she turned and rubbed her buttocks against it, her
bare breasts shaking ecstatically. Her wet red lips were parted
as though she were gasping, her pearly teeth glistened in the
blue light. Her nostrils quivered. She was creating the illusion
of being seduced by a bale of cotton.

Dead silence reigned in the audience. Women stared at her
greedily, enviously, with glittering eyes. Men stared lustfully, lids
lowered to hide their thoughts. The dance quickened and people
squirmed. Billie threw her body against the cotton with mad
desire. Bodies of women in the audience shook uncontrollably
from compulsive motivation. Lust rose in the room like miasma.

The act was working to a climax. Billie was twisting her
body and rolling her hips with shocking rapidity. She worked
completely around the bale of cotton, then, facing the audience, flung her arms wide apart and gave her hips a final shake.
"Ohhh, daddy cotton!" she cried.

Abruptly the lights came on and the audience went wild
with applause. Billie's smooth voluptuous body was wet with
sweat. It gleamed like a lecher's dream of hot flesh. Her breasts
were heaving, the nipples pointing like selecting fingers.

"And now," she said, slightly panting when the applause
died down, "I shall auction this bale of cotton for the actors'
benefit fund." She smiled, panting, and looked down at a
nervous young white man with his girl at a ringside table. "If
you're scared, go home," she challenged, taunting him with a
movement of her body. He reddened. A titter arose. "Who'll
bid a thousand dollars?" she said.

Silence fell.

From two tables back someone said in a level southern drawl,
"One thousand."

Eyes pivoted.

A lean-faced white man with long silvery hair, a white moustache and goatee, wearing a black frock coat and black string bow, sat at a table with a young blond white man wearing a white tuxedo jacket and a dubonnet-colored bow.

"The mother-raper," Coffin Ed said.

Grave Digger gestured for silence.

"A gentleman from the Old South!" Billie cried. "I'll bet you're a Kentucky Colonel."

The man stood up, tall and stately, and bowed. "Colonel Calhoun, at your service, from Alabama," he drawled.

Someone in the audience clapped. "A brother of yours, Colonel," Billie cried delightedly. "He's attracted by this cotton too. Stand up, brother."

A big black man stood up. The colored people in the audience roared with laughter.

"What you bid, brother rat?" Billie asked.

"He bids fifteen hundred," a voice cried jubilantly.

"Let him bid for himself," Billie snapped.

"I don't bid nothing," the man said. "You just asted me to stand up, is all."

"Well, sit down then," Billie said.

The man sat down self-consciously.

"Going," Billie said. "Going. This fine bale of natural-grown Alabama field cotton going for one thousand—and maybe I'll go with it. Any other bids?"

Only silence came.

"Cheapskates," Billie sneered. "You're going to close your eyes and imagine it's me, but it ain't going to be the same. Last chance. Going, going, gone. And look how many actors will benefit." She winked brazenly, then said, "Colonel Calhoun, suh, come forward and take possession of it."

"Of what?" some wit cracked.

"Guess, you idiot," Billie sneered.

The Colonel arose and went forward to the platform, a tall, straight, confident white man, and handed Billie ten one-hundred-dollar bank notes. "I deem it an honor, Miss Billie, to purchase this cotton from a beautiful nigra girl who might also be from those happy lands—"

"Not me, Colonel," Billie interrupted.

"—and in so doing benefit many deserving nigra actors," the Colonel finished.

There was a scattering of applause.

Billie ran and pulled handfuls of cotton from the bale and the Colonel tensed momentarily, but as quickly relaxed when she came running back and showered the strands of cotton on to his silvery head.

"I hereby ordain you as King of Cotton, Colonel," she said. "And may this cotton bring you wealth and fame."

"Thank you," the Colonel said gallantly. "I'm sure it will," and then signaled to the stage door opposite Grave Digger and Coffin Ed.

Two ordinary-looking colored workmen came forward with a hand truck and took the bale of cotton away.

Grave Digger and Cotton Ed hurried towards the street, limping like soul-brothers with duck feet. The truckmen brought out the bale of cotton and put it in back of an open delivery truck, and the Colonel followed leisurely and spoke to them and got into his black limousine.

Grave Digger and Coffin Ed were already in their panel truck parked a half-block back.

"So he found his car," Coffin Ed remarked.

"One gets you two it was never lost."

"That's a sucker's bet."

When the truck drove off they followed it openly. It went up Seventh Avenue and drew to the curb in front of the Back-to-the-Southland office. Grave Digger drove past and turned into the driveway of a repair garage, closed for the night, and Coffin Ed got out and began picking the lock of the roll-up door as though he worked there. He was working at the lock when the Colonel's limousine pulled up behind the truck across the street and the Colonel got out and looked about. He got the lock open and was rolling up the door by the time the Colonel had unlocked the door to his own office and the truckmen began easing the bale of cotton down onto the sidewalk. Grave Digger drove the panel truck into the strange garage and cut the lights and got out beside Coffin Ed. They stood in the dark doorway, checking their pistols, and watched the truckmen wheel the bale of cotton into the brightly lighted office and drop it in the center of the floor. They saw the Colonel pay them and speak to the blond young man, and when the truckmen left, the two of them spoke briefly again and the blond young man returned to the limousine while the Colonel turned out the lights and locked the door and followed him.

When they drove off, Grave Digger and Coffin Ed hurried across the street, and Coffin Ed began picking the lock to the Back-to-the-Southland office while Grave Digger shielded him.

"How long is it going to take?" Grave Digger asked.

"Not long. It's an ordinary store lock but I got to get the right tumbler."

"Don't take too long."

The next moment the lock clicked. Coffin Ed turned the knob and the door came open. They went inside and locked the door behind them and moved quickly through the darkness to a small broom closet at the rear. It was hot in the closet and they began to sweat. They kept their pistols in their hands and their palms became wet. They wanted to talk but were afraid to risk it. They had to let the Colonel get the money from the bale of cotton himself.

They didn't have long to wait. In less than fifteen minutes there was the sound of a key in the lock. The door opened and two pairs of footsteps entered and the door closed.

They heard the Colonel say, "Pull down the shades."

They heard the sounds of the shades covering the front windows and the door being pulled to the bottom and latched. Then there was the click of the light switch and the keyhole in the closet had sudden dimensions.

"Do you think that'll be enough?" a voice questioned. "Anyone can see there's a light on inside."

"There's no risk, son, everything is covered," the Colonel said. "Let's don't be too secretive. We pay the rent here."

There was the sound of the bale of cotton being shifted, probably being turned over, Grave Digger thought.

"Just give me that knife and keep the bag ready," the Colonel said.

Grave Digger felt in the darkness of the closet for the door-knob, and squeezed it hard and pulled it. But he waited until he heard the sound of the knife cut into the bale of cotton before turning it. Soundlessly he opened the door a crack and released the knob with the same caution.

Now through the crack they could see the Colonel engrossed in his work. He was cutting through the cotton with a sharp hunting knife and pulling out the fibers with a double-pronged hook. The blond young man stood to one side, watching intently, holding open a Gladstone bag. Neither looked around.

Grave Digger and Coffin Ed breathed silently through their mouths as they watched the hole grow larger and deeper. Loose cotton began piling up on the floor. The Colonel's face began sweating. The blond young man looked increasingly anxious. A frown appeared between his eyes.

"Have you got the right side?" he asked.

"Certainly, it shows where we opened it," the Colonel said in a controlled voice, but his expression and his haste expressed his own growing anxiety.

The blond young man's breathing had become labored. "You should be down to the money," he said finally.

The Colonel stopped digging. He put his arm into the hole to measure its depth. He straightened up and looked at the blond young man as though he didn't see him. For a long moment he seemed lost in thought.

"Incredible!" he said.

"What?" the blond young man blurted.

"There isn't any money."

The blond young man's mouth flew open. Shock stretched his eyes and he grunted as though someone had hit him in the solar plexus.

"Impossible," he gasped.

Suddenly the Colonel went berserk. He began stabbing the bale of cotton with the hunting knife as though it were human and he was trying to kill it. He slashed it and raked it with the hook. His face had turned bright red and foam collected in the corners of his mouth. His blue eyes looked stone crazy.

"Gawdammit, I tell you there isn't any money!" he shouted accusingly, as though it were the young man's fault.

Grave Digger pushed open the closet door and stepped into the room, his long-barreled, nickel-plated .38 revolver leveled on the Colonel's heart and glinting deadly in the bright light.

"That's just too mother-raping bad," he said and Coffin Ed followed him.

The Colonel and the young man froze, suspended in motion. Their eyes mirrored shock. The Colonel was the first to regain his composure. "What does this mean?" he asked in a controlled voice.

"It means you're under arrest," Grave Digger said.

"Arrest? For preparing a bale of cotton to exhibit during our rally tomorrow?"

"When you hijacked the Back-to-Africa meeting you hid the money in this bale of cotton during your getaway, then lost it. We wondered what made this bale of cotton so important."

"Nonsense," the Colonel said. "You're having a pipe dream. If you think I had anything to do with that robbery, you go ahead and arrest me and I'll sue you and the city for false arrest."

"Who said for robbery?" Coffin Ed said. "We're arresting you for murder."

"Murder! What murder?"

"The murder of a junkyard laborer named Joshua Peavine," Grave Digger said. "That's where the cotton fits in. He took you to Goodman's junkyard looking for this cotton and you had him murdered."

"I suppose you're going to have this Goodman identify this cotton," the Colonel said sarcastically. "Don't you know there are seven hundred million acres of cotton just like this?"

"Cotton is graded," Grave Digger said. "It can be identified. There were fibers from this bale of cotton left in Goodman's junkyard where the boy was murdered."

"Fibers? What fibers?" the Colonel challenged.

Grave Digger stepped to the pile of cotton on the floor and picked up a handful and held it out to the Colonel. "These fibers."

The Colonel paled. He still held the knife and hook in his hands but his body was controlled with great effort. The blond young man was sweating and trembling all over.

"Drop the gadgets, Colonel," Coffin Ed said, motioning with his gun.

The Colonel tossed the knife and hook into the hole in the bale of cotton.

"Turn around and walk over and put your hands to the wall," Coffin Ed went on.

The Colonel looked at him scornfully. "Don't be afraid, my boy, we're unarmed."

The tic came into Coffin Ed's face. "And just don't be too mother-raping cute," he warned.

The white men read the danger in his face and obeyed. Grave Digger frisked them. "They're clean."

"All right, turn around," Coffin Ed ordered.

They turned around impassively.

"Just remember who're the *men* here," Coffin Ed said.

No one replied.

"You were seen picking up the laborer, Joshua, by the side of the 125th Street railroad station just before he was murdered," Grave Digger continued from before.

"Impossible! There was only a blind man there!" the blond young man blurted involuntarily.

With a quick violent motion the Colonel turned and slapped him.

Coffin Ed chuckled. He drew a photograph from his inside pocket and passed it to the Colonel. "The blind man saw you— and took this picture."

The Colonel studied it for a long moment, then handed it back. His hand was steady but his nostrils were white along the edges. "Do you believe a jury would convict me on this evidence?" he said.

"This ain't Alabama," Coffin Ed said. "This is New York, and this colored man has been murdered by a white man in Harlem. We have the evidence. We'll give it to the Negro press and all the Negro political groups. When we get through, no jury would dare acquit you; and no governor would dare pardon you. Get the picture, Colonel?"

The Colonel had turned white as a sheet and his face looked pinched. Finally he said, "Every man's got his price, what's yours?"

"You're lucky to have any teeth left by now, or even dentures," Grave Digger said. "But you asked me a straight question, and I'll give you a straight answer. Eighty-seven thousand dollars."

The blond young man's mouth popped wide open again and he flushed bright red. But the Colonel only stared at Grave Digger to see if he was joking. Then disbelief came to his face, and finally astonishment.

"Incredible! You're going to give them back their money?"

"That's right, the families."

"Incredible! Is it because they are nigras and you're nigras too?"

"That's right."

"Incredible!" The Colonel looked as though he had got the shock of his life. "If that's true, you win," he conceded. "What will it buy me?"

"Twenty-four hours," Grave Digger said.

The Colonel kept staring at him as though he were a four-headed baby. "And will you really keep your bargain?"

"That's right. A gentleman's agreement."

A flicker of a smile showed at the corners of the Colonel's mouth.

"A gentleman's agreement," he echoed. "I'll give you a cheque drawn on the committee."

"We're going to wait right here behind drawn shades until the banks open in the morning and you send and get the cash," Grave Digger said.

"I'll have to send my assistant here," the Colonel said. "Will you trust him?"

"That ain't the question," Grave Digger said. "Will *you* trust him? It's *your* mother-raping life."

XXII

TUESDAY PASSED. COLONEL Calhoun and his nephew had disappeared. So had Grave Digger and Coffin Ed. The entire police force was searching for them. The panel truck had been found abandoned beside the cemetery at 155th Street and Broadway, but no trace of their whereabouts. Their wives were frantic. Lieutenant Anderson had personally joined in the search.

But they had simply ditched the panel truck and limped over to the Lincoln Hotel on St. Nicholas Avenue, operated by their old friend, took adjoining rooms and went to bed. They had slept around the clock.

Now it was Wednesday morning, and they had come down to the precinct station in a taxi, wearing bedroom slippers on bandaged feet, to turn in their report.

At sight of them the captain turned purple. He looked on the verge of an apoplectic stroke. He wouldn't speak to them, wouldn't look at them again. He gave orders for them to wait in the detectives' room and telephoned the commissioner. The other detectives looked at them and grinned sympathetically, but no one spoke; no one dared speak, they were hotter than a pussy with the pox.

The commissioner arrived and they were called into the captain's office. The commissioner was distinctly cool, but he had himself well under control, like a man just keeping from biting his nails. He let them stand while he read their report. He leafed through the eighty-seven thousand dollars in cash they had turned in.

"Now, men, I just want the facts," he said, looking about as though searching for the facts he wanted. "How was it possible that Colonel Calhoun escaped while you were guarding him?" he asked finally.

"You haven't read our report correctly, sir," Grave Digger said with great control. "We said we were waiting for him to come back so we could catch him red-handed taking the money from the bale of cotton. But when he started to unlock the door his nephew said something and they rushed back to their limousine and took off. That was the last we saw of them. We tried to chase them but their car was too fast. They must have had some gadget on the lock to tell them if it had been tampered with."

"What kind of gadget?"

"We don't know, sir."

The commissioner frowned. "Why didn't you report his escape and let the force catch him? Obviously, we have departments better equipped for it—or don't you think so?" he added sarcastically.

"That's right, sir," Grave Digger said. "But they didn't catch the two gunmen of Deke's and they had two full days before these same gunmen show up here, in the precinct station, and kill two officers and spring Deke."

"We figured we'd have a better chance of getting him by ourselves. We figured he'd come back for the money sooner or later, so we just hid there waiting for him," Coffin Ed added with a straight face.

"For one whole day?" the commissioner asked.

"Yes, sir. Time didn't matter," Grave Digger said.

The captain cleared his throat angrily but said nothing.

But the commissioner reddened with anger. "There is no place on this Force for grandstanding," he said hotly.

Coffin Ed blew up. "We found Deke and his two killers, didn't we? We gave back Iris, didn't we? We found the money, didn't we? We've got the evidence against the Colonel, haven't we? That's what we're paid for, isn't it? You call that grandstanding?"

"And how did you do it?" the commissioner flared.

Grave Digger spoke quickly, heading Coffin Ed off. "We did what we thought best, sir," Grave Digger said amenably. "You said you'd give us a free hand."

"Umph," the commissioner growled, scanning the report in front of him. "How did this girl, this dancer, Billie Belle, get hold of the cotton?"

"We don't know, sir, we haven't asked her," Grave Digger said. "We thought they'd get it out of Iris, they had her all yesterday."

The captain reddened. "Iris wouldn't talk," he said defensively. "And we didn't know about Billie Belle."

"Where does she live?" the commissioner asked.

"On 115th Street, not far," Grave Digger said.

"Get her in here now," the commissioner ordered.

The captain sent two white detectives for her, glad to get off so easily.

Billie didn't have time for her elaborate onstage make-up and she looked young and demure, almost innocent, without it, like all lesbian sexpots. Her full soft lips were a natural rose color, and without mascara her eyes looked brighter, smaller and rounder. She wore black linen slacks and a white cotton blouse and she looked like anything but a sophisticated belly dancer. She was relaxed and slightly on the flip side.

"It was just a whim," she said. "I saw Uncle Bud sleeping in his empty cart when I was driving down beneath the bridge to see about my yawt, and somehow his nappy white head made me think of cotton. I stopped and asked him if he could get me a bale of cotton for my cotton dance; I don't know why, just 'cause if he cut his hair it'd make a bale, I suppose, and he said, 'Gimme fifty dollars and I'll git you a bale of cotton, Miss Billie,' and I gave him the fifty right then and there, knowing I'd get it back from the club. And sure enough, that same night, he delivered it."

"Where?" the commissioner asked.

"At the club," she said, lifting her eyebrows. "What could I do with a bale of cotton in my home?"

"When?" Grave Digger asked.

"I don't know," she said, becoming impatient with these senseless questions. "Before I came at ten. He had left it in the stage entrance where it was in the way and I had it moved to my dressing room until I wanted it on the stage."

"When did you see Uncle Bud again?" Grave Digger asked.

"I had already paid him," she said. "There wasn't any need of seeing him again."

"Have you ever seen him again?" Grave Digger persisted.

"Why ever should I see him again?" she snapped.

"Think," Grave Digger said. "It's important."

She thought for a moment, then said, "No, that was the last time I saw him."

"Did the bale of cotton look as though it had been tampered with?" Coffin Ed asked.

"How the hell would she know?" Grave Digger said.

"I'd never seen a bale of cotton before in my life," she confessed.

"How did Iris find out about it?" the commissioner asked.

"I don't really know," she said musingly. "She must have heard me telephoning. I saw a want ad in the *Sentinel* for a bale of cotton and called the number. Some man with a southern accent answered and said he was Colonel Calhoun of the Back-to-the-Southland movement and he needed a bale of cotton for a rally he was planning to have. I thought he was some smart alec making a joke and I asked him where this rally was taking place. When he said on Seventh Avenue, I was sure he was joking then. I said I was having a cotton rally on Seventh Avenue myself, at the Cotton Club, and he could come to see it, and he said he would. Anyway, I know I was joking when I asked him for a thousand dollars for my bale of cotton."

"Where was Iris when you were talking on the telephone?" the commissioner persisted.

"I thought she was still in the bathroom, soaking, but she must have come into the dining room in her bare feet. I was in the sitting room lying on the divan with my back to the dining room door and I didn't hear her. She could have just stood there and eavesdropped and I wouldn't have known it." She had her little secret smile on again. "That would be just like Iris. Anyway, I would have told her all about it if she had asked, but she would rather eavesdrop."

"Didn't you know she had escaped from prison?" the commissioner asked softly.

There was silence for a moment and Billie's eyes stretched. "She told me that detectives Jones and Johnson had let her out to look for Deke. I didn't approve of it but it wasn't my business."

Dead silence reigned. The commissioner looked hard at the captain, but the captain wouldn't meet his gaze. Coffin Ed grunted, but Grave Digger kept a straight and solemn face.

Billie noticed the strange looks on everyone and asked innocently, "What was so important about the bale of cotton?"

Coffin Ed said jubilantly, "It had the eighty-seven thousand dollars hijacked from Deke's Back-to-Africa pitch hidden inside of it."

"Ohhhh," Billie gasped. Her eyes rolled back. Grave Digger caught her as she fell.

Now a week had passed. Harlem had lived notoriously on the front pages of the tabloids. Saucy brown chicks and insane killers were integrated with southern colonels and two mad Harlem detectives for the entertainment of the public. Lurid accounts of robberies and killings pictured Harlem as a criminal inferno. Deke O'Hara and Iris were dished up with the breakfast cereal; both had been indicted for conspiracy to defraud and second-degree murder. Iris screamed in bold black print that she had been double-crossed by the police. The Back-to-Africa movement vied with the Back-to-the-Southland movement for space and sympathy.

Everyone considered the dead gunmen as good gunmen and Grave Digger and Coffin Ed were congratulated for being alive.

Colonel Calhoun and his nephew, Ronald Compton, had been indicted for the murder of Joshua Peavine, a Harlem Negro laborer. But the State of Alabama refused to extradite them on the grounds that killing a Negro did not constitute murder under Alabama law.

The families of the Back-to-Africa group of O'Malley's who had gotten their money back staged an outdoor testimonial for Grave Digger and Coffin Ed in the same lot where they had lost it. Six hogs were barbecued whole and the detectives were presented with souvenir maps of Africa. Grave Digger was called upon to speak. He stood up and looked at his map and said, "Brothers, this map is older than me. If you go back to this Africa you got to go by way of the grave." No one understood what he meant, but they applauded anyway.

The next day Harlem's ace detectives were cited by the commissioner for bravery beyond the call of duty, but no raise came forth.

Undertaker H. Exodus Clay was kept busy all week burying the dead, which turned out to be so profitable he gave his chauffeur and handyman, Jackson, a bonus which enabled Jackson to marry his fiancée, Imabelle, with whom he had been living off and on for six years.

It was a quiet Wednesday midnight a week later and Grave Digger, Coffin Ed and Lieutenant Anderson were gathered in the captain's office, drinking beer and shooting the breeze.

"I don't dig Colonel Calhoun," Anderson said. "Was his object to break up the Back-to-Africa movement or just to rob them? Was he a man with a cause or just a thief?"

"He's a dedicated man," Grave Digger said. "Dedicated to the idea of keeping the black man picking cotton in the South."

"Yeah, the Colonel thought the Back-to-Africa movement was as sinful and un-American as bolshevism and should be stamped out at any cost," Coffin Ed added.

"I suppose he thought it was the American thing to do to rob those colored people out of their money," Anderson said sarcastically.

"Well, ain't it?" Coffin Ed said.

Anderson reddened.

"Hell, you don't know the Colonel," Grave Digger said pacifyingly. "He intended to give them back the money if they went south and picked cotton for a year or so. He's a benevolent man."

Anderson nodded knowingly. "It figures," he said. "That's why he hid the money in a bale of cotton. It was a symbol."

Grave Digger stared at Anderson and then looked over at Coffin Ed. Coffin Ed didn't get it either.

But Grave Digger replied with a straight face, "I know just what you mean."

"Anyway it made it easier for me and Digger to find," Coffin Ed said.

"How?" Anderson asked.

"How?" Coffin Ed echoed. The question threw him.

"Because it was still there," Grave Digger said, coming to his rescue.

Anderson blinked uncomprehendingly.

Coffin Ed chuckled. "Damn right," he said, adding under his breath, "That throws you too."

Grave Digger said, "I'm hungry," breaking it up.

Mammy Louise had barbecued an opossum especially for them and with the fat yellow meat she served candied yams, collard greens and okra, and left them to themselves to enjoy it.

"It's a damn good thing those southern crackers gave Colonel Calhoun enough money to spend to get us back south or we'd still be looking for the Back-to-Africa loot," Coffin Ed remarked.

"Be a lot of trouble, anyway," Grave Digger agreed.

"How you reckon he figured it out?" Coffin Ed asked.

"Hell, man, how you think he was going to miss seeing the bale had been tampered with," Grave Digger said. "As much cotton as he's handled in his lifetime."

"You think we should go after him?"

"Man, we've already recovered the stolen money. How're we going to explain another eighty-seven grand?"

"Anyway, let's find out where he's gone."

Two days later they got a verification from *Air France* that they had flown a very old colored man with a passport issued to Cotton Bud of New York City by way of Paris to Dakar.

They wired the prefecture in Dakar:

WHAT DO YOU HAVE ON OLD COTTON HEADED U.S. NEGRO ... NEW YORK TO DAKAR BY AIR FRANCE ... Jones, Harlem Precinct, New York City.

SENSATIONAL STUPENDOUS INCROYABLE ... M. COTTON HEADED BUD BUYS 500 CATTLE HIRES 6 HERDSMEN 2 GUIDES 1 WITCH DOCTEUR ... TOOK TO THE BRUSH ... WOMEN FAINTED ... THREW SELVES INTO SEA ... M. le Prefect, Dakar.

FOR MILK OR MEAT ... Jones, Harlem.

MONSIEUR QUELLE QUESTION ... FOR WIVES WHAT ELSE ... Prefect, Dakar.

HOW MANY WIVES WILL 500 CATTLE BUY ... Jones, Harlem.

M. COTTON HEADED BUD ALSO HAS MUCH MONEY ... M. BUD HAS BOUGHT 100 WIVES OF MOYEN QUALITE ... NOW SHOPPING FOR BEST ... WANTS LA MEME NUMERO AS SOLOMAN ... Prefect, Dakar.

STOP HIM QUICK ... HE WILL DROP DEAD BEFORE SAMPLING ... Jones, Harlem.

SHOULD HUSBAND DIE WIVES MAKE BEST MOURNERS ... Prefect, Dakar.

"Well, at least Uncle Bud got to Africa," Coffin Ed said.

"Hell, the way that old mother-raper is behaving, he might have come from Africa," Grave Digger said.

CHINUA ACHEBE
The African Trilogy
Things Fall Apart

AESCHYLUS
The Oresteia

ISABEL ALLENDE
The House of the Spirits

MARTIN AMIS
London Fields

IVO ANDRIĆ
The Bridge on the Drina

THE ARABIAN NIGHTS

ISAAC ASIMOV
Foundation
Foundation and Empire
Second Foundation
(in 1 vol.)

MARGARET ATWOOD
The Handmaid's Tale

JOHN JAMES AUDUBON
The Audubon Reader

AUGUSTINE
The Confessions

JANE AUSTEN
Emma
Mansfield Park
Northanger Abbey
Persuasion
Pride and Prejudice
Sanditon and Other Stories
Sense and Sensibility

THE BABUR NAMA

JAMES BALDWIN
The Fire Next Time,
Nobody Knows My Name,
No Name in the Street,
The Devil Finds Work
(in 1 vol.)
Giovanni's Room
Go Tell It on the Mountain

HONORÉ DE BALZAC
Cousin Bette
Eugénie Grandet
Old Goriot

MIKLÓS BÁNFFY
The Transylvanian Trilogy
(in 2 vols)

JOHN BANVILLE
The Book of Evidence
The Sea (in 1 vol.)

JULIAN BARNES
Flaubert's Parrot
A History of the World in
10½ Chapters (in 1 vol.)

GIORGIO BASSANI
The Garden of the Finzi-Continis

SIMONE DE BEAUVOIR
The Second Sex

SAMUEL BECKETT
Molloy, Malone Dies,
The Unnamable

SAUL BELLOW
The Adventures of Augie March

HECTOR BERLIOZ
The Memoirs of Hector Berlioz

THE BIBLE
(King James Version)
The Old Testament
The New Testament

WILLIAM BLAKE
Poems and Prophecies

GIOVANNI BOCCACCIO
Decameron

JORGE LUIS BORGES
Ficciones

JAMES BOSWELL
The Life of Samuel Johnson
The Journal of a Tour to
the Hebrides

ELIZABETH BOWEN
Collected Stories

RAY BRADBURY
The Stories of Ray Bradbury

JEAN ANTHELME
BRILLAT-SAVARIN
The Physiology of Taste

This book is set in BEMBO which was cut
by the punch-cutter Francesco Griffo
for the Venetian printer-publisher
Aldus Manutius in early 1495
and first used in a pamphlet
by a young scholar
named Pietro
Bembo.